PROSPERO REGAINED

TOR BOOKS BY
L. JAGI LAMPLIGHTER

Prospero Lost
Prospero in Hell
Prospero Regained

PROSPERO REGAINED

L. Jagi Lamplighter

A TOM DOHERTY ASSOCIATES BOOK
NEW YORK

This is a work of fiction. All of the characters, organizations, and events portrayed in this novel are either products of the author's imagination or are used fictitiously.

PROSPERO REGAINED

Edited by James Frenkel

The author wishes to thank Peter Atkins for permission to reprint his poem "Expectant Father to His Unborn Son." Copyright © 1998 by Peter Atkins. First published in *Weird Tales,* Fall 1998.

A Tor Book
Published by Tom Doherty Associates, LLC
175 Fifth Avenue
New York, NY 10010

www.tor-forge.com

Tor® is a registered trademark of Tom Doherty Associates, LLC.

Library of Congress Cataloging-in-Publication Data

Lamplighter, L. Jagi.
    Prospero regained / L. Jagi Lamplighter.—1st ed.
        p. cm.—(Prospero's daughter ; bk. 3)
    "A Tom Doherty Associates book."
    ISBN 978-0-7653-1931-9
    1. Prospero (Fictitious character)—Fiction.   2. Magicians—Fiction.
3. Hell—Fiction.   I. Title.
PS3612.A547435P79 2011
813'.6—dc23

2011024294

First Edition: September 2011

Printed in the United States of America

0 9 8 7 6 5 4 3 2 1

To Franchezzo and A. Farnese,
whomever you may be,
with much gratitude!

CONTENTS

PROSPERO REGAINED

Once More Back into the Swamp

"What we need now is a cheer weasel!" My brother Erasmus pulled his boot out of the thick ooze with a sucking *pop*. Mud spattered across his dark green breeches, his justacorps, and the hem of Mab's trench coat. Erasmus winced. "Sorry about that, Company Detective. This not-letting-go-of-each-other business makes things rather cramped." He lifted Mab's right hand, which he held in his own. "Still, beats being led astray by demonic illusions, I suppose."

"What in tarna . . ." Mab muttered in his Bronx accent. He glanced nervously at the infernal landscape that stretched around us in all directions: the dreary swamps, the cypresses dripping with dead moss, the lurid red sky, the Wall of Flame burning in the far distance. His left palm, slick with sweat, was slippery in my grasp. "What in Creation is a 'cheer weasel'?"

"It's something Mephisto says when people are glum: 'Nothing a good whack with a cheer weasel won't fix!' " Erasmus tentatively stepped onto a shaggy gray hummock. The lump of dead grass sank beneath his weight. Pulling his foot back, which now dripped with more goo, he made a face. "I have no idea if it's a modern pop-culture reference or an invention of my brother's deranged brain. Either way, I think I might benefit from a whack of the old cheer weasel about now. Might increase the appeal of being trapped in Hell, searching for my lost family members with my brother the former pope, an Aerie One trapped in a human body who thinks he's Humphrey Bogart, and the sister I hate."

"Not Bogart." Mab glanced up at his fedora—he would have pulled it low over his eyes, but he did not have a free hand. Under his breath, he muttered, "Well . . . maybe Philip Marlowe."

Erasmus, Mab, Gregor, and I moved slowly through the Swamp of Uncleanness—where dwelt the souls of those who had fallen prey to the sin of lust. Walking hand in hand was easy enough on a paved road. When the ground underfoot was spongy and sinking, it became both treacherous and aggravating, particularly for those of us who were in the middle. We could neither wipe sweat from our faces nor pinch our noses to block out the horrendous stench.

It was so hot here that steam rose from beneath our feet. Worse than the stench were the sinners themselves. Yet, we could not lower our eyes and ignore them, as if wearing imaginary blinders. Instead, we had to peer into every nook and cranny, searching for our missing brother.

And our presence here was entirely my fault.

On my other side, my brother Gregor stuck his staff, a length of ebony carved with blood red runes, under his arm, and gave my hand a comforting squeeze. His crimson cardinal's robes, with their billowing half cape, stood out against the landscape, a bright spot in the literally God-forsaken gloom.

For most of his life, Gregor had been a bulky, almost brutish, bully of a man, consumed by hatred, mainly toward the Protestants. Our youngest brother Ulysses, to save himself from the demon Abaddon, imprisoned Gregor for many years. Yesterday, we discovered this and rescued him. We found him a changed man. The new, more contemplative Gregor was slender. He had dark, shoulder-length wavy hair and a calm, almost saintly, expression. What sparked this change in Brother Gregor, we did not yet know. I had to admit to myself that I was curious about what had happened during his imprisonment to bring about this transformation. It had to be something more significant than losing four stone of weight.

Gregor slipped his arm up so that our elbows were hooked together. This freed his hands, which he cupped around his mouth with its close-trimmed black beard.

"Mephisto!" Gregor shouted for the umpteenth time. Lowering his hands, he spoke, his voice hoarse and breathy due to a magical mishap in his youth. "I do not see him anywhere. Are you certain he is here, Miranda?" Then, looking across the swamp, he called out again, "Mephisto! Mephistopheles Prospero!"

"No sign of him, Ma'am. I'm with Father Gregor, here. Are we sure this is where the Harebrain landed?" Mab muttered. His "this" sounded like "dis."

"In the vision the angel showed me, his besetting sin was lust." Sweat ran into my eyes. I blinked rapidly. The heat still was opressive, but the memory of the angel and the sense of peace she brought momentarily lifted my spirits.

"That means the Hellwinds would have dropped him here. So, he's here . . . somewhere. Unless he's found his way out on his own."

We glanced across the tremendous expanse of swamp that stretched out in every direction as far as the eye could see.

"It's hopeless," sighed Erasmus.

AROUND us, fetid quagmires, dotted by bracken-covered islands, stretched beneath a lurid sky crisscrossed with bands of steely gray. Souls damned for excessive lust floundered in the muck, crying out for succor—until they were dragged down by their more licentious compatriots. On the larger is-lands, groups of the damned engaged in massive orgies, resembling a battle more than any erotic acts. Others clambered onto smaller islands, upon which great corpulent demons disported with them. On one nearby isle, a six-horned demon whipped the damned until they dropped to their knees and performed acts of obscene obeisance.

The whole sordid scene, with its noxious gases that left the four of us reeling and retching, was made even worse because we now knew that the liquid in the swamp was not water but the accumulated drippings of the wanton desires of those on earth. Qualities that were merely spiritual upon the material plane had a physical nature here. Just the memory of having had to swim through the stuff left me queasy, and here I was, voluntarily walking into it again.

I would not have done it, not for any price, had there been another way to find my missing siblings and rescue our father. But there was not, and I could not leave my family stranded in Hell forever.

Gritting my teeth, I choked back my gag reflex and forced myself to scour the unseemly landscape, searching each passion-contorted face for the features of my brother Mephisto . . . the brother who held the crystal ball that could lead us to the others.

Beside me, Gregor bent his head in low, breathy prayer, "Lord Jesus, hear my prayer. Help us in our hour of need."

"Don't be ridiculous," Erasmus scoffed. He stood ankle deep in reddish mud waiting for the rest of us to jump onto the next hummock. His staff was strapped diagonally across his back. His Urim gauntlet hung on his belt. When we first set out, he had worn it in order to be ready in case of attack. But since he could not use the *Staff of Decay* while standing so close to the rest of us, he eventually decided there was no point in wearing the hot, un-yielding gauntlet. "God does not heed the prayers of those in Hell."

"Why shouldn't He heed ours?" I countered. "We are not damned. We're still alive."

"Gregor may not be damned," Erasmus granted, "but sisters who betray their family are another issue."

"I beg your pardon?"

"Surely you don't expect me to believe you summoned up the Hell-winds by mistake? I will remind you that Abaddon warned us there was a traitor in our family."

"Careful, Professor Prospero!" Mab jerked his head, trying to push back the brim of his fedora, which was now falling across his eyes. "It does not pay to listen to demons!"

"That's what you told us," Erasmus replied mildly, "right before your Miss Miranda, here, scattered our family to the four quarters of Hell. Or perhaps I should say, to the Nine Circles of Hell."

"It's not like she did it on purpose," Mab countered.

"I fear, Spirit Detective, my dear sister has deceived you as to her nature and intent. Either that, or you plotted with her." Erasmus turned his head and regarded our other brother through his lank dark hair. "Really, Gregor. Out of our whole family, the only other person you managed to save was Miranda? Couldn't you have given her a push and rescued someone worth-while?"

The terrible regret that had tormented me ever since I accidentally sum-moned up the Hellwinds, which caused us to lose six of my siblings—seven if one counted Caliban—gave way to wrath. Anger rushed through me like a tidal wave beating against an unprotected shore.

Surely, there was no one in all the world as horrible as Erasmus! It seemed a cruel irony that Theophrastus, whom I loved so dearly, had been ripped from my grasp and carried away, while Erasmus, of all people, had been saved.

Erasmus clearly felt the same way about me.

"I saved whomever I could," Gregor replied gravely. He nodded toward Mab and me, his silky black hair spilling over his crimson-clad shoulders. "Clearly the hand of Providence was upon us. Without Miranda, we would be lost. She is the only one who can see through the illusionary pleasure garden that lies over this Circle of Hell. It befuddles us whenever we are not touching her, leading us astray. Without her, we would have lost our way an hour ago."

"I like the pleasure garden," Erasmus grumbled. He released Mab's hand and gazed around at the alternate landscape. Mab quickly took the opportunity to use his free hand to adjust his hat and to wipe his face with a monogrammed handkerchief.

Erasmus smiled and drew a deep breath, as if inhaling fresh garden air. "It's pleasant, with cool fountains and dancing girls wearing veils and harem outfits. The air smells like . . ."—he sniffed again—"cherry petals."

I sighed, wishing that I, too, could experience that false utopia. I disliked the idea of volunteering to be fooled, but I was bone-weary and soul-tired. A few breaths of something that did not smell noxious—even if it *was* actually noxious—would have been a welcome relief.

But, it was not to be. I could not see the infernal illusions. I was not sure why, but I suspected that it had something to do with the two wings of emerald light—like impressionistic brushstrokes—that stretched from the shoulders of my enchanted tea gown. Perhaps, if I stripped off my emerald dress and donned a garment not steeped in protective enchantments, I, too, could have fallen prey to the deceits of Hell. But I was not about to pull off my gown in the midst of the prison for the torment of the overly lustful.

Besides, it was not in my nature to deliberately fool myself. I had not served Eurynome, the White Lady of Spiral Wisdom, for five hundred years, just to throw away all the wisdom I had learned for a few moments of relief.

The memories of my years as a Handmaiden to the Unicorn and of the reason for my having been demoted from those honored ranks returned to me. A tear trickled down my cheek, but I could not free my hand to wipe it away.

Erasmus grabbed Mab again, smiling regretfully. "The real picture is far less rosy, of course. What appears to be a fountain is actually oozing sewage. The dancing girl is a giant, bloated spider dripping with poison." He pointed at another island where a creature such as he described hung upon a gigantic web. "As to the smell . . ."—he started to sniff the real air and coughed, nearly gagging—"I will not even begin to elaborate."

"By Titania! Why a pleasure garden?" Mab scratched his eternal five o'clock shadow with the hand that clasped Erasmus's. "It makes no sense!"

"Wish I knew," Erasmus responded wistfully.

"Ma'am." Mab pointed my hand at the horizon. "What's that?"

In the distance, a single point of light shone above the swamp waters. Unlike the steely gray bands amidst the lurid reds of the sky, it was pure and silvery, like starlight. A spark of hope stirred within me, as if I beheld some fragile and heavenly thing that gave wings to my heart.

"Beware," Mab growled. "Could be a trick."

"It is no trick," Gregor replied. "It is holy."

"How could there be something holy in Hell?" Erasmus scoffed, peering into the gloom. "It's a will-o'-the-wisp, sent to lead us to our doom."

"We're already in Hell; how much more doomed could we be?" muttered Mab.

"There are worse places than this one." Erasmus kicked the water. It splashed thickly, clinging to his shoe like gelatin.

"It is a holy light," Gregor repeated, and he began to walk.

"How do you know?" asked Erasmus, as we waded back into the swamp, all still holding hands.

Gregor gave him a grave, contemplative look. "What worries me is how you could not know."

WARILY, we approached the tiny silver star, sometimes walking along narrow islets, sometimes wading through mud, sometimes swimming in the awful goop itself. The silvery light proved to be farther away than it had first looked. After a time, it winked out.

"Told you," Erasmus murmured, faintly amused. Gregor merely continued walking in the same direction.

The longer we walked, the heavier my heart became, until it seemed that my flagging spirits were physically dragging me deeper into the mire. I hated the putrid smell, the eerie green fires burning above the marshes, the gray light cast by the bands of steely luminescent clouds streaked across the ruddy skies, the acts of crudity taking place around us, all of which seemed to involve violence rather than pleasure. I, who so hated rapists—who had been robbed of all that was dearest to me by that violent crime—was trapped in the country of eternal rape. I felt like a claustrophobe whose path to salvation lay through a narrow closet the length of the Grand Canyon. I tried to avert my gaze, to look only at faces and not see what the bodies were doing, but it was a futile effort. Each time I failed, it was as if I came face-to-face again with the monster Osae and all that he had taken from me.

My fists clenched, making Mab and Gregor, whose hands I was holding, grunt in surprise. How it galled me to know that my attacker, this same Osae the Red, currently lay with his head resting upon the knee of Lilith, the demon Queen of Air and Darkness. She fed him dainty morsels from her own hand as a reward for his treatment of me—for having successfully robbed the Prospero Family of my Lady's counsel.

Without my Lady's help, how were we ever going to find Mephisto in this vast place?

But even that was easier to face than the question that truly worried me: what had happen to the others? Erasmus spoke the truth when he said that there were far worse places in Hell than this swamp. Where was Theo, and what awful torture was he suffering? And what condition would he be in when we found him?

To keep from dwelling on such painful matters, I let my mind roam, leaping from subject to subject. I considered briefly a dozen topics: the fate of my father, what was happening back on earth, how Prospero, Inc., was doing back home; et cetera. Eventually, all my thoughts drifted to the elf lord, Astreus Stormwind.

I pictured Astreus: his joyful triumphant laugh when I accepted the *Book of the Sibyl* from his hand; the outrage I had felt when he asked me to kill him and then would not explain himself; and the way his irises had burned with a golden fire when he admitted that, before the Fall, he had been an angel, and not just any angel but of the Eighth Choir of Cherubim. How eerie his gaze had been—that wild yet calculating fierceness—when we flew above his palace in Hyperboria, and he offered to drop me from a great height, so that, when my brains were dashed upon the ground, my soul might be sped upon its way to Heaven. Most of all, I recalled his parting words, as I stood before the storm playing my flute.

Because I would have my last memory be of the two things I most loved.

Surely, he did not mean me?

He was an elf. I was merely a mortal maid. Such a pairing was, in his own words, as likely as a hawk wedding a dove. He loathed me for being a slave owner because I would not break my magic flute and set free the Aerie Ones, Mab's race. He despised me so much for this—even though setting the Aerie Ones free would mean the death of millions of human beings—that he decided I was not worthy to slay him.

He could not have meant me.

If he did not, then to which two things did he refer: the sky and my flute? The sky and music?

The mere thought that he might have intended the words to include me caused my cheeks to burn. How foolish could I be? For five hundred years, I had remained distant, pure, and virginal. Osae the Red had seen to it that I was no longer the latter but that did not excuse a flurry of foolish girlish emotions. That I might allow myself to become enamored again, so soon after my humiliation at the hands of the fake Ferdinand—which led to Osea's attack, to the loss of my Lady's patronage and of the Water of Life that keeps my family immortal, and, ultimately, to the destruction of the Family Prospero and all that we stand for—was shameful.

Of course, the fake Ferdinand had actually been Astreus, too, but in his demonic guise.

My only consolation was that, since I would never see Astreus again, this foolishness would soon pass. Surely, the image of the smiling elf, currently constantly reoccurring in my thoughts, must have been caused by the influence of this swamp. As soon as we departed from this horrible place of torture for the lustful, my mind would grow calm again.

And yet, as I remembered the tone of his voice when he had spoken those parting words, an odd and glorious tingle spread through me that reminded me strangely of joy. It did much to drive back the gloom.

AHEAD stretched one last narrow island and then an expanse of oily murk dotted here and there by large rocks occupied by fat spiders or ugly lizards. A series of hummocks formed a bridge between our current location and this last isle. To cross them, we had to let go of each other and leap from one to another in single file.

My heart dropped at the thought that at the end of this next island, we would have to climb back into the swamp. I shivered at the memory of that awful slime oozing along my skin. Muttering darkly under my breath, I leapt onto a hummock that stood between me and the island, cursing when I slipped and landed hard on my knee. As my other leg dropped into the slimy mire, something snaked out of the water and grabbed it, dragging me backward into the mire.

Greasy ooze slid over my face and skin. Grasping hands reached underneath my gown, groping at my thighs and tugging at my underclothes. I twisted angrily, my motions made awkward by the viscous liquid, and kicked free.

Through the semitransparent murk, I faced three leering dead men. The damned souls grabbed at me hungrily. Something ugly burned in their dead eyes. Behind them, a fat, grinning demon floated naked in the filth. I averted my eyes at once, but the brief horrifying glimpse remained burned in my mind, causing me to squirm and retch.

The demon wielded a cat-o'-nine-tails, with which he scoured the men. Whenever they approached me, the demon trembled with pleasure. Whenever the men lost their grip on me, he hissed, dismayed. When he cracked his whip, the men convulsed, crying out with pain and greater hunger. This, too, caused the demon convulsions of pleasure.

They came at me from three sides, seeking to crush me between their naked bodies. I kicked and punched, struck at them with my four-foot-long pinewood flute—the same instrument that had so recently betrayed me by accidentally summoning the Hellwinds. I grabbed for my fighting fan, but the gunk around me kept drawing my shoulder bag away from my grasp, and I could not reach the weapon.

My attackers were weak, but my blows merely passed through them. Wherever the cloth of my enchanted emerald tea gown brushed them, however, they were repelled, making my elbows and knees better weapons than my fist or foot. As I turned, the mysterious winglike brushstrokes of emerald light coming from the shoulders of my dress touched the spirit-flesh of one of my attackers, causing him to reel back, screaming in pain.

I had a new weapon!

I spun about. The three men recoiled, their arms and faces burnt where my wings had caught them. Eagerly, I sought to take advantage of my momentary freedom and rise. My meager supply of air was nearly depleted. When I swam in the direction I thought was up, I found only more water and more copulating pairs, one or two of whom caught sight of my struggle and left their ravaged partners to pursue me.

Desperate for air, I circled in the murky slime, hoping for some glimpse of the lurid red of the sky. Spinning kept the damned souls at bay, for they quickly learned to fear the wings of emerald light, but out of the corner of my eye, I saw the demon itself approaching.

It floated forward, leering lasciviously. A twelve-foot tongue protruded from its wide mouth and snaked through the water. Slipping beneath my gown, the black tongue slithered up my stomach with its forked tip. I jerked backward, resisting the urge to cry out.

I turned to my Lady for help . . . but of course, She was no longer there.

The urge to scream grew stronger, but I dared not open my mouth. The memory of the taste—like fat drippings mixed with rotting corpses and feces—still filled me with horror.

Desperate, my heart pounding, I struck out. I struggled and swirled, badgering the crude horror with my wings. The glowing emerald light seared its skin as it had the dead men's, but this merely excited the demon. Again and again, it lashed out with its terrible whip, causing the dead souls to

twitch and dance. Despite the pain my wings had caused them, they clawed
at the slime to get back to where I swam, as if only by doing so could they
sate some terrible inner hunger that tormented them.

The curling tongue, prodding my flesh, sent shivers of revulsion across
my body. It triggered memories of Osae's attack. That, combined with lack
of oxygen, was too much. I panicked, thrashing wildly, my limbs flailing.
I was sure I was about to lose consciousness and die, drowned in the discarded sludge of human lusts.

In my delirium, I dreamt that Mab hovered above the demon's head, his
lead pipe rebounding off the creature's thick skull. Then everything went red,
and the demon's face twisted and decayed before my hallucinating eyes.

STRONG arms, unharmed by my wings, hauled me through the ooze.
Gasping, I kicked and punched, determined to win my way to freedom.
My elbow slammed into something, causing a loud crack and a scream.

Dumping me unceremoniously on the bracken, my brother Erasmus
howled with pain, holding his bloody nose. His humming staff fell to one
side, and all the bracken for ten feet in every direction turned gray and
withered away to dust. I quickly jumped away from where the *Staff of Decay*
buzzed unattended.

"You see what comes from helping her?" Erasmus shouted when he could
speak. "I told you we should have left her down there! Would have served her
right, ending her days as the doxy of a demon! She would have been following
in her dam's footsteps!"

Behind him, Mab and Gregor emerged from the swamp, dripping with
dead vegetable matter and scum. They both came over and touched me.
Gregor gagged and let go again. He tried to wipe off the scum he could not
see.

"Ugh, but that's foul!" Mab swore, squatting beside me. "Don't listen to
him, Ma'am. He didn't say any such thing—about leaving you in there, I
mean. He just screamed like a banshee and leapt right in after you."

"Oh, don't tell her that! It will go to her head," moaned Erasmus. He
gingerly poked the swollen bridge of his nose with his pinky fingers. "Well,"
he added presently, "I guess every cloud has its silver lining. When I came
out of that . . . stuff, I thought I would be ill again. But the pain in my nose
had put that entirely out of my mind."

"That was . . . horrible," I gasped for lack of a better word, shaking with
revulsion. Frantically, I brushed at my body, trying to rid myself of the

lingering goo. As I wrung the slime out of my hair, its shining black color gave me a shock. I had forgotten Erasmus had restored its original color. I had expected to see the silver-blond locks that had been mine for so many centuries.

Erasmus glanced over at me, his mouth and chin bloody, his eyes accusing.

"Thank you, Erasmus. You saved my life," I gushed, overwhelmed by gratitude for both my brothers and Mab. "I'm so very sorry about your nose. I thought you were another one of them."

I reached out to touch his arm as I talked, but he pushed me away.

"Humph!" Turning his back, my brother used his white Urim gauntlet, which had once been part of an angel's armor, to pick up the humming length of his staff. The gauntlet would not wither, though it was pitted and dull. All other Urim I had ever seen shone like living moonlight. Once back in Erasmus's hand, the *Staff of Decay* stopped its deadly humming. Its whirling gray length slowed and fell still, becoming a long, rectangular staff, the sides of which were painted alternately black and white.

"Don't know what possessed me," Erasmus continued. "Amazingly stupid idea, traveling around here with a woman. What were we thinking? We should have left her on the bridge, taken our chances without her."

"We would never find Mephistopheles that way," Gregor observed. "We would have been sucked in by some pleasant-looking evil, or perhaps walked right past him, his face hidden from us behind a dream."

"True," Mab said, mopping his craggy brow. "When she fell in, everything turned nice again. Made it kind of hard to find the baddies who were attacking her. I had to bonk a dapper gentleman in a tuxedo on the head with my trusty lead pipe, and punch right in their kissers a couple of swains, who were offering her flowers and chocolates."

"Dapper gentleman!" I cried. "That horrible bloated . . . well, on second thought, maybe it's better you didn't see it." I shivered again, suddenly cold.

"Wish it could have been me instead of you who saw him, Ma'am," Mab replied humbly.

"We won't find Mephisto this way either," Erasmus complained. "All this walking around on the surface. We're only seeing a small percentage of this place. When we first came through the gate, it seemed to Miranda as if we were under the swamp, slime and ooze in all directions. What if Mephisto is down there, like the things that tried to drag her into the depth? We'll never find him if we're up here!"

"What else can we do?" I countered. "Without Mephisto, we can't rescue any of the others."

"So that's it." Erasmus plopped down and folded his arms behind his head. "This is how I shall end my days, slogging through the Swamp of Uncleanness, searching aimlessly for my brother who had the Ball of Getting-Us-the-Hell-Out-of-Hell, in the company of the sister I hate more than any other—whose fault it is we're stuck here to begin with—until I die, most likely from complications stemming from an infected broken nose. Appropriate way to go, I suppose, killed by Miranda."

"Enough." Gregor's head had been bowed in prayer. Now, he straightened, his voice calm yet stern. "We are in Hell, Brother, where the malicious burn upon the fires of their wrath and envy. One might hope their example would teach you civility."

"I have proven remarkably hard to teach," Erasmus replied blithely.

"That is not a trait of which I would boast," Gregor said, his voice again stern.

Much to my surprise, Erasmus looked chagrined.

"You're probably right," he murmured, wiping his face on his sleeve. The red of his blood showed brightly against the subdued landscape. From the left, there came a *kerplunk,* as if something large had slid into the water.

Mab frowned. "There are things down here that feed on blood. Wraiths, demons, and servants of demons! Vile things! Maybe we'd better get moving!"

Hopping back across the hummocks, he stooped and picked up his fedora. Apparently, he had thrown it aside when he leapt in to save me. Frowning down at the water, to make certain no demon waited to grab his foot, he hopped back.

We held hands again and started walking, slower than before. We were thirsty and tired. It was hot here, and it stank. The vile acts and general repulsiveness worsened as we continued. Demons, some hideous, some gorgeous to behold, moved among the damned souls, inciting them to yet greater excesses. Nearby, an emaciated man moaned pitifully as he tried to sate some burning hunger upon a fat lizard.

In the distance rose a vast cylindrical tower with a round mushroom-like cap, constructed from something living that writhed and squirmed. I decided not to examine it any more closely, but Erasmus did and, apparently, regretted it. With a grunt of sympathetic pain, he drew his legs together and cupped his free hand protectively over his groin.

"Oh, that's ghastly!" he said.

"Don't look, Ma'am," Mab advised. "It's not a sight for ladies."

"Nothing here is fit for ladies." Gregor's voice sounded even more gravelly than usual.

"Good thing our dear sister isn't one," Erasmus replied, a note of cheerfulness in his weary voice. When Gregor gave him a quelling look, he pointed at his swollen nose with his free hand. "Would a lady do this?"

"No true lady yields her virtue without a fight." Gregor used his ebony staff as a walking stick, swinging it, planting it, striding forward, and swinging it again. Its blood red runes glittered eerily as it swung.

"But our good sister already lost her virtue to a demon," objected Erasmus. "Why bring my nose into it?"

"It was an accident," I snapped back, more harshly than I had intended. "I already apologized. No one 'brought your nose into it.' At the time, I thought you were a demon."

"A likely story," muttered Erasmus.

Gregor halted and leaned heavily upon his staff. With his free hand, he wiped sweat from his face. "Is it my imagination, or have we been walking for hours?"

"Certainly seems like hours," replied Mab.

"We must rest," Gregor said. "We cannot continue as we are."

EVENTUALLY, we found refuge on a sandy flat isle that to me seemed completely exposed, but which my brothers and Mab, when they released my arms, assured me was surrounded by high arbors of black roses.

"Does anyone have something to eat?" Erasmus asked sadly. "The food I brought has been ruined by the swamp."

I looked through the contents of my shoulder bag, but swamp water had soaked through it. Nothing remained edible. I carefully wiped off my mirrored fighting fan, my figurine of Astreus, and my tightly sealed vial of Water of Life. A wistful action really; the bag would probably just get drenched again the next time we started moving.

To my great dismay, I discovered that the silver and horn circlet Father Christmas had given me was gone. With it, I could return Astreus's memory to him. Apparently, it had fallen out of my bag during the fray. That meant it now lay at the bottom of the Swamp of Uncleanness, if there was a bottom. If not, it drifted ever downward and, with it, my hope of ever seeing Astreus again.

For without it, even if the elf lord still lingered somewhere within the sooty depths of the demon Seir of the Shadows, I would never know.

Mab's food had fared better than the rest of ours. From the pockets of his trench coat, he pulled a number of Ziploc bags. Inside the sealed plastic, his bread and cheese was squashed but fresh. He shared the food among us. Hungry as we were, neither Erasmus nor I could bring ourselves to eat much. Erasmus shared some fresh water from a canteen.

"I'll never look at another woman again," murmured Erasmus. He was lying down with his head resting on some object that was invisible to me, so that his head seemed to be floating in mid-air. He covered his eyes with his hands. "Ever! My womanizing ways are a thing of the past! Oh, to think . . . ugh!"

"If you had not done so previously, you would not be in such a sorry state," Gregor observed. "I find the place no more wearing than any other unpleasant location."

Erasmus raised his head. His eyes glittered black with malice. "Forgive me if I don't happen to be a priest, a spirit, or an ex-virgin whose only experience with love has been demon-rape. Some of us are men and must live like men."

"And shall suffer, after death, like unto what you call 'men,'" Gregor thundered back in his preaching-from-the-pulpit voice, steady yet booming. "Had you chosen a virtuous life, you would not now be obliged to pay the wages of sin."

"Oh, and you'll do so well when we come to the country of one of your besetting sins, will you?" Erasmus snapped.

"The angel said Gregor was closest of all of us to overcoming his vice," I offered, my spirits again buoyed by the mere memory of the angelic encounter.

"You would come in on his side." Erasmus closed his eyes and let his head drop back until it again rested upon his invisible pillow. "You shouldn't have repeated that where Brother Gregor could hear you—the pride it engenders will mar his good record."

"He is right." Gregor nodded. "Pride is a difficult enemy to defeat, and those who succumb to it suffer in a far lower place than this."

Looking around, it was hard to imagine that there were places worse than this. But that was where my sins would have dragged me, to the place where pride was punished. I shivered, suddenly extraordinarily grateful for Gregor and his staff.

Erasmus looked out over the swamp, staring out at the dead cypress trees dripping with slimy gray moss. He murmured again, "It's hopeless."

"Rest, Brother." Gregor's voice was gentle despite its gruffness. "Let us examine the matter again when we are rested."

"Very well." He shut his eyes. "I'll rest, rise, and look forward to another day of looking for Mephisto on an empty stomach. We'll be lucky if we don't draw the attention of the other Mephistopheles with all this shouting . . . the demonic one."

Mab and I exchanged glances, but neither of us had the strength to speak, much less to explain to my brother that there was no other Mephistopheles, just our brother, the demon. Besides, we did not know how Gregor, the Catholic priest, would take it.

We took turns sleeping. For a time, the horrors of Hell were replaced by the terrors of nightmares. I awoke, sweating, to find reality worse than my dream, and sat, alone in the sweltering heat, in the squalor and stink of Hell.

Mab sat up suddenly. "Look, Ma'am! Our holy star is back!"

It was, and much closer now. Rousing the others, we had a brief discussion about what to do next. Erasmus and Mab were still wary of the star, and after my recent encounter, I was as well, but Gregor continued to insist that the light was holy. He started toward it, walking with long strides, and the rest of us were forced to abandon him or follow.

Pushing onward, we soon came upon a wide flat area, rather like a beach. There, we saw a strange sight.

The Late Lord of Arden

A robed figure stood upon the beach, his face hidden by a voluminous hood. Seated about him were two men and a woman, whose decrepit garments dripped with swamp scum, as if they had just come from the sludge. The woman wept joyfully; the men's faces showed wonder, gratitude, and weary relief.

The figure's arm was outstretched. Upon his palm rested a point of pure silvery light, like a tiny star.

We approached cautiously. It was pleasant to step onto that beach. The sand, though it sank slightly beneath our steps, was firm and solid compared to the spongy hummocks and squishy swamplands through which we had been trudging. The air was still hot enough to make sweat drip down the back of my neck, but the heat seemed less oppressive. The constant moaning of tortured souls sounded muted and far away. Nearby, frogs croaked in a stagnant pool.

I had to give Gregor this much. The star certainly did not feel wicked.

Coming closer, we could see more of the hooded figure. A golden belt encircled his waist, and emblazoned in matching gold on the left sleeve of his deep blue robe was an anchor, a star, and the words: HOPE IS ETERNAL.

"That's not something you see every day . . . in Hell," murmured Erasmus.

The robed figure reached up and pushed back his hood, revealing a young man with a dark curling forelock above slender Merovingian features. As the light of the silvery star fell upon his face, Erasmus shouted with joy. Letting go of Mab, he ran toward him.

"Malagigi!"

"Could it be?" I whispered, surprised.

"Maugris!" Gregor growled in his low, gravelly voice. He leaned upon

his staff, his brow narrowing with disapproval. Upon his face, his new serenity warred with his lifelong disapproval of practitioners of black magic.

"Uh . . . Mala-who-ha?" Mab mopped his face with his handkerchief.

"Maugris d'Aygremont, an unsavory sorcerer of the worst ilk," Gregor
replied. Tightening his grip on my hand, my brother stepped forward, so
that he stood protectively between Malagigi and me. "It does not surprise
me to meet his sort in Hell."

Mab released my other hand and trudged forward until he came up
beside Erasmus. Pushing back the brim of his fedora, he peered carefully
into the face of the man carrying the shining star. The Frenchman gave
him a welcoming smile and a little shrug before turning his attention to
Gregor.

"Ah, *oui,* Brother-in-Law. Still angry about my not being good enough
for your twin, hmm?" Malagigi said, for I saw now that it really was him—
either that or a shade had assumed his semblance. He looked much as I recalled from the last time I had seen him, at the Eighteenth-Century
Centennial Ball. The Centennial Ball was an event where all the Earth's
immortals gathered to dance and swap news. As the name implied, it was
held once a century.

Malagigi still had the slight mustache that emphasized the smiling lips
that had once talked my sister Logistilla into marrying him. No wonder
Gregor had not been happy to see him. Gregor had always been extremely
protective of his twin sister. Apparently, that had not changed.

"But I assure you, Père Gregor," he continued, graciously acknowledg-
ing Gregor's religious rank, "three years as a boar taught me a great deal. As
for who I am"—he made Mab a flourishing bow—"I am Malagigi of the
Brotherhood of Hope, formerly a Sorcerer of the land now called France
where I once was the lord of a forest called Arden."

"Ah . . ." Mab looked through his notebook, carefully pulling apart the
wet pages and peering at the blurred ink. He frowned at it in dismay. "Ah,
right . . ." Finding what he wanted, he tapped his finger against the soggy
paper. "You're one of 'Charlemagne's Brood,' the magicians who helped the
French sack Milan in 1499, driving Prospero and his children—including
Miranda and Erasmus here—out of their ancestral home."

"*Vraiment.* It is very true!" Malagigi's mouth curled with amusement at
the old nickname.

"You had a brother named Eliaures, who specialized in making sticks turn
into snakes," Mab read from his notes, "and three sisters: Alcina, Falerina, and

Melusine. The last one, Melusine, was your half sister, who sometime had a serpent's tail instead of legs, if I recall."

"But, of course! That is quite accurate, though I'm not sure I would say Eliaures specialized in turning sticks into snakes," Malagigi corrected. "Making men believe that sticks had turned into snakes—poisonous snakes. So that they died from their own fear. Now *that* was one of his tricks!"

Gregor released my hand and clasped it again. He did this twice more before inclining his head toward me and whispering, "No pleasure garden. The silvery light must dispel the illusion. Did I not tell you it was holy?"

"How did a holy thing come to be in this place?" I whispered back to him.

Gregor shook his head. "That I cannot fathom. Perhaps Erasmus is right about it being a trick, like the light of an angler fish, held out to lure us in. Though, that Maugris can hold it is a promising sign—he cannot be all wicked and bear such as that. Still, I remain suspicious of his motives."

"Who are these people?" Erasmus regarded the three dripping souls of the dead who crouched upon the beach before us.

"Erasmus! How amazing that it is really you!" The Frenchman threw out his arms. "I would not have thought lust to be your sin. Or are you here with us?"

The two men tried to embrace, but Erasmus's hands passed through the other man's body. Malagigi, on the other hand, was able to touch Erasmus's enchanted garments. Thus, they were able to give each other an awkward hug.

"*Sacrebleu!*" Malagigi cried, repeatedly poking his finger through Erasmus's face. My brother tried to fend off the immaterial hand and failed. Malagigi poked through both his hand and his swollen nose. "You are still alive! What are you doing here?"

"I could ask you the same thing," Erasmus replied. Next to the neatly groomed monk, my brother looked bedraggled, his dark hair, damp with sweat, lanker than usual as it fell across his eyes. His handsome jacket and waistcoat were so muddy that I could hardly make out that they had once been green. "I remember quite clearly that you cleaned up your act with women after your marriage to my sister resulted in you spending a year as a goat or a moose or something . . ."

"Boar. Did I not mention having been turned into a boar, only moments ago? Really, Erasmus, you should be more attentive!"

"Must be the shock of seeing you," Erasmus replied blithely, his spirits clearly lifting. "I have a living body to worry about, after all."

"True. And your nose! It looks awful! No wonder you are distracted. With your nose puffed up like a baguette!"

"My red badge of courage." Erasmus tapped his nose and winced. He shot me a withering look. "As I was saying, by the time you lost your head to Madame la Guillotine, you were rather respectable in the passion department. Shouldn't that have put you in another borough, so to speak?"

Any remark Malagigi might have made was lost as Gregor strode up and fixed his penetrating gaze upon him. My brother the former pope made an imposing figure with his dark hair flowing upon the shoulders of his crimson robes and the *Staff of Darkness* in his hand.

"You said 'Are you here with us'?" Gregor asked hoarsely. "Who is 'us'?"

"The angels," whispered the woman who sat upon the sand at Malagigi's feet.

"But no! The Brotherhood of Hope," Malagigi corrected the woman quickly. He gave her a smile that was both charming and kind. "We are not angels—*pas du tout*! We are fellow travelers hoping to make our way to a better place. Angels are creatures of pure spirit, beings of light whose very presence heralds Heaven. Where they step, the world recalls God's holiness and rejoices.

"Even here, in the Uttermost Pit, the footsteps of angels bring blessings. It is said that the King of the Angels, our Lord, once harrowed Hell with the Angelic Host at his side, and that if you can find their footsteps and walk where these blessed ones walked, you can follow them out of Hell, and no demon can touch you while you tread therein. Of course, one must have love in one's heart to see the footstep of an angel.

"As for us," Malagigi continued more humbly, "we of the Brotherhood of Hope are sinners like yourself, trying to earn our way up Mount Purgatory by doing good deeds. You may think of us as the angels' lowly helpers, if you wish." Turning to Gregor, Malagigi concluded, "Did I not say, when I introduced myself to this man in the hat, that I was with the Brotherhood of Hope. Really, you sons of Prospero do not listen. You should attend to your surroundings."

I came forward. "You're helping the angels harrow Hell? Do they come regularly? Or was that just that once, two thousand years ago?"

I recalled Ferdinand's story of having been turned to stone before the

City of Dis and later rescued by angels. Ferdinand had proved a fake but that did not mean that there were not elements of truth to the story the incubus Seir of the Shadows had told while he was impersonating my long dead love. As Mab had pointed out, demons often wove truth in among their lies to make them more believable.

Malagigi turned to greet me and froze, his eyes widening slowly in amazed joy. Crying out, he threw himself down on the sand and hid his face, though the hand with the tiny star still held it steadily before of him. The three shades also scuttled backward, bowing until their faces were pressed against the beach.

"An angel," breathed Malagigi. "A real angel!"

I spun around, but there was nothing behind me except gloom and marsh. The frogs croaked loudly.

Turning back, I found Erasmus covering his face in mock shame. "Please get up. That is not an angel. It is just my sister. She has a . . . a magic dress."

Oh. I had forgotten about the wisps of emerald light coming from my shoulders. In the silvery light of the star, their glow was less prominent.

Malagigi remained kneeling, but he tilted his head to allow himself to squint up at me, his eyes narrowing thoughtfully. "Psst. Erasmus, this is not my beloved Shrew. Is she the Icicle or a new one?"

Chuckling, I extended my hand to help him rise. "The Icicle. Nowadays, people just call me Miranda."

"'O brave new world, that has such people in't,'" Malagigi quoted, laughing. He reached up but his hand passed through mine. Smiling ruefully, he rose under his own power and bowed over my hand, his dancing eyes examining my face. "We've met before, only your hair was different . . . like ice."

Erasmus shaded his eyes and turned away, as if he was too embarrassed to glance in our direction. "How can you even look at a woman after seeing this place, much less kiss her hand? Aren't you afraid of ending up here, Man?"

"Damned for kissing a hand? Which—as you have witnessed—I did not do." Malagigi raised a chiseled eyebrow. "Nonsense. Seen a bit too much of this place, have you, *mon ami*? Here, hold the star. You will feel better." He moved quickly to Erasmus's side and, holding his hand above Erasmus's, slid the tiny silver light onto my brother's palm.

"I say," breathed Erasmus, as he watched the tiny star of hope glitter on his outstretched hand. "That's . . ."

"Refreshing?" Malagigi suggested. "But, of course! What a tale you four must have to tell! But first, let me speak with my new friends and send them on their way." He turned to the other three, who were still cowed on the ground, gazing at me in mingled awe and fear. Helping them up, he said, "You are free to go. If you wish to escape from this place, you can only do so by helping others. Anyone who can see you and who can see the truth of his or her own condition is a candidate for rescue. But do not waste your strength trying to help those who cannot see you or who do not ask for help. They are not ready yet and will only cause you grief."

"Is there nothing we can do to repay you, Gracious Monk?" asked one of the men as he rose.

"Pray for me." Malagigi lowered his head and pressed his hands together. "We all benefit from prayer."

Behind him, I could see Gregor's shoulders relax. Apparently, Malagigi's piousness assuaged my brother's skepticism. He nodded his head in approval as he leaned upon his staff, at peace again.

"We will pray!" one of the men promised.

Malagigi helped the woman to her feet, and the three spirits of the dead departed together, each helping the other two along. Turning, Malagigi clasped Erasmus's enchanted sleeve, laughing.

"I hate to break up this nice reunion," growled Mab, "but decent folk like Mr. Theophrastus may be burning as we speak." Mab wiped his brow with his handkerchief then tipped his bedraggled hat toward Malagigi. "Begging your pardon, Harrower, but we're looking for a guy who's down here somewhere." He gestured vaguely at the swamps and mires. "Any chance you could help us find him?"

"Is he alive like you?" When Erasmus nodded, Malagigi chuckled. "That should be easy. Wait a moment, while I ask."

Malagigi bowed his head and knelt in prayer. A hush fell over the little beach. Gregor shifted his weight and prayed as well. Gregor praying was a common sight, but it was a bit odd to see the dashing French enchanter petitioning the Lord so humbly.

Looking up presently, Malagigi said, "But of course! Your brother, Mephistopheles! The Greatest Swordsman in Christendom! He is this way. Follow me!"

MALAGIGI led us across the beach and onto a thin causeway that looped in and out of the many islands within the swamp. The sights and smells were as awful as before, but they seemed less onerous in the company of the Brotherhood of Hope. Malagigi insisted each of us should take a turn holding the star. So, after a time, Erasmus reluctantly slipped the silvery light to me. The shining silvery point began to sink through my hand, but I found that if I concentrated, I could keep it upon my palm. Despite its brightness, it felt cool and refreshing. A feeling of hope suffused my limbs and buoyed my spirits. For the first time since my Lady's departure, I felt whole.

WE followed Malagigi and came to a gray, weathered dock that protruded over the swamp. A gondola was moored beside it, the rope creaking as the craft moved with the current. Its bottom was wider and flatter than the gondolas I remembered from Venice, but it had the same high, curled *dolfin* and *risso* rising up at the bow and stern respectively. Malagigi unhooked a long pole-oar that hung on one of the pylons and stepped onto the boat.

"Are you sure this will hold us? We're not dead, you know." Erasmus prodded the gondola with his foot. It pushed out away from the dock and then drifted back. Erasmus put his hand on my arm and squinted, checking to see if the vessel changed its nature, if anything he was seeing were illusionary. Apparently, it stayed the same.

"But of course, I know you are not dead! Unlike some people, I attend!" Malagigi jumped onto the gondola and gestured for us to follow. "This boat is made from wood that grows here. You can touch it for the same reason that you walk on this island or swim in the waters."

"That's not very reassuring," Mab grumped. He stared dubiously at the boat . "It's not going to suddenly turn on us, like those mangrove trees, is it?"

Malagigi chuckled. "Ran into those, did you? But surely you knew enough to remain calm, yes? Nothing in Hell can hurt you, so long as you remain calm. Trap you, yes, but not harm you. If you give in to passion, though— anger, fear, lust—then you become vulnerable, and . . . well, Heaven help you!"

"Is that why I can't touch you, but the men in the swamp were able to grab my foot—because I was annoyed?" I waved my hand through Malagigi's shoulder as I stepped lightly onto the gondola. It bobbed but held my weight.

"Anger gives them power over you." Malagigi supported my elbow as I boarded, resting his fingers on my satiny sleeve. "Also, apparently, they can touch your magic dress, yes?"

"As you see." I smiled and sat down on a low flat bench.

"Fear makes us vulnerable, then?" Gregor asked.

"Really, you do not attend! I already mentioned fear." Malagigi *tsked* as he politely moved backward to allow Gregor to step aboard, his scarlet robes swirling about him. "Though a little healthy apprehension is allowable."

"Good safety tip," murmured Erasmus. The boat moved unsteadily when he boarded. He sat down quickly. Mab followed him and sat beside me.

"Let me see if I understand the system," Mab said. "Anything we do that demonstrates that we believe the dangers going on around us are real—like feel afraid—sucks us in and makes us vulnerable?"

"Exactly." Malagigi twisted a finger through his forelock. "As long as we remain aloof, we are safe from the dead. Nothing here can harm us. But if we allow ourselves to be tempted or cowed, we are dragged down to their level and can fall under their power. This includes anger and fear, but also eating, drinking, or even accepting rest . . . of course, this applies to us Brotherhood brethren. I am not sure about you living folk. The shades of the dead will not be able to harm you if you are peaceful, but there may be other things here that are more dangerous to living flesh."

"You mean like giant spiders and demons with pitchforks?" I asked, thinking of some of the horrors we had encountered before we were scattered.

Malagigi nodded, adding enigmatically, "Among other things."

"So the dead cannot hurt us if we are calm, but with demons all bets are off?" Erasmus clarified.

"Exactly." Malagigi bowed and extended his hand, as if handing Erasmus a diploma.

We pushed off into the swampy river, Malagigi poling us past swirling clumps of long reed that seemed to reach for us as we sailed near them. Dead cypresses rose from the water, and a lone fig tree stood desolate, leaves gray, branches devoid of fruit. The stink of dead vegetation was everywhere.

"Christ sent that one down here," Malagigi commented as we poled by the fig tree. "Got impatient with it for not producing fruit. Pointed his finger at it and, *zup*, it appeared here."

"And this is that *very* fig tree?" Gregor shot to his feet and leaned over to get a better look at the tree, causing the craft to rock violently.

"It was but a little joke," Malagigi apologized with a shrug, as he tried valiantly to steady us with his pole-oar. Gregor did not look amused, but he resumed his seat.

"SO, you were the Lord of Ardennes! I don't think I knew that, Malagigi," Erasmus mused. He was leaning over the edge, poking at things beneath the water with his staff. He had taken his dull and pitted Urim gauntlet from his belt and donned it rather than hold the staff in his bare hand.

"Ah, that was long, long ago, long before you were born, *mon ami*."

"Ardennes?" Mab opened his notebook, made a face at the soggy paper, and closed it again. "I thought you said the Forest of Arden."

"Arden. Ardennes." Malagigi shrugged. "They are both the same."

"Long before I was born?" Erasmus objected. "I am over five hundred!" He smirked. "I have the wisdom born of age."

"I was older than that when we took Milan. I had passed my seventh century," Malagigi replied. "So, do not speak to me of wisdom born of age! Recall that I was the son of Charlemagne, who ruled until the year 814. Really, you Prosperos have no proper sense of history. Most likely, you did not attend your instructors as children."

"Either that, or the *Orbis Suleimani* mucked with the facts," Mab muttered.

Malagigi continued. "As I said, it was long ago. Back in the days when faeries still ruled much of the earth." He poled us forward, gazing off into the distance, his hood still resting on his shoulders. "My mother, Morgana La Fay, ceded part of the faery forest of Broceliande to my control. I lived there, bespelling rogues and raising unnaturally wise horses."

"Raised horses, did you?" Mab commented. "Something you have in common with Miss Logistilla."

"Ah . . . Logistilla! Her eyes! Her thighs!" Malagigi threw up a hand as if to ward off Gregor's frown of brotherly disapproval. "No disrespect intended! Ours was a love that was not meant to last. She found me a bore and decided that form should follow function."

Erasmus snorted with amusement, and even Gregor shook his head ruefully.

Malagigi continued, "Still, many lessons did I learn during my sylvan apprenticeship. The enchanted horses I raised after my indentureship as a beast of the wood made the wise Bayard look as ignorant as a babe . . . but, alas, the age of knighthood had passed, and there was no one to ride my fair steeds to fame, as my cousin Renaud once did. Instead, my noble steeds lived and died on some French battlefield amidst a thousand other steeds. The days of enchanted horses and magical swords had passed.

"But what days those were!" Malagigi gazed off into the distance, as if he could see through time to an earlier age. "Days of magic and fire, not as they are remembered now in history books. What fine beasts, my horses." He turned to Erasmus. "Do you know your uncle Antonio had one of my horses? A distant descendant of Veillantif, one of my finest. He rode it the day we sacked Milan?"

"The day he died," Erasmus murmured.

Malagigi shrugged again. "That was not the fault of my steed." He was silent a moment and then added, "Antonio hungered after our magic like a dog after his master's bone. He had no powers of his own but claimed the secrets he had once possessed that had been stolen from him. Perhaps, he lied, and yet . . . in life, I walked paths no one else could walk and spoke to spirits who would speak only to me . . . but Antonio, he knew things even I had never heard tell of! A charming man, he was, too. To hear it from him, he was innocent, and it was your father who was in the wrong."

"Poor Uncle Antonio. I wonder what became of him," mused Erasmus.

"He is here." Malagigi spread an arm indicating Hell. "Not in the swamp, but lower."

"He is?" we cried.

"Two times I have spoken to him," Malagigi said. "The first time was when I was newly a shade. The second time was after I had joined the Brotherhood of Hope. I found him enthroned in some infernal palace and urged him to repent and come away with me. But he would not listen. He said . . ."—Malagigi shrugged his shoulders. "Eh . . . he was too caught up in the illusion of his past to come away."

Erasmus frowned down at his hands. I recalled his fondness for our uncle and how it had been Erasmus who found Uncle Antonio when the latter was dying upon the battlefield—Antonio, who confessed to Erasmus that he had killed my first love, Ferdinand.

I recalled, as well, how earlier the same day, upon that battlefield in Milan, Uncle Antonio had accused Father of robbing a sacred library. After centuries of maligning him, I now had to admit that my uncle had been telling the truth. Father had stolen the enchanted tomes from the *Orbis Suleimani*. Apparently, most of Antonio's magic had depended upon those books, even as ours now depended upon the staffs into which the books had been transformed.

Only, thanks to Seir of the Shadows, I now knew that each of those
volumes had contained a demon bound within its pages, the same demons
that now were bound within my brothers' and sister's staffs.

That the incubus Seir was actually Lord Astreus, who had been tithed
to Hell by Queen Maeve for helping my brother Mephisto, I pushed from
my mind. I could not allow my thoughts to dwell upon the elf lord again
while I remained in this horrible swamp.

Seir of the Shadows claimed that my father and Antonio had been
about to set the nine great demons free, when Father suffered a change of
heart. Rather than release the demons that King Solomon had so carefully
bound, my father stole the books and fled into exile, taking my infant self
with him . . .

. . . Or so I had thought, until Mephisto revealed I was the daughter of
the wizened old witch Sycorax, Caliban's mother, and not of Father's beloved wife, Lady Portia. So, apparently, I joined Father later, once he was
already living on Prospero's Island.

Father's journal suggested that he had a supernatural ally in these matters, a "Fair Queen" whom he called "M." This woman may have helped
him escape with the magical, demon-infused tomes. My great fear was that
"M" stood for Maeve, the Queen of the Elves—because I now knew that
Maeve was merely a disguise of Lilith, the Queen of Air and Darkness, one
of the Seven Rulers of Hell.

If Father's "Fair Queen" was Lilith, what did that suggest about Father's
motives? Was he an accomplice, robbing the *Orbis Suleimani* of the demon
tomes to help the Queen of Air and Darkness carry out her evil plans? Or
had he been tricked by the Elf Queen, believing her to be only whom she
appeared to be?

Could Father be our traitor? That made no sense, since he was the one
who had been captured, and whom we had come to rescue. Was it possible
that he had not been captured at all, but had merely led us into Hell to our
doom? No, the idea was ridiculous. If Father wished to destroy us, he could
have merely asked us to walk into Hell, and we all would have gathered our
things and gone. There would have been no need for all this rigmarole.

No, Father could not be a traitor!

Besides, if Father were the traitor, he would have let the demons go,
rather than bind them into staffs and guard them for five hundred more
years. More likely, Mab was right, and Abaddon, Angel of the Bottomless
Pit, was lying. There was no traitor.

The very fact that, after five centuries, Father had never freed the demons, cut against my theory about the identity of "M." This thought lifted my spirits, until I recalled what Mab had said about demons disliking each other. Perhaps, the Queen of Air and Darkness wished to keep these nine great demons imprisoned so as to increase her own glory. Or, perhaps, she wanted them in our hands. According to the essays in Father's journal, exposure to infernal influences warped the human soul. Perhaps, Lilith believed that if the Family Prospero, the Heirs of Solomon and the Defenders of the Earth, were constantly in the presence of these demonic influences, the ill we would do, even involuntarily, would be greater than what these demons might achieve on their own, were they free.

All this was speculation. Much as I would have appreciated Mab's input and that of my brothers, I did not feel an open gondola in the middle of the Swamp of Uncleanness was the proper place to discuss these matters. Father had kept all this secret for so long, it would be foolish of me to blurt it out where random demons might overhear us without first learning his reasons for secrecy.

Malagigi yelped and pointed at Erasmus's sword belt. He leaned forward eagerly. "What is this? Is that not *Durandel,* the unbreakable sword of Orlando?" He tossed back his head, laughing aloud. "Legends still live!"

Malagigi turned to Mab. "Do you know *Durandel*? What a sword! Forged by fairies, they say. It once cut a pass through the Pyrenees! Originally, it was the sword of Hector of Troy, that noble knight who was slain by the deceitful Greeks. Hector's mother threw it into the sea after he was slain, but when Roland, Orlando as you call him, needed a blade, I called up a mermaid to fetch it and bring it to him."

"I thought you gave him the sword you won from the Saracen admiral, the flaming sword," I said.

"*Flamberge*? But no! I gave *Flamberge* to my cousin Renaud." Malagigi smoothed his mustache. "But enough ancient history. How is Logistilla?"

We glanced at one another.

"We don't know," Erasmus said bluntly.

"Oh?"

"Our sister, here"—Erasmus gestured at me—"summoned up the Hellwinds and scattered our brothers and sister across the length and breadth of Hell."

"But why?" Malagigi gazed at me in astonishment.

"It was an accident," I explained stiffly, as a fresh burst of resentment toward Erasmus assailed me. "I didn't intend to call the Hellwinds. I just . . ." I hefted my four-foot pinewood flute and let my arm fall again. "I just played my flute."

"She says that now," Erasmus murmured, "but we have been told that there is a traitor in the family, and Miranda is the only one who fits the bill."

"Professor Prospero," Mab growled, "I told you not to put any faith in what Abaddon said. He's a *demon*!"

"But you said yourself that these predictions often have some truth in them," Erasmus countered.

Gregor leaned forward. "Isn't it more likely that Abaddon meant Ulysses? The Angel of the Bottomless Pit thought I was dead. He must have believed Ulysses was loyal to him."

"Ulysses?" asked Malagigi.

"Our youngest brother." Erasmus explained. "Born after your death. He fell into the clutches of Abaddon, who ordered him to harm our family, to ensorcell Theophrastus, to kill Gregor . . ."

"To make sure that Gregor was no longer 'a living man upon the earth.'" Mab read from his waterlogged notebook.

"So, Ulysses got Logistilla to turn Gregor here into a panther; he remained that way for eighty some years," Erasmus finished.

"Actually, I spent the last few decades in an underground bunker on Mars," Gregor interjected.

"Mars?" Malagigi looked up, though only lurid reds and clouds of steely gray were overhead. "Upon a spot of light gleaming in the night sky?"

"That's why I left the Mars part out," Erasmus commented blithely to Gregor. "Mars is a place, Malagigi. There's a planet there . . . I mean the planet is a place, like France. Not a planet in the ancient sense of a dot of light in the sky. Earth is a planet. So is Mars."

"But of course! And the sun is a place like Egypt." Malagigi scoffed. "Come, my friend, are you sure that the noxious gases of the Swamp are not affecting you adversely?"

"Only our noses." Mab sniffed dubiously and then crinkled his nose against the putrid stench he had just inhaled.

"I am quite well," Erasmus replied. "Not my fault if you got yourself beheaded before the rise of modern science."

"Whatever that may be." Malagigi waved a hand airily. He nodded encouragingly at Gregor, who was currently holding the silver star. Gregor lifted his hand up higher, so that the silvery light surrounded the gondola.

"So, you were going along about your day, troubling no one, when your sister called up the Hellwinds. Where? On the streets of Edinburgh?"

"We were on the Bridge across the River Styx," I said.

"You were in Hell? All of you?" He glanced around as if to see which of us were not present. "Theo? Titus? Cornelius? Logistilla, too? *Pourquoi?*"

I said, "My father has been captured by demons. The Queen of Air and Darkness holds him prisoner. She plans to kill him on Twelfth Night, which, unless I have completely lost track of time, is the day after tomorrow. We were trying to rescue him," I finished grimly.

"The great and dread magician Prospero? This is astonishing news indeed! And you all came to rescue him! Amazing! How lucky that you have Miranda's Lady to guide you, for I cannot see how mortals could hope to make such a trip without the supernatural help of the Bearer of the Lightning Bolt!"

"Actually . . ." My tongue would not move in my mouth. I hid my face in my hands.

"My sister was defiled by a demon," Gregor said bluntly. "The White Lady of Spiral Wisdom no longer heeds her."

Thank you, Gregor, that was tactful, I thought. *I hope that's not how you handled your parishioners during confession.* Tears threatened to well up, but my eyes remained dry. The peace the star brought sustained me.

"Ah . . . this is dire news!" Malagigi's eyes grew round and watery as the implications sunk in. "But did not your family rely upon Water of Life for your immortality? Without a Handmaiden of Eurynome to travel to the Well at the World's End, how will you maintain your eternal youth?"

"We won't," Erasmus replied, his voice flat. "In a mere few decades, we will all grow old and die."

"I sorrow for you all!" Malagigi lowered his head in silent prayer. Looking up, he said, his voice serious, "You know, of course, that without Divine Eurynome to guide you through Hell, you have no chance."

"An angel told us to come," I replied defiantly. "She said we had the tools we needed to succeed."

"Mephisto has the scrying ball of John Dee—Merlin's ball, the one Solomon used when he came down here disguised as Asmodeus," Erasmus explained. "If we can find Mephisto, we can use it to find Father and the others. And, of course, we have our staffs."

"Ah!" Malagigi's eyes flickered over the three staffs of power we carried— the staffs that were our Prospero Family legacy: Gregor's *Staff of Darkness*,

Erasmus's *Staff of Decay,* and my flute, the *Staff of the Winds*—before coming to rest upon *Durandel* riding in its sheath at Erasmus's side. Softly, he murmured, "Maybe, with Heaven's help, you have a chance after all."

"Yeah," muttered Mab, "a snowball's chance!"

Narrowing his eyes, Mab began surveying our surroundings carefully, as if attempting to discern exactly what the proverbial ball of frost's chances might be.

The Greatest Swordsman of Christendom

"A traitor lurks in your midst," Malagigi mused as he poled, "and, yet, you do not fear Mephistopheles, Prince of Hell? We are certain, are we not, that when we find him, he will refrain from sticking us upon his pitchfork and roasting us over the coals, yes?"

"Our brother is not the same individual as the demon of that name," Gregor corrected him in his calm, gruff voice. He was peering at the silver star, which he held in his outstretched hand.

Mab and I exchanged nervous glances again. Malagigi watched this carefully. He stroked his mustache and then gave a quick shrug, as if to say: "What is this to me?"

As we punted underneath a growth of diseased palms filled with spiderwebs, Mab leaned over, all the while keeping a wary eye on the web's inhabitants, spiders as large as cats, with the faces of women.

"Begging your pardon, Ma'am," he whispered in my ear, "but are we certain that the Harebrain is on the level? He is, after all, a demon. Maybe that's what Abaddon meant by there being a traitor in the family."

"You told us not to worry about Abaddon's warning!" I whispered back.

"True," Mab allowed softly, "but I wasn't thinking about the fact that you had a demon in the family. Demons love ratting each other out."

Mab pulled out his waterlogged notebook, frowned at it, and stuck it back in his trench coat. Searching his pockets, he pulled out the notebook Father Christmas had given him, the pages of which were waterproof. With a quick shake and a wipe with his handkerchief, it was as good as new. To his delight, the Space Pen he had received upon the same occasion worked, too.

Flipping the waterproof notebook open, Mab quickly wrote out a list of my siblings' names, with Mephistopheles at the top. Above this, he scribbled: POSSIBLE TRAITORS.

Meanwhile, Malagigi, who was pushing through the sticky white tangles with his pole, was speaking to my brothers. "Ah, Mephistopheles Prospero! What a fine swordsman your brother was! It was a pleasure to watch him, which is much to say as he was cutting down my men! Of course, I did not know any of those men personally. It had been several centuries since I had ventured from Ardennes, except to visit my siblings in our tower in the vale of Orgagna, but I cared for them on principle, since they were Merovingians . . . I mean . . . what is the new word? . . . Frenchmen. Still, Mephistopheles was a wonder!"

Mab drew a square around Mephisto's name and then drew out one of his waterlogged notebooks. He carefully turned the pages, slowly separating one from another until he found what he wanted. He read what he had written and then, looking up, asked, "Several times now, I've heard people call the Harebrain the 'Greatest Swordsman in Christendom.' I gather it's a title. How did he get it?"

"I'm not sure . . ." I glanced at Erasmus.

"His real prowess lay upon the battlefield, of course," Erasmus replied, "but sword fighting as a military art stopped meaning much once muskets and rifles began replacing swords. And Mephisto has never achieved the same degree of mastery with a gun that he has with a blade."

"Ulysses has the distinction of being the best shot in the family," Gregor commented, "perhaps, because he was the only one of us who would not have preferred to be a swordsman."

Erasmus gave a contemptuous shrug. "Be that as it may . . . the title 'Greatest Swordsman in Christendom' was presented to Mephisto by Queen Elizabeth, upon the occasion of his match against Salvador Fabris, who was then considered the greatest swordsman in the world at the time."

"Fabris! Even I have heard of him!" Malagigi replied, impressed. "This duel, did you see it?"

Erasmus and I shook our heads.

"Alas, we were in Italy," Erasmus explained. "Theo was in the audience, though. He was serving as a knight for Queen Bess under the Earl of Essex at the time."

"I was a child of six growing up in Milan." Gregor leaned forward with uncharacteristic enthusiasm. "So, no, I was not able to attend. But I do recall Mephisto reenacting the match for Logistilla and me. My brother played both parts with great thrusts and flurries and a good deal of shouting that I, in retrospect, suspect was not part of the original. I was so impressed, I insisted on swinging around a long wooden spoon for some months, to the dismay of my nanny."

"I did get to see him fight the great Ridolfo Capa Ferro," I said, recalling that long-ago afternoon upon the fish-boned bricks of the Piazza del Campo in Sienna when I had watched some of the world's greatest fencers strut about beneath the hot Italian sun. It had been an unusual treat for me to leave my cloistered chapel and spend an afternoon with my family. I still remember the spicy taste of the sausages sold by a street vender at the far side of the shell-shaped market square and the sound of the crowd as they cheered for their favorites.

"Ah, yes!" Erasmus's eyes sparkled at the memory. "Old Ironhead announced he and his students would face all comers—propaganda for his fencing school, of course. Only Mephisto beat them all. After that, Capa Ferro used to come by to wheedle trade secrets out of our elder brother. They became great friends."

"That event I do remember!" Gregor's dark eyes glowed with the warmth of golden memories. "By that time, I was twelve and so disappointed that none of the grown men would fence with me—at that age I had no notion yet that I was destined for the church. You won a few matches yourself, if I recall, Big Brother."

"Well . . . yes," Erasmus replied, looking down at his hands in an uncharacteristic moment of humility. He played with his fingers. "I did my part for the family honor."

Gregor gave Erasmus a rare fond smile. "I remember your son Sebastian cheering for you. He told everyone within earshot that the winner was his father. Your poor wife was quite beside herself with embarrassment."

It was so unusual to see the somber Gregor smiling openly that I felt oddly disorientated, as if I were seeing a brother I had not known I had. Maybe Gregor really had changed during his imprisonment. I wondered how it came about. I hoped that Erasmus would accept this olive branch, acknowledge Gregor's enthusiasm, and give him with some encouragement, but Erasmus merely turned away and stared off through the tangled webs at the cypress trees beyond, his face tight and drawn.

Another spasm of irritation at my pigheaded brother ricocheted through me. What was wrong with him? Was not the misery around us enough motivation to bridge the gap between himself and his brother?

I clenched my fists, resisting the urge to push him over the side of the gondola into the swamp, where he belonged.

As if he could hear my thoughts, Erasmus suddenly turned around, but he was not looking at me. He grinned at Malagigi. "Those show bouts of Mephistos are all well and fine, but none of them compares with my brother's greatest match."

"You mean the match he and Cesare fought over that pretty girl?" I asked, recalling the event. I added enthusiastically, "I saw part of it, the part that could be seen from the *Filarete* tower. Didn't they fight some of it on a staircase?"

"It was the sort of thing you'd see in a film." Erasmus laughed with glee; the shadow that had fallen over his face moments before vanished as he recalled this incident from his early youth. "Up and down stairs, over tables, in and out of doorways, across the parade grounds . . . that's the part Miranda caught. It was unbelievable! In my whole life, I've never seen its like! Two of the best swordsmen in Italy fighting over things worth fighting about: women and money!"

"I have heard about this duel my whole life, Maugris!" Gregor exclaimed. Again there was a rare flash of boyishness in his smile. "Mephisto and Theo have acted it out for us dozens of times. And, once, when we were invited to visit the *Castello Sforzesco* for some public festival—the castle that had belonged to my family when Father was Duke, before—" Gregor laughed as if suddenly putting two and two together. "It was you and your siblings, who took it away from him, wasn't it?"

Malagigi gave a shrug. "It was your uncle Antonio who convinced the French king to attack. We merely came along to lend a hand. A dashing figure, your uncle. A pity he died that day."

"That was before I was born. I never met him. Anyway, we visited the *castello* for some public celebration, and Erasmus blocked out the whole fight for Sebastian and me, showing us where various parts of the fight had taken place, where first blood had been drawn and where Cesare finally conceded. There was even a faint blotch on the stone that Erasmus claimed was Mephisto's blood, shed when Cesare stabbed our brother in the shoulder after refusing to yield when first blood was called."

"Ah, yes!" Malagigi laughed. "Even I have heard of this match!"

"You?" Gregor asked, taken aback.

"But of course!" Malagigi replied. "Your uncle Antonio described it to us. He was very fond of Mephisto. When we first met, he still hoped Mephisto and Erasmus could be turned, that they would eventually join him against Prospero."

"Really!" I nearly shouted in surprise. "What an extraordinary idea!"

"It may not have seemed that extraordinary to Uncle Antonio," Erasmus admitted. "Mephisto and I did admire him greatly. He had turned against Father. It only made sense that he might think others would, too."

"Would you have?" I asked, shocked.

Beside me, Mab pulled out his list of Traitor suspects and drew a box around Erasmus's name.

"Of course not!" Erasmus replied, a touch of both humor and sadness in his voice. "But how was Antonio to understand that?"

MALAGIGI poled us forward as the rest of us sat quietly, basking in the light of the silver star. The swamp here was littered with debris from rotting trees. Ahead, a wide log floated between two cypresses, blocking our way. Malagigi switched his pole-oar to the nearer side of the gondola, so as to maneuver us around the log.

Erasmus leaned back and gazed at the silver star. "He isn't a bad brother, all in all. Mephisto, I mean. He fought a couple of times on my behalf over the years. His trusty blade has defended you, too, Miranda, as I recall."

"A few times," I admitted. "Usually it was Theo who sprang to my defense. In fact, Theo once dueled Mephisto for the right to defend me. After that, Mephisto let Theo be my champion. But there were a few times when Theo was not around, and some young blood troubled me. Mephisto was quick to put the upstart in his place!"

"Mephisto fought Theo? Did Theo win?" Erasmus asked, surprised. "I mean Theo's good, but . . ."

"I don't know. They did not fight the duel in front of me . . ." I rested my nose against my folded fingers. "I've always assumed Theo won."

"Just like Mephisto to win and then let Theo have his way," chuckled Erasmus. "Or even to let Theo win, if he thought Theo really wanted it."

"I doubt it." Gregor's voice grated. "Mephisto would not have trusted his sister's safety to another unless he thought Theo could do the job. Theophrastus must have pushed himself upon this occasion and bested our elder brother."

I tried to remember more details, but the events were lost in the mists of time. I was sure that the fight had taken place at our estates in Scotland, but during which of our stays there, I could not say. It had been centuries since I had thought of the incident. Looking back, it struck me as sweet that my brothers would go to such an effort. It made me love them both all the more.

My heart swelled until my chest felt tight. Fear for both of them seized me. Mephisto I was not as worried about; he could turn into a demon. But Theo was somewhere in Hell, alone. His face, his look of desperation as his fingers were ripped away from mine, hung before me like a specter.

"Mephistopheles fought several duels on my behalf." Gregor put his foot up on the bench in front of him and stared ahead of us. "Once he even went to a duel looking like me, with the help of Logistilla's *Staff of Transmogrification*. I was against this, mind you. After Logistilla turned me into the cardinal, she was never quite able to return me back the way I had been." He pointed at his throat to indicate his voice, which had been hoarse and raspy ever since that incident. "And I worried that something similar would happen to Mephisto. But she insisted she had mastered her staff since then. So, Mephisto went ahead and let her change him."

Erasmus leaned forward, intrigued. "What did he do, then?"

"He waited for the thugs who were trying to squeeze money out of my church and bested their leader. They thought I had done it, so they left me alone after that." Gregor was quiet for a moment, lost in the swirling pools of distant memory. "The other times, he appeared as himself. He always won, of course."

"Were these incidents all before your brother went bonkers?" Mab asked.

Gregor tapped the tips of his fingers together, thinking. Then he shook his head. "He has come to my defense as recently as the early nineteenth century. I had a parish in Suffolk then. Mephisto made quick work of a band of ruffians who were preying upon my parishioners. That was nearly two hundred years after his mind went."

"Much as it pains me to say this"—Mab screwed up his face and carefully drew a single line through Mephisto's name, where it topped the list of sibling suspects in his notebook—"I think we can rule out the Harebrain as a possible traitor. Wouldn't make sense to keep defending you all and then stab you in the back. After all, Ma'am, if Mephisto wanted you dead, all he would have had to do was not rescue you, either in the warehouse or when we were in the plane being attacked by the dragon."

"That's a very good point!" I exclaimed. It had not occurred to me that I owed my life to Mephisto twice over.

"Too bad. Would have been an easy thing to blame Mephistopheles, an open-and-shut case . . . Alas, it's not to be. In fact, I'm beginning to think your older brother . . ." Mab's voice trailed off. He flipped to another section of his older soggy notebook and ran his finger across the page, reading what was written there and harrumphing to himself.

Gregor cleared his throat. After a lengthy pause, he spoke in a whisper even more breathy than normal. "For years, I have worried that it was having spent time as me that led to his madness, that Logistilla never turned him back correctly. The incident where he impersonated me happened not long before he lost his mind."

"It wasn't you." I touched Gregor's arm gently. "He drank from the Lethe."

"Well, that was stupid!" Erasmus thumped his staff against the boards of the gondola. "Can it be undone?"

Mab frowned. "I don't think that would be such a good idea, Professor Prospero. I think . . ." Mab paused and peered across the water at the souls of the dead on the next island. "What are they doing? Trying to marry a rock?"

Beyond the stand of trees, a large group of shades attempted to embrace a large rock. On another island, more tormented souls bowed and scraped, worshipping an enormous spiderweb inhabited by giant woman-faced spiders. Farther still, other unexceptional or repulsive objects received obeisance or undue attention from the dead.

"How peculiar," murmured Erasmus. "I wonder what they are seeing."

Malagigi turned to Gregor, whose turn it was to hold the star. "If you close your hand, the rest of us will be able to see what the locals see."

Gregor grunted and closed his hand slowly, as if he did not think this was a wise course of action. As the light of the star faded, the pleasant warmth became an oppressive heat. The whine of mosquitoes filled my ears along with the ever-present moans of the dead. The humidity caused my hair to stick to my face. Even worse was the terrible stench of sewage. Together, the heat, humidity, and horrid odor made it hard to breathe.

"Oh my!" Erasmus had risen up to get a good look at the islands, his free hand pressed against his nose, plugging his nostrils. He winced at the pain.

Of course, to me, everything still looked the same.

"Please hurry!" I batted at the air around me but could not seem to shoo the mosquitoes making the irritating whine. My hand went right through them. "I can't see what you are looking at anyway. Neither can Gregor so long as he's holding the star."

Erasmus sat down rapidly. "You can open your hand, Brother. I've seen enough."

Mab, who had turned in his seat in order to see better, scrunched up his face. He had tilted his head one way and then the other. Finally, he shrugged. "Sorry . . . don't get it."

"What did you see?" Gregor opened his hand, bathing the gondola in silvery light. The temperature suddenly seemed more pleasant, the air more breathable, and the stench less offensive. The mosquitoes vanished.

Mab peered, frowning. "They're all panting around a lady's shoe and over there was some underclothes and stuff. Looked as weird with the illusion as without. Weirder, in fact."

"Fetishists," Erasmus said. "That rock is a high-heeled shoe, and those spiderwebs are a bra and a pair of silken undies. I won't even describe the rest of them."

Gregor said ponderously, "What we are seeing are the souls of those who directed their lust at a symbol instead of the real thing. Their punishment is, apparently, to be allowed to live out their empty fantasies."

Erasmus shuddered. "Fitting, yet creepy."

Mab stared at my brothers for a long time. He lowered the brim of his fedora and muttered, "Sorry. Still don't get it."

"Rejoice," Malagigi replied. "There is much about the darker side of humanity that it would be better not to understand."

"What about the illusions my brothers and Mab could see?" I asked. "What is their purpose?"

"To fool the lost souls," Malagigi replied.

"Why in tarnation . . . and, in this case, I mean exactly that . . . why, here, in tarnation, would anyone bother?" Mab asked. "The souls are already damned, aren't they?"

"Not as damned as they could be." Malagigi's voice was unexpectedly grave.

"What do you mean?" asked Gregor.

"This"—Malagigi spread his arms indicating the swamps—"is not the lowest level of Hell. There are lower levels. Those on Earth are told that once a man dies, his spirit dwells forever in the same place, but it is not the case in either direction. Not only can those in Hell be saved, but the fallen can fall still farther. The more they indulge and debauch themselves—the more they prey upon their fellows—the heavier their souls become. Soon, their souls grow so heavy that they are caught up by the next sweep of the Hellwinds." Malagigi's hands worried the golden knot of his belt.

"Ridiculous!" exclaimed Erasmus. "You're pulling our leg, right?"

"I wish I were, *mon ami,* but it happened to me."

We all stared at him.

"It did?" I leaned forward with great interest. Gregor's gaze also was fixed upon the ex-sorcerer's face.

Malagigi met Gregor's disbelieving stare evenly before continuing. "After I died, instead of repenting—as any sensible sinner would have—I sought revenge for the destruction of my family. I called upon my friends—elemental spirits of the fire, air, and water who owed allegiance to me alone—and set them upon those who were responsible for dragging us from our home. Only . . . spirits are not wise. They cannot see the world clearly. Without me there to direct them . . ." He slapped his forehead. "*Zut alors!* Did it go awry!"

"Oh! Never turn revenge over to spirits!" Mab shook his head mournfully. "They'll muck it up. Take it from me, I know!"

"Needing guidance, they picked a man who could vaguely hear them and influenced him to kill those who were responsible. Only they did not know who was responsible—we humans look much alike to them. Unless they have a drop of blood or a piece of hair to identify a particular soul, they have trouble telling us apart. So, they prodded this man, Maximilien his name was, to kill many people . . . many, many people."

I could feel my eyes grow round with horror. "Not Maximilien Robespierre?"

"That was it." Malagigi's voice trembled softly.

"You mean the terrible bloodshed and violence of the reign of Robespierre was your fault?" I cried. "The glory of France was destroyed . . . by you?"

Malagigi's shoulders slumped. An immaterial tear slid down his narrow cheek. "I received my revenge, *biensur*, and with it, my just deserts—incarceration in a lower circle of Hell than my initial sins had earned me.

"Only at this point," Malagigi explained, his voice heavy with self-mocking pity, "did I begin to repent. Finally, after torments too horrible to tell, a fellow of the Brotherhood of Hope named Benedetto found me—he was rescuing others to earn off his own sins. Since then, I have devoted myself to this order and to helping others. I dwell in hopes of earning forgiveness for my transgressions. I especially try to save souls who were killed because of the urgings of my elementals."

"So, you yourself were a damned soul who was saved!" Gregor marveled. "Then it is true!"

"Indeed." Malagigi spread his arms. "I am living proof." Then, he chuckled. "Or proof, at any rate. The 'living' part is a matter of opinion."

Erasmus sighed wearily. "You mean we are expected to pray and to be contrite even if we find ourselves in Hell? That hardly seems fair. I thought the one virtue of Hell was that it gave rest to those who were tired of such nonsense. That there were no churchmen to prod you."

"It depends," Malagigi answered cheerfully, "on whether or not you wish to get out again."

"It would be well to keep that in mind." Gregor shot a calm but penetrating look at Erasmus, who arched a single eyebrow.

"What worries me is that a soul in Hell had the leeway to call up spirits and cast spells on the living," Mab muttered. "Don't seem right. This place is supposed to be the biggest, toughest slammer around—you'd think the security would be tighter."

As we sailed the gondola, the silvery light of the tiny star shining around us, I contemplated what Malagigi had told us. On the one hand, his story seemed astonishing to me, so alien was the notion of the Brotherhood of Hope to my Protestant beliefs. On the other hand, some part of me did not find it surprising. As was recounted by Father Christmas and in the *Book of the Sibyl,* my Lady Eurynome had left High Heaven to free mankind from the Garden made by the demons. It was not so difficult to believe that others might strive to save those who still remained the playthings of those demons.

A FLOATING log among the cypresses to our right lifted abruptly, revealing a row of yellow razor-sharp teeth. The teeth opened into a maw that gaped nearly as large as our gondola.

"Sea monster!" I leapt to my feet and pointed.

The monster reared out of the swamp with a loud pop. Water sluiced off its scaly back. A huge green monstrosity with wide fins to either side of its neck slashed at us with webbed fingers armed with cruel, curving claws.

In one fluid motion, Erasmus leapt to his feet and drew *Durendel.* Meanwhile, Malagigi gave his pole a violent shove, propelling us quickly backward. Erasmus would have pitched overboard into the filth, but Mab caught his green doublet and pulled. Gregor rose slowly to his feet as well.

Bracing my feet, I drew my fighting fan and then looked from it to the sea monster. True, the moon-silver slats that made up its blade had been forged by the Japanese smith god Amatsumaru, but it was still a puny weapon against so great a foe. Yet, neither of the greater weapons I was accustomed to wielding—my flute and my Lady's aid—could help me now. Unfortunately, without my Lady to inspire my steps and my blows, I was not a particularly good fighter. I suddenly felt helpless and realized how dependent I was upon the chivalry of my brothers and Mab.

It was not a feeling I liked.

"We could use the Greatest Swordsman in Christendom about now!" Malagigi exclaimed as he poled vigorously.

The motion of the gondola caused Gregor to lose his footing and stumble backward. Arms flailing, he grabbed the high curl of the *risso* rising from the stern and steadied himself. Still clutching the stern iron, he growled, "Why are we fleeing? Did you not say that nothing could harm us unless we became angered or afeared?"

"Nothing dead," Malagigi corrected quickly as the gondola slid rapidly backward. "This is a living monster. They wander down here by accident occasionally."

"Monsters wander into Hell by accident?" Mab threw down his hat. "Since when?"

"Since time immemorial."

"Can it hurt you, Malagigi?" I asked. "You are made of spirit."

"Probably not." Malagigi did not look entirely confident.

Picking up his hat again, Mab clambered forward and hunched over, peering intently at this new enemy as it reared from the frothy waters, roaring at us. "It's a sea monster all right." He slapped his lead pipe against his hand. "I recognize the species from the old days. Same kind Hercules stopped from munching on some Trojan princess."

"A Ketos?" Erasmus hung on to the *dolfin,* where the bow iron rose above the rest of the gondola. The unbreakable blade *Durandel* shone in his hand, gleaming with a holy light too bright to look upon directly. "The same breed that the Greek hero Perseus slew to win his bride, Andromeda. Theo fought one in the Caspian Sea once. Were you with him, Gregor?"

"No. Must have been Titus. I think I had not been born yet." Gregor frowned, looking from the monster to the golden ring on his hand. "I don't believe the Seal of Solomon is of any use against living monsters."

"Here it comes!" Erasmus shouted.

It was upon us.

We all leapt backward. The sea monster's jaws closed on the gondola, just missing Erasmus. As it clenched its teeth, the high, curved bow iron broke with a resounding crack. The jagged broken tip drove into the top of the creature's mouth like a spike, forcing its jaws open. This saved our boat from being snapped in half but did not protect us from the beast's fetid stifling breath.

Shouting some ancient war cry, Erasmus swung at the creature's head. He was not the swordsman that Mephisto and Theo were; his first blow bounced off the creature's tough scales.

"Damn!" Erasmus exclaimed, adding as he swung again, "or should I be saying the opposite? Is there a verb form for being sent to heaven?"

"Redeem!" Gregor shouted, a priestlike gleam shining in his eyes. He hit the creature with the *Staff of Darkness*. A *crunch* of cartilage followed the *whack* of his blow.

Fan in hand, I lunged forward and swiped at the monstrous head. The fan sliced through the monster's nose as if it were a well-roasted turkey. The fore part of the nostril fell away revealing pale reptilian flesh. This infuriated the beast but did little serious damage.

It roared and yanked its head free of the gondola, shaking us all. Pale ichor dripped from the wound in the roof of its mouth and from its severed nose.

Mab leapt across the boat, his trench coat whipping about him. Landing on the monster's head, he hit it repeatedly with his lead pipe. The pipe bounced off the thick scales. Scowling, Mab leaned forward precariously and thrust his pipe into the soft tissue of the beast's eye.

The monster bellowed in pain, throwing its head this way and that. Mab slid backward and grabbed hold of the pointy green frills behind the creature's head. Below, its thrashings exposed the creature's throat. Erasmus took advantage of this and struck again.

This time his blow was true. *Durandel* sunk deeply into the soft neck. Flailing, the beast knocked the gondola into a spin. Gregor and I were thrown forward.

I came to rest across the side of the gondola, the wooden *forcola* digging into my ribs. The creature loomed over me like a great green and yellow wall, my nose pushed up against its leathery scales. I had landed hard with my fan arm pinned beneath me and the wind knocked from my lungs. When I could breathe again, the monster's hot, lizardy odor caused me to cough. It was like being trapped in the reptile house at the zoo.

Beside me, Gregor had regained his feet. He hefted the *Staff of Darkness,* blocking the monster's arm as it reached for us. While he struggled with it, I climbed to my knees. My fan had become embedded in the gondola. I struggled to pull it free.

The boat rocked, and Gregor was thrown backward. The sea monster took a swipe at me. Helplessly, I watched as the fistful of razorlike claws came at my face. Just as the shiny black tips drew near my eye, I yanked free my fan and swung.

The silvery fan of the Japanese forge god sliced through the wrist of the ketos. Its webbed hand flew free of its arm. I ducked to one side, but a claw raked my cheek as it fell. My face stung, but I had done the thing some serious damage. With some relief, I noted that it was not regenerating. You can never tell ahead of time with sea monsters.

In the center of the boat, Malagigi knelt in prayer, the silver star resting upon his palm. For an instant, I felt angry that this magician, who had been such a terror on the battlefield when he fought us in Milan, now chose to sit by doing nothing. But, of course, none of his tricks—wise horses and illusionary shades of the dead—would have been of any use here, even if he could have performed them. Most likely, we were better served by his prayers.

The monstrous reptile screamed in rage. Looking up, I saw Mab had wounded the other eye. The creature was now blind. It tossed its head, waving its good claws and its stump. Its neck frills flapped. Pale ichor splattered the gondola. Ironically, the smell of it was more pleasant than that of the surrounding swamp.

"Not a good thing, all these wounds," Mab called as he clung to the beast's tossing head, his arms wrapped around a hornlike protrusion. "Blood calls stuff. Not sure I'd want to see what it calls here in . . . What the Hell is that!"

There was rush and a *swoosh*. Something was racing toward us under the swamp, something big—very, very big.

The ripple grew closer. An island rose into the air. Long curved roots the color of ivory hung down from the bottom.

No. Those were not roots. They were teeth.

In the Belly of the Kronosaur

I grabbed my flute from the strap that secured it to my back and then remembered. With my useless flute in one hand and my puny fan in the other hand, I gazed open-mouthed down a throat the length of a turnpike exit.

"Run!" screamed Mab.

Erasmus, who was standing on the broken bow of the gondola, whacking at the sea monster with *Durandel,* glanced over his shoulder at our trembling little boat in the midst of the algae-covered swamp and called casually, "Run where?"

Then, the gondola rose up into the air, and all went dark, except for the gleam of emerald light from the winglike wisps coming from the shoulders of my gown, and the bright beam issuing from Erasmus's sword. We tumbled for a time, sliding and falling, as if we were on some amusement-park water slide. I clung to one of the low benches with both arms. Finally, we came to rest, right side up. The gondola undulated beneath us, and a *sizzle,* like the sound of eggs cooking, came from several directions, along with a disturbing loud squishy noise that sounded like a cross between walking in wet galoshes and being stuck inside of a giant washing machine.

Wherever we were, it was hot and stank of bile and bleach. It stank so badly I could hardly breathe. In the semidarkness, I heard the sound of retching. At least one of my companions lost what little food his stomach held.

"What happened?" I called hesitantly.

"A cavern enclosed around us, I think." Mab's voice came from far away. "By Setabos, the air is foul in here!"

There was a *whoosh* of wind, and a cold gust from some unknown source blew against my face. This cooler air smelled sweeter, like a late winter's day when the ice was beginning to thaw, but it only lasted a moment before the humid and putrid air overwhelmed it.

"We've been swallowed." Gregor coughed, then choked out stoically. "Apparently, Maugris here was right about monsters wandering down here since time immemorial. We have been swallowed by a kronosaur."

"A whosawhatzit?" called Mab, trying to shout over the general cacophony, the galoshes-washing machine *whooshing*.

My head swam, but an examination did not reveal any bumps or sore spots. So, perhaps the disorientation was caused by the shock of having been swallowed by an enormous, ocean-dwelling reptile. In the dark, with nothing else to distract me from the sting of my wounded cheek, I felt as if there were a line of fire across my face.

"Ah, Ma'am?" Mab shouted. "The wounded Ketos is in here with us and alive . . . and I'm still on it! Anybody got a light?"

Beams of brightness streamed through the darkness, illuminating the bits of the inside of the stomach in which we now dwelt. Erasmus held *Durandel* aloft over his head, its blade gleaming with a holy light. Finally, we could see our surroundings.

The gondola was partially cracked across the middle and flooding quickly. It bumped against a half-digested skull of something large. Above our heads, huge curved bones arched like the ribs of a cathedral ceiling. Farther away, beyond this skeleton of a recent dinner, slumped our sea monster, with Mab still clinging to one of its gill-like neck frills. As the thing stirred and slowly began moving its head, Mab lowered himself down and touched a toe to the liquid beneath him. His shoe hissed and steamed in the pooled digestive acids. Quickly, Mab clambered up toward the top of the sea monster's head.

Malagigi stood on the cracked gondola gazing in disgust at his broken pole-oar. Then, he opened his other hand. Upon it, the silver star shone brightly. Suddenly hopeful, I took a deep breath, which I immediately regretted. Bile and ammonia raked my lungs, causing me to double over. My innards writhed in disgust.

The starlight revealed giant folds of soft tissue around us, pale and bloodless like the innards of a fish. These flaps of stomach flesh undulated and rubbed against each other, causing the disconcerting squishy sound. They pushed up against our boat and the skeleton and the sea monster on every side, leaving us with very little room to maneuver. In two places, it pulled together to form a pucker. Most likely, one led to the throat and the other to the intestines. There was no indication as to which way might be which.

As the ketos woke and shifted, it had to shove aside curtains of stomach wall. This angered the sea monster it. Roaring, it thrashed its tail and bit at the thick muscular folds of flesh.

"This is not good!" Mab cried, during one of the moments when he reappeared from where he had been being smothered by the folds of stomach lining the sea monster attacked. "If Old Gill-Frill here keeps this up, he's going to infuriate our host!"

As the blinded sea monster twisted about again, Mab jumped free. He sailed across the intervening space to grab one of the rib bones of the half-digested skeleton. Clambering from rib to rib, he reached the dome of the skull, next to which floated our quickly flooding gondola.

"Phew! Glad to be off of there," Mab declared as he slid onto the sinking gondola. "Besides, the thing didn't have any more eyes for me to blind."

My shoes hissed as the rapidly rising liquid splashed over them. I backed up.

"Let's kill it before it gets us," Erasmus gasped as he recovered from a bile-induced coughing bout. He lowered his arm, depriving us of the pillar of holy light that streamed from *Durandel,* and strode forward, leaping up onto the skull and shimmying across the vertebrae toward the sea monster. "Bad enough to be in one monster's stomach without having to be eaten by a second one, too."

"What?" called Gregor, cupping his hand to his ear, straining to hear over the roar.

"I said, 'Get the bad monster!'" Erasmus shouted back.

Gregor nodded and started forward. I paused to examine the cracked gondola. "This is going to sink into the stomach acid, and we're going to lose it." I jumped up onto the skull to stand beside Mab. "Let's pull it out of the digestive juices."

Mab, Malagigi, and I hauled the heavy craft up onto the skull of the whatever-it-once-was, while Gregor and Erasmus continued the fight against the sea monster. I had intended to leave the fight to them, but as I leaned over to steady the boat, the sea monster's long sinuous tail struck me.

I flew backward off the skull and bounced against the folds of the kronosaur's stomach. The squishy lining molded to my body, engulfing me. I felt as if I was falling into a huge wall of wet, stinking, rubber foam. The spongy surface dripped with juices that burned my wounded cheek and sizzled against my hair and enchanted gown. Soft painful stuff engulfed my face, smothering me.

And, oh, the smell!

My heart beat like it thought it could save me by racing. I flailed, seeking to breathe. My fan was still in my hand. I slid it open but thought better of it; wounding our host might cause worse troubles. Instead, I elbowed the springy stuff, pushing it aside as if I were swimming. Moving thus, I was able to wriggle out from the stomach wall and grab hold of a rib of the skeleton.

My brothers battled the sea monster. Erasmus hacked at its throat with *Durandel*. Mab had stuck his trusty lead pipe through the wide gill-flaps to the left of the creature's head and pulled with both hands. Only he had done his work too well. The pipe ripped through the membranes of the frill, so that Mab now dangled dangerously close to the churning stomach acids below. Helpless, he kicked his feet.

Gregor had taken up the gondola's broken *dolfin* as a weapon. He was trying to drive it into the creature's heart; however, each time he thrust it against the monster's chest, it bounced off.

Staring at this battle, I wet my lips. This proved to be a mistake. The acid that burned my face now blistered my tongue. I wiped my face angrily with my sleeve and peered at the battle more closely, searching for a way to help my brothers. If I could reach the far curve of the rib upon which I stood, the sea monster would be within arm's reach. Though what I could do once I was there, I did not know.

I jumped onto the floating vertebrae that had once connected the two ivory curves. It wobbled beneath my foot. The silvery shadows my body cast swayed to and fro against the great folds of the stomach. Quickly, I leapt to the far rib, throwing my arms around it and hugging it until my footing became steady. Sliding my fan open again, I hooked an arm around the smooth white bone and leaned out precariously.

With one graceful stroke, I slit the sea monster's chest. The green scaly hide parted, peeling away from my blade.

"Gregor!" I waved. "Stab him here!"

Gregor lifted the broken bow iron and shoved it into the wound. He was not at a good angle, though, and the makeshift spike did not impale the creature very deeply. Grabbing the rib tightly, I kicked off. Like a child swinging on a tree branch, I whipped my feet through the air and slammed them against the curving top of the *dolfin*, driving it home into the creature's heart.

The Ketos thrashed violently. Then, it twitched three times and was still. Wiping the blades of my fan clean against the monster's scales, I looked around. Mab was nowhere to be seen, though I could hear his voice, swearing. Erasmus's feet protruded from a fold of stomach wall. Gregor held up the

Staff of Darkness and was experimenting to see the effect of the Hellshadow that issued from it upon the stomach of our host. Malagigi sat cross-legged upon the dome of the skull, the silver star resting upon his open palm.

"Olley-olley-Ome-free!" I shouted, grabbing Erasmus's legs and pulling. "I got it. You can all come out now."

"NO good." Erasmus lowered his staff, which vibrated and hummed in his pitted Urim gauntlet. He gagged, covering his tender nose with his free hand. When he recovered and could shout again, he called, "Look at that stomach fold! Instead of withering it, I just made the thing bigger!"

"It's a dinosaur!" I shouted over the noise of digestion. I rested against one of the ribs, rubbing my damaged lips with an antiseptic wipe Erasmus had given me from his bag. It did not seem to soothe the burning at all. I could not keep from wondering whether Erasmus had intended to aid me when he gave it to me. At least the smell of it helped keep the odor of the digestion going on about me at bay.

"Kronosaurs are not dinosaurs," Gregor interrupted. His voice came from a pool of shadow issuing from his staff. "They are short-necked plesiosaurs."

"A plesiosaur, then," I continued. "These creatures don't die of old age; they just grow larger. That's what some reptiles on earth today do, anyhow. They don't have a natural adult size like mammals; they just keep getting bigger until something kills them—a predator, disease, or lack of food. Down here, without any natural predators, this thing has apparently just kept growing—since the Cretaceous Period!"

"Then my staff is useless," Erasmus concluded. He came back over to sit close to Gregor and me, so that he could speak without shouting. "It's cut our way out or die the death of digestion. What are you doing in there, Gregor? The silver star too bright for you?"

"I prefer the mild brimstone scent of the Hellshadow to the stench of vomit and bile," Gregor replied. The reminder of the smell caused Erasmus to gag again.

"Ugh!" Mab groaned. "This is a bad business!"

"But, of course, now we know firsthand how Jonah felt," Malagigi offered from where he sat atop the skull, star in hand.

"We can't afford to stay here three days!" I pounded my hand against the skull, rocking the boat. "Father is going to be killed on Twelfth Night. We had five days left when we set out, and that was at least a day ago, maybe two. Not to mention what could be happening to the rest of our family!"

"We wouldn't be worried about the rest of the family, if someone hadn't summoned the Hellwinds." Erasmus gave me an accusatory stare. "We'd be past the Wall of Flame by now, not sitting in the stinking belly of some prehistoric whale."

"Enough, Erasmus." Gregor's voice called from the ball of darkness. "We have more important things to do than snipe at one another. We must work together to get out of here."

"What about crawling out the throat or the anus?" Mab asked.

"We could go up the throat—if we knew which way it was and had some method to keep the kronosaur from swallowing us again—but the other way is a no-no." Erasmus shuddered. "Can you imagine how long the intestines would be in a thing this size? Miles, perhaps hundreds of miles, depending upon how advanced the creature's innards are. We'd probably founder somewhere and end our days smothered by plesiosaur poop, if the stench didn't get us first."

"If I could be killed by stench, I would be dead already," I murmured.

It seemed a shame that my awful swim through the Swamp of Uncleanness when we first entered Hell had not inured me to unpleasant smells. At the time, I had thought that no odor would ever disturb me again. Apparently, that was not how one's nose operates.

"Could we cut our way out?" the ball of brimstony Hellshadow asked calmly in Gregor's voice.

"I doubt it." Erasmus patted *Durandel*. "Even if we were capable of physically hacking our way through what is probably at least two dozen feet of meat, bone, and gristle, it's unlikely we could survive being caught inside the wound-tunnel, once the creature began writhing from the pain. We'd be squashed."

"Let me get this straight." Mab scratched his eternal beard stubble and then counted the points on his fingers. "We can't wither it. We can't cut our way out. The *Staff of Darkness* doesn't do squat down here, except protect us from the stench, assuming we want to trade light and a bad odor for darkness; neither does the Seal of Solomon. And calling the Hellwinds inside this big oaf's stomach . . . Bad idea, right?"

"Right." Erasmus nodded.

"What's left?" Mab asked.

"Slow death by digestive juices?" Erasmus suggested.

"Can you help us, Mage Monk?" Mab turned to Malagigi.

"Mais non." The Frenchman shook his head. "I am able to walk through

the monster's flesh, so I could leave, were I willing to abandon the star. But I could not take any of you with me." He smiled ruefully. "Rather like the old days, when I knew all manner of secret paths but could not walk them unless I went alone."

"Could you go for help?" Mab asked.

"Go where?" Malagigi gave a very Gallic shrug. "No one out there would be willing to help, even if they could. As for the Brotherhood of Hope, my people won't be back for days. Hell is hard for us to reach. The masters brought us here and will not come back for us up until we have given what aid we may. Even if they were to come early, what could they do for you? You are not dead.

"It is at moments like these," the ex-sorcerer Malagigi opined eloquently, spreading his arms, "that I wish I could call up my old friends to help me. But even if they would come, I would not call them here. They were ethereal creatures, all. Elementals. This place would harm them. Merely being in Hell would corrupt the purity of their natures."

I leaned against the nearest rib and considered our situation. There had to be a way out. I recalled the angel Muriel Sophia, with her warmth and golden light, and how her visit had banished all uncertainties from my heart. She could not have sent us all into Hell just to have it end like this. I could not turn to my Lady for ideas so I glanced around at the great folds of bloodless flesh, searching for inspiration from other less spiritual sources. How huge and intimidating they looked, like great, slimy, smelly curtains. And Erasmus was right. He had made them even larger.

"Hey!" I exclaimed. "How about making the kronosaurus younger?"

"Come again?" asked Erasmus.

"Make it younger! If aging makes it grow, wouldn't making it younger make it shrink?" I asked. "Either it would throw us up when we became too big for its stomach, or we could cut our way through the narrower side."

"If you made it small enough, it would break open around us," Mab offered. "Er . . . if we didn't get squished first."

"You know, Miranda, I think you may have finally had a good idea," Erasmus said as he tapped his staff. It began to hum and buzz in his gauntlet again and to emit a blue glow. "How amazing! I suppose there's a first time for everything."

SHRINKING the kronosaurus small proved a lengthy process. While we waited, we built ourselves a sort of makeshift lean-to to protect us from the churning and stench of the stomach. First, we cut the skull of the mystery beast free from its skeleton, flipped it over so that it formed a giant white cup. Next, we wedged it inside its own curving ribs—the only things down here that were too large to be routinely tossed about by action of the stomach. This, we bound together with rope from Mab's bag. Then, we placed the cracked gondola inside the upside-down skull, giving us a place to sit. Finally, using pieces of Malagigi's broken pole as tent poles, we strung Gregor's enchanted crimson robes over our heads, to protect us from the digestive juices. Like my tea gown, Gregor's robes had been woven by Logistilla's magical process and could not be damaged by ordinary means. This was why he still wore them, even though he had not been a cardinal for centuries and preferred to dress in black.

So we all huddled together in our makeshift hideout and waited. Erasmus lay on his stomach beside the gondola, stretched out on the edge of the upturned skull. His arm was extended beyond our small enclosure, so that the tip of his staff pushed against the stomach wall. I was not privy to the secrets of the *Staff of Decay*, but he seemed to have some directional control over its effect.

Beside him, Gregor was now dressed in the black turtleneck and slacks he had been wearing beneath his robes. Using the *Staff of Darkness*, he wreathed the outside of our hideout in the thick shadowy stuff that issued from his staff, in the hope that it might protect us from the terrible smell.

I sat next to Mab, who was rereading his notes in the light of the silver star. The star rested on my hand, so long as I concentrated upon it. Malagigi, who was not encumbered by the monster's flesh, flitted in and out of the kronosaurus, reporting to Erasmus upon his progress.

From time to time, Erasmus would take a break from shrinking the plesiosaur to age the digestive juices that had gathered beneath us. The giant reptile might merely grow larger when withered, but the juices in it stomach could be aged until they were no longer active. With time, new juices gathered, but Erasmus's actions gave us a bit of leeway. When the smell became overwhelming, Mab would open his mouth and puff, creating a cool fresh breeze and blowing away the putrid odor. This, I now realized, was the source of the fresh air I had momentarily breathed when we first entered the stomach. After a time, the fresh air would leak out, the stench return, and Mab would do it again.

Mab had been hunched over his notes. Now, he glanced at me and chuckled.

"What's so amusing?" I called. Despite our close quarters, it was still difficult to hear one another, due to the near-deafening *whirr* and *squish* of digestion around us.

"Er . . . nothing, Ma'am." Mab lowered the brim of his hat. "Just that I may have figured out something about all those Post-It notes we found at your brother's place. Don't want to say anything yet, though, as I'm still forming my theory." Returning to his notes, he murmured something to himself. I could not quite make out his words, but it sounded like: "If I'm right, I'm going to owe the Harebrain some kind of apology."

Closing his notebook about fifteen minutes later, Mab took a length of rope and, exiting our lean-to, began measuring the stomach folds and their shrinkage times, coordinating his findings with Malagigi's. As his watch was not working, he asked Gregor and me to count seconds, to help him gauge time. After ten minutes, he announced that he thought it would take approximately five hours to shrink the creature sufficiently to allow for our escape.

"Which isn't so bad," Mab concluded, "if you consider that the creature has been growing for over a hundred and thirty *million* years!"

Five hours! Increasingly, I found myself worrying about Father and the rest of the family. Father, at least, was in a prison somewhere, and, while Lilith might be torturing him, she would not kill him until Twelfth Night. So, in an odd sort of way, he was safe.

But Theo? Mephisto? Titus? Logistilla? Cornelius, and Ulysses? Oh, and Caliban? Who knew where the Hellwinds had deposited them. The Hellwinds were designed to bring souls to the part of Hell most appropriate to their sins. If my siblings were dumped headlong in the places designed to torment them for their worst vices, what chance did they have of surviving?

Dread and foreboding gripped my heart, and cold sweat ran down the back of my neck. These sensations grew worse whenever I had to resist my five-hundred-year-old habit of turning to my Lady for solace. My only comfort was the light of the little star. Somehow, seeing its cheerful silvery glow, it was impossible to be entirely glum.

THE waiting dragged on and on. I am not ordinarily claustrophobic, but the narrow confines of the acid-filled stomach began to oppress me. I contemplated the future should we fail to escape this living prison. Many things troubled me: the fate of my family, our unanswered questions, plans that I had not completed. What bothered me most was that Prospero, Inc., would be left with no one at the helm, leaving mankind with less protection than they had received for the last five centuries.

My heart went out to the Aerie Ones we employed and to the billions of human beings who benefited from our services. It seemed unfair that, should I perish here—never returning to ensure that Prospero, Inc., continued to honor its obligations—the spirits would eventually break free of the covenants that enforced the laws upon which modern science depended, and mankind would be plunged into another dark age.

Seemed like a terrible price: I die in the belly of a kronosaur; all mankind suffers.

EVENTUALLY, Gregor suggested we take this opportunity to get some sleep. Since we had just two days ago imbibed our yearly drop of Water of Life, which rejuvenated our bodies and extended our life, we were at our heartiest. We could do without food or sleep for some time. As we did not know what would come next, however, it seemed wise not to strain our resources. Erasmus had to stay awake to operate his staff, but Malagigi offered to sit with him and let the rest of us, who still lived in flesh, sleep.

Mab, Gregor, and I arranged ourselves about the small vessel as best we could, using the hardwood benches as our pillows. We spent a few hours in fitful sleep, tossing and turning and suffering from nightmares. They were so terrifying that waking up to discover I was merely in the stomach of a kronosaurus in the depths of Hell was a relief. Perhaps Gregor's dreams were similarly nightmarish, for he also gave up on sleeping and, instead, knelt in prayer. Mab and I continued to wrest what repose we could from the occasion. The hard surface and uncomfortable position conspired to make this difficult, but I eventually drifted off with visions of elf lords dancing in my head.

I AWOKE sore and stiff. Mab woke, too, stretching and grumbling. He muttered something about coffee, to which Erasmus replied with a chuckle. "This is Hell, my man. You need to go to Heaven for good coffee."

We sat in silence for a time, huddled like children at summer camp—assuming that they had pitched their camp inside the world's largest living laundry machine during the wash cycle.

Gregor, who was watching the process around us intently, asked, "How did this creature come to be so great? It is far greater than the kronosaurus of Earth. They were only forty-five feet long."

Erasmus glanced back from where he lay stretched out upon his stomach, his staff extended. "Why do we assume that the biggest ones got stuck in tar pits? Those limits we read about—thirty-five feet, fifty-five feet— that's the length of the largest specimen we've found . . . Who knows how big the ones we didn't find were? Can you imagine trying to figure out what humans were like by measuring remains discovered in bogs?"

"That's a mildly disturbing thought," murmured Gregor. I doubt the others could hear him over the roar of digestion, but he was seated right beside me.

The air had begun to grow blue around Erasmus, as his staff continued to whirl. He quickly thrust his arm away from himself and toward the kronosaurus, but not before he removed at least ten years from himself. He now looked rather young for a professor.

"Oh, I saw 'em," Mab reported loudly. "The dinosaurs, I mean. They were big! Bigger than your museums account for . . . but of course, I was a wind at the time, so it's hard to give exact measurements. Wasn't really interested in measuring, in fact, until I got this fleshly body."

"Why are they called kronosaurus?" asked Malagigi. Somehow, his voice always carried, despite the noise. "Is it because they are so old, it is as if they were the masters of time?"

"No. They were named thus after the Greek Titan who ate his own children. I believe the thought was that this reptile had a mouth so big, it could swallow anything," Gregor explained.

"Even us," muttered Mab.

"What?" Gregor leaned forward.

"Even us," Mab shouted.

"Ah." Gregor nodded.

"How do you know so much about kronosauruses?" Erasmus called. "An evolution scoffer like you?"

"Ulysses was an admirer of dinosaurs. He took me to see a kronosaurus skull once, back in 1897," Gregor shouted back, a difficult thing for a man who spoke in a hoarse, raspy voice. "A man had done a painting of what he thought the living creature might have looked like. Not a bad likeness, though he got the shape of the brow ridge wrong."

I said, "But I thought you didn't believed in evolution."

"I don't," Gregor replied. "I believed dinosaur bones were a trap to lead men away from the faith, a tool of the devil. Clearly, I was right. The presence of this creature proves my point. Dinosaurs and their relatives come from Hell."

"That does not necessarily follow—" I began, but Mab interrupted me.

"There was an age when dinosaurs roamed the earth, all right, if that's what you are arguing about," he assured us. "Big massive slowpokes that used to stomp around. You had to really get up speed to blow them over, but once you got one of those big ones down, they'd roll around for hours, days sometimes, making their weird, undulating sound. We used to love to . . . er, never mind." Mab trailed off.

Erasmus chuckled. "Who would have imagined it? Our Company Detective was a prehistoric cow-tipper!"

"A what?" called Gregor. Malagigi seemed puzzled as well.

"Cow-tipper," Erasmus called back. "As in, tipping cows?"

"Dripping trout?" shouted Gregor.

"Oh, never mind!"

A look of incredulity came over Erasmus. Adjusting his staff, he brought it close to his face, aging himself until he looked like a distinguished professor again. Grinning, he pushed several times upon his nose, which had healed during the aging process. He put his staff back to work, murmuring softly, "Why hadn't I thought of that before?"

"But what is the kronosaur doing here?" I called. "It's too old to be something drawn out of the nightmares of the damned." I turned to Malagigi. "Did you say it came here from earth?"

Malagigi nodded. "It must have swum into the spirit world back in its day, and it is still living here. One swam out a few years back. Not a kronosaur but a similar creature with a thinner neck. Some mortal magician ripped an opening in the spirit world and one of the ancient beasts escaped."

"Yes, I know who you mean," I said. "That fellow Theo hated so much, the black sorcerer who lived beside a Scottish loch. That particular plesiosaur works for Mephisto now. He's got it on his staff. He calls it Nessie."

"What do they do down here?" Erasmus mused. "What do they eat?"

"Other monsters." Malagigi shrugged. "Each other. People like you."

"Can't be too many of those," Erasmus replied. "Not really the thing, you know, coming bodily into Hell. As a rule, tourist agencies warn against such excursions."

I started to comment on Ferdinand's period of bodily incarceration in Hell but then recalled that had been a hoax. Luckily, I remembered before

I spoke. Otherwise, I might have discovered firsthand whether or not it was possible to die of embarrassment.

Malagigi stuck his hands in his voluminous sleeves, reminding me of dozens of monks I had known in my youth. "As to why the creature is here, I know not. Perhaps, it has become part of the punishments inflicted here, or it may not even be aware that Hell had grown up where its old stomping grounds used to be."

That was an eerie thought! I straightened up. "What was Hell? I mean, before there were men to punish?"

"A jail for fallen angels until Judgment Day," Gregor replied gruffly.

"But what about this swamp?" I continued. "Was this particular area used to imprison fallen angels? Did it exist previously, and the Seven who rule Hell just built over it? I thought Mephisto said human passions brought this swamp into being?"

"Je ne sais pas." Malagigi shrugged. "When I next see my master in the Brotherhood of Hope, I will ask him. He has a master of his own, who lives near the top of Mount Purgatory. From time to time, that master is able to question the saints."

"The Church may be wrong about dinosaurs," Erasmus called casually, his dark eyes watching Gregor avidly from beneath his lank hair. "The pope admitted the existence of evolution recently."

"*What*? Blasphemy!" Gregor cried. Then, his brow furloughed. "So, Teilhard de Chardinon won our bet did he? I owe him a drink . . . only he's probably dead now, isn't he? How sad."

"The Church was wrong about harrowers, too," I said. "Apparently, eternal torment is not eternal."

"I knew the Church was wrong on a great many points, but you think they would have gotten that right," Erasmus murmured.

"For any who do not repent, it is eternal. For them, the flames will burn eternally, or the swamp will stink." Malagigi pinched his nostrils shut with his hand. "But would God be just or good if he did not hear men's prayers, even when uttered in the bowels of Hell? Remember, the Bible promises us, 'If I make my bed in Hell, behold, thou art there.'"

"So all this time, the Church has been scaring our socks off with tales of Hell, and they haven't been true?" Erasmus turned to Gregor and shouted over the digestive roar, "When you were pope, Brother, did you ever hear tell of such a thing?"

Gregor nodded. "We knew."

Erasmus shot up into a sitting position and stared at Gregor, his whirling staff ignored in his hand. His head brushed against the crimson roof. "Come again?"

"We knew." Gregor assumed his grave and ponderous churchman aspect. "It is recorded in a document called the *Apocalypse of Peter.*"

"*Apocalypse of . . .*" called Mab. "What's that—the End of Pete?"

"*Apocalypse* means 'revelation,'" Gregor explained hoarsely. "In this case, a revelation supposedly witnessed by Simon Bar Jonah, though no one believes Saint Peter wrote it himself."

"How come no one has ever heard of this document?" Erasmus asked suspiciously.

"Churchmen have," Gregor replied gravely. "When the Church Fathers put the Bible together, they debated whether the holy script should end with the *Revelations of Saint John* or the *Apocalypse of Peter.* Eusebius of Caesarea, the man who drew up the original list for what books should appear in the Bible, was uncertain about *Revelations.* He preferred the *Apocalypse of Peter,* but in the end the Church Fathers chose Saint John's writings to enter the Scripture."

"Any idea why?" Mab asked, pen poised.

"Partially for reasons of authenticity and partially because in Saint Peter's book, Our Lord Jesus tells Saint Peter that at the end of time, if those in Heaven pray for those in Hell, God will let all the sufferers out. But, he asks Saint Peter not to tell anyone." Gregor raised his voice so we could all hear him over the background noise. "The Church Fathers felt any suggestion of a way out of Hell might encourage men not to take virtue seriously. Besides, as it was Our Lord himself who requested the matter be kept secret, they felt his wishes should be honored."

"So, they knew that if we should ever find ourselves in Hell for real, we should keep praying? That's sort of an important point, don't you think!" Erasmus looked shaken. Then, his expression grew more skeptical. "Are you sure you didn't just make this up?"

"It's all true. You can look it up, if you like," Gregor replied stoically. "Or you could, last time I was out and about. I am assuming that the *Orbis Suleimani* has not altered the records since. If they had not done so in nineteen hundred years, they are unlikely to have done so while I was imprisoned."

"The *Orbis Suleimani!*" Malagigi's eyes had grown round. "*Sacrebleu!* They are sorcerer-hunting madmen of the worst sort! Their name alone strikes terror into the hearts of every practitioner of the subtle arts!"

"That is because they defend mankind from the menace of magic." Erasmus leaned forward, grinning wolfishly. "That's how humans got to be the way they are today, you know . . . masters of the earth: because of the *Orbis Suleimani*. Because of us!"

"Enough about the *Orbis Suleimani*. They give me the creeps," Mab announced. "Caught a—well, you'd call it a cousin—of mine once, several millennia back, and he's still in a vial in the Vault under Prospero's Mansion." Mab gave me a level look. "If we survive this, Ma'am, I think you should give him back to me. Call it 'hazard pay.' "

"Very well, Mab. If we get out of here alive, you may have him," I promised firmly, silencing the objections in my brothers' faces with a stern glance.

The look of astonishment upon Mab's face, when he heard he had gotten his way, was priceless.

As we crouched together beneath our makeshift tarp, the silvery light of the tiny star illuminating our faces, I thought of my brother Theophrastus who had left the family for decades, allowing himself to suffer and grow old, due to his fear that continued exposure to magic would damn him.

"Does Theo know all this," I asked, "about there being hope, even in Hell?"

"I do not know." Gregor's long hair rippled over his broad shoulders as he shrugged. "Why?"

I tried to swallow, but my mouth was too dry. "Someone should tell him."

CHAPTER
FIVE

Some Are Born with Souls . . .

"Your turn to take the star." Malagigi extended the silver spark toward Mab, who sat hunched down upon the floor between the seats of the broken gondola, doodling in his notebook.

"I don't know about this," Mab muttered. "I'm not like the rest of you . . . I don't got one of those soul things."

"Excuse me?" Malagigi inclined his ear.

"He's not a human," Erasmus explained from where he lay on his back now, his arm and staff extended outside our hideout. "He's an Aerie Spirit, one of the servants of my father, the magician."

"You mean, like my elementals?" Malagigi's features lit up. He leaned toward Mab, his face appearing more substantial in the silvery light. "Do you know that God will grant you a soul, if you ask for one in prayer? My master in the Brotherhood of Hope explained this to me. I told my elemental friends and one of them, a sylph, was granted a soul!" He frowned, absentmindedly brushing at the anchor symbol upon his shoulder. "The others would not ask."

Mab frowned dubiously and pulled his hat lower over his eyes. He turned to me where I sat cramped atop one of the gondola benches, my head ducked to avoid bumping the robes that made up the roof above me. "Is that true, Ma'am? Can a creature without a soul be granted one?"

"It can," Gregor responded before I could answer. "Father once told me he believed putting Aerie Ones into bodies might make it possible for them to acquire souls."

"What!" I cried, leaping up. My head pushed upon the robes above us, causing acid that had pooled in the folds of the fabric to stream down on all sides.

"Why would that be?" Erasmus poked his head up. "Elves have bodies, and they do not have souls."

"It was not the body per se," Gregor called back, "but the interaction with mankind. It was living among human beings and interacting with us that Father believed would bring about this transformation. Elves do not live like men. Nothing in their society—if you can even call it that—encourages compassion, consideration, love, or good deeds."

"Really?" I sat down again, hard.

The world seemed to spin around me—or maybe it actually was spinning—as this missing piece fell into the puzzle that was my father's secret plans. So, Aerie Ones could gain souls! Was that why Mab and Caurus seemed so civil, while Boreas—who dwelt in a body but seldom interacted with men—did not?

Mab had not been civil back in his windy days. The Greeks had considered the Northeast the worst of all winds, and sailors knew to fear the notorious Nor'easter. Could the Aerie Ones who interact with humans on a regular basis be joining the Company of Men, of which Astreus had spoken—a term he had used to refer to a gathering of human beings, the way one might say, a pack of wolves or a herd of deer.

My thoughts returned to the cavern of naked Italians beneath Logistilla's house—bodies I suspected Father had instructed her to create for the purpose of housing Aerie Ones. Could Father's plan be to give souls to all the Aerie Ones? Was such a thing possible? Had he hoped they would gain souls before he was required to free them at the end of their thousand years of service?

What of the *oreads* and the *oni*? The sylphs and the salamanders? Could they gain souls, too, if they spent time in a body? The possibilities were mind-boggling!

"Mr. Prospero told me this, too." Mab shrugged. "But I don't feel any different, so I've been figuring it didn't work. What will happen if I don't have a soul? Can I still hold the star?"

Malagigi shook his head sadly. "It will either burn you or fall through your hand."

"Best not to tempt fate," Gregor said hoarsely. "We cannot risk either wounding you or losing the star."

Mab nodded glumly and stuck his hands in his pockets.

"Nonsense." Malagigi went to wave his hand through Mab's arm and was surprised to find it somewhat substantial to him. He patted Mab's shoulder, his hand sinking into Mab's coat. "When else will you get such a chance?

And besides, if you don't have a soul, you needn't lose hope, it could still come! Here, take it. I'll snatch it away again, instantly, if you start to burn."

Malagigi knelt upon the seat of the gondola and pulled Mab's hand from the pocket of the trench coat. The Frenchman dropped the star just above Mab's palm, while cupping his other hand under Mab's, ready to catch the star, should it fall through Mab.

As we sat hunched within our tent and watched the twinkle of silver fall, time seemed to stand still. Gregor, still seated, leaned against his black staff, watching intently. Erasmus had turned off his staff and sat up. Now, he squatted beside Mab, eager for a better view. Mab himself stood rooted in place, his face screwed up. I wondered if he was saying a prayer.

My heart hammered oddly, as if playing a melody against my ribs. Even though there was no reason for my reaction, I felt certain that a great deal rode upon this test. Father had told different stories to various of his children, none of which I knew for certain to be true. If Father's theory about Aerie Ones receiving souls by inhabiting bodies and interacting with men was true, then maybe other things Father had claimed might be true as well.

Maybe, despite all the evidence otherwise, I was not the child of the witch Sycorax. Maybe Father's great love for my mother was not a lie. Maybe Father had never enchanted me, or used me cruelly.

Were the star to burn Mab or fall through his hand, it would be the death knell of all my hopes—as if I would then know for certain that Father was a liar, I a slave, and my entire long life a fraud.

The little star reached Mab's hand. He cried out, gasping, and flinched backward.

My eyes filled with tears. I turned my head away.

"Look!" Malagigi leapt up and danced. He pointed with great excitement. "It's staying!"

I snapped my head up. It was true! The tiny silver star rested upon Mab's palm: it did not burn his flesh.

"Feels . . . sort of weird," Mab voiced hesitantly. Then, slowly, a smile crept across his stony features until it became a wide, jubilant grin. He held his hand up high. The little star shone upon it. Its silvery light flooded the entire hideout, illuminating the cardinal robes above, the gondola below, and the rim of the huge skull.

Erasmus laughed. Malagigi clapped his hands, and even Gregor allowed himself a slight smile. As for me, I cried tears of joy.

Of course, as there was no evidence to support my intuition—no Lady who could have sent it—Mab's catching the star was not really proof of anything.

Yet, my heart sang.

"IT's definitely getting smaller in here." Erasmus's shout jarred me from the waking dream into which I had slipped. He knelt on the edge of the skull with his head sticking back inside our tent. "The ribs have been pushed together, for one thing, with the vertebra all sort of knocked together in a pile. We'd be squished in the mix, too, if it weren't for this skull. We should begin preparing for the next step."

I stretched my stiff limbs and tried not to gag as the stench of digestion assailed me anew. The roaring and grinding were nearly deafening now, and the inside of our makeshift tent was sweltering. My face and neck dripped with perspiration. I wondered that I could have slept through this at all.

Gregor looked up from the middle of the gondola, where he and Malagigi had been kneeling together in prayer. "What did you have in mind, Brother?"

"I think, with my expert knowledge of medicine, the steps I have taken should induce the creature to vomit. I doubt the kronosaurs on earth had a regurgitation reflex, but this creature seems to, so I won't argue with providence.

"Once it throws us up, we'll need to sail on something when we get out. Or, at the very least, hold on to something. Any idea how to go about this?" Erasmus asked. He lifted the crimson robe that formed our tarp, scooted inside the tent, and then tucked the robe back into place, insulating us somewhat from the violence of the stomach. "I'm assuming we'll be spit out into the midst of the swamp rather than near land. Of course, we might be spit out into the depths of the ocean of slime, and all asphyxiate before we reach the surface—in which case, we won't need a boat. Assuming we do need a boat, however, what are we going to do about the gondola?"

We studied our vessel, moving the silver star here and there, to facilitate the examination. I ran my hand along the damaged area, feeling the break in the otherwise smooth wood. "It's cracked, but not split. The *dolfin* has broken off the bow, of course, but that will not affect its water-worthiness. If we had some oakum, we could patch it."

"Didn't think to bring any," Mab mumbled apologetically. He looked puzzled when the rest of us laughed.

"How about securing it to the skull?" I suggested. "We already know that the skull can float a bit; maybe the two of them together could stay afloat."

Erasmus laughed derisively. "Oh, that will work, I'm sure! I can just see us now, floating through Hell in an upside-down skull." Smiling, he tipped back his head and recited:

They went to sea in a Sieve, they did,
In a Sieve they went to sea:
In spite of all their friends could say,
On a winter's morn, on a stormy day,
In a Sieve they went to sea!

"If I recall," Gregor said, humor twinkling in his eyes, "'they' returned twenty years later, hale and whole, having 'been to the Lakes, and the Terrible Zone, And the hills of the Chankly Bore.'"

Mab shuddered. "If this is the Lakes, then I guess we have the Terrible Zone to look forward to. Hope it doesn't take us twenty years to get back, though. That would be bad for Mr. Prospero. Don't much like the sound of Chankly Bore, either."

Erasmus chuckled. "I didn't know you could quote Edward Lear, Gregor. You never cease to surprise me! Very well, let's lash our gondola to the sieve and throw our fate in with The Jumblies. May we be as lucky as they, and our sieve float."

"UH . . . people!" Mab peered out from under the robe as we completed the task of binding the gondola to the skull. "That sea monster we killed? I don't think it's dead!"

"Of course!" Malagigi slapped his forehead. "We never saw its spirit leave its body and depart for some other place! Why didn't I think of that! Bad, Maugris! *Mal!*"

"Perhaps, you should attend more," Erasmus chided mockingly.

"Ah! *Touché!*" Malagigi made a show of clutching his heart as if he had been stabbed.

"Is that what would usually happen?" I asked. "We would see the spirit depart from the body?"

"If a living creature died, yes." Malagigi sat down beside me. "Unlike the kronosaur, however, the sea monster may not be a creature that swam, living, from Earth. It may be one of those nightmares that serves the demons and preys upon the Lustful. If so, then it is bound by the rules that govern the damned. When spirits are damaged here, they lay in a stupor for a time and then regenerate to suffer the same torment again—or to inflict it, if they are one of the torturers."

"So, what do we do now?" I asked, readying my fan.

"Easy enough," Erasmus declared. "We 'kill' it again!"

Mab frowned. "This place gives 'kill' a whole new meaning."

Putting his hand on the hilt of *Durandel,* Erasmus lifted the crimson robe. Then, the world turned upside down. We were all thrown willy-nilly, bouncing off my brother's garments and slamming repeatedly into the gondola, until my head, back, and shins were all stinging. From all around came thuds and shouts of pain. Erasmus, who had been partway out, nearly slid over the edge of the skull, but Gregor managed to grab his foot and yank him back in. Eventually, all of us were able to grab on to the seats.

"Malagigi!" I shouted, once I had wedged my feet under the far seat, so that I now flopped around with the skull-boat rather than in it. "Go up and see what is going on!"

The blue-robed Frenchman flitted away, reappearing soon after.

"La! I believe the creature is trying to disgorge us."

"Finally," Gregor croaked hoarsely.

"That answers any questions about its vomit reflex." Erasmus clung to the upside-down gondola seat. "Quick! Cut the ties that are holding us to the ribs!"

Around and around, we spun, like fair-goers trapped in a children's ride. I managed to open my fan and slice through the rope securing us to the ribs nearest to me. I could only hope that the others had done the same.

Then, we were right side up again, rushing along on a river of bile. The crimson robe had pulled free in several places; it fluttered wildly. Through the openings, we could see that we were in the mouth rushing toward the creature's teeth. The wet roof of the mouth was only a little ways above our head, and the teeth were now only the size of fence posts—nowhere as large as the sharpened columns we had passed on our way in, but still big enough to pierce us through the middle. As we careened toward them, the jaws began to close.

We were heading directly toward a picket fence of death. The river of stomach fluids that bore us forward poured over the lower teeth, but the gleaming tips of the upper teeth descended rapidly.

"It's going to bite us!" I cried.

"Down in front!" Erasmus cried. "Everybody duck!"

Erasmus drew the sword *Durandel.* Rising in a place where the ropes had come free, he balanced on our unsteady craft like a surfer, the blade raised behind his head.

We shot forward just as the jaws descended. Shouting, Erasmus swung. His sword struck through two teeth with the full force of his strongest blow. They cracked, spraying splinters of ivory enamel right and left. Erasmus threw himself down onto the crimson robe, squashing the rest of us, and we sailed through the gap to freedom.

The force of our ejection from the kronosaurus propelled us some distance across the scum-covered swamp. Luckily for us, the plesiosaur had surfaced before disgorging us, so we could breathe. However, there was no way for us to escape, should it decide to pursue us. As it dived, we held our breath, waiting to see if it would resurface. Our skull-boat bobbed lopsidedly, but it did not sink.

"Any sign of it?" Mab peered off into the gloom, looking this way and that.

"None," Erasmus replied after another tense minute had passed. "I see our other friend over there, the sea monster. It's floundering about, but it looks as if its eyes are healing. Perhaps, we should run before it recovers more fully."

"Run, how?" I asked. "Our pole-oar is broken."

"Ah! As to that!" Malagigi pulled free the two pieces that had been used to support the tent. Closing his eyes and bringing his hands together, he prayed over them. When he lifted his head, he was holding the full-sized pole again.

"Well . . . that's convenient!" Erasmus declared. "Nicest thing that's happened all day!"

MALAGIGI poled us through the swamp. Mab held the silver star, grinning like a jack-o-lantern. The swamp was horrible, ugly, and stank, true, but it beat being digested by an ancient dinosaur.

"Now we are back where we were," Malagigi said cheerfully as he poled, "seeking the Greatest Swordsman in Christendom. Ah, what a fighter he was in his prime! Come, Erasmus, distract us from the horrors around us. Tell us more of this famous duel that your brother fought."

Erasmus obliged, describing the duel between Mephisto and Cesare in some detail, adding, "It was a great rivalry. Both young men were handsome

and talented. They moved in the same circles and were fighting over a beautiful girl. Antonio set the whole thing up. He made a mint off the match. Everyone had bet on the higher-ranking, better-known Cesare, of course."

"Higher-ranking?" Mab paused. "Wasn't Mephisto's father the Duke in
an independent Duchy?"

"Cesare's father was pope," I replied.

"Pope!" Mab exclaimed. "I thought popes weren't allowed to be fathers . . .
except in the spiritual sense, of course."

"That is the normal way of things," Erasmus replied airily. "This pope
was different."

A deep inarticulate noise made me glance Gregor's way. Slowly, my
brother rose until he stood precariously in the gondola, his red cardinal's
robes billowing about him. He glared down at the rest of us, his face so suffused with wrath that his normally olive complexion appeared ruddy.

It was the old Gregor again, the Gregor from before his imprisonment,
the harsh and brutish man I could never bring myself to like.

"Are you telling me"—his hoarse voice sounded softer and more menacing than I had ever heard him—"that the Cesare Mephisto fought was
Cesare Borgia?"

"Didn't you know?" Erasmus asked in surprise.

"No! No one mentioned it."

"I take it you've heard of this Borgia guy?" asked Mab.

"Heard of him? *Borgias!*" Gregor spat, his eyes glittering with the memory of countless hateful offenses. "If ever there was a family I abhor, it is the
Borgias! Everything that went wrong in Western Civilization since the fif-
teenth century was the fault of the Borgias! All this . . ."—he spread his
arms, indicating the Swamp of Uncleanness beyond; the silver star wobbled
about on his hand—"harkens back to them!"

"That seems a bit extreme," Mab said cautiously.

"When people speak of the abuses of the Church," Gregor continued,
"they are referring to the reign of the Borgias! The Reformation was brought
on by the excesses of the Borgias! No wonder the blackguard broke his
word to Mephisto and continued fighting after first blood! A blacker scoundrel never walked the earth, except perhaps for his father! I hope Pope
Alexander burns in Hell!"

The wrath in Gregor's eyes flickered suddenly and drained away as he
glanced around at our surroundings. He stroked his beard thoughtfully. "I
wonder if we'll see him here."

"I suspect he is farther down, in a lower Circle," Malagigi replied graciously, his eyes watching the star and the rocking motion of the gondola. "I could inquire if you like."

"No . . . no matter." Gregor sat down again, leaning on his staff as he did so, his hoarse voice steady again. "These Borgias corrupted the Church with decadence, performing every imaginable offense. Cesare was the man after whom Machiavelli modeled his book, *The Prince*.

"And the greatest irony?" Gregor continued sadly. "Several Renaissance artists used Cesare Borgia as their model when painting Jesus. Because of this, to this day, portraits of Our Lord continue to resemble this unscrupulous villain! He was a murderer who threw his rape victims into the Tiber, and his is the face of our Savior!" Gregor shook his head at the tragedy of it. "This is the kind of man with whom our brother consorted? This sword partner of Mephisto's was even accused of having committed the heinous crime of incest, fathering a son upon his own sister."

"Gregor, my lad, maybe we Prosperos shouldn't throw rocks at other glass houses," Erasmus cautioned gently.

Gregor gave Erasmus a puzzled glance, and I realized that my brother, the former pope, had not understood whose children Teleron and Typhon were. The argument between Titus and Logistilla back on Prospero's Island must not have made much sense to him, but then, having just returned from three decades of imprisonment upon Mars, probably much that we said did not make sense to him. I wondered if Titus would have married Logistilla if he had known Brother Gregor was still alive.

"Besides," Erasmus added, "Pope Alexander VI did get the trains running on time." He waved his hand. "Or whatever it was that needed done back then. He ran a tight ship of state, which is more than can be said for Mussolini, who is credited with getting his trains to run on time, but never did." When he saw me gawking at him, Erasmus added with a shrug, "Ulysses told me. You know what a train nut Ulysses is."

Malagigi said, "Young Cesare was a follower of Antonio's, I believe, rather than a friend of Mephisto's. He looked up to Antonio because your uncle was reputed to be a sorcerer."

I said, "Theophrastus believed that the stories of Cesare's sister, Lucrezia Borgia, poisoning people were actually a cover for the spells that Antonio taught her and her brother."

Gregor nodded. "Among the inner circles of the Church, it was well known that she practiced black magic of the worst sort."

"But that might not have been Antonio's fault," Erasmus warned. "The Borgias were *Orbis Suleimani,* too. So—like Antonio and Father—they had access to the magic they were supposed to be stopping. How do you think the popes in Rome got all that loot we appropriated from them in 1623? The Spear of Longinus? The Ark of the Covenant? The two Borgia popes, Cesare's father and his great uncle, robbed the *Orbis Suleimani* treasure house to get all those goodies."

"Indeed. That was the reason I supported Father's raid on the Vatican, despite my reservations." Gregor spoke gravely. "Father was entirely correct. Access to unholy magic was ruining the Church. The quality of the churchmen improved greatly after we removed those accursed talisman. Only we should not have taken the Ark of the Covenant. I told Father this at the time, but he would not listen. The events that followed proved me right."

I straightened, startled. Gregor believed that Cornelius's blindness had been a punishment for our having stolen the Ark from the holy church? I wondered if there were any truth to his theory.

"Borgias!" Gregor shuddered. Despite the great heat, he chafed his arms as if he was cold. "They must all be down here somewhere, Cesare and Lucrezia, too."

"She was a very lovely woman, Lucrezia." Erasmus sighed.

"You knew her?" Gregor's eyes flicked over him disapprovingly.

"Only in passing," Erasmus murmured. "Though Mephisto fought a duel on her behalf when he was Duke of Milan. She married one of our cousins, you know."

"The Harebrain was duke, once?" Mab asked.

"After our guide"—Erasmus indicated Malagigi—"and his siblings drove us out of Milan, our family regrouped and returned about fifteen years later. Both Mephisto and I had a chance to be duke for a bit, before the Hapsburgs finally threw us out for good in 1535."

"Hadn't realized that. Maybe I should be calling you, 'Your Grace.'" Mab scribbled a note.

"It was long ago," Erasmus allowed. "If you won't call me Erasmus, please stick with Professor."

"And this great duel between your brother and Cesare: it was all over a girl?" Malagigi asked eventually, when the going got easier for him. "How *romantique!*"

Erasmus chuckled. He leaned over the side of the boat and peered into the swampy waters below us. "Cesare claimed Mephisto had trifled with her and alienated her affections. Only it had not been Mephisto at all . . ."

"Really? Who was it?" I had never heard this part of the story.

Erasmus had the decency to look sheepish. "It was I."

"You!" I scrambled to sit straight in my astonishment. "And Mephisto fought Cesare to cover for you?"

Erasmus actually blushed. "I was four years his junior and still clumsy with a sword. Mephisto knew I had no chance." He chuckled again. "I was so innocent back then. Bianca and I had met by the Elephant Door, alone, and I had kissed her on the cheek. I thought myself so very naughty."

"All these years, Mephisto never said a word!" I laughed.

CHAPTER
SIX

The Hellwinds Cometh

After we had poled our skull-boat for about a quarter of an hour, Malagigi pointed to a large island upon which succubi cavorted with the souls of the dead. As we approached the shore, horned women swept out of the sky, calling to Mab, Malagigi, and my brothers, smiling and cooing. They had naked breasts and long straight hair. One extended her long finger, with its blood-red nail, and crooked it at me, pursing her lips invitingly. I jerked back, revolted. Gregor placed his staff over his forearm, forming a cross. Hissing, she flew away.

Landing, we followed Malagigi around a large boulder. On the far side, a great black demon lay stretched out on a couchlike rock. Rotting, emaciated women fawned upon him, kissing his marble-like limbs and performing acts I did not study closely enough to identify. Nearby, other women, equally repulsive, danced jerkily or sang. Their music was a horrible cacophony of nauseating sound.

Before I could avert my gaze, the demon turned its many-horned head and regarded me with glowing sapphire eyes. I recognized my brother.

"Ugh, Mephisto," I cried in disgust, raising a hand to block my vision. "Really!"

"Mephisto?" Erasmus frowned, glancing about. "Where?"

"Sister?" The demon chuckled, half-rising, so that he reclined like a Roman. "Care to join us?"

Mab strode in to the midst of the revelers and grabbed the crystal ball from where a damned soul had been trying to commit an unnatural act with it. He crossed to where Mephistopheles lay and shoved the silver star near his face so that the true nature of his paramours became clear to him. Roaring with revulsion, my brother the demon leapt to his feet, scattering the fawning damned like mice before a lion. His staff, still handcuffed to his arm, swung about freely.

"Fool, Sorcerer," Gregor shouted. "You have brought us to the wrong Mephistopheles. I warned you all that we should not trust Maugris."

Gregor turned toward Malagigi. With calm determination, he raised the hand bearing the Seal of Solomon. I did not know if the Seal could harm a good shade such as our guide, but I did not want to risk finding out. I leapt in front of the Frenchman and spread my arms, blocking my brother's way.

"No, Gregor! That *is* Mephisto!"

" 'Is' in what meaning of the word?" murmured Erasmus, his brow furrowed. He stood poised, as if waiting for the situation to resolve into some kind of sense.

Overhead, the flying succubi screamed and reeled, dashing away into the lurid red sky in their attempt to flee the dreaded Seal of Solomon. Gregor, meanwhile, had turned his makeshift cross on our family demon.

"Come now, Brother. That will not work on me." Mephistopheles laughed, though he winced and took a step back.

"What does this mean?" Gregor's raspy voice was so harsh I could hardly make out his words. "Why does this demon call me 'Brother'?"

"Because that demon is the Harebrain in his alternate form," Mab explained as he returned from poking around the stone couch, Mephisto's clothing dripping from his arms. He handed the long royal blue surcoat to Mephistopheles, muttering. "Here. Don this to cover your nakedness. There are ladies present." Mab glanced with disgust at the now cowering souls of the damned. "One, anyway."

"So, our brother has an alternate form . . . rather like Bruce Banner and the Hulk?" Erasmus asked faintly.

Gregor stared at him blankly.

"Doctor Jekyll and Mr. Hyde," explained Erasmus.

"Yeah, only I don't think any science experiments were involved," Mab quipped.

Gregor was unable to follow their conversation. He scowled at them both. "I like this not! How did Mephisto become a demon?"

Mephistopheles stepped forward, now dressed in his surcoat. Malagigi and Erasmus both took a careful step backward. Gregor, Mab, and I stood our ground.

Looming over them, my brother the demon pointed at the crystal globe in Mab's hands. "The Mystic Eye of John Dee can see into the depths of Hell. With it, I beheld dastardly deeds and black treacheries committed by the denizens who dwelt here. Demons are forever committing crimes they do not want their superiors to discover. By observing these crimes and informing them that they had been observed, I gained their support. In this manner, I moved up through the ranks until I had acquired the prestige and powers of a Prince of Hell. Once I had this power at my fingertips, I used it to forge new compacts." He hefted his staff, which was a good foot longer than it had been in our youth. "To create new bindings so that I could summon more creatures."

"Despicable," hissed Gregor, his old churchman ways rising to the fore.

"Gaining power in Hell—by blackmail. Doesn't God burn you twice for that?" Erasmus's voice was light, but there was a tremor to it. Mephistopheles turned his many-horned head toward Erasmus. His sapphire eyes glittered icily. He took a menacing step forward.

"Let he who is without sin cast the first stone," urged Malagigi, stepping hastily between them and raising his hands, though I did not know what kind of a barrier his insubstantial body would have made.

"So, this is what drove you mad." Gregor leaned against his staff and nodded as if some ancient suspicion had been confirmed. "Consorting with the Powers of Hell!"

"No, Brother, that was caused by . . . Arghh!" Mephistopheles tipped back his horned head and howled at the lurid sky. "Fools! You have caused me to recall what I must not!"

Above, the sky rumbled.

"Flee, fools!" Mephistopheles raised his arms toward the sky. "The Queen of Air and Darkness approaches!"

The lurid red sky rolled back like a scroll, showing a foggy gray beyond. From this mist streamed a horde of demons, imps, demi-goblins, and cacodemons followed by a black chariot pulled by skeletal lions. Within the chariot, whip in hand, stood a figure of beauty and malice, cold as death, pale as bone.

Alarmed, we Prosperos raised our staffs. Hellshadow seeped from Gregor's staff and Erasmus's began to hum. Unconcerned, Malagigi walked calmly to Mab and held out his hand. Reluctantly, Mab parted with the little silver star. Retreating until he stood a short distance from the rest of us, Malagigi bent his head in prayer and raised his hand, so that the light upon his palm shone brightly. Starless, Mab pulled out his lead pipe.

Erasmus held his whirling, humming staff at arm's length, wincing slightly because of the stiffness in his arm, tired after hours spent withering the plesiosaur. "Would it be out of place of me to ask why Lilith is attacking us?" he asked airily. "Is it just a general she's-evil-we're-good thing? Or is it personal?"

"It's personal," Mab replied. "She owns your brother . . . but only when he remembers that she does . . . which is why he drank from the Lethe."

"And Gregor just made him remember. Got it. Good going, Greggie-Poo."

The demon Mephistopheles turned his head and regarded us. "How did you four escape the Hellwinds? How did you stay together?"

"Gregor's staff," I replied. "It protected us."

Mephistopheles's head swiveled until his glowing eyes fixed on Gregor. "Protect us, Brother, for only the Hellwinds will save us now!"

"Brothers, to me!" Gregor grabbed me about the waist with one arm, as he planted his feet and raised his staff. Darkness poured from its black, rune-carved length. Erasmus and Mab lunged for Gregor, each grabbing on to the crimson robes.

Mephistopheles cried, "Play, Sister! Call up the Hellwinds and blow the Queen of Air and Darkness from the sky!"

"What?" I cried, The specter of Theo's face as he was torn from my grasp rose before my thoughts. "I can't! It will go badly again! I'll lose you all!"

"Great," Erasmus murmured. "She's only willing to play her flute when it's going to harm her own family. Can't bear to hurt the poor Queen of Air and Darkness. That wouldn't be nice."

By God, sometimes I hated Erasmus! With an angry jerk, I shook the grime and mud from my flute and lifted it to my lips.

As the marvelous music issued forth, Mephistopheles crossed his arms, lowered his head, and shrank, until he was Mephisto again. He looked wildly right and left and then dived toward Gregor, landing full out on his stomach where he hugged Gregor's right leg, his staff clattering beside him. Malagigi glanced up from his prayers, smiled, and lowered his head again. Apparently, the Hellwinds did not worry him.

The song of the flute rang out across the swamp, evoking memories of birds in flight and spring mornings washed clean by fresh warm rain. All around us, the demons and the damned turned toward the music. Some came toward me, wondering, imploring, as if drawn against their will.

Others recoiled, covering their ears and yowling. Not even the slightest breeze blew, however, and I feared the Hellwinds would not heed my command.

Could it have been an accident that the Hellwinds came the first time, not my doing after all? A great sense of relief washed over me.

Then, we heard it, a roar like unto a thousand jet engines, bearing straight down upon us. The Hellwinds had come.

Darkness billowed out of Gregor's staff, obscuring much of our view. Through it, we could barely make out the clouds of inky soot as they bore down upon the flying horde. Lilith's entourage, now terrified, turned and fled. Some of the quicker ones darted to safety, but the rest were caught up and carried away.

The Queen of Air and Darkness held up her hand, and the Hellwinds parted around her. Those of her servants who were behind her quickly moved into the safety of her wake. Slowly, the area of calmness around her spread, and she continued her advance.

"Geesh!" whispered Mab. "That's not good!"

Just then, a fleeing cacodemon, desperate to escape the dark winds, crashed into Lilith, knocking her backward. The moment she ceased commanding them, the Hellwinds bore down upon her. The clouds of billowing darkness caught up her carriage and tumbled it over and over again. Then all was quiet and dark.

"SHE's gone. You can emerge." Malagigi's voice calmly cut through the darkness. The Hellwinds were gone, and all was quiet again, save for the moans of the damned. The smell of brimstone was strong in the air.

Mephisto rose to his feet and cheered, punching the air. "Yah! Yippee!" Turning to Malagigi, he threw his arms out wide and cried, "Hi, I'm Mephisto. Don't you recognize me?"

"Yes, I know who you are," Malagigi responded.

Mephisto began to say something else, but paused when he saw Erasmus's and Gregor's expressions.

"What? What did I do now?" He looked down. "Why am I naked except for my surcoat?"

"Too busy orgying with the likes of them." Erasmus gestured at the emaciated men and women groveling on the island about us. It was less crowded than before. Apparently, a few of the locals had been caught up in the Hellwinds, along with Lilith's entourage and moved to some other place. Those who remained cowered on the ground; one or two gazed with fascination at Malagigi's star.

"Yuck!" Mephisto clapped his knees together and waved his hands about excitedly, his staff flying freely. "Ewww!" Then, he straightened and looked down at the rest of his clothes, which Mab thrust at him. "Why'd I do that?"

Gregor moved toward Mephisto, his expression serene, but his staff upraised menacingly. I stepped in his way.

"He doesn't remember, Gregor. He doesn't remember anything about it. That's how he protects himself from his oath to . . ." I paused and wet my lips, pointing up at where the Queen of Air and Darkness had just departed. "From the person who just came after us. There's no use questioning him. He doesn't remember a thing."

Gregor regarded Mephisto who was busily trying to get dressed—a process that involved undoing and reattaching the handcuffs.

"Is this true?" Gregor asked hoarsely.

"Is what true?" Mephisto looked happily between our faces, frowning slightly when he saw Gregor's scowl. "What?"

"Bah!" Gregor spat and turned away. He stood with his back to Mephisto, his arms crossed. Then, his shoulders relaxed. He shook his head and chuckled softly. "It just does not pay to become upset. Not even when one's family members become demons."

I gawked at Gregor. Was this the same thundering brother I remembered? Boy, had he changed!

"Just get dressed, Harebrain," muttered Mab, "and be thankful that it was these guys who found you, and not Mr. Theophrastus and the *Staff of Devastation*!"

AS we waited for Mephisto to dress, Malagigi joined us, his tiny star gleaming on the palm of his outstretched hand. "I must part with you all. Miranda's music has stirred memories of better things in a few of these poor souls. There may be good I can do here."

"It has been a pleasure to see you, Malagigi," Erasmus replied sincerely. "Particularly, to see you in that"—he indicated the blue robe with the anchor and star on its shoulder—"rather than in this." He gestured toward the swamp and Hell beyond.

"It is not a bad life—for life is what we of the Brotherhood of Hope call it, even though, for us, the word does not have the same meaning it does for you," Malagigi replied. "In many ways, my life is better now than it was on Earth."

"How so?" Gregor came forward, his crimson robes billowing about him. He leaned upon his staff, watching Mephisto.

"I had become callous." Malagigi tucked his hands in his sleeves. "As a youth, I was raised by a good Christian fairy—there are some, you know," he added when Gregor frowned skeptically. "I was taught to help others and do good. But, I could not seem to do good. Those I helped turned out to be the villains, or they died of old age despite my best efforts. After a time, my enthusiasm waned. Now, finally, I can help others, because I can see exactly what is good and what is not!"

Erasmus snorted with contempt. Malagigi arched his very French eyebrow.

"*Mais non?* You think I cannot?" he asked. "Good moves you up. Evil moves you down. It is all very obvious and straightforward . . ."

"You make it sound so easy," Erasmus said dubiously.

"Oh, no! It is difficult! This work is difficult, too." He gave a shamefaced smile. "Difficult and humbling. In my day, I had been the master of secrets, walking paths only I could walk and speaking to friends with whom only I could converse. Now, I am no longer unique. Everyone in the Brotherhood, except the most abject novices, can walk the hidden ways and talk to elementals. I, who lived by subterfuge and mystery, have no more secrets to sustain me. I am stripped bare."

Malagigi untied his golden belt and slowly opened his blue robe. Underneath, he wore a garment of glimmering white, only the cloth was stained, as if it had had been dipped in blood and gore. Erasmus recoiled visibly; his gaze fixed upon the gruesome blots that marred the robe's purity.

"Ew!" Mephisto cried from where he hopped about trying to get his leg into his pants. "Yucky! Pewwy!"

Malagigi hung his head sheepishly. "Every time I help someone I've harmed, a stain fades; so now, as those who attended will recall, I seek out those who are here due to the French Revolution. But the damage done to France by the Reign of Terror still goes on, and new stains appear even as the old ones fade.

"And then there are stains for those who were damaged by my students," he added, sighing heavily.

"You suffer for your students' sins?" Gregor asked.

Malagigi shook his head. "Only for the harm done with secrets that were not mine to share. It is the penalty I must pay for having divulged mysteries I had been told to keep privy."

"I don't remember you doing much teaching." Erasmus leaned forward with interest. "Did you take many students?"

"Only a few. None after Theophrastus betrayed me." Seeing our glares, he cried, "*Mais non!* Not your brother Theo! I was speaking of Philippus Aureolus Theophrastus Bombastus Von Hohenheim."

"Oh, him!" Mephisto nodded knowingly.

"Philippus-wha-who?" Mab asked.

"A student of mine wrote down the secrets I taught him and published them before all the world." Malagigi sighed again.

"He means Paracelsus," Erasmus drawled. "Though, in his defense, Paracelsus is still much revered by the medical community for his contributions to the healing arts."

"That perp I've heard of! Paved the way for no end of trouble, he did." Mab slapped his lead pipe against his fist. "Letting on about the existence of sylphs, for instance. Mortals and spirits shouldn't mix. No good will come of it."

"Paracelsus was a dodo head," Mephisto declared. "He confused gnomes with *oreads*."

"Actually, I did that," Erasmus admitted airily, examining his fingernails. "I was a member of the Paracelsus Obscuration Team—though we did not call it that, at the time. His work had been spread too widely for the *Orbis Suleimani* to squelch it entirely, but we could alter it, make it less effective. We made changes to the original and to some primary copies. Later, our false version was taken as the true copy and proliferated. Of course, having the wrong information led to some would-be magicians making deadly errors but . . ." Erasmus shrugged. "Better the magician than his victims."

Mab pulled out his notebook. "Why gnomes instead of *oreads*?"

"Gnomes can't cause earthquakes."

"Ah . . . good point!"

Malagigi shivered. "Even now, the Circle of Solomon fills me with terror. Perhaps, more so now, since I would be a shade to them and vulnerable to their exorcists!" He drew his robes together. Then, with a quick little smile, he opened them again and pointed to a splotch like an old bruise over his hip. "This one is our attack on Milan."

Erasmus had trouble finding his voice. "Whatever my part of that, I forgive you."

A tiny portion of the stain, nearly imperceptible, faded.

"Dear God!" whispered Erasmus. He looked more shaken than I had ever seen him.

"And I!" I stepped forward. "I forgive you, too."

"And me! Me, too! Oh, oh, pick me!" Mephisto jumped around with his hand in the air, the sleeve of his half-donned shirt flailing wildly about his head. "I want to forgive!"

"And mine for what it's worth, though I was not there," rumbled Gregor.

As we watched, tiny bits of the purple and green bruise that was the attack of Charlemagne's Brood on Milan vanished, leaving slightly more of the robe white and pure.

"Glorious!" Gregor whispered hoarsely. "To have seen it with my own eyes."

"Come on, Detective!" Mephisto pulled on Mab's coat. "Join in!"

"What?" Mab drew back, outraged. "I didn't contribute to that stain! I've never even been to Milan. Not that I remember, anyway." Turning to Malagigi, he added, "But I want to keep this new soul of mine clean, so if there is anything I can forgive you of, I do."

Malagigi drew his dark blue garments closed, hiding the stained robe, and fastened his golden belt. His eyes filled with tears. "My one great regret is that I cannot share this knowledge—that redemption is possible even here, in Hell—with my brother, Eliaures. I cannot find him. I have spoken to my sister Melusine. She is too caught up in her spite to hear me yet, but I pray for her daily. Never underestimate the power of prayer, nor cease to pray for your loved ones, whether alive or no!"

"If I see 'em, I'll let 'em know," Mab promised.

"What of your other sisters?" I asked.

"Alcina and Falerina are above." Malagigi pointed up. "They were never as wicked as the rest of us, so they could find it in their hearts to forgive our murderers. I see them occasionally, when they descend to the foot of Mount Purgatory to visit me. But Eliaures, I cannot find."

"Your wish is my command," Mephisto chirped, snatching the crystal sphere back from Mab. "Ball, show me Eliaures."

Within, we saw a group of souls carrying great boulders as they walked along a raised causeway. Recognizing his brother among them, Malagigi cried out with joy.

"He's on the Pathway of Pride at the foot of the Mountains of Misery," Mephisto said. "We're going that way."

"If you see him, tell him my story! Tell him that redemption still awaits!"

"We will do so," Erasmus promised, clasping the Frenchman's hand one last time.

"God go with you, Prosperos!" Malagigi's face shone. "Go in peace, and may your family be reunited! Should you have need of the Brotherhood of Hope, pray. We will not be able to help you in your quest, but if you find someone worthy of our attentions, we will come.

"Blessings to you, too, Souled Elemental! Bright this day will remain in my mind: the day I saw that even the living air can be accepted into the bosom of God!"

Mab returned a crooked grin, then frowned. "What if Lilith returns?" He slapped his lead pipe menacingly across his palm. "Will you be okay?"

"She cannot hurt me, so long as I neither fear nor desire her," Malagigi replied, smiling. "And after the glories I have seen Above, nothing here holds the power to tempt me."

"May God bless thee and watch over thee, my Son." Gregor made the sign of the cross over Malagigi.

"Thank you, Most Holy Father."

Gregor blessed him as he had blessed countless thousands. Unlike when he performed this ritual on earth, the half cape of his crimson robes billowed, as if an invisible wind stirred the fabric. A halo of golden light appeared above his head. Awed, Malagigi bowed his head reverently.

All around the damned paused. Most then fled, screaming. A few stumbled toward my brother, their hands raised before their eyes, as if they longed for the holiness that they recognized, but could not bear the brightness of the light that radiated from him.

"Wow!" Mab gaped.

"Well, he was pope," Erasmus murmured. "Once a pope always a pope, you know."

"Just like the kings and queens of Narnia!" Mephisto exclaimed in delight. When the rest of us glanced at him in puzzlement, he just smiled.

The golden light faded slowly. Then, Gregor was merely Gregor again, but few lost souls approaching him were not daunted. They came toward him, one even daring to touch the hem of his robes. Gregor blessed them, too, and the strange phenomena of light and holy breeze happened again.

MALAGIGI moved forward to speak to the souls who had been blessed by Gregor, while the rest of us walked back toward our skull-boat. Overhead, the sky had rolled back, and the ruddy sky streaked with bands of gray had returned.

We drew near the shore and began dragging the skull-boat back into the swampy waters. Mephisto kept poking at the boat, making it rock. He leapt up and danced around the rim of the skull, his hands spread like an acrobat on a high wire. The rest of us stood, wearily, urging him to stop so that we could come aboard.

Eventually, Gregor and Erasmus manhandled him into a seat and climbed in themselves. The thought of setting out over these waters again filled me with dread. Without the star, the heat was oppressive, and the smell made me nauseous. I let Mab climb in ahead of me.

As I prepared to join my brothers, Malagigi appeared behind us, beside the big rock at the top of the slope.

"Miranda?" he called. "A word, *s'il vous plait?*"

Eager for one more moment in the light of the silver star, I hurried back to the Frenchman. One or two of the decrepit shades came around the edge of the giant boulder, but Malagigi dismissed them with a gesture. He beckoned me close, as if he did not wish anyone else to overhear us.

"Yes?" I inclined my ear toward him.

"This is not a place for one such as you." Malagigi whispered urgently. "You must go back to the surface! If you will not return to the world of the living, go back to the Gate of False Dreams and await your family there, in Limbo."

"That is sweet of you," I began, touched by his chivalric concern. He cut me off with a curt shake of his head.

"Sweet? *Non!* You do not attend!"

"Excuse me?"

"I saw you with the star!" He held out the tiny silver spark. "It would not stay upon your palm. You had to work some enchantment to keep it from sinking through your hand."

"I just concentrated," I objected.

"You should not have had to do so," Malagigi replied, his eyes searching my face, as if he were expecting to see the answer to what puzzled him there.

"W-what does this mean?" I asked haltingly.

"It means something is *wrong* with your soul."

An icy sensation crept down the back of my neck, despite the surrounding heat. I felt strange, as if I were floating, as if I had just awakened from an unpleasant dream and was not yet oriented as to my surroundings.

"My soul!" My hands flew to my chest. "How could anything be wrong with it?"

"I know not, but incomplete it is," Malagigi replied. "Hell is a dangerous place for those blessed by Grace. For those who lack Grace's gifts . . . there is no hope. They have not what is needed to resist the hazards that will face them. If my elemental friends, my sylphs and undines, came here, their pure nature would be tainted by the filth of this place, and they would become fallen, demonic. If you go forward, the person you think of as Miranda will not return. You will literally suffer a fate worse than death."

In my mind's eye, I saw an elf with eyes the color of storms explaining to me what Hell was like for those who had no soul, and why I should slit his throat rather than allow him to suffer such a fate.

"But . . . how could this be?" I cried. A terrible sensation gripped my heart, a dragging, sinking dread. The ground beneath my feet seemed to draw me downward. It amazed me that I was still standing.

I tried to approach the matter rationally. "It must have some cause. My father . . . Theo thinks Father has me under a spell, a spell that impedes my free will. Could enchantment such as this cause . . . soul damage?"

It made me cringe terribly to reveal such aspersions against my father to someone who was practically a stranger.

Malagigi frowned thoughtfully, tracing his mustache with his finger. "I would have to ask my master to be sure, but I do not believe so. Slavery can cause a man many harms, but it cannot rob him of his humanity, no matter what his masters may believe. No, something much more dire is at work here."

"Erasmus believes my mother to be Sycorax, the witch."

Malagigi meditated upon this a time before answering. Meanwhile, the tiny star shone brightly, mocking me with its buoyant cheer. "I recall Sycorax, a slender girl with wide imploring eyes who served some Pagan god." I blinked, startled at the contrast between our memories of Caliban's mother.

Malagigi must have met her when she was young. "Was she not a human witch?" he asked.

"Part-ogre, I believe," I offered quickly.

"Possible." Malagigi frowned dubiously. "But unlikely . . . A human mother would pass a human soul to her child. No, this strikes me as more serious. Your mother must have been truly supernatural, a sylph, or a mermaid— something altogether lacking in a soul."

CHAPTER
SEVEN

The Black Bog of the Sullen and Slothful

"Operate that oversized marble, would you, Harebrain?" Mab asked as I
climbed shakily into the skull-boat. "We can't go any farther until we know
where the rest of your family is. Luckily, the Sphere shows us the real version instead of the primrose version. Or unluckily, depending on how horrible the truth is." He cocked his head and regarded me from beneath the
brim of his fedora. "There wasn't any other member of your family whose
sin was lust, was there, Ma'am?"

I shook my head. "We were each quite different."

"Okay." Mephisto pulled out the crystal ball that had once belonged to
the Elizabethan magician John Dee. He rolled the delicate sphere up and
down his arm, which he undulated like a hula dancer. Mab and Erasmus
flinched as they imagined the precious object rolling off his arm and sinking into the swamp. "Who do you want me to look for first?"

"We could head for whomever is closest," suggested Gregor.

"We should go to whomever is most in need," Erasmus countered.

"Hey, Ball-io." Mephisto caught the glass globe in his hand and looked
into it. "Show me the member of my family who needs our help the most."

Mist swirled in the depth of the crystal ball, clearing to reveal a bank of
hardened lava. Two burnt hulks of flesh were visible in the crystal. One lay on
the ground, a breastplate and helmet of shining white Urim burnt into his
black and bubbling flesh, the *Staff of Devastation* on the ground beside him.
The second stood over him, brandishing a club, the wood of which was, surprisingly, untouched. Soot rained down upon them, sticking to their open
blisters.

The world swayed before my vision.

Someone was screaming. The shrill, horror-filled voice was very close to my ear. It was only when my throat began to ache that I realized the voice yelling my brother's name over and over was mine.

"Theo! Theo! Theo!"

Gregor's strong hands gripped my shoulders. He peered into my face. When he saw that my eyes focused on him, he pulled me roughly against his chest in an embrace that was meant to be comforting, but did not leave much room to breathe. Perhaps, he had intended that because without air in my lungs, I could not scream anymore.

Where was my life? The one I left a month ago? Where was the mother that Father had so loved? Where was my soul? Where was the brother who, above all the others, had made my life worth living?

Where was my Lady?

How could all these things have been taken away so quickly?

The shock of Malagigi's revelation had been bad. Once his parting words had sunk in, however, I had actually felt buoyed up. The possibility of having a mermaid or maybe even an Aerie One for a mother was preferable to being the daughter of the witch Sycorax. And while the information that something was not right with my soul terrified me, it also gave me hope. If I was not human, maybe Father was justified in enchanting me. Maybe I could earn a complete soul, as Mab had. Though if I had not earned one yet—after over five hundred years of living among men—I was not sure what else I could do to merit one.

Discovering one's soul was imperiled, however, was nothing compared to the horror of seeing the person one held most dear unrecognizably burnt and writhing in pain! At least, I was assuming that blackened hulk was Theo—from the breastplate, helmet, and staff. If this was someone else with Theo's gear, and the real Theophrastus were around the corner, I could not have told the difference, so damaged was his body.

As I pulled away from Gregor and looked at the ball again, all concern for myself left my mind; my only thoughts were of how to reach Theo.

"Courage, Sister. He still lives." Gregor squeezed my shoulder; his face was as pale as the mist rising over the swamp.

"Dear God!" Erasmus's voice wavered, as if the ghosts of memories haunted him. He shivered unconsciously. "Burns . . . Those are horrible wounds."

"Ball, show us how to get there from here!" cried Mephisto. His hands were shaking so that he nearly dropped the crystal globe.

Mist swirled in its depth, followed by images of the swamp, the Bridge Across the Styx, and the Wall of Flame.

Panicked, I shook off Gregor and grabbed Mephisto's shoulder. "If you turn back into your big form, you could fly us!"

"No good, Ma'am." Mab shook his head reluctantly. "I'm as eager to save Mr. Theophrastus as anyone—him being such a decent guy—but summoning up Lilith won't help us. We'd just waste time fighting her again."

"But, Theo! He's dying!"

"He will not die today," Gregor replied firmly. "Not a mere day or two after he took the Water of Life. He is suffering, surely, but I can see him moving. If he is alive now, and he receives no additional wounds, he will endure another day. Besides, it looks as if Caliban is with him."

"*And in those days shall men seek death, and shall not find it; and shall desire to die, and death shall flee from them,*" Erasmus quoted softly. He stood, his gaze unfocused, his hands chafing his own arms, as if he was cold.

"Er, thanks, Professor Prospero." Mab gave Erasmus a worried look. "I'm sure that is supposed to make us all feel better."

"But you must be able to do something?" I cried. My voice sounded unnaturally shrill. I could not understand how the others could be sitting so still. "We've got to do something! Gregor! Pole faster!"

"I am moving us as quickly as I can, Sister, but I must know where to go." Gregor spoke calmly, but his hoarse voice had a slight tremor to it.

He poled our little craft forward quickly as he could push. No one spoke. I clutched the edge of the gondola and stared ahead, as if by dint of effort I could see straight through to where Theo lay. Simple objects loomed large in my sight. The dilapidated fig tree to our left had mottled peachy swirls amidst the gray of its bark. The rope tying the gondola to the skull had frayed in places, so that tiny beige hairs stood out from it, as if it had goose bumps. Beyond that, to me, nothing more existed.

Eventually, Mephisto's voice broke the spell. "I'm not afraid of old Lilly-poo, not when Theo's at stake! And I can call up some of my friends to help!" he declared bravely. Then his proud shoulders slumped. "Only flying wouldn't help. The Wall of Flame has no top. I couldn't fly you over it. Do you all think you can get through it?"

"What was the Wall again?" asked Mab.

"A towering inferno of passions. You walk into it and get buffeted by all sorts of emotions: rage, lust, overeagerness. You have to be able to will your-self to be calm to pass through." Mephisto squinted and scrunched up his face, as if to demonstrate the effort of will involved.

Gregor and I insisted we could make it through, but Mab and Erasmus did not seem so confident.

Erasmus glanced back at the Swamp of Uncleanness and said haltingly, "Perhaps, you had better go on without me."

"Don't know what I can do now that I got this soul," Mab muttered. He held his fedora in his hands, twisting the brim. "Could be I can. Could be I can't."

"Come to think of it," Mephisto piped up suddenly, "I'm not sure I can go through without . . . well, you know: whatever it is that I do that I don't remember that you were just talking about that calls you-know-who."

"Is there another way?" asked Erasmus.

"The *Staff of Silence* can stop the raging passions and part the flames," Mephisto replied.

"In that case," Gregor said gruffly, "let us all pray that Titus and his staff are still on this side of the Wall."

THE crystal ball, thank goodness, showed Titus to be on our side of the Wall of Flame. He lay asleep among the bogs on the far bank of the Styx. Luckily for us, he was not actually underneath the peat. Erasmus wanted to call up Mephisto's winged beasts and fly directly to Titus, but Mephisto insisted we pass over the Bridge across the River Styx on foot. Crossing the Styx might rob some of his friends of flight, he explained, and we would not want to find this out halfway.

We rapidly poled our way to the nearest solid island. Once there, Me-phisto tapped his staff, and I began to imagine we were surrounded by great winged beasts. Then, they were among us: the handsome winged steed, Pega-sus; a golden lion with shining mane and downy wings; a gryphon; and the gigantic magnificent roc. Mephisto leapt atop the winged lion. Gregor and I clambered onto Pegasus. Erasmus claimed the gryphon, leaving Mab to sit upon the giant talon of the enormous roc.

Mounted on these creatures, we flew across the swamp. Normally, the joy of flight was my primary delight. Today, however, even the exhilaration of winging along on the back of Pegasus—the terrible swamp passing harm-lessly below—eluded me. It could not drive away the image of my charred and scalded brother.

No matter how hard I urged Pegasus on, he did not go fast enough.

Reaching the bridge, we landed and dismounted. Then, we all held hands and ran, Mephisto's friends padding noisily behind us. Gregor was on the right, his staff ready should the Hellwinds return. With my flute silent, however, all was still. We gained the far side without losing anything more than our breath.

As my feet stepped onto the packed earth, I paused for a single instant to glance back at the bridge.

Had it been only a day ago that we had tried to cross the first time? It seemed like another lifetime.

How exuberant we had been after our victory over Abaddon. We had been laughing, singing even. It had been our first truly happy moment together since the Christmas of 1666.

What could we have been thinking, trespassing upon the Inferno with lighthearted cheer? If only we had not been so hubristic! If we had shown proper respect for our surroundings, we might have succeeded. By now, we might have found Father and been safely back home.

ONCE on the far side of the Styx, we mounted our supernatural steeds again and flew over the marshy earth. We used John Dee's crystal ball as our guide. No illusions dazzled the others here. The view I saw and that showed in the ball was the same view the others beheld.

Each foot, each yard that flashed beneath us, I wished was a thousand more. We flew with the speed of eagles, but it was not fast enough to satisfy my sisterly heart.

"These are the Black Bogs of the Styx," Mephisto called to us from the back of the winged lion. "If you look down long enough, you'll catch a glimpse of the bodies asleep beneath the surface."

"How can you see anything?" Mab shaded his eyes as he attempted to peer over the roc's foot and into the water. "The water is *black* as pitch!"

"They're there, even if we can't see 'em," Mephisto called back. "Though wouldn't it be eerier if we could? I've always thought sleeping beneath the water was eerie. What about you, Miranda?"

"Please, Mephisto," Erasmus objected, yawning. He was slipping slightly to the one side atop the gryphon. "This place is terrible enough without you telling ghost stories to make it creepier."

"It's not a ghost story," Mephisto insisted. He yawned as well, giving a big wide stretch. "They are actually down there."

"All the more reason not to dramatize it," Erasmus called back.

I had been nodding tiredly, my thoughts caught up in fearing for Theo, when suddenly a feeling of free fall in the pit of my stomach made me look up. The flying horse had lowered its head. Its eyes were closed, and it had stopped beating its wings.

We were plummeting.

"Pegasus!" I screamed, yanking on his mane.

The winged steed pulled up and began flapping again, but he careened to the left. I felt as if I was flying on a drunken horse.

Around me, the other winged beasts struggled as well. The roc listed sideways. The winged lion yawned. The gryphon had fallen behind.

"Mephisto," I cried, "your friends are falling asleep!"

Mephisto craned his head to see. "We have to land! I've got to send them away!"

"You mean we have to walk through the bog?" Erasmus cried, aghast. "Don't you have anything that can help us? I mean this is Theophrastus we're talking about! The Old Man needs us!"

"And Titus as well," murmured Gregor.

Mephisto shook his head sadly. "My friends are animals. They don't have the kind of souls you need to resist the ravages of Hell!"

"What about the angel?" Mab called. "Didn't you brag about having one that would act like a valet?"

"Angel in Hell . . . bad idea!" Mephisto squeaked back. "Let's just say things would get worse, not better."

A frisson of fear went through me as I thought about Mephisto's reasoning. I thought about Malagigi's words: *They have not what is needed to resist the hazards that will face them.* If Mephisto's creatures could not survive here, what of me? Would I be able to stay awake?

Soul or no soul, I vowed silently, I would not fail Theo!

WE landed and dismounted, and Mephisto sent his friends home. The ground here was boggy and smelled of peat. Except for the boiling clouds of inky soot overhead and the weird multicolored flames, which ignited intermittently above the bogs before quickly burning out, this could almost be a place on Earth. My brothers and Mab did not report any troubling illusions here, so we no longer needed to hold hands.

We ran, our feet sinking into the spongy earth with each step. It was slow going, and time after time, one of us stumbled. Here and there, pools dotted the landscape with bodies visible in the black water. Some floated face down; others stared at us open-eyed. One or two began to reach out toward us imploringly. Before they could sit up, however, their eyelids sank down, and they returned to sleep.

"Who are they?" Mab panted. He reached for his notebook, but did not pull it out, as he was running.

"The Sullen and Slothful," offered Mephisto. "People who didn't do enough with their lives . . . you know, the kind of guys who go on welfare and drink beer and watch TV all day, never even lifting a finger to brush a fly from their nose? Guys who waste their lives, never doing any good for anyone but never really hurting anybody, either."

"The Angel said Titus's sin was sloth," I commented wearily, hardly aware that I was speaking. The wonderful effect that recalling the angel had had upon my spirits had faded. In the same way that I had not been able to think of fear when she was present, I now could no longer remember the lightness of spirit that had accompanied her. I recalled that it had been present, but I could not remember what it had been like.

"Explains why Titus is here," Gregor's gravelly voice growled as he ran. Despite his serene expression, his face was red from the exertion. It was unlikely he had gotten much exercise while living in his Martian prison.

"Has anyone explained to Gregor about the demons in our staffs?" I gasped, pressing my hands against the stitch in my side. My legs felt like they were made of waterlogged wood, stiff and sluggish.

"The what in our staffs?" Gregor stopped short and gazed at the length of black ebony carved with blood red runes in his hand. While my mind cried out indignantly against the delay, I felt gratified to learn I was not the only one in the family who had been in the dark.

"Our staffs are powered by demons that Solomon stole from Hell," Erasmus said. He, too, was panting. Taking advantage of Gregor's pause, he leaned over and rested, his hands resting on his thighs. "Prolonged exposure to demons warps the human soul. Titus's makes him slothful."

"Why did Father give us these accursed things?" Gregor raised his arm as if to throw his from him. Erasmus lunged and grabbed the staff just as it left Gregor's hand.

"Because someone had to keep them safe—as in: out of the hands of the Rulers of Hell!" Erasmus shouted. He shoved the length of ebony back at Gregor. "Have you gone crazy? Or would you like me to give this back to the Three Shadowed Ones for you?"

Gregor glared at Erasmus, his face red, his nostrils flared. For a moment, I feared he would strike him. Instead, he closed his eyes. Perhaps he was praying. When he opened them again, his face was calm, though still flushed. He retrieved his staff from Erasmus's hand.

"Which demons?" he panted.

"Powerful entities," Erasmus replied. "Princes and Dukes of the Pit, lords of their respective realms. Their loss was a heavy blow to the Inferno, and many a man has been saved due to their absence."

"Indeed? I wish Father had told me." Gregor's husky voice was curt. He shook his head hard, as if to clear it, causing his shoulder-length hair to spread about him like a silky black mane. Continuing forward, he moved at a rapid walk. "Am I the only one he left in ignorance?"

I shook my head, taking big steps to keep up with him. "I only just found out myself."

Erasmus smirked. "Father reserved many of his secrets for those of us who joined the *Orbis Suleimani*."

The landscape grew more boggy, and it became impossible to run. Our feet disappeared into the springy mat of the rusty sphagnum moss. Hundreds of lakes and ponds covered the countryside, peat floating on the black water, thick and dark. Here and there, a hand or a knee protruded through the brown mat of dead vegetation. Where the ground grew firmer, we had to push our way through thorny brambles.

Insects swarmed thick above the surface of the bog. My dress repelled them, but they passed through my face and hands, which I found disconcerting. Their immateriality did not protect us from their unpleasant, high-pitched, buzzing drone. Erasmus tried to swat a few, annoyed by their noise. Irritated, he found he was able to catch one. He squished it between his fingers with a satisfied sigh.

Immediately, he was mobbed by swarms of mosquito-like creatures, all of which were able to draw his blood. Swearing, he activated his staff. The insects about him vanished. He swung his staff near the rest of us, and the irritating buzz ceased, leaving only the soft *whir* of the *Staff of Decay*.

Erasmus's staff was not the only thing preying upon the insects. The landscape was dotted by lank-leaved butterworts and sundews fringed with hundreds of slender tendrils, each tipped with a blood-red dot. Each was spotted with gnats, mosquitoes, and dragonflies, still writhing and alive but unable to escape the sticky grasp of the carnivorous plants. I shivered.

So tired . . .

My limbs felt heavy. My eyes were closing. If only I could rest and do this later, rest even the littlest bit . . .

With a hiss of determination, I threw off the suggestion of fatigue. I was not a person inclined to sloth. I could not have been C.E.O. of Prospero, Inc., had I not been willing to drive myself above and beyond what the next person would do. Certainly, I might be drowsy, but there was work to be done, siblings to be saved.

Around me, my traveling companions fought their own battles with fatigue. Gregor grimly strode forward, but Mab and Erasmus stumbled, and Mephisto walked with his eyes shut, his hands stretched out in front of him like a blind man. I remembered that Erasmus had not slept in the Kronosaur.

"Help! Please, I beg you, help me!" A middle-aged man struggled to free himself from the bog, pushing against the spongy peat. He waved his arms imploringly. "You there! Please, I beg you!"

"Well . . . what do we do now?" Mab asked uneasily. He rubbed his eyes and the back of his neck, blinking tiredly.

"We keep going!" I snapped.

"Probably a trick anyway," Mephisto replied airily. He yawned again and stretched. "Anyone up for nap? All that debauchery back on the island tired me out."

"Fool!" Mab spat. "It's this place! You told us yourself about the bodies sleeping beneath these waters. If you fall asleep here, you'll never wake!" He glanced worriedly at the man struggling toward us. The stranger waved more frantically, but he was sinking. "I think he can see us. Shouldn't we try to help him? What if he's like those people Malagigi was able to rescue?"

"What if he's an evil scum?" Mephisto countered.

"He does seem able to see us." Erasmus took advantage of the conversation to pause. He leaned heavily upon his staff.

"I'm going after him," Mab declared.

"Wait!" I cried. "Mab! We can't afford to stop and help him! Besides, it could be a trick!"

"Ma'am, it's a chance I'll have to take. Until I caught that star, I didn't know about my soul, so I was free to act as I pleased. But now I know. A soul is a big responsibility, Ma'am! What happens if I sully it?" Mab glanced at the dreary landscape around us and shuddered. "I can't allow that to happen, Ma'am, so I've got to do the right thing, whatever presents itself. Leaving a helpless man to flounder in the black marshes of doom can't be the right thing."

"Oh, what the heck," Erasmus muttered. "I'll go."

Erasmus strode forward. He moved quickly around the pool to where the man thrashed about, and offered his hand. The stranger in the bog reached out and caught it. To Erasmus's surprise, he was able to grasp it. He pulled, and the man began to come free of the peat.

The sod around Erasmus and the stranger yawned open, revealing a pool beneath. From beneath the waters rose a gigantic sundew, its shiny yellowish petals speckled with thousands of slender tendrils, each glistening with what looked like a drop of blood. The stranger yanked back, catapulting Erasmus directly into the clutches of the flesh-eating plant.

The tendrils reached blindly toward Erasmus, sticking to his body. As he yelped and struggled, tearing the tendrils from his hands and clothes, the long petal itself rolled up like a yellowish tongue. Erasmus was now caught in the plant's embrace, wrapped up like a living hors d'oeuvre.

"Told you it was a trick," Mephisto's tired yet cheerful voice sang out as he tapped his staff, calling up reinforcements.

It flashed through my mind what a great relief it would be never to be teased by Erasmus again. We had to save Theo. We could not pause to rescue another family member who had gone astray.

Immediately, I rejected such nonsense, but not before Erasmus caught sight of my expression. As he disappeared beneath the black waters, a sneer of ironic amusement came over his features.

Shaking myself, I leapt into action. Mab was already creeping along the peat toward Erasmus's last known position, reaching blindly under the surface with his lead pipe. Gregor strode along the spongy stuff and slapped the shade that had tricked Erasmus with the Seal of Solomon. The stranger screamed and shivered. Then, his eyes closed, and he fell down and began to sink into the bog. As I ran forward, I imagined that a long, sinuous hamadryad slid along the peat beside me.

"Here, follow Kaa and Soupy! They'll take you to him!" Mephisto cried, indicating the two snakes, now slinking their way across the brown peat, the great hooded hamadryad and the slender, green, grass snake I had last seen wrapped around the waist of the Queen of the Maenads.

I grabbed the tail of the slender green Soupy, who happened to be closer, and dived in, pushing through the peat and letting the snake be my guide. Beside me, Gregor pulled off his heavy crimson robes and grabbed hold of the king cobra, diving in as well.

The black water looked ominous, but after the Swamp of Uncleanness, it seemed almost wholesome. It was thicker than normal water and black. If I had not been holding on to the snake, I would have been utterly lost. Soupy seemed to know where he was going, however, so I gripped his smooth, scaly, length tightly and pressed on.

Following the snake through the thick black water was nerve-wracking. First, I feared I would run out of air before I found Erasmus. Then, I became afraid that this black liquid was actually water from the Styx. If so, it was not something into which I should have immersed my whole body. Achilles's mother was careful to keep his ankle out so that his skin would have a place to breathe. It would be sad to live through my encounter with the impurities of the Swamp of Uncleanness only to perish in the Styx.

Before I could fret further, however, my hand encountered Erasmus's leg. At least, I was pretty sure it was Erasmus's leg. At least, I hoped . . .

Opening my war fan, I slid it forward until it rested on the pulpy stem of the sundew petal. Very carefully, so as not to harm my brother, I slit the stem, freeing him from the plant. I could feel the sundew tremble and recoil.

Grabbing his leg, I swam upward. Only Erasmus's leg suddenly pulled off to the left. I yanked back. His foot moved toward me then away again. Somehow, I had lost my hold on Soupy, so I dared not let go of Erasmus. Desperate for air now, I moved in the direction Erasmus was being dragged and swam upward.

I broke the surface of the water beneath the peat. The soft spongy stuff sat on my head like a hat the size of a rug. In the darkness, something splashed and sputtered. I heard a hoarse indrawn breath.

"Gregor?" I cried hopefully.

"Quick, help me!" he gasped. "I have Erasmus by the arm. The plant must still have a hold on him, though, because every time I pull him toward me, he snaps back."

"That was me!" I exclaimed. "I've got his leg. I thought something was trying to take him away from me!"

"*Jesu!* If it's not one thing, it's another!" he exclaimed. Then he burst into laughter. Despite the horrific images still dancing in my mind, I could not help but join him.

Laughing, we drew the unconscious Erasmus out of the water, so that his face was in the small air pocket we made by pushing the peat up with our heads. Luckily, his staff was still in his hand. Gregor split the peat above our heads, and after many false starts and much splashing about, we managed to drag our brother out of the bog and onto a bramble-covered island. I snagged Gregor's robes from Mephisto, who lay sleeping (some guard he turned out to be), and spread it over the thorny thicket to make a place to stretch out Erasmus. Gregor, meanwhile, worked on getting the water out of our brother's lungs.

Finally, after numerous attempts to rouse him, Gregor declared, "I am not the physician Erasmus is, but I believe he is asleep . . . rather than unconscious or in a coma."

"Mephisto is sleeping, too." I glanced across the miles of brown fens with their eerie will-o'-the-wisps glowing here and there. There was no sign of the snakes, either. I hoped they would be okay. "What do we do now? Mab?"

Mab, who had managed to remain awake while we were below, crawled slowly to our position, head drooping.

"No good, Ma'am," he slurred sleepily. "Sloth isn't much of a threat to a wind, but this fleshly body isn't fully under my control . . ." He began to slump over. "I could leave it, if you want me to, abandon the body, but . . ." His eyes closed and his head fell forward. He began to snore.

Gregor, lean and taut in his wet black garments, with his hair slicked back, glanced toward where we believed Titus lay, and then down at our sleeping companions.

"There is no point in waking the sleepers just to drag them farther into this bog," he said. "The effect will only grow stronger as we continue, and they will succumb again. One of us will have to go take Mephisto's ball and go after Titus. The other one will have to stay here and guard the sleepers."

"We've got to hurry!" I cried. "Theo!"

"Perhaps I should go. You may have trouble moving Titus."

I looked around me. Erasmus lay asleep on the crimson cardinal's robes, Mab sat slumped over, snoring gently, and Mephisto lay sprawled out with his mouth open; staffs and gear were scattered around him.

"No. You stay here. You can protect them should the Hellwinds come," I declared. "I'll find some way to rouse Titus."

To Sleep, Perchance to Dream . . .

I trekked across the fen, my flute strapped to my back. The crystal ball still showed "the quickest way to reach Titus safely." I followed it, pushing through brambles. They slid along the enchanted fabric of my gown with an eerie zipping sound but cut the backs of my hands. Blood welled out of the little scratches, drawing hordes of insects. Apparently, I did not need to be angry for them to sip my blood, once it was spilt. Or perhaps my frustration with the brambles was enough to make me vulnerable to the locals.

Like the barghests Mab and I had fought in the warehouse, which now seemed like an eon ago, the insects drew substance from my blood. Human blood granted solidity to creatures of the spirit world when they drank it, which is why the ancients were always feeding it to ghosts whom they called up from the underworld. The insects that supped off my bleeding scrapes became so solid that they could then bite my face and ears.

The carpet of peat beneath my feet rose and fell occasionally, as if something moved beneath it. I began to feel exposed. Worse things might be attracted by blood in this place than insects. There was nowhere to run, nowhere to hide.

So I went forward.

I shrugged off my fatigue, until the thought occurred to me that I might be legitimately tired, as I did not know how long it had been since I had last had a good night's sleep. The moment a legitimate reason for my weariness occurred to me, I could hardly keep my eyes open. My eyelids drooped. My limbs grew heavy.

I stumbled.

The first three times I righted myself. Soon, however, my legs would no longer hold me. I had to put the crystal ball in my shoulder bag and crawl forward, first on my knees, then on my stomach. My arms trembled from the exertion of pulling along my body.

It seemed pointless, stupid, to crawl along across this spongy, yielding substance, my mouth filled with little twists of dry sphagnum moss I could not seem to spit out. What was I going to do when I reached Titus? Pull myself back with my fingers while I dragged him behind me with my toes?

And yet, I would not give up. The very idea of yielding to sloth was so offensive that I refused to stop, refused to give in, refused to lay my head down as every aching muscle begged me to do.

Besides, Theo needed help, and we needed Titus to reach Theo.

Hours I crawled, hauling my body across the bog, dragging myself through prickers, swimming through dark waters. My hair was wet and lank. I began to shiver.

How much more of this could I take?

I rejoiced when I finally laid eyes on my great titan of a brother. There was Titus, in the distance, asleep on the fen, just where the ball showed him to be. But my joy was brief. It was still a long way to go, and my brother was slowly sinking into the peat. If he went under, I would have no chance of finding him, and even if I did, I would not be strong enough to drag him up again.

I crawled on and on and on. Funny to be crawling across the fens to Titus. All my best memories of fens involved Titus. The loamy smell mixed with the scent of mold brought those memories vividly streaming back. Titus had been the first to return to Scotland after resigning his commission under Marlborough; this was while Logistilla and I were still living in frosty Denmark. Only, instead of returning to our estate, Titus married a country maid and took up a job as a collier cutting turf. When the rest of us arrived, some years later, Titus chose to stay with his wife and his work. Peat was the main source of fuel and warmth for much of the British Isles at the time, and Titus felt he was contributing to the quality of life of ordinary people.

I used to visit him occasionally, sometimes bringing goodies from Edinburgh, sweets and finery, for him and his family. I remembered watching him come walking across the fen after a day's work, with the long handles of his flaughter and his tusker, his turf-cutting tools, slung over his back. He would wave at us with one of his big hands as he strode confidentially along whistling "Farewell to Lochaber."

Sometimes, he and I would hike the fens together, talking of days past or gathering plants for him to press and sketch. Upon one occasion, I even joined his wife and his "wee lad and lassie" in laying out the cut turf to dry. We would stop for lunch sitting amidst the storrows, the pyramids made from stacks of the dried peat. Peat made a beautiful fire, I recalled; it glowed rather than burned. Titus often declared that food cooked over peat tasted better than the finest cooking at the best clubs in London.

This idyllic period of Titus's life came to an abrupt halt when his wife, Birdie, and the little ones fell prey to smallpox. Titus sweated out the illness himself but the rest of his family did not make it. When he recovered, he burned their cottage to the ground and returned to our family estate, a sadder and quieter man.

I once overheard Erasmus asking him why he did not use his Water of Life to save his family from the illness that claimed their lives. Titus shook his head sadly and replied: "That is not what the Water is for. I gave my family into God's hands . . . and God took them."

From thoughts of Titus's family, my mind meandered aimlessly, so weary was I from my exertions. Thoughts I would rather not contemplate snuck around my guard. Was Astreus gone already, consumed by wickedness and hate? Or did some part of him linger on in Seir, dwindling with each passing hour?

No. I could not think about that now. It was too sad. My heart would break.

Memories of my childhood seemed safer. Portraits of Father and his young family drifted by my mind's eye: my father, Lady Portia, and my infant self. How sweet and tinged with the gold of happy memories did these recollections seem, until I recalled that it had never been so, and the gold-tinged images burst like the filmy bubbles that children blow.

For Lady Portia, the great love of Father's life, was not my mother . . . if there had even been a great love of Father's life. If that was not a lie, as well.

Had Father loved her? I wondered. Or Sycorax, or the mermaid, or sylph, or maybe a river sprite—the woman who had given birth to me? Whomever he had summoned the first time he used the great spell that now powered Mephisto's staff. Who had he known back then upon whom he might have fathered me? Whom had he called upon?

"M."

I sat straight up and swung my legs around before me, my bottom sinking into the spongy moss. "M," Father's "Fair Queen." If my mother was not Sycorax, then it must be the mysterious supernatural benefactor who helped Father arrange his return to power.

I would have no proper soul if I were a child of the Queen of Air and Darkness!

I did not know for certain the identity of "M." It could be someone else: Malagigi's sister, the serpentine enchantress Melusine, or even his mother, Morgana La Fey. But could either of those beings arrange for the King of Naples to be sailing near our island during a storm? Melusine certainly could not. Morgana? Perhaps, but I believe she had already retreated from our world by then, departing to dwell in Avalon.

But Maeve, Queen of the Elves, who was secretly the demon Lilith? She could have done it. Only the Powers of Heaven had more sway over the mortal world than she!

TWO hours later, or perhaps two minutes, but it certainly seemed like a long time, I reached the end of my strength. I willed myself to go forward, but my limbs did not move. I could still see, but only through the thinnest cracks in my eyelids.

So close. I could make out the pattern of Titus's plaid jacket and the cedar *Y* that was the top of the *Staff of Silence* sticking up beside him. But it was no good. I could not continue. I should not be surprised, I told myself. Malagigi had warned me that my soul was flawed. Like Astreus, like Mephisto's friends, I did not have whatever it took to hold out against the terrible fatigue.

Only, as my eyes slid mercifully closed, a stray thought drifted through my mind: *How come I made it this far?*

My brothers had surrendered, except for Gregor. Why was I still moving?

I gritted my teeth. It could not end like this! Theo could not be abandoned to die in agony and Father to be tortured to death by demons because the rest of us fell asleep!

If my soul could not help me, what of my sins? Why bear the Pride of Angels, if I could not use it to goad me forward?

I turned to my Lady, something I had remembered not to do until now. Of course, nothing was there, but I prayed anyway. Then, gathering the very last of my strength, I shouted.

"Help! Please!"

It seemed a foolish thing to do, but maybe someone else from Malagigi's Brotherhood of Hope would hear me. On the other hand, something far less pleasant might hear me. But it was all I could think of. My limbs were too tired even to tremble. I lay there no more able to rise than if I had been made of lead.

That was it. It was over.

Gazing through my lashes, I saw a flicker of motion. Ahead of me, Titus stirred. My brother sat up, then rose, moving slowly and sluggishly. Bog muck dripped from his garments. His Highland jacket was splotched with mud, and the once-white socks beneath his green and black kilt were black and filthy. He paused, his knees bending as if he might sink down and rest. However, he caught himself, pulling himself forward with his staff.

He came across the fens, one ponderous step at a time. His face was ruddy with exertion. His eyelids drooped, threatening to close, but he did not slow down.

I could not believe it. Titus? Lazy, sleepy Titus? From where did this stamina come?

He reached me and offered his hand. I smiled but was too tired to talk. Using the last of my strength, I reached up. Wordlessly, he heaved me up over his back and wrapped my arms about his great neck. Then, he began plodding forward.

I bounced on his back, sometimes watching, sometimes dozing. At times, we sank into the water, and Titus was forced to swim—I chuckled sleepily at this. Bog snorkeling was a favorite sport of his, though he had never had to do it while lugging a sister. At other times, he walked through brambles as if they were nothing, despite that the thorns must have scratched his legs beneath his kilt. Perhaps Logistilla had knitted him enchanted knee socks.

With Herculean effort, I handed him the ball. With it, he located the others.

When we reached the others, Titus scooped up both Mephisto and Mab, leaving Gregor to carry Erasmus. Gregor had been resting with his head upon his staff, but he roused himself, lifted our brother, and retrieved his robes. By this time, I had revived some. Titus put me down. I found I could walk again, though shakily. I walked beside him, while he continued with Mab over his back and Mephisto in his arms.

Finally, an eternity later, Mab began to stir. Titus and Gregor lay down their burdens and rested. Mephisto and Erasmus still slept.

"Sorry, Ma'am," Mab mumbled sleepily.

"We need to rouse them," Gregor said hoarsely. "Too bad we don't have any smelling salts."

"Ah, but we do!" I laughed suddenly. Drawing out my vial of Water of Life, I uncorked it and waved it briefly under the noses of the sleeping men.

A wondrous scent, more beautiful than any rose garden at dawn, filled the air. My eyes opened, and I realized that they had been half closed for hours. For an instant, I felt that I was not in Hell at all, but someplace glorious and holy.

Then, I saw Erasmus staring at me. He did not say anything, but his eyes were black with hatred.

I knew what he was thinking, of course. He was replaying in his mind the last thing he had seen before he went under: me, just standing still, watching him get dragged under the sod. I thought of telling him what happened next, how I had leapt in after him, but decided against it. He would only turn it against me anyway, and there was Theo to rescue.

Mab and Mephisto were both rising.

"Let's go!" I cried. "Theo needs our help!"

Mephisto tapped his staff, calling back the two snakes, both of whom were asleep, and sending them safely home. "Titus, we need your help to get through the . . . Titus?"

My great titan of a brother fell facedown upon the spongy loam.

"He's fallen asleep! After all that!" I laughed and knelt beside him with my vial in my hand. "Help me turn him over."

Gregor and Erasmus rolled Titus over, but he was not asleep. His eyes were open, almost fixedly so, and his face was deathly pale.

"You must go on without me." Titus spoke with great effort. "I cannot continue. I have done all that I . . ." He grabbed at his chest and his upper arm, moaning. "I have saved you. I can do no more."

"Don't be silly!" I said, beginning to open the vial further, but Titus shook his head.

"It will take too much Water to save me now. Water you will need to protect Mankind. Go."

"That's ridiculous!" I cried. "You just saved my life! You saved us all! I'm not going to leave you here!"

"I have done my part," Titus whispered.

"Actually, you're not done yet," Erasmus drawled. "Theophrasatus has been burnt from head to toe. We can't reach him to save him unless you get us through the Wall of Flame."

"Yeah, you dodo head! We still need you, so there!" Mephisto squatted down beside him and hammered on Titus's chest with his fists. Then, he knelt and listened to Titus's heart.

"Miranda," Mephisto cried, rising. His face was now as pale as Titus's. "Give him some Water! Quick!"

Mephisto began tapping his staff again and again, calling up one beast after another and sending them away almost as quickly. Anything large enough to carry Titus was either asleep already or began to fall asleep once it arrived.

Titus moaned. "Very well. I can manage one more task, if it will save Theo."

He struggled to sit up but was unable to do so. Mephisto and Gregor helped him to sit. I offered him Water again, but he shook his head, clutching his chest.

Mab leaned down beside him and said softly, "Mr. Titus, you don't want to die here! Who knows how long it will take the angels to find out that your soul isn't in its right place?"

Reluctantly, Titus opened his mouth. I gave him a single drop of Water. The marvelous fragrance filled the air again. The sod beneath our feet trembled as nearby sleepers stirred. Spiky red flowers and little five petaled white ones opened on some nearby brush.

We stood around peering hopefully. Titus struggled to rise but fell back again before reaching his feet.

"It is no good," he whispered. "I can go no farther. Even with the Water you sacrificed. You will have to find a way to save Theo without me."

"We cannot just leave you here!" Erasmus exclaimed.

"You will have to," Titus replied, his Scottish brogue more pronounced than normal. "I canna go on. You canna carry me." He smiled wanly. "You may tell me that you will collect me on the return trip, if it will make you feel better."

Erasmus squatted down. "We both know that we may never make it back. For one thing, we had been planning to teleport out, once we found Father . . . assuming we ever find Ulysses again."

"Don't be silly! We're not leaving anybody!" Mephisto stamped his foot, causing the ground to undulate. Lifting his staff, he peered at its carvings. "I'll have one of my friends carry you. There must be someone who is not asleep."

"Please . . ." whispered Titus.

"But why, Titus?" I asked. "It's as if you don't want to continue."

Titus sat quiet for a time, pale and sweating. Then, finally, he said, "The rest of you cannot imagine what life is like for me."

"We can imagine a great deal," said Gregor, of all people. "What in particular do you mean?"

Titus's breath was coming unevenly, and a hand was still pressed against his chest. He sat for a time with his head resting on his other hand. Finally, he looked up. A single drop of Water would preserve him from death, but it apparently was not enough to cure what ailed him. I clutched the vial in my hand, debating whether to give him more.

"Explain yourself!" Mephisto snapped curtly.

My head snapped up, startled. I could not remember the last time Mephisto had been short with anyone. Titus seemed startled as well. He looked at Mephisto. Then, hanging his head again, he said, "Perhaps, I should start at the beginning."

"The beginning of what?" I asked.

"The beginning of the *Orbis Suleimani*."

"This, I got to hear!" Mab whipped out his notebook and pen.

"But what about Theo?" I cried. "We've got to . . ."

"Shhh." Gregor put a calming hand on my shoulder. "Hear him out. If Theo has lasted this long, he can wait a few more minutes."

Mephisto took the crystal sphere from me.

"Theo's still alive!" he announced. "The other guy with the club—I assume it's Caliban, because it's Caliban's club—is watching over him. Theo's still . . ." Mephisto bent close over the ball. ". . . still breathing!"

"Very well." Gregor knelt beside Titus. "Speak, Brother."

"When the demons fell, they formed an infernal council," Titus whispered, "and swore an oath of obedience to their dark masters. Among other things, they promised to be still and silent when the Great Seven of Hell called upon them to do so—so that the matter of attacking Heaven could be discussed. The right to enforce this oath was given into the hands of the Devil's bailiff, a demon named Gaap, of the rank of president—which, of course, existed as a rank of office before it became associated with the United States. Gaap is this demon who resides in my staff.

"Hell lost a great deal of power the day King Solomon captured Gaap. So long as Gaap remains restrained, the Great Seven cannot call their people to order. They cannot force them to listen, or fall silent, or to cease their debauched antics in order to organize them toward any useful purpose. Or toward any purpose whatsoever."

"That's great," Mab said enthusiastically. "What a victory that was for the Forces of Good!"

"It is," Titus replied heavily, "but there's a price. Because the power my staff draws upon Gaap's office, rather than a natural power he possesses, he could not be bound as tightly as the other demons. The result is that the power of the staff seeps out, stilling and quelling whatever is nearby. And what's 'nearby' happens to be me."

Titus raised his weary head and looked at us imploringly. "Do any of you even remember what I was like, before I grew tired, and weary, and slow?"

"Certainly," Mephisto announced with great zeal. "You were as strong as a bull, as fierce as a bear, and as deadly as a boar!"

Titus's face broke into a wide grin but it soon faded.

"I was a hero," he said quietly. "A hero admired by my fellow men and adored by ladies. 'Titus the Titan,' they called me, the same way some still call Theo, 'Theophrastus the Demonslayer.'" He looked down at where his big hands lay in his lap. "It was that hero whom Logistilla wanted. She still recalled me from her youth, my power, my prowess." He spread his hands indicating himself. "I'm afraid the truth was a great disappointment to her."

"What has that to do with anything?" Gregor asked, frowning.

"If it's so hard on you, why don't you give it up?" asked Mab. "The staff, I mean?"

"Give it to whom?" asked Titus. "If I can hardly endure it, I who could run all day and wrestle a wild horse to the ground? What would it do to my less-enduring siblings? No, it is my cross to bear, and I shall bear it . . . so long as I do not become a bear again." He chuckled wanly at his own humor and added more cheerfully, "Though perhaps, I should thank Logistilla, for I feel my two years away from the staff have done me good. I am stronger and more alert since I've returned to being a man. More so than I have felt for years. I could never have heeded Miranda's call just now, if I had not had those two years' respite."

"I know how you feel," Gregor smiled. "I remember the day I turned back from being a leopard to find myself in my buried cell on Mars. I was in this dingy, tiny apartment, but my thoughts were filled with a peace I had not experienced during all those years spent carrying the *Staff of Darkness*." He leaned his head back against a rock, reminiscing. "It was glorious! Of course, I didn't know it was because there had been a demon in my staff poisoning my soul."

"My two years away from the staff helped me save you all, but they were not enough to save me." Titus's chin sagged. He face was still an unhealthy putty color. "The hero in me lives no more . . . or perhaps he slumbers the sleep of no return, back there under the black waters. What is left of me . . . canna go on. I have not the courage, the resolve, needed to continue to face the power of Gaap. My staff is too heavy. I canna do it. The demon has won. I am done."

We were silent a time, except for Mephisto, who was crying noisily. He hugged Titus and would not let go of him. Erasmus blew his nose on a handkerchief Mab offered him. My eyes, too, were wet with tears. I wiped them away quickly. Gregor, clad again in his crimson cardinal robes, bowed his head in prayer.

Then, Gregor raised his head. There was a light in his dark eyes. He touched Titus's shoulder. "Brother," he said hoarsely, "I have a solution for you!"

"And what is that?" Titus's voice was nearly inaudible.

"We trade."

"Wh-what?"

"Sloth is a vice I do not fear," Gregor smiled. "Had it been able to conquer me, it would have done so during my many years of imprisonment. Instead, I have defeated it."

"So, you say, Brother," Titus said gently, "but what proof do we have of this?"

"Proof?" Gregor scowled, outraged. "Why, how about the fact that I am fit, when I could have been flabby and rotund from lack of exertion. How about . . ." Gregor threw back his head and gave a short laugh. He gestured grandly toward the swamp. "You have seen the proof with your own eyes. I stood watch over these"—he gestured at Mab, Erasmus, and Mephisto— "and I did not sleep. If sloth could conquer me, this would have been the time and place. Give your staff to me, Titus. I will carry it now."

With that, he extended the *Staff of Darkness* to Titus.

A spark of hope came into Titus's brown eyes, and he straightened, breathing more easily. Reaching out his big hand, he clasped Gregor's tightly. Then, very slowly, very reluctantly, he extended his staff.

Partway, he paused and asked uncertainly, "The *Staff of Darkness* . . . what is its vice?"

"I do not know," Gregor admitted.

"The angel's vision showed Gregor's sin as hatred," I said.

"Of course!" Gregor slapped his forehead with a resounding crack. "Of course! Malice. Bigotry. Hatred." His eyes grew round with awe. "Was all that—my great struggle—because of the demon in the *Staff of Darkness*?"

Titus threw back his head and laughed, a deep booming sound like the Titus of old. "Those are vices I can well bear, Brother, vices I can well bear."

Smiling, my brothers exchanged their staffs.

"I WONDER what it would be like to be a body lying under the water," Mephisto asked sleepily, as our feet finally stepped onto firmer ground. He yawned and stretched, raising his arms way above his head. "Oh well, some things we'll just never know! Really helps to have friends, you know! Especially when in a tight spot." He tapped his staff against his boot. "Pegasus."

The winged steed appeared, but it stood with its head down, its white eyelids shut. Nothing Mephisto did would rouse it. The same was true of the gryphon and the roc. Mephisto sent them home again.

"No one is staying awake!" Mephisto stamped his foot. "I must have some flying friend who doesn't sleep. One who's not an angel, anyway. As I think I mentioned, angels have a funny effect on Hell. Oh! I know!" He tapped his staff again. "Svart Kara! She won't fall asleep. She never sleeps."

I rubbed my eyes, worried that I might be hallucinating from fatigue. The black waters were beginning to look like the black swan Astreus and I had ridden through the stars on Christmas night.

And then it was here. A huge black swan, the size of a sailboat, whose feathers shone with the silvery light of stars—the living embodiment of a constellation from an alien sky. The great swan bent her feathered head and rubbed it against Mephisto, who threw an arm around her thick neck and swung up onto her back.

I recalled how Astreus had offered to give me her name as his wager, claiming that, with it, I could call her from the sky to ride upon her. Who would have guessed that Mephisto already knew her? Perhaps Astreus had introduced them, too, long ago.

"Grab on, folks!" Mephisto cried. "No better place to sleep than the soft back of a swan. We'll nip over and pick up Theo. I dare not keep her here too long. The infernal vapors are not good for her, but I'm sure she won't mind taking us for a quick flight. Right, Svart Kara? Good swan!" He stroked the short silky feathers along her throat.

We helped each other onto the back of the swan, and the great black bird launched itself into the sky. High above the ground we soared, gazing down at the Styx, the bridge, and the vast bogs. Bodies floated among the peat, some faceup, some facedown, pale and eerie in the dark waters. The place we had just been stood out from the rest, a tiny island of red and white flowers amid the relentless brown.

Mephisto asked the ball to show him Theo and then showed the image within to Svart Kara.

We soared through lurid clouds and the strange steely gray light, which Mephisto claimed was the glow of perverted reason, emanating from sharp-minded souls who turned their intellects away from Heaven. The swan flew smoothly. Her feathers were soft and pillowlike, and the air about them smelled of stardust. I nestled into the place where the wing rose from the back and slumbered, dreaming of another ride in the arms of a stardust-covered elf.

In the Bowels of Hell

I dreamt I flew through the midst of a swirling inferno and woke to the trumpeting of the great swan. Soot and molten sparks danced in the unpleasantly hot air. Smoke curled up around me, bringing the scent of hot metals and burning cartilage. The swan poked at us with her hard beak. Its eyes were wide and rimmed with white.

Her wings were on fire!

Mephisto, waking sleepily, put out a hand to soothe her, but the terrified bird would have none of it. She landed upon a black island separated from the islands around it by a river of lava and rose up on her legs, beating her burning wings and trumpeting again.

This fanned the flames, terrifying her more.

The sleeping Erasmus and Gregor were dumped unceremoniously onto the island. The thin skin of volcanic glass atop the hardened lava broke under the impact, cutting their skin where it was not protected by magical clothes, so they woke with shouts of pain. Mab jumped clear, landing heavily on his feet. Mephisto, Titus, and I still clung to the swan, Mephisto and Titus to her neck, and I to the base of one wing. Slowly, Titus and I slid down her body and landed beside my tumbled brothers. Mephisto made a soothing sound once more, then tapped his staff again. The great black swan vanished like a dream.

I saw no sign of Mephisto. Had he vanished with her, as he had with the chimera back on St. Thomas, taking the crystal sphere and abandoning us in Hell without any means of finding our way?

Then, I caught sight of him, still in midair, where the swan's neck had just been. He somersaulted as he fell and landed lightly, his arms spread, the crystal ball in one hand and his staff in the other.

"Ta-da! Poor Svart Kara! Turning back into a constellation should put out the fire, but I hope we haven't hurt her. I'd feel really bad if catching on fire made one of her stars burn out or something! I'd hate to be the cause of a supernova. Too much karmic responsibility."

"Please, Mephisto, it's too early." Erasmus dabbed at the scrape on his cheek. "Blood again? And our fair sister is fine, I see. Why must it always be me?"

I ignored him. We were surrounded by uneven, ropy black rock as far as the eye could see. Rivers of lava divided the vast flat expanse into islands. Here and there, geysers erupted out of the rivers, splashing against the ash-dark sky like red-orange fireworks. The heat was stifling, like a sauna where the temperature had been turned up well beyond the safety zone. It smelled of hot rock, reminding me of Shoeing Day, when we would bring our horses to the blacksmith's forge.

In the distance burned the Wall of Flame. Apparently, we had passed through it on swan-back while we slept. I had a vague, dreamlike memory of Gregor tapping his new staff, and the fire parting harmlessly around us in absolute silence. The swan had been unscathed after we passed through. Her feathers must have been ignited by the smoldering cinders in the air.

"Look! We're on the Burning Plains." Mephisto pointed. "Eew!"

On the next island over lay two burnt hulks of what had once been human beings. One wore Theo's helmet, goggles and breastplate; the other held a wooden club.

"Theo!" I cried, running forward.

The smooth obsidian-coated twists of the hardened lava flow underfoot made for poor footing. I fell, managing to twist as I did so, so my enchanted gown, rather than my exposed flesh, struck the ground. Landing, I slid on my side for a yard or two over bumpy ropes of rock before the next rise slowed my motion, the cloth of my enchanted dress my only protection against the sharp volcanic glass. I lay there, in shock, until Titus offered me a hand, pulling me slowly to my feet. Bruised and embarrassed, I resumed moving forward, though more gingerly.

Together, we picked our way across the *pahoehoe* lava. The hardened flow rose and fell unevenly. Its ropy texture resembled the folds and wrinkles of beaten batter—if the batter was the color of charcoal ash. This folded, twisted quality gave the landscape an eerie and forbidding quality, as if we were beholding the petrified innards of Earth.

"This really is the bowels of Hell." Gregor brushed a molten cinder out of my hair. His own forehead was bleeding.

Mephisto opened his mouth cheerfully as if to offer a goofy rejoinder but then fell silent, his eyes resting on our charred brother. Sweat poured down his brow, and a burn mark marred his cheek. Mephisto wiped the perspiration from his eyes and said nothing.

Mab gazed at the surface beneath his feet, spooked. "This is lava, isn't it? It looks uncomfortably like the petrified arm of a Nuckelavee or some other skinless monster."

"Ugh! You're right!" Erasmus lifted one foot and then the other, as if he could somehow put distance between himself and the ground. "I really wish you hadn't said that! Now, I can't get that image out of my head."

We rushed as best we could across the slick yet uneven ground, stumbling and catching our balance. It would have helped if I could have paid attention to my footing, but I could think of nothing but Theo. It was so terrible that he should be in pain. He did not deserve this!

My brother Theophrastus was our knight in shining armor, the most decent one among us. In family meetings, he was our conscience, the one who reminded the rest of us when our plans strayed beyond what a good man should do, who insisted we live up to a high standard. And, most of the time, we listened to him.

We knew that, of all of us, he was the closest to Heaven—which is why it had taken me so many years to consider seriously his threat to give up magic so as to avoid Hell.

How could Theo, of all people, be afraid of Hell?

A memory came back to me: Theo insisting we take food to the poor on the Feast of St. Steven, even during the winter when we ourselves were starving. I recalled following him through a heavy snow, a cold wind cutting my face, my arms full of the last of our provisions. The two of us were singing "Good King Wenceslas" and we both dissolved into laughter when we got to a stanza that neither of us knew. But we reached those who were in need, and Theo saw to it that they were fed and given warm blankets against the cold. He carried a cord of firewood the whole way on his back.

Other memories came tumbling after: Theo charging into battle, fearless, sunlight gleaming off his visor; Theo at the tiller, the wind blowing his hair, bleached blond in front from the blast of his staff; Theo, in waistcoat and shirtsleeves, building a new barn for a tenant; Theo thrashing husbands who beat their wives. He got in a great deal of trouble for this once, when he made an example of a man who turned out to be of higher rank. But it did not stop him. A few years later, he was back at it again. There were at least a few women I had met who gave him credit for saving their lives.

Erasmus might love humanity, but he seldom cared for individual people. Theo loved people. He was friendly and outgoing. He always knew our neighbors and what they were up to: who was expecting a baby, whose cow had calved, who needed a new drain. Sometimes, he would spontaneously go over and fix a pipe or build a new shed, performing tasks that were needed without ever having been asked. He just saw that it was needed and did it—without asking or expecting anything in return.

The others occasionally mocked me, claiming that I liked Theo best merely because he admired me so. That was just nonsense.

I loved Theo because he was the best of us.

A TEN-FOOT gap separated us from the island where Theo lay. As we approached it, we began to hear screams. They were high and faint, nearly inaudible over the noise of bubbling lava. Reaching the edge, we discovered the hard surface we stood upon was only three feet thick. Beneath it, the rock wall glowed like a live ember. A river of lava flowed in the space between the two walls.

Gregor grunted. "We'll have to leap the gap between this island and the next."

I moved closer to the gap, which looked awfully broad for leaping over, and peered down. A shiver went through me despite the heat, which was causing sweat to drip down the back of my neck. People, blistered and burning, swam in the molten river. Some had facial bones as black as cinders, the tissue and muscle having long ago burnt away; others had a melted liquid dripping from where their eyeballs had been. Yet, no matter how they screamed and burned, they were not entirely consumed.

"I don't get it," said Mab. "How come they don't just climb out? It's only about a yard to the surface. Any two or three of them working together should be able to escape."

"Ah . . ." Erasmus's smile had little to do with humor. "Working together . . . now there's the rub. Isn't it?"

Whenever the souls struggling in the molten river drifted near one another, they fought. Burning and suffering though they were, they ignored their own peril to get one last swipe in at their neighbor. They ripped, punched, and clawed at each other. Yet, none of them seemed to notice that the blows they struck, with their thin, weak, skeletal arms, devoid of muscle or flesh, did no lasting damage. Nor did they care that no matter how much harm they inflicted, they never killed their opponent.

The harder they fought, the more heated their wrath, the hotter the air and lava around them became. A brawl sent a spray of lava flying through the air. Where two combatants wrestled, grabbing each other around the neck in an attempt to strangle each other, the river became so hot that the lava bubbled.

"I wonder if they know they are dead," mused Titus.

"Nope, most of them don't," Mephisto replied cheerfully. "Sad, isn't it? I feel for them, the poor dopes. Guess that's why Theo and Caliban are here. They're angry fellows."

Anger, of course. This was the Burning Plains, where the Wrathful suffered for their lives of anger and rage. Theo's weakness had always been his hot head.

"How do we cross?" I concentrated on the supine form that was Theo, willing him to move, so I would know he was not . . .

"Like this," said Titus. He picked me up and threw me across the gap.

I flew through the air, limbs flailing. Plummeting down on the other side, I covered my face with my arms and rolled across the uneven ground. The obsidian crunched beneath my weight.

I stood up gingerly and brushed myself off. Erasmus and Mab flew through the air and crashed to a landing. They also rose, looking a bit worse for the trip. Mephisto, on the other hand, did a triple flip as he soared and landed lightly on his feet. Gregor shook his head, refusing Titus's attempt to lift him. There was not even a chance that Gregor could throw Titus.

"We will wait here," Titus called. "Save our brother."

"Wait there?" muttered Erasmus, as we started forward. Sweat ran down his brow. "What makes him think we're capable of making it back across?"

"Don't be a sourpuss," Mephisto replied cheerfully. He held up his staff. "Svart Kara won't return, I bet, but I still have other friends. Maybe we can crawl across the gap on the back of Kaa."

"Oh, that sounds just dandy," growled Mab.

"Thank the stars! You've come!" croaked the second burnt figure in a hoarse mockery of Caliban's voice. He rose shakily to a kneeling position, propping himself up with his club. Beside him, a charred skinless form with an Urim helmet and breastplate embedded in his burnt flesh, gasped for air.

"Theo . . ." I whispered.

Pelting across the uneven landscape, I fell to my knees beside him. My brother still wore his goggles, which appeared unharmed, so his unscathed eyes looked out from his blackened and blistered skinless face. Bile rose in my throat, and I feared I would vomit. The smell of charred flesh and burnt hair was nearly unbearable.

Could this mass of smoldering flesh be my beloved brother? My mind balked when equating this charred monstrosity with the handsome youth he had been: the fierce courageous young man that Mephisto had portrayed in the white marble statue that had stood for centuries in the Great Hall of Prospero's Mansion.

Belatedly, I recalled that Seir's attack had damaged Theo's statue. That face, too, had been lost.

It would take more than a drop or two of Water of Life to fix this damage. Five drops, at least, likely even more. But if I did not heal him quickly, if his body were allowed to remain like this, then even Water would not wash away such scars.

The world could not spare that much Water.

Was this to be my brother, then? A smoldering husk. Would he remain like this forever, a ghastly horror to make children shriek?

Unbidden, the image of little Theo, the solid small boy with lithe brown limbs and a head of black curls, rose in my mind, and I recalled the first words he ever spoke to me, the night when, at the age of four, he had followed me up the stairs of the *Filarete* tower: *Sistah, Mephto told me we can see whole world from up here. Is it true?*

I yanked out the precious crystal vial and splashed nine or ten drops of Water of Life into Theo's mouth. A scent, more beautiful than blooming lilacs after a morning rain filled the air, driving away all other odors. The fist of fear that clenched my heart opened. I found I could breathe again. I had not even been aware I had been holding my breath.

There was no outward change, but immediately, the pain went from his eyes. His skinless mouth opened as if he were trying to smile.

"Theo," I cried. "Thank God!"

Charred muscles along his face and legs regained their reddish meaty look. A bit of skin spread over his cheeks.

But that was all.

All that Water—ten to forty more years more that one of us could have lived on to continue the fight against the denizens of Hell—and it had not been enough.

Behind me, Erasmus's staff whirled. He said calmly, "Out of the way, Sister. It's my turn now."

Kneeling beside Theo, he yanked the helmet and breastplate from Theo's chest with an awful *thwak*. Something was stuck to the inside of the breast-plate. Amid the flesh and grime, I caught a glimmer of gold. Too worried about my brother to investigate further, I moved to the side to make room for Erasmus.

Erasmus's staff hummed in his dull white gauntlet. He knelt and passed it over our brother's body. The air around Theo grew reddish and warm. New flesh grew before our eyes as Erasmus's staff sped up the regeneration process. Slowly, it spread until it covered his whole body. His nose returned; his lips grew back. His arms and legs became as firm and smooth as baby's skin.

Theo stood up, naked, but young and whole again. Rushing forward, I embraced him, tears running down my cheeks. He hugged me back fiercely, laughing and spinning me about. Setting me gently on my feet, he kissed my cheek. Then, he gave Mephisto and Erasmus a bear hug and shook Mab's hand vigorously.

Pulling off his goggles, Theo wiped his eyes. Then, realizing his state of undress, he held his breastplate sheepishly before his groin. Mab shrugged off his trench coat and held it out. Theo quickly donned it, thanking him.

"I've lost the rest of my armor," he explained. "The heat of the lava was too much for it. Too hot even for the enchanted garments I wore beneath. Both melted. I must thank Logistilla, though, as her handiwork saved my life, allowing me to live long enough to swim to the edge, where Caliban was able to reach me. Where is Logistilla?" He looked around.

"We haven't rescued her yet." Erasmus held his staff at arm's length. It was still whirring. Mephisto, Mab, and I took a careful step back. "That lava must be something! I've never heard of anything that could damage Logistilla's cloth!"

"Erasmus, can you do the same to Caliban as you did for me?" Theo tapped the new skin of his arm with some pleasure.

"Only if Miranda gives him some Water of Life," Erasmus replied. "All the *Staff of Decay* can do is speed up the normal healing process. Without the Water to regenerate him, my staff will scar him for life . . . if it doesn't just kill him outright."

They all looked at me.

The sharp edges of the tiny crystal vial bit into my hand as my fingers clenched around it. There was so little Water left. It was so rare now, so vital! Each drop represented years of life for one of my brothers, years that Theo or Mephisto or Titus would lose if I gave out what was necessary to help Caliban. Nor would a single drop do. Or rather, one drop would stabilize him, but it would leave him ugly and fleshless. It had taken four drops to heal the airy, bodiless Zephyrus, after he had been attacked by angry djinn. Caliban would undoubtedly require more.

If I refused, Caliban would die. My would-be-rapist, my ancient enemy, would perish, never to set foot upon the face of the Earth again. True, I said I forgave him, but did that erase his crimes? Father had saved me that day, but how many other women had he raped down through the years, before Mephisto managed to tame him and make a mockery of a gentleman out of him?

How many women had not been saved, as I had not been saved on New Year's Day?

My old hatred rose a hundredfold. For centuries, his savage violence had haunted my dreams. I remembered the awful smell, the groping hands, the pain when he broke my forearm, snapping it in two—it had tingled when the weather changed for years afterward—until my first trip to the Well at the World's End put a stop to mortal aches and pains.

My broken arm, with all its aches, was insignificant compared to the betrayal—the terrible, awful knowledge that a friend could not be trusted. This first betrayal now cut me afresh. I saw it as the harbinger of all the betrayals that had followed . . . including my father's.

I could not turn on my father. I could not destroy Hell and the many demons whose temptations had ruined my family, but I could put an end to this one, first traitor.

Caliban knelt on the sharp obsidian, chest heaving, most of his weight resting on his club. As he gazed at me with his blackened blistered face, hope slowly drained from his eyes.

"Hurry up, Miranda," whined Mephisto. "Fix my Bully Boy!"

Mephisto gave me an encouraging smile, but Caliban knew better. He nodded, once, and lowered his head.

My head throbbed oddly as time seemed to stand still. To leave another human being like this was unthinkable, and yet I could not raise my hand to offer him the Water.

I forced myself to look at my surroundings. All around us lay the stark, inhuman landscape of twisted and writhing stone. Rivers of lava, with their cargo of burning souls, flowed between the islands, and jets of red-orange flame shot up against the blackened sky. The Hellwinds had brought Caliban here. Was this where his soul would rest if he died now? Would he be trapped here forever, burning, suffering?

If so, could I condemn a man to this? Condemn him for a crime attempted five hundred years ago? Did not forgiveness mean one washed the slate clean and started anew? I recalled the kindly things Caliban had said about me when I overheard him speaking to Erasmus near Eurynome's Chapel on Father's Island. Suddenly, I felt chagrined.

"She's not going to do it." Erasmus smirked. "She didn't rescue me, either."

It brought me an iota of comfort to know that I had already moved to kneel beside Caliban before Erasmus spoke.

With Herculean effort, I pulled the stopper from the little vial. At first, my hand would hardly obey me. Only the firmest pride and discipline forced the motion of my arm. But then, as I lifted the stopper, and the glorious smell again assailed us, a warmth crept into my heart. As my spirits rose, a huge burden was lifted from my shoulders. I felt so light, I feared my feet might lose contact with the ground.

Overcome by this strange fierce joy, I let six drops fall into Caliban's mouth. Startled, he jerked his head, and the first drop missed him, splashing against the ashen rock.

A single green sprout broke through the volcanic glass with a *crack*. Then, a second and a third, then a dozen, and then fifty. Obsidian crackled all around us. Vines grew and sprouted, making a soft rustling noise, like leaves in the wind. Morning glories, ferns, lily of the valley, and soft green moss spread outward, until our entire island was a garden wonderland, such as I had seldom seen even in the most beautiful gardens of Old Europe. Across the river of lava, I could see Gregor and Titus gaping in astonishment.

A little breeze stirred, cooling our sweaty faces.

"How beautiful," whispered Theo.

Kneeling, he put his hands together and bowed his head. Mab took off his hat and held it over his heart.

"Ma'am, this is bad," Mab muttered, despite his clear delight at the change of scenery. "Even up on top, Water of Life attracts stuff. But, down here? Only . . ." He paused, searching for the name of one of his gods by which to swear. After mopping his brow, he threw up a hand to signify defeat. "Heck, none of the guys I call upon know what might be attracted down here!"

From the distance came a crash. One of the other volcanic islands heaved, splitting apart into a geyser of lava. Then, another island rose and cracked, and then a third. Something big moved beneath the surface of the lava. Guessing from the landmasses it displaced, it was even bigger than our kronosaur, and it was coming this way! Overhead, flocks of bat-winged imps rose into the air, swarming toward us. They were followed by larger flying demons.

"Time to go!" Erasmus swung his humming staff near Caliban, whose flesh leapt across his body, causing the large man to cry out in agony. Quickly, I gave him one more drop and then put the vial away.

Grabbing Caliban's hand, I ran through the lilies and wisteria to the edge of our island. My brothers and Mab ran with us.

"How are we going to get across?" I released the large man, who received a bear hug from Mephisto, who then gave him his blue *fleur-de-lis* surcoat to cover Caliban's nakedness. "What about Mephisto's friends?"

Behind us, though still some distance away, another island rose and fell as the whatever-it-was grew closer.

"No good. Most of them are afraid of fire." Mephisto wiped sweat from his eyes. "The ones big enough to carry us, anyway. Besides, I checked while you were helping Theo, and the bigger ones are still asleep, even the snake."

"Then, how?" Gregor asked hoarsely.

"Caliban can throw us," Mephisto shouted confidently. "He's practiced. He's been in the circus."

"How will he cross?" cried Theo, as Caliban hefted Mephisto and tossed him across the lava-filled gap.

Tumbling through the air, Mephisto shouted back, "He'll have to juuump!"

Great, I thought, as my turn came to be flung across the great fiery gulch. *He'll fall in the lava, and all that Water I just gave him will have been wasted.*

I flew through the air, cinders catching in my hair. The glass-coated ground rushed at me far too quickly. I threw up my hands to protect my face, only the ground never made it. Instead, something caught me by the waist, and I found myself hanging upside down. With a toss, Titus threw me into the air and spun me about, righting me. Then he put me gently on my feet.

"Thank you, Titus. Very kind of you," I murmured as he reached up to catch Theo.

Caliban threw Erasmus and then Mab. Titus caught them, stumbling a bit the last time. When we were all on our feet, Caliban drew back, preparing to run. As he charged, his foot slipped on the uneven ground, and he fell heavily, slicing open his naked arm and thigh on the sharp obsidian. Sheepishly, he rose to his feet and tried again. This time, when he slipped, he managed, arms windmilling, to catch himself before he fell. After a few more false starts, Caliban walked to the very edge of the gap, his naked body dripping with blood, and called:

"It's no good. I'm going to have to jump without a running start."

"Ridiculous," snapped Erasmus.

"What else can he do?" asked Titus.

Mephisto slapped his hand against his head and tapped his staff. I began to imagine that Caliban was no longer crouched on the far side preparing to jump, rather that he stood next to Mephisto. Then he was here, next to Mephisto, smiling broadly.

"Well," Erasmus laughed, "that was amazingly easy. Really nice being a Prospero, isn't it?"

"It is, indeed." Mephisto hugged his staff to his chest and rubbed his cheek against the winged lion that topped it.

"A very nice staff, Mephisto, though I like mine . . ."—Gregor paused, glanced between his hand and Titus's, and frowned—". . . better."

"What now?" rumbled Titus.

We looked around. We were surrounded, for as far as the eye could see, by black islands separated by rivers of lava. The great island-crushing thing and the flocks of demons were quickly approaching.

"Hey, Harebrain? Any chance of calling back that big black bird?" asked Mab.

"After we burned her?" Mephisto shook his head. "Not a chance! She'd be as likely to join their side as to help us." He pointed toward the nearest flock of imps with his elbow as he said "their side." Then, he pulled off the scarf he had wrapped around his neck and handed it to Caliban.

"Here, this will make a nice loincloth."

"Loincloth," Gregor snorted. "That is hardly more decent than nakedness. Here, let me take off my outer garment."

"Sorry, there's nothing I can do about your feet . . . D'oh!" Mephisto slapped his forehead again. "What a dope I am! I shouldn't have called Caliban to me. I should have sent him home, back to where I'd first called him from. He could have picked up a few things for us before I called him back."

"Can't you send him back now?" Mab asked.

"I could," Mephisto replied, "but now he'd appear back on the other side of the lava river, where I just called him from. But it does give me an idea!"

As Gregor removed his crimson robe, Mephisto tapped his staff. I began to imagine seven rough-looking young men in jeans, hooded sweatshirts, and a few spiked leather jackets, each with a great deal of gold jewelry hanging about his neck. Then, they were here. The seven young men looked around and clung to one another, wailing and wide-eyed with terror.

"Hi, there! It's me. Remember me? The guy who pays for all your bling-bling?" Mephisto spread his arms, giving them a cheerful smile. Then, he pointed toward the biggest one, and another one who was about Theo's size. "You! You! Strip! That's right, take off all your clothes. Hurry, boys, you don't want to stay in Hell a moment longer than you have to, do you? *Vite! Vite!*"

"Holy Croesus! His staff can actually call seven thugs from D.C." Mab whistled. He scratched his stubble, grimacing. "He mentioned this when we first met him, during the drive to Vermont to visit Mr. Theophrastus, but all this time, I thought that was his idea of a joke."

Quickly, two of the young men stripped down to their underwear, which Theo insisted they be allowed to keep. Their companions huddled together, the hoods of their sweatshirts pulled over their heads to protect them from the ash and cinders. As soon as their clothing was on the ground, Mephisto tapped his staff and sent the terrified hoodlums home.

"How did you acquire such unsavory servants?" Gregor asked disapprovingly.

"They mugged me," Mephisto explained. "After I had my friends"—he patted the figurines on his staff fondly—"explain things to them, they agreed to come work for me."

"Hardly nice to bring them to a place like this . . . even if they are mug-gers," Erasmus said. He ducked his head as the sky rained cinders. "On the other hand, this place would make one heck of a Scared Straight program!"

"I'll give 'em a bonus," Mephisto said confidently. "Maybe a Lear jet or a Humvee." As he handed the sweatshirts, jeans, and sneakers to Theo and Caliban, I could not help wondering who Mephisto expected would pay for these new toys.

Mab wondered the same thing, only he did it out loud. "Hey, Harebrain, how do you pay for all this stuff you give them if you are always broke?"

"Why do you think I go broke so quickly?" Mephisto answered cheer-fully. "I am a rich, stock-owning Prospero, after all. But by the time I get done feeding and taking care of all my friends, I seldom have anything left. I do have a lot of friends, you know." He patted his staff. "That and taking pretty girls on expensive dates. That eats up the lucre, too."

Caliban squeezed into the larger thug's jeans and Nikes but not the leather jacket, which was too small. He managed to pull on one of the sweatshirts. Theo received a hooded sweatshirt, jeans, and a pair of black boots. He put on the leather jacket Caliban had discarded and ripped the hooded sweatshirt into strips which he used to strap on his breastplate. Then, he took charge.

Coolly, in his best Theophrastus the Demonslayer voice, my brother instructed: "Mephisto, find us a path out of here. Erasmus and Titus—Gregor, keep your staves ready. Gregor, unlimber the *Staff of Darkness* and get us some cover!" He glanced in puzzlement at Titus, who held up Gregor's old staff. Theo shrugged and clicked his goggles, which were, amazingly, still working, and a low noise, like a dynamo beginning to spin, reverberated from his staff. "As for the rest of you, stay behind me!"

Spreading his legs and setting his feet on the bumpy ground, he shouldered the *Staff of Devastation* and took aim.

Promises of Marriage

Fifteen minutes later, blazing sunlight, more brilliant than the eye could tolerate, flooded the lava tube where we had paused, hiding and waiting for Theo and Gregor to catch up. It was warm here, but only pleasantly so, not like the oppressive heat of the lava fields we had just fled. We stood around Mephisto who was attempting to use John Dee's crystal globe to provide light.

"Show me the sun," he had instructed the ball.

"Too bright! Too bright!" several of us shouted as a brilliant glow lit the room, hurting our eyes.

"Daylight, Harebrain, not the sun itself!" Mab had turned his back and covered his face with his arms. "You wanna blind us all?"

"Show me daylight." Mephisto's voice came cheerfully.

A moment later, a pleasant glow poured out of the glass sphere, illuminating the cruel points of the stalactites hanging overhead and the pumice floor, which crunched beneath our step.

Behind us, Theo and Gregor came running down the tube. When they reached the rest of us, they stopped, panting. Theo's staff still hummed and vibrated in his hand.

"Got him," Theo said. "At least, I think I did, but I had to shoot him twice." He paused while Erasmus whistled in astonishment. "I've never had to shoot anything twice before. Must have been something big, in all senses of the word!"

"What about the flying flocks?" asked Caliban.

"Scattered after the first blast, those that didn't immediately crisp," Theo replied. He twisted his white metallic staff, and the whirring dynamo noise fell silent. He then separated it and slipped the two parts into the holster on his back.

Gregor said, "It's a very good thing we found the lava tube before Theo fired at full-strength. When the glare cleared from the first shot, the entire landscape—islands, demons, sinners, and all—had been transformed into one giant glassy crater, which promptly sank with a loud pop, lava pouring over its lip. This sent a wave of molten magma over the place where we had all been standing." He shook his head. "I am not a soft man, but even I feel sorry for the sinners caught in that blast. True, they will return eventually, but pain is still painful, even in Hell."

"Good thing the ball showed us the tube," Mab said. "Not sure I could have taken much more of that squiggly landscape that looked like weird petrified intestines."

"Speaking of this tube," asked Titus, "where does it come out, do we know?"

"In the country of Gluttons," Mephisto confided, smiling down at the glowing ball, so that his face was suffused with light. "I peeked ahead."

"Sounds unpleasant." Gregor shook his head. "Especially since my stomach is so empty, the burning wine Maugris spoke about is beginning to sound appealing."

Titus removed his pack. "I have some rations still. Oh, wait, they've been dipped in the bog. Is that going to harm them?"

"Let's take a look," insisted Erasmus, opening Titus's pack.

Titus's food turned out to have been mainly prewrapped or in sealed bags. The bread and chocolate were ruined, but there were various nuts, summer sausage, a bag of baby carrots, and some protein bars, which he kindly shared among the eight of us, along with three cans of soda pop. The smell of sausage and grape soda pop made my mouth water. I sat on the pumice and eagerly devoured my share. I could not recall having been this hungry since the late seventeenth century, the time I had spent three days trapped in a fallen house.

"Best not to go into the Hell of the Gluttons hungry, if we can help it," observed Mab, munching on a handful of carrots.

I bit into a carrot. I could not recall the last time I had eaten something that tasted so good. One benefit of our recent traumas was that my thoughts were no longer obsessed with Astreus. I felt sane again; my mind was my own.

Even better, as we sat and ate, the self-cleaning enchantments woven into our garments had an opportunity to work their magic. Within a short time, Gregor, Titus, Erasmus, Mephisto, and I all wore clean clothes. Theo and Caliban were dressed in garments taken from Mephisto's thugs. That meant only Mab still looked bedraggled, his trench coat and fedora caked with mud and stained with bog water.

Titus took a bite of one of the protein bars. "Riding on that bird got me thinking . . . all those swan maidens you brought home, Erasmus. How did you find them? You must know something about dealing with Fairyland. Any chance of seducing someone who could bring us more Water of Life from the elvish court?"

"No luck there," Erasmus replied. "Not unless I could seduce one of the Queen's Ladies, or the Queen herself. The kind of girl you can trap by sneaking up and stealing her cloak isn't given access to Water of Life."

"Not a good idea." Mephisto slumped down until he was practically lying across the tube.

"The Elf Queen Maeve is actually the Queen of Air and Darkness in disguise," Mab said glumly.

I managed to take a sip of soda and pass the can to Theo without spilling the precious liquid. Mephisto was not so lucky. He sat up, spitting his grape soda across the tunnel.

"How did you find out!" He looked about frantically. "I don't think I'm supposed to know about this!" He stuck his fingers in his ears. "Not listening. Not listening. Not listening."

"Is she really?" Erasmus cut himself a slice of sausage. "How amazing! The same woman we saw up in the sky in that flying chariot? The one who's after Mephisto?"

Mab glanced at Mephisto nervously. "Harebrain's right. It might be better if we didn't talk about the Queen of Demons in his presence."

Lilith, the Queen of Air and Darkness, seemed to rise like a specter before me. Was she my mother? Was I some half-demon monstrosity who had to be controlled by Father's magic lest I turn and rend my family?

No. I did not believe it!

I would not believe it.

Unfortunately, this hypothesis fit the facts. It explained "M," and Theo's theory and Malagigi's observations. And yet, deep down, I did not believe it. Deep down, I believed in Father. I believed he was not the sort of man who would cast a spell upon his beloved daughter, and I believed that no Demon Queen could fool him, at least not for very long.

But I could be wrong. I had been wrong about Ferdinand, about Ulysses, about so many things.

I deliberately returned to Titus's subject. "What about Fiachra? I saw him at the New Year's party. Could he help?"

Erasmus shook his head. "Not highly ranked enough."

"We could try their quests. I, for one, still think that's a splendid idea." Theo patted his staff. "There must be some task on their Questing Board that we could accomplish."

"What's a Questing Board?" whispered Caliban to Mephisto, but the latter still had his fingers in his ears.

Mab whispered back, "It's where the elven court posts tasks they want done. If you accomplish them successfully, they reward you with Water of Life."

"Don't know how they'd take our getting involved." Erasmus took a bite of sausage. "What we need is the backing of a member of the High Council. I can't really help there, but maybe we could sell them our sister. She's damaged goods anyway." He turned toward me. "How long do you have to wait until you find out if you're pregnant with a half-demon bastard?"

With no preliminary warning, Theo hit him. He punched Erasmus in the face. I cheered, but this did not take away the feeling of having been slapped. Silently, I prayed to whatever power was listening that there would be no unpleasant consequences from Osae's attack.

"Not the nose again!" Erasmus cried as blood gushed down his lips and chin. "What are you hitting me for? I'm not the one who's responsible!"

"You do not talk about our sister that way." Theo crossed his arms and glared down at Erasmus. "Ever."

Erasmus started to reach for his staff, but the rest of the family was glaring at him as well. He slumped back against the wall of the lava tube, one hand pressed against his face.

"I would make a big deal about this," Erasmus muttered, "except I've decided to give you a pass for having just lived through a dunking in the Lava of Wrath. Really, though, Theo, after seeing where anger can lead a person, it might behoove you to curb your temper."

"Maybe Miranda could marry her elf!" Mephisto suggested, paying Erasmus and Theo no heed. He had taken his fingers from his ears and was shoveling nuts into his mouth. "She saw him at Christmas, you know. They danced together and then slipped off into the night . . . alone!"

"You have your own elf?" Gregor looked up from the protein bar he had begun to unwrap. He had stopped to read the ingredients and had been puzzling over some of the substances listed. Whatever Ulysses had fed him on Mars, apparently it had not come in brightly colored packages.

Mab frowned at me. "Never did get to ask you where you went that night at Santa's."

"Astreus took me on the back of that same star-swan Mephisto just called up. We flew to Hyperborea, where he gave me a copy of the *Book of the Sibyl*," I said.

The Elf Lord's name tasted sweet in my mouth, and my heart soared at the chance to speak it—so much for having put him from my mind!

"The *Book of the Sibyl*!" Theo cried. "After all this time!" Then, he winced as he recalled why I no longer needed it. "Quite decent of him. Any idea why he did this?"

"The Lord of the Winds had heard a prophecy that a Sibyl of Eurynome would free the elves from their oath to Hell." My voice dropped. "He was hoping that Sibyl would be me."

"Wow!" Mab whispered. "You didn't tell me about this, Ma'am! Released from the tithe to Hell. Could a Sibyl do that?"

"Sibyls can absolve oaths," I replied.

"Wouldn't that be glorious?" Theo's eyes glittered. "What a coup that would be for the Powers of Good!"

"Well, then. It's settled." Titus gave a big smile. "When we go back, our sister can marry this elf. No reason for her not to, anymore. Surely, a member of the High Council will have access to Water of Life."

"Let's just hope that he is not as stingy with giving it out to his relatives as Miranda is," Erasmus quipped, but he was smiling with almost no trace of his customary smirk.

"I don't know," Theo growled. "Is this elf good enough for our sister? We'll have to check him out."

"Take it from me," Mephisto cried cheerfully. "He's the best!"

A lump the size of one of those boulders we had seen souls of the dead carrying formed in my throat. Twice, I opened my mouth to explain that Astreus was dead, subsumed by Seir, but somehow I could not, not here under these awful conditions. Should we make it home in one piece, there would be time enough for Mab to mourn his dead lord.

"Freed from the tithe!" Mab murmured, awed. "Lost a lot of my people to the tithe over the years. I had a—well, you'd call it a cousin—who got tithed many millennia ago. Never heard from him again. The elven monarchs picked on us for a time, used to tithe us Aerie Ones exclusively." He lowered his head. "Lord Astreus saved us. He gave up all chance of returning to Heaven in order to protect us."

A warmth spread through me that had nothing to do with our proximity to the lava fields. So, Astreus had been telling the truth! He had told me that he endured a thousand years being tortured in the Tower of Thorns—a place where I could not have lasted for ten minutes—rather than forswear Heaven, only to yield to his captors' demands when they threatened to tithe his people, the spirits of the air, to Hell.

Mab himself was one of those saved by his selfless act.

Theo turned to Gregor. "If their oath to Hell were absolved, could the elves return to Heaven?"

"Theoretically." My brother the former pope stroked his neatly trimmed beard. "The doctrine on the redemption of elves is sketchy at best."

"There's doctrine on the redemption of the elves?" Erasmus laughed.

"Of course," Gregor replied. The rest of us exchanged glances and laughed.

No wonder Astreus took the time to copy the Sibyl's book by hand! I recalled the way he had spoken of Heaven and how his eyes had burned with golden fire when he described how he had once been an angel. So great was his desire to return that even the slight hope that I might some-day become a Sibyl who could absolve his oath had been enough to stave off the darkness that otherwise would have devoured him.

Suddenly, I wished fervently that Astreus were not dead! Or that I had not squandered our last minutes together quarreling with him.

"I'm no use to him anymore." I hung my head in shame. "Nor would he have married me, for he cared nothing for me. He was only interested in finding a Sibyl."

"He did so care!" insisted Mephisto. "He promised me he'd marry you. I wasn't going to have my sister seduced and abandoned by an elf!"

"Promised you?" My jaw dropped. "When was this?"

"I must say I'm impressed." Erasmus cupped his newly injured nose; his voice sounded odd. "I had no idea you had an elf suitor, Miranda. And a member of the High Council, too! Good work!"

"Might have been a marriage worthy of you," Gregor acknowledged with a curt nod.

In all my years, my brothers had never approved of any suitor for my hand. I did not know what to make of it.

"Can elves marry?" Caliban asked, as he shoved an entire protein bar into his mouth. "The fairy tales and literature all emphasize their capriciousness. Are they capable of being faithful?"

Erasmus tipped his head back, still trying to stem the flow of blood. "There's been at least one tremendously successful marriage between elves and men, you know. Back in the twelfth century, Fincunir the Clever married a mortal maid named Oonagh, said to be among the most beautiful women ever to grace the earth. Last I heard from Fiachra, they were still together."

"When did Astreus promise this?" I asked again.

"When we first met," Mephisto responded.

"Back in 1627?" My mind reeled at Mephisto's news. "How strange! But he told me elves no more woo mortals than hawks court doves."

Mephisto frowned, and Mab cleared his throat.

"Begging your pardon, Ma'am, but that doesn't quite make sense. Lord Astreus has . . . well, a bit of a reputation for romancing mortal maids. A number of the great artists and poets of the world are descended from him."

"Really?" That stung a bit.

No wonder he had come forward so quickly to dance with me that first summer's night. I recalled how he had laughed, mocking his fellows for not seizing the opportunity.

What would it have been like, I wondered, being Lady Astreus Stormwind? I pictured us flying among the stars, or sipping elfwine on a balcony of his palace in Hyperborea, or diving over the edge of the world, hand in hand, to see what brave new worlds might lie beyond the brink.

Delightful as these images were, however, the idea became less enticing when I considered our life at home. I imagined him pacing, bored, while I worked in my office, or, worse, sitting cross-legged atop the back of an armchair, his intent, ever-changing eyes intimidating the shareholders at a board meeting of Prospero, Inc.

On the other hand, I would have loved to see the expressions of our supernatural clients, the gnomes and nymphs, and even the troublesome djinn, when we showed up for contract negotiations with a Lord of the High Council!

As for home life, what would it be like to hear the halls of Prospero's Mansion ringing with the laughing voices and pattering footsteps of little elflets—elflets from whom future world-renowned artists and poets might spring? So, subtle, clever Fincunir had been married to the same woman for nearly a thousand years! Could we have done as well?

No, I realized sadly, it would not have been like that for us, because Oonagh gave up the mortal world to dwell in fairyland, but I was constrained to stay on earth and run Prospero, Inc., in order to protect mankind. I might have been able to fit in a trip to wonderland once a century or so. The rest of my time would be spent in Oregon, running Prospero, Inc., while Astreus gallivanted about the universe, appearing on my doorstep only when it suited him—if it suited him at all.

After all, he was an elf. Once he departed, I would never know whether or not he would return. Would he remember me? Or get caught up in the moment and tarry elsewhere, perhaps with some fresh mortal maid—forgetting me as Erasmus feared his son Fiachra might forget, were he not constrained to visit every New Year's Day.

I sighed and closed my eyes. It was all a dream, of course, a flight of fancy. There was no future for Astreus and me. Even if some miracle restored him to the sunlit realms, such a union—seeing him for a few days here and there, never knowing if he would return to me—would be unbearable, especially once the Water ran out and I rapidly grew older.

I might come to love him, and he might grow to love me, but happiness would be impossible.

"I wonder why Astreus said such a thing?" I mused aloud. "About hawks and doves, I mean."

"To throw you off guard," Mephisto chirped. "That's trick seventeen from the *Book of Seduction*. You take some girl who would normally want to send you packing and convince her you couldn't possibly be interested, so that she starts wondering 'Why not?' Next thing you know, she's eating out of your hand like a trained deer. Works every time."

That lying elven devil! My cheeks grew red as my brothers regarded me in amusement. How dare he toy with me! And how dare he be dead, and thus conveniently escape my wrath!

"It's not very easy to train deer," mused Titus.

"*Book of Seduction?*" Caliban lowered his slice of sausage. "Where can I get a copy?"

"Just a joke." Mephisto giggled as Caliban's face fell. "Besides, Astreus wouldn't have wanted to seduce you, Miranda! Then you would not have been a Handmaiden anymore. He was biding his time."

Oh! As if that made it better! Why had I not taken the opportunity to slit his throat when he had offered it!

"Aren't you going to make a speech about not cavorting with elves,

Bodyguard?" Mephisto had gone over to Titus's bag and was rummaging around, pulling out a squished candy bar, which he quickly consumed.

Mab cleaned his ear with his pinky. "Well, funny thing about that. Mortals marrying elves, bad business. No good can come of it. But frankly, we now know Miss Miranda isn't a mortal. She's half witch or something." He turned to Caliban. "Your mother wasn't merely a human witch, was she?"

"She was part human, but only part," Caliban replied. "Her father was an ogre."

"If you're one of us, Ma'am . . . that changes a lot."

Ah, the irony! How nice the idea of having Sycorax as my mother now seemed. No matter how repugnant that heritage, it was preferable to being the daughter of the Queen of Air and Darkness!

"Where are the others?" Titus interrupted, licking the last of the chocolate coating from his protein bar off his fingers. "Where are Logistilla, Ulysses, and Cornelius?"

"We don't know yet," I replied. "You four are as far as we've gotten." I turned toward the others. "I recommend we do the same thing we did before, and go next to whomever most needs our help."

"I think we should go after Cornelius next," Erasmus said, wiping his mouth. "It must be terrifying to be in Hell and not be able to see your way around." He paused and cocked his head. "On second thought, might be nice to not be able to see the sights. If he's not in pain, he might have no idea how bad things are."

"I hate to think of Logistilla all alone in this terrible place," Titus said quietly. "She must be frightened."

"But doesn't that make you happy?" Mephisto asked, confused. "I thought you hated her!"

"Not at all," Titus objected, surprised. "One doesn't start hating one's wife just because she turns one into a bear for a few years. I was just angry about the children."

The rest of us stared at him.

"If you say so," murmured Erasmus. "Though I could hate someone for far more frivolous reasons."

"Wife?" Gregor glanced from one face to another. "I thought we were talking about our sister—my twin!"

Erasmus held up a staying hand. "Don't ask!"

Gregor's brow darkened. He and Titus regarded one another suspiciously. Again, his protectiveness toward Logistilla warred with his hard-won serenity. Erasmus shook his head, dark hair falling into his eyes. He brushed it aside, muttering. "Oh, this isn't good!"

"Ball, show me the member of our family who is in the most trouble." Mephisto quickly shoved the ball between Gregor and Titus. Immediately, the light illuminating the tunnel winked out. Instead, the crystal globe showed an image of a naked Ulysses running over a steep rocky landscape. Behind him, the ground seemed to be writhing.

"Ulysses next, then," Theo said decisively, as Mephisto instructed the ball to show us daylight; a pleasant glow again illuminated the lava tube.

"Theo and Caliban," Titus asked as he rose, stretching, "what happened to you when the Hellwinds hit?"

Caliban said, "We held on to each other as the winds drew us together and dropped us in the lava. I climbed out almost immediately but had to go back in to help Theophrastus. After that, there was nothing to do but wait and pray."

An wave of affection for the big man swept over me when he described voluntarily jumping in to the bubbling lava to rescue Theo. I was glad I had given him the extra Water.

"How could you survive in that heat, even for an instant?" asked Gregor, aghast.

"Far as I can tell," Caliban answered slowly, "there was no real lava, only burning wrath. The calmer I became, the cooler it got around me." He lowered his head, chagrined. "Unfortunately, I am prone to wrath, so I did not escape unscathed."

"What amazes me," commented Erasmus between bites, his eyes resting speculatively on the bog-dipped chocolate, "is that your club survived. Isn't it just made of wood? I would have expected it to go up like a match."

"I held it up over my head, so it would not fall in," Caliban explained, still chewing. "What of the rest of you?"

The four of us who had sought out Mephisto together met each other's eyes.

Gregor spoke up hoarsely, "Best not to talk of it."

The Battlefield of Wasted Lives

Titus's generosity in sharing his supplies allowed us to pass through the place of punishment for the Gluttons without undue temptation. This was a good thing, for while I saw fat men and obese women gorging themselves on badly rotten fare, or worse, upon other Gluttons, my brothers reported scrumptious mouthwatering feasts as far as the eye could see. They walked blithely, restraining the desire to sample some tasty morsel, while I was forced to watch ungainly damned souls shovel filth into their mouths and guzzle the wine, which, far from whetting their palate, left them writhing upon the ground, clutching their throats, as if they had drunk a vial of acid.

Eventually, the appetizing dishes began to tempt my siblings. One and then another reached over to touch my shoulder, so that they might see my version and know the truth. After a time, we were all walking together, arm in arm.

Several times during this walk, Mephisto called up Pegasus or the roc and tried to rouse them, but the creatures remained asleep. Gregor suggested opening the vial of Water of Life and holding it beneath their nostrils, as I had done earlier; however, we decided not to risk it while surrounded by hungry souls. They might not be able to hurt us—assuming we remained calm— but they could touch our garments. None of us wished to find ourselves bodysurfing over an angry crowd of the gluttonous dead. Who knows what delicacies we might resemble in their eyes.

Once he called the black swan, but when she arrived she pecked him angrily. He promised not to call her again while Below.

As we walked, my brothers chatted cheerfully with Caliban and Mab, but my thoughts kept returning to the conversation in the lava tube.

That cur! That cad! That rakehell! That bounder! That *fringuellone*! *Che donnaiolo*! *Che farfallone*!

So, Astreus had a reputation for dallying with mortal maids, did he? And I had fallen for his cool elvin charm. As if my recent humiliation by the false Ferdinand in front of my family was not enough! Ooh! I was glad he was dead, the exasperating elf! If he knelt before me now, I would slit his throat in an instant!

AHEAD of us, a curtain of what looked like black gauze stretched across the landscape, fluttering gently to either side of a large gateway made of bone. As we drew closer, what we had taken for gauze turned out to be woven human hair with eye balls strung along it like beads. These eyes were still alive and swiveled to follow our movements. They gazed at us imploringly, as if they hoped we would offer some aid or comfort.

"Ugh!" I cried, recoiling. "What is this?"

"It's a gate. It leads to the next circle down. You know, where badder baddies get paddled. I think this is the Fifth Circle we're entering," Mephisto explained. He then added, "For each pair of eyes hanging here, some poor twerp of a dead guy is wandering around blind, trapped in eternal darkness."

"Dear God! What a terrible fate," Gregor exclaimed, expressing aloud what the rest of us felt, though he then added piously, "No doubt their sins were black enough to deserve such a punishment."

"Haven't we seen this somewhere before?" I whispered to Mab.

"Yes, Ma'am, on the carved wall at Mephisto's mansion. I would say that clinches the theory about the Harebrain being a demon who visits Hell occasionally, but that would be like mentioning the barn door is open after the horse has trampled your head."

WE slowly approached the gate in the veil of hair and eyes. The demon guarding it had the thick horn and stubby legs of a rhinoceros with a huge bulbous body between. He sat upon a great, bloated reptile much like those we had seen in the Swamp of Uncleanness, only larger. He kept a constant vigil, prodding souls who tried to pass him with his pitchfork to drive them off. The few that came too close, he skewered and ate.

"I'll get this one. I know what to do!" Mephisto tapped his staff.

I began to imagine that a cockatrice strutted before the gate. Then, the demon saw it, too. He roared and charged the poisonous creature, his lizard mount leaping comically as it charged the prey. The cockatrice stood its ground defiantly, spitting streams of poison, until it realized the demon was immune to its venomous gaze. Then, it turned and fled.

Bellowing with glee, the demon spurred its lizard and rode after it. Meanwhile, the eight of us quickly sneaked through the unguarded gateway. As soon as we were safely away, Mephisto tapped his staff again, and the cockatrice vanished like a dream, leaving the angry demon to stomp back to his post empty-handed.

On the far side of the bone gate stretched a vast barren plain, beyond which rose the Mountains of Misery, where John Dee's ball had displayed Ulysses cavorting. The plain was as featureless as a salt flat. Every step we took kicked up soot and dust, which Mephisto claimed were the ashes of blighted, wasted lives. Great clouds of black smoke tinged with sulfurous flames hung overhead; we seemed to walk beneath upside-down volcanoes that stank of rotten eggs. As if the stench were not bad enough, the air was so oppressive we could scarcely breathe.

After a time, we began to hear an unnatural din. In the distance, two mighty hosts of damned souls battled. They came at each other like ravaging wolves, fighting with teeth and fists, for they had no proper weapons. They fastened upon one another's throats and tore at their enemies with fingernails as long as claws, scratching and biting like angry jackals. The demons who marshaled these berserk troops drove chariots pulled by the spirits of dead men, whom they lashed with whips of flame, urging them ever faster.

The battle cries of the combatants, the thunder of their conflict, and the shrieks of the wounded made an eerie wild music that urged us all to fight or flee. More than once, I had to close my eyes and breathe deeply, despite the stifling atmosphere, to keep from bolting in fear. My brothers, clearly uncomfortable, hunched their shoulders against the sound of it. Theo and Erasmus held a tight grip on their staffs; both hummed, ready. Mab put in his earplugs. So caught up in their fray were these demons and their troops that they did not notice our passing.

Now that my mind was no longer occupied with the revolting nature of the Swamp of Uncleanness or fear for Theo's life, the true horror of our surroundings began to dawn upon me. Every soul I had seen since I arrived—every victim of lust in the swamp, every sleeper beneath the Styx, every burning hulk who attacked his neighbors rather than escape from the molten lava, every partaker at the feast of gore, and every soldier in the two clashing hordes—had once been a living person—a person who could have escaped this wretched place had he chosen to live a better life. Every one of them had once been somebody—once, somebody's sister or brother, somebody's father or mother, somebody's beloved little child.

How did they all come to this?

Even more disturbing was: where did they come from? There were always a few people whom everyone agreed would be damned: Hitler, Napoleon, the Borgias, my uncle Antonio. But no one really expected ordinary people to go to Hell. Yet, we had passed thousands of damned souls, possibly millions, and that was just in the few sections through which we had traveled. There must be hundreds of millions beside, maybe billions. Would even a single one of these sufferers have chosen to be here, if he understood what was waiting for him?

The irony, the sorrow, the sheer waste, appalled me.

WE no longer held hands, for here there were no illusions. The others were trapped in the same dismal landscape as I. The Plain of Wasted Lives, with its dark roiling sky, spread away from us in every direction.

We walked for hours, each step kicking up dust, which got in our hair, our eyelashes, our mouths. Bones crunched beneath our feet, and often we had to step over rusted breastplates and cracked helmets. It was like every battlefield I had ever walked, except this dreary plain lacked the stink of carnage. That should have made it less unpleasant; instead, it seemed more ghostly, a phantom battlefield, emphasizing the waste and loss, without a single reminder of life, even the unpleasant ones.

As the clouds of dust and smog grew around us, my mind drifted to the wasted opportunities of my own life. I had never known love, never been a wife or a mother. With the Water of Life running out, I would die never having known any of these things.

I had so wanted children!

How ironic that Astreus was lost to me just when I could have accepted his suit. Of course, I would have refused him—unless he was offering me his head on a pike! But, even if he had been what I first took him for, he would not have wanted a sullied mortal woman. It was the Handmaiden of Eurynome he had wanted. Or, rather, the Sibyl!

Sibyl . . . a low tortured sigh escaped my lips as the reality sank in slowly. I would never be a Sibyl. All that work, prayer, obedience, loneliness, all in the hope of gaining a prize that would never be mine. Since that day, at the age of five, when Father consecrated me to the service of the Unicorn, I dreamt of rising to the highest ranks of Her servants and gaining the Gifts of the Sibyl: opening locks, creating Water of Life at will, commanding the lightning! And, most of all, absolving oaths.

Had I become a Sibyl, I could have freed Mephisto from his oath to the Elf Queen, Ulysses and Logistilla from their oaths to Abaddon, and the elves from their oaths to Hell. All this good I could have done, and I still, to this day, did not know why the rank of Sibyl had been denied to me.

Oh, I had theories aplenty: it was because I held the Aerie Ones captive, or because I had held Her consort Ophion as a prisoner in my flute. But, neither of those theories really made sense. Had that been all that was needed, my Lady would merely have told me to set them free. No, whatever was lacking had to be something in me, some quality in myself, something like . . .

A soul!

Maybe my Lady did not want women with damaged souls to serve her.

My limbs grew cold, almost numb. It was to guard against *lilim,* the seductive temptresses that served the Queen of Air and Darkness, that Eurynome required her Handmaidens to be virgins. Lilith was Eurynome's great enemy, bent upon Her destruction. The Demon Queen had been the one who furnished the enchanted weapons to the Unicorn Hunters of old, and Lilith was the one who tricked Mephisto into promising to bring her the Unicorn's head, a promise he had sacrificed his sanity to escape.

And I . . . I might be Lilith's daughter!

Had Father dedicated me to Eurynome as some kind of a ploy, an attempt to harm my Lady? But if so, why had it taken so long to accomplish? Could Father have been waiting patiently all this time, like a spider in its lair, for me to become a Sibyl so that he and his "M" could hatch some dastardly plan?

It made no sense. Eurynome would never accept a daughter of Lilith as one of Her Sibyls. I could have served Her until the end of time—I could have been the best Handmaiden there ever was—and I would never have achieved my desire. If, in truth, Lilith were my mother, then throughout my long life, all my hopes and dreams had always been for nothing.

Tears flowed down my cheeks, a hot trickle that quickly became a torrent. I wept bitterly and could not stop. I wept for the life that I had wasted. I wept for the love that I had lost—for I had loved the real Ferdinand well and truly. Had Astreus and I had more time . . . well, who could guess what might have come?

But it was not to be.

Theo's arms came around me, holding me tightly, comforting me. I threw myself against him, crying on his shoulder.

"Oh, Theo!"

He held me for a bit, swaying gently back and forth, while the rest of our party moved on ahead of us. Tears splashed against his shirt and his breastplate.

He smoothed my hair. "I am so sorry. It is all my fault."

"Sorry for what?" I looked up, my face tearstained.

"Osae . . ." His voice faltered. "I arrived too late."

I hugged him fondly with a hiccup and a sniff. "How could you have known?"

"But that's just it." Theo's face looked so young and sincere peering out from his helmet, so like the dear brother I had thought lost forever, that my heart ached. I feared I would begin bawling all over again. "In my excitement at seeing Gregor again, I hesitated when the Voice spoke." He lowered his head in shame. "I had gotten out of the habit of listening to it during my long years of exile, when I had distanced myself from the family. By the time I heeded it and ran to get my staff, it was too late."

"Voice?" I asked, startled. "What Voice?"

"The one that tells me when family members are in trouble. It's not a voice, really." He blushed. "I mean, not an audible sound another could hear."

"Have you always heard this Voice?"

"Always? No . . . The first time was while we were taming Vesuvius. The Voice warned me that the local oreads had betrayed us and had dropped Titus into a crevasse. That was in 1631."

"Funny, you've come to rescue me so many times, and yet it never occurred to me to ask you how you knew to be there. In Venice, remember when those men trapped me in that alley?"

Theo laughed. "What I remember was the time in Paris, when you jumped off the bridge into the Seine! If I'd been any later, that boat would have cut you in two!" He grew suddenly serious. "And that angry mob in Lisbon—I hate firing my staff at ordinary human beings. I wish there had been another way out!"

"Well, I was very glad you had your staff the time that Welsh wyvern woke up a decade early! Otherwise, I'd be rather crisper today!" I patted his arm. "Wait, just recently, when you saved me from Osae the Bear at the gas station in Vermont and then later, from Osae the Mab at Father's mansion. Was that . . . ?" Theo nodded. "Amazing! All this time, I just thought that showing up when you were needed was part of who you were."

"Your man Mab asked me about it, and Mephisto seemed to know something about it, too. I've wanted to question him further, but . . . well, you know what it's like getting information out of Mephisto!"

"What does this Voice sound like?"

"A flute speaking words."

"I know that voice!" I laughed in delight.

"Do you?" Theo looked thunderstruck.

"Yes! It is the guardian angel of the *Orbis Suleimani*!"

"Really?" Theo cried, astonished. "Why would their angel come to me? I am not a member of their mystical mumbo-jumbo organization!" He made a face expressing his disapproval.

"Erasmus asked me a similar question when I told him she had visited me," I replied. "I don't know the answer. Maybe we made ourselves available when others did not."

We began walking again, not wanting the others to get too far ahead of us. Mab was already looking back suspiciously. Theo took my hand, and we walked in silence for a time. Bones cracked underfoot, and clouds of black ash boiled overhead. The place stank.

"I was a goner, Miranda. The Hellwinds dropped me into that lava and . . . I was angry at everything. Everything was so unfair. I cursed the wrath of God! Then, Caliban's voice cut through all that, calling me back to my duty, reminding me that the family needed me." He smiled sheepishly. "My old argument of fearing I'd end up burning in Hell didn't hold water anymore!

"Funny, how life is. For decades now, I—who for most of my life feared nothing—have lived in terror, afraid of dying, afraid of burning in Hell. And now?" He laughed joyously, such a contrast to the creepy landscape around us. "Now, it's happened! I've burned in Hell and lived to talk about it. Better yet, I'm still alive, and I'm happier than I've been in years."

"Happier?" I wiped mud—born of tears and dust—from my cheek and then looked over the dismal plain, dotted with pointless battles that represented the death of so many hopes. "Here?"

"It's as if I've woken up from a dream." Theo shook his head as if clearing away cobwebs, a distant light in his eyes. "It could have been yesterday we all gathered at Gregor's graveside, and I took the vow to turn my back on magic, even if it meant that I would age and die. The intervening time, the years of loneliness and suffering—it's as if I have suddenly awakened, and they never happened. All my old firmness of purpose has returned and now burns in my breast like a shining star."

"Now, you sound like Theophrastus!" I smiled in delight, despite the lump of sorrow and regret still lodged in my heart.

Theo's eyes blazed. "I hope we live through this adventure. There are a thousand things that need doing! The monsoons still need binding, as do the many oreads. I did get around to those along the San Andreas Fault, but other faults await. The weather has been crazy of late. A firmer hand is needed.

"Then, there's the immorality and indulgence of modern society. Clearly some demons have escaped onto the surface and are influencing public opinion—most likely they're in Hollywood. That's where I'll start looking, anyway. And then there are the modern witches that have popped up everywhere. Gregor and I—or maybe it will be Titus and I, since the two of them have apparently changed staffs; I assume they'll tell me why at some point—are going to have quite a time sorting out which ones are innocent and which ones are doing real harm."

"It's good to have you back!" I hugged him. Another great weight lifted from my shoulders.

How odd and astonishing that this plain of wasted purpose brought out the best in Theophrastus, that he—of all people—would be immune to its lure.

Suddenly, I realized why I had found his behavior so puzzling over the last few decades. While Theo may have made and broken vows down through the years—regarding eschewing wine, women, and magic—he had never swerved in his pursuit of virtue and right. I kept expecting his love of righteousness to assert itself and compel him to act. I had not taken the *Staff of Persuasion* into account.

Yet, sorrow over paths untaken was not one of Theo's vices; he was too active, too purposeful. He might regret his impulsiveness but never his lack of action. He had not wasted his life! It was the magic of Cornelius's staff, not his own will, that had drawn him away from us these last decades. As soon as he had thrown off the external coercion from the staff, the real Theophrastus had reemerged, as idealistic and determined as ever.

My brother laughed again, squeezing my hand tightly. "It feels good to be back!" Then he frowned his serious, chivalric frown and wagged his finger at me. "But, you should not have wasted so much Water of Life on me! It was an excess we can't presently afford!!"

"Oh, Theo!" Tears welled up in my eyes again. I gripped his hand as tightly as I was able.

*   *   *

AHEAD of us a long trench cut across our path. I slid down the dusty bank, along with Mab, Theo, Erasmus, and Gregor. Mephisto opted to have Caliban throw him over the gap. He did a flip in midair and landed lightly on his feet, throwing his hands up like gymnast and shouting "Ta-da!" Caliban then leapt the trench, followed by Titus, whose foot slipped on sandbags piled on the far side, causing him to slide down the steep bank on his stomach, breathlessly joining the rest of us at the bottom.

Beside us, in the gloom, beady eyes gleamed. If that was not bad enough, the ground beneath my feet swarmed with thousands of horned beetles, all clicking their mandibles. As I shrieked in surprise, a rat the size of a large cat poked its nose out of the shadows.

"This is one of those moments when I wish Logistilla were here with her staff. Those creatures would look so much less disturbing if they were toads or dogs." Erasmus paused. "No, on second thought, being down here surrounded by packs of ugly toads or angry dogs would not be a great improvement."

Caliban knelt and extended his hand, which I quickly accepted, allowing him to haul me up onto the sandbags. He then helped Titus, and the two of them aided the others, until we were all out of the trench.

Ahead of us stretched more trenches, each separated from the next by waist-high barbed wire.

"Great." Mab's Bronx accent seemed unusually pronounced. "This is where we should have used the horse. From now on, we should check out the terrain ahead of us with the marble."

"The Seeing Sphere of Horus the Wise—also known as the Gazing Stone of King Solomon, or the crystal ball of Merlin the Magician, and that of the Renaissance wise man John Dee—might not appreciate being called a marble," Mephisto replied cheerfully, patting the crystal sphere.

"How exactly does this ball of yours work, Mephisto?" Erasmus asked as we climbed over the first of the barbed wire. "Can it answer any question? Show me tomorrow's winning lottery numbers? Show me the secret combination to a safe?"

Mephisto walked up to the fence, measured it with his eyes, took three long steps backwards, and ran. Leaping, he threw his body straight up, so that he rotated his heels over his shoulders without his head altering its height. He landed lightly on the far side of the fence.

Lounging against the protruding gun barrel of a rusting tank, he balanced the crystal ball on his fingers, rolling it back and forth, while watching the rest of us clamber awkwardly over the fence. "Nope. It only shows things I could see if I spent long enough looking myself. So if, right now, someone is writing down tomorrow's lottery numbers or the combination to the safe, it could show that. Otherwise, no luck."

"How does it define trouble, when it picks who is in the most trouble?" Gregor eyed the crystal ball suspiciously as he untangled his crimson robes from several barbs. "That seems a rather complicated concept."

Mephisto petted it as if it were a small animal. "It can't, really. It can only show us who looks to be in the most trouble. If a danger is invisible or in the person's head, the ball can't help. When I first got it, it had trouble judging even obvious visible problems. I had to train it."

"So, you couldn't just ask the ball who the traitor was, then?" Erasmus looked faintly disappointed. He stepped over the next trench, which luckily was only two feet wide.

"Are you back on that dopey traitor theory? Nope. It couldn't help us unless someone was committing an act of treachery against us right now." Mephisto hefted the ball up to his eye level. "Ball, show me any of my goofy brothers who are committing acts of treason." We all peered at the ball, but the mist continued to swirl. "There, you see?"

"Or sisters," Erasmus pressed.

"Or sisters," Mephisto added to the ball. Again, there was no change within the crystal.

"Jiminy Christmas!" Mab exclaimed, as we all approached the next fence. "It's not like Miss Miranda would be plotting against you right now as we're walking along. If she were, you wouldn't need a ball. You'd be able to see with your naked eye!"

"Is there a traitor?" Gregor paused and glared at the rest of us warily. "If so, it cannot be Caliban here, or Mab, because they are not family, but as for the rest of us . . ." He stared grimly into each of our faces. "If it should turn out that there is a traitor, I want that person to know that Theo and I will kill you."

"What if it's Theo?" asked Erasmus.

Gregor snorted, refusing to dignify Erasmus's comment with an answer.

"Show me Theo being a dopey traitor," sang Mephisto. Featureless mist continued to swirl in the ball.

"What of Ulysses?" Titus asked. He picked me up by my waist and deposited me on the far side of the next barbed wire. Then, he stepped over it with ease. Mephisto handed him the crystal ball and did a back handspring over the fence. Titus handed the ball back to him. "Are we certain he will not betray us again?"

"He did not kill me when he could have," Gregor replied in his gravelly voice. "In fact, he went to great lengths to keep me alive. He may be weak and foolish, but I believe his heart is in the right place."

"But he is still bound by his oath to Abaddon," Titus continued, walking again. A narrow board covered the next trench. We all teetered across this rickety bridge in single file. "What if Abaddon reaches him while Ulysses is off on his own? Could that be the danger the ball warned of?"

"We sent Abaddon down in the depths of Hell, into the ice at the very bottom where Satan is entrapped," Theo said with some satisfaction. "He won't be back anytime soon."

"Are we sure?" Erasmus asked. "Mephisto, check the ball."

"Show me Abaddon," Mephisto said, speaking to the ball. The mist swirled revealing the great demon's legs and feet. His head, shoulders, and chest were embedded in a sheet of unpleasant-looking green ice.

"Well, at least we don't have to worry about him." Erasmus chuckled. "We can go back to worrying about Miranda and, maybe, Mephisto."

"Show me myself being a dopey traitor," Mephisto asked the ball as he hopped over a line of barbed wire. The picture of Abaddon vanished, replaced by swirling mist.

Erasmus's supercilious attitude grated on my nerves. I longed to slap him and wipe that smug sneer off his face, but slapping him would, of course, solve nothing. Gregor and Theo, however, eyed Mephisto warily.

"We mustn't start distrusting each other," I urged, climbing carefully over the next fence. "That is what the demons want. It is their weapon against us!"

"How convenient, Sister," Erasmus purred, as he made his way over beside me, "that virtue and goodness compel us to fall right into your trap."

"Show me virtue and goodness," Mephisto asked the ball but received no response.

"Professor Prospero, you got to listen to her!" Mab spoke up. The tail of his trench coat had caught on the fence. He wrestled with it, trying to work it free. "I know demons, better than you folks. Your family unity is the biggest advantage you have over the Forces of Hell—they never work together. Not for long anyway. And they can't take this unity away from you unless you give it up freely!"

"Yes, little spiritling. We know you are loyal to Miranda."

"Why must you be so spiteful, Erasmus!" I snapped. "What have Mab or I ever done to you?"

"Show me why Erasmus is so spiteful," Mephisto chirped cheerfully.

"Mephisto, will you please cut that out, you're . . ." Theo reached out as if to yank the crystal globe away, and then he froze. Within the ball, the mist cleared and an image formed.

A simple stone altar stood in the midst of a pentacle. Atop the altar, two dolls had been poised. One was dressed in doublet and hose of green and black and a cavalier's hat, much like the one Mephisto currently carried on his back. Its right hand was covered by a white gauntlet, and it held a white and black staff. The other was feminine, silver-haired, and garbed in a satin gown the color of emeralds. In her right hand, she carried a flute. Both dolls held tiny swords in their left hand, with which they stabbed the opposite doll through the chest.

Mab hissed at the image, as if it were poisonous. "Sympathetic magic, Ma'am. Bad stuff!"

"What are they? Voodoo dolls?" Erasmus peered closer. "Hey, that's me! That's supposed to be Miranda and me. Are we . . . are we stabbing each other?"

"Yes," I said numbly, aghast. "But where is this? Who . . . who did such a thing?"

I glanced at Erasmus and felt the familiar rush of hatred flow throw my veins. Could that sensation, which I suffered nearly every time I thought of Erasmus, be caused by the spell these voodoo dolls represented? If so, how long had the spell been going on? Years? Generations? Centuries?

A horripilation of dread spread along my arms. Someone had cast a spell intended to harm me: a spell I had had no chance of knowing about, much less stopping. The horror of it reminded me, yet again of Seir's first attack on Prospero's Mansion. I felt as if something inviolate had suddenly been ripped open and defiled.

"Ball, show me who made these dolls," Mephisto asked. The ball showed a red demon with long bat ears and delicate fingers. Mephisto snorted with annoyance. "Show me who this demon works for."

An image formed of another demon, this one had a black-and-gray pie-bald hide and large incisors. Mephisto rolled his eyes, annoyed. "Show me who gave the command to make the dolls."

The mist swirled, showing yet another demon, bright blue with a wide mouth full of crocodile teeth.

Mephisto hissed in annoyance. "Those idiots! They do this on purpose, layers and layers of command, just to stop guys like me. I could keep asking right up to their ultimate boss, but whoever really originated the orders might not even be in the official line of command. Ball, show me where the dolls are."

The mist swirled and showed the dolls again. Then, the picture pulled back, showing a familiar structure with towers rising over reddish stone walls.

"The *Castello Sforzesco* in Milan!" I cried.

"Dear God!" Erasmus leaned forward. "Why are the walls running with blood?"

"Are they?" Mephisto peered closer. "Oh, they are! This must be in Infernal Milan."

"Infernal Milan?" several of us asked.

"Most cities have an infernal version," Mephisto replied. "I like to think of it as the city's evil twin! Every time anyone sins on earth, a bit of wickedness drips down into Hell. The more sinful the people in the city, the more solid the evil dark twin becomes. You think Milan looks bad, you should see Rome!"

"Or New York," murmured Erasmus.

Mephisto shook his head. "New York's in a category by itself."

I gripped Theo's arm. "You are saying these dolls of us are here, in Hell?"

"Yep, in the infernal version of our granddaddy's castle," Mephisto declared.

"Look around," Mab pressed. "Maybe the perpetrator has left some clues. Might even be on the premises."

"Ball, show me the rest of the *castello*." Mephisto held the ball atop his hand for us to see. "Oh, my!"

The crystal sphere moved through the hallways and into the ducal presence chamber. Upon the throne sat Logistilla.

CHAPTER TWELVE

There Once Was a Girl Named Maria

"So, we've found the culprit at last," Mab exclaimed with some satisfaction. We had stopped for a rest and were seated on the dusty plain.

"My question," Erasmus asked as he recovered from a fit of dust-induced coughing, "is why encourage me to fight with Miranda? I thought Logistilla liked me."

"My bet's been on her all along." Mab grinned like a cop about to make a bust. "I told you her place stank of the Devil."

"That must have been Abaddon!" I said.

"Never thought to ask her what else the Angel of the Bottomless Pit might have gotten her to do," Erasmus mused. "Makes sense that if he made a play for Theo and Gregor through Ulysses, he wouldn't leave Miranda and me out entirely."

"Bet this has something to do with that cavern of undead Italians," Mab crowed, delighted at having his suspicions proven true. Several of the others gave him startled looks, but Erasmus merely chuckled.

"Those are intended for Aerie Ones, such as yourself." Erasmus's tone was light and cheery, as if he spoke of some obvious thing that everyone knew.

So, I was right about the bodies! Yet, my pleasure was short-lived. I may have figured out Father's plan, but Erasmus had been privy to it all along. And to think that I had believed I was the one in whom Father confided!

Thinking back, I realized that Erasmus had never liked me. It was not until the early 1600s, however, just after Logistilla and Gregor came on the scene, that he became intolerable. But then, it was about that time, as well, that he stopped studying art and swordplay and threw himself into sorcery. That could hardly be the fault of the then young Logistilla.

If these dolls dated from the period of Logistilla's youth, then they might indeed be the cause of our enmity. If they were recent, then they were of little interest, for, by now, they would merely be icing on the cake of mutual hostility.

Could Logistilla have been setting us against each other all her life? The idea of young Logistilla behaving in such a fashion was laughable. What would have motivated her to do such a thing?

I ran my finger through the dust. "I don't think this could be Logistilla's doing. It doesn't make any sense."

Titus looked relieved. "Miranda's judgment is always good."

"No," Erasmus drawled maliciously, "*Eurynome's* judgment is good. But the Unicorn no longer informs our sister's decisions."

Erasmus was right. Without my Lady to guide me, my judgment had proved faulty. I hesitated, uncertain.

Gregor leaned over and gave my shoulder a comforting pat. He said hoarsely, "It is for the best. Your soul is safer now that you have put that blasphemy behind you."

That was the last straw. I was in Hell, in the midst of dust and ash, having scattered my family and lost my Lady, and my brother had the nerve to be less than respectful to Her!

I screamed. "My Lady is a loyal servant of your God! The one and only God! There are more things in heaven and earth, Gregor, than are dreamt of in your theology!"

Taken aback, Gregor stepped away from me. His face betraying his startlement.

"Whoa!" Erasmus threw up his arms as if to ward me off. "The wildcat has unsheathed her claws."

"Enough with you!" I turned on him. "Didn't you see the vision in Mephisto's globe? Don't you realize you are being manipulated by magic? You would think that, upon learning this, you might make some kind of effort to restrain yourself. But no! You're just as malicious as ever! What is wrong with you, Erasmus?"

Theo's firm grip came down on my shoulder. "What's wrong with him is that he's under a spell, just as I was. Forgive him."

I shrugged his hand off and continued, glaring at my family. "As to Logistilla, I say she is innocent! She is petty, and she turns people into animals, I grant you that, but I do not believe she would do something like this to us. Nor do I believe—" I turned on Theo—"that Father would cast a spell upon me, or any of us! I believe in our family! We might fight. We might annoy each other, we might even fake each other's deaths or turn each other into bears, but when it really comes down to it, we are faithful, loyal!"

The others were staring at me as if I had sprouted wings from my ears. My tirade had impressed them, so seldom had they seen me get truly upset.

Erasmus spoke in his calm, oily voice. "I'm sure Father felt the same way about Antonio."

If he had slapped me, I could not have felt more shocked.

He was right. Surely that betrayal had been as shocking as Logistilla's would be to me. More so, for Father and Uncle Antonio had once loved each other dearly.

WE walked until Mephisto dropped midstep onto his face and lay snoring gently, as the dust formed puffs about him. The rest of us were too exhausted to drag him back to his feet, so the others insisted on making camp. I argued that we needed to keep pushing onward, to reach the others, to save Father, but Theo pointed out gently that if we dropped from fatigue before we made it to Father, we would not do him any good.

Mab snuck the crystal ball out of Mephisto's pocket and asked it to show him the date. It was still the third of January. We had three days left, and the distance from Ulysses to Father did not seem very far. The only question remaining was how long it would take to rescue the other three—Ulysses, Logistilla, and Cornelius. But as the others were already falling asleep, the point was moot.

Gregor took off his crimson robes and insisted that I, being the lady, rest upon them. I spread them out so that I slept upon one side, leaving the other side open for someone else. None of the men wanted to be the one to take the softer surface while the rest of them proved their manliness by sleeping on the hard ground. Finally, they dragged the sleeping Mephisto onto the robe and went off to make up their own beds with their jackets and bags.

We lay upon the hard ground, our mouths dry with dust. Except for Theo, who merely looked tired, and Mephisto, who was asleep, the others were looking gaunt and harried, as if haunted by personal ghosts.

"So much time lost," Gregor murmured hoarsely, from where he lay, his head resting on a broken helmet. "Tell me, Brothers, Sister, Spirit with a Soul: what have I missed during my absence?"

We all spoke at once, eager to dispel the gloom by describing how the world had changed since 1921. There was so much to say. We touched on a few highlights: the First and Second World Wars, the Space Age, Hollywood, the

Internet, improvements in technology that had changed the world. Gregor listened to these matters impassively, then turned the discussion to the matter of most interest to him—the Catholic Church and how it had fared during his internment.

Most of us had little to say about this topic, not having kept track of such things. It was not a subject I had any interest in. Titus went as far as to sneer with distaste, displaying his loyalty to his native Scottish Protestantism. Theo, however, was able to answer many of Gregor's questions, albeit in layman's terms and not in the detail Gregor would have liked. Erasmus had not been a religious man in many years, but as a scholar, he kept abreast of the times and could fill in explanations or offer background that Theo did not know. And from time to time, Caliban, who lay on his back with his head resting across his club, spoke up, surprising everyone with the answer to some esoteric question that Theo and Erasmus could not answer.

Much of what was said distressed Gregor. He was horrified to hear of recent scandals and the loss of faith among the modern public, though he was just as horrified to hear that mass was no longer being said in Latin. He was cautiously hopeful to hear that the church had taken a gentler tone toward heretics, but withheld his final judgment, saying that until he saw how the documents were worded and how their mandates were being carried out, he could not give his approval. Certain niceties of the relationship between the bishops and the pope caused him great distress, until he sighed and shook his head, smiling sadly.

"It is not meet for me to trouble myself about these things. Especially now, when I have only hearsay to go on. If I should survive to see the light of day again, I will investigate this matter myself. God willing, I will find myself at peace with it. If not, I can always hover nearby waiting for a cardinal to die and, with Logistilla's help, work my way back up to being pope again."

"I don't suppose it would occur to you to work your way up, like everyone else," Erasmus asked wryly.

Gregor eyed him skeptically. "What past would I show them? Do you plan to turn me into a baby and have me grow up again? The life of a pope gets scrutinized. I can hardly come forward and present myself as a member of the heretical and blasphemous witchcraft-practicing Prospero Clan." He settled back again, his arms crossed behind his head. "Besides, while it is true that I rose to power upon the laurels of a better man the first time, the second time I started as quite a young man and worked my way up to pope on my own merit. But enough of this. Tell me more about this new modern world."

We talked some more, describing some of the wonders that mankind had wrought in the last century.

"Television?" Gregor interrupted after a time. "Is that the same as 'telly'? Ulysses furnished my prison with a fancy magic lantern containing moving images which he called by that name."

"The very same!" Erasmus had taken off his long, green outer justacorps to use as a pillow. He lay on the dust in his shirtsleeves and waistcoat. "So, Ulysses gave you a television, did he? I'm glad to hear it. Maybe you are not as far behind the modern world as I first feared. Did what you see seem shocking?"

Gregor grimaced as if pained. "The women acted brazenly and dressed outrageously. I prayed constantly that this pageant was worse than the reality it sought to represent."

"Might be it was, if it was MTV," Erasmus allowed. "Though the reality is pretty bad nowadays. Do you remember the name of the program?"

"Ulysses called it, *I Love Lucy*."

"Dear Jesus!" Erasmus bent over and pressed his hand against his mouth to restrain his mirth. Mab lowered the brim of his fedora until it hid his face in shadow. Theo, Titus, Caliban, and I were not so lucky. We burst into laughter.

"Do not take the Lord's name in vain," Gregor snapped. "Something I said amuse you?"

"Only that *I Love Lucy* is tame by modern standards," I replied, chuckling sadly.

"Ah, so those prayers went unheeded." He nodded.

Erasmus chuckled. "I fear you will have to weather a few shocks when you get home."

"You think it a laughing matter, Brother?" Gregor frowned. "I pity those who walk the earth today. So many of them will be led astray by false promises and vice masquerading as virtue. And this"—he gestured out over the dreary battlefield—"will be their reward."

Gregor's words were harsh and chilling. In their wake, I found myself considering the modern world in a new light; many things that had formerly struck me as quaint or eccentric took on menacing overtones.

"I have missed so much." Gregor sounded slightly stunned. "The loss of time, of opportunity . . . the sheer waste! And yet, I am not sure I would alter events, were I able. I would never have come to grips with my hatred had I not been forced to confront my own thoughts for years on end. I would still be as angry and as bitter as I had been before my captivity."

"Were you as bad as that?" I asked, very curious about what had caused this amazing change in my brother. I leaned forward, eager to finally learn what had caused his transformation.

"I was," Gregor admitted. "The worst of it came after I had been on Mars for about eight years. My confinement had begun to oppress me, and I was seized by hatred, loathing, and wrath such as even I had never suffered before. I hated the Protestants for stealing from us! For robbing so many of eternal life. If it had not been for Luther, Calvin, and others . . . or perhaps, if it had not been for the Borgias, who gave them the fodder they needed to sway the masses . . . we, the Church, would have had the Puritans!"

"I beg your pardon?" Erasmus leaned forward.

"If the new Puritanical order," Gregor continued hoarsely, "had been embraced by the Church—as it had other orders had before it: the Benedictines and the Jesuits, the Dominicans and the Franciscans—I could have participated. Instead? What happened? This good human impulse slipped through our fingers, all those virtuous folks who followed it were lost to Hell, and the Council of Trent, which was supposed to conciliate the dissenters, made things more opulent and ceremonial! The purity and simplicity I craved were forever forbidden to me!"

"This makes sense of many things," Erasmus murmured.

I felt the same way. Gregor had always reminded me of the Puritans; I had wondered why he had not joined their movement. Now I saw: he had wanted to be a Puritan . . . but only so long as the Puritans were under the jurisdiction of his beloved Catholic Church.

"My hatred and rage grew so great that I became ill," Gregor continued, sitting up, a black form against the dull gray skies of the plain. "I grew feverish and delirious. Days passed. Ulysses sometimes forgot me for months at a time, so I began to fear that I would die of my illness before he returned to aid me. I lay there, fretting about the Reformation and the sins of Luther and Pope Alexander II. Then, in the midst of my delirium, I beheld a vision."

His voice became hushed, awed. "As I lay within my bed, a woman descended from Heaven clothed in a robe woven from the sun. She stood upon a crescent moon, and upon her head was a crown of twelve stars. She revealed to me that she was the embodiment of the Great Church, the Church our Lord the Savior founded upon the rock of Saint Peter.

"'Rise up!' I cried in my rabid state. 'Seize the malefactors! Rend them! Reveal to them the error of their sinful ways!'

"Gazing at me with pity, she pointed at her sun-bright robes and asked me sternly if I could see any rents in her garments. I acknowledged that there was none. She then announced that she took no cognizance of the split caused by the Reformation."

Gregor paused and shook his head, astonishment evident upon his face. "Can you imagine? She thought the differences between the Lutherans and the True Church was no greater than that between . . . between the Benedictines and the Jesuits! As if our great religious wars were nothing but a squabble among children, in which their mother took no side! It was utterly astonishing!"

"And you believe this to have been a true vision?" Erasmus asked from where he lay stretched out on the dirt, atop his coat, his arms crossed behind his head.

"Bah! Of course not." Gregor waved his hand dismissively and lay down. "It was the delirium of a sick man." He added, his voice intent, "But it made me *think*!"

I AWOKE before my brethren and lay for a time staring up at the black billowing smoke shot through with red-orange flames. It was hard to convince my body it was morning—morning being a relative term here—but I eventually rose and, finding my shoulder bag, drew out a brush. Sitting down upon Gregor's robe, I brushed out my raven-dark hair.

Behind me, a voice was speaking softly. I turned, stifling a scream when I saw someone standing within our camp. The light was dim, and the figure's back was to me. I could not make out who it was. He stood, motionless, as if gazing at the battle of the dead raging in the distance. Even before my eyes made out who he was, I had determined his identity; for now I could make out the words:

Since Death has all my brethren tak'n
He will not long me leave alone
On force I must his next prey be;
Timor Mortis conturbat me.

Since for the dead remedy is none
Best is that we for death dispone

After our death that live may we;
Timor Mortis conturbat me.

Erasmus turned, smiling his self-mocking smile through the lank dark
hair that fell over his eyes. "Seems appropriate to the place, does it not?
Frighteningly appropriate, even."

As he walked away and retrieved his long green coat, I had the oddest
feeling that he had not actually recognized me. Perhaps, this was true, for
he did not pause to say something disagreeable.

MY respite from malice was fleeting.

"Up early, are you, O Get of Sycorax?" Erasmus asked almost cheerfully.

I sighed. "Erasmus, now that we know about the dolls and their spell,
don't you think that it would behoove you to make some effort to resist the
spell-induced hatred? You are deliberately allowing yourself to be influenced by dark enchantments."

A wave of antipathy overwhelmed me, but I dismissed it sternly. It was
a magical attack and not my own feelings. I did not need to bow to it. I
briefly recalled Theo's admonition to forgive Erasmus but could not bring
myself to go that far.

"My disdain for you, Sister dear, does not come from any spell. Logistilla, or whomever cast the spell, was merely taking advantage of an enmity
that was already present."

"Then why do you hate me so?" I repeated the question I had asked him
when we were sipping Mango juice back in Boston—what now seemed like
a lifetime ago.

"Maria, of course," he answered.

I caught myself before I blurted "who"? Clearly, this person was important to my brother and he expected me to remember her. Maria? The name
sounded vaguely familiar. Father had had a nurse named Maria during his
illness after Gregor's "death," but I could not recall that Erasmus had much
to do with her.

I vaguely recalled Erasmus's first wife, a sweet young woman with a
round face, long legs, and a colt's large brown eyes. Her name had been
Maria, I was nearly certain, but I had hardly known her. How could I have
offended her?

I waited, hoping he would say more.

"Because of Mother and my Maria," he continued.

"Your mother?" I asked, astonished. Could this quarrel of his be so old as Isabella Medici? Both Isabella Medici and Erasmus's first wife had died centuries ago. "What do they have to do with me?"

"You murdered them," he replied.

"I?" I exclaimed. "I was not even present! Your mother choked on a chicken bone at a dinner served by her own great-niece—a party to which I had not even been invited—and your wife, if I recall, died in childbirth."

"Exactly," replied Erasmus. "You weren't there."

I sighed with exasperation. "Don't tell me this is the old Water of Life argument again! Life with an immortal Isabella Medici would have been intolerable!"

"She was my mother! What if it had been Lady Portia, whom you apparently continue to insist Father adored. Would you have saved her?"

"Of course. Father loved her."

"Well, I loved Maria."

"You would have tired of her eventually," I repeated by rote what Father had told me.

Only now, the words sounded flat to my ears. I recalled, for some reason, the old lady I had seen crossing the overpass in Chicago. If matters had been different, and Ferdinand had lived, might it have been me who lay dying upon a birthing bed, as Maria had? I felt strangely disoriented, as if familiar objects had suddenly transformed into an unfamiliar landscape.

"Is that so?" Erasmus said. "Funny, I never have tired of her memory. In all the years since, I've never met a woman who compared with her. No woman since has been as sweet, as gentle, as faithful. No woman, again, has made me feel as complete."

When I did not answer, he continued, "She died in my arms, you know, her sweet brown eyes calling out to me to help her, to stop the pain. Her blood ran through my fingers . . . all my scholarly learning could not help me stanch its flow. And all I could think of, as my love's life ebbed away, was that a single drop of Water from the lily-white hand of my older sister could save her, could stop the pain . . . could save the child, the fruit of our love. A single drop. They both died that night, the mother and the child, leaving me to grieve and our four older children motherless." He paused momentarily unable to go on.

Eventually, he continued, speaking haltingly. "You've tried to take my family from me, but you have failed. Do you know I've kept track of them all? Every single offshoot of my and Maria's love down unto the twenty-third generation? They number in the ten thousands now, yet I know the name and location of every one. That boy you saw guiding Cornelius, is the twenty-third of my line, the twenty-second eldest son in a direct line from my eldest son Sebastian."

That was why the young boy who had been guiding my brother Cornelius around back at Erasmus's house had showed up when Mab and I asked the Santa's Naughty and Nice pool to show us children who were members of our family. How strange and disconcerting to think that I had thousands of great-great-nephews of whom I knew nothing. Worse, Mr. Mustache had probably been one of these descendants, too. This meant that the man I had led to his death when he had tried to chase my sailboat at night on our way to Logistilla's had been not only innocent, but also a family member!

Erasmus was speaking again. "In those wee hours, as my Maria's life seeped inevitably away, I cursed you in my heart, and I have never forgiven you. You are the murderer of my love as surely as if you had killed her with your own hands."

"A ridiculous supposition, Erasmus. Do you also hold me responsible for every other person who had died between then and now? Theoretically, I could have gotten the Water to them as well."

"What do *I* care about *them*?" he rasped. "You could have saved my Maria and my baby! *My* wife and *my* child—I never even discovered whether I lost a boy or a girl. It would have cost you nothing! As Maria lay dying, I left her, even though she called out to me not to leave her alone, and spent some of our precious last minutes together begging Father on my knees to force you to help her. But, he refused. He said the Water was yours, and only you could decide how it would be used."

"Father said that?" I whispered, shocked. "How strange . . ."

Something in my tone caught my brother's attention. Erasmus halted his diatribe and peered at me. "How so?"

"Because Father was the one who told me not to give it to you."

"What . . . ?" Erasmus leaned forward, his eyes glittering.

"Do you think that I, a young woman with no husband, could have known anything of love? How could I have made the judgement that you would tire of Maria? I know nothing of the ways of men and women."

"I thought that was precisely why you did it . . . because you were bitter over Ferdinand and wanted others to suffer," he said, a touch of uncertainty creeping into his voice.

"Certainly not!" I objected. "I would not be motivated by such pettiness! I merely did what I always did. . . . I obeyed Father's wishes."

For a moment, Erasmus looked pained, then he laughed harshly. "Very cunning of you, Sister, to try and frame Father when he is not here to defend himself. I am not fooled. You cannot blame your crimes on him. Nor do I buy Theo's theory that Father has enchanted you. You are the culprit behind all our family ills, and here, in Hell, the truth shall come out!"

CHAPTER THIRTEEN

Bite the Angel's Finger!

Mephisto awoke and summoned up his friends again. Pegasus proved bright-eyed and whinnying, but the others remained fast asleep.

"Ma'am, didn't you once tell me that Pegasus was a magic horse who could carry your whole family?" Mab asked, yawning. He stretched, trying to straighten a crick in his back caused by having slept on a rock.

"Yes!" I laughed and turned to Mephisto. "Shall we ride?"

"All aboard!" Mephisto gleefully threw his arms out. "But keep in mind that Peggie gets tired easily when he carries everyone. I don't know how far he'll be able to take us."

"Anything is better than walking the whole way," Erasmus murmured gratefully.

So all eight of us mounted the magic horse. Mephisto took the reins. I sat behind him, with Theo behind me, then Mab, Gregor, Erasmus, Titus, and finally, upon the haunches, Caliban. None of us knew how Pegasus could bear such a burden; it must have been part of his magic, and we gloried in it.

What a joy to fly, to leave the dust and din of the plain below us and soar through the air. True it was smoggy, sulfurous, and we had to fly quite low to avoid the black boiling clouds, but it was a pleasure to see the ground fly by beneath our feet.

Several times, Mephisto checked on Ulysses in the crystal ball, but Ulysses was always somewhere in the same rugged landscape, running naked along cliffs and rocky ramparts.

We flew on, squished together like living spoons, the ground flashing by beneath us. As I watched it fly by, I was reminded of the Aerie Ones, for whom seeing solid land flash by beneath them was an ordinary occurrence.

I thought of Mustardseed and Windflower and the others back at the company and wondered how they were coping without me.

This past month was the longest break I had taken from my corporate duties, since the last time I had left on the year-and-a-day journey to the Well at the World's End to fetch more Water of Life, sometime back in the 1960s. Back then, my absence had not mattered as much, as Father had still been in charge.

Ah, Prospero, Inc. I chafed to be back at the helm. I missed the office, the buzz of Aerie Ones about their business, the challenges of keeping everything moving smoothly. It was a life I loved, work I understood. I could not wait to get back.

Mentally, I reviewed the Priority contracts soon to come due. Again worry gnawed at my innards. Could Mustardseed handle everything on his own? The Priority contracts seldom came due without some complication that required my direct action. I hoped this time would prove the exception, that they would carry on competently without me.

We flew for hours but eventually our ride came to an end. Our flying steed grew weary and could no longer bear our burden. He landed and trotted for a time. When even that became too much for him, we dismounted, and Mephisto sent him home. Then, he briefly called up his maenad, Queen Agave, and gave her instructions to see that the winged horse was properly curried and fed.

We set out on foot again, sore from our ride but rejoicing at the territory covered. The jagged purple peaks of the Mountains of Misery now loomed above us. Beneath them rolled their foothills, where Ulysses waited, only a few miles away. And, yet, our every footstep still kicked up a cloud of dust that made the already oppressive air even harder to breathe. Some of my brothers began wheezing.

A loud *rat-a-tat-tat* reverberated across the landscape. Ahead, a group of damned souls manned a machine-gun nest, strafing the countryside.

"How do we get past this?" Titus asked.

"We walk. Aren't we safe so long as we do not become upset?" asked Erasmus.

"Perhaps, but what about our garments? Will the enchanted cloth resist the spiritual bullets?" Titus fingered the cloth of his ruffled shirt.

"What bullets?" Erasmus scoffed at Titus. "They could not possibly have bullets. Where would they get them?"

"A strange time to quibble with the reality of all this, isn't it, Brother?" Theo gestured at the tanks, the barbed wire, the broken-down Jeeps. "Where do they get any of these things?"

"That's different," Erasmus replied smoothly. "I can imagine being in Hell with barbed wire. I cannot imagine being in Hell and having enough bullets."

With that, Erasmus walked jauntily across the gunners' fields of fire. The rest of us watched intently, uncertain how to rescue him if the impact of spiritual bullets upon his garments should fling him to the ground. He strolled across the entire field of fire. The huge guns worked noisily, strafing the area. My brother remained untouched. He moved confidently to the next trench, beyond the range of the gun nest. Turning back toward us, he waved.

Mephisto, who had been gaping in astonishment, pushed his jaw shut with his hand and declared, "I may be insane, but he's crazy!"

EVENTUALLY, the rest of us found the courage to walk through the machine-gun fire. On the far side, Caliban stood in the shallow trench and lifted us over, except for Titus whose legs were long enough to step across by himself. Beyond that, more flat, featureless plain stretched toward the rolling foothills, which grew closer as we trekked onward.

"So, I have a question, Brother Gregor," Erasmus announced as we trudged onward, dust forming little eddies around us. Beside him, Mephisto was walking on his hands. Apparently, merely strolling on flat sandy earth was not difficult enough for him.

"And what is that, Brother Erasmus?" Gregor replied in his low gravelly voice. His crimson robes swished about his long legs.

"How come the Church lied to us about Hell?"

"How is that?"

"You said so. That they knew that people could get out of Hell, from some document purported to have been written by St. Peter, but that they decided to lie to us." Erasmus cocked his head. "Is that the proper behavior of people who claim to be followers of Our Lord?"

The others, those who had not been there for the original conversation, looked at Gregor with some interest, Theo in particular.

"People can get out of Hell?" he echoed.

"Of course, they can," Mephisto chirped from where he walked beside us on his hands. "Didn't Christ himself go down and break some guys out? While he was dead, no less!"

"That was a one-time thing," Theo argued. "The Harrowing of Hell, when Christ saved the patriarchs and the Virtuous Pagans of Old."

"Says who?" Mephisto asked. "Angels come down here and Harrow all the time." He turned his upside-down head toward me. "Ferdie mentioned it, remember?"

"'Ferdie' was an incubus," I drawled. "He was probably lying."

"It may be that some souls can escape Hell," Gregor replied carefully, ignoring Mephisto. "With prayer and help. But the Church Fathers were not certain. They had hints that this might be the case but felt it was better to err on the side of caution. So, after much debate, they made the choice to hide these references from their flock."

"Well that's . . ." Theo's voice trailed off. His face had grown pale, as if he had just had a sudden shock. He pressed a hand against his chest. I touched his arm, concerned. He did not even seem to notice me.

"As to our following the example of Our Savior," Gregor continued, "He himself hid His meaning a great deal of the time. He taught in parables instead of speaking openly, and He told those healed to tell no one what had occurred. He even said . . ."

Gregor spoke in Latin. Erasmus merrily repeated the passage in English. "*Because it is given unto you to know the mysteries of the kingdom of heaven, but to them it is not given . . . For this people's heart is waxed gross, and their ears are dull of hearing, and their eyes they have closed; lest at any time they should see with their eyes, and hear with their ears, and should understand with their heart, and should be converted, and I should heal them.'*"

"You can quote the Bible?" Caliban asked, surprised. He swung his club as he walked, occasionally striking the ground, where his weapon kicked up a minor dust storm while leaving a shallow trench where it contacted the ground. "I thought you were an agnostic scoffer."

"Man, no one who works for an angel can doubt their existence. I merely doubt the truth of certain . . ."—Erasmus gestured with his hands—"metaphysical claims." He flashed a sudden grin that transformed his face, making him look uncharacteristically handsome. "Besides, I wrote that passage."

"Blasphemy," Gregor growled.

Mab took off his hat and straightened the brim, which had gotten bent when it caught on some barbed wire. "I thought those words came from that nice guy you mortals hung up on a tree."

"He spoke them, true, but I am the one who chose that particular phrasing." Erasmus waved a hand at himself. "We in the Second Oxford Company were responsible for translating the Four Gospels and Acts and Revelations—the best parts of the New Testament, I've always thought. Of course, the Cambridge Company got Psalms, those lucky dogs—though I was able to get Dr. Andrew Bing to use a few of my suggested phrasings."

"Who-how, now?" Mab scratched his head.

"Translators on the King James Version of the Bible," Theo explained. His face had recovered its normal color, but a deep furrow still marred his brow. "Erasmus was one of their number."

"Indeed, I was," Erasmus stated airily. "Though, of course, Cornelius insisted on having my name removed from the historical records. Actually, only the second half of that quote is mine. Sir Henry Savile and Dr. James Harmar worked out the wording for the first half."

Titus snorted in disbelief, "After all these years, you still remember who wrote what?"

Erasmus chuckled. "Only passages I worked especially hard on . . . or in places where we had massive arguments, which I won."

"Speaking of Cornelius and changing history," Gregor mused, stroking his beard, "it is interesting that you, of all people, would complain about the caution of the Church. Your *Orbis Suleimani* has raised hiding evidence to an art form. You fake historical records, forge documents. Hardly the heralds of truth."

"Ah, but look at the good we have done," Erasmus countered, spreading his arms. "Before we hid the existence of the Kings of the Elements and their many supernatural servants, humans thought they had to worship these forces. We put an end to all that. Now, we humans are the masters of the natural world. Our work has done wonders for their quality of life, not to mention their souls.

"When men believe in the lesser supernatural, they lose all reason. They either cower with fear, worship the nymphs and satyrs and try to act like them, or try to learn forbidden secrets and use them to gain power over their fellows. And elves and djinn are not like angels. They are perfectly willing to make secret deals, to promote one man above another, to distrpt the balance of power. Technological tyrannies may be bad, but believe me, they are nothing compared to supernatural ones. Weapons may be expensive, but any man can shoot a gun. If your king or dictator makes a deal with a demon, only he can throw fireballs, or read minds, or blow up your head. And, somehow, it always comes down to demons . . . because they are the ones that try the hardest to reach men. By hiding magic, we have sealed the demons back into Hell—saving countless lives."

"If you approve of keeping these secrets," Gregor argued, "how is the decision of the Church Fathers any different?"

"We don't work for Mr. I-am-the-Way,-the-Truth,-and-the-Life," Erasmus countered. "We work for an angel. Angels are famous for telling men to keep quiet."

"Are they?" Gregor frowned.

"Oh yes. Angels are the keepers of the Secrets of Heaven." Erasmus said, "I think their secretive nature was summed up best by a poet named Peter Atkins in his poem, 'Expectant Father to His Unborn Son':

My Jewish friends have told me that a child,
Before it slides its way to being born,
Possesses these: The secret names of God;
The hidden sources of heaven; All the wild
Fulfilling wisdom that its parents mourn
Their foolish loss of. It is not the rod
Of education nor the chains of work
That rob us of the Marvelous, but the spite
Of Angels: For a stroking finger seals
The child's mouth into silence. Thus some clerk,
Some Bureaucrat of God, denies our right
To Wonder, as around us life congeals.
Sweet child, resist. Deny that curtain's fall:
Bite the Angel's finger. Tell me all."

We all chuckled but none as loud or as long as Theo. His bark of laughter momentarily drowned out the *rat-a-tat-tat* of machine guns behind us.

"Hear! Hear!" Theo cried. "Good for him!"

"How is that?" Gregor asked gently. "When you know first hand what good the angel's admonition to secrecy has accomplished. You have worked for Father, helping keep secrets, for centuries."

"True, and perhaps there is good in it," Theo replied fiercely, a knightly gleam in his eye. "But that doesn't mean that I have to like it. I believe in honesty. I believe in Truth. Someday, I would like to live in the world where every child chomped down on his shushing angel and escaped unsilenced into the world."

WE left the trench-riddled land behind us, but more wasteland lay ahead. After several hours of trudging through this, we rested. Titus shared the last swallows from his canteen, but the tiny sip only served to turn the grime in my mouth to mud. Sighing, we climbed heavily back to our feet and pushed onward.

"Boy, this place is dusty." Mab coughed, waving his hand in front of his face. "Reminds me of that time I got stuck in a bag."

"Wandered in and couldn't get out, did you?" Erasmus teased Mab.

Mab shook his head. "Nah. Wasn't that kind of thing. You see, the elves had invited my—well, you'd call 'em brothers—and I to a party. Nice affair. Lots of ambrosia flowing. Some fairies, tiny tykes, started a game of tag. I admit we winds got a little rowdy. Knocked over a few trees, a spire or two, maybe the odd tower, but that was nothing big for us. How were we to know those trees had sprouted during the original creation?"

"So, your punishment was to be stuck in a bag?" I chuckled.

"Nothing so tame, Ma'am! Our punishment would have been much, much worse! Except the boss interceded upon our behalf, played his harp. You see, the Elf King had some kind of 'in' with the King of the Gods, and if the matter had been put before Old Sky Beard, we would have been in hot water indeed!"

"The Elf King is the King of the Gods," I said.

"Really!" Mab asked, flabbergasted. "Well . . . that explains a lot!"

Erasmus leaned forward. "Interesting! Where did you hear this?"

"From Tybalt," I replied.

Mab groaned, disappointed. "Aw, Ma'am! You can't believe everything that furball tells you!"

"I gather this boss of yours played well?" Caliban asked Mab. "Did he charm the Elf King with his song, as Orpheus charmed the King of the Dead?"

Mab walked in silence for a few steps, scratching his eternal stubble. "Er . . . not exactly. You see, we winds know the secret of music, and we had shared this with our boss. So, as he sat before the court, he began playing faster and faster. Soon, all the court was dancing—well everyone except

Fincunir, he's too clever to get caught by this kind of trick—and, more importantly, they couldn't stop dancing."

"A red-shoes moment?" Erasmus asked.

"Exactly!" Mab agreed. "Finally, the queen—the old queen, Titania— begged him to let them go. Well, the boss replied that here was the whole court wildly whirling about, bumping into things and the like, which was all we winds had done. So, it seemed wrong to treat us overly harshly. Queen Titania agreed, and between them, they cooked up this idea of putting us in a bag and giving us to some mortal ship captain."

"I believe I've read that story." Caliban laughed. "The sailors on that ship opened the bag and let you go, did they?"

"Yeah, only the Greeks didn't include the part where the boss descended on a black swan in the dead of the night and slipped among the sailors, whispering to them that the bag was filled with treasure."

"Black swan!" I repeated, startled. I recalled visions of shipwrecks wrought by the winds and their master that I had once seen while falling from just such a bird. "Mab, this boss of yours . . ."

"Lord Astreus, of course," Mab replied. "Thought you knew that, Ma'am. That I used to work for him, I mean."

"I did," I said slowly. "I just hadn't put the two together."

Stories I had heard over the years drifted back to me: scraps of tales told to me by Tybalt, rumors passed along by Mephisto, or dusty passages I had come upon in Father's old tomes. Astreus Stormwind, the tricky and clever Lord of the High Counsel who once bested the old lord of the trolls by so beguiling him with music that he forgot to depart at sun up, turning to stone with the first ray of dawn light; or who once stole the sky, rolling it up like a carpet and refusing to return it, until the Lord of Winter let the sun out of a bottle; or who once fenced the Lord of the Doldrums in a great duel that lasted nine days and nine nights and only ended when the Becalmer agreed never again to leave the borders of his sea kingdom.

Somehow, I had forgotten that this trickster figure was my Astreus. Or, rather, the Astreus that I knew. He was not my Astreus. I wanted nothing to do with him! And yet, I could not help admiring him for his loyalty to his people. Few supernatural creatures were like that.

"Ma'am"—Mab broke through my reverie—"if what Tybalt told you about the Sky God is true . . ."

"It may be," Erasmus interrupted. "Alastor, the name of the King of the Elves, is an old epithet for Zeus."

Mab continued, "Well then, if Mr. Prospero's *Eleusinian* spell actually worked, and he really did get adopted by the Earth Goddess Demeter . . . would that make you the Elf King's grandniece?"

"I have no idea, Mab." I laughed. "I don't even know if Father ever cast that spell."

"What spell was this?" Erasmus's interest was piqued. He was always interested in sorcery.

"Father was working on a re-creation of the old Eleusinian spell that allowed the Eleusinians to get out of the land of the dead with their memories intact. We think it was part of the process for making his new staff, the *Staff of Eternity*," I said.

"Huh! Did it work?" Erasmus looked quite intrigued. "Ah, but you already said that you did not know. Interesting . . . interesting. Wonder if he could pull it off."

A conversation struck up between Erasmus, Theo, and Mephisto about the likelihood of Father being able to carry off such a project. I took advantage of their preoccupation to pose a few questions I was very curious about to Mab.

As casually as I was able, I asked, "Tell me, Mab, what kind of a master was Astreus?"

"The boss? Oh, he was a bag load of fun, Ma'am. Really looked out for us winds!"

"Did he have any faults?" I pressed.

Mab thought about this for a while. "He was quixotic, Ma'am; he would change his mind at the drop of a hat. All elves are like that, but Lord Astreus was capricious even by elvish standards—though he acted rather differently the last time I saw him—at Santa's place." Mab frowned. "Also, he didn't understand about humans; I mean how frail they are and all that. Course, I didn't know back then, either." Mab paused again. "All things being equal, Ma'am, I'd rather be working for you."

I was so touched that, for a moment, I could not speak.

My brother Gregor, who had apparently been listening, stepped closer and posed a question to Mab. "So, you prefer your current life to your past?"

"No, Sir, I'd prefer to be free. But if I were free and had to have a boss, I'd rather it were Miss Miranda."

"SHE hasn't moved," Titus announced.

"Who, Miranda?" Theo asked. "She's moving just fine."

Titus pointed at the crystal ball, which Mephisto was balancing on the back of his arm, rolling it between his shoulder and his elbow. "Logistilla. I have been having Mephisto look in on her regularly. All this time, while we made our way through trenches, slept, flew on Pegasus, et cetera, she has not so much as turned her head or twitched a finger."

We gathered around Mephisto, peering into the ball. Logistilla sat upon the infernal version of the throne that had once belonged to my father, as handsome and regal as any queen. Yet, Titus was correct. She sat unmoving. She stared straight before her, holding some bit of broken crockery as if it were a scepter. The *Staff of Transmogrification* lay ignored atop the debris beside her seat. On the dais, next to her, huddled an emaciated old man who hugged his own piece of crockery. He looked a bit like Old Theo, before Erasmus made him young again—if Theo had stopped eating for centuries. I could not place the man, but it was obvious he was a member of my family.

"Who's that other guy?" asked Mab.

"Galeazzo Lucretius di Rizzo," Erasmus said. He glared at me. "Logistilla's third son. He died a bitter death, consumed with envy for his mother's immortality."

"Envy," I whispered. "Logistilla's vice is envy, too."

"Miranda's right," Gregor said finally. "Logistilla could not have made those dolls. She is a prisoner here, a captive of her vices."

"Maybe she was carrying the dolls in her purse, and they fell out when the Hellwinds deposited her," Caliban offered.

"Fell out onto an altar in the middle of a pentacle? Sorry, Buster, I'd like the perp to be Miss Logistilla as much as the next guy, but this just doesn't add up." Mab yanked out his notebook, licked his finger, and started flipping pages. He glared at Mephisto. "I'm updating my list of suspects."

"If it was not Logistilla," Erasmus said, "there must be someone else in the *castello*."

"Show us who else is in the *castello*, other than our sister and her dopey son, I mean." Mephisto held the crystal ball up for us to see, but it merely grew misty again. "If someone else comes there, they aren't present at the moment."

THE ground began to rise sharply. Large boulders and deep sinkholes made footing treacherous. Ahead, we could see the rounded tops of the foothills. Beyond them stood the Mountains of Misery themselves, their peaks sharp and stark against the fiery red-orange sky.

The air grew colder, almost frigid. Our breath left our mouths in white clouds, which immediately distinguished us from the rest of the inhabitants, sad baggy-eyed souls who toted the great boulders, carrying them up the slopes upon their shoulders.

We hiked up a steep rise and paused at the top, most of us panting. Ahead was a series of rocky outcroppings with small ledges upon which damned souls balanced, looking nervously this way and that. Just ahead, nestled between the rocks, was a large sinkhole, as big as a pond, from which issued a constant hissing. In the darkness of its depths, something writhed.

Most of us moved away from the opening, but Mephisto squatted down on the edge of the sinkhole and peered into it.

"Snakes!" Mephisto leapt up, waving his arms wildly. "Why did it have to be snakes? I hate snakes!" Mid-gesticulation, he paused and tapped a finger against his chin, thinking. "No, wait, that was Indiana Jones. I like snakes." And he leaned over, offering his hand toward the nearest serpent as it slithered up over the rim of the sinkhole, hissing. "Hi there, Little Fella!"

Gregor, who had been staring darkly at the pit, grabbed Mephisto and yanked him back, just as one of the serpents struck, barely missing my brother's hand. "Those are not snakes. They are souls of the damned. I do not know what will happen if one bites you, but it could not be good. Let us move away, quickly!"

Hauling Mephisto along, Gregor strode some hundred yards before he stopped. The rest of us followed quickly. Behind us, hundreds of snakes came pouring out of the pit, converging on our previous position.

"How did you know they were the souls of the damned?" Caliban asked curiously, his breath forming bright white puffs.

"I can hear them speaking."

"You can speak to snakes?" Mephisto's eyes narrowed. He pointed a finger at Gregor. "You're a parselmouth, aren't you? I bet you're in Slytherin!"

The comment meant nothing to Gregor or to me, but Erasmus and Caliban laughed heartily. Gregor gestured at the heavy golden ring he wore on his right hand. "The Seal of Solomon grants the gift of speech with beasts. These creatures speak in the language of beasts, but they talk of things no beasts would mention. They wish to steal our shapes."

"Oh!" Mephisto exclaimed, nodding sagely. "So that's where we are! Makes sense Ulysses would be here."

"Where, exactly, is here?" Mab chafed his arms against the cold.

"It's one of the places of punishment for thieves," Mephisto explained.

"There are lots of thieves, but not enough human bodies. The snaky guys slink around trying to sneak up on the human-looking guys. If they can bite them, they get to steal their shape. Then, the previously snaky guy gets the human shape, and the guy who got bitten becomes a snake."

"How do you know all this?" Theo asked, eyeing Mephisto suspiciously.

"Dante describes something like that in Canto 25." Caliban spoke up from where he stood with his club resting on his shoulder. "Only he described red and black lizards, with feet, rather than snakes. Shall I quote the passage?"

Erasmus arched an eyebrow. "You can quote Dante?"

Caliban shrugged and smiled.

Mab, who had been scanning the hillside, suddenly pointed. "Hey, isn't that the perp? Er . . . I mean, your brother?"

High above us, a naked Ulysses stood nervously on a tiny rock shelf, kicking at serpents who tried to come over the ledge. Theo called out to him, and Mephisto jumped up and down, waving his arms and his staff, but Ulysses did not seem to notice us.

"Where's his staff?" I asked, squinting at the figure of my brother. "I don't see it."

"Then, it is unlikely that this is our brother," Gregor replied hoarsely. "Someone has stolen his shape."

Mephisto raised the crystal globe. "Ball, show me my brother Ulysses!"

The ball showed the naked Ulysses kicking snakes on the ledge.

Mephisto frowned and then asked, "Ball, where is my brother's staff?"

Mist swirled in the glass sphere, then cleared to show the *Staff of Transportation* lying between two boulders, a green and yellow snake wrapped tightly around its length. Following the images in the crystal ball, we pinpointed where this was relative to our current position.

"How are we going to retrieve him?" Titus asked. "That area is crawling with snakes."

Caliban stepped forward. "Allow me."

Swinging himself onto the nearest boulder, the large man who might or might not be my half-brother jumped from rock to rock, covering distances I would have sworn no human could leap. Each time, he landed as lightly as a gymnast, sweeping snakes out of his way with his club. To aid him, Gregor tapped his new staff. The incessant hissing and faint cries and curses in the distance all vanished, leaving an empty silence. The snakes swayed aimlessly as if stunned.

Caliban swooped up the *Staff of Transportation*. A moment later, he landed beside us, carrying a leather bag, and the staff, the green and yellow snake wrapped tightly about it. There was no sign of Ulysse's clothes. Some thief's soul must have made off with them.

Caliban dropped the bag at our feet and drew the serpent from the staff, holding it by its tail. When Gregor turned off his staff and the sound and hissing had returned, Mab came forward to peer at it.

"Ma'am, I think this is him. Notice the little yellow mask around the eyes." Just like that domino mask your brother always wears."

Sure enough, the snake had a yellow figure eight about the eyes against the otherwise grass green head. Gregor held up his ring and leaned toward the serpent, careful to stay out of biting range.

"Ulysses? Is that you? . . . Ah, yes. We came as quickly as we could. There were others in greater need . . . No, we did not abandon you out of spite and revenge. I told you I have forgiven you. Did you not believe me? Well, 'tis no matter. Your body? Good question." Gregor turned toward the rest of us. "Any ideas?"

We all began talking at once.

IN the end, we concluded that we had to rescue Logistilla first. We would head to Infernal Milan, investigate the voodoo dolls, and then return here with Logistilla's staff to recover Ulysses's shape. With the *Staff of Transmogrification,* we could both restore Ulysses and turn the serpents into something less dangerous—something without sharp teeth. Mephisto suggested bunnies, then acted out some kind of a skit involving a baby rabbit that ripped out the throats of knights, which, I must admit, was rather amusing, even if it was against the whole point of taking away the snakes' teeth.

When Mephisto finished his theatrics, we touched Ulysses's staff to the ground, to allow us to return to this spot instantly, and then set off following the crystal ball. Ulysses rode curled around Gregor's neck. Mab, the only one who did not already have a staff or club, carried the *Staff of Teleportation.* Titus leaned over and explained to my brother the snake that he had better not bite Gregor, or Titus would personally tear him to shreds. Perhaps Ulysses believed him. Either way, he was very well behaved.

The ball led us over one of the smaller foothills and into a dense forest of twisted, repulsive trees with crooked grasping branches. The leafless boughs, like claw-fingered arms, gripped the struggling damned in a tight woody embrace. Thick gluey sap oozed from the dark trunks, holding fast anything that so much as brushed against it. From time to time, we caught a glimpse of the forest's prisoners: men and women with wild eyes and tangled hair who writhed and screamed, ever trying to tear themselves free of the viselike grip that held them immobilized. Even Mephisto did not know what their crimes had been.

As we entered this nightmarish wood, long ropelike roots stretched out, attempting to trip us or wrap about our ankles, and great shrouds of some dark moss, hanging from the branches, tangled in our hair and garments. The air was unpleasantly dank, and, from time to time, the flapping of leather-winged horrors startled the trapped dead, causing them to scream. Gregor tapped the *Staff of Silence,* and the moans and muffled cries that had become our constant companions fled, along with the disturbing flapping. Within the range of his effect, the unnatural trees froze, allowing us to walk among them unhindered.

The walk through the forest seemed interminable. We were able to free a few of the poor souls trapped among its branches. They escaped when Gregor's staff froze the trees that had been imprisoning them. We could not hear their words, but the lip and hand gestures of some indicated that they were grateful. Yet, many others remained as they had been before we freed them, writhing and silently screaming, unaware that they could escape.

Those who were aware of their new freedom followed us, staying within the range of Gregor's staff, lest they be caught again. After what seemed like hours, possibly days, we rested and ate some of the meager provisions we found in Ulysses's bag: canned caviar, water crackers, and grapes, strange fare for Hell. We took turns sleeping, while those who remained awake kept a watchful eye on our new spirit companions.

Two of the damned tried to attack the sleeping Erasmus but were driven back by Gregor, who brandished Solomon's Ring at them, driving them out of the safety of the silence and back into the forest, where the trees soon trapped them again. After that, the remaining shades did not cause any trouble. We were forced to move on sooner than we would have wished, however, because the flapping horrors had ringed our position and appeared to be cawing for reinforcements.

Finally, we reached the far edge of the terrible forest. As we came out into a landscape of barren rolling hills, our spirit followers dispersed, going their separate ways. Our group continued forward, picking up the pace. Several attempts were made to start a conversation, but they foundered.

For the most part, we kept to ourselves.

❧✦❧

The Duchess of Infernal Milan

We passed over rolling hillsides covered with dead and moldering grapevines. The lay of the land was familiar; the longer we walked, the more I recognized it. Even so, I was not prepared for what I saw as we crested a hill.

Before me lay Milan, but it was not the Milan of my childhood. The familiar skyline of towers, domes, and steeples had not changed, apart from a few newer skyscrapers. Yet, everything was different.

An enormous fungus sprouted from the magnificent dome of the Duomo, the cathedral where I once had waited in vain for the murdered Ferdinand. The *Castello Sforzesco,* my childhood home, was dark and corroded, its walls dripping with blood. The *Filarete* Tower, where I had first spoken to little Theo, looked rotten and swollen, like an overripe fruit. The *Arco Della Pace,* which I had seen in pictures, though never in person, as I had not returned to Milan since it had been built, dripped with moss and shiny poisonous-looking vines.

Oh, my poor Milan!

Looking at it nearly broke my heart. I felt new sympathy for Astreus and his memories of lost heaven. Being trapped here, in this twisted reflection of the place I had loved, would be a far worse punishment than any physical torture.

Nor was I the only one affected.

Gregor drew back. "What horror is this?"

"It looks like home," Theo cried, "only horribly wrong."

"It's the skyscrapers. They're new," Mephisto suggested cheerfully.

Theo turned on him angrily, and Mephisto shrank back. Eager to redeem himself, Mephisto made a fist and shook it at the pale sickly yellow-gray sky. "Oh dastardly demons, to have done such a thing to our town!"

Again, he glanced at the city before us, and his cheerful demeanor slipped, showing a brief glimpse of grim, bleak sorrow. Then, he perked up, smiling. Slipping his arm through mine, he pulled me forward. "No time like the present! Let's go!"

WALKING the streets of this dark Milan, we stared about us like passersby at a train wreck. Black oily mud oozed up through the cobblestones, as if the city were sinking into a swamp. The streets, the parks, and the *Piazza Mercanti* all crawled with damned souls, literally. Bright red imps with flaming whips drove the unfortunate about on all fours, like cattle. Dark, insubstantial spirits, which Mephisto identified as vengeance-seeking wraiths, hovered everywhere, floating through walls. Some clustered about Erasmus and Theo and would not leave them. They tried to cluster around Gregor as well, but he made the sign of the cross, and a sudden gust of wind drove them away. One tall wisp of a shade even tried to attach itself to me. My wings flared brightly, and it fled, wailing.

The *Naviglio Grande* flowed with crimson blood instead of water. On its banks were strewn thousands of skeletons, which Mephisto said were reminders of victims murdered by the rulers of the city, either openly or in secret. Many of the remains were child-sized; the tiny skulls and hand bones of babies, slain by the rulers of their households, perhaps, lest a different sin be discovered.

The air here was thick with droplets of blood and stank horribly, like spoiled meat. We were all relieved when our path took us away from the waterway.

As we ducked around a particularly large growth of fungus, we came face to face with a brigade of demons. The infernal soldiers had goat legs and corroded tridents. They cackled, a high horrible sound, and poked things with their weapons: pillars, walls, passing souls. Whatever they touched corroded, as if eaten away by some deadly acid. The first demon to spot us screeched eagerly. He and his companions charged toward us.

Erasmus and Theo both began warming up their staffs, but neither could act immediately. Titus and Caliban could wield theirs like ordinary weapons, but they were reluctant to do so, as they did not want them to become corroded. Mab pulled out his lead pipe, I drew out my razor-edged fighting fan, and Mephisto tapped his staff, laughing. Out of the corner of my eye, I began to imagine that half a dozen fanciful creatures were bounding around on the muddy street. Not winged creatures, such had carried us across the swamps, but the chimera and the cockatrice and other deadly beasts.

It was Gregor who saved us.

He strode forward, his hair flowing about his shoulders, and brandished the Seal of Solomon. Laughter, a strange grating sound we seldom heard, issued from his throat. He cried in a great voice, "Back, foul vermin! Or suffer my wrath! For I have been crowned Pope of the One True Church and have, at my beck and call, all the Armies of Heaven!"

Gregor's crimson robes billowed, and a golden halo shone above his head. The demons drew back.

Then, they sneered mockingly and rushed at him.

My brother moved with rapid grace. Wielding his new staff like a rapier, he dipped it beneath the leading trident's prongs and then rose to strike the haft, knocking the weapon aside. Facing the foremost demon, he slapped it in the face with the back of his free hand. Solomon's Ring grazed its skin. Immediately, it withered into a tiny ball.

Gregor pulled a glass vial from under his robes, popped the shrunken remains of the demon inside, and capped it. He held it up for the rest to see. Cowed, they turned and scattered, gibbering. Gregor sealed the vial with his ring and replaced it beneath his robes.

Sighing, Mephisto sent his various friends away. "Gregor gets all the fun."

Erasmus clapped. "Oh, bravo! Shouldn't you blow across the top of the ring like a gunslinger, or something?"

Theo, his staff now humming and buzzing, looked Gregor up and down. "That was impressive, Little Brother. Where did you learn to fight like that?"

Gregor bowed respectfully to Theo. "You taught me, Older Brother. Right there." He extended his staff and pointed at an area of rotting vegetation behind the *Castello Sforzesco*, where the *Parco Sempione* now stood in modern Milan.

Theo barked out a laugh. "And so I did!"

Titus, however, was frowning. "Be careful, Brother Gregor. Remember what you told us about not becoming angry."

"Angry?" Gregor rasped, grinning. "I haven't had such a good time in years! Brings back the old vampire hunting days, does it not, old friend?" He asked the snake, who was still curled about his neck. The snake hissed, and Gregor laughed again. "Pshaw. You were never in any danger."

WE found Logistilla inside the *castello*. She sat upon the throne in the ducal presence chamber exactly as we had seen her in the crystal globe, a shard of crockery held in her hand as a scepter.

Gregor strode over the rubbish strewn across the floor of the chamber and offered his hand to Logistilla. "Come, Sister," he said gently, "let us be gone from this place."

"Noooo!" Logistilla shrieked, drawing herself up. "It is mine! It was always meant to be mine! I was meant to live here! You can't take me away!"

Gregor went pale with fear. He lunged out and seized her shoulder. Then, his head sank forward, his face slack with relief. To the rest of us, he said merely, "I feared she had died."

He tried to draw her to her feet, but she would have none of it. She beat on his hand with her sharp piece of pottery, drawing blood. The old man who huddled beside her on the dais looked up from his shard with some interest.

"Mine," he intoned in a querulous voice. "Mine! Mine! Mine!"

"Definitely envy," Theo poked at the debris on the floor with the butt of his staff. "She always wanted to live in the *castello*."

"So, you all know this place?" Mab asked, looking about at the vast structure with its handsome courtyards. He gestured at the walls. "This reddish stone beneath the blood—it looks familiar. Isn't the Great Hall back in Prospero's Mansion built from this same stuff?"

I nodded. "The *castello* was our old home in Milan. Mephisto, Theo, and Erasmus were born here—or in the real version of which this is a dark copy . . ."

"Not copy!" interrupted Mephisto. "Evil twin!"

"By the time Logistilla was born," I continued, "the Spaniards had taken over and were using the *castello* as their headquarters. So Logistilla grew up in a modest villa. She has always envied the rest of us for having once lived in the grandest place of which she knew."

"And now she is here." Titus frowned. "We should not have left her alone so long. Women are weaker than men." He moved to where she sat and squatted down, gazing at her.

"And this other guy"—Mab jerked his thumb toward the old man—"you said he was her son?" Erasmus and Gregor nodded. Mab made a note. Then, he sniffed, grimacing. "This place smells bad, Ma'am," he said, his voice low. "*Really* bad."

"Of course it does, Dopey-head!" Mephisto replied. "The whole city is stinky!"

Mab shook his head, his expression quite serious. "Not rotten bad, Harebrain, evil bad. Someone's been casting some vile magic here." He cocked his head. "I'm gonna take a look around. Harebrain, where'd that fancy marble of yours show those voodoo dolls?"

Mab began moving slowly through the presence chamber, sniffing the air, and poking at things with his pipe.

As he moved away, I gazed at the familiar walls, shivering slightly. How strange to see them again, or to see their dark reflection, stranger still when I contemplated the time that had elapsed since last I lived in the *castello*. A month ago, I would have congratulated myself on how far I had come, on my many great achievements in the intervening centuries. But now? All the aspects of my life that I might have praised were either lost or proven an illusion.

Had I gained nothing in the intervening years?

Squatting, Titus took Logistilla's hand and spoke to her softly.

"Titus?" She looked up hopefully. Comprehension began to dawn behind her eyes and then fled away. "No. He disappointed me. He would never do anything but watch TV. I turned him into a bear."

"True," Titus growled, sounding very much like a bear indeed, "but then you turned me back, and here I am."

"I never turn my animals back," Logistilla pouted. "At least, I would not have to if Cornelius hadn't refused to help me anymore, the snake."

"Actually, Ulysses is the snake," Mephisto said gaily, pointing at the serpent curled around Gregor's neck. "Cornelius is more of a bat or a mole."

So, that was why Logistilla was angry at Cornelius!

I recalled her casting aspersions upon him when we visited her on her island. So, he had been using the *Staff of Persuasion* to influence her customers and then thought better of it. Good for him. Who would have guessed Cornelius would develop scruples?

Gregor hunched his shoulders like a wrestler taking a fighting stance and curled back his lip menacingly, a look I remembered well. It was as if New Gregor had vanished and Old Gregor stood in his place. "Titus," he asked hoarsely, "why—precisely—did our sister turn you into a bear?"

"You will have to ask her," Titus replied brusquely. His eyes were upon Logistilla, and he did not spare Gregor a glance.

"Because he was a couch potato!" Mephisto confided conspiratorially. "She doesn't think much of lovers who only exercise their channel-surfing finger."

"Lover?" Gregor repeated. He made a face as if the word tasted bad to him. "Titus, why would Mephisto refer to you as our sister's lover?"

"Now, Gregor," Theo began, stepping forward.

"Off with you, Theo." Gregor shoved him away. "If I need your help, I'll ask for it."

"Uh-oh. He's reverted to Old Gregor, hasn't he?" Erasmus murmured to Mephisto. "I hope it's a temporary change, like calling up Shazam or something. I was getting to like the new Gregor."

"You and me both!" Mephisto responded. "Old Gregor can be a royal pain in the patooshie!"

Gregor stalked forward, but Titus did not spare him a glance.

"I have no time for your theatrics, Little Brother," Titus growled. "Saving Logistilla is more important than your moral qualms. I have already explained myself to the others. Logistilla turned me into a bear because she was disappointed with my performance as her husband. Apparently, she wanted a more active man. Though I recall her turning several husbands into toads or boars for the crime of being too active, in one way or another."

"Husband?" That caught Gregor up short. "You *married* our sister?"

"You have a problem with that?" Titus stood and glared down. He towered above Gregor. "Historically, there are precedents for marriage between brothers and sisters. The gods did it. The Egyptian pharaohs."

"Pagans," Gregor spat.

The two men glared at each other. The rest of us backed away, except for Theo, who stood lightly upon his feet, ready to dive in, if necessary.

But what could Theo do? He could not threaten his brothers with his staff. Like an atomic bomb, the *Staff of Devastation* was of little use as a weapon of deterrent when dealing with one's own. True, Theo was a decent fighter, but he was out of shape, and the others had both height and breadth over him.

If Titus got his hands on Gregor, any fight would be over. On the other hand, Gregor was faster and meaner. He might try maneuvers from which Titus would never think to protect himself.

The two of them circled each other. Titus loomed like a Scottish giant, clad in his highland jacket and tartan kilt with a lacy jabot collar at his throat. Gregor moved lithely, his splendid crimson robes and half cape swirling about him. The chamber grew entirely silent, except for their footsteps and the *swoosh* of kilt and robe. Around his neck, Ulysses the Snake hissed.

The tension in the room made my skin crawl. My mouth had gone dry, but I felt as if I dared not move even to swallow.

"Enough!" Theo snapped.

Theo looked at Mephisto. Mephisto looked at Caliban, who was even brawnier than Titus. Caliban cracked his knuckles and stepped forward, ready to knock heads.

Gregor and Titus ignored him, their eyes locked on each other. Titus's big meaty hands slowly closed into fists. His arm drew back. Caliban stepped forward, grinning.

This was about to turn into an all-out brawl.

With a bellow, Gregor struck Titus with a right cross, taking the big man by surprise. Titus's head snapped back, but he recovered quickly. He waded forward, shaking the blood from his mouth and grinning. Gregor backpedaled quickly, throwing out jabs at Titus's face and chest, but Titus merely raised his massive arms, and the blows bounced off the huge muscles of his shoulders and arms like tennis balls off the side of a tank.

Titus lunged, expecting Gregor to dart backwards, but Gregor closed with him and pummeled his stomach repeatedly with solid punches. Titus *oophed* and then did a leg sweep and a hip throw.

It was a simple jujitsu move. But Gregor had disappeared from the face of the earth before the martial arts of the East became all the rage. None of the ruffians he boxed during his days as a priest in Ireland had used moves like that.

"What in the world was that?" Gregor yelped unceremoniously, from where he lay on his back.

Titus slammed his enormous meaty fist into his hand and moved toward the prone Gregor.

"Titus!" I croaked, "What's the point of being the easy-going guy, if you can't walk away from a fight when your wife needs you?"

Titus blinked sleepily. He thrust forth the *Staff of Darkness*, and asked, "Do you want your staff back?"

With this reminder of his recent good deed, the wrath drained from Gregor's eyes. When he stood up, he looked less like a brute and more like a Spanish poet again. Frowning, he stroked his short-cropped beard.

"Did you get married in a church, at least?" he asked gruffly, brushing of his robes.

"We were wed at St. George's Episcopal in the British Virgin Islands."

"Anglican . . ." Gregor frowned and then shrugged, muttering, "could have been worse."

"What about your Great Church Lady, from your vision? Doesn't she approve of all denominations?" Erasmus asked mockingly. Gregor spun around and glared at him, his shoulders hunching forward again.

"Right." Erasmus made a casual gesture in the air. "Forget I said anything."

Mab called from the far side of the room, "Mr. Theophrastus! Come take a look at this!" Theo gave his brothers one last stern look. Excusing himself, he went to join Mab. That left the rest of us to puzzle over Logistilla.

Walking forward, I lay my hand on Logistilla's shoulder, hoping to dispel the illusion that gripped her, but my touch had no effect. She remained upright and unseeing, a regal duchess before her imaginary subjects, unaware of the squalor about her in this pathetic mockery of our ancient home.

Apparently, it was not an illusion of the senses that gripped her, but one of her own mind's making.

Watching Logistilla sit like a noble sovereign reminded me of her real reign as Duchess of Saxe-Weimar, one of the tiny Germanic states. Her husband had died young—or perhaps he was the one she turned into a stag after he had strayed with a particularly comely lady-in-waiting. I had trouble keeping Logistilla's husbands straight—after which she ruled, first as regent and then through her son, for over fifty years. My sister had proved a fine sovereign. Under her reign, the kingdom expanded, the laws were enforced, and the people grew richer.

True, a few of her political rivals had gone hunting never to return, at least not in human shape, and a few hostile neighbors had abruptly withdrawn their threats after a visit from her brother. (Napoleon, who forced the duchy of Saxe-Eisenach to combine with Saxe-Weimar and then handed control of both duchies over to Logistilla's son, was recorded as having remarked: "A charming man, the dowager duchess's brother; a pity that he is blind in both eyes.") All in all, however, her people had been pleased with her.

What a shame that Logistilla had not yet been born when our family ruled Milan. There would have been such a natural meeting of minds between Father, who wished to rule in name only, and Logistilla, who cared little for titles, desiring instead to preside over the details, to rule in truth. All my other siblings either wanted the prestige of being duke or had no interest in ruling whatsoever.

It was too late, of course, as the days of dukes and princes were no more. Nowadays, my sister's competence as a ruler was a wasted talent, of no use to a recluse who made her livelihood by selling new shapes to criminals and cripples.

Suddenly, I wondered if Logistilla, too, realized what a help she could have been to Father. Could that be the reason she disliked me so? Because she resented Father's reliance upon me when, in her mind, she could have done a better job? Unappreciated talents could become a heavy burden. I felt unexpectedly sorry for her.

"I do not know what to do," Titus admitted, his voice low. "Miranda, could you ask your La . . ." His voice trailed off and he flushed. He lowered his head again, muttering, "Er . . . sorry."

I turned away, my eyes wet with unshed tears.

"Honey, can you hear me?" Titus asked, chaffing Logistilla's arm.

"I will not leave! I belong here! You cannot make me think otherwise!" cried Logistilla. "It is my due!"

"Here?" Titus rumbled. "In this dilapidated shack? With no servants? No running water? None of the comforts of home? Ha! Woman, you can have it and with my blessing. Me? I'm going back to our real home. Remember our house? A beautiful mansion with heat and air conditioning and all the benefits of modern life! Handsome furniture, electric lights, and our children. Children who will not grow old and die, but who will live as long as we do, so long as the Water lasts."

"Argh!" The withered old man who clawed at Logistilla's throne gave an inarticulate cry and lunged at Titus, slapping at him weakly. "Water! Water!" he cried in his high shrill voice. "Life! Life! Why should your other children have it, if it is denied to me? Why?"

"Cease, Galeazzo," Logistilla cried. Apparently, she was aware of him. "He is not your enemy. My sister Miranda is! She is the one who slew you! She is the one who has everything, when I have nothing. She is the one who lived in this glorious home, a princess! While I was barred outside, forced to live in obscurity."

This dark version of Milan, the loss of my Lady, and horrors I had seen all crowded around me, closing in as if to smother me. On top of all this, my sister's accusations were unbearable.

"This heap?" I cried. "This prison? I did live here—if you can call my existence here 'living'—but hardly as a princess! Once, Father suggested I make myself scarce, and so I did so. I lived here, haunting the halls, without speaking to my stepmother, my uncles, our guests, or even to my wise Aunt Ippolita, whom I tremendously admired. I spoke to no one, unless directly spoken to, except the Aerie Ones, the servants, and . . ."—I glanced back toward where my brother and Mab crouched before a pile of debris—"and little Theo." My voice dropped to a whisper. ". . . For fifteen years."

There. The truth had finally come out. I did not think I had known it myself consciously until I had spoken.

My brothers stared at me, appalled.

"Fifteen years?" Erasmus repeated. "You did not speak to anyone? Not Mother? Not Ludovico? Because of one stray comment from Father?"

I bowed my head, ashamed.

"God's Teeth, Miranda, I had no idea!" Logistilla exclaimed. She looked directly at me. An unfamiliar emotion—could it be pity?—filled her dark eyes. Suddenly, she threw the broken pottery shard from her and, standing, snatched up her shoulder bag and the *Staff of Transmogrification*. "What is this filthy place? Get me out of here!"

Gregor and Titus both rushed forward to help her. Logistilla looked back and forth between them, frowning. Stepping away, she slid her arm through that of the rather startled Caliban, who glanced around warily, clearly not wishing to provoke my brothers.

Erasmus, meanwhile, confronted me, demanding, "Are you telling the truth?" I nodded. "Then, Father really did have you under a spell!" His face had gone strangely pale. "And all the time I was growing up, I never noticed!"

I could not answer. I wondered why I had never noticed Father's influence over me, and yet, it seemed so normal to do exactly as he said. I had always done so.

I pictured my father, the wise and brilliant man who had guided my life and kept our family on an even keel. How could I reconcile this man with the subtle sorcerer who hid secrets and ensorcelled his children? My current image of my father seemed as transformed from what it had been a month ago as this bloodstained, fungus-covered hall was from the *castello* I remembered. I wept.

"Oh, dastardly Daddy!" Mephisto hugged me. "He should never have done that."

Logistilla's withered son batted helplessly at our shoulders, wailing and bemoaning. Logistilla turned and saw him. She pulled away from Caliban and ran forward, wringing her hands.

"Galeazzo!" she cried. "Oh, my poor son!"

The five of us (I did not count Ulysses the Snake) tried to speak to Galeazzo, to tell him of heaven and the Brotherhood of Hope, all to no avail. Feeling sorry for Logistilla, who was weeping now, I gave Galeazzo a drop of Water. The sweet scent that filled the air raised our spirits and Galeazzo's substance seemed less ephemeral; however, there was no change to his state of mind. The Water invigorated him, but he used this new strength to rage and spit curses at heaven. Finally, even Gregor, who had been making the greatest effort of all, admitted defeat.

Lowering his head and pressing his hands together, he said, "All we can do now is pray."

"MIRANDA? Erasmus? You'll want to see this," Theo's voice called brusquely. "Logistilla, do you know anything of this?"

We joined Theo in the next chamber, where Mab was noting something down on his list of Possible Traitors. A pentacle had been etched into the floor, at the center of which stood the stone altar with the miniature images of Erasmus and me impaling each other. Other tools and accoutrements of the arcane arts were on display as well. Near the window, a red and black lizard had been sacrificed upon a second altar. It was pinned down by several stakes and wriggled lethargically, unable to break free.

"What is this place?" Logistilla walked into the chamber. She uttered a little gasp when she saw the dolls. "Oh, how horrible! Oh, that poor lizard! I hope that thing wasn't a man once!"

"Did you do this?" Mab confronted Logistilla.

"Me? With what, my staff and some rubble? I need models, you know. I couldn't make a doll that looked like Erasmus out of nothing. The only person I have saved in my staff is Gregor. Besides, why would I do such a thing? Do you think I *want* my siblings to quarrel? I mean, I admit it is amusing from time to time, but, really, there is a limit!"

"Then who?" growled Mab. He looked so disappointed at not having found the perpetrator that I felt sorry for him.

Erasmus asked, "How long have these been here, Detective? Can you tell?"

Mab shook his head. "Can't tell because Hell covers its tracks. Makes stuff look like anything it wants. Not like up on the surface, where cause leads to effect.

"If I had to make a guess," Mab continued, "based on the dust and the number of bones and such, I'd say a long time. Decades? Centuries? Hard to tell, 'cause matter doesn't behave right here. Dust could settle in seconds equal to what would take years to accumulate above, just cause it's, well, Hellish. But I can list our suspects."

"Really?" Erasmus glanced at me sidewise. "And who would they be?"

"If it wasn't Miss Logistilla, the only obvious candidates are Mephisto and Ulysses," Mab replied directly.

"Why them?"

"They're the ones who have had access to this place, the only ones who have traveled in Hell before—so far as we know. My first guess would be the Harebrain, because he recognized this place and seemed to know all about it, meaning he could have been here before. But then, the Perp is currently a snake, so if his snaky face showed recognition or guilt, I didn't have the animal-whispering skills necessary to detect it."

"I understand how Ulysses could be a suspect," Theo said slowly, "since he has access to Hell with his staff, but why Mephisto?"

"Ix-nay on the emon-day uff-stay!" Mephisto whispered loudly, making a gesture with his finger across his neck. "No reason," he said more loudly, "the detective just thinks I get around."

Theo gave him an odd look but did not inquire further. "Is there anyone else it could be? What about Abaddon? He was the cause of a great deal of our misery." Behind him, Gregor and Logistilla both nodded.

Mab lifted his head and sniffed the air carefully. He answered slowly, "Could be . . . Abaddon is the one who brought up the idea of a traitor . . . could be he did it himself to plant suspicion. However, it doesn't smell like him . . . not that same stink I remember from Miss Logistilla's house. Begging your pardon, Ma'am." Logistilla huffed at him. Mab continued, "Besides, demons almost never do this kind of stuff themselves. Something to do with the Heaven/Hell compact. Usually, they get human servants to do it for them." He sniffed again. "Smells like a human . . . but not one I can put my finger on. Too old."

"Any other clues?" asked Erasmus.

"Not that I can recognize as such. No footprints or useful hints like that," Mab snorted and shook his head. "Hell is no place for a detective."

"Hell is no place for any of us," Gregor replied solemnly.

From Mab's expression, I could tell that he did not like dropping the matter of who might have put the dolls here, but neither did he want to be the one who told Theophrastus the Demonslayer that we had a demon in the family.

He turned to me. "Before you got here, Ma'am, we were just discussing how best to disenchant the dolls. Spells like this have to be dismantled carefully. Doing it properly could take hours."

"Or, I could blow up the whole chamber with my staff," Theo offered.

"What is the downside of that?" Erasmus asked.

Mab said, "It might cause you and Professor Erasmus some discomfort."

"Discomfort as in we might suddenly combust?" Erasmus asked.

"Nah," Mab replied. "If Mister Gre . . . Mister Titus surrounds you with that darkness stuff, you should be okay. You might feel kind of funny, though, when the spell breaks—tingly or something."

"I'm willing to risk it." I stepped forward. "Erasmus?"

"Oh, certainly!" He gazed with distaste at the dolls. "The sooner the better."

I turned to Mephisto. "You're the local expert. Will damaging this building harm the earthly Milan?"

"Quite the opposite," Mephisto chimed in cheerfully. "The less similarity between the two, the less sway the evil twin has over the original."

"In that case, Theo, be my guest." Erasmus gestured at the altar. "Blow this place to Hell."

Mab touched his arm. "We're already in Hell, Professor."

"Quite right." A quirk of a smile twitched at Erasmus's lips. "Blow the place to Kingdom come!"

Operating the *Staff of Darkness* for the first time, Titus surrounded us with a circle of Hellshadow. Then, Theo unlimbered his staff again from where he carried it upon his back and pointed it at the occult chamber. He had strapped his breastplate back on with the strips of sweatshirt and wore it now over his jeans and heavy metal T-shirt. Slipping his goggles back over his eyes, he spread his legs, set his stance, raised the *Staff of Devastation,* and fired.

The world erupted into fiery wrath, and the ground beneath us shook. As the altar and the wall behind it evaporated, a wave of hatred and despair struck me such as nothing I have ever felt. I cried out in agony, certain that everything precious in the universe was lost, corrupted, of destroyed. The desire for revenge gripped me. Then, just as quickly, it was gone, as if it had never been. My thoughts cleared.

So that was the spell breaking! I was grateful to be free of it. Perhaps, things could be different between Erasmus and me from now on.

Theo regarded the chamber in disgust. "Any reason why I should leave a stone of this revolting place standing? No? Good!"

Theo turned his staff toward the outer wall and fired, instantly destroying it. Like a fireman struggling with an unwieldy hose, he moved the shining ray of deadly light across the corroded, bloodstained landscape. As the white beam touched each building, it exploded into pure brilliance.

Wind from the explosion blew his hair about his head and his shirt rippled over his taut chest. I could not see his face, but I knew he was smiling bravely, showing his teeth. Between the earthshaking booms, I heard his triumphant laughter.

The city exploded. The walls and the towers and domes beyond disappeared behind a brilliant white light. The air was filled with that hot ozony odor I associated only with Theo's staff. Then, the brilliance faded, and Dark Milan had been replaced by craters of smooth featureless glass.

When all was calm again, the presence chamber stood alone, surrounded by a vast glassy expanse, from which little streamers of steam rose up, hissing.

Theo walked back in, his face around his goggles a deep tan, his forelock bleached a pale blond. His clothes, too, whatever was not covered by the breastplate, had lost some of their color, and were now faded as if they had been too long in the sun. When he pushed his goggles back, there was a raccoon mask of pale skin about his eyes. He grinned, his face alight.

"Move outside." Theo gestured at the courtyard, the one place, other than this room, that was not glowing and hot. "I'll blow this room up, too."

"No!" Logistilla leapt protectively before the dilapidated throne beside which the pathetic shade of my dead nephew crouched. She spread her arms. "Galeazzo! Don't hurt Galeazzo!"

Theo immediately twisted his staff, and the dynamo hum fell silent. He shouldered it again, frowning. "Hope I didn't blow up any other family members out there." He walked over to the withered shade of his nephew. "Galeazzo, are you sure that you do not want to come with us?"

Galeazzo hugged his pile of ceramic shards and cried in a high thin voice, "Mine! Mine!"

Theo turned away, frowning sadly.

"Ma'am, I suggest we get going now." Mab held up the *Staff of Transportation*. "Before the big guys send someone to survey the damage."

Leader of the Family Prospero

"Let's get this over with," Logistilla fumed, as a landscape of sinkholes and boulders appeared around the ten of us. "Where's Ulysses?"

"Right here." Gregor held up the snake by the middle, its head and tail flopping unceremoniously.

Titus, who had been peering up the hill, now pointed. "There's his body. Still on the same ledge."

"Put him there, on that rock," commanded Logistilla, pointing at a low, flat boulder. Gregor did so. Logistilla angled the globe nestled into the top of her staff, held in place by seven prongs, each carved to look like a different animal, until she caught the reflection of the soul who was shaped like Ulysses. There was a flash of jade-colored fire. Then, Ulysses stood on the rock, naked and blinking sheepishly. Gregor quickly covered his naked body with his crimson robe.

Narrowing her eyes, Logistilla pointed her staff at the figure of Ulysses still on the ledge. Her staff glowed again. Then, where Ulysses had seemed to be, a large pink pig grunted.

"That'll confuse them!" my sister chortled.

The pig squealed in alarm and fell some thirty yards to the rocks below. Immediately, it was swarmed by serpents, biting its legs and exposed under-belly. The soul with the shape of a pig collapsed, becoming one snake among many, and another pig grew in the midst of the serpents. Then, it was bitten and shrank, and yet another took the shape of the pig. This was repeated numerous times, before one of the pig-shaped souls managed to break free and run.

"Good show, old chaps!" Ulysses cried, hugging Titus and Theo, who happened to be nearest to him. "Glad to be back!" He gave a little laugh and snatched his staff back from Mab. "Thank you for carrying that for me! I'll take it now. So, where to?"

"Away from here," Erasmus said. "Ulysses, can you take us farther from the snakes?"

Mab spoke up. "I touched the staff to the ground on the plains approaching Infernal Milan. Seemed like a relatively harmless place, as places down here go."

"Can do!" Ulysses held out his free hand toward the rest of us.

"Great," said Mab. "Let's go! The snakes are coming!"

Sure enough, the ground ahead of us seemed to writhe as a wave of hissing serpents flowed over the rocks toward us, eager to steal our shapes. Ulysses held up his staff and spread out his arm. We all grabbed on, and the snake pits vanished in a flash of white light.

THE *Staff of Transportation* set us down in the midst of a field of sickly, moldy-smelling grapes. The place seemed empty. In the distance, a tower or two and a few half-ruined buildings stood where Infernal Milan had risen.

"Mephisto," I said, "ask the ball what the date is, please?"

"Ball, show me the date," commanded Mephisto.

The mist swirled. Within, we could see a tear-away calendar on a receptionist's desk in some hotel or hospital. The date read: January 4th.

"Father dies tomorrow night," I whispered shakily.

"Who are we missing?" asked Ulysses.

"Only Cornelius," Erasmus said. "Mephisto, where is Cornelius?"

"Show me Cornelius," Mephisto announced happily. He bent over the ball. Then, his face went slack and the color drained from it, until he looked surprisingly pale. "H-he's in the City of Dis! Even if we could reach Dis, we'll never get past the gates, the guards, and the gorgons. Not before tomorrow, anyway. Oh, poor Corny!"

"We don't have to get by all that nonsense to reach Dis," Ulysses replied smugly.

"Oh, and why is that?" Mab glared at Ulysses suspiciously, as if expecting him to start picking our pockets.

"Remember I told you how I got into trouble by asking my staff to take me to the first place it had ever been? Well, that place happens to be spot in the middle of the City of Dis. We can go right there. No walls. No guards.

No gorgons." Frowning he tried to rearrange the long robes so that they did not drag. "Though I should tell you, it's not a very pleasant place."

"Let's go!" Erasmus stepped forward. "Cornelius needs us."

"Wait!" I cried. Everyone turned and looked at me. "Mephisto, does Cornelius seem to be in any trouble or pain?"

Mephisto shook his head. "Nope. He's just sort of sitting still. No one is near him."

"Then, let's get Father first! Cornelius seems to be safe, while Father is slated to die. We don't even know how far away Father is from here." I looked to Mephisto, who gazed into the ball, jerking his head away and blinking rapidly when he got too close to the dreaded eye-damaging thorns.

Bent over the ball, Mephisto reported, "If we start back by the Snake Pit, we go up the Paths of Pride, through the pass over the Mountains of Misery, over the Glacier of Hatred, and to near the foot of the Tower of Pain. I say it should take us about a day, including stopping for a nap, but not a really long one."

"Is it the morning of the Fourth, now? Or the evening?" I asked.

Mephisto peered over the ball again. "It's the morning in Boston and afternoon at Daddy's island."

Erasmus jumped in. "So, Father is to die at midnight tomorrow, and we have thirty to forty hours to reach him, depending upon what time zone Lilith operates in. If Mephisto says it will take us approximately twenty-four, that leaves us an extra six hours or maybe more to get Cornelius! Let's go!"

"No! Wait!" I cried. "What if we run into trouble? Either in Dis or on the way to Father, and it takes longer. Shouldn't we save Father first, and then get Cornelius?"

"Cornelius is a blind man stranded alone in Hell," Erasmus shot back angrily. "And Ulysses here says he can take us right there. It would be a crime to leave him any longer than we have to, especially as we don't know what is happening to him!"

An argument broke out, with various members of the family joining in to support either myself or Erasmus. Mab weighed in on my side. Caliban said nothing. He strode back and forth with his club on his shoulder, on the lookout for trouble.

Finally, Caliban came over, lowered his club and addressed the rest of us. "Beg your pardon, Prosperos, but you seem to be wasting precious time arguing. Why don't you put the matter up to a vote?"

"Ooo, a vote, goody, goody!" Mephisto, who had not been paying attention, raised his hand. "Me! Pick me!"

He began dancing around and spinning in a circle in the middle of a row of grapes. His staff fell free of his hand and circled wildly around his head upon its handcuff.

"Exactly what are we voting on?" Logistilla asked acerbically. She had let her long hair down and was brushing it out with a brush she had taken from her shoulder bag. "Whom to rescue first?"

"No," Erasmus stated, "let's vote on who is in charge. That way, whoever wins decides our future course of action, and we never have to go through this again."

"I'm with Miranda." Theo came and stood at my shoulder. "While I admit she can be a bit wonky on matters relating to Father's instructions, she has proven wise and level-headed in all other matters."

"And if she should go bad?" Ulysses asked, glancing at me nervously.

Theo shrugged. "We'll deal with that if we come to it."

"I am with Miranda, too, for what it is worth," added Caliban.

Mab pulled his hat over his eyes and hunkered down. "Me, too . . . not that any of the rest of you care."

"Erasmus's the only one among us with any sense." Logistilla stood and walked to stand beside him. "I, at least, will look to him."

Titus rose slowly. "I am with him as well. I love our sister Miranda dearly, and I think she is kinder than she often pretends. But, if it is a matter of whose hands into which I wish to place the rest of my life? I stand with Erasmus."

"Well, then," Erasmus began, "I think that about decides—"

"I stand with Miranda," Gregor's husky voice interrupted. Dressed merely in his black turtleneck and black pants, he looked like a spy from a foreign movie. "You're a good man, Erasmus, but if it were not for Miranda, I would still be on Mars."

"I assume you'll grant me Cornelius?" Erasmus asked me. "We all know where he would be standing were he here." He glanced at where Mephisto was doing his best imitation of a whirling dervish and added, "I'll grant you Mephisto, just to be decent."

I nodded and looked around. Theo, Gregor, Mephisto, Mab, and Caliban supported me, though I doubted Erasmus counted the last two, since this was a matter of who would lead the family. Logistilla, Cornelius, and Titus supported Erasmus. That left Ulysses. Erasmus and I turned to face him.

"Looks like it comes down to you." Erasmus crossed his arms.

"W-what? Me?" Ulysses cried, startled.

"We're going to let him vote?" objected Logistilla. "The man who imprisoned Gregor?"

"You're one to talk, woman!" muttered Titus.

"He's a member of the family," Gregor replied gravely. "Ulysses? Choose wisely. Our future, and that of mankind, may depend on your choice."

Ulysses looked back and forth between Erasmus and me. "Um . . ."

Mephisto left off dancing and came skipping back to join us. "What are we doing?"

"We're voting on who is the head of the family," replied Theo.

"But I'm the head of the family!" Mephisto pointed at himself with his thumb, his staff flying outwards. Erasmus and I both ducked. "I'm the eldest son."

"Saved by the raving older brother," Ulysses murmured, taking a slight step back.

"You've been disqualified on grounds of insanity," Erasmus explained to Mephisto.

Mephisto planted his staff on the ground before him and leaned on it. He stated surprisingly cogently, "It is possible to disqualify a person upon grounds of insanity, but that requires a legal action, and no such action has been performed."

Theo turned to Mephisto. "Come on, Brother. Don't be foolish. We're in a hurry. Father's life is on the line."

Mephisto pointed at himself. "But I am the head of the family."

"Now, Mephisto, don't make a fuss." Theo moved toward him.

"No! I think I will make a fuss!" Mephisto stabbed his finger at Theo. "And who are you, of all people, to lecture me, Mr. Think-I'll-run-away-and-shirk-my-duty! I may be crazy, true, but I have never run away, and I have never shirked my duties!"

Erasmus laughed aloud. "What have you ever done for the family?"

Mephisto cocked his head. "What have you ever done for the family, Mr. I'm-too-busy-to-follow-up-on-Daddy's-distress-note? Normal people, sure. But Miranda? Ulysses? If we had to wait for you to look out for us, we'd still be waiting, and I'd still be staffless!"

"And what are these duties you've performed?" Erasmus frowned severely at Mephisto, much as one might regard a disobedient child.

"Oh, let's see, shall we?" Mephisto counted off his points on the fingers of his left hand, starting with his thumb. "First, I kept tabs on everyone.

Bodyguard, over there, thinks it's because I wanted to hit you all up for money. That's not true. I mean, money helps, but why would I hit Theo up for money? Or Titus? They're poor!

"I kept track of everyone, because that's what older brothers do, especially older brothers in families where the father is absentminded and can disappear into his study for years, forgetting to tell his enchanted daughter to eat or something. I kept track of you all back when I was sane. You expected it of me then, and I still do it now—even if I'm not as good at it as I used to be." He looked down, his eyes sad.

"And that's why we should follow you? Because you knew where we all were?" Erasmus sneered.

"I'm not done." Mephisto moved on to his index finger. "Second, I took care of Logistilla the time she broke her leg. Fed her animals and stuff." He pinched his nose. "Phew! Do they stink!"

Titus looked at Logistilla in concern. "I didn't know you broke your leg!"

"It was a few decades back." She played with the strap of her shoulder bag. "Before you and I were an item."

"Third, I kept track of Titus, until the bear thing, which even I couldn't have anticipated. And, even while he was gone, I did what I could. I gave his kids presents every birthday, and I spent Easter and Christmas with them while he was missing, and most of summer vacation. Well, except for this Christmas, because I was at the North Pole. But I made sure Santa brought them something good."

Mab had been looking through his notebook. Now he looked up, a gleam in his eye. "'For T.C.' That stood for 'Titus's Children,' didn't it?"

"Yep!" Mephisto put his hands on his hips. His staff shot out sideways, nearly hitting Logistilla in the lip. "How do you know about my private code?"

"I visited your house, remember?" Mab turned to me. "Turns out my theory was right, Ma'am, the one I mentioned in the belly of the thing-awhatsy? Those notes at the Harebrain's place? They were reminders to look in on the rest of the family." He glanced down again. "What did 'For E.D.' mean? On the other box of Christmas stuff."

"Erasmus's Descendents," Mephisto replied. "I give them Christmas presents, too. Not all of them, of course; not even I am that good. Just the children."

Erasmus gasped in surprise. "You know about my descendents? Yo-you give them presents?"

"Sure. Why not? They're family, after all. But, I'm not done." It took Mephisto an obvious effort to keep his thoughts focused. His brow was furrowed as if in great concentration. "Fourth, I kept an eye on Miranda, dropped by from time to time to make sure Daddy remembered her. She hasn't really needed my help during the last fifty years or so, ever since Daddy put her in charge of Prospero, Inc. She's sort of been looking out for herself, but I check up on her anyway. Even if she does have me thrown out half the time."

I gaped at him, flabbergasted. All this time I had thought of myself as so cool and self-sufficient, the idea that somebody—or even worse, my ditzy, mad brother—felt I was so fragile and inept that I needed looking in on wrenched my view of my life so severely that I feared it would never be the same.

"But . . ." Theo sputtered in astonishment. "You knew? Father had Miranda under a spell, and you didn't say anything?"

Mephisto shrugged. "I have no idea why she is the way she is. I asked Daddy once, but all he said was that he was doing the best he could for her. Who am I to question the paternal font of wisdom? I'm not in charge when Daddy's here."

"There's going to be a whole lot of questioning of the paternal font of wisdom, if we live," growled Erasmus.

"The note on the flute referred to her, didn't it?" Mab asked. Mephisto nodded, and Mab chuckled wryly.

"What did it say?" I asked. I recalled a Post-it on a flute, but that was all.

" 'Bonehead, monthly,' " Mab drawled. "I assume that meant to look in on Miranda once a month."

"Yep!"

"Bonehead!" I objected.

"Oh, that's precious!" Erasmus burst out laughing.

"What were a few of the others?" I asked.

Mab opened his notebook: "Pillbox marked: CHECK ON THIS ONCE A WEEK?"

Mephisto grinned. "That meant check on Theo."

"Golf bag marked TAP with . . ."

"NEVER STOP LOOKING! I remember that one." Mephisto thumped Titus on the arm. "That meant I wasn't going to give up on my big lug of a brother until I found him. Shame I didn't know to look for a bear."

"STIRRUP FROM THE STEPPE. CHECK MONTHLY?" Mab continued.

"Check on Logistilla, that was from one of her horses."

"Horses! Again!" wailed Logistilla.

Mab ignored her outcry. "Wind this bandana in January, May, and September."

"Cornelius." Mephisto pantomimed putting a bandana over his eyes. "He had a group of good guys watching after him, so I didn't feel I needed to check him as often. But after Titus disappeared, I felt I should keep closer tabs."

Mab read: "*This is a mnemonic. Do not move?*"

Mephisto scratched his head. "Don't remember." Mab snorted.

Titus hung his head. "Mephisto really was looking out for all of us."

"Yeppers. Okay, back to the point. Fifth—" Mephisto continued onto his pinky—"I tried to help Erasmus by doing some of Theo's and Gregor's tasks for him before he got to them." He looked sheepish. "I didn't always do them right, sometimes I made things worse . . . but I tried."

"And this is supposed to recommend you?" Theo frowned.

Mephisto turned on Theo, holding up the thumb of his right hand. "Oh, and six, I went by and checked on Theo from time to time, keeping an eye on him. And when he was really sick, I sneaked a drop of Water of Life into his chicken broth. Just to make sure he didn't die just because he was a being a pigheaded idiot." He glared at Theo. "Remember the time you had pneumonia, and the time you got gored by the bull? Good thing I did too, considering it turned out you were ensorcelled!"

"How dare you!" Theo cried.

"Leanna was in on it, too." Mephisto put his hands on his hips. Leanna, I gathered, was the woman from the photos at the farmhouse, Theo's dead wife. "She didn't know about the Water of Life, of course. But I convinced her to call me any time you were in a really bad way. She came from a big family, and it made her sad that you were estranged from yours. So, she'd call me secretly whenever things were really bad. Oh, and I was the one who paid off the loan after that really big storm blew the apples down too early. I got the money from Daddy, of course, but I arranged the whole thing. Daddy never knew what I used it for. He just thought I'd been profligate again."

Theo stared at Mephisto with his mouth hanging open. "I-I had no idea!"

The rest of us were equally astonished. I felt both touched and disoriented. Mab looked more thunderstruck than anyone else. Ulysses quickly stepped up behind Mephisto, followed by Caliban.

"Guess I shouldn't call him Harebrain anymore," Mab muttered.

"But you're crazy, Mephisto!" Erasmus shouted.

"True." Mephisto's old characteristic quirk of a half smile, which I had not seen in over three hundred years, appeared upon his lips. "But I'm not partial!"

Erasmus drew back startled.

"Good point," Titus murmured. He left Erasmus and moved behind Mephisto.

Erasmus turned on Titus. "How so?"

"Impartiality is an important quality in a leader," Titus replied with his customary patience.

Mephisto put his hands on his hips and looked around, gazing at each of us in turn. "The job of the head of the family is to look out for the family. The whole family, not just the members of it you happen to like. And I"—he raised a hand and pointed at himself—"am the only one who has been doing that. Half of you haven't spoken to each other in years, and most of you didn't even know about . . . well, never mind about that.

"Of everyone in the family, Miranda and Erasmus are the least qualified to lead us because they hate each other! Even if the spell that originally caused their hatred has been destroyed, they still don't think clearly when it comes to each other. Who can trust them to be fair? Well, actually Miranda would probably be fair, despite hating Erasmus, but Erasmus would constantly claim she wasn't being fair, which would be just as annoying to the rest of us as if she really wasn't." Erasmus gave Mephisto a startled hurt look.

"Hear! Hear!" cried Ulysses. "I can't abide the two of them bickering all the time."

Mephisto continued, "I, on the other hand, am fond of each and every one of you—at least when you're not irking me. But, I do like most of you all the time, and all of you some of the time, which is probably more than anyone else here can say, except perhaps Titus.

"Besides"—Mephisto walked over and slapped Theo on the back—"even if I were disqualified, the job would pass to Theophrastus here. He's the second born son. You, Erasmus, aren't even in the running."

Logistilla gave a haughty sniff. "And women don't count, I suppose?"

Mephisto cocked his head, his quirk of a half-smile returning again. "Are you arguing in favor of my handing the family reins over to Big Sister Miranda? She is the oldest."

"I concede the point," Logistilla replied quickly.

"Oh, and I kept an eye on all of you with the crystal ball, too." Mephisto tossed the glass orb in the air. Then he frowned at it. "Only it wouldn't show me Titus the Bear for some reason, so I was worried about him. I've spent the majority of the last two years looking for him."

"My staff alters people enough to hide them from scrying devices," murmured Logistilla. "That's why we originally turned Gregor into a leopard—to keep the demons from finding him with their magical mirrors."

Mephisto hefted the crystal ball and then began rolling it up and down his hand. "It wouldn't show me Gregor, either, which was weird, come to think of it. I knew the ball would look into Hell. After our heavenly communication spell went awry in 1949—when Daddy was so worried about where Gregor's soul went—I should have been able to figure out that Gregor was not here. I wonder why I didn't catch on that something was out of place. I guess 'my brother was turned into a leopard by my sister' just doesn't come quickly to mind."

Turning to Mab and me, Mephisto balanced the glass sphere on his fingertips. "This was how I really found out about the Three Shadowed Ones attacking your plane, Miranda. I saw it in my crystal ball and used a trick with my staff to move myself to my butterfly, who was hidden on Snosae the Sned."

Logistilla clapped her hands. "Well done, Mephisto!" She moved to stand behind him, much to Erasmus's astonishment. "I guess that settles it. Big brother Mephistopheles is the head of the family. He also saved us from Baelor, by the way. I thought our goose was cooked until he came somersaulting out of nowhere and stabbed the demon through the eye."

"I did that?" Mephisto scratched his head.

"Are you all crazy?" Erasmus cried, gesturing at Mephisto and glaring at the rest of us. "He's insane, and he's a demon!"

I glanced nervously at Theo, but he did not appear to have noticed. Perhaps he thought Erasmus was speaking metaphorically.

"Oh, stuff it, Erasmus," Logistilla responded. "You've lost. Get over it." Turning to Mephisto, she asked, "So, Big Brother, what do we do now?"

Mephisto cocked his head and tapped his finger against his chin thoughtfully. Finally, he said, "We go to Dis. If we can rescue Cornelius quickly, we do. If not, or if we get into trouble, we bug out with Ulysses's staff and go rescue Daddy."

The City of Dis

Arriving in the City of Dis was like jumping into a furnace. The very air itself seemed to burn. We threw our hands before our faces, and Ulysses let out a keening wail, for his feet were bare and the street beneath us was scorching hot. He would have teleported away again, had Gregor not had a strong grip on him.

Mephisto tapped his staff, and I began to imagine an eight-foot-tall primate with thick, curly, white fur standing beside him. Then, the yeti was here with us, exuding a very pleasing cold. We huddled close to him, grateful for some relief from the heat. The abominable snowman whimpered imploringly, dazed by the warmth and unfamiliar surroundings. Mephisto took his big pawlike hand and gave him an encouraging smile. Eager to please my brother, the yeti trudged along with us, producing what cold he could muster.

It soon became evident that the heat was too much for the yeti, whose ability to shed cold was merely a side talent he had been taught by his old master, the Winter Wizard. The poor creature was panting, its pink tongue extruding from its mouth. Mephisto tapped his staff again, and I began to imagine that the p-son-en, the great bird of ice we had fought on our way home from Father Christmas's, circled over head. Then, the snowbird cawed and dived, breathing frigid Arctic air upon us.

"It's . . . that thing that nearly froze us!" Mab exclaimed.

"Went back and got it, of course," Mephisto declared happily to Mab and me. "I call it P-san, like a Japanese guy."

The heat was too intense for the p-son-en; the bird began to melt. Mephisto coaxed it to rest upon the shoulder of the yeti, one huge talon on each hairy shoulder. Together, the two beasts were able to protect each other and to keep us reasonably cool.

There was not much we could do about Ulysses's bare feet, though Logistilla did offer to turn him back into a snake, or at least a toad. Grunting, Caliban leaned down and lifted Ulysses onto his shoulders, as if he was a small child.

"This heat is nothing," Theo scoffed, teasingly as he strode beside them, smiling up at Ulysses. "Caliban and I had to swim through lava."

"Be glad it is just your feet," Caliban grunted cheerfully.

"Burned in lava," Ulysses shuddered from his perch on Caliban's shoulder. "You poor blokes! That's much worse than having to spend a spot of time as a snake."

"Thank God this all happened right after New Year," Theo said more seriously. "No ordinary man could have survived what we went through. Even with the Water we just drank, I would not have made it without Caliban's quick thinking." He shook his head sheepishly.

Moving over beside me, Theo whispered softly. "To think my life was saved by the same man who, for centuries, I dreamt of hunting down and killing."

"You, too?" I asked, wiping sweat from my eyes.

"I wanted to bring you his head as a trophy."

I swallowed and squeezed Theo's arm. "Back then, I would have liked that. In retrospect, though, I'm glad you didn't!" I recalled my uncharitable thoughts toward Caliban on the lava flow and felt chagrined. "What amazes me is that Caliban, of all people, had the mental wherewithal to remain calm while he was burning. That's . . . just astonishing!"

Theo was silent, an odd expression on his face. "Strange. I realize I was probably delirious, but I could have sworn that, as the lava boiled around us, I heard a great voice cry out, telling Caliban that if he remained calm, all would be well."

We moved along the streets as quickly as we could without actually running, passing between enormous towers that rose, pitch-black and windowless, from the red-hot street. Far above us, their boxlike tops were silhouetted against a fiery orange sky. In the same way one knows things in dreams, we knew this was New York City.

"So, this is the Big Apple's evil twin?" Erasmus took off his jacket and his waistcoat and opened his shirt collar.

"This is the City of Dis." Mephisto's usually cheeriness was subdued. He looked about with a steady wariness. "Dis looks like whatever city most people on earth associate with iniquity."

Ulysses spoke from Caliban's shoulders. "When I first came here, it looked like Paris."

Mephisto nodded. "It's been London, too. I hear in the past, it's looked like Rome and Babylon and all those decadent cities from the old days." He added, "New York's not as important nowadays as it was, not as decadent as it used to be either. Bet Dis is going to change again soon. Maybe Los Angeles or some Far East city like Mumble—or whatever they are calling Bombay these days. I bet L.A, if Hollywood keeps getting worse."

Erasmus groaned. "Something will be seriously wrong with mankind when the largest city in Hell is the City of Angels."

We went around a corner and found a street lit by blue streetlights, despite the brightness of the day.

"Ah, there it is." Ulysses sighed. "Isn't it a beaut?"

He pointed up at a street lamp. Beneath the shade, where the lightbulb should be, hung a star-sapphire the size of a large man's fist.

"Is that it?" Logistilla's voice rose sharply. "Is that the *thing* that kept you from fleeing, like any sane creature would do, the first time you came here?"

Glancing down the street, I saw that all the lights were like this. The gem that caused Ulysses's undoing was just one of hundreds.

"Would have nicked it, too, if Abaddon's goons had not caught me." Ulysses looked warily this way and that, relaxing when he saw nothing alarming. He gazed at the gem longingly. "Hey, I don't suppose we might . . . I mean, while we're here, anyway—" He reached toward the lamp, leaning precariously to one side. When the rest of us glared at him, he shrank back, clutching Caliban more tightly. "Er . . . no. Forget I asked."

"You must be crazy!" Logistilla cried.

Ulysses sighed again. "I suppose trying now, after all the trouble it's caused, makes me as big of a git as that Bilbo fellow, when he asks to see the ring again, after that whole, horribly long book about getting rid of it."

I had no notion what Ulysses was referring to, but Erasmus laughed. He added, "You read, Ulysses? I'm surprised."

"You bet your head. I read the whole thing." My youngest brother huffed, adding philosophically, "Well, except for the boring parts, of course."

Erasmus, the book-lover, snorted in disgust. "Philistine."

COMING around the next corner, we encountered people. Men and women stood motionless, as if frozen in the act of crossing the street or stopping to buy coffee. Many crowded together around the street corners, wearing suits and dresses from the early twentieth century. Everyone seemed to be wearing their Sunday best. The ladies wore spring bonnets and the men top hats or skimmers. The inhabitants were not actually frozen—we saw a few shift their position—but they held so still otherwise that we felt as if we were walking through a diorama at a wax museum.

Nearing a street corner, we discovered that the people had gathered beneath a loudspeaker. Even those in the streets had their heads cocked, as if they were listening. Over the speakers, which were posted on every corner, came an authoritative, cultured, masculine voice. This voice was so calm and soothing, it was easy to be lulled into listening, even into believing it.

This constantly droning voice was eerily reassuring, but in all the wrong ways. It was as if one was being comforted for one's worst faults by being told they were virtues. The voice promised:

We love you.
We adore you.
Think only on us.
Think only on yourself.
Everyone adores you, your mother, your brother, the woman on the street corner.
They love you so much they want you to kill them.
They want to give you the gift of their lives.
Surely, they are not so selfish as to object to you murdering them?
How dare they be so unsupportive! So uncaring!
Don't they love you?
How could God punish you for doing what comes so naturally to you?
God is your enemy!
Abhor God!
We love you.
Love only us!

Many of those who were listening wore guilty, yet hopeful expressions, as if they knew they had done some terrible thing but would like to believe that they had been justified because they were the real victims. This strange message made no sense to me, until I remembered Malagigi's explanation for the illusions we ran into in the higher circles. Perhaps, there were worse places one could go than Dis.

"I do not like this city," Titus murmured, covering his ears.

"Nor I," Gregor whispered in his gruff voice. "This may be the worst place we've come to yet. Let us find Cornelius and leave."

"You can say that again." Ulysses looked about furtively, then lowered his head, hiding his face behind his hand. "I'm afraid one of the guards will wander by and recognize me. Wish I had my mask!"

"Weren't you wearing it last time you were here?" Logistilla asked tartly.

"Oh, good point." Ulysses straightened up and gestured at the overly long crimson robe he had borrowed from Gregor. "They'll never recognize me without it, especially dressed like this!"

I walked rapidly beside my brothers in the sweltering heat, feeling as if I was melting within my gown. Of course, I should have been grateful. This heat was nothing compared to the lava! I was still amazed that Caliban had made such an effort to save his club when his body was burning. I wondered if it was for sentimental reasons, or because he was certain he would be needing a weapon.

And what about the voice that Theo had thought he had heard instructing Caliban to remain calm? Could it have been the same voice that warned us of the corrosive nature of the armor of the demon Focalor during the battle by the Bridge across the Styx, just before we were separated?

But who had warned us? And why?

WE followed the crystal ball, seeking Cornelius. Soon, the air became slightly cooler, and Mephisto sent the woeful yeti and melting p-son-en home. I was so grateful for the help the creatures had given us that I promptly forgave Mephisto for burying me under ten feet of snow the time he first befriended the giant shaggy creature.

As we passed men standing motionless on street corners and women holding parasols, we began to notice quieter voices, each one different, as if we were hearing the inner monologues of those trapped here.

A voice above a man standing by the curb: *Charles had it coming. Charles asked for it. Charles wanted it this way, or he would have shaped up!*

A voice near a woman seated in a doorway: *You should have seen him. You should have been there. You would have done the same!*

A hot-dog vender standing motionless beneath an unreadable street sign: *It's not my fault. I didn't want to do it! He made me! If only he had been more reasonable!*

"Murderers!" Logistilla's voice rose shrilly. "Why is Cornelius here? Whom did he murder?"

"Maybe Cornelius *is* our traitor," Theo whispered.

"It doesn't make sense," I replied. "The angel said his sin was ambition."

"Maybe he has killed too many in his scramble for the top?" Logistilla covered her eyes like an actress in a melodrama.

"Cut the theatrics," Erasmus snapped back. "This has nothing to do with Cornelius."

Theo frowned at him. "How could it not?"

"I read in some ancient tome of Father's that the City of Dis was once the kingdom of King Paimon, the demon who powers the *Staff of Persuasion*." Erasmus's voice was uncharacteristically emotionless. "Our brother was pulled off course by the sins of his staff."

"Can that happen?" I asked.

Erasmus replied, "I once asked Father why he used to carry the *Staff of Persuasion*, since he seldom tried to persuade anyone. He said it was because Paimon was the worst of the demons, far wickeder than all the rest put together. He wanted to keep an eye on it."

WE continued down the narrow, boxed-in streets as quickly as we could, breaking into a run at times, with Caliban's heavy steps thundering beside mine, as he kept up with ease, despite bearing the burden of Ulysses. Twice, Mephisto directed the ball away from Cornelius's location to check the time, so we could keep track of how long we had until midnight on Twelfth Night. Only a quarter of an hour had passed so far, but it seemed like we had been here for days.

We broke into a run, darting across streets and down alleys. Soon, we were too winded to carry on much conversation. My thoughts returned instead to the issue of Father and secrecy. There were so many things Father had not mentioned—demons in the staffs, Logistilla's secret project, the issue of Aerie Ones and souls—that I no longer knew how to guess what he did and did not know.

Did Father know about Logistilla's and Ulysses's involvement with Abaddon? If so, that might shed light upon his insistence for secrecy. Or did this desire have a more sinister root? According to Seir of the Shadows, Father and his brother Antonio had been best of friends before their encounter with demons. Then, a demon named King Vinae had tempted young Father. Vinae, and the same King Paimon of whom Erasmus had just spoken, tempted Uncle Antonio. The demons convinced Father and Antonio to betray the *Orbis*

Suleimani and release the nine great demons King Solomon had labored so hard to trap.

Only at the last moment, Father changed his mind. He stole all the demons and fled, leaving his brother Antonio behind.

Had this falling out with Antonio scarred Father so much that, to this day, he found himself unable to trust anyone? Even us? Even me? The idea was disturbing. Though, of course, if Abaddon was right, and there was a traitor in the family, then Father was right to distrust us.

But was there a traitor? Or was that just another lie intended to set us at odds with one another?

What was I thinking?! Someone had set up those dolls of Erasmus and me. Funny, while Erasmus still irritated me, I no longer felt the hatred that used to rush through me like a flood every time I saw or even thought of him. For centuries, this had occurred. I thought back but could not remember when it had started. Usually, I had fought it off by turning to my Lady. How much worse must it have been for Erasmus, who never had a Lady to help him?

But who had cast this spell? Logistilla? Caliban? Erasmus himself? Theoretically, it had to be someone who could have reached Infernal Milan. Ulysses? He could have gotten there with his staff. But, that idea was ludicrous; Ulysses was no magician. Besides, he was not old enough. If that spell caused the rush of hate, it had been going on for centuries, well before Ulysses's birth!

Mephisto? He had both the means to reach Infernal Milan and the magical know-how to set up that chamber. Yet, if his recent protestations were to be believed—and the evidence Mab had found in Mephisto's mansion supported him—then he spent much of his time looking out for the family. Why would he waste time attacking us?

Theo? Titus? Cornelius? Gregor? None of those options made any sense. Could it have been Father? That made no sense at all. Father would never . . .

But did I even know Father?

I reviewed the other matters of which Father stood accused. Sending Ferdinand to Hell? He had never done that. Lying to me about my mother? That was harder to explain. He had led me to believe she had been the love that transformed his life. Instead, she was a vile witch whose very name he cursed, or perhaps worse. Binding my will? If he offered the explanation that I would have otherwise grown to be a monster, could I forgive him?

The idea of Father ensorcelling me still struck me as ridiculous. But, how else could I explain the strange attacks of empathy that had been assailing me ever since I discovered Father's disappearance? If they were not caused by the weakening of some spell, what could they be?

What if it happened here? The thought of suddenly seeing life from the point of view of a lost soul filled me with terror. True, something like that had already happened when I had entered Astreus's dream and found myself in the Tower of Pain, but that only increased my trepidation. I dreaded the thought of experiencing even a single moment of such horror again.

If only these unexpected glimpses into other people's souls were because of the weakening of some spell Father had cast upon me. Then, once we finally rescued Father, I could beg him to restore it!

All the hope that had buoyed me since the tiny silver star had rested upon Mab's hand fled. I could remember how seeing the star on his palm had cheered me, but I could not recall why I had felt it was significant. No one doubted that Father was a wise and splendid magician. So, why should it be important that he had learned the trick of giving elemental spirits souls? Did that mean that he was honest with his children? Or that he always used his knowledge for good?

No. It meant nothing.

In retrospect, I felt very grateful to have met Malagigi and to have learned about the Brotherhood of Hope. If I had been forced to walk through this accursed place while believing that every man and woman here had been damned by God for eternity, I feared the horror of it would have been too cruel to bear.

I thought of Eurynome, descending from Heaven to save mankind in the Garden. For the first time, I wondered: why had God breathed life into the homunculi the demons had made—the ones that became mankind? Were we not damned from the start because we lived so near the corrupting nature of the demons, whose mere proximity harms the human soul? It was almost enough to make me want to believe the more traditional version of the Garden of Eden story.

How ironic, I thought sadly. *The* Book of the Sibyl *claimed Bitter Wisdom was the Handmaiden of Eurynome. By that definition, I should be far more qualified to serve my Lady now than I had been in my innocence.*

AHEAD loomed the towering columns of the Dis Stock Exchange. Far above, the sculpted Classical figures upon the building's pediment buried their faces in their hands or pulled at their hair, expressing sorrow and woe.

Some did worse things, such as tearing out their own eyes or gnawing off their own arms. We gazed up in silent horror and then followed the crystal ball between the enormous Corinthian columns and into the building.

The trading floor in New York City had once been the grandest indoor space in the nation, but this chamber dwarfed even its earthly counterpart. Nonetheless, it was tremendously crowded, with well-dressed men and women in gloves and gowns gathered around all the circular podiums. They stood motionless: their heads tilted, listening. The only movement came from ghostly paper tickets that skittered across the smoldering, polished, wide-beam wood floor. Here and there, they burst into curls of flame. The chamber was filled with the scent of burnt paper.

We found Cornelius sitting against a marble wall, motionless. His staff was in his hand, and a bowler hat lay upon his lap. He was dressed in a double-breasted suit with a white collar and a narrow tie. After so many years of seeing him with a bandage across his face, it was strange to see his pale, lifeless eyes. They made him seem older and yet more vulnerable.

As we crossed the floor to him, our heels clicking against the hot, smoldering wood, I thought about his recent falling-out with Logistilla, who used to be one of his closest cronies. I had never thought of Cornelius as principled, yet he had drawn the line at helping Logistilla cheat crooks and cripples. Perhaps, he had a core of integrity after all. I certainly hoped so, considering the substantial influence he had over the movers and shakers of the world.

In my mind's eye, I always saw my brother Cornelius leaning over to whisper into the ear of some sovereign, aristocrat, company owner, or C.E.O., the amber atop his staff—later remade into a white blind-man's cane—glittering brightly. Those in power soon came to realize my brother's worth, and he had often served as an ambassador, either secretly or publicly.

The story of Cornelius's life was the story of the Powers that Be, of secret deals, unrevealed reasons, all the unseen things that really moved the cogs of business and politics. While the inner workings of the *Orbis Suleimani* were a mystery to me, I knew this subtle, secretive, globe-spanning organization, which decided how history would be viewed by humankind, was under the sway of Cornelius. What my brother lacked in sight, he often made up for in foresight.

It had been Cornelius who first came up with the idea of our family forming a company. He had been the one who suggested the idea of hiding our dealings with the supernatural world under a veneer of mundane business. This had not been so important back in the early seventeenth century when the Prospero Transport Company first received its royal charter. Now, however, with modern surveillance and taxation methods, it was essential.

No wonder Cornelius would not sell me his shares! Over the last fifty years, as I had labored to build up and improve Prospero, Inc., I had come to think of the business as mine. Cornelius, on the other hand, must still think of it as his. He conceived the very concept of the company and then made it a reality. Between that and his cautious concern for the future, he would not want to let go of his portion of Prospero, Inc.

This revelation brought understanding, but not sympathy. Cornelius was a cold, calculating man. I respected him, but I could not bring myself to like him much. I understood why he might value Prospero, Inc., but that created no desire to share it with him.

As we neared him, his voice spoke from above us: *They won't come for me. No one in the family ever remembers me. That is the reward I have earned for all my years of selfless service. I'll be all alone, forgotten. Forever dwelling in the dark.*

"Don't be an ass!" Erasmus bent down and yanked him to his feet.

"Erasmus? Is that you? Thank Heavens!" Cornelius, the calmest and least demonstrative of my brothers, grabbed Erasmus's hand tightly. Titus rushed forward and grabbed both Erasmus and Cornelius in a bear hug. The three of them embraced, laughing. Cornelius reached up and touched their faces.

I looked around but could see neither an indication of how he came to be dressed in out-of-fashion garments nor any sign of his original belongings. That was too bad. We had all been hoping Cornelius might have some food left among his things.

My brother stooped and picked up his staff, a slender blind-man's cane with a sphere of amber set into the top—its white length was still tied with a black warding ribbon Erasmus had placed upon it to keep the dangerous King Paimon from influencing us without our knowledge—and set his bowler upon his head.

"Ready when you are, Brothers," Cornelius spoke with a note of cheer I had seldom heard in his voice.

I looked around at the group of us, and it struck me. We were all together! I paused a moment and glanced at each sibling, drinking in their faces. If, in the troubles to come, anything should happen to some of us, I wanted to be able to remember the family at this moment.

Gregor stood in the midst of the Exchange. Without his red robes, the difference between his lithe present self and the stockier physique of his past was more pronounced. He held his new staff before him with both hands, as a priest might carry a cross, his expression calm and prayerful. To his left, Ulysses sat upon Caliban's shoulders with Mephisto standing just beside them. Ulysses and Mephisto both seemed to be in good spirits. The former usually took things lightly, but he had seemed particularly cheerful since Logistilla had restored his true shape. The latter had a distant wistful smile. Funny to see the two of them together, both slender, wiry, and light-heartedly. I had never before noticed how similar they were.

Erasmus was still grinning at Cornelius. He took Cornelius's arm and hooked it over his own. The two of them looked so natural together, with Titus, Cornelius's full brother, smiling beside them. Theo waited stalwartly beside me, his eyes alert, keeping watch for dangers. He had not forgotten that we were in Hell or that Ulysses had originally been captured by demons not far from here. Mab stood beside him, scratching his stubble. Next to him was Logistilla, who had been staring down her nose fastidiously at the men who stood frozen in the exchange around us. As Titus came to stand calmly beside her, his hand resting protectively upon her shoulder, Logistilla shrieked. A moment later, she covered her mouth with her hand, but her eyes were peering fervently upward.

I looked around, seeing nothing. Then, listening, I heard it, too. As if from the air above our heads, our own voices were speaking.

Logistilla's voice said: *So, Big Sister lived like a prisoner in her own castle? Why does that make me feel sooo good?*

Titus's voice growled: *If Caliban looks at her that way again, I don't care if he's Mephisto's man, I'm going to crack his skull, squeeze it like an orange until the juices run out!*

A rich bass spoke that sounded familiar. It took me a moment to realize it was Gregor's real voice, not his damaged gravelly whisper: *What a sorry lot we Prosperos are. How many of us, by right, deserve to remain in this God-forsaken place? Maybe I should slay us all and do Heaven a favor.*

Caliban's voice mused: *My nose is stuffed up again. Wonder if I could pick it without anyone noticing?*

Ulysses's spoke idly: *This robe really doesn't suit me. Wonder if Gregor could be conned into giving me his turtleneck and slacks. I'd look far better in them than he does. Or better yet, Cornelius's suit. Now that's sharp!*

Cornelius's voice was repeating in a soft, stunned tone. *They're here. They came. I can't believe it!*

Erasmus's voice cried in despair: *My life is a field strewn with ash, like that wasteland we crossed. Oh, Maria, how I have failed you!*

Theo's voice chuckled: *Boy, I looked fine when I fired my staff! Wonder if Miranda noticed?*

Mab's voice said: *What the . . . ?*

Mephisto's voice chirped: *I'm hungry. Wonder if anybody brought cheese?*

And my voice . . . To my dismay, I heard my own voice repeating aloud the dour thoughts running through the back of my mind—the kind of thoughts I usually dismissed: *First Father, now these Voodoo dolls. Do I have any thoughts of my own? Oh, my lost love! Would that you had not been cruelly murdered!*

Beside me, Theo's face slowly turned red. Mephisto lowered his head, concentrating. He hugged his arms and hummed a song. Above us, his voice fell silent. Noticing this, a panicked-looking Gregor immediately began to pray. His voice stopped as well. Logistilla tried to pray, but her voice-over continued:

Our Father . . . Darn! How does that prayer go? What's the point of praying anyway? God never listens or answers. If there even is a God. Would a God of Goodness leave Galeazzo in that forsaken hellhole? I wonder if he was happy to see his mother. Oh, wait! I'm supposed to be praying! Oh, how my mind does wander!

Then, Titus touched Gregor's shoulder. Gregor tapped his new staff. Blessed silence fell.

The souls of the damned in the range of his staff's effect stirred and looked about. Several approached us, attempting to join our group. They tried to speak to us or gesticulated imploringly, two of them doffing their black bowlers and holding them meekly before their chests. But, of course, we could not hear what they said. Gregor threatened them with the Seal of Solomon, and they quickly retreated. As we moved toward the door, and the effect of the *Staff of Silence* passed beyond them, they froze again and stood motionless listening to the Voice.

The eerie thing was that Gregor's staff did not silence only the outside voices. The monologue that had been berating me both in my head—the voice I had assumed was my own—fell quiet, too. I could think positive, practical thoughts and could consider negative consequences, but no self-effacing repulsive thoughts rose to confound me.

The *Staff of Silence* may always have had this effect, only I had never had a reason to notice before.

As I wound my way through the finely dressed locals, who milled about, bewildered, within the effect of the silence, I thought about my voice-over. Lost love? Since when had I began thinking of Astreus as my love?

I blushed a dark crimson. A better question might be: Why had I assumed that I had meant the Elf Lord instead of Ferdinand?

Then it struck me. The demons were affecting our thoughts.

Our very minds were not our own. What actions we had taken in our lives, what mistakes we had made, had been at their urging? I knew my anger at Erasmus was fanned by them, but what else? Had it been my idea to stay at home when London was burning, back in 1666, or was that thought caused by demons? Had it been my idea to play my flute on the bridge, or had that come from them, too?

The whole subject made me feel as if something were crawling on the inside of my skin. I shivered and shook my head as if I could shake out the bad thoughts. The others must have come to similar conclusions, for their faces were pale and their expressions ranged from baffled to disturbed.

As we reached a sparsely populated area near one of the bronze-colored round booths, Ulysses gestured from Caliban's back for everyone to come together. We began gathering about the *Staff of Transportation,* preparing to depart.

A pile of colored tickets near our feet burst into flame. It burned without a crackle, though the scent of burning paper grew stronger. Erasmus blithely stepped over it and put his arm on Ulysses's shoulder. Then, he abruptly pulled back and motioned to Gregor, moving his finger across his throat and pointing at the *Staff of Silence.* Gregor nodded and tapped his staff. Sound came rushing back.

"This is too good an opportunity to miss." Erasmus pointed at Mephisto, who was lounging against the booth, clicking his fingers in his ear to hear the noise of it. "Are you the family traitor?"

"No, you dope!" Mephisto exclaimed. From above, a voice that sounded like Mephisto's replied: *No, you dope. I'm the family savior.*

"Bit of a savior complex, perhaps, but no guilt." Erasmus spun nearly sliding on the polished wooden floor and pointed his finger at Theo, who stood nearest to Mephisto. "Are you the traitor?"

"Don't be an ass." Theo repeated the words Erasmus had just spoken to Cornelius. Above, his voice said: *I have failed my family. I allowed the demons to trick me and sway me from my duty. What greater treachery could there be?*

Erasmus snorted. "Right! Next?"

One by one, Erasmus called upon each of the others, Caliban and Mab included, and Mab questioned Erasmus as well. While one or two voice-overs were embarrassing, no one revealed treachery. Erasmus and Mab both grilled Gregor, questioning him about the comment we had heard overhead about him killing us all.

Gregor's face reddened, but he replied fiercely. "I would never harm any of you! Those thoughts of mine you heard—they were the sort a man knows better than to listen to. When I was in constant prayer, back in my cell, I had rid myself of such thoughts. Here in the heart of the Inferno, it is harder to discipline one's mind . . ."

"We know," Mephisto replied cheerfully. "Didn't you notice all these evil thoughts went away when Titus did his silence thing? That means they aren't even our thoughts, They are evil thoughts sent by bad demons. For instance, I'm sure Calvin would never think about picking his nose, were it not for bad demon thoughts," Mephisto said, using Caliban's modern name. He slapped his Bully Boy on the back, and Caliban's face grew rather red. Then, Mephisto paused and tilted his head. "But I really would like some cheese."

Overhead, Gregor's real voice cried: *What if they don't believe me? What if they think I am the traitor and lock me up again?* and Mephisto's said dreamily: *Maybe with some salami.*

Erasmus finished with the others and turned to me, an unpleasant gleam in his dark eyes. From his air of suppressed glee, I realized this was the moment he had been anticipating. My brother truly believed I was the traitor, and he thought he was about to prove it to everyone.

"Finally, the truth, Dear Sister!" Overhead, Erasmus's voice chortled: *At last!*

"It's not me," I replied. "Why would I cast a spell on myself?" Above us, my voice said: *Hurry! We've got to hurry, or Father will be dead! Unless Father is the traitor!*

I blushed to have the others overhear me doubting Father. Theo and Titus both frowned severely at me, and Logistilla gasped in outrage at the very thought. Erasmus merely grinned wolfishly and stepped closer. As he opened his mouth, however, all sound fled.

Frowning with great annoyance, Erasmus gestured to Gregor to cut the silence again. This time, Gregor shook his head, indicating again that we should all gather together by Ulysses, and tapping his left breast. It took me a moment to realize that he was making a gesture to indicate a pocket watch. He was trying to say that we had to get moving and save Father.

Relieved, I stepped obediently toward Ulysses. Erasmus was far from pleased. He stomped forward, frowning angrily. Then, he changed direction and charged at me.

Striking my stomach with his head, he threw me over his shoulder, then, as I gasped, he sprinted across the chamber until we were outside the effect of the *Staff of Silence.* Throwing me to the smoldering floor, he grabbed me by the throat. "Here, of all places, you cannot lie! For God's sake! Tell me the truth! What are you?" Above him, his voice-over cried out plaintively: *All this time, they've been taken in by her, believed her lies. Finally, we shall learn the truth!*

Coughing, I tried to tear his hands from my throat, but he had the same advantages of extraordinary strength as I did, and he was the stronger of us. The heat of the floor scalded my back. I kicked at Erasmus, trying to lift as much of my body off the wood planks as possible; however, he quickly knelt atop me, pinning my legs. Above us, to my dismay, my voice cried out pathetically: *Erasmus, can't you see that I am innocent? I am nothing but a pawn to whom Father told lies. Stop hurting me!*

"No!" he cried. "You lied about Ferdinand. You've kept the Water from us. You killed Maria. You chortled, laughing as you lauded your victories over us!"

The same words were repeated in the air above his head.

My vision was growing dark around the edges. I struggled, desperate for air, pulling on my brother's hands. My voice-over cried:

I am innocent! I shall die having failed my father . . . having failed my Lady . . . and never having known love.

"Stop!" Theo charged toward Erasmus like a knight on horseback. Mephisto's face bobbed over Theo's shoulder, his staff swinging about as if ready to strike. Before they arrived, however, Mab appeared and hit Erasmus over the head with his lead pipe. The great chamber resounded with the loud *whack.*

Erasmus released me and grabbed his head, yowling. Theo tackled him, knocking him hard against the floor. Theo knelt on Erasmus's chest, shouting, "Stop hurting her! Can't you see she's just a victim?"

Above, Theo's voice-over cried: *If he kills her, after she saved me, brought me back to life . . . Oh, please live, Miranda! Please live!*

"Ow! For Heaven's sake! I'm not going to kill her!" Erasmus shouted back. "I just want to know the truth!"

Reluctantly, Theo released Erasmus and stood, glaring down at him.

His face ashen, Erasmus held his head where Mab had struck him and rocked back and forth, his features contorted with pain.

"Ouch! That hurts!"

"Serves you right, bothering Miss Miranda like that when she's never done anything to you," Mab growled.

Erasmus scooted backward, away from Theo, and rose to his feet. "But that's just it! She has harmed me. She's harming us all. She's lying! She's a fake like . . . like those false wings she's been parading about," Erasmus spat, turning on me as I rose shakily to my feet, my hands pressed against my throbbing throat. "Prancing about as if you're an angel, when we all know you're nothing but a witch's bastard! See!"

Overhead, his voice cried: *She's lying. She has to be. I will prove it!*

Crossing the distance between us again in two large steps, Erasmus grabbed my shoulder and spun me around so that my back was to my family. As Theo bear-hugged him about the middle and dragged him away, Erasmus unlatched the enchanted clasp that released the fastenings on my enchanted dress. My gown fell open in back, baring my shoulders before my family and the population of the Exchange.

Theo swung Erasmus around, knocking the latter's head into the nearest circular booth. My gown began sliding off my shoulders. Crossing my arms to keep it from slipping further, I noticed that no wisps of emerald light sprang from the loose flaps of enchanted cloth now. Opening the fastening must have broken the spell that had produced the wings.

Overhead my voice exclaimed: *I hope they reappear when I close my gown. They were useful!*

At the same time, Erasmus's voice-over cried shrilly: *No! I don't believe it! How can this be?*

To my left, Theo had forced Erasmus to his knees, his hands gripping Erasmus's shoulders. But he was no longer looking at Erasmus. Instead, he stared at me. Erasmus stared at me, too, ignoring the trickle of blood running down his temple into his eye. Caliban, Mephisto, and Mab stood about them, ready to jump in if necessary. Yet, they were gawking at me, as well. Farther away, the rest of my family also stared in astonishment.

The floor had been very hot. Perhaps my skin had blistered, and they were aghast at the horror of it? I grew faint with shame. How mortifying that I—who would not even swim without a proper bathing costume—was now so flagrantly exposed.

No man, save Father, has ever seen my back. I shall die of shame!

Bracing myself, I twisted, resolved to see what held their attention so raptly. And then, I, too, gaped in wonder.

Wings of emerald light flared behind me as brightly as ever. Only they did not come from my enchanted gown. They sprang directly from my shoulder blades.

Overhead, Erasmus's voice cried out: *This cannot be! Can I have been wrong all this time? But your mother was an evil witch! Why else would Father have put you under a spell?*

Like the traitor Erasmus accused me to be, the overhead voice that sounded so deceptively like my own betrayed me. It blurted out my secret fear. It did not do it meekly or with shame, as I might, but in a most blatant and arrogant fashion: *Fool! That wretched witch was never my mother. My mother is the Queen of Air and Darkness!*

Oh, no. My heart stopped beating. My chest froze. I opened my mouth, gasping for air that did not come.

Erasmus's jaw dropped open so far that I feared it had become unhinged. He looked at me with a mixture of astonishment and triumph. Theo took a stumbling step back. Caliban, who had just arrived, went pale. Even Mab's face scrunched into an incredulous grimace.

From down the street came the tromping of demon feet.

"Okay, let's skidaddle! We can discuss this later." Mephisto yanked Ulysses toward me and grabbed my shoulder. "Everyone hold on!"

CHAPTER SEVENTEEN

Sycorax's Child

"Snakes!"

This time, the serpents were waiting for us. We arrived in a flash of light back at the foothills of the Mountains of Misery. The rock we had marked with the *Staff of Transportation* had been far from the snakes the first two times. The locals had caught on to where we appeared and disappeared, however, and had slithered over to wait for us.

They swarmed over our feet, biting us mercilessly. Caliban and Mephisto wore boots. Ulysses still sat on Caliban's shoulders. Mab made quick use of his trusty pipe to send snakes flying in all directions. Cornelius, who had missed all the recent family drama because he had been within the effect of the *Staff of Silence,* and Logistilla, who had immensely enjoyed the spectacle of Erasmus attacking me, both were in such good moods that—true to Malagigi's predictions—the snake bites could not affect them.

The rest of us were not so lucky.

I found myself slithering along in the dark on my very long stomach. Approaching a crack of light, I peeked out from the folds of my gown in time to see someone who resembled me skipping away over the ramparts, displaying far more of my naked body than merely the shoulders. I feared I might shrivel up from sheer embarrassment and blow away like the dust on the Plain of Wasted Lives. Luckily, most of my brothers were too busy hissing and slithering to notice, but Mephisto had the gall to wolf-whistle.

My burning desire to wreak revenge by slithering up his boot and biting his knee was thwarted by the realization that I would then look like Mephisto—most likely, if I understood the system, a naked Mephisto—a fate I fervently wished to avoid.

To my delight, however, I noticed the wings of emerald light had stayed with me. They now protruded from my sinuous length. This cheered me so much that I found the magnanimity to forgive the impertinence of my wolf-whistling brother.

Soon, Erasmus, Theo, Gregor, Titus, and I slid along on our tummies—a disorienting sensation—while pale greenish light from the globe at the top of the *Staff of Transmogrification* glowed all around us. Next, hopping toads crowded the rocks, and I found myself towering above my brethren in Titus's bulky form, displaying more of Titus than I would ever care to see. A tense moment followed, during which I looked like naked Erasmus, and he looked like me, before Logistilla restored everyone to their proper shape.

Then, I was myself, naked, in a field of toads.

"WHOSE idea was it to come back to the snake pit?" Logistilla cried, when we were again dressed and out of Snakeland. "Of course, there would be snakes there!"

We were following the crystal ball along a raised causeway of black obsidian that Mephisto had identified as the Paths of Pride. To either side yawned an enormous chasm from which noxious vapors leaked. Ahead, the Paths led to the foothills and on to the rocky slopes of the Mountains of Misery. Behind, a great plain stretched away as far as the eye could see, broken in places by the forbidding forest we had passed through on our way to get Logistilla.

"Wasn't a matter of ideas," Ulysses replied from Caliban's shoulders. He now wore Gregor's black turtleneck and slacks, which he managed to make look stylish—despite their being several sizes too big for him—and Gregor was back in his crimson cardinal's robes. However, Ulysses still did not have any shoes. "It was either walk out of Dis—through the gorgons and all—or use the staff. And, of places the staff has memorized, this is the closest to our pater." Leaning precariously to one side, he reached past Caliban's shoulders and tapped his staff against a rock, memorizing this location. Straightening, he addressed me. "So, your mum is some demon, then?"

"No!" I cried, exasperated. "I have no idea who my mother is! Father's journal and what he told Mephisto both point to Sycorax. But Malagigi thought my mother was something . . . more supernatural, like a mermaid or a sylph. . . ." I drew the line at explaining Malagigi's reasoning. "Then, as I was crawling through the bog to rescue Titus, it occurred to me that Lilith was a possibility. But it was just a passing thought! And I am definitely not happy about it, much less proud!"

"That's what she says now." Erasmus flipped his staff in the air, catching it by the end and tossing it again. I noticed that he had used his staff to fix his face, yet again. His temples had gone more gray. "When we cannot hear the truth."

My fists clenched, and I considered asking Theo to punch him again. Or, better yet, I could stride over and punch him myself! Now that would be satisfying. What a shame I had broken his nose accidentally when I was half-conscious. I strained, thinking back, but could find no memory of having heard the *crunch*. Instead, I replayed for myself several times my memory of the moment when Theo punched him in the lava tube, as well as Theo slamming Erasmus's head into the bronze booth in Dis.

What an irritating man Erasmus was! No matter how much evidence mounted that I was innocent, he simply refused to see it. Granted, his hatred had been enflamed by a spell, but that was over. What excuse did he have now?

Since the fateful encounter in Dis, our family had tacitly broken into two groups. Mephisto, Gregor, Theo, Mab, and I walked to one side; Erasmus, Cornelius, and Logistilla had moved to the other. Titus was walking near Logistilla, though he did not seem very happy about the whole situation. Caliban, with Ulysses on his shoulders, strolled in the middle between the two warring camps. I was not certain if he did this on purpose, at Mephisto's urging, or if he was unaware of the tension.

"Those voices are just demons talking," Mephisto insisted. "Servants of Paimon. Erasmus's a pickle-head for listening to them."

"They seemed accurate enough to me," Erasmus said. "At least mine was accurate."

"That just means you're a pickle-head who listens to what demons say to you!"

"I suppose that's a possibility." Erasmus missed the end of his staff, and it clattered against the obsidian. He shot me a dark glance, as if I had somehow caused him to drop it. I glared back. He picked it up and asked, "What about the wings, though? Doesn't that imply that her mother was some sort of demon? Or at least a succubus?"

"Look over there! It's the Train to Nowhere!" Mephisto cried, pointing, obviously attempting to interrupt us before another argument started.

Only, there really was a Train to Nowhere.

To the left of the forest lay the battlefields we had crossed to reach

Ulysses. On the far side, to the forest's right, train tracks cut across the red-dish earth; an engine pulling a line of cars chugged along them. The tracks continued into the distance as far as the eye could see.

Beyond the tracks rose an immense, curving structure of bridges and exits. The roads looped back upon one another like a four-dimensional figure eight. Many vehicles traveled these roads, some lengths of which were jammed with traffic. Yet, not a single stretch of highway made its way across the plains, away from these endlessly intertwined exits. Only the train left, and it apparently went to Nowhere.

"What's that?" I asked, pointing.

"The Cloverleaf from Hell!" Mephisto replied cheerfully. "And the Eternal Traffic Jam. Many people end up on that one in their nightmares."

"People come to Hell in their dreams?" Ulysses exclaimed in disbelief.

"Nah," Mephisto responded, "but Hell is on the far side of the Gate of False Dreams. Images from here often drift into people's nightmares."

Ulysses pointed at a single-file line of people stretching as far as the eye could see. "What's that? The Endless Queue?"

"Exactly!"

Ulysses shuttered. "I'd rather be a snake then end up there! I hate waiting!"

THE closer we drew to where the Mountains of Misery rose in the distance, stark and sharp against the red flaming sky, the chillier it grew. Walking beside us were the tortured dead. We drew close to one another, skirting to the left or right to avoid lone men with great loads upon their backs, bent old women walking so bowed over that they crawled along like beasts, and gangs of slaves wearing heavy iron collars linked together by a great chain. These last were driven by imps with flaming whips, who hovered above them or rode upon the back of one of their number, spurring him on with their long venomous claws.

"Slavers," Mephisto said sadly. "Guys who sold slaves in life or who were really nasty to the ones they owned."

"They deserve every minute of it!" Mab glowered, glaring at my flute.

"Look! The Train to Nowhere!" Mephisto pointed again, apparently hoping to forestall another argument. Yet, we all looked again. The sight was still equally dreary.

"Why is Gregor carrying Titus's staff?" Logistilla asked. Cornelius, who had not known this was the case, cocked his head, curious. Theo and Caliban looked on in interest as well.

"We swapped," Titus said.

"A shift of burdens, so to speak," Gregor replied serenely in his husky voice.

Logistilla hugged her staff tightly. "A revolting idea! I mean, I do admire Cornelius's staff, and Erasmus's is nice, too. But I like mine better."

The others, I noticed, were holding their staffs close as well, as if horrified at the thought of possibly losing them. I felt only sympathy. I certainly would not have wanted to give up my staff. It made me admire Gregor's gesture to Titus all the more.

Though I could not help wonder whether there was a reason why the only two who seemed willing to consider changing staffs were the two who had been forced to take a vacation from them in recent years. It was hard to imagine that I would feel differently about my staff if parted with it for a time, but I had been wrong about other things. Of course, mine did not have a demon.

"By the way, Caliban," Logistilla said as she stepped up close beside him and rested her hand admiringly upon his huge bicep, "who is your father? Shakespeare is mute on that matter."

Caliban glanced down at Logistilla who gave him a sultry look. He blushed, Titus growled, and Gregor grimaced.

"Don't know," Caliban admitted.

Erasmus was a few steps ahead of them. "You never asked your mother?"

"It would never have come up." Caliban looked chagrined. "Back when she was alive I thought Master Prospero was my father. She used to go on about how he had fancied her the first few times he summoned her. Then, she'd rail against him, cursing him for his fickleness."

"First few times? He summoned her more than once?" Mab had come over to join us; now he drew his damaged older notebook from his pocket and flipped through it quickly, circling something with his Space Pen.

"Oh yes," stated Caliban. "She told me he had a statue, much like the figures on Mephisto's staff. When he tapped it, she would appear."

"Huh!" Mab scratched his six o'clock shadow.

I thought of the two wooden dolls in my room on Prospero's Island, the ones I had played with as a child. Could one of them be the figurine that summoned Sycorax?

"Oh, do come!" Ulysses exclaimed from Caliban's shoulders. "It's obvious who this big brute's father is! Just look at his chin. It's practically the same as Gregor's, only larger."

Caliban moved to stand beside Gregor and jutted out his chin. Gregor stuck out his bearded jaw as well. To our astonishment, Ulysses was right! In fact, I recalled noticing the similarity between him and Gregor the first time I saw Caliban.

Erasmus laughed. "You mean that bratty child of Sycorax's Father complained about in his journal was Caliban?"

"Why else would Father have kept him alive all these years?" Ulysses asked. "It's a wonder he didn't give him a staff, too."

Caliban and Mephisto exchanged surreptitious glances, smirking.

"You mean he's family? Oh, phooey!" Logistilla threw up her hands. "All the best ones are." She stepped beside Titus and tucked her arm through his. "Well, if I must love a brother, I might as well stick with the one I already have." Titus put an arm around her, his grin practically splitting his face in two. Ahead of them, Gregor's face contorted with disgust.

Caliban, for his part, looked enormously pleased. "You mean I've got a family?" He gave Mephisto a friendly punch. "Brother!"

"Brother!" Mephisto shouted back, giving him a hug.

"Whoa!" cried Ulysses, who swayed precariously atop Caliban's shoulders.

Cornelius, who was being helped along by Erasmus, asked, "But wasn't Caliban older than Miranda? Didn't he come to the Island with Sycorax?"

Caliban shook his head. "Not that I remember. When I was little, I thought Master Prospero was my father, and Miranda was my older sister. He even let me call him Father until . . . well . . ." He glanced at me, then looked down, ashamed.

I thought back, using the picture of my little self from Father's journal as a reference to sift through the mists of time to the original memories. I said slowly, "I remember when Caliban was smaller than me. It must have been Shakespeare who introduced the other idea."

"Most likely," Ulysses snickered. "Father never would have told the Bard the truth about Caliban's origins. Too embarrassing."

"Does that make Caliban our Fearless Leader?" Logistilla asked. "If he's the oldest, I mean?"

Caliban looked at Mephisto, who shrugged. Gregor shook his head. "Right now, we are only speculating. Unless Father confirms our theory, Mephisto is still the eldest."

Erasmus stared at me speculatively. "I see now how you arrived at the conclusion that the Queen of Air and Darkness might be your mother."

"And how was that, Brother?" Cornelius tilted his head, listening.

"If Caliban is Sycorax's child, then Sycorax was not the first creature Father summoned—the one he told Mephisto had given him Miranda," Erasmus explained. "So, who could Miranda's mother be?"

"In his journal," Erasmus continued, "Father speaks a great deal about 'M,' whom he refers to as his 'fair queen.' My guess is that, if it was not Sycorax, then this mysterious benefactor of his was probably the first being Father ever summoned. I have long suspected the identity of the fair queen 'M,' and while Father had never confirmed my suspicions, he has not contradicted me, either. Q.E.D., the first being Father ever summoned, and thus, Miranda's mother, must have been the elf queen, Maeve!"

"O dastardly Daddy, stealing my elf queen!" Mephisto cried. "No wonder he warned me away from her. Oh . . . wait." He cocked his head, tapping his forehead thoughtfully. "Didn't she turn out to be someone icky?"

"Lilith, in fact," purred Erasmus.

Mephisto stuck his fingers in his ears. "I didn't hear that! I'm not listening!"

"Maeve is Lillith? When did we learn this?" Cornelius asked, baffled. Logistilla and Ulysses were staring in amazement as well.

"Um . . ." Erasmus glanced at Mephisto. "Long story. Unwise to explain now. When we get home, I'll tell you whatever parts you haven't worked out for yourself."

Theo leaned forward. He held his staff, his knuckles white. "Maybe it wasn't Father who cast a spell on Miranda . . ."

Erasmus finished the thought with a chuckle. ". . . maybe it was her mother."

"Disturbing," I said slowly, "but unlikely, as Eurynome would certainly have destroyed any spell cast by her great enemy."

"Course, we don't know for sure that 'M' is Maeve," Mab muttered as he scribbled something down in his notebook. "Pays to keep track of what is fact and what is speculation."

"Oh, I think we can be pretty sure," Erasmus said. "I've referred to 'M' as Queen Maeve numerous times, and Father has never corrected me."

"Is that so?" Mab drawled. "Funny, Miss Miranda referred to her mother as Lady Portia, numerous times, and Mr. Prospero never corrected her, either."

Erasmus chuckled. "Touché."

"I say," Ulysses leaned over sideways from Caliban's shoulder and spoke

softly to Cornelius. "You once told me that Father's journals said he consecrated Miranda to her Lady to restrain some kind of baser nature. Now
that she's no longer in the Unicorn's service, is that baser nature going to
reassert itself?"

Even Ulysses knew about this? I was torn between shame and annoyance.

"We are hoping not," Cornelius replied as he tapped his way along the
obsidian road with his black-wrapped cane, "but nobody knows. According
to Erasmus, Father reported in his journal that she was a terror. Or . . .
wait . . . was that Caliban?"

"Sorry about that." Caliban hung his head sheepishly.

The last of my resentment toward Caliban dissolved, and I felt as fondly
toward him as I did toward Gregor or Titus. True, he had once attacked me,
but only out of ignorant brutish lust, not deliberately and maliciously, like
Erasmus. And he certainly seemed to have changed in the intervening five
hundred and some odd years. I had been glad that I spent the extra Water to
save him and return his strength when I heard how he had saved Theo. Now
I was doubly glad. To have discovered later that I abandoned a family member in need . . . it would have been unthinkable!

But it still left the matter of my mother.

My parentage was changing so quickly it was as if I was being hit in the
face by the revolving door of heritage. So, Sycorax was not my mother! And
yet, Caliban was still my brother, and Father's son! No wonder Father had
kept him alive! One of the great mysteries of my youth, why Father did not
want to kill Caliban after he attempted to rape me, was finally solved. It
was not in Father's nature to slay his own son.

If Sycorax was not my mother, however, my chances of escaping the fate
of being the daughter of the Queen of Air and Darkness looked bleak indeed. And what about Ulysses's fear that, without the influence of my Lady,
I might begin to revert to some kind of demonic monster? This concept had
been introduced before, but it seemed all the more disturbing if I was the
daughter of one of the Seven Rulers of Hell! The notion was sobering, and
I resolved to watch my thoughts and actions more carefully.

"So, you're family!" Ulysses gave Caliban's head a pat. "That means
Miranda would have won, if Mephisto hadn't butted into the vote."

"Who would have you voted for?" Erasmus glanced up at Ulysses from
where he held Cornelius's arm.

"Oh, come! That is hardly sportingly!" Ulysses objected.

"Seriously," Erasmus's eyes narrowed.

"Neither of you! That's for sure! The two of you are the ones who got me into all this trouble!"

"That's hardly fair," I cried, nearly walking into a band of slavers. The leader recoiled from my gown. "We may have driven you away from Prospero, Inc., but we hardly forced you to swear an oath to Abaddon."

"Our fault? How so?" asked Erasmus.

"It was just after the Guvnor gave me my staff," Ulysses replied, "and I had come up with this brill idea of finding out if it could go any places we hadn't visited. I didn't know the staffs contained demons from Hell! I thought they came from Fairyland or some such.

"Anyway, I showed up at the family lodgings to see if I could get a couple of sibs to come along, just in case there was a spot of aggro . . . you know, trouble," he added when he saw we were unable to follow his modern British slang. "But, I couldn't get a word in edgewise. Erasmus and Miranda were going at it, bickering about who knows what, as they always did. Wouldn't even give me the time of day. So, I went on my own, met Abaddon, and the rest is history."

Mab stepped up beside me and whispered, "Didn't you tell me it was Ulysses's going off on his own that broke up the family business?"

Stunned, I nodded, whispering back, "I kept asking Father to stop him, but he would not. He must have known Ulysses's reasons. But he didn't breathe a word to me! The family came apart just after that. Gregor died, Theo left; soon there was no one."

All this time, had I been blaming everyone else for the family desertion of Prospero, Inc., when all along, it had been largely my fault? Or at least half my fault. How tremendously humiliating! How right the angel had been when she said that my greatest vice was pride.

"Let me get this straight," Mab said aloud, scribbling a note. "We're down here because Mr. Prospero got captured. Mr. Prospero got captured trying to rescue Mr. Gregor and, indirectly, Mr. Theo. Mr. Gregor and Mr. Theo were in trouble because the Perp here, er . . . Mr. Ulysses . . ."

"The Perp?" Ulysses laughed. "That's a fine how-do-you-do!"

Mab glared at him. "As I was saying: 'cause Mr. Ulysses swore an oath to the Angel of the Bottomless Pit. Mr. Ulysses swore the oath because he came down here by himself and got into trouble. He came by himself because Miss Miranda and Professor Prospero were bickering. And those two were bickering 'cause of those voodoo dolls we found back at Infernal Milan. Did I leave anything out?"

"No." Erasmus looked as stunned as I. "I think that about covers it."

Mab raised his voice so that the others could hear him. "Which brings us back to the question of the traitor—the joker who encouraged you and the Professor here to bicker. Let's assume for the moment that Erasmus's trick with the overheard voices in the city of Dis worked—no real reason to assume that. Those overhead voices were probably liars, but let's just grant it for the moment. If the trick in Dis worked, the traitor is not a member of the family—whatever Abaddon might have said."

"What about . . ."—Logistilla swallowed—"Father?"

Mab snorted. "If Mr. Prospero wanted to hand you all over to Hell, he would have just put out a silver platter and told you all to jump on. And you would have, too."

"If Father were the traitor," I said, "he would not have bothered teaching us to love good and eschew evil."

"So, who is it?" asked Erasmus.

Mab scratched his eternal stubble. "At this point? Hard to say . . . but my guess is Seir or one of the other Three Shadowed Ones. They've been after you all since 1623. Even if they don't have the thaumaturgic skills necessary to make those dolls, they must know plenty of demons who do. Thaumaturgy being a specialty of demons."

"Why Erasmus and Miranda?" Logistilla walked with her head resting against Titus's shoulder.

"No idea. Maybe they already disliked each other? Maybe that's whose hair they happened to gain access to the day they snuck in the bathing pool. Could be anything."

"Any other possibilities?" Cornelius tapped along beside Erasmus.

"Can't think of anyone else who's in a position to get down here. Beyond that, it could be anybody: including Erasmus, or even Caliban, here. Could be me. I could be working for the Man-in-the-Moon, out to get anyone who lives on a substance other than cheese. Or anyone who eats cheese." He gave Mephisto a long look. Mephisto glanced innocently this way and that, whistling.

"Of course, you Prosperos have lived a long time, by mortal standards. You might have many enemies no one has thought to mention to me. Piss off any gods of the underworld? Rogue Archmages? Wayfarers? Elves? There are a lot of beings who could do something like this. . . . most of them wouldn't do it down here, though. That kind of limits it to demons and their ilk."

"Or dead people," I added.

"Dead people?" Ulysses laughed. "How could they do anything? They're . . . dead."

"Malagigi caused the Reign of Terror in France after he died," I replied. "Apparently, magical knowledge doesn't go away once you're dead. If you know something, you still know it. There's nothing about being in Hell that keeps a person from casting spells."

"Great," grumbled Erasmus. "Now we have to make a list of everyone we know who is dead."

"Everyone who didn't like us, anyway," Mephisto said.

Erasmus rolled his eyes. "It's going to be a long list!"

"Hey! Speaking of Malagigi," Mab interrupted suddenly. "We're on the Paths of Pride. Isn't that where Malagigi's brother is supposed to be? Let's look for him!"

Mephisto immediately pulled out the crystal ball and asked to see Eliaures, brother of Malagigi. He peered over the ball, scrunching up his face and turning this way and that, as he tried to figure out exactly where the spot it showed him was in relation to our current position.

"He's back that way." Mephisto pointed down the raised obsidian causeway, back the way we came. "Closer to the plains."

"Too bad!" I exclaimed. "If we'd only remembered earlier, we might have been able to angle our path that way to meet him."

Mab looked at me, appalled. "But, Ma'am! We can't just leave him. We promised!"

"We said we'd try."

"Ma'am, if we can rescue someone, it's our duty to try! I'm not going to break my promise and sully my new soul."

"Or his new shoes, either," Ulysses murmured.

"Enough with the clothes!" demanded Logistilla. "All right. I'll make you a set of your own when we get home. And some for Theo, too, assuming Daddy will give me more Styx water."

"No good," I said. "The King of the Djinn spilled it all."

Logistilla pouted. "No chance you tapped on that bridge by the Styx, is there, Ulysses?"

"Indeed there is." Ulysses leaned over precariously and tapped the mahogany staff against the obsidian pathway. "But you'll have to go back and get it by yourself. If I get out of here alive, I ain't never coming back!"

"Even if it means you have to mend your ways and begin leading a virtuous life?" asked Gregor.

"Even then," Ulysses replied firmly, and he made, perhaps for the first time in his life, the sign of the cross. Gregor snorted, but he looked thoughtfully at our youngest brother.

Mab barged ahead before anyone else could speak. "Back to Malagigi's brother. I gave my word. I've got to at least give the guy his brother's message."

"No, Mab!" I said sternly.

"Yes, Ma'am." Mab crossed his arms.

"After we rescue Father, we can—" I began.

Mab cut me off, "No good, Ma'am. We both know it'll never happen. We'll be running from Lilith or something. If we're going to reach him, we've got to do it now."

"Mab! We can't take the chance," I cried. "What if we arrived even a minute too late to save Father's life? We'd never forgive ourselves!"

Mab shook his head stubbornly. "Ma'am, even if you're not going to go, I am. I'll catch up somehow. Or you can come look for me later . . . if you feel like it."

"Mab . . ." I whispered, torn. I did not want this to turn into another battle of wills such as what had happened aboard the *Happy Gambit*. And yet, I hated the thought of leaving him, a lone Aerie One with a soul, trapped in Hell with nothing except a lead pipe.

"I'll go with you, Detective," offered Erasmus.

"For Heaven's sake! Erasmus!" I cried. "You are just doing this to exasperate me!"

"Not at all. I also promised Malagigi. After seeing his robe, I want to keep my promise." He smiled spitefully. "Not everything is about you, you know."

Theo asked, "Mephisto, how much time has gone by—in Boston—since we set out to get Cornelius?"

Mephisto peered into the ball, looking several places. "Three hours."

"What?" I cried in surprise. "Only three hours? Our whole trip to Dis, the snakes . . . everything?"

"Seemed like a lifetime," murmured Logistilla.

Erasmus said, "So we still have thirty-four hours Boston time. Why don't you wait here, Sister. We'll go find him and come back." He peered into the globe which Mephisto had set upon Eliaures again. "Shouldn't take much more than an hour to get down there and back."

"I'm going, too." Theo unlimbered his staff and began fitting the two parts together.

"Why don't we all go?" Mephisto tapped his staff. "I'm sure Peggie's rested by now!"

THE winged steed danced about nervously, his hooves clacking against the hard roadway. His eyes were wide and showed white, but he did not buck as all eleven of us mounted. He trotted briefly and then broke into a canter that became a gallop. Then, he ran off the side of the pathway.

For a stomach-dropping second, he veered downward, and I could smell the noxious vapors from the pits below. Then, his wings opened, and he soared upward, carrying us aloft.

Guided by the crystal ball, we flew for fifteen minutes. Then, Logistilla shouted, pointing out her ex-husband below. She had been married—at different times in different centuries—to both Malagigi and his brother. Mephisto reined in Pegasus, and we dived.

Eliaures walked along the raised obsidian causeway bearing a huge boulder upon his back. The French sorcerer was delighted to see us, especially Logistilla, whom he had loved in life. From the winged horse, Mab and Erasmus yelled to him, telling him about Malagigi and the Brotherhood of Hope, and how he could summon their help by praying. After hearing our story, he tried to throw his boulder aside, but could not.

"Here, allow me!" Theo slid from the back of the horse and knelt on the obsidian. Aiming carefully, he fired his staff so that the hot white beam struck the top of the boulder. There was a terrible blast. The upper portion of the rock exploded into white light. The remaining section split down the middle and fell from the terrified Eliaures's shoulders.

"*Sacrebleu!*" Eliaures cried in his charming French accent. Standing, he kissed Theo near both cheeks. Then, approaching the horse, he kissed Logistilla's hand fervently, though his lips slipped through her fingers. Titus glared at him, but he did not notice. "I have suffered under the weight of my own pride for so long! What must I do to be saved?"

"Help others," Gregor replied gravely.

"And we know just the guy for you to start with!" chimed Mephisto.

Using the crystal ball, Mephisto found a route for Eliaures to travel to

Infernal Milan that did not take him through the nightmarish forest. Eager
to begin his life of charity, by offering assistance to his ex-stepson, Galeazzo,
Eliaures wished us Godspeed. Then, he set off, marching down the black
obsidian road, whistling—rather inappropriately, considering the manner
of his demise—the *Marseillaise*.

ULYSSES's staff took us back to the highest place we had reached on the
Paths of Pride, and the winged horse carried us onward toward the mountains. After about an hour, the obsidian causeway ended, and we flew over
the rocky slopes of the Mountains of Misery themselves. Almost immediately, Pegasus began to tremble, his coat slick with sweat. Mephisto brought
him down and sent the steed home, again summoning the Maenad and instructing her to care for him. This time, Queen Agave brought her cutting
board. Holding it up before us, she scraped it with her fingers. Milk, honey,
and wine flowed freely.

Eagerly, we used the wine to wash our canteens and wineskins clean, and
then we filled them. After that, we took turns lapping fresh, creamy milk,
scooping up the thick golden honey, and sipping ruby-dark wine from the
board. In all my life, I could not recall ever having tasted anything so wonderful, except perhaps the Water that flowed from the Well at the World's
End. The milk was sweet and sustaining; the honey melted upon the tongue;
and the wine lent us an inner warmth against the chilly air.

Eventually, Mephisto announced that the landscape was affecting the
Maenad queen, who was shivering violently. He tapped his staff, and she
vanished like a dream. Happily, we packed away our newly filled containers
and set off again. It is unlikely that a more contented band had ever hiked
into the Mountains of Misery.

The Mountains of Misery

"Wish I had some shoes." Ulysses sighed from his perch upon Caliban's shoulders as we started up the first slope. "No offense to your shoulders, old chap, but I hardly think you'll be able to carry me the whole way. Besides, my bum's getting a bit sore. All in all, I'd rather be legging it."

"Your wish is my command!" Mephisto tapped his staff, and I began to imagine his seven young hoodlum friends were among us. When they appeared, quaking with terror, Mephisto eyed their size and pointed at one, announcing cheerfully. "You. Give my brother your shoes."

As the young man hurried to obey, Mephisto continued. "Go buy some better shoes for my brother here, ones that actually fit him, and something for that guy to wear under his robe." He pointed at Ulysses and Gregor in turn, "Oh, and a bandana, and some food. Cheese would be good. I'll call you back in a few hours." Then, with a second tap, he sent them away again.

"That's size nine on the shoe, and make sure they're top drawer!" Ulysses called after the vanishing thugs.

"There you go again!" Logistilla cried. "We're stuck in Hell, with Erasmus strangling Miranda—great show by the way, Brother! I do hope there will be a repeat—and all you can think about, Ulysses, is whether or not you're a fashion plate! The sheer shallowness of your secret inner self appalls me!"

"In my defense, it was not while our brother was strangling our sister—basely done, Erasmus, roughing up a girl; really!—that I thought about my garments, but while we were walking through the exchange with all those well-dressed nobs," Ulysses objected. "It was a natural thought."

Logistilla looked at Ulysses and ran her fingers over her staff, as if contemplating what to change him into.

At the far side of our small band, Erasmus was helping Cornelius over the rocks. With a sudden lurch, I realized that, with all the excitement as we left Dis, we had forgotten to look for Cornelius's enchanted robes. Now he was unprotected, dressed only in the formal suit and tie we found him in.

Walking cautiously along the rocky way, his staff tapping before him and Erasmus, Titus, or Theo helping him over the rougher bits, Cornelius inclined his head to address Erasmus. I was close enough that I could hear them, though I did not let on. "What is all this about you strangling Miranda? I assume the words were meant figuratively?"

"No." Erasmus's voice was muted. "I literally tried to strangle her."

Cornelius was quiet for a time, digesting this: "I assume you had a good reason, Brother?"

"I thought I did at the time."

"Are you all right?" Cornelius's voice expressed concern.

"As well as can be expected."

Neither of them, I noted, asked after me.

WE hiked the Mountains of Misery, which Mephisto reported were hewn from selfishness and oppression. The dead here kept to themselves. They scurried away if we drew too near.

The slopes were steep and bitterly cold; many of us developed painful blisters. At first we walked jauntily, buoyed up by honey and wine, but the sheer misery of our situation, the cold, the blisters, the unending, difficult climb, soon took its toll upon our spirits.

Turning my thoughts away from the cold and the chafing of my shoes, I was able to keep my spirits up by thinking of delightful things. I contemplated my love of flying and how much I had enjoyed our recent rides on Pegasus. I thought about that feeling of satisfaction in a job well done that came each time Prospero, Inc., successfully negotiated a new Priority contract or met the conditions of a standing one. What a pleasure it was to do work that was truly useful, to know that my help made modern science and all the advances of mankind possible.

When that paled, I turned my thoughts to my flute and how much I loved playing it—under ordinary circumstances, when it called sylphs and Aerie Ones, rather than the Hellwinds. Even the knowledge that the Serpent of the Wind dwelled within could not dim my delight, particularly since I was not entirely sure if his presence there was a bad thing. I mean, if my Lady did not object, why should I? Perhaps, he was happier in my flute than he would have been had Father left him in the jar where King Solomon had imprisoned him. After all, he got to blow things about and occasionally call up storms.

I recalled the tempest I had played the morning that I summoned Astreus and discovered he was Seir of the Shadows. How the winds had raged, and the mountainside shook. Rain had fallen upon the island like spears of water, striking every leaf and blade. Great billowing thunderheads, dark as sin, had raced though the sky, only to be split by tridents of lightning. And the thunder! The whole earth had groaned at its force. What a storm it had been!

I was midstep over a low flat rock, my thoughts filled with the joys of storms, when the thought struck me. My heart froze in my chest, and my limbs went cold. I struggled for breath, the chilly air raking my lungs painfully.

Mab had a soul. Caurus must have a soul, too. And Windflower? How many Aerie Ones with souls had I compelled with the flute?

Slowly, I turned and looked down from our great height at the figures, now tiny, who moved upon the Paths of Pride. I could make out a band of men and some women, roped together and suffering under the scourge of their driver imp.

Slavers.

The morality of commanding spirits, fickle soulless things, could be argued *ad nauseum,* but there was no debating the wrongness of enslaving creatures with souls.

Tears stung my eyes. I reached back and touched my flute lovingly. After we rescued Father and were safely home, I could approach the family magicians about whether it would be possible to release Mab and the other souled Aerie Ones from the flute's control without breaking it. If so, wonderful. If not . . . there would be time enough to think about that then. In the interim, I could hand out a lot of earplugs!

After this, my attempts to cheer myself failed. Soon, I could hardly bring a happy thought to mind. Instead, my thoughts were filled with the misery of our situation, the futility of our task, the irony of Astreus's death, the burden of my true parentage, how much I wanted to knock Erasmus's head into the sharp-edged rocks—the arrogant bastard! How dare he manhandle me!—and other topics equally glum, all of which clamored for my attention as I plodded slowly upward along the narrow trail.

WE rested briefly several times. Despite Logistilla's repeated requests for a longer break, I insisted we push on. We did not know how much time it would take us to cross the mountains, or what obstacles might wait beyond.

The longer I walked, the more miserable I felt. Then, as I stumbled on a loose boulder, an unpleasant sensation gripped me. It was that horrible feeling that comes when one suddenly realizes that one has forgotten something of extreme urgency, as if the previously solid ground beneath one's feet suddenly transformed into shifting sands.

These plans for the Aerie Ones—these stratagems involving bodies and souls—it was all for naught. Everything that Father had set in motion depended upon one thing: time—long, uninterrupted durations of time. And time, we no longer had.

We were living in the heyday of humanity, the best of times. The dreams of better times that men cherish in their hearts—often expressed as visions of sleek, silver spaceships and world-encompassing peace—these dreams would never come. For, when the spirits broke loose, modern science would fail, and mankind would be cast back into an earlier age.

Columbus sailed to America in 1492. There was a reason why no one had reached the New World before him—before Father bound up the winds and commanded them to serve man's sails instead of smashing any ship that crossed the equator. The more winds Father captured, the more superior grew man's control of the sea and skies. The age of the explorers, of clipper ships, and even ocean liners and airplanes, all grew out of the Prospero Family's mastery of the winds.

What was going to happen in a hundred years or so when we all died of old age, freeing the Aerie Ones from their oath?

Had we had years enough, perhaps we could have given them souls, and perhaps they would have developed good souls and choose not to do harm, and perhaps pigs would have learned how to fly . . .

But we did not have enough Water for any of us to live long enough to complete that project.

Had their service run out while we still lived, any wind who misbehaved would have been hunted down by my brothers and forced to swear a new oath. Most likely, the Aerie Ones would have been given the same kind of deal Prospero, Inc., offered the other spirits, where we provided them with something they wanted in return for them living up to a set of laws— what scientists called the "Laws of Nature"—and limiting the harm they did to mankind. There might have been a short period of dire havoc, but it all would have been well in the end.

Only, now, when the Aerie Ones got free, my brothers would be dead.

True, the *Orbis Suleimani* would still exist, but without us, they would be hard pressed just to keep guard over the demons in the staffs. Running

Prospero, Inc.—without Water of Life or the help of the Aerie Ones—was out of the question.

So, mankind would be cast back to the days before sea travel or air travel. And that was assuming that the other sprites we had bound did not all rebel when Prospero, Inc., stopped honoring its contracts. If that happened, it would not be the Renaissance civilization fell back to, but the Dark Ages.

Should the *Orbis Suleimani* fail, on the other hand, the results would be far worse than the Dark Ages. It would set mankind back to the time before Solomon bound the elements. Back before fire would smelt iron! Back to the days of volcano kami who demanded virgin sacrifices, and rivers who would rise up at their whim and outrage maidens; back to the days before mankind ruled the earth.

This wonderful world that man had built, where so many ate, so many lived in comfort, so many lived without slavery or fear of imminent death, it would all be gone in a twinkling of an eye. And it would be all my fault!

If I had not been taken in by Seir, if I had not trusted the false Ferdinand, the future would still be shining and bright. I covered my face with my hands and wept as if the sorrow of my heart were a river that would never run dry.

We were living in the last days.

WE continued, silent, cold, and miserable. The three peaks we had already climbed eclipsed much of our view. Occasionally, we caught glimpses of the Plain of Wasted Lives, the nightmarish forest, and, in the far, far distance beneath a red-orange sky, infernal towers rising from behind the dark wall of the City of Dis.

The trek was wearying and depressing. Luckily, I had a secret weapon. Every time I felt too sorrowful, I glanced back at Theo, walking among us, hale and strong. Just the fact that he looked himself again, with his fierce gaze and his chiseled cheekbones—that he was the most handsome of my brothers was generally agreed by both men and women, though there were those among the fairer sex who preferred Mephisto, who was the prettier of the two—lifted my spirits, if only a notch or two.

To my right, the Mountains of Misery trailed away into the distance, growing ever taller. Gazing at them, I forgot, for an instant, that I was in Hell, regarding peaks hewn from sorrow and misery. During that instant, the vista seemed breathtakingly beautiful, complete with "purple mountain majesties."

The sight stirred long-buried memories. I had almost forgotten how much I had loved to journey to new places. In my first few centuries, my family had traveled a great deal. I recalled wind-tossed sea voyages into unknown waters, cresting the Rhipaeans to catch my first glimpse of the ever-dawn of Hyperborea, our first visit to Japan and the Far East. Best of all, of course, had been the secret and wonderful journey of a year and a day to the Well at the World's End—a journey, I realized with a sudden pang of sorrow, I would never make again.

It was a journey upon which no human could accompany me, but I seldom went alone. In my youth, I would travel with a dog, whichever of the family's curs or hunting hounds I was fondest of at the time. Later, after Father had presented us with our familiars, I made the trip with my familiar, Tybalt, Prince of Cats.

All that had ended once I took over Prospero, Inc. The pressures of running the company crowded in upon me, and there was no time for frivolities such as journeys to unknown lands. And yet, I still longed to discover what was beyond the horizons I knew: to visit the halls of Forestholme; to cross the arched bridge between Mount Urnath and Mount Amaranth in fell Avernus; to see the silver fields where my Lady walked; and, of course, to behold the wonders that Astreus had tried to tempt me with at Father Christmas's mansion, the wonders that only seven had seen beyond the Brink of the World.

But, it was not to be.

With the eerie certainty that comes from glimpsing the present as if it were a far distant age, I realized that, assuming I lived, this grueling and heart-racking trek across Hell would one day be numbered among my most cherished memories. While it was true that I had been made uncomfortable, injured and humiliated—not to mention living in constant terror for Father and my other loved ones—this journey had granted my heart's dearest wish: our family worked and traveled together once again!

AFTER seven hours, we finally surrendered to fatigue and made camp. Titus and I still wanted to continue, but Logistilla, Cornelius, and Mephisto were nearly dropping from exhaustion. Truth be told, I was so tired I could not properly focus my eyes.

Mephisto tapped his staff, and again the seven young hoodlums appeared among us, their arms overflowing with bags of fast food and clothes. Mephisto sent them home immediately, instructing them to collect bedding for us. He handed a pair of shiny new Nikes to Ulysses and the bandana to Cornelius, who immediately tied it around his head, covering his eyes. Then, Mephisto divvied up the food: hamburgers and fries, tacos, a bag of nachos smothered in liquid cheese, and a bag of carrots. When combined with our wine, milk, and honey, it proved a surprisingly satisfactory meal.

By the time Mephisto summoned the seven young men back again, they had gathered six sleeping bags, four blankets, a linen bedspread, some towels, a tablecloth and a shower curtain. We spread the shower curtain over a flat ledge that was tucked under an overhang, facing away from the wind. Then, we made do as best we could with the rest.

Though totally exhausted, I lay awake upon my sleeping bag for a time, contemplating what was to come. A little over a day and a half from now, either all would be lost, or Father would be safe, and I would be home again. I pictured what I would do, visiting the office, reading by the fireplace in the lesser hall, with Tybalt curled up on a silken pillow, the phoenix lamp emitting its cinnamony fragrance.

Only, for the first time, I felt dissatisfied. What would I read by the light of the phoenix lamp? All my studying thus far had been in pursuit of Sibylhood. Without that search to sustain me, what purpose did my life have?

Even my Prospero, Inc., duties—which heretofore I had enjoyed immensely—evoked no sense of excitement. After our trek through Hell, returning to the daily toil of running a company suddenly seemed like a step backward, as if a graduate were to return to college the following fall, instead of setting out to make his way in the world.

As I drifted off to sleep, I dreamt I was the Sibyl destined to free the elves from their oath to Hell, but that I was unable to pursue this goal because there was no one else to run Prospero, Inc.

SLEEPING atop the hard rock of solidified misery, I slipped in and out of nightmares. Once, I thought I had awakened but perhaps that, too, was a dream. In the dream, Mephistopheles the demon stood beside me, his head lowered so he could fit beneath the overhang. He spoke with a man made entirely of shadow who crouched near me, watching me with blood red eyes.

"I hear you are no longer recognized," said the shadowy form.

"And with whom do you side, Incubus? With myself, or the Queen?" My brother the demon spread his wings and flexed his glowing ruby claws.

The sable incubus did not so much as glance at Mephistopheles. "I have always been one who acknowledges the Powers that Be, Great Prince! While

I am here, where you are, I am certain you are a Prince of the Sixth Circle, with all the requisite honors!"

"As well you should be." Mephistopheles chuckled. He leaned over until he was practically breathing down the smaller demon's neck. "I do not like the way you are looking at my sister."

"I cannot help it." The incubus's eyes remained fixed upon me. "My other self thought of nothing but her for almost four hundred years, and now I, too, can think of nothing else."

They paused a moment and regarded me in silence.

Leaning forward, the incubus extended his hand toward the emerald light of my left wing. "You must not let Lilith have her! The Queen of Air and Darkness wishes to bring Miranda to the Tower of Thorns, and, once there, to do unspeakable things to her—by which I mean, literally, 'things for which we have no words.' My beautiful dove will not survive." His fingers brushed my wings and he yanked them back, as if they stung, putting them in his mouth. "Though perhaps she is not a dove, after all."

This last was spoken by a third voice, familiar and airy, that belonged to neither demon, though the mouth of the sable one moved. Hearing it made my heart sing, as if, amidst the winding labyrinths of dreaming, I had come upon a lost portion of my soul that I had not realized was missing.

"My sister is stronger than she appears," replied Mephistopheles.

"Not strong enough. Last time, she could hardly bear the Tower, even for a few moments," countered the third voice.

"Miranda has been in the Tower of Thorns?"

"I brought her there in a dream."

"For that, I should rend you."

"It was not my intention to bring her. Besides"—the voice sounded like the incubus's again—"you have already rent me once. Perhaps, that will do?"

"Perhaps."

The incubus's blood-red eyes drank in my face. "If Lilith captures her, call upon me. I will save her!"

"You?" laughed my brother. "Resist Lilith?"

The sable incubus rose catlike to his feet. "Thanks to your sister, I have a power far greater than Lilith on my side."

"And what power could that be?"

As he faded away, his voice lingered behind him: "Ask King Vinae!"

Before slipping into deeper dreaming, I wondered what secret Seir of the Shadows could know, that he could boast of resisting the Queen of Air and Darkness herself.

I WOKE to find that everyone else was asleep except for Titus, who stood watch. Apparently, my brothers had set a watch among themselves without including me in the roster. Not that I minded the extra rest, but it galled me to know that they had done this because they did not trust me.

Rising, I glanced down, and my heart stopped in my chest. In the small rocks and dust beside my sleeping bag were the tracks of demon feet, a large set and a smaller set.

It had not been a dream.

I moved to the ledge and sat gazing out at the mountains below. What was out there, I do not know, for my mind never beheld what my eyes saw. I was too busy contemplating other things.

Could Astreus still live? Could he have held out against the darkness, even without hope? Surely, that was his voice I had heard.

Such joy rose in me. I felt as if the peaks had fallen away, and I was flying; as if my wings could pick me up and carry me; or, perhaps, as if the sheer force of my exaltation was so great as to repel all misery, throwing me thus into the heavens.

The realization I had rejected in the City of Dis could no longer be denied. *I loved him.*

When had it happened? I had thought myself wiser than to fall in love with an elf. And yet, in the midst of this ecstasy born of hope, I could not find fault with my choice. I loved the elf who wished to free all others from the clutches of Hell. Who could be more fitting?

My joyous flight of fancy faltered. I had seen Mephistopheles and Seir. I remembered where they had been standing. This means my eyes must have been open, at least briefly—which meant that Seir could have seen that I was awake.

My heart dropped like a stone. I had not soared. I was still anchored firmly upon the ledge of misery. I had gone nowhere.

Was it so astonishing that the demon who had once been Astreus could reproduce the dead elf's voice? Seir had played yet another trick upon me. Most likely, he hoped I might be led to believe that some part of Astreus still lived within him so he could lead me to some harm—which meant Astreus Stormwind really was dead.

He must be dead, or Seir would not have allowed me to hear his voice. Seir would not have given me hope, if hope was real. He was a demon.

Once before, I had allowed Seir to pluck my heartstrings, when he resurrected the image of my dead first love. My error, in trusting the false Ferdinand, had stripped my family of their immortality.

I would not fall for his blandishments again.

But I still loved him.

Eventually, others began to stir. I rose to join them, folding up my blankets and putting them into a backpack which Mephisto had requisitioned from his seven hoods. The milk had spoiled during the night, despite the cold weather, but the wine and honey were welcome.

As I licked honey from my fingers, the latter part of the dreamlike conversation returned to me. A power stronger than Lilith? Ask King Vinae? What did it all mean? Vinae was one of the nine demons King Solomon originally captured—the one that had supposedly powered my staff—only instead, Ophion, the Serpent of the Wind, the ancient consort of my Lady, dwelled within my flute.

So, where was King Vinae?

CHAPTER NINETEEN

Prospero's Purposes

We pushed on, climbing and descending these heartless peaks. The mountains were an unrelenting gray-brown, the monotony broken only by changes in the type of terrain: sheer cliff sides of which to be wary, jagged boulders to scramble over, or loose rocks to avoid. As we struggled to navigate each new landscape, we reassured each other that the next stretch of path would be easier. Only, it never was. After a time, our muscles burned, our feet ached, and our supply of wine had run low.

A strange rumbling sounded, and rain began to fall. At first, this raised my spirits. I loved rain and anticipated that the coolness would be refreshing.

Icy cold slush fell from the sky. I loved weather, all weather . . . except for freezing rain. One never seems to be able to keep it away from one's skin, no matter how one dresses. It dripped under my collar, sending freezing slivers down the back of my neck.

I cringed all the more when I recalled that whatever was falling was, most likely, the product of some human sin and not water at all.

"Oh, this is just too much!" Logistilla cried. She beat her hands about her head as if she could drive off the rain. "How can we have weather in Hell?"

"Dante mentioned 'foul icy rain.'" Caliban had hunched his shoulders against the inclement weather but it did not seem to be doing much good. Water dripped from his nose. "But he puts it in the Third Circle with the Gluttons."

"Maybe it moves, like real weather," offered Ulysses.

"He said it was ceaseless," Caliban said.

"If so, we missed that, for which I am grateful," Erasmus sighed. "Let's find a place to get out of this and see if it passes."

* * *

WE found an overhanging ledge and huddled against the rough stone. The sleet barely missed us. Occasional gusts of wind blew the cold spray into our faces.

Gregor growled. "To quote Erasmus quoting Mephisto: what I need right now is a good whack from a cheer weasel."

"Of course!" Mephisto tapped his staff. "The cheer weasel! Why didn't I think of that?"

"You mean there really is such a thing?" Erasmus looked up in surprise.

I began to imagine that a rainbow-colored length of something leapt about upon the dreary gray rocks. Moments later, it was with us. The cheer weasel was as long as an ordinary weasel, but it was much fluffier, like the Persian cat of ferrets. Instead of brown or white fur, it had horizontal stripes of bright rainbow colors. It had eyes like shiny black beads, and its ears were unusually large. Instead of a little black nose, it had a huge red ball. All in all, it looked like a weasel designed by a clown.

"How . . . ghastly!" Logistilla drew back. Yet, after a cursory examination of the creature, she could not help chuckling.

"Here goes!" Mephisto called out, and he whacked Gregor across the face with the cheer weasel.

The cheer weasel elongated as it swung. Imagine swinging a creature made out of pompoms strung together by elastic. Its nose swelled, becoming even larger, and it let out a delightful noise like a child's squeaky toy. Gregor's face disappeared behind rainbow-colored fur.

Gregor squawked. Then, a smile began lurking at the corner of his mouth. A moment later, his face relaxed into an actual grin. "Interesting!"

"Does it really work?" asked Erasmus.

"Here, try it yourself." Mephisto whacked Erasmus across the face with the cheer weasel.

WHAT followed was a cheer weasel free-for-all, with occasional gusts of icy rain blowing this way and that. Each of us grabbed the weasel and whacked someone else with it. Being whacked with the thing produced a giddy sensation. First, I received a face-full of soft fur. Next, a happy tingly feeling started at the top of my head and spread down my spine until even my blistered feet felt cheerier. Two hits, and we were singing with glee.

And, once I got my hands on the thing, it was great fun to swing it and feel it stretch out as it struck someone else's face, emitting its funny, squeaking sound. I had the most fun whacking Mab and Theo and Titus . . . though the noise Ulysses made when I caught him full in the mouth with the rainbow fur was one I will remember for years to come. I would have liked to smack Erasmus with the thing, too, but the weasel must have sensed that there was not enough cheer in that particular desire, for it wiggled out of my grip. Then, Ulysses had it, and he was whacking Cornelius, who sat down, giggling like a schoolboy who had been caught doing something naughty.

After a time, our sides ached from laughing. Mephisto reclaimed the cheer weasel and draped it about his neck like a multicolored furry muffler. The rain had finally stopped. We set off again at a good clip, talking in overly loud voices, all speaking at once, as we discussed what had happened to each of us since the bridge. Whenever one of us began to lag, Mephisto would whip the weasel off his neck and smack the malingerer across the face with a mouthful of multicolored fur.

Conversation stopped for a time as the slope became steeper. We crested the saddle between twin peaks. It was cold and snowy, and there was no life anywhere: neither bird nor insect nor a single soul of the damned. Just rock and snow and horizon. Far below, we could see the curving highways of the Cloverleaf from Hell and some of the greenery of the nightmarish forest. Beyond that rose towns such as Infernal Milan, all of which looked like tiny models in a museum diorama.

Starting down again, we headed at a brisk pace for a pass Mephisto had seen in the ball. We surfed down a section of loose scree and then found ourselves on a downhill path that zigzagged back and forth across the slope. The long, shallow switchbacks made our downward progress extremely slow, but they also made this stretch of the path far easier than what had come before. We found we had some breath available for conversation.

Mab pulled out his notebook and flipped open to a blank page. "It occurs to me that this might be a good time to ask some questions."

"What did you have in mind, Detective?" Erasmus asked. He walked behind Cornelius, prodding him gently with his staff whenever the latter veered off the path. Our group still traveled in two sections, with Theo and Erasmus exchanging dark looks whenever they came near each other. "Anything is better than being left alone to contemplate our personal miseries in silence."

"I want to compile a list of the tasks Mr. Prospero gave each of you," Mab explained, scribbling as he walked. "Miss Miranda's duties, I know. She's in charge of Prospero, Inc. The company is responsible for making and maintaining contracts with spirits so as to subdue them and make the earth more amenable to human beings. Am I right? Or is there something else, too?"

"No," I laughed, though the cold wind cutting across my face did much to reduce my good mood. "That is quite enough."

"And you, Miss Logistilla?"

Cornelius cleared his throat. "I hate to curb your enthusiasm, Spirit Creature, but is this conversation wise? Would it not be better that we each keep our own counsel? Especially here in Hell, where our words could be overheard?"

"I wouldn't worry about that, Mr. Cornelius. Just take a look around." Mab gestured toward the empty barren rocks. "Even the demons don't seem to like it here. Not an imp or an incubus in sight! Might be the only privacy we get down here."

"Still," Cornelius continued, "I must counsel against spilling family secrets. There may be reasons why Father did not want us to share them."

Mab scratched his eternal five o'clock shadow. He now looked less unkempt than many of my brothers, since they had not shaved in several days. "I understand your reluctance, Mr. Cornelius, and I hate to be a harbinger of doom, but if we fail to rescue Mr. Prospero, and something happens to one of you . . . well, knowing what the dead guy's duties had been might become important to the survivors—and the human race."

Cornelius walked along tapping the stony path before him with his long cane. His head was tilted, as if in concentration. Finally, he spoke. "You have convinced me, Spiritling. The needs of the future outweigh any consideration of secrecy. Carry on."

"Good!" Mab grinned. "Miss Logistilla?"

"I make bodies for Father's 'great project.' Ouch!" Logistilla cried as Titus stepped on her foot. A buffeting with the weasel combined with the winds had loosened her hairpins. Her long black hair now flowed freely down her back. Titus braided it for her as they walked, except this meant that he kept treading on the back of her shoe. "I have to design each so that it matches pictures Cornelius brings me. I've gathered quite a collection of them now, waiting against the day when Father asks for them."

"Interesting." Mab made a note. "And the Perp . . . er . . . I mean Mr. Ulysses?"

"I nick stuff," Ulysses offered. Of all of us, he seemed the least disturbed by the cold and miserable conditions. He was shivering, but he seemed as cheerful as ever.

"You steal for Mr. Prospero?"

Ulysses shrugged. "You know how keen the Orbies are on keeping magic talismans out of circulation? Well, someone's got to be the one to pinch them from the current owners and put them in the Vault. That someone happens to be me."

Seeing us all staring at him, Ulysses gestured at his *Staff of Transportation*. "You don't think the Guv'nor gave me this old thing so I could impress ladies with the Hope Diamond at parties and imprison my favorite brother on Mars, do you?"

"How could Father condone such a thing?" Gregor demanded. "Stealing is a sin! It is breaking a Commandment!"

"Father seems to condone a great deal of things that don't sit well with the Commandments," murmured Theo.

Mab said, "Rewriting history, for instance. Isn't that Bearing False Witness?"

"I leave money!" Ulysses objected hotly. "Of course, I get to decide what the thing is worth, but I've taken quite a few appraisal courses, and I fancy myself a fair hand at estimating the value of things.

"As for the Commandments, I've never really put much stock in that sort of truck." Ulysses paused to glance around nervously at the striated rocks of solid misery. "Of course, I'll give it a great deal more thought, now! Definitely don't want to have to come back here! Still, I think I nab things for a good cause. 'Salvation of Mankind' and all that."

"How can you call yourself a Prospero and not honor the Commandments?" Gregor shook his head in disgust. Theo also looked appalled, but Erasmus chuckled. Theo frowned severely at Erasmus, and the two glared at each other until a turn of the path put a rock wall between them.

It was one thing for Erasmus and me to bicker; it was quite a different thing for Theo to be angry with him. While Theo was often grumpy, he was seldom on bad terms with anyone, except Mephisto—the two of them were forever sniping at each other, but it was a brotherly sniping, usually born of Theo's concern for Mephisto. This new tension between him and Erasmus, since we left Dis, was beginning to disturb me.

Meanwhile, Ulysses was saying, "Oh, I was devout enough when I was a lad, back when I lived with Guv'nor. But, then, all this traveling around . . . I'm good with places, but not with times—this was before these modern alarm watches—I started missing the occasional church service. Then, every other one and then, I plum forgot to go.

"Then, one day," Ulysses continued, "I read this article that explained how little independent evidence exists for the Bible, the New Testament anyway. Apparently, we don't have any contemporary sources, other than the Bible, for the existence of this Jesus chap. He's mentioned in some ancient books, Josephus and the like, but scholars discovered those references were forgeries added several hundred years later. So, I began thinking maybe this Savior chap never existed at all. Why should I have to go sit on a hard bench and hear some old bloke drone on about him?"

"That is our fault," Cornelius sighed. Then, he gasped as the rainbow-colored weasel whacked him in the face.

"No sighing or pouting!" Mephisto declared, wrapping the little creature about his shoulders again and feeding it a bit of honey from his pocket, which he had apparently filled with the sticky stuff. The creature nuzzled Mephisto's ear with its big red nose and licked him fondly with a thin black tongue. Meanwhile, Cornelius chuckled in spite of himself.

"The crime you're talking about, Corney, took place nearly two thousand years ago," Ulysses objected. "I'm still shy of my two hundredth year. You can't pin that one on me!"

"Me neither!" Mephisto shouted gleefully. He put honey on his nose and giggled raucously as the cheer weasel licked it off.

"By 'our,' I meant the *Orbis Suleimani,* which would include you, too, if you ever showed up for meetings." Cornelius addressed Ulysses. He tried to speak sternly but, due to the weasel's lingering influence, a smile kept creeping onto his face.

"Sorry, old boy, the schedule thing . . ." Ulysses waved a hand. "What do the Orbies have to do with all this Jesus stuff?"

"In the early days of the Christian movement, the *Orbis Suleimani* removed references to Christ and His miracles from historical documents, the same way they have removed references to other gods and magic," Cornelius began.

"The *Orbis Suleimani* weren't Christians back then?" Ulysses interrupted, surprised.

Cornelius halted in disbelief, his cane still dangling before him. "The organization was started by King Solomon of Israel!"

"Oh. Quite."

"As I was saying," Cornelius regained his dignity. "In the third century, a leader of the *Orbis Suleimani* known as Claudius Nocturnus was healed of a club foot. Claudius converted to Christianity and took the rest of the *Orbis Suleimani* with him. Once they became Christians, they regretted the work their predecessors had done covering Christ's trail—including editing Josephus—so they sought to undo the damage by putting back what had been removed. Only they had not kept proper records of the original wording, so they wrote their own version."

"So it was a forgery, but only because they were trying to replace the original reference, which they had removed?" Ulysses shook his head. "Far too confusing for the likes of me!"

THE easy but very long switchbacks ended, and we began traipsing straight downhill in single file. Across the valley into which we descended was the entrance to the pass for which we headed. It seemed such a shame that we had to descend all that way just to rise up again, but even with the influence of the cheer weasel, Mephisto could not get any of his winged friends to fly here. The moment he summoned them up, they began shrieking or shivering or curled up into a ball. The only animal he summoned up that seemed unaffected by the Mountains of Misery was the weasel.

Disappointed, we started down into the valley. Once we were underway again, Mab returned to his subject again. "So, Mr. Ulysses, you collect magical talismans?"

Ulysses nodded. "Exactly, taking them out of the hands of men and demons alike!"

"That is where the new items in the Vault came from!" I exclaimed suddenly, thunderstruck as his words finally registered with me.

"Right-o!"

"Wow. That's . . . amazing," I choked out.

A great many explanations for how new talismans, such as Gungnir, were making their way into the Vault had occurred to me. None of them had included the possibility that my wayward youngest brother was out there doing his part for the family.

Titus rumbled. "Ulysses finds them, and I guard them, making sure that no one, including Ulysses, can steal them. I also go to the location of a magical disturbance and stop it with the antimagical aspects of my staff . . .

Gregor's staff, now . . . but only if it's such a massive disturbance that it will still be going on once I get there, which is seldom the case, nowadays. Unless Ulysses happens to be nearby and can give me a ride."

"This job you were doing, keeping the magic guarded"—Mab fixed his eye on Titus—"it wouldn't happen to involve a dollhouse?"

Titus looked rapidly around at the silent skyscrapers, as if to make certain no one was listening. "Shhh! Do not speak of that here! It's your duty, now, Gregor. I'll tell you all about it, if we get out of here alive."

"Very well." Gregor nodded grimly.

"The Vault!" Titus struck his forehead with his palm. "Damn you, Logistilla! What a fool of a woman!"

"Please do not wish my sister any closer to Hell than she already is," Gregor growled, moving closer to Logistilla, who raised her nose in the air, giving Titus the cut direct.

Titus turned, towering over Gregor. "Did anyone explain to you that when *your sister* turned me into a bear, she left me that way for *two years*? During those two years, the work I was doing for Father went undone. I had been using my staff to guard the Vault and keep the demons from it. Who knows what might have gotten in there while I was gone."

"Seir of the Shadows, for one," I murmured.

"If Father had only told the rest of us about this," Theo frowned, "Logistilla might have known enough to see to the problem."

"Or she might have told Ulysses, and the demon they worked for," Erasmus countered smugly. "And they might have tried to kill Titus, too."

"Oh!" Theo looked embarrassed. "Good point."

As we climbed a steep incline, I thought about my recent trip to the Vault. At the time, I had wondered why the fourth pedestal in the Elemental Chamber was empty. Now, I knew where Ophion, the Serpent of the Wind, was. Rather than solving matters, however, this discovery had opened the question of what had happen to the demon whom everyone thought had been in the instrument.

If Father felt that each of Solomon's demons needed a keeper, so much so that when he decided to give up the *Staff of Transportation,* he went to the trouble of siring a son, Ulysses, solely for the purpose of giving the staff to him, then he cannot have left Vinae just lying around somewhere. He would have bound him into some object and given it to a family member for safekeeping.

Oh. Of course.

"It was King Vinae!" I declared.

Two things happened simultaneously. First, Erasmus spun around and stared at me, a gleam of great interest in his eye. Second, Caliban bent his head, so that his cheek and nose rubbed against his club, and made a low *shushing* noise.

"Yes?" Erasmus left the path and moved closer, over dangerously loose rocks. The gleam in his eye unnerved me. "What about him?"

"I was just trying to remember his name," I equivocated.

"Ah, Vinae." Erasmus stepped back onto the path. He pushed his dark hair from his eyes and smiled dreamily. "What I could have learned, what I could have achieved, if Father had allowed me even a few minutes with him! But Father feared Vinae. He'd had some kind of bad experience with the demon in his youth, and didn't trust either himself or me to be anywhere near him. Which is why I thought Father had relegated Vinae to his lesser function of calling up storms, trapping him in the *Staff of Winds*.

"Only, if Baelor's correct—and under the circumstance, there's no reason not to believe him—Vinae's not in your flute." Erasmus gave a light self-mocking smile. "And to think that all these years I envied you and coveted that instrument. What a waste of my energy! Still," he concluded, "King Vinae would have made an excellent *Staff of Wisdom*."

"There should be a lesson for you in there," Gregor said.

"I wonder where Father put him," rumbled Titus.

"Let us hope we find Father and can ask him," Gregor replied gravely. "The thought that there might be a demon lying about someplace unguarded strikes terror into my heart."

"Perhaps it's in the Vault," suggested Theo.

Out of the corner of my eye, I watched Caliban continue to pat his club and whisper to it surreptitiously.

So, I was right. It had been Vinae's voice that Theo heard instructing Caliban on how to escape from the lava. No wonder Caliban had struggled to save the club!

It made sense. Only someone with little curiosity and no interest in intellectual pursuits could be trusted in the presence of King Vinae. Oddly, it seemed as if the effect of carrying the *Staff of Wisdom*—the very same influence that might have led Erasmus, or even Father, to ruin—had inspired the dull-witted Caliban, until he grew to think and consider like any ordinary man. If so, in one elegant move, Father had civilized Caliban and hidden Vinae from Erasmus, trusting the whole matter, instead, to Mephisto.

Clearly, Father had not wanted Erasmus to know where King Vinae was, so I did not reveal the secret. Yet, I resolved to find a chance to get Caliban alone and question the club. Perhaps, I could get it to tell me what secret Seir possessed that made him believe he could stand up to Lilith.

Mab had been scribbling in his notebook as he walked. Now, he looked up. "Let's see, where were we? Anything else you do, Mr. Titus?" Mab asked. Titus shook his head. "Nope? Next . . ."

Mephisto raised his hand. "Ooo, oooh, pick me! Pick me! I catch stuff. You could call me the family recruiter. I tame monsters and get them to join our side. If I can tame 'em, they live. If not, it's off to Theophrastus the Demonslayer!"

As he walked, Theo was staring grimly at the gray rocks beneath his feet. "I grow apples."

Whack! Mephisto whipped the weasel off his shoulder, smacked it across Theo's face, and flipped it back again with a single motion of his wrist. The weasel issued its happy, toylike squeak.

"Ah! Mephisto, for Heaven's sake!" Theo laughed, rubbing his nose as if it still tingled. "What a startling sensation!"

Turning to Mab, he chuckled. "Before I became a farmer, I slew demons, monsters that Mephisto could not tame, and really nasty sorcerers. I also used to help intimidate spirits into submitting to Prospero, Inc.'s contracts. A lot of things were afraid of me for some reason."

"I wonder why . . ." Mab muttered beneath his breath.

Gregor held up a hand in front of his face, as if to block any incoming weasels. "Before my imprisonment, I fought witches, ghouls, zombies, vampires, and other foul creatures who could be driven back by holy means. I was also the official Prospero, Inc., oath binder. I officiated over the oaths sworn by our clients—a job that belongs to Titus now."

"Mr. Cornelius?" asked Mab.

Cornelius took a moment to answer. In the silence, his cane tapped regularly from side to side, feeling for the trail. "I run the *Orbis Suleimani,* which is charged with the task of upholding King Solomon's legacy and protecting mankind from magic. I also arrange for policy in various countries to favor us, when necessary." He jiggled his cane. "Recently, however, I have been spending more and more of my time growing identities for Father's 'great project.'"

"Growing identities?" Mab looked up from where he had been making notes. "What's that mean?"

"You know about Logistilla's part of the project?" Cornelius asked.

"The cavern of naked Italians? Yeah."

Erasmus snorted with amusement at that, and Logistilla sniffed in disapproval. Mephisto eyed Logistilla and pointed meaningfully at the weasel, nodding his head knowingly. She gave him a wide, fake grin. Apparently, that was enough to hold off the dreaded weasel whack.

"My job." Cornelius started to speak and then paused as the path dipped down into a shallow dell and then straightened again. When he had successfully negotiated the dip, he continued, "is to produce IDs for those bodies. Only, with computers and private detectives, providing a watertight identity is so complicated that Erasmus finally came up with the idea of starting each persona off as a baby. This way, we produce the correct paperwork at the correct age, so as to create a legitimate paper trail. When the imaginary person is an adult, the Aerie One who enters the body will never have any trouble producing valid ID.

"This sounds reasonable in theory," Cornelius continued. "In practice, it has turned out to be a nightmare. Each month, I must go down to a hospital and ensorcel a nurse into signing release papers for a nonexistent baby. Then, each of the nonexistent babies must have birth certificates, doctors' records, Social Security numbers, school records, et cetera. Many of which require that someone be ensorcelled with the *Staff of Persuasion,* which I must do in person." He held up his black wrapped staff.

"I could not do this without Erasmus's family. They do a great deal of the work. The doctors among them sign much of the paper work, and two are clerks in large public schools, which is a tremendous help. Nowadays, with the home schooling fad, it's become a bit easier—fewer people to enchant, but still, the whole project takes a great deal of effort and cuts into my regular work."

"That's why they're all Italians! Because they're all meant to look like part of Erasmus's extended family!" I exclaimed. My own identification was badly out of date. I wondered if Cornelius would help me obtain a new ID.

"Exactly," replied Cornelius.

"Congratulations, Erasmus." Mephisto raised a nonexistent glass. "Don't you owe us, like, a hundred cigars? I'd like mine to be chocolate."

Erasmus chuckled. "Mephisto, if we make it back alive, I will personally buy you one hundred chocolate cigars."

"And my buddies Theo and Calvin too!" Mephisto put an arm around Theophrastus and Caliban.

"I don't want one." Theo hunched his shoulders, shrugging off Mephisto's arm. "That molester of women can keep his cigars."

"And all your buddies, Mephisto, all one thousand of them," Erasmus promised kindly, but something sinister leapt in his dark eyes as they rested on Theo.

We had finished our descent and were climbing again. The pass lay just above us. The path ascended steeply upward. We began climbing. Within only a few steps, our thighs were burning.

We climbed for an hour and twenty minutes without speaking, pausing to rest only when we finally reached the pass.

As we rested, sipping wine, Mab reviewed his notes. "I never heard from you, Professor Erasmus."

"Me?" Erasmus leaned back. He was licking honey from the inside of a Ziploc bag Mab had lent him when the Maenad was among us. "I used to be the family sorcerer, seeking new arcane knowledge, locating wayward spirits for Prospero, Inc., to intimidate, and finding the talismans Father sends Ulysses to collect. I was also the family enchanter, hence 'Erasmus the Enchanter,' as I was called in yesteryear. I made magical talismans when we had need of them.

"I've hardly had time for that over the last few decades; however," he continued, "as I am Father's replacement for Theo and Gregor . . . so I've been fighting witches and slaying demons, for which I must admit I am sadly unsuited. Very good to have you back, by the way!" He bowed toward Gregor and Theo.

"You? I had no idea!" Theo blurted, red-faced.

"Surely, you didn't think Father was just going to let matters slide while you putzed around on that farm of yours? Oh, how important! Apples! Someone had to do your dirty work . . . Whoa! Not me! I wasn't complaining!" Erasmus cried as Mephisto whacked him with the cheer weasel. His voice rose into a high chuckle from behind the rainbow creature.

"I guess I thought it would be . . ." Theo paused, frowning.

"The *Orbis Suleimani*? Exactly right!" Still chuckling, Erasmus gestured toward himself. He pulled a piece of bright orange fur from his mouth. "And they gave the job to me!"

Gregor bowed in return. "Thank you, Erasmus. I believe Ulysses owes you some time. Feel free to call on him for assistance."

Ulysses opened his mouth to object, but then thought better of it and clamped it shut again.

Which Way I Fly Is Hell

We set off again, making our way over the large boulders that littered the pass. Here and there, a dead soul sat dejectedly, kicking his feet, or hunched against the bitter wind, brooding. A few huddled in crude rock huts.

We jumped from rock to rock, some of which were unsteady and flipped up under our weight, throwing us backward. In this fashion, I skinned my knee, Erasmus injured his ankle, and Ulysses banged his head rather badly.

After the ramparts came a very steep ridge. A path had been worn into the side of the ridge, but it was quite narrow and covered with loose sand that slid beneath one's feet. Beyond the path, the cliff fell away in a sheer drop. We hugged the wall, stepping with great care. Cornelius, who was used to being very careful with his feet, did better than the rest of us. But several of my siblings, particularly the ones who were not wearing their own shoes, slipped, nearly plummeting to their death. After the third misstep, Mephisto called up the hamadryad Kaa and made everyone hold on to him or wrap him around our waist. The snake's eyes rolled back immediately, and he slipped into a comatose state, but this did not impinge upon his usefulness as a rope.

We would have been lost without the cheer weasel. Several times, Logistilla burst into tears. Once, Ulysses began bawling, throwing his arms around Gregor and apologizing over and over again. Gregor patted his head and assured him that all was forgiven, but Ulysses continued to cling until Mephisto whacked him across the side of the head with the furry rainbow muffler. Another time, I noticed silent tears seeping out from under Cornelius's bandana. I nudged Mephisto and glanced Cornelius's way, and he, too, received a whack with the weasel. The tears stopped, but there were still two damp spots on the bandana just below his eyes.

I inched my way along the cliffside, impatient to be beyond these mountains and on to Father. To distract myself from the wretchedness of our situation, I contemplated the information that Mab had gleaned from my siblings. The entire exchange had been eye-opening. Not only Ulysses, but all of my siblings had been laboring away at tasks Father had set them. Yet, every time I criticized them to Father, he had said nothing!

Why had he not told me they were about his work?

A terrible feeling of loneliness and misery settled upon me, as if there were a rent in my soul—assuming I had a soul to rend. All these years, I had labored for Father, doing his bidding, carrying out his will, even when his instructions required that I address no one for fifteen years, or remain in a house while the city burned around it. And my reward for this exemplary service, I believed, had been that I was Father's confidant, the one with whom he shared his secrets, the one he relied on to carry out his most important work.

But that was a lie.

Whatever else I might learn from this point forth about my mother, my soul, whether or not I was under a spell, etc.—even if Father should turn out to be innocent of all other charges, myself free from spells, and his great love, Lady Portia, was my mother after all, the companionship I believed Father and I shared, where I served him, and he trusted me, would remain a lie. Nothing Erasmus could do—mock, sneer, or even strangle me—could hurt as much as this.

Smack! Soft fur that smelled of raspberry and licorice tickled my face, sending jolts of tingly cheer though my limbs. Despite the pain in my heart, I could not help laughing.

We had reached the highest point of the pass and were back on firmer ground. A knife-edged ridge ran between our current position and the last mountain we would need to tackle before we could descend. Unfortunately, a stiff wind buffeted the ridge, making the otherwise simple crossing quite dangerous. The sight was daunting. Nonetheless I could not seem to stop giggling.

"What a funny creature that weasel is." Logistilla observed me as if I were a subject in a scientific experiment. "Where did you get it, Mephisto?"

"At Santa's house," Mephisto replied, adding when Mab raised his eyebrow, "Not this time. One of the other times, when I went to talk to Astreus."

"Then, you knew?" I cried.

"Knew what?" Mephisto asked as he stepped out onto the ridge walking with his arms stretched wide like a tightrope walker.

I followed him, and the bitter wind hit me, ripping tears from my eyes. Suddenly, it was all too much. Tears poured down my cheeks that had nothing to do with the weather.

Here on the ridge, Mephisto dared not strike me with the weasel, which was beginning to look rather bedraggled. Its fur was now limp, and its big ears were sagging. Mephisto examined it, pouting. He kissed it gently. Then, he tapped his staff, sending it away.

"You knew that . . . t-that he'd been tithed!" I cried.

"Tithed who?" Mab inched along behind me. "What are you talking about, Ma'am?"

"Astreus!"

"Astreus Stormwind? The Lord of the Winds?" Erasmus barked a laugh. He was behind Mab, balancing carefully with his arms outstretched. "Don't be an idiot, Miranda. The elves don't tithe members of the High Council."

"They did so!" cried Mephisto, his voice filled with anguish.

"They tithed Lord Astreus?" Mab demanded. "Who did? When?"

I had forgotten that Mab did not know. He should have learned of this in a gentler manner, not shouted over the wind in the midst of Hell.

"Mab," I spoke loudly over the wind. I wiped my face with my satiny sleeve, which did nothing but spread the salty liquid around. "Pass me your earplugs. I'll give them to Mephisto. Mephisto, put them in your ears."

This took some careful maneuvering, but when it was done, Mephisto could not hear us.

I explained, "Mephisto swore an oath to Queen Maeve to bring him any part from any animal she chose. She asked for the head of Eurynome."

There was a collective gasp all the way back along the ridge, as each of my siblings grasped the significance of what I had just revealed. I paused briefly to let them digest the news and then continued. "In order to save him, Astreus brought Mephisto water from the Lethe, so that he would forget his oath. This protected him from Lilith's power. Should he remember, the oath becomes enforceable, and Mephisto becomes her slave."

"Which is why our brother is so scatterbrained!" Cornelius exclaimed from somewhere behind me. A glance back showed that he was crawling. Titus carried his cane. "And why he resisted all my attempts to teach him the Ancient Art of Memory. Every time his memory improved, he must have recalled the truth and sabotaged my efforts to help him!"

"Exactly," Mab replied.

"Lilith's arrival in the Swamp of Uncleanness now makes a great deal more sense," Erasmus opined.

"To punish Astreus for keeping Mephisto from her, Lilith tithed him," I continued.

"But . . . how could she! The High Council would never have allowed it," Mab cried. "They didn't know anything about Lord Astreus having been tithed at Christmas dinner!"

"They don't know," I choked, tears flowing freely. "Maeve threw a big party and announced that Hell had forgiven the tithe that Sevenyear. Then, she paid the tithe secretly . . . with Astreus."

"No! That's terrible!" Mab cried. "We've got to save him!"

I sank down until I knelt atop the ridge, stricken. Mephisto must have glimpsed me sinking down out of the corner of his eye, because he pulled out the earplugs and leaned over to comfort me. He had no trouble with the narrowness of the ridge, and could balance perfectly despite bending over.

"There, there," he said kindly, patting my shoulder. "Don't cry. There, there."

"We can't save Astreus," I bawled. "He's dead!"

"No! That can't be true!" insisted Mab.

Mephisto's face went very pale, and he grabbed my arm in a grip so tight it was painful. "What makes you say that?"

"Only hope kept him from falling prey to the darkness, hope that I would become a Sibyl and free him from his oath. When he learned about Osae . . ." I could not go on.

Burying my face in my hands, I wept.

SOMEHOW, we made it across the narrow razor's edge to where the ridge widened and we could walk two or three abreast. Our main problem was Mephisto, who had begun to move more and more slowly. His eyes became hollow, his expression blank. And a cold terror gripped us, for we had all seen this before. This was Mephisto in Slump, the dark morose phase of his erratic highs and lows; a phase that sometimes lasted for months.

We managed to shoulder him along over the more dangerous portion of the ridge, wrapping the limp snake around him to make sure we did not lose him over the side. Then the freezing rain returned. Icy water drizzled down our faces, finding its way inside our clothing. My hair lay slicked against my scalp and neck. I felt like a wet cat.

When we reached the safer ground, Mephisto mewed softly and collapsed. Once on the cold wet rock, he curled up into a ball, arms wrapped around his head. Nothing we did or said budged him.

We stood there, sopping wet, looking down at him where he lay, next to a boulder. Loose stones were scattered over the rock underfoot, which was striated with pale and dark gray, broken here and there by veins of quartz. The ridge was wide enough for four men to stand abreast. At the edge of the ridge behind us, the cliff sloped away sharply for some thirty feet before plunging, straight and sheer, down to the valley far below.

The rain let up, but we were still miserably cold. A gray mist hemmed us in on all sides, its dampness clinging to the backs of our necks. The wind gusted, granting us short glimpses of other peaks rising like stone ghosts. When it blew, it whistled loudly, an empty hollow sound.

"Let me carry him." Caliban bent over Mephisto; he touched his forehead and checked his pulse. "I have helped him through such fits before."

"No good." Erasmus shook his head. "Or rather, it's okay now, but what if the footing becomes more precarious? It's one thing to slink along a ridge or jump from rock to rock with someone clinging to your back. It's quite another thing to do so while carrying someone in your arms."

"Well, at least it's a start," snapped Theo, "and quite decent of him to offer. I haven't seen you suggest a better idea!"

Ulysses tapped his staff on a large flat rock. "I say, we could break into two groups. I could hike ahead with one group, touch my staff to some place up there. Then, I could come back here in the blink of an eye, gather you all, and take you instantly to the spot up ahead."

"That's a wonderful idea!" Logistilla clapped her hands. "Do go ahead, Ulysses. Take Theo, Miranda, and the rest. Titus and I will take care of Mephisto." She sat down on the boulder beside Mephisto.

"I'll stay here and help." Erasmus sat down beside Logistilla. The boulder sloped off on one side. He braced himself with his legs.

"I think not." Theo took a menacing step toward Erasmus. His shoulders rose into a wolfish hunch. "You'll come with me."

"Oh?" Erasmus got up slowly until he and Theo stood eye to eye. "Why is that?"

They stood too close together. Theo glowered at him; Erasmus's face remained calm. Both their eyes held that gleam men got when they saw a brawl in the offing and could not wait to charge out and meet it.

"Because neither of our sisters should have to make the extra trek, and, frankly, I don't trust you near Miranda," Theo said.

"Is your precious sister too fragile to make the journey, then?" Erasmus sneered. "Funny, I would think the daughter of the Queen of Demons would be heartier than the rest of us? Or are you afraid I'm going to mug her for her Water of Life?"

"Now, boys!" Logistilla laughed with false gaiety. She chafed her arms, sending water spraying from her wet garments. "Let's not fight, hmm?"

My brothers ignored her. They stood facing each other on the barren rocky ridge, teeth bared like mad dogs. The wind whistled past them. Theo's spiked black leather jacket made him look like a bristling timber wolf crouching before the attack, while Erasmus grinned like a sleek panther, the tails of his dark green jacket whipping noisily behind him.

"Now, brothers, let's not . . ." Titus's voice trailed off. He looked to our family leader, who lay curled up in a ball. Then, he turned to me.

"Should I stop them, Miranda?" he rumbled. "I could grab one of them, and Caliban the other."

I opened my mouth, but my throat was too dry to speak. I nodded. Beside me, Mab slowly drew out his lead pipe and laid it across his palm.

"Butt out, Titus." Erasmus did not glance toward us. "This is between Theo and me."

Nonetheless, Titus moved around until he stood behind Theo. Caliban, however, remained beside the curled-up Mephisto, oblivious to the brewing conflict.

Cornelius stretched out his staff, lightly tapping those who stood nearest to him. He wished to intervene, but there was nothing he could do. He could not see the conflict, and he could not use his warded staff to force his brothers to behave.

"Brother?" he called hopefully. "Erasmus? Theophrastus? I beg you. Do nothing foolish."

"What kind of a man attacks a woman?" Theo growled, ignoring Cornelius. "Your own sister, for Christ's sake!"

"It would be nice if family connections made a person immune from treachery, but we have Uncle Antonio's example to assure us that this is not so." Erasmus's voice dripped with spite like poison drips from a snake's fang. "Frankly, I'm glad I did it. Otherwise, we would not have known that our sister was a little demon bitch, who might revert to her mother's evil ways at any moment."

"You're crazy!" Theo shouted. His voice was shockingly loud in the hush of the damp mist.

The rest of us took a step back, even Titus. Cornelius flinched and threw up his hands as if to block a blow.

Erasmus, however, just sneered. "Am I? Look what she just did! She deliberately upset Mephisto and made him go catatonic, so as to slow us down. I wonder if she wants us to reach Father at all?"

I gave an involuntary cry of outrage. Though Theo did not turn his head, he heard me. A noise halfway between a steaming locomotive and an angry bear erupted from his throat. It rose in pitch like the whistle of a tea kettle. Cornelius covered both his ears.

Theo swung a fist at Erasmus. Titus caught Theo in a viselike hug, trapping both arms.

"This is for the lava tube." Erasmus punched him full in the face. Without pausing, he hit him again. "And this is for banging my head into the wall!"

Theo's head snapped back against Titus's plaid chest, once, then again. Blood poured down his face from his nose. His lip had split.

Shaking his arms free of the chagrined Titus, Theo murmured, "I'll get you later."

Titus was a head and a half taller than Theo and nearly twice as broad, yet his large face crumpled with fear.

"I didn't mean for him to hit you!" he cried. "I thought Caliban was going to stop him!"

Theo lunged forward. Erasmus backpedaled. A glance behind him showed that the ridge's edge was perilously close. With a sickly grin, Erasmus grabbed his staff from the boulder beside Logistilla. In the lull between gusts, we could all hear the familiar *hum*.

I gasped, unable to think of any way I could help Theo. My stomach clenched so tightly my abdomen felt as if it had turned to steel.

Erasmus flourished the *Staff of Decay* before him like a whirling gray sword. Snarling, Theo drew the metallic fore piece of his staff from off his back and parried. He knocked aside Erasmus's first thrust. Whatever the *Staff of Devastation* was made of, the metal did not dent or tarnish.

"Two can play at that game, Brother," Theo's teeth widened into a fierce grin, "and my staff is bigger."

"An empty boast, Old Man," Erasmus said, "as you would never use your staff on a family member. But I, on the other hand . . . I made you young; I can make you old again."

Theo reached up over his back for the lower portion of his staff.

"Titus, grab Theo again!" I barked out, my voice hoarse from tension.

Titus grabbed his arms at the shoulders. Theo's face fell. He had the look of a dog whose master had just betrayed him. All this had been his way of defending my honor against Erasmus.

"Father is waiting!" I gestured wildly toward the path ahead. "When we have rescued him, you can fight with Erasmus to your heart's content. I will even sew you a favor, if you like."

"Good enough," Theo said, his face suddenly sober. Titus let him go, and he started to resheath his staff.

Erasmus lunged forward, the *hum* of his staff audible to us all. With a bellow, Gregor knocked his shoulder into Erasmus. Gregor's red robes billowed about him like standards upon a battlefield. The blow threw Erasmus several feet. He stumbled, sliding on the loose rocks. Skidding right to the edge of the ridge, he windmilled on the brink, desperate to regain his balance.

Aghast, Gregor ran toward him, followed closely by Ulysses and Mab. Then, before any of us could reach him, Erasmus fell backward.

Hearing the commotion, Cornelius cried out, "Brothers? Sisters? What is happening?"

Erasmus rolled head over heels four times down the steep slope before sliding an additional twenty feet. He caught hold of a small ledge and clung to it. Half a body's length beyond, the cliff fell sharply away, and there was only mist.

I ran to the edge and threw him the snake. Erasmus glanced from the limp cobra tail to me and laughed, a cold unhappy sound.

"If you think I am going to trust my life to you, you have another think coming, Sweet Sister! I'd rather trust Theo!"

"Oh, let me do it!" Logistilla snatched Kaa from me and dangled the mottled brown hamadryad down the slope toward Erasmus. Titus stepped up behind her, put his arms around her waist, and grabbed the snake as well with his big hands.

"Actually, this is my bailiwick." Ulysses stuck his staff through his belt. He flinched as he laid his hand on the cold skin of the serpent, perhaps remembering his recent stint in the snake pit. "Logistilla, Titus, see to it you hold on tight."

Ulysses grabbed the snake with both hands and slid down the cliff. He let the slick reptile slide through his hands at high speed. My heart leapt into my mouth. He was about to slide right past Erasmus and plummet down the mountain. How could he possibly stop in time?

As Ulysses sped along, he reached down. Erasmus lunged for him. They grasped hands. My stomach clenched, waiting to see what snazzy maneuver Ulysses used to slow them down.

Only Ulysses did nothing.

They kept sliding. Ulysses pulled a startled Erasmus off the ledge and down with him. There was no way the hamadryad could stop their fall now, not without great harm to Kaa anyway. Ulysses was doomed, and he was dragging Erasmus with him.

The snake's tail came to an end, and my brothers plunged into midair, falling. My stomach dropped with them. Below, a long, long way down, mist swirled over a valley of rock and sharp boulders. I peered closer. Was it my eyes, or were the two of them glowing with a white light?

There was a brilliant swirl, and they vanished. A moment later, a second flash appeared atop the flat rock Ulysses had marked with his staff. Then, Erasmus and Ulysses stood among us.

Mab drew down the rim of his fedora, hiding his face. "Shoulda seen that coming."

"Me, too," I whispered weakly.

Titus gave a snort of amusement. "Come now. It was obvious."

Limbs shaky with relief, I rushed toward them. We all crowded around. Logistilla ran and hugged them both, the unconscious snake flapping behind her.

Erasmus hugged Ulysses as well, which took my younger brother by surprise.

"Thank you," Erasmus gasped. He was panting hard. The blood that had fled his face had not yet returned. His unfocused eyes were wild and unsteady, as if he were still seeing the rocky valley beneath him. "Though weren't you cutting it a bit close? What if your staff had not activated in time?"

"Nonsense." Ulysses brushed some chips of rock from his lapel. "I pull stunts like that all the time."

"My apologies, Brother." Gregor bowed from the waist. "I did not mean to strike you so hard, but it is unwise to use our staffs upon each other." Straightening, he lectured pedantically, "Remember what Malagigi told us. We must attempt to remain calm."

Erasmus had remained calm the whole time he fought Theo. He had remained calm while he slid backward and tumbled down the hill. He had remained calm while he hung from the tiny ledge. Upon hearing Gregor's admonishing words, however, the cords of his anger finally escaped his grip, flying off into the wind.

"Calm!" He raged. "Why? How much worse can it get? We are in Hell! Wherever we go is Hell! Every way we look is Hell!" He spread his arms wide indicating the ghostly mountains. A gust of wind lifted his dark hair and the lower portion of his dark green justacorps, around his hips and legs, so that he appeared to be soaring. "*Which way I fly is Hell; myself am Hell!*"

His voice rang throughout the hills, cutting through the damp mist and echoing back to us again and again: *Myself am Hell! Hell! Hell!*

With his lank hair blowing in his eyes and his handsome, pale features, Erasmus looked very much like Milton's wretched hero. Several of my siblings drew back.

I strove to keep my voice even. "If we work together, we can get out of here."

"Oh? Is that so? And for how long? A week, a year, a century, till the Water runs out?" Erasmus bellowed, the muscles of his face straining. I had never seen him so angry. "Don't you get it? We're all coming back here. That's the price of carrying our staffs. That's the price Father agreed to for saving humanity! All his children go to Hell!"

"That's not true!" gasped Logistilla.

"No, it's not. Don't listen to him," Theo commanded firmly.

"Yes it is," Erasmus shouted back. "Father told me this when I complained about not sharing the Water with the rest of mankind. He explained that magic was harmful to men."

"Told ya," Mab muttered to no one in particular.

Erasmus strove to control the volume of his voice, his effort visible upon his features. "Father's only giving it to us because he needs someone to carry the staffs. But he knows the price. Those who dwell too close to demons are damned. He put his own soul on the line to save mankind, and he signed us right up to serve beside him. When we die, we all come here—except maybe Miranda, who will come here anyway, due to her own infernal nature. That's probably why Father didn't give her a staff with a demon in it. Figured she'd be joining us in the family roasting pit anyway!"

For a brief instant, I felt sad that my staff was the only one without a demon, that I alone was excluded from this bond the rest of my siblings shared. It was a nonsensical thought, but the heart is a nonsensical organ.

No wonder Erasmus had stooped to drunkenness when he learned that the family supply of Water would run out! He thought all was lost. He believed that nothing waited for him in return for all his years of service but Hell. The angel had showed me that Erasmus's sin was despair. If what we had just glimpsed was the world he lived in, I was astonished that he could get out of bed in the morning, much less continue the brave fight against our infernal foes.

"Father couldn't have carried them all himself," Theo objected. "He would have been overwhelmed years ago. Someone had to help him."

"You!" Erasmus turned on Theo, screaming, "You coward! You chickened out. Too good for the rest of us, are you? You broke your promise when we needed you! Is your soul so important that all mankind should perish? Father didn't think so!"

Theo drew back, wiping away some of the blood that still flowed from his nose.

Gregor's voice sounded even more hoarse than usual. "We're not damned yet. So long as we walk the earth, there may be a way out."

"I thought so," Erasmus spat back, "until the hero ran out on us. I looked up to you, Theo! I trusted you! Mephisto's crazy. That made you the eldest . . . and you ran! Like a coward! What now? Is it all up to me? Then we're all certainly doomed!"

"You're right! I was an ass." Theo stepped forward until he stood nose to nose with Erasmus again. "I've come back. What about you?"

"What about me?" Erasmus asked, but for the first time, he sounded uncertain.

"What of this Brotherhood of Hope you and Mab told Eliaures about?" Theo continued, a hand pressed against his nose. "If what you told the Frenchman is true, then we are never really doomed. There is always a way out."

"Perhaps . . ." Erasmus's voice wavered.

"Of course there are ways!" Mephisto declared, his voice chipper and bright. "Angels help us!"

"Mephisto," Erasmus spun in surprise. "Y-you came around!"

Mephisto stood up and stretched, yawning. "You started acting like such a doinker, Erasmus, that I had to. I should spank your lily white tushie!"

"I've always thought mine was more of an off-peach," Erasmus replied dryly, his temper again under control.

"So, you would say your tushie is peachy?" Mephisto asked.

"Enough," Gregor interrupted, "there are ladies present!"

Logistilla laid her hand on Gregor's arm. "Oh, do let them prattle on, Brother Dear. It's impossible to be thoroughly miserable when people are talking about tushies."

From Hell's Heart, 1 Stab at Thee!

We crested the last peak. The mist had lifted. Overhead hung smoggy clouds illuminated by the same steely gray glow we had come upon elsewhere; only, beyond the Mountains of Misery, it was far brighter, moving across the sky like a silvery aurora borealis. Looking down, we could see a barren rocky slope covered with patches of dark fog and dirty snow. The snowy spots grew more and more numerous until they merged, forming a glacier. In the distance, rising from this icy expanse, stood the Tower of Thorns.

I screamed and clutched my eyes, which burned as if they had suddenly become filled with hot pepper. Several others screamed as well. Trembling, I wiped my eyes. Pulling my hands away, I found blood on my fingers, as I had in Astreus's dream. The thorns were so painful that merely the act of looking at them had caused harm. It was a good half an hour before I could see clearly again. The memory of my brief visit to that tower in Astreus's dream, when he accidentally swept me into his memory of having been tortured there, returned to me—with its terrible wrongness and unspeakable alien desires. A cold clammy terror gripped me.

WE rapidly descended the rocky slopes, stepping at last onto flat ground. What a pleasure to walk without having to check one's footing every step. I gave a great sigh of relief and rejoiced. Finally, we would be able to move more quickly.

According to the ball, we had spent over twenty-two hours in the Mountains of Misery and now had approximately twelve hours until midnight. By Mephisto's estimate, we were about three hours from where Father was being held, but that was assuming we could make good time crossing the field of ice.

A low moaning wind swept across the barren rock, pushing dark patches of fog in its wake. Its breezes carried an icy bite. Luckily our enchanted garments dried quickly, though I felt sorry for Theo, Ulysses, and Caliban, who wore ordinary cloth. They were shivering. Ulysses's lips had turned blue.

Overhead, hordes of horned goblins thundered by. Sometimes, they carried with them damned souls who dangled helplessly from their claws. Once, a great winged demon with the head of a fanged beast began circling the valley. Mab and Mephisto identified him as Sitri, a Prince of the Seventh Circle. Titus tapped his new staff, producing a dark fogbank of our own, and we headed out under the cover of darkness.

The rock underfoot soon changed to snow and then packed ice. The air grew colder, too. Icy winds bit into the back of my neck, sending goose bumps up and down my arms. The spells in our enchanted garments protected us from the worst of it, but Ulysses's teeth soon chattered so loudly that Mephisto began composing a song to the beat. Theo, who was shivering as well threw him a dark look. With an exaggerated sigh, Mephisto summoned up his Bully Boys and instructed them to fetch parkas. Twenty minutes later, he summoned them again. They dropped off three parkas, some sweaters, some hats and gloves, and a few scarves. Mephisto handed out the bounty, and the constant *ch-ch-ch* of teeth finally fell silent.

By then, we had reached the glacier proper. Unfortunately, travel across this icy terrain proved to be slow and treacherous. Fissures hidden beneath the icy surface constantly threatened to engulf us. We clambered over undulating wave ogives, rising to cross their snowy mounds and descending to pass over their dark rocky gullies. This was both dangerous and exhausting. More than once someone slipped, limbs sprawling as their feet slid out from under them.

We could hear the moans of sinners, but we could not see them. We were hemmed in by tall, pyramid-topped, blindingly white seracs that made it seem as if we were walking through the snowfields where frost giants grew the blades for their weapons. Some individual icy spires rose over a hundred feet.

My turn to slip came as I clambered down a particularly slick ogive. I would have fallen straight backward and smashed my head on the ice had Theo not caught my arm, steadying me. He looked a mess in his overly large parka. His eyes were black and blue, his nose and lips were swollen. Yet, to me, he appeared as dear as ever! Reaching over, I squeezed his hand. He squeezed mine back and smiled, though this caused him to wince. The

two of us continued together, helping each other across the more treacherous stretches.

As we crested one frozen wave, a ghostly serpent came slithering across
the snow.

"The Shape Stealers! They've found us!" Ulysses leapt onto Caliban,
who caught him, holding him like a child.

The serpent raised its head and swayed back and forth, hissing. Approaching it, Gregor knelt and inclined his ear, listening. His face was a
study of calm serenity.

"It is a messenger from Eliaures." Gregor stood again. "The Frenchman
sends the following message: '*Reached Milan. Our mutual friend here before
me. Headed your way. Big procession. Be wary.*'"

"That's clear as mud," Erasmus stuck his icy hands in his pockets. He
had not been lucky enough to score gloves, though he did have a red and
blue sweater and a green hat with a pompom. "Eliaures would have been a
menace had he lived until the age of telegrams."

"What in tar . . . creation does it mean?" asked Mab.

"By 'our mutual friend' does he mean Malagigi or Galeazzo?" I asked.

Theo frowned, "By 'headed your way' does he mean he, Eliaures, is
headed our way? Or that the 'mutual friend' is headed our way? In either
case, why should we be wary?"

"Why would Galeazzo have a big procession?" asked Logistilla.

Gregor questioned the snake again and then shrugged. "It is a sending,
not a real creature. I can get no more from it." Even as Gregor spoke, it
vanished, fading like mist.

"What was that snake thingamajiggy?" Mab bent down and sniffed the
ice where the thing had been.

I said, "One of the serpent sendings Eliaures was able to summon in life,
when he was a sorcerer."

"It's creepy, really, how many magicians seem to keep their skills after
they are dead," Mab shivered. "Don't seem right, somehow."

THE third time Logistilla slid and fell, landing hard on her bottom, she began to cry. Gregor and Titus went to her, trying to comfort her but mainly
getting in each other's way. Ulysses gave her a silken handkerchief upon
which to blow her nose.

"Oh, get away, all of you," she cried, driving back Gregor and Titus by
brandishing the greenish globe atop her staff at them. "You're a useless

bunch! Mephisto's the worst of all. Doesn't the *Staff of Summoning* have anything that could carry us over this horrible landscape?"

"As a matter of fact, it does!" Mephisto tapped his staff. "What a good idea! Don't know why I didn't think of that!"

I began to imagine a wall of matted fur rose from the glacier. Then, Mephisto's mammoth stood before us, the one I had glimpsed out in back of his house. It was a great brown furry creature with round ears as big as a large dinner plate and huge curving tusks as tall as a person. Its long flexible trunk ended in two almost fingerlike knobs. Immediately, it wrapped this appendage around Mephisto, embracing him mammoth-style and trumpeting its joy at their reunion.

Mephisto asked the creature to kneel, and we all climbed aboard, trying to find a comfortable spot. The creature's back, from the dome of its head to its rump, was a good twelve feet long and at least three feet wide. Eventually, we found that if we sat back to back and clung to the thick, woolly hair, we could steady ourselves and keep our seats. This was important, because when the creature rose ponderously to its feet, we found ourselves a good ten feet in the air.

The effort was worth it. The mammoth moved across the uneven field of ice with surefooted ease. Once we became used to the undulating motion, we found ourselves traveling in relative comfort, with the warmth of one another's backs to lean against, except for Mephisto, who rode astride the beast's head. Only the strong musky aroma of the oily wool kept the ride from being ideal, though after some of the stenches we had encountered in the last few days, the smell of mammoth seemed rather pleasant.

I was seated between Ulysses and Mab, with my back against Theo's. To my left, Mab surveyed the countryside; suspiciously, his eyes took in the miles of ice and snow.

After a time, he leaned over so that his mouth was near my ear. "A snowball'd have a better chance down here than I had thought, Ma'am."

"I WAS just thinking," Erasmus opined, after we had been swaying along on mammoth-back for half an hour, "about Ulysses's comment back on the Paths of Pride, when he said he was glad to have ended up among the snakes and not in the Endless Queue? Interesting, Ulysses, that you didn't end up in the Queue. Apparently, Hell is not about living our worst fears."

"I don't think it's even about punishment." Ulysses lounged against Caliban, with one crossed leg resting atop the other knee.

"Really? How so?" I asked. "It certainly seems like a ghastly place, all the torture and such."

Ulysses toyed with the fur cuff of his borrowed parka. "Certainly, there are individuals being tortured by demons and the like. But, I can't help feeling that it looks more like the strong preying on the weak, and less like the Big Bearded Guv'nor In The Sky picks on Mere Wormlike Mortal."

"Then what do you call all this?" Erasmus gestured at the snowy landscape, with its ogives and moraines.

"Wish fulfillment."

"Come again?" Erasmus jerked upright, causing Cornelius, who sat behind him, to throw his arms out and dig his fingers into the mammoth's long wool.

Ulysses shrugged. "It just seems as if everyone's being given what they asked for. You want to steal? Sure, go ahead. But everybody else around you wants to steal, too. You want to fight? You want to rule? Go ahead! But that's all you get. You don't get any of the good that, on earth, we expect to come along with it—the end we think these behaviors will gain us. Because all the good is up there." He pointed up. "To get good, you have to give it, too, or some rot like that."

"That's a rather deep thought for you," Gregor rumbled from where he leaned against Logistilla. His hands were folded in his lap.

Ulysses smiled and gave Gregor a friendly punch on the arm. "I jolly well couldn't have hung around with you all these years and not picked up something."

Gregor did not reply, but a slight wintry smile disturbed the grim symmetry of his face.

THE *click* of Theo's goggles woke me from a light trance. "I see a procession of some sort off to the left. It's traveling basically the same direction we are. I can't tell much about it from here, though. They seem to be carrying someone in a chair."

"Is it Galeazzo?" Logistilla asked hopefully.

A few more clicks, and Theo replied, "Can't tell. The angle's wrong. But, looking ahead, I estimate that our path will cross theirs in about . . . twenty minutes."

WE heard them before we saw them, a weird, eerie sound, like a marching band that played out-of-tune pipes and broken drums. The music was wild and sensual, such as a siren might sing to lure her victim, and yet it brought with it a sensation of fear and repulsion. No music on earth could have been simultaneously so beautiful and horrible.

I covered my ears, aghast.

Marching across the ice came a procession of men and women in ragged uniforms of various offices and walks of life. In their midst, a regal figure rode upon a sedan chair carried by brutish figures. Unlike the bestial and wraithlike procession members, this enthroned man was handsome, almost dashing—or he would have been, had part of his face not rotted away. I recalled that Abaddon had had a similar affliction.

Then, I made out his features, and I knew.

I knew who it was that had set Erasmus and me against each other; who Eliaures had found when he reached the ruins of Infernal Milan; who the Angel of the Bottomless Pit had meant when he claimed a traitor lurked within our family. As Mab had suspected, Abaddon had lied, and yet . . . there had been truth in his words.

"By all that's holy!" breathed Erasmus. He leaned forward for a closer look and nearly slid off the mammoth. "It's Uncle Antonio!"

I URGED the others to push forward without stopping. I wanted nothing to stand between us and saving Father. Mephisto, however, signaled to the mammoth to kneel. So we all slid off and moved awkwardly over the ice toward the procession. Uncle Antonio's bearers lowered his chair to the ground, and he rose to meet us.

"Nephews!" Uncle Antonio waved. He spoke in Italian. "Nieces. How fortuitous!"

Erasmus bowed respectfully. Mephisto jumped up and down, waving. Theo leaned on his staff and frowned. The others stayed back, never having met Uncle Antonio, who died before they were born.

I saw all this with my eyes, but my mind, which seemed to be moving slowly, as if in a cart pulled by a very elderly donkey, could not grasp it. My brothers were speaking to him? They were smiling at him? Had they forgotten that his was the hand that had slain my only hope of escaping a joyless, barren life?

Trembling with rage, I strode forward to confront him. My heart pounded in my ears, as if hatred had a sound like rushing waters. "Murderer! Vile monster! You killed Ferdinand! You exiled Father to that tiny

island, you plotted against the King of Naples, and you murdered his son!"
I thought but did not add "and my love!"

"Remain calm," Gregor whispered gently under his breath. "Remember
Malagigi's warning."

"So, you finally enlightened her, did you?" Uncle Antonio directed his
magnetic smile upon Erasmus, pulling my brother in like an iron filing. To
me, he merely gave a courtly flourish of the hand. "Guilty as charged. I did
slay the young whelp, and I plotted against his father, the King of Naples,
that I admit.

"But, exile Prospero? Quite the opposite! Prospero betrayed us! He tucked
you under his arm and crept away under the cover of night, taking with him
all our treasures. I had no objections to him taking Vinae, but he could have
left Paimon for me. Selfish knave. Would not even share with own his brother!"

"Father wasn't exiled?" Theo asked.

"Exiled? By whom?" My uncle spread his arms in an expansive Italian
shrug. "He was the duke. Milan was a sovereign state. Who was there to exile
him? No. He ran, the coward. He ran and hid and gathered his power. Then,
armed with his newfound knowledge, he came back, and used magic to wage
war against us, until he had remade the *Orbis Suleimani* in his own image."

"Why did Father do all this?" Gregor came up beside us, his face impassive. His half cape billowed in the icy wind.

"You must be one of the young ones." Uncle Antonio bowed. "I am Antonio, your uncle." He nodded toward the others whom he had not met, Cornelius, Titus, Caliban, Ulysses, Mab, and, finally, Logistilla, at whom he flashed
a charming smile. Logistilla lowered her dark lashes and smiled mysteriously.

Watching this exchange, I wondered if some illusion showed the others the missing portions of his face. I reached out and touched my sister's
shoulder. She gave a little gasp and jerked away from Uncle Antonio, repulsed.

Uncle Antonio turned back to Gregor and shrugged. "I know no more of
Prospero's musings than you, less most likely. At first, I thought King Vinae,
in some effort to put himself above his fellow demons in glory, had offered
my brother yet another gift. Later, we learned otherwise. Apparently, Prospero used the summoning magic Vinae taught him to call up some abomina-
tion. This wicked creature offered him yet more power, if he would betray the
rest of us. Probably, it was that witch who could control the moon, the one
whose bastard we found living on the island where Prospero was hiding."

"Or Lilith," Erasmus murmured softly, his dark malicious glance resting on me.

"While this is fascinating," I spoke through gritted teeth, held rigidly due to both anger and cold, "you killed Ferdinand!"

"And I am here to pay for my sins." Uncle Antonio gestured as if to take in all of Hell. "What more would you require of me?"

I stood mute, not knowing what to say to that.

"What is your position here, Uncle?" Theo eyed the motley procession with distaste.

"I am Duke of Infernal Milan."

"How is it that you are a duke, Uncle?" Erasmus asked. "That hardly seems like a vile torment."

"I am glad you asked," my uncle smiled at Erasmus as if they were comrades at a drinking party, "for it is thanks to you, Nephew."

"Me?" Erasmus asked, surprised and pleased.

"Indeed. Do you recall the kindness you did me on the battlefield, as I lay dying, my innards spilling out upon the earth? You soothed my brow and gave me a drink from your own wineskin. A bond was forged between us by your kindness. Because of that kindness, I escaped my torment, after many years spent trapped and freezing in a field of ice."

"Did my brother pray for you?" Gregor gazed at Erasmus with newfound approval.

"Not quite." Uncle Antonio smirked. "Not one to leave a kind turn unrewarded, I bent my will and sorcery to aid you, Erasmus. All the best moments of your life, I was with you."

Erasmus brushed his lank hair from his eyes and straightened his shoulders. Something hopeful flickered across his face, like the first breath of spring breeze after a particularly harsh winter. "Thank you, Uncle."

My uncle gave my brother a smile I did not like. "When your pride in your ancestry ruled your actions, I was with you. When you treated your soulless seal wives cruelly, as such creatures deserve, I was with you. When you denounced your scheming sister as a witch and a harridan, I was with you."

The color drained from Erasmus's face. "Those were hardly my best moments . . ." His voice faltered. His throat convulsed. "In fact, one might argue they were my worst. I learned during this trip that those poor faery women might have gained souls had I treated them with human kindness."

Uncle Antonio shrugged. "If God meant such creatures to have souls, would he not have granted them souls at the hour of their creation? Surely, you are doing His work by keeping such women from growing a human heart."

"You are vile!" Erasmus backed away, sliding on the slick ice. "This 'kindness' of yours has done me nothing but harm!"

Theo caught him, steadying him. I reached over and touched Erasmus's arm. He shrugged me off, but not before his back stiffened. He had seen what I had wanted him to see.

Uncle Antonio swaggered forward. "Shall I tell you how you helped me, Nephew? Oh, this will amuse you, of that I am certain! Listen closely and learn how you have benefited your fond uncle.

"When first I awoke, after my death, I found myself in the freezing ice fields where traitors are punished—not this ice. It's smooth and bluish and much, much colder. A wasted and inhuman place, where no care or human affection ever lingers. Not a place men, even dead men, should ever be." His face took on a strange, haunted gauntness as he spoke of his torture. I almost felt sorry for him. "For a hundred years, maybe twice that, I suffered thus. Then, one day—in the midst of this numb nothingness of ice—a woman of incomparable grace and beauty appeared. She came to me and spoke words of comfort, saying she would set me free, grant me power and honors, and make me Duke of Infernal Milan, if I would only agree to help her. All that was required was that I help destroy my hated brother Prospero and his despicable daughter.

"She explained she was Lilith, the Queen of Air and Darkness, one of the Seven Rulers of Hell. She wished to strike a blow against her nemesis, the White Lady of Spiral Wisdom. To do this, she needed a damned soul that had some bond of blood or affection tying him to Prospero and his daughter, her enemy's Handmaiden. Since I had in my heart a drop of affection for Prospero's youngest son, Erasmus, and since, even more importantly, Erasmus was fond of me but hated Miranda, I would do splendidly.

"The Queen of Air and Darkness was as good as her word. She freed me from the ice and made me the duke here. All she required in return was that I breathe hatred into my nephew and turn his heart against my loathsome niece. I objected when I learned that my actions might cause you discomfort, Nephew, for I am genuinely fond of you. You were kind to me, when you might have been otherwise, and made my last moments more bearable. However, Lilith made it clear that if I refused, I would return to that ice, forever. Reluctantly, I agreed.

"Thus, my sorcery restored, I have spent my days ruling over those damned souls who dwell here and working my magic against my traitor of a brother. I have whispered to you day and night, inflaming your hatred, reminding you how Miranda had robbed you, had stolen what was yours, had lied and abused and defamed you. Anything you might believe."

"My sister . . ." Erasmus swallowed as if his mouth were too dry to continue. "Did . . . did she do any of those things?"

Uncle Antonio raised his shoulders in another elaborate Italian shrug. "How would I know? Most likely, as she is her father's daughter, and he was a traitorous cur."

"But you don't know for sure?" Erasmus looked as if he had been punched in the solar plexus.

"Come, Nephew!" Uncle Antonio chided. "You should be grateful. I saved your life."

"How so?"

"Without the hatred I breed in your heart to give your life focus, how would you resist the terrible despair that threatens daily to consume you?"

Erasmus was now as pale as the souls of the dead in the procession. His eyes glanced about wildly, as if hoping that the rest of us had not heard this. Perhaps, he feared we would mock him, but I did not mock him. Instead, I remembered the afternoon on Father's island when all that had kept me from desolation had been my hatred of him. If he lived his life like that all the time, I felt very sorry for him indeed.

Our eyes met, and I saw him sway, as if one of the mainstays that held him up had been cut. It was not mockery he dreaded, but pity.

Uncle Antonio turned to the others, glancing from face to face. "Where is the blind one? I wish to pay my respects to King Paimon."

"I am here, but he cannot hear you." Cornelius tapped his way forward. He looked somewhat incongruous in his tailored suit and with a bright red and white bandana wrapped around his eyes. "He is bound and warded. Neither you nor I shall benefit by his company today."

"Ah, a pity." Uncle Antonio stared at the black-wrapped cane like a man coming upon the lover who had spurned him years before, choosing another in his stead.

"When . . . when did this start?" Erasmus croaked, his voice nearly too dry to hear. "This 'help' you have been giving me?"

"After Maria died," Uncle Antonio replied. "Before that you were not accessible to the Darker Powers." He leaned his head back and laughed.

"Oh, Sweet Maria. What good she has done our cause, and how she has suffered for it!"

"What do you mean?" Erasmus cried. "Surely, she is not down . . ." His voice trailed off.

"Down here? No. She is on earth. She lives in Poland, where she is a sixty-three-year-old widow, mother of four."

"Excuse me?" Erasmus asked, shocked.

Uncle Antonio leaned toward him, his dead eyes filled with malice. "Maria loved you so much. Such pity did she feel for your sorrow over her death that she had herself reborn and came back to be with you."

"People can live more than one life?" Gregor interrupted skeptically.

"Some do," Uncle Antonio replied with a shrug. Turning to Erasmus, he continued, "This was in the early eighteenth century. You met, but you spurned her because she reminded you of your lost love, and you could not bear the pain of it. She spent the remaining days of that life in a convent."

"What?" Erasmus pressed the back of his hand to his mouth. He seemed to be swaying. "Oh! If I had only . . ."

"Oh, there's more," Uncle Antonio continued. "Undaunted, she tried again. The second time, you married her—remember Helena?—but you treated her coldly because you felt she did not measure up to your real wife, her previous self. The third time, you used her cruelly and would not wed her. Her name was Natalia then. Ah, I see you remember her, too. After that, Maria gave up. She asked to be granted a life that had nothing to do with you."

"No!" My brother's legs wobbled and then gave out. He collapsed to the dirty snow. Hiding his face in his hands, he wept, a harsh and heart-raking sound.

Much as I hated him, my heart ached for him. Learning that he had spurned the very woman he had loved so all-consumingly was very possibly the worst moment of his long, immortal life.

Uncle Antonio leaned over my weeping brother. He seemed taller, as if Erasmus's defeat gave him strength. "That was my greatest victory," he chortled, "hardening your heart toward her. Had you allowed yourself to love again, you would have been lost to me!"

Erasmus pounded on the snow. Sharp shards of ice cut his hands. Red blood stained the ever-present white.

Mephisto stepped between Erasmus and my uncle. "That's enough, you bully! You leave my little brother alone!"

"Ah, Mephisto. Lost your marbles, have you? A shame. You had such promise in your youth! And look at you now, pale and pathetic. An insult to the demon after whom you were named!"

Mephisto held up a finger, objecting. "Um, actually, I think he was named after me."

Ignoring Mephisto, Uncle Antonio sneered at Erasmus. "You could have been great, Erasmus, had you not allowed despair to rule you. You could still be great, if you listen only to me." He leaned around Mephisto. "All other hope has been lost. Why not throw in with me? Join me, as my right-hand man. All I ask in return is one little thing, that you surrender your whole soul to hatred."

Erasmus, his face in his hands, rocked back and forth, wailing. Cornelius moved forward and sought to comfort him, but Erasmus's rocking shoulder kept escaping his hand.

Mephisto gazed at Erasmus. His face darkened. Putting his hand beneath his enchanted surcoat, he shoved Uncle Antonio through the enchanted cloth, sending him sprawling. Servants from the procession rushed forward and helped my uncle to his feet. As Uncle Antonio rose, Mephisto seemed to grow taller. His hair stood on end, and his eyes shone with a sapphire light.

In a great voice, he cried: "Leave my little brother alone!"

Uncle Antonio stepped back, alarmed. "What witchery is this?"

Gregor stepped forward and laid a hand on Mephisto's arm. "Calm yourself, brother."

"Worry not!" Uncle Antonio told Gregor. "I fear not this lunatic. What weaklings Prospero bred! Even from here, from the depths of Hell, my magic has proven the stronger! He always was a fool, my brother. He shall die a traitor's death, and I shall be the victor!"

"Victor over what?" I gestured at our horrible surroundings. "This?"

"You visited my Infernal Milan. Have you ever seen a finer kingdom?" My uncle's eyes glittered with pride and something else, as if he was rejoicing in having won away from us a kingdom he thought was ours. "Or a handsomer people. Oh, I grant you that your Theophrastus has done it a poor turn, but I am assured it will soon be restored as it should be. And, tonight, I finally realize my long-sought dream! Lilith has promised that mine shall be the hand that kills Prospero!"

He could not see it! The city we had seen with the blood and fungus and horror was invisible to him. In his deluded eyes, Infernal Milan was as beautiful as real Milan, with healthy and prosperous citizens.

My heart ached. My uncle was a murderer and a practitioner of the dark arts. He had set Erasmus and me against each other, nearly causing the downfall of our family and of the entire human race. And yet, in the end, he was still family. A bone-freezing cold, worse than the biting wind of the glaciers of hell, froze my limbs. I hated the demons for what they had done to him.

Stepping forward, I put my hand on his shoulder. My hand sank into him, but it had the desired effect.

Uncle Antonio stumbled backward as he beheld his procession, crying wildly, "What horror is this?"

"These? These are your subjects." I spoke forcefully. "You kingdom looked just as dilapidated, even before Theo destroyed it! These followers are what you have gained in return for betraying your kin. Was it worth it, Uncle Antonio? Was this worth betraying your family? Was it worth Ferdinand's life?"

Uncle Antonio stared around in revulsion, gasping in horror as his hand came in contact with his damaged face. His words barely escaped his horror-strangled throat. "She tricked me! Lilith has tricked me. No! It cannot be!"

His eyes then focused upon me. "It must be you who is tricking me. You sly daughter of a witch! You shall never be a Sibyl, you stupid girl. I have seen to that! No woman who is consumed with hatred for her own brother will ever feel the grand compassion required of Sibyls! Thanks to Queen Lilith and her Unicorn Hunters, Eurynome shall never have another Sibyl—not you, not anyone!—and the elves shall pay their tithe to Hell forever!"

He slapped me across the face. It did no damage, of course. His hand passed through me, but the sensation was unpleasant. My wings flared more brightly. Behind me, I heard the soft hum of Theo warming up his staff. But Mephisto acted first.

Bellowing, he swelled up. His skin turned dark. His clothes ripped. Dozens of sharp curling horns sprouted from his head and wings sprang from his back. Shaking off Gregor's hand, he pushed Gregor and me behind him. Then, he spread his enormous bat wings, shielding all of us.

"Prince Mephistopheles!" My uncle's damaged face trembled with awe. "But you cannot be!"

"Finally. Someone has recognized me!" My brother the demon took a menacing step forward. He raised a jet hand tipped with claws of glowing ruby.

Uncle Antonio threw his arms before his face, crying, "Lilith! Aid me!"

Leaping back into his sedan chair, he gestured frantically for his bearers to lift him.

"Run!" he cried. "Quickly, my people, run!"

The very notion of this large ponderous procession fleeing was a farce. They were surrounded on all sides by uneven ice floes. With a single beat of his great bat wings, Mephistopheles could have descended upon Uncle Antonio and his entire entourage, if he had wished to. He did not. Instead, as the procession turned and darted away, their disturbing music even more discordant as they rushed to put distance between us and them, my brother the demon swiveled and fixed his glowing sapphire eyes upon us.

"Come, Brethren, we must flee! Our uncle has called the Queen of Air and Darkness."

The rest of us, except for Erasmus and Theo, ran toward the mammoth, but Theo raised the *Staff of Devastation* and pointed it steadily at Mephistopheles's heart. "Tell me why I shouldn't send you to Kingdom Come as well, Demon?"

Rushing back, I jumped in front of Mephistopheles, spreading my arms. "Theo! It's Mephisto!"

Theo scowled. "Miranda. It's a demon."

"But that demon is our brother!"

"Then, Abaddon was right. There is a traitor in our family," Theo said.

"Yes!" I screamed, pointing at the fleeing crowd. "It's Uncle Antonio!"

Mephistopheles crossed his great black arms. "Shoot if you wish, Good Brother, and I will go to the Kingdom of which you speak, in which case, I will not be of much use to anyone down here, will I?"

"A demon? To Heaven?" Gregor came back to stand beside the fallen Erasmus, whose blood was still seeping from his lacerated hands.

Mephistopheles swiveled his horned head and fixed his sapphire eyes on Gregor. "You think because the Hellwinds set me in the Swamp of Uncleanness, that my end will be that unpleasant place? My soul is weighted with lust, it is true, but my sins are not so heavy as to draw me Below. Purgatory, maybe, but no lower. I am Heaven's servant through and through." My brother smiled, showing sharp white fangs. "You may consider me a double agent."

"Impossible!" Theo insisted. "Don't listen to him. He's trying some kind of trick."

"Shall I tell you how it came about?" Mephistopheles asked. "After I used the Seeing Sphere of Horus the Wise"—he hefted the crystal ball—"to achieve a position in Hell, I found myself upon a downward spiral. For it was not enough to gain a position in Hell, one must be consistently sinning and showing one's badge of crimes and ills in order to maintain one's rank. Very quickly, I found myself within traps from which I could not extricate myself. My clever plan had proved foolish and empty. I was lost.

"And yet, despite the crimes I was committing, my allegiance was still to Heaven. I wanted to do good, to help mankind, and, most of all, to protect my family. The next time the angels harrowed Hell, I threw myself down upon my face before them and asked for forgiveness.

"They raised me up and took me to another of their order, a five-winged Virtue, whom they said was responsible for my soul. She sat enthroned upon a scallop shell, with crowns of cloud and sea spray hovering above her brow. In her lap, the way a mundane king might hold a scepter, she held the earth. Gazing upon it, I could see the motion of the clouds and the tides.

"It burned me to be near her, and the light of her halo was fearsome to behold, for it was too bright for my eyes. Yet, I stood my ground, waiting to hear what fate she held in store for me.

"In a voice like unto a living flute, she greeted me as one of Solomon's Heirs. Those who dwelled Above, she explained, had great trouble approaching those who dwelt in Hell. Either the damned were unable to see them, or the angels were too bright for their sinful eyes to look upon. However, the angels, ever vigilant, have not turned aside from their duty to guard and lead mankind.

"In order to aid those whom they could not reach themselves, the angels employed emissaries, individuals who have not yet left their sins behind, who can be seen and heard by those below. The Brotherhood of Hope is one such effort.

"The angel gave me a choice: I could depart, leaving my infernal princedom behind and return to the world of the daystar. Or, I could remain a Prince of Hell and serve the angels, addressing those who could not hear them directly upon their behalf. The choice was mine.

"I struggled with this choice. On the one hand, I wished to serve the angels and undo some of the damage I had done. On the other hand, my duty to my family weighed keenly upon me. When I was Below, I was unable to protect them, to watch over them—and some of them dearly needed watching over!" Mephistopheles's great sapphire eyes rested upon myself and Erasmus. "So, I sought a boon. I asked that if I agreed to become their servant, and spend some of my time below, doing their bidding, that they would undertake to aid me in my effort to protect my family.

"The angel agreed. When my family was in danger, she promised, angels would warn Theophrastus, who—of all my siblings—could hear their celestial voices the most clearly."

"M-me?" Theo's arms holding the staff sagged. His jaw literally hung open. "You mean the Voice that tells me when family members are in danger? All these years, I've been listening to the voice of an angel sent by Mephisto? Mephisto!!"

Theo stood a moment longer, stunned with wonder and confusion. Then, he fiddled with the control collar of his staff, separated it back into two pieces, and stuck it back over his shoulder.

"So that's how you knew when to come rescue Miss Miranda!" Mab exclaimed. He had come up behind me. "I remember Mephisto said something about it having been angels. But then Mephisto says a lot of things."

"Mephisto?" Theo murmured for a third time, flabbergasted.

Caliban came crunching across the snow. He walked up and laid a big meaty hand kindly upon the demon's shoulder. "Time to come back to earth, Master."

Putting his hands behind his back, Caliban took a deep breath and sang:

> *The master, the swabber, the boatswain and I,*
> *The gunner and his mate*
> *Lov'd Mall, Meg and Marian and Margery,*
> *But none of us car'd for Kate;*
> *For she has a tongue with a tang,*
> *Would cry to a sailor, Go hang!*

Mephistopheles cocked his head to listen to the singing. As he listened, a playful smile shanghaied his demon face. He grew smaller and pinker until he was his normal self again, puzzled and blinking. Lifting his voice, Mephisto joined in, singing the song, made immortal by *The Tempest*, the song he had been singing when Mab and I first encountered him in Chicago:

> *She lov'd not the savor of tar nor of pitch,*
> *Yet a tailor might scratch her where'er she did itch:*
> *Then to sea, boys, and let her go hang!*
> *Then come kiss me, sweet and twenty,*
> *Youth's a stuff will not endure.*

Cornelius came tapping across the ice and joined in the song. Logistilla did, too. She knelt beside Erasmus, hugging his shoulders. When he lifted his head, much surprised, she wiped his face with Ulysses's handkerchief, which she pulled from her sleeve.

"There, there, Dear Brother," she cooed. "We all have bad centuries now and then."

CHAPTER TWENTY-TWO

The Staff of Wisdom

As we began lumbering forward on mammoth-back, moving across the glacier, a great voice cried out: *"Beware! The Queen of Air and Darkness approaches!"*

Immediately, Titus tapped his staff on the sole of his shoe; black fog smelling of newly lit matches billowed from the *Staff of Darkness*. Mephisto signaled for the mammoth to kneel. Once we were on the ice, he sent it away, so that we did not need to hide it as well.

We crouched together, peering up nervously. Before the dark cloud thickened, we caught glimpses of Lilith in her horrible chariot flying across the gray sky.

"Whose voice was that?" Erasmus whispered urgently. "Who warned us just now?"

No one answered, but Caliban crouched near me. I could make out his silhouette in the green light shed by my wings. From the sounds he made, I suspected he was hiding his club behind his back.

We knelt on the snow, shivering in the darkness, though there was an emerald glow around my wings and the top of Logistilla's staff. Theo crawled up beside me and pulled me against him, so that my head rested on his shoulder. He rubbed my back fondly, his face angled up, as if he were straining to catch sight of any threat through the darkness. Mab sat nearby, flipping his lead pipe in his hand. I could hear the *swack, thlip, swack* as he caught it, released it, and caught it again.

Overhead, some flying thing screeched, followed by a rush of wings. We held our breath. Should Lilith detect that our cloud was somehow different from the other black fogs, we would be sitting ducks, unable to see her coming.

Twice, then three times, the screeches and flapping grew near, as if the

Queen of Air and Darkness were circling the valley. We waited, silent and motionless, except for Ulysses, who gave a low moan of fear. I wondered if one of our siblings had taken away his staff, as he did not teleport away.

Eventually, the flapping retreated.

"Is the coast clear?" Caliban asked.

"*Lilith has departed*," boomed the great voice.

I recognized the voice. It was the voice that had cried out during the battle by the Bridge over the River Styx, warning us of the corrosive properties of Focalor's armor.

Titus rapped his staff against the stone, turning it off. The darkness would soon disperse in the breeze.

"Yahoo, Lilith's gone! She doesn't know where we are, nana nana boo boo!" sang Mephisto. I could hear his feet tapping on the stones as he danced.

A new voice spoke out of the darkness, soft as silk, sending sensual ripples from the crown of my head to the soles of my feet. "I shall tell her though . . . unless you return what should be mine."

"Seir of the Shadows!" Mab hissed.

I drew my fighting fan and leapt to my feet. Around me, I could hear the others pulling their weapons and readying themselves. Theo grabbed my arm and maneuvered me behind him, so that we stood back to back, facing in opposite directions. Mab stepped into the emerald glow cast by my wings and joined us. Now, the three of us stood with our backs to one another, facing outward.

"Go away, Inkie!" shouted Mephisto. "Nothing here belongs to you."

Seir's voice came lilting through the gloom. "Oh, but it does. A certain darkness-issuing staff that I accidentally left in Miranda's boudoir. If I do not return with it, I will be severely punished. I am sure that the argument 'but I was overwhelmed by the sweet charms of a certain lady' will not go far with the Queen of Air and Darkness."

"What was an incubus doing in your bedroom?" Logistilla cried, appalled. "Don't tell me you succumbed to his blandishments!"

"Certainly not!" I exclaimed, exasperated.

Seir laughed. "Oh, but we did spend the night together, did we not, my sweet? I remember it all so well: the firelight, the taste of your kisses, the intimate details about your family you confided to me, the secrets of the *Orbis Suleimani* you whispered into my ear . . ."

I heard Cornelius's sharp indrawn breath.

Theo stiffened. I felt him move, and heard the soft whine as his staff began warming up. "Enough of this. Stop besmirching my sister's name!"

"Did you really kiss him?" Mephisto chimed in. "What was it like? I hear kissing Inkies is just glorious!"

"I thought he was Ferdinand." My cheeks grew uncomfortably hot.

"Tricked by an incubus, really!" Logistilla huffed.

"Seir suckered!" Mephisto responded gleefully.

"You could not have had Gregor's staff all that time, Miranda!" Erasmus exclaimed. "I carried your things from my house myself. It was not among them."

"No, Seir left the staff on Father's Island, just before the angel came."

"Was that the same angel you told me about?" Seir's voice flowed as sweetly as syrup. "What was her name? Oh, yes: Muriel Sophia."

"Miranda! You didn't!" Erasmus shouted.

Cornelius's voice shook with rage. "Since the time of Solomon, we have kept secret the name of the guardian of our order, and you blurted it out to the enemy?"

"No, Cornelius." I pressed a cool hand against my burning cheeks. "All I said was that I met her once."

"She speaks the truth, my blind buffoon. I had no notion that this was the coveted name of the angel who protects the Circle of Solomon until you told me yourself, just now." Seir's voice had moved closer. "But I thank you for sharing this pearl of wisdom with me. Queen Lilith will be pleased. So pleased, she may forgive me for losing the *Staff of Darkness*. So, I shall depart, for I doubt words alone—even my honeyed words—shall win me back the staff."

"Where is he?" Theo asked. His staff began to hum. "It's pitch-black over there. Is everyone out of the way in that direction?"

Logistilla said, "Are you crazy, Theo? How in the would could we tell what direction you mean by 'that' one?"

"So for now, Miranda," Seir sighed, "I will away, but know that each moment we are parted, I shall be planning for our next delight. For I love you with all my heart and cannot do otherwise . . ." His voice softened, "Being who I am."

"All Inkies love all women. Isn't it romantic?" Mephisto piped cheerfully, but I was left with the eeriest feeling Seir had meant something else entirely.

The wind picked up, and the darkness began to blow away. I found myself face-to-face with Erasmus and Cornelius. My cheeks still aflame, I asked roughly, "Is there even any point in my trying to defend myself?"

"All these many years, all our precautions, all for naught." Cornelius wrung his hands. There was a tear upon his cheek, just below the bandana, which was damp below his eyes. "If the demons know which angel we call, they can trick and beguile us, coming to us in her guise and misleading us with false prophecies. We are lost."

I expected venom and fireworks from Erasmus. But he merely sat down on a boulder and leaned forward, resting his head on his knees. He looked haggard, as if he had turned his staff upon himself and aged two decades.

He said flatly, "I don't know what to think anymore."

MEPHISTO summoned up the mammoth again, and we continued our trek toward Father. We moved more quickly this time, for the mammoth found a medial moraine running the direction we wanted to go. Climbing up onto this icy ridge, it walked along its flat rounded length at a good clip, much more quickly than a man could cross this terrain. Very soon, Antonio's procession fell away behind us.

Eurynome shall never have another Sibyl, and the elves shall be forced to pay their tithe to Hell forever.

It was not just me. The existence of all Sibyls was under attack. No wonder I had not been able to find any Sibyls, even though their access to Water of Life should have made them immortal. The Queen of Air and Darkness had murdered them!

She had even tried to kill me, or her Unicorn Hunters had, back during the reign of Queen Elizabeth the First. Only the vigilance of my brothers and the might of their staffs had saved me. How many other attacks upon me through the centuries might have been orchestrated by Lilith? I wept the death of my fellow servants of Eurynome, all those brave Sibyls and Handmaidens who had not been so fortunate as to have a staff-wielding family— not to mention a guardian angel—to protect them.

If Lilith was my mother, she did not seem to be happy about it. Could it be that she did not know? I could understand how fathers might not know their own children, but mothers? You think they would at least have a clue.

One phrase of Antonio's echoed through my thoughts again: *No woman who is consumed with hatred for her own brother could ever feel the grand compassion required of Sibyls.*

I thought back to the young boy who had guided Cornelius, the boy who was apparently Erasmus's direct descendant, to Caurus, to the elf maid in Father Christmas's kitchen, to the young woman in the plum parka at the Lincoln Memorial, to the old lady crossing the highway in Chicago . . . all the way back to the moment in the Great Hall when I decided to save Mab. The words of the *Book of the Sibyl* returned to me: *To look into the eyes of another and see one's self: this is the greatest of gifts, the true Gift of the Sibyl.*

After five hundred years, I had finally gained one of the necessary pre-requisites for Sibylhood: the great compassion—empathy for others. And to think that I had feared I was under some kind of attack!

Hot tears streamed down my cheeks. Softly, I cursed Osae the Red for what he had stolen from me. Then, I cursed Seir, for I would never have al-lowed Osae to approach, had he not looked like Ferdinand. Of course, I would never have trusted Ferdinand, if flashes of Astreus had not shone through—I thought of the moment by the hearth at Prospero's Mansion, when his Ferdinand mask slipped, and he spoke of "the time when the truth would be known about the queen." That was what betrayed me. I recognized that as a moment of true sincerity and, thus, was taken in by the rest.

And yet, I could not bring myself to curse Astreus.

THE white expanse of snow went on and on. I stared ahead into the icy vista, squinting, as if that could somehow help me see Father more quickly. I could not wait to see his dear face, and yet, thinking of my father left me confused and disoriented. Whom should I be picturing in my mind: the wise, loving man I thought I knew? Or the subtle, deceptive man whom others claimed him to be?

Father had devoted his life to keeping the supernatural from dominat-ing mankind. This duty ran counter to his true interest, which was to delve into the secrets of the universe and uncover the hidden nature of things. For him, subduing spirits and dangerous entities was not difficult, but pro-tecting humans from magic also meant stopping others from using sorcery.

Father was a compassionate man. He found this obligation especially burdensome and often grumbled to me about it. He understood exactly why a man or woman might wish to delve into the mysteries of the occult, and he hated to put an end to such pursuits. At times, a budding sorcerer could be embraced within the *Orbis Suleimani*. Not everyone was suited to join; how-ever, some were too independent, too selfish, too unwilling to hide their successes from the eyes of their fellows, or merely female. Women were not allowed. Then Father faced the quandary of having to prevent another from doing what he himself loved best.

This weighed upon him, and yet he did not allow it to diminish his *joie de vivre*. He had a keen sense of humor and was a huge fan of practical jokes, a quality unfortunately inherited by both Titus and Ulysses. One favorite Father used many times was to enchant a cow so that its milk ran green or purple or even blood red, depending upon the season of the year and who he was attempting to startle. We lost more dairy maids that way, though once he managed to convince the whole village that St. Patrick had blessed our cows upon his holy day. Another time he had some poor sweet thing leaving elaborate gifts for the local leprechauns, though he rewarded her in the end by leaving her clues to a real pot of gold (made by Logistilla, of course). Erasmus still holds that a similar incident during our stay in Koln, Germany, led to the tale of the *Elves and the Shoemaker*.

Father loved using his magic to startle the ignorant, especially if he felt the person was deliberately obtuse. He was generous as well, and often rewarded anyone who responded with spirit or gumption. I objected to this behavior, cautioning that frightening the locals was a good way to get us burned or at least run out of town, but he always seemed to know exactly how far he could go—a gift he did not manage to pass on to his children, several of whom have gotten us into serious trouble due to their lack of Father's perspicacity.

While his sense of humor occasionally distressed me, I could not think of any time that his actions had been more than mischievous. He also used his sorcery for great good. At times, he took it upon himself to act as an unofficial judge, following in the shoes of Solomon. If a neighbor were committing a crime and getting away with it, Father would use his magic to plague the man until the objectionable behavior ceased. Or if someone was unjustly harmed, Father would use his powers to put things right. Other times, however, equally objectionable things would go on around us, and Father would take no interest. I was never able to discover the criteria by which he decided when to interfere.

Erasmus's exclamation broke my reverie. "Oh! This is excruciating!" He sat hunched over with his legs crossed, drumming his fingers against his knees. "There must be something we can do to pass the time. Anyone for chess?"

Several of my siblings volunteered, but as there was no way to keep even a makeshift board balanced atop the mammoth, limiting his opponents to those of us who could play chess in their head. Titus and Logistilla both made a go at it. Erasmus crushed both of them.

Erasmus began drumming his fingers again while staring impatiently at the unrelenting white expanse strafed with rocks and mud before us. Finally, Theo growled, "Erasmus, why don't you stop torturing the rest of us and just play Miranda."

"Because I swore I would never play Miranda again," Erasmus replied.

Silence ensued. We rode along, the emptiness wearing upon us as we all squinted ahead, seeking any sign of Father. All was bleak, flat, and icy. Finally, Erasmus sighed, "Dash it all! Miranda, Queen's Knight Attack."

It had been so long since I had had a decent opponent that I could not help smiling. Interlacing my fingers, I stretched my hands and replied, "Pawn to Queen's Four."

In this manner, we passed quite a bit of our undulating mammoth ride, before Erasmus finally forced me to tip my figurative king.

WE came over an icy hill to find a forest of cages made of ice spread out upon the glacier before us. Within, men and women hunkered down, withdrawn, or stood with their hands frozen to the bars, shouting at the world. What little we could hear of their ravings overflowed with spite.

Some of the cages stood alone, while others were surrounded by a flurry of wraiths striving to enter the cage and seize their inhabitants. The wraiths appeared to fall into two types: souls of the dead who stabbed and grabbed at the incarcerated figures, and fainter ghosts who whipped about the cages. A few cages had so many of the latter that they were ringed like the planet Saturn.

Ulysses tilted his head back and spoke to Caliban, who was behind him. Pointing at the bar of an empty cage, he hissed, "Psst, Old Chap! I dare you to slide off the old mammoth and lick that pole."

"I may be an ex-wild-man-of-the-wood, but I am not an idiot," Caliban replied. His chin rested upon his club, which he held between his legs.

"Oh, come on. I'll give you a quid!"

"What's a quid?" Caliban asked.

"Americans!" Ulysses exclaimed in exasperation. Leaning forward, he asked, "What are those things anyway? Those flying blokes?"

"The faint ghostly ones are memories of the victims, harmed by the people in the cages," Mephisto explained.

"What are the more solid ones?" I asked.

"The victims themselves. People harmed by the one within the cage they circle. They are so consumed by rage and revenge that they continue to be bound to him, haunting and tormenting him, rather than going on to their final resting places," Mephisto said. "In those cases, the cages are as much a protection as a prison."

"What is the sin of those within?" Gregor asked.

"Hatred," Mephisto replied. "They cut themselves off from others, leaving their lives a barren Arctic waste."

"Ah-ha!" Theo exclaimed.

"What is it?" I asked.

Theo chuckled sadly, "It's just that I finally understand why Mephisto knows all these things. I'd been wondering when he took up the study of the circle of Hell."

Beside me atop the musky mammoth, Mab had opened his notebook to his Possible Traitors page. He circled Antonio and drew lines through the other names on his list.

"You had Antonio on there already?" I asked, surprised. "When did you add him?"

"In that dratted Milan place, when I saw the throne. I remembered Malagigi saying that he came upon your uncle 'enthroned in some infernal palace.' I couldn't help wondering if that was the spot. Never got around to mentioning it, though, because other stuff came up. Lots of other stuff."

ERASMUS snapped his fingers and moaned. Logistilla had wrapped handkerchiefs around his bloody hands, but that did not dull the pain when he moved them. "I knew I recognized the voice that cried out in warning! So he is here! Miranda, why did you lie to us?"

"Lie about what?" I asked, confused. The rhythmic motion of the mammoth had been lulling me to sleep. "Really, Erasmus, now that we have had the truth from Uncle Antonio, it would be nice if you stopped accusing me of everything that pops into your head."

I might not have known what Erasmus was talking about, but Caliban did. He spoke up. "She did not lie. It is I who am carrying him."

Erasmus barked out a short laugh of utter amazement. "You mean instead of a staff, King Vinae now resides in the *Club of Wisdom*? Oh, that sounds like Father's sense of humor!"

"No wonder you didn't let your weapon get burned up in the lava." I laughed, giving Caliban an encouraging smile. He smiled back sheepishly.

Erasmus then asked wistfully, "I don't suppose you could ask King Vinae whether the Philosopher's Stone requires two parts zinc or three?"

"Master Prospero ordered me not to let you talk to him." Caliban sounded apologetic.

"More's the pity." Erasmus sighed dejectedly.

"What do you need the Philosopher's Stone for?" I interjected. "The golden donkey of King Midas—or King Midas himself transformed into a donkey, I'm not sure which—is in the Vault. Our family shall never again want for gold." I shuddered as I recalled my encounter with the thing and how close I had come to being added to the family treasure store myself.

"You stay out of this." Erasmus sounded almost cheerful for the first time since his encounter with Uncle Antonio. "It's not the gold; it's the principle of the matter. I've spent more decades pursuing the Philosopher's Stone than most sages get to live. Someday, I'd like to crack the secret." He paused. "The donkey of King Midas? When did that come to be there?"

"Must have been Ulysses," I replied.

"Guilty as charged, old girl." Ulysses casually took a bite of an apple left from what Mephisto's hoodlums had brought the night before. There was also a bit of honey left and a bag of carrots. They were being passed around the mammoth. "Though Father had to help me with the donkey. That was a tricky one!" he added. "Thought I was a goner for a minute there! Could have spent the rest of my existence as one of those golden knickknacks on display in Erasmus's mansion."

"Just realized I never got to ask Caliban what his task was." Mab flipped open his notebook to his Family Duties and wrote "Caliban" beneath his list of other names. "What do you do, Bully Boy? Other than run errands for the Hare . . . er, Mr. Mephisto?"

"I talk to the *Staff of Wisdom*," Caliban said. "That's my job. I talk to it, and I make sure no one else talks to it."

"Whatever do you talk about?" asked Logistilla.

"Art, poetry, literature, the ballet." Caliban gave the club a fond smile. "He's not such a bad companion really. I've learned a great deal. Sometimes, I bring home questions my students have asked me, and we chat about them, so I have an answer for the students in the morning. Isn't that right, Club?"

"Indeed," replied the voice of King Vinae. *"Incidentally,"* added the demon, *"not that anyone asked me, but I do so love to impart wisdom. If Caliban instructs me to give warning should something approach or overhear you, you will be relatively safe and free to talk."*

"Thank you, and I instruct you to do that," Caliban replied, "but you should not volunteer information. You know that."

"Just trying to help."

Gregor leaned forward, clearly puzzled. "Your students?"

Caliban said, "I am a professor at NYU." At Gregor's blank look, he elaborated, "New York University? In the city?" When Gregor nodded, he continued, "I teach poetry, English literature, and, occasionally, Italian."

Caliban cleared his throat and addressed the club, announcing solemnly, "Please warn us of any dangers, if anyone is listening, or if anything is approaching our position."

"I understand and shall obey."

Logistilla leaned forward. "Why isn't he supposed to volunteer information?"

"He gets uppity." Caliban tucked the club under his arm.

"I was just thinking how useful it would be to have a staff that talks," murmured Cornelius.

"Really?" Erasmus gave a low chuckle. "I was just thinking how pleasant it was that mine did not. Not that I wouldn't enjoy questioning Vinae, mind you, but talking back, all the time?"

"I heard that," murmured the club.

THE hatred frozen within the landscape began to affect the mammoth. It trumpeted and stomped around, tossing its great tusks. Mephisto nearly fell off. He ended up dangling beside the creature's head, hanging on to its ears. He had to kick off the tusk and do a flip to get back up again. Titus and Logistilla were not so lucky. During a particularly violent stamp, they slid off the rump. Titus grabbed the beast's tail, and Logistilla grabbed Titus about the waist. She then bounced against Titus as her feet were dragged along the ice.

"Sorry, folks, that's the end of the mammoth line," Mephisto called out. He had some trouble getting the creature to kneel. Theo leapt off and, coming around the woolly beast, caught me as I slid from its back. Only he lost his balance and we both fell onto the snow. We stayed there—laughing—until Mab came tumbling down on top of us.

Mephisto sent the mammoth home, and we began walking. The glacier here was foliated, with layers of ice and rock creating striations, so that we seemed to be traveling over a gigantic box of vanilla fudge swirl topped with little cages of rock crystal sugar. It was beautiful but creepy.

I fell in step beside Caliban. Mab walked beside me, the collar of his trench coat turned up against the chill.

"Caliban?" I kept my voice low. "Did Father forbid me from asking questions of the *Staff of Wisdom*?"

"You, Miss Miranda?" Caliban scratched his head. "No. Not that I recall."

"May I address it?" I asked. Beside me, Mab quickly pulled out his Space Pen and waterproof notebook.

"Certainly!" Caliban inclined his head toward his club. "Psst. Keep your voice down. No need to broadcast your answers to the entire landscape!"

I leaned toward the club, speaking softly. "Seir implied there is a power stronger than Lilith, and that you know what it is."

A low but deep chuckling came from the wood. *"You of all people, Servant of She Whom We Cannot Name, need to ask this of me?"*

"Ex-servant," I muttered under my breath.

"Oh? Do you serve Her no longer?"

My face burned. "I have had my station ripped from me."

"So you have lost your rank. Have you turned your back upon your Mistress, as well?"

"No . . ."

"Then, you are still her servant, are you not?"

"Ah . . . yes?" I said, taken aback. It had not occurred to me I might continue to serve my Lady's purposes, even if I could not hear Her.

"Surely, then, you know what you have Above that we lack here Below," continued the voice from the club. *"In the dark, a candle is very bright, a fire more so, and a bonfire draws all attention. Compared to sunlight, however, they are puny.*

"Living in darkness, we fallen angels have grown much impressed by the Seven Rulers of Hell: Satan, Lucifer, Asmodeus, Lilith, Beelzebub, Belphegor, and Abaddon. We believe them great and terrible, able to rip down the pillars of Heaven and plunge all the universe into night.

"What fools, we!" The voice laughed contemptuously. *"And I was among the most foolish of them. How puffed up with myself I was, how fooled by the very lies I doled out to others! Even my imprisonment by Solomon did not enlighten me. It took my great nemesis to rip the blinders from my eyes and show me the truth."* Softly, almost as if to himself, he added, *"For what else could have enticed him, to whom I had offered all, except the one thing no demon could offer?*

"Far from being torn down and dismantled," the voice continued, *"as the Great Seven claim, Heaven has not been even so much as touched by our rebel-*

lion. *We have accomplished nothing except to make our own lives miserable. We are kings of emptiness.*

"*In my ignorance and vanity, I was like one who, having lived always in the shadow of Mount Everest, believed that mountain the greatest thing in the universe. From its base, it may so appear. However, should one compare it with a mountain range, a continent, a planet, the solar system, galaxies, clusters of galaxies, and so on, it is as nothing! And all these true wonders are held together by that one power of which we in Hell know not.*"

"And that power is?" I asked.

"*Come, Little Servant of the Most High . . . What did the man from the Brotherhood of Hope teach those whom he rescued? What did they need in order to escape Hell?*"

"How do you know about that?" I asked. "You weren't there?"

The staff made a sound much like a snort. "*Some Demon of Wisdom I would be if my knowledge was restricted to what happened near this club! What did Malagigi tell them they needed if they wished to be free?*"

"To be nice to each other?"

"*Precisely!*" the voice speaking from the club agreed. "*To be free they must practice Charity.*"

I replayed in my mind the conversation between Mephistopheles and Seir but could make no sense of how Seir might defeat the Queen of Air and Darkness with charity. He hardly seemed the charitable sort. I wondered if Seir had referred to something else, some other secret Vinae knew. I questioned him some more, but he offered no other explanation.

"One last question," I asked. "You mentioned 'your great nemesis.' Who is that?"

"*She from whom I learned the depth of my own foolishness.*" The voice chuckled again. "*The Angel of Bitter Wisdom.*"

There was an *angel* of Bitter Wisdom? Was this the same Bitter Wisdom who was the Handmaiden of Eurynome?

Startled, I failed to match Caliban's long steps and dropped behind him. Mab fell into step beside me, but he kept his thoughts to himself.

Such Stuff as Nightmares Are Made Of

As the tower grew closer, the cages of ice were replaced by thorny prisons, too terrible to gaze upon. A quick glance out of the corner of one's eye caused little pain, however, so we could catch brief glimpses of the inhabitants.

A few cages held cruel haggard men, twisted from unnatural appetites. One had gouged out his eyes upon the thorns, reminding me, in the sickening way that one recalls a passion the morning after an indulgence, of a similar desire that had taken hold of me during my dream of the tower. Two others were so terribly twisted, contorted into some kind of knot like yogis, with arms and legs protruding where they should not be, that I could not find their heads and wondered if they were human at all. Yet another writhed and moaned, foaming at the mouth as if in the grip of a fit.

Most of the inmates were not human. We passed a minotaur, a three-headed ogre, two harpies, three tattered-winged entities, and a giant who was sunk in the ice to his waist. He reached for us, banging upon the glacier in an attempt to collapse a fissure beneath us when we proved to be out of his reach.

Those were the more decent sort of prisoners. Many others were more dreadful and less recognizable, with membranes, tentacles, or additional appendages, the uses of which I could not discern. Some were repulsive to the eye or offensive to some unknown sense of moral rightness. One vulgar monstrosity puffed its ugly membranes, spewing a thick syrupy fluid across the snow, staining it a disturbing reddish pink. The gesture, while meaningless to humans, was clearly intended to be rebellious or perhaps lewd.

In the next cage, a blond man with wild bloodshot eyes and scars along his stomach and chest—perhaps he had been gouging himself with his own overgrown fingernails—hyperventilated. He laughed maniacally and spit furiously, as if trying to imitate the excesses of his horrendous neighbor. This I found more horrible than these alien creatures.

To our right, a series of big cages dripped with icicles. Imprisoned within them were extremely tall men with symmetrical faces. These creatures would have been handsome, possibly even beautiful, had their faces held even a hint of kindness or virtue. Instead, anger, hatred, lust, greed, and other destructive emotions warred upon their faces, making them cruel and disturbing to behold.

Erasmus turned to Ulysses. "Rather undercuts your theory about there being no divine punishment, doesn't it?"

"Not at all," Ulysses replied. "I'm not sure about the cages of ice, but this place looks like demons punishing demons."

"Yep," Mephisto agreed. "This is where the demons punish their enemies: fallen angels, other monsters, *Orbis Suleimani* agents who foolishly didn't keep their souls clean."

"So, Father's nearby?" I cried hopefully.

Mephisto nodded. Donning Theo's goggles, which were apparently on a setting that protected his eyes from the pain of the thorns, he peered into the crystal ball. "Shouldn't be long now. Maybe an hour."

"Club, how long until midnight?" Caliban asked.

"Seven hours."

"Great!" Mephisto smiled. "We have loads of time!"

Theo looked around nervously and then said in a hushed voice, "I wouldn't be too cocky, Mephisto. Who knows what we will need to face when we get there . . . if Father is even still sane."

That was a frightening thought! I began to walk faster.

"What are those . . . things?" Logistilla stared, clearly both attracted and repulsed.

Mephisto put Theo's goggles on again and squinted at them. "Nephilim. You know, from the Bible."

" 'There were giants in the earth in those days . . . mighty men of renown,' " Gregor quoted from the Book of Genesis. "During the Flood, all the monsters and abominations were swept from the earth. This must be where God imprisoned them."

"Or someone imprisoned them, anyway." Erasmus took a turn with the goggles and then regarded me thoughtfully. "After our uncle's revelations, I hate to be the one to point this out, but I can't help noticing these abominations have something in common with our dear sister. Here, take a look."

He handed me the goggles. I held them to my eyes and, no longer fearing the thorny bars of their cages, peered more closely at the tormented giants, though these were merely some ten or fifteen feet tall, not nearly so big as the three-hundred-foot-tall creature who pounded the ice a little ways back. With a strange sinking sensation in the pit of my stomach, I saw what Erasmus had meant.

Wings, much like mine, spread from their shoulders. Like mine, they were mere impressions, as if dashed off quickly by an impatient artist. Only, these wings were made of palpable darkness, rather than light.

I handed Theo back his goggles and turned away, recalling the insults the King of Fire had spat at me. *Vile half-breed! Accursed Nephilim!* At the time, I had thought he was talking to Caurus, but he had been looking right at me.

I turned to Mephisto. "What exactly is a nephilim? I know they're supposed to be half-supernatural creatures, but what specifically are they?"

It was Gregor who answered. "The full quotation from Genesis 6:4 reads thus: 'There were giants in the earth in those days; and also after that, when the sons of God came in unto the daughters of men, and they bore children to them, the same became mighty men which were of old, men of renown.' The word translated as 'giant' in the King James version is *nephilim*."

"So they are the children of men and angels?" I asked. They were half-breeds—children of men and fallen angels—and they had wings like mine.

"That's one tradition," Erasmus said. "Another tradition claims all those antediluvian monsters—nephilim, *lilim*, gibborim, and the like—were the children of Lilith and Cain." He chuckled, though his heart did not seem to be in it. "Looks like that voice of yours in Dis told the truth about your mother after all."

WE walked on, passing more thorn cages and leaving the nephilim behind. As I climbed up the side of a moraine, I got a pebble in my boot. The others moved ahead while I pulled off my shoe, shook it out, and put it back on again.

As I caught up with the others again, a hand touched my shoulder. Turning, I found myself looking into blood-red eyes set in a sable face. Seir of the Shadows stood just behind me, only inches from both Theo and Mab. My heart hammered like a drumroll, but my brother had turned to speak to Titus, and Mab was paging through his notebook; though why I wanted to preserve this demon from Theo's wrath, I hardly knew.

"What are you doing here?" I whispered, clutching my flute close to my chest.

"I could not stay away," Seir whispered back. He dropped a kiss on the spot where my neck met my shoulder. "Know that I am jealous of my other self. I intend to win you for my own."

"He is dead," I mouthed.

"Not as dead as I might wish." He touched his hand to his sable lips and blew me a kiss.

Then, like a shadow before the rising sun, he was gone.

The encounter left me shaken—until I recalled that the purpose of demons was to deceive. How transparent I must be if Seir could trick me again with the same ploy of pretending to be my dead, lost love. But then, he was an incubus, and incubi had only one trick. Obviously, I would not give in to his blandishments. So, his only choice was to lure me into believing Astreus was not dead.

A clever ploy. Only now I had caught on, so I was wary.

Still, I was impressed by his daring. Had he been a real lover and not a false seeming, the act of risking his life and limb to come and see me while my brothers walked just beside me would have impressed me, very much so. How sad that the very signs of love could be so easily imitated by one whose heart was bent upon treachery and deception.

THE blisters on my feet had begun to ache. I wished I could put something cool and soothing on the wounds, or at the very least, lick them. Yes, lick them and drink the clear blood-sweet goo within; that would be pleasant. I pictured myself sipping from my foot . . .

Horrified, I shook my head as if the motion could clear away the unpleasant image. Glancing around, I noticed that Mephisto was trying to eat a rock, Logistilla cooed like a mother bird while attempting to feed Titus a carrot she had prechewed for him, and Ulysses was gnawing on his own elbow.

"Stop! Wake up!" I cried. "Pay attention to what you are doing!" Everyone stopped and quite a few of them looked suddenly startled or guilty. "It's the influence of the Tower of Thorns, I think. Strange appetites to which men should not be prey emanate from there. We must resist them!"

"That explains a lot." Titus wiped carrot off his cheek. "I was suffering from the weirdest desire to piss on the sun."

"Er, sorry, Gregor, Old Boy, I seemed to have chewed a hole in your turtleneck." Ulysses pulled sheepishly at the unraveling threads at the elbow of his shirt.

"What is this horrible place?" Theo's face had gone rather pale.

"This part of Hell isn't meant for people," Mephisto chimed in. "Some people are kept here, but it's really for punishing other creatures: elves, Titans, giants, primordial beings from before the birth of stars. The things they desire, such as to defile the sun, don't make much sense to human beings, so we interpret them in weird ways. Yuck!" He tossed aside the rock he had bitten and rubbed his teeth.

"Ma'am, this is downright unpleasant." Mab grimaced in disgust. "Bad enough to be stuck with all these body-related desires, without getting socked with a group of new ones as well. Anyone else suffering from the desire to meld with noodles? No?" He pushed the brim of his hat down over his eyes. "Sorry I brought it up."

"Guess it's back to you, Gregor." Erasmus was looking off into the distance, a expression of faint distaste on his face.

"Please," Cornelius begged while he walked guided by Erasmus's arm, "not the silence again. I beg of you!"

Gregor said, "Then, I will put it up briefly every ten minutes, to help wake us up, should we fall prey to something unpleasant. Otherwise, it's up to each of us to resist."

GREGOR was as good as his word, but, in my opinion, the silences did not come often enough. Despite my best attempts at vigilance, I wasted time dwelling on the pleasures of being ground into paste and eaten by ants. Or how good I would feel if only I could impale my stinger in Erasmus and pump poison into his bloodstream—the promised gratification of poison pumping was particularly enticing. I longed to emit sparks that would drink in the essence of my surroundings, consuming the virtue of what they touched and conveying it to me, leaving behind empty and sullied husks.

The fact that I was incapable of doing these last two things did not diminish my desire for them one iota. Nor were my brethren better off. I could not tell what went on in their minds, but from their mingled expressions of longing and disgust, they, too, struggled in the battle against senseless unnatural emotions.

I could defend myself, I discovered, by indulging in some powerful negative emotion. If I concentrated upon a desire for revenge against Erasmus, and how I wanted to torment him with the appendages I did have, that helped keep the alien desires at bay. Yet, I did not particularly care to indulge my hatred. Nor, as I pictured myself strangling Erasmus while simultaneously kneeing him in the groin, his purple face contorted with outrage and pain, could I entirely escape that desire to pump him full of poison. It would make such a fitting end to all his arrogance and abuse.

TO distract myself, I let my thoughts wander to a subject I had been deliberately skirting: Astreus and Seir.

Why would the incubus risk his life to pop in and visit me? To taunt me? To kiss my neck? Was he spying on us? What could he have possibly learned?

Or was this just the way of incubi, that they acted like outrageous lovers, imitating actions they thought might impress their victims. After all, he had succeeded in hoodwinking me with Ferdinand. Did he think, after my trusting Ferdinand led to my losing everything, that I would turn around and trust him again, if he only made a show of having maintained Astreus's attentiveness?

It was all nonsense. Astreus never had been as fascinated with me as the incubus pretended. Seir was just saying these things in an attempt to beguile me.

The words Astreus had spoken by the hearth, while in the guise of Ferdinand, echoed in my thoughts. *You must excuse me, Miranda. When you have lived above and now must dwell below, and your only crime was the chaste love of a virtuous woman, the affections of that woman take on immense significance.*

I had felt in my soul—or what I took at the time for my soul—that he had been sincere. And, as I had just admitted to myself, it was because of my faith in this speech—because of the way it had touched me and stirred something within me—that I had trusted Ferdinand, trusted Seir, and, to my eternal shame, trusted the Ferdinand that turned out to be Osae the Red.

Were these words true, regardless? Had Astreus loved me, too? Or was I merely easily misled?

Of course, I had also believed Astreus's protestations about hawks and doves. But then, of course I would. The incompatibility of elves and men had been drummed into me since infancy. But did Astreus believe the two were incompatible? Apparently not, if he had a reputation for seducing mortal maids, a fact which suggested he did not love me but had been merely dallying.

Only he had not attempted to press his advantage, which also suggested that he did not love me. Except that he had kissed me—while we were falling from the black swan to his towers in Hyperborea. No, wait, I blushed, embarrassed yet again. That had been my imagination.

Or, had it?

I had no ability to dream waking dreams. Why had I believed his suggestion that I was the one responsible for imagining our kiss? Astreus had kissed me!

I pressed my fingers against my lips and then moved them to wipe away the tear that ran down my cheek. Finally, I admitted the truth to myself. He had kissed me, and he had been speaking of me when he spoke of the "two things he most loved"—those two things had been myself and the sky.

The Elf Lord had loved me!

One kiss. It was not much to hold on to, to carry me forward for the rest of my life, as I slowly grew mortal, old, and weak.

But it was better than no kiss at all.

MORE than once, Caliban's club called out a warning, and we hid beneath a cloud of darkness until the sentinel imp flew away. Once, when the darkness cleared, we found Mephisto had pulled up his shirt and surcoat and was, with careful concentration, pushing the tip of a carrot into his belly button. Seeing us watching, he quickly stood, letting his garments fall. "I've had the oddest craving to eat things the original way . . . the way we did in the womb. Do you think if this went in my belly button, it could be digested directly into my bloodstream?"

Erasmus snatched the carrot from his hand. "Adults can't do that."

"Oh. Right," Mephisto said cheerfully, but I caught him eyeing the bag of carrots slyly.

OF course, I told myself as we continued, Astreus might be alive. After all, what evidence did I have that he would be gone, except his own word? And who could trust the word of an elf?

How did death by sorrow work, anyway? Did losing hope kill an elf instantly? Might not the habit of hope keep him alive a few days? A week? A year? If I had not lost the crown, could I have revived him? What if I tapped on the figurine and asked to borrow Mephisto's hat?

I reached for the little wooden figure of Astreus, which was still in my bag. That was when my heart broke. Because it did not matter anymore.

Astreus could be alive; he could be within Seir, striving against him right now; he could come walking over the snow and announce that he had defeated Seir and had come to declare his undying love, but it was of no account, because I—who could not tell when my father was lying or whether Ferdinand was a fake—could never afford to believe him . . . because what looked like Astreus might actually be Seir.

No matter how sincere he seemed; no matter how truthful he sounded; no matter how my heart ached, I could never again trust that any form of Astreus who approached me was not another Ferdinand, a false face put on by Seir in order to deal my family another blow.

True, the worst damage had already been done, but that did not mean there were not still secrets to be wheedled out of us, or staffs to be stolen, or praise to claim from Lilith for delivering me, hog-tied, to be handed over to the Torturers.

The mere thought of my brief stay in the Tower caused spasms of fear to pass through my body. What would become of me were I one of its inhabitants, I dared not surmise! The Elf Lord, and with him any chance I might have had at love, was lost to me forever.

Slowly, my heart as heavy as an anvil, I took the little wooden figurine that my brother Mephisto had made for me so long ago and threw it into the snow.

AS we drew closer to the Tower of Thorns itself, the unnatural desires grew greater and more disturbing. Nothing outside of us seemed threatening, but the danger that we might be driven to harm ourselves increased. Fear of the approaching tower made me jumpy, which caused me to slip on the ice more than once. One time, I tumbled down an ogive, striking my elbow hard on a protruding rock. It throbbed uncomfortably for about an hour, making my mood even bleaker.

Around me, my siblings, too, struggled with strange impulses. Logistilla beat Ulysses about the head with her staff after she caught him during a brief break trying to gnaw on her leg. A fistfight broke out between, of all people, Theo and Gregor. The two of them rolled about in the snow and pummeled each other for about a minute before Caliban and Titus were able to tear them apart. Then, Mephisto curled up in a ball and crooned mournfully. It took us nearly twenty minutes to uncurl him.

Caliban carried him for part of the time, but even he had trouble moving along the ice holding a full-grown man as if he were a bag of groceries. We even argued about trying to use Mephisto's staff to summon up the cheer weasel. Then, as quick as it had begun, Mephisto snapped out of whatever had been troubling him and continued forward as cheerfully as before. It occurred to me that Father Christmas may have given Mephisto that silly creature for a good reason.

WE made our way down an icefall, jumping carefully from curving stair to stair, then across a field of glacial suncups, carefully stepping over the bumps and trying to avoid the deeper craters, some of which were filled with slick black ice.

Ahead, one of the thorny cages had a ring of angry wraiths such as we had seen around the cages of ice. Within, a proud man with a hawklike nose was dressed in the rich but tattered garments of a high official of the Church. He glared out while nimbly dodging spears of ice thrust at him by the more solid of his tormentors. I dared not glance at the cage for too long, but in my quick glimpse I saw no sign of wings or horns. Apparently, he had once been human.

"Theo, quick, give me your glasses!" Gregor tore the goggles off Theo's face. Putting them on, he peered toward the cage and then gasped. "It's him! The fiend!"

"Him, who?" Logistilla asked.

"Borgia!" Gregor bellowed, his face contorting with wrath. Breaking away from us, he leapt over the bumpy terrain and charged the cage. Seizing an icy javelin from one of the tormenting wraiths, my brother began to jab at the man within the cage, whom I now recognized from my brief, fleeting glances as Pope Alexander VI, the father of Cesare Borgia, whom Mephisto had once bested in a duel.

The prisoner's nimble movements allowed him to escape the sharp tines of his ethereal oppressors, but Gregor was not so easily dodged. Once and then again, his blows struck home, stabbing the former pope's shoulder and thigh.

The rest of us chased after him, though we crossed the uneven terrain more cautiously.

"So, this is the same guy Mr. Gregor was complaining about back in the swamp? How weird that we'd just stumble upon him!" Mab whistled.

"Not at all," Cornelius replied from Caliban's shoulders. The latter had scooped him up when the terrain had become too uneven. "Mephisto told us that this is where the fallen *Orbis Suleimani* are held. Roderic Borgia was a member of our great cause."

"Yeah . . . I remember the Professor saying something about that," Mab grunted.

Gregor screamed in rage, his face dark and blotchy with hate. He shouted accusations about how the horrors of the Reformation and the iniquity of today were all the fault of Pope Alexander's decadent ways. As when he had faced Titus in Infernal Milan, he seemed larger and more brutal, more like the Gregor I had disliked of old, and less like the wiser brother who had returned from Mars. He thrust his bloody javelin into the cage with great accuracy, stabbing Pope Alexander VI again and again. Intellectually, I realized that the man was already dead, but it was still disconcerting to see my brother attack him thus.

"Perhaps, I should . . ." Logistilla began moving forward.

Titus blocked her way, his Scottish brogue unusually strong. "No good, Woman. In that state, he won't even know ye."

"Psst, Mephisto," I hissed. "What about the cheer weasel?"

Mephisto shook his head. "No good against a really rip-roaring anger. Just helps with depression. Gregor's gone bye-bye. He's flipped out like a ninja."

We had to keep going. We had no time to waste. We did not dare delay, so close to Father, but nor could we continue without Gregor.

One by one, each of my siblings went forward and tried to reason with Gregor. For the most part, he ignored them in his rage. They shook him, shouted at him or, in Mephisto's case, tried telling jokes. It was not clear if he even heard them. Once or twice, one or another of them got in his way and he pushed them aside without even looking at them. Logistilla got the worst of it, she went flying backward and slid across the uneven ice on her backside. She sat there, weeping bitterly, until Titus went and picked her up, giving her a big bear hug, which she returned grudgingly.

Finally, everyone had tried except Caliban, Mab, and me. I stood thinking carefully: what did I know about Gregor that might help? There must be something that would snap him out of whatever had overcome him. Ah!

I walked up to where Gregor stood, stabbing and shouting. In a gentle but clear voice, I quoted back to Gregor the words he had said to me the morning after Osae's attack. " 'You think your present sorrow is solid, like a sphere of diamond encasing your soul. But, the nature of sorrow is closer to that of ice. Ice melts when warmth is applied.' "

Gregor turned his head toward me. His eyes were red with hatred.

I met his gaze. "You said that to me. When I was drowning in sorrow after Osae's attack, you said that to save me."

Comprehension returned to Gregor's face. He turned his head slowly, regarding his surroundings. When he saw the javelin in his hand, he threw it from him.

"No!" Gregor cried, looking at his hands, which were raw from the cold and ice. "But, I had forgiven my enemies! I had overcome my hatred!"

Erasmus leaned over so that he stood nose to nose with Gregor. "If you start bemoaning and carrying on, I'm going to join in, and I have so much more to bemoan than you do!"

"We can't have that," Gregor answered hoarsely. He managed a weak attempt at a smile.

"Let's keep going, folks," called Mephisto. "It's not long now. Almost there! Just a little bit longer, and it will all be over. We can all go home, soak our feet, and have a long round with the cheer weasel."

OUR periods of silence grew longer, though this made things much more difficult for Cornelius. After Caliban fell and injured his knee, Cornelius was forced to walk again. Without the sound cues he was used to, he became disoriented. He slipped once and slid nearly three yards, scraping his cheek and chin. Finally, Gregor objected. He feared relying on the *Staff of Silence* was not wholesome. For one thing, it tended to make us sleepy. He urged us, instead, to pray, claiming this kept his mind clear.

A few minutes later, Logistilla complained, "Praying is no good. My thoughts keep drifting back to the many joys of sublimation."

"Sublimation, as in going directly from a solid to a gaseous state?" Erasmus eyed her quizzically.

Logistilla's eyes flashed. "Oh go ahead and mock me, you arrogant lout! I bet your impulses are so much nobler."

Erasmus wisely fell silent.

Gregor eyed me speculatively. "Miranda, can you play a hymn on your flute? An ordinary hymn which will not affect the weather?"

"If she can't, I can make it so she can!" Erasmus sprang forward and put his hand on Cornelius's arm. When Cornelius raised his staff, Erasmus unwrapped a short length of the black warding cloth surrounding the *Staff of Persuasion* and cut it with a pocketknife. Then, he tied the piece around the haft of my flute like a black bow. "This will do it!"

Gregor bowed his head. "Then, in the name of all that's holy, play!"

Raising my instrument to my lips, I chose a selection of hymns I had learned during the reign of Queen Elizabeth the First. I had played them many times in my life, but always upon mundane flutes, never upon the *Staff of Winds*. I played them cautiously, so as not to accidentally call up a storm.

The sacred music swelled and flowed over the landscape, sweeping before it all wrathful and inhuman thoughts. My fear vanished, replaced by a calm sense of buoyant well-being. So beautiful was the sound that, for an instant, I felt as if I had been transported back to the black swan and lay listening to the Music of the Spheres, or as if I stood before a choir of a thousand angels as they sang a new world out of the Sea of Chaos.

Around me, peace and hope replaced the tense wariness that had been gripping my family. Logistilla gazed about serenely, Cornelius's slumped shoulders straightened, and Gregor went so far as to smile grimly. He and Theo shook hands, both claiming they could not recall why they had become angry. Theo hugged Titus, announcing that he forgave him for the incident on the ridge during the fight with Erasmus. Bursting into song, Mab took off his hat and held it over his heart.

Around us, the prisoners also responded. A minotaur's bellowing fell silent, as did the screams of three dog-faced women. Several large monstrosities hunkered down, cocking their heads to listen. Even the nephilim seemed moved, a touch of something like unto sorrow touching their coldly perfect faces.

There were few humans in this area besides us, but those that were there ceased their contortions. They stood upright in their cages, as men were meant to stand, listening with calm expressions. One bedraggled yet stalwart man, who had been standing upright already, seemed particularly moved. Despite that the warped bars of his thorny cage had collapsed, constricting about him and inhibiting him from moving, he lifted his voice and joined in, singing the words.

I recognized his voice. I knew it as well as my own.

CHAPTER TWENTY-FOUR

Master of a Full Poor Cell

"Father!"

We broke into a run, all shouting at once. As we neared Father's cage, those in the front began to slide. Logistilla and Cornelius skittered helplessly across the slick snow. Ulysses tumbled onto his bottom, gliding over the glacier toward an incline to the right of the cage. Mephisto called up Kaa and threw Ulysses the comatose snake's tail. Grabbing the body of the serpent, Theo pulled Ulysses up the slope. The moment he regained his feet, my brother touched the butt of his staff to the snow; if he slipped again, he could teleport back to that spot. Mephisto sent away the hamadryad.

After that, we proceeded with more caution.

The slickness came from water running over the snow. The glacier here was melting, and there was a smell like springtime in the air. Now that I was no longer playing, I could hear the tinkling of tiny streams and the *drip-drip* of icicles hanging from Father's cage, though, perhaps cage was no longer the right word.

The other prisoners were confined behind straight thorny bars. Father, on the other hand, was ensnared in something that might once have been a cage, but was now a jumble of twisted, thorny vines. Only one remained fairly straight, warping in only slightly, so that it was still a good two feet from his body. The other eight curled about him like hungry vines, pressing their painful barbs into the flesh of his shoulders and chest. His arms were trapped, and he could barely move his head. Scratches and scabs marred his cheeks. If these thorns were even a tiny bit as painful upon physical contact as they were to our eyes when we looked at them, it was a wonder Father was even conscious, much less smiling.

Father looked ghastly. His face was gaunt and pale and scratched in many places. His gray hair and beard had grown long and unkempt. His clothes were in tatters and through the holes the bones of his ribs were clearly discernable beneath his skin. His eyes, however, were as fierce and intelligent as ever. They lit with delight upon Gregor and the youthful Theo.

"It worked!" His voice was but a faint shadow of his normal robust baritone. "Gregor lives!"

Gregor planted his staff and shook his head. "No, Father, I was never dead." With the briefest glance at Ulysses and Logistilla, he added, "It is too long a story to tell now. Sufficient to say I was held against my will but was rescued by the family at Miranda's insistence."

Father turned to me, and his eyes rested on the green wings of light protruding from my shoulders. He did not seem surprised. "They match your eyes nicely!"

"We'll have plenty of time to talk back home." Erasmus came to stand near the cage, averting his face so as not to look directly at the bars. While I had not heard him scream, he must have looked at the thorns, for there were tears of blood on his cheeks. "How do we get you out of here?"

"That should be easy enough." Theo grinned and unlimbered his staff.

Father's welcoming smile faded. He shook his head. "I am in a trap from which there is no escape. It was noble of you children to come here to rescue me. Foolish, but noble! Yet, I fear it was futile." The thorn-bars constricted him terribly, but he turned his head the little bit he could and glanced toward the Tower. "Quickly. You must leave now, before the Torturers come. Hurry!"

Erasmus barked a laugh. "You can't seriously think we'd come all this way and leave without freeing you!"

Theo spoke brusquely. His tone reminded me of his soldiering days. "Describe the situation in detail, Father. Perhaps we can find a way out you haven't considered."

"Quite unlikely," snorted Father, "but I suppose you deserve that much for your efforts. Here is the situation: I am in a cage with nine bars. Each bar is made from a hair off the head of one of you. The hairs have been enchanted so they are in a magical sympathy with your staffs. Every time you use your staff, the corresponding bar contracts."

"Oh, is that what they did with those hairs?" Ulysses murmured. "Smeg!"

Several of my siblings glared at Ulysses. Father continued, "One of the bars—I do not know to which staff it belongs—is currently embedded into my flesh, poised to drive a thorn directly into my heart. If its corresponding staff is used again, I will die. If a bar near it contracts too much, I will be forced onto the thorn and die. If you use your staffs to free me . . . you will kill me."

Mab had borrowed Theo's goggles and was peering at the cage. "This bar by itself, the one that is still mostly straight, must be for the *Staff of Devastation*," he said, returning the goggles. "Mr. Theophrastus is the only one who hasn't used his staff a great deal. He should be able to fire it off a bunch more times, without endangering you, Sir." Mab turned to Theo. "Mr. Theophrastus, can you blow up the top of the cage without hurting your father?"

"Mab! You're here? How odd!" Father did not pause to hear any answer Mab might make but continued rapidly. "Theo, whatever you do, do not fire! My explanation is not finished!

"The only way to free me from this trap would be to break your staffs. This I forbid! The purpose of my life has been to keep Solomon's demons trapped and away from mankind. I fail to see the point of undoing all my life's work, just to save my life. Besides, if you did break a staff, the newly released demon would probably slay me before you could rescue me, making the whole exercise moot."

"What you are saying is: we can't get you out without killing you in the process," Erasmus said.

"That's the speed of it." Father nodded crisply, wincing as one of the thorns scratched his face. "It's been a good life. I don't mind leaving it. I trust you all to carry on."

"We won't be carrying on much longer." Titus lowered his great head. "Osae the Red raped Miranda. We no longer have a source of Water of Life."

Only three times have I seen my father cry: at Gregor's graveside, at the death of our infant sister born between Cornelius and Titus, and over the corpse of his brother Antonio. Yet, now, tears welled up in his keen eyes, tears he could not reach up to wipe away. Logistilla, who was closest to his head, pulled out Ulysses's handkerchief, now stained with Erasmus's blood. Reaching carefully between the thorny bars, she gently wiped his cheeks.

"Oh, those are grim tidings indeed!" He gazed upon my face, stricken. The fortitude that had allowed him to resist the thorns seemed to be failing. In Italian, he whispered, "My poor darling, what will become of you now?"

I knelt beside the cage, holding his fingers where they stuck through the twisting, vine-like bars. Tears ran down my cheeks, too. I wished bitterly that Titus had not told him. Could Father not have been spared learning of my terrible shame? On the other hand, I supposed if he truly was not going to come back with us, he needed to know, in case there was some last-minute instructions he wished to give us.

The notion that, after all this, we might lose him was too much to bear. We had come all this way, endured so much; surely we could not fail now! Could life even go on without him? Father had been the mainstay of my existence for over five hundred years. I could not imagine the world without him.

Why had the angel sent me, if the task was impossible?

And yet, was he even what I thought him to be? I raised my head wearily. "Father, why did you tell me my mother was Lady Portia Lucia Gardello?"

My heart beat with hope. *Please,* I prayed, *dispel the whole theory with a snort of merry laughter. Let it vanish like a bad dream!*

But he did not laugh. Instead, his eyes filled with sorrow.

"From whom did you hear that name, Child? Did it ever pass my lips?"

I thought back, using the picture of Ferdinand and me on the ship from Father's journal as a launching point, striving to search the real past, not some later fancy invented by Shakespeare. As far as I could recall, Father had only ever referred to my mother as "your mother" or "my fair love."

"It was Ferdinand who told me the name of your wife."

"And you assumed she was your mother. I never said that she was. I only told you that she had owned the silver locket in which you carry your splinter of Unicorn horn."

"But . . ." Tears threatened to spill down my cheeks. "You told me you loved her! You described how she changed your life! Shakespeare even quoted you as saying: '*Thy mother was a piece of virtue!*'"

Father drew his bushy eyebrows together. "Shakespeare was an overly wordy man!"

I wanted to say more, to ask him who my mother was, but Mephisto interrupted me.

"Daddy, you actually 'pooned Sycorax?" He blurted out. "What was it like? Did she smell bad? How do you 'poon a hoop?"

Father actually blushed. "She was not yet grown into a hoop when I first encountered her." He glanced at Caliban speculatively. "She was rather lovely, in fact."

"Then, Caliban is our brother?" I asked.

My father was silent a time, gazing off toward the general vicinity of the Tower of Thorns, his cheeks bright red. I had never before seen him so ashamed that he could not find his tongue. Finally, with great difficulty, he admitted, "He is."

Behind us, Ulysses let out a strangled moan. Blood ran down both of his cheeks. He clutched at his eyes. Titus, who was beside him, took his arm and helped him to sit down on a dry patch of snow. After a moment, Ulysses blinked and managed a smile.

"Trying to find a way to free Father. I'm rather good at casing joints with an eye to escape, but I have to be able to see the situation to assess it."

"For God's sake, Ulysses! Think!" Father frowned at him. "Use Theo's lenses!"

Theo whipped off his goggles and handed them to Ulysses, who rose shakily to his feet.

"Right-ho. Just let me get a good look at Father's position." Ulysses put the goggles on, though he was still blinking from the pain of his previous try. "I'll let you chaps know whether the situation allows for any hope." He began tracing each convoluted bar, circling the cage as he did so. As he stepped around the far side, he nearly lost his footing again. "Aw, bollocks! Would be a darn sight easier if it weren't so slippery! Why is it so wet here?"

Father chuckled and pointed off toward the incline, down which the little rivulets were rushing. "My captors made the error of allowing me to hold on to my staff, thinking that they could take it from me when we arrived here and use it to resurrect armies of evil dead. The fools!"

"What happened?" asked Ulysses.

Father's eyes sparkled merrily at the memory. "They cannot touch it. Not even to pick it up and move it from the spot where I dropped it."

Mab flipped open his old ruined notebook and squinted at something. He looked up. "Because it came from a piece of the True Cross?"

"Exactly," Father said with a smile. "Hell cannot exist where that staff is. Even here, down in the Seventh Circle, it brings life. Should it remain there, over time the glacier will melt away around it, and trees will grow."

Theo approached the bars. "Father, I must ask you to answer a question: Did you put Miranda under a spell?"

"I beg your pardon?" Father sounded quite startled.

Erasmus said, "Theo believes you ensorcelled her to make her pliant and obedient."

Father looked from Erasmus to Theo to me, his face inscrutable. Then, he stated rather tartly, "I would think the answer to that would be obvious!"

Before we could question him further, Ulysses spoke up. "Doesn't look good, chaps! If we could break even one of the eight bars that are close in around him, even a single one I could get him out, but as it is, he hasn't any leeway." He sighed and handed the goggles back to Theo. "Even if we used Logistilla's staff to turn him into something small enough to climb through the bars, there's a good chance the thorn that's already piercing his chest would get his heart before the change was complete. Ordinarily, I'd be game to try it, figuring we could always patch him up afterwards with Water of Life, but with these thorns . . . Well, they give me the willies! I rather think they might kill him instantly."

"Could we bring him back with the *Staff of Eternity*?" Cornelius asked.

"Unlikely, if I die on the thorns," Father replied. "They would convey me directly into the hands of the Torturers."

Glancing toward the Tower of Thorns, which was about a quarter of a mile away, Father's bushy brows drew together. I could only glance that direction briefly, and even that filled me with dread and loathing. Out of the corner of my eye I saw a door open in the bottom of the tower from which some figures in long hooded brown robes emerged.

Father gazed at each of us, as if trying to memorize our features. "You should not have come, Children, and yet I will go to my grave more easily having looked this last time upon your faces. Now, you must leave me. I will be dead within half a day. Queen Lilith has promised to come in person to watch me die. I am to be slain at the stroke of midnight. If I am not mistaken, it is currently somewhere in the vicinity of vespers—one can track time here by how often the Torturers come out of their tower to visit their charges. They are due any minute now. Please obey this last wish of mine and save yourselves. My whole life will be for naught if you perish here beside me."

Erasmus said, "Father, we met Uncle Antonio. He had been casting spells upon me for generations, working through me to derail your plans!" He fell to his knees beside the cage. He reached up as if to grab the bars but thought better of it at the last minute. "I am so sorry. I have failed the family, and I have failed you." He covered his face with his hands.

"Buck up, son. You've time to put it right." My father spoke firmly. "Now, go!"

Erasmus did not rise. Instead, he bowed his head. "I didn't even respond to the message you sent by Phoenix-script! It would have gone ignored had Miranda not stumbled upon it."

"Cried wolf one too many times, did I? That will teach me not to be so dramatic." Father gave a grim smile. His fingers moved toward Erasmus's head, but could not reach it. "Fret not, Son, we all make mistakes. I'm sure

Miranda's Lady must have drawn my message to her attention. Besides, all is well that ends well.

"As to Antonio"—Father sighed—"I am saddened to hear this but not surprised. Lilith must be behind it. It was she who set up this trap for me, and she who sent the Three Shadowed Ones." He looked at me again, his eyes glistening brightly. "So, we have lost the Water of Life. Everything will depend on the *Orbis Suleimani* now. Do your best, Children, while you can. It will be a tragedy if, after all we have done, the Queen of Air and Darkness succeeds."

A soft whisper, like a snake's hiss, came from the brown robed figures, who were covering the distance between the tower and Father's cage very quickly. In their hands, they carried mist-gray sickles. I remembered these creatures from Astreus's dream. When they opened their mouths, what issued forth was pain rather than words.

"Go!" commanded Father. "Now!"

I jumped up, pulling at Mab and Mephisto, who were closest to me. "We must go!"

Theo turned on Father. "Look! She does exactly what you say, even when it is absurd. This may be our last chance, Father! How do we set her free from the spell you've cast upon her?"

"Theo, do not be ridiculous. The Torturers are coming!" I shouted. The mere sight of their awful sickles brought back to me all the terror that the hymns had banished. "Let us at least withdraw until we come up with a plan."

"She has a point!" Ulysses twirled his staff impatiently. "And, furthermore, we cannot use our staffs—well, except for Theo who has quite a bit of leeway—unless we wish to be responsible for murdering our own father. Which means we have to walk out of here!" He paused. "Amazing that we just so happened to have used our staffs just the right amount so that we arrived to find put you in mortal peril but not so much as to have slain you!"

"It's no coincidence," Father replied. "Lilith and the Torturers control the constriction of the bars. I am certain they arranged things so that you all would find me alive and be unable to extract me from my predicament. Lilith would like nothing more than to have me slain by my own children. That kind of perversity appeals to her—but only if you all were aware you were committing patricide and did so because you were forced to pick your own well-being over mine.

"That being said," he added, "I urge you to do just that. Take Ulysses's

staff and go home! Flee this terrible place! If even a single one of you perished trying to walk out of here . . ." He paused, his eyes traveling over each
of our faces. "Please! Save yourselves!"

"We will go but not by staff," Gregor replied. "Lilith may slay you, but
our father's blood shall not be upon our hands."

Theo stepped forward again. "Father, about Miranda?"

Father's fierce eyes filled with sadness. "I cannot help her, Theo. I have
done all I knew to do. Apparently, it was not enough." He looked at me.
"Miranda, I cannot be there for you any longer. Neither, apparently, can
the Lady whom I hoped would save you. You must listen to your brothers
from now on. Now, go, Children, and may God grant you speed!"

"But, Father—" Theo began.

The Torturers were growing larger in size as they approached: ten feet
tall, fifteen feet, twenty. They began to wail, a sickly sound, like a knife
scraping across glass. Cornelius gave a cry and covered his ears.

"Go!" commanded Father, shouting.

We ran.

THE brown cowled robes of the Torturers opened. From beneath them
streamed bat-winged monstrosities. They flew above us, until the sky was
black with them, and from everywhere we heard the *thwak-thwak* of moist
leathery wings. Ducking our heads, we ran. Logistilla raised her staff to
transform them into something more amenable, but Titus yanked it from
her hand, shouting that no wife of his would be the one who killed Father.
After that, we just ran.

From out of the sky came a flying thing three times as large as the rest.
It grabbed me by my hair, yanking me upward. I slashed at its leg with my
fighting fan, slicing one leg clear through. The severed limb, still clutching
my hair, fell forward and whacked me in the face. My victory was short-
lived, as the creature produced more legs, four or five in all. One was
shaped like a crab's pinchers. It grabbed my arms and legs. Croaking a most
horrible sound, it turned and began flapping toward the Tower of Thorns.

Theo raised his staff, then lowered it, no doubt fearing he would hit me,
too. Leaping prodigiously into the air, he grabbed one of the larger flying creatures, swung himself onto its back. Grabbing it by some sensitive membrane,
he forced it to pursue me. The creature flapped toward me, Theo's arms tightly
about its neck. It was not fast enough, however, to catch up while bearing my
brother's weight. Theo and his bird-monstrosity fell behind.

Below us, more bird monstrosities dive-bombed my siblings. Logistilla was curled up in a ball, screaming. Titus stood over her, punching the creatures out of the air with his big meaty fist. Cornelius screamed as one plowed into him, razor-sharp beak first. Glancing back and forth between me and the others, Theo saw that he was not going to reach me but he might still do some good on the ground. Casting one last anguished look in my direction, he turned his captive mount and dived down to rescue our siblings.

Ice and cages rushed past beneath me. The Tower of Thorns grew closer and closer. Rising around its base, I could see mist the color of dead flesh. A strong desire to sully innocence possessed me, and I began to imagine, in vivid detail, ways I could desecrate my own purity. Killing my father would be the easiest, of course, a quick plunge into the world of sin, and my soul would never be clean again. All I need do was play my flute.

Panic seized me, and I gasped for breath, hyperventilating. I could not return to that tower! I could not bear it! I would rather die. I struggled, trying to tear myself free. The crab claw slithered against my enchanted gown as I writhed.

Despairing, I prayed.

"Beareth all things, believeth all things, hopeth all things, endureth all things." The words echoed in my thoughts almost as if someone had spoken them. I knew they were from the Bible, but I did not recall their significance. My captor dived, drawing nearer to the tower, and I accidentally glanced at the thorns. As I screamed, blood running down my cheeks, I remembered what it was that beareth all things and endureth all things.

Charity.

King Vinae had not meant charity as modern men used the word. Vinae was referring to its older meaning: love.

My next idea was crazy, but I did not have time for reason and forethought.

"Seir!" I recalled from the séance on the sailboat—how long ago that seemed now—that just calling his name was enough to summon him. "Seir! Help me!"

After I cried out, I felt quite foolish. Trusting an incubus because of a stray comment made in a dream was ridiculous. If he did come, he would certainly carry me off to some infernal love nest. Yet, even that would be preferable to the Tower of Thorns!

Yet, lo and behold, he came.

He appeared beneath me, emerging in the shadow the creature and I cast, and entwined his arms about me, his blood-red eyes gazing into mine. Immediately, a heady sensation swept over me, as if I had downed a glass of strong wine too quickly—but at least this giddy passion drowned out the more depraved desires emanating from the tower.

"Good, My Sweet," he whispered. "You have called me at last! Now, we can be together forever, our bodies entwined in sensuous love."

"Not unless you get rid of that!" I glanced upward, grimacing, for one leg still gripped my hair painfully.

"Ah. Easy enough."

Seir vanished, appearing beneath the creature. Clinging to its many legs, he began to remove its talons from my body. The winged monstrosity screeched and began pecking at him with its razor-sharp vulture beak. A fight ensued, most of the details of which I could not see as they took place behind me.

More creatures came, smaller ones that dived at Seir. Drops of red blood and black demon ichor splattered over me. Then there was a hoarse screech and a scream, and I was falling.

I waited for Seir to catch me.

He did not.

I struck the ice headfirst.

I CAME to in a blur of pain. Mab was standing over me, brandishing his trusty lead pipe, which ran black with ichor. Bits of claws and leathery wings from some of the smaller creatures were scattered upon the snow to either side.

"Head wounds are becoming a habit," I whispered, lying back with blood running into my eyes.

"Hold on, Ma'am. Help is coming." Mab crouched down beside me. He looked so concerned, so tenderly worried, that tears came to my eyes.

"Is it true?" I coughed through a red haze.

"Is what true?"

"Caurus says the Aerie Ones love me."

Mab's stony face broke into a lopsided grin. "Caurus talks entirely too much, Ma'am. Now, you rest until your brothers get here." He brushed the matted hair from my brow and planted a solemn kiss upon my forehead.

As he turned away, he paused suddenly and, pulling something from his pocket, pressed it into my hand. "You dropped this, Ma'am, back when we were hiking across the glacier. I picked it up for you."

It was my little wooden figurine of Astreus Stormwind.

* * *

MY family came around me. Titus lifted me gently and carried me like a baby. While my other brothers defended us, using their staffs like clubs, Theo rifled through my shoulder bag and gave me a tiny drop of Water from my crystal vial. Some of the pain went away and I knew now that I would live. One drop was not enough to bring me back to full consciousness, however, which scared me. Blearily, I realized my head wound must have been very bad indeed.

We traveled for a time. I passed in and out of consciousness. I remembered seeing Caliban swat creatures from the sky as if they were softballs, and a brilliant white explosion that could only have been Theo's staff. Even Logistilla insisted on getting in on the action, impaling a flying thing with the pointy bottom of her staff.

This was the last thing I remembered that made sense. After that, things became stranger. I ran along the black-and-white glacier that soon became pages of musical notation. This enormous scroll of sheet music reached up into the sky, curling above a range of sleeping mountains. The faster I went, however, the slower I moved, until I was practically motionless, arms and legs barely able to respond to my instructions. The path of notes beneath me slid sideways, and I fell into a darkness filled with hungry eyes and cruel shiny teeth. They moved in toward me, fangs chomping rhythmically. I wanted to run, but the desire to be devoured, to be torn limb from limb for no useful purpose, oppressed me. Expending immense effort of will, I dashed away through clouds of weeping color. The ravenous things gave chase.

In the gloom ahead of me shone two tiny golden moons. As I approached, the darkness coalesced about them, forming a feline shape. It came forward and rubbed against my leg.

"You have wandered too far, Mistress," purred a familiar voice. "Come. I will lead you back to your body."

Tybalt, Prince of Cats, led me through strange delusions I could not later clearly recall. We pressed on, together, undaunted by the bizarreness. Eventually, we found our way back to more peaceful dreaming.

"*This* is what familiars are for." The black cat's eyes glittered in the darkness. As I fell into a dreamless slumber, I heard a soft feline voice murmur, "Fetch a cup of tea, indeed!"

WAKING, I found myself lying in one of the sleeping bags Mephisto's hoodlums had given us. Our attackers were nowhere to be seen. My brethren were arguing over how much Water of Life to spend on me. Finally, they decided to give me one additional drop, bind my head, and see how I was in the morning, as the rest of them were too tired to push on anyway. If I could not travel by they time they awoke, they concluded, they would have to give me still more Water.

The others left, except for Erasmus and Theo. I knew it was them from the sound of their voices, but I still could not open my eyes. I could hear Erasmus packing away the first-aid kit.

Theo spoke in his rich tenor, asking, "How soon can we move her?"

"We could move her now," Erasmus grunted. It sounded as if he was struggling with something. "But I think it better to wait. Most of the others have fallen asleep. While it is true that we should get out of Hell as soon as possible, I think the chances of at least a few of us making it out alive go up if we are rested and alert. Besides . . ."

"Besides what . . . ?"

"I just had a thought in regard to Father's situation. It probably would not work, but . . . I need some time to think about it."

"You think there might be something we could do to help Father?" Theo's voice trembled with hope.

"Maybe. As I said, I need some time to think it through . . . to see if we brought what we would need." There was a rustle that sounded like Erasmus fastening his bag and standing up. "She looks so beautiful when she's asleep." Erasmus sounded wistful. "Like an angel."

"She always looks like an angel to me," Theo replied.

"I have hated her for so long." Erasmus's voice was low. "Loathed her and despised her, and now I'm beginning to think it was all in my mind, that I ascribed to her terrible motivations she never had, that the person I hated does not even exist. Who is this Miranda? She does not seem to be the sniveling conniving witch I took her for."

"Do you think it was all Uncle Antonio's doing?" asked Theo.

"No. I thought badly of her even back when he was alive. He just took advantage of the antipathy I already felt. When I was young, I disliked her because Mother did. Then, after Uncle Antonio admitted to murdering Ferdinand, I just assumed that everything else she said was a lie, too. Just goes to show the damage one little lie can do."

"Mother was jealous."

"Of Miranda's beauty?" Erasmus asked. "Well, I can't blame her for that. If our dear sister had not been spellbound into making herself scarce, she would have been a heartbreaker. Mother had a knack for sniffing out potential threats."

Theo snorted. "Not of her beauty, of her place in Father's affection. Mother wanted to rule Father. When she could not, she blamed Miranda, whom she could tell was involved with the portion of Father's life over which she could not gain control. But what Mother did not understand was that it was not Miranda who was her rival, but Father's books, his studies. As caught up as she was in politics and power, Mother could not fathom the lure of knowledge."

The men were silent for a time.

"You love her, don't you?" Erasmus said presently.

"Of course. She's my sister!"

"That's not what I meant, and you know it!" Erasmus scoffed. "You've always loved her. Ever since we were children." He paused. "You could marry her, you know. If nothing else, Titus and Logistilla have proven that. She's going to need someone to look after her."

Theo knelt down. I felt him stroke my cheek.

"I do love her," he said presently, "but not in the way you think. I love her as a knight loves his liege lord's lady—a true knight, not some traitor like Lancelot. I may love her more than brothers ordinarily love their sisters, but it is a pure, exalted, chaste love; a longing to serve and protect. I do not love her the way I have loved my wives."

"Pure and chaste?" Erasmus mocked. "You've never once wanted to clasp her to your chest, or kiss her ruby lips?"

"It's not like that," Theo insisted. He sounded flustered. I could picture him blushing.

"If you say so," Erasmus replied lightly.

Theo shifted his weight. I guessed that he had just stood up. "What about you? You could marry her."

"Me?" Erasmus exclaimed in abject horror.

"Titus and Logistilla got married," Theo said lightly, "and the two of you have much in common. You're both intellectuals. You love books. If you pooled your resources, shared the arcane tomes Father has parceled out to each of you, you'd have quite a library."

"Tempting as that may be," Erasmus's voice dripped with sarcasm, "I will remind you that I have hated her my whole life, and she despises me."

"She only dislikes you because you are cruel to her." Theo paused. "Don't you think you might be able to put that behind you now?"

"Perhaps . . ." Erasmus mused. There was a pause as if he were thinking. "Perhaps. But only in a normal, brotherly sort of way."

"You'd make a fine couple," Theo insisted. I could detect a slight tension in his voice that I knew, from years of experience, indicated suppressed humor. "Don't you want someone to bring you your slippers while you read your magic books?"

"Come now. Our dear sister is hardly the slipper-bringing type!" Erasmus's voice sparked with indignation.

"Admit it, Erasmus"—Theo's voice became grave—"you've always been jealous of her affection for me."

"I beg your pardon!" Erasmus exclaimed, outraged. "I admit, if she were not my sister, I might have pursued her. Who wouldn't? She's exquisite! But that is hardly the basis for a happy marriage! Besides, she is my sister. One just doesn't think that way about one's sister!"

I heard an odd muffled sound. Was someone choking? I struggled to rise, to wake, but could not shake the lethargy that lay upon me like a heavy blanket.

"You're mocking me!" Erasmus barked, astonished, as Theo's muffled snorts dissolved into full-blown laughter.

"Do you think I'd let her settle for the likes of you?" Theo chortled. "After centuries of being ribbed about this by you all, I figured it was time for you to have a taste of your own cooking—to see how unpalatable it is. Maybe we can put the whole sordid subject behind us for good now." There was another robust burst of laughter. "But, oh, the look on your face!"

Erasmus snorted in disgust and then chuckled himself. Suddenly, he stopped. "I pray to God Miranda's actually unconscious! If she's overheard us . . . Dear Lord!"

As my brothers departed, Erasmus murmured something about going to check to see what supplies we had on hand. They sent Mab to stand guard over me. As Theo's laughter trailed off into the distance, I lay there, unable to speak or rise, and contemplated what I had just chanced to overhear. I had known for centuries of Theo's affection for me. His adoration shone clearly in his eyes each time he rode back from a war and presented me with some token of his bravery. Our brothers often teased him about this, accusing him of harboring unholy desires for me, but I had never heard Theo speak of what was truly in his heart. His revelation relieved and delighted me. While I loved him greatly, it was a sisterly love. It was a joy to discover his heart mirrored mine.

Erasmus's outrage and his chagrin at the thought of my having over-heard them amused me, even if I found the whole subject rather appalling. But the best part was that Theo was teasing Erasmus. This meant that the two of them were talking easily to one another again. They had always been close. I would have felt terrible if the matter in Dis had come permanently between them.

Wonderful as it was to have us all working together again, my heart ached at the thought that Father was not to appreciate it.

And Erasmus was wrong, I thought as I drifted off again, I was per-fectly good at fetching slippers. I had been doing it for Father for centuries.

Thy Mother Was a Piece of Virtue

I dreamt I danced with a man made of shadow, his black opera cape billowing about us in time to the music. In my dream, he kissed me and apologized for losing me. In the way of dreams, I knew he was wounded, though no wounds were visible.

The dream changed, and I danced with Ferdinand before the hearth in Prospero's Mansion. Then, it changed again, and I danced with Astreus in a glade of ferns. Astreus pulled away and gazed about him, frowning.

"I thought I was dead."

"You are," I answered sadly. "This is your ghost."

"Nay." Astreus's eyes were the somber purple of a late evening sky. "So, Seir has called me up, has he? More the fool! He may not find me so easy to put down again." He looked at me, as if only now noticing that I was present. "To what purpose did he call me? To dally with you?"

"To beguile me," I replied firmly, pushing him away. "To confound and confuse me. But I am not fooled, Seir of the Shadows. You may take any guise you please; I shall not trust you again!"

"Indeed." Astreus's eyes sparkled a merry green. "A wise course for a mortal maid: to never leave yourself unguarded, never offer your heart. And you shall reap the harvest you sow. You shall go to your grave, safe and unmourned, finding eternal repose beneath the epitaph: 'She trusted no one.' Oh, how wise the daughter of Prospero; how wise and how alone."

I AWOKE to find my family preparing to cast a spell. Pentagrams and triangles had been drawn into the snow. All our staffs had been thrown into a pile; they had even taken my flute. Mephisto still wore his handcuffs, but the part that had held his staff now dangled, empty. The only person still who had not been disarmed was Caliban, who sat with his club leaning against his knees.

Mab stood guard over me; a smile of delight crossed his craggy face when he saw I was awake. I rose gingerly and found that, though my head was sore, I could see clearly again.

"Glad to see you up and about!" Theo leaned over and gave me a quick kiss on the cheek. Offering me his hand, he helped me to my feet.

Logistilla was addressing the others, waving her arms about in great gesticulations. "We'll never make it. The Hellwinds will get us again, and again, and again, until we all die and are tortured here for real."

"Not to worry, we have a solution to the Hellwinds . . ." Erasmus called, from where he was putting the finishing touches on one of the summoning triangles. Then, he paused, raising a finger. "Oh, wait . . . requires use of the *Staff of Darkness*. No. You're right, Sister. We're doomed."

"So, what have you all done while I slept?" I asked, as I shook out my hair and took a stab at straightening it with a comb from my bag.

Mab was chomping on a carrot. "Prepared the Professor's spell to save your Father."

"Save Father?" I cried out, my forgotten comb flying from my hands. Ulysses politely fetched it for me. "We've found a way?"

"Erasmus says he has," Logistilla replied, "but he won't tell the rest of us what it is."

Mab scratched his eternal stubble. "Just in case this spell doesn't work, Ma'am. I think you should know that I investigated the matter of how Lilith managed to set up that trap for your Father. Turns out the Perp gave them the hairs."

"In my defense," Ulysses said, sitting down beside me on one of the outstretched sleeping bags. "They were going to kill me if I didn't. It was an easy matter to get the hairs. I came by, visited each sibling, touched the ground, teleported back in the dark of the night, and stole a few from a brush in the bathroom. Theo, Erasmus, and Cornelius were the most difficult. Being familiar with magic, they guarded themselves, but eventually I outwitted . . . I worked it out."

I looked nervously at my comb, wrapped my hair up as it was, and pinned it behind my head.

Ulysses continued, "At the time, I thought the fact that my life was in danger justified everything. Now that I've seen Father in action—I mean, the

Gov'nor's willing to die rather than let the demons go . . ." He hung his head sheepishly, "I realize I've been a royal git."

Logistilla patted his hand. "Don't despair. Father knew you'd grow up eventually."

"Point is, Ma'am, Ulysses got your hair instead of Caliban's—him not knowing which demon was in which staff and all." Mab looked down at his fedora, which he was worrying between his fingers. "I . . . er . . . I thought you should know, seeing as Mr. Prospero is your father and all."

"Spirit-man, I would thank you to keep your wild hunches to yourself!" Logistilla huffed. "We don't understand a word you are saying!"

But I did. I understood exactly.

I MUNCHED on the few remaining carrots and tried to stay out from underfoot. I sat upon a blanket, which did little to protect me from the icy chill of the glacier, my most-recent dream weighing upon my thoughts. Were I to trust it, I might allow myself to hope. But that could not be.

Still, Astreus's taunt about not trusting had struck home. How had he known my thoughts? Oh, because I had told him.

And because it was a demon's duty to sow doubt and fear.

The dull ache in my heart became an open, gaping wound that threatened to tear apart my whole being. Disgusted, I reminded myself coldly that even had none of this happened, there would never have been a chance for us. Humans did not mesh with elves. Astreus would never have been happy living in the mortal world. As for me, I could hardly leave Prospero, Inc., to go gallivanting about with elves—no matter how much I might wish otherwise . . .

No, better that I mourn him, than that I tempt myself with false hopes and fall prey to Seir's machinations again.

Of course, Seir had come to rescue me. Could that mean there was some truth to his claim that Astreus's affection for me lived on in his dark heart?

I shook my head, amazed at my own schoolgirl-like naiveté. What incubus would not come when called by a woman he pursued? His coming signified nothing.

ERASMUS came over to where the rest of us were gathered. "Everything's ready to save Father. Only, I need a volunteer and . . . an ounce of Water."

"An ounce!" we all cried.

"A whole ounce? That's at least forty drops!" I declared. "Would Father want that, under the circumstances? He ordered us to leave him."

"Forty drops could keep one of us hale and strong for forty years, twice or three times that if we ingested it sparingly." Cornelius spoke up from where he had sat in quiet meditation. "That was eighty or even a hundred and twenty more years that Father's projects could be watched over and brought to fruition. Eighty to a hundred years more guiding the *Orbis Suleimani* and making sure they are on the right path. Which would Father want more? His life? Or another century for one of us?"

"But he told us not to . . ." I began and then let my voice trail off.

Theo frowned down at me. "You're only saying that because you are under a spell."

I swayed and sat down, startled.

Was that true? It certainly did not sound like me to argue in favor of abandoning Father. What was I thinking?

And yet, it seemed so obvious. Father had told us to leave. It was his last wish. He wanted his family to survive and carry on. We should not do anything that endangered our ability to carry out that last wish.

I frowned, remembering the false voices in the City of Dis. I turned to Gregor to ask him to put up the zone of silence briefly, so that I could determine whether or not these thoughts were intrusions such as we heard in Dis. Just as my mouth opened, I remembered that he could not use his staff.

I felt certain, absolutely certain, this was the right course . . . in exactly the same way I had felt certain, during the Great Fire of London, that I should remain in the house—even though all London was burning—because Father had told me to mind it until he returned.

Oh my.

"It's not a spell, it's an imprinting," Logistilla declared. She lay with her head in Titus's lap.

"How do you know?" asked Theo.

"It must be so." Logistilla spoke to the rest of us like a schoolmarm addressing her charges. "Remember when Theo asked if Miranda was under a spell? Father said the answer was obvious. Well, I've been thinking: what about the situation would Father consider obvious? I believe I have figured out what he meant.

"I've looked into the Unicorn quite a bit you know," she continued primly. "I, too, considered joining her service once. Miranda could not pos-

sibly be under a spell that controlled her free will—not while serving the
Lady of Free Will, Herself. Any such spell would have broken long ago. I'm
sure that is what Father meant when he said it was obvious. No, if Miranda
cannot disobey Father, it is not because of a spell!"

Gregor spoke in his hoarse grave tones. "Angels have no free will of their
own. Their attention is fixed upon God, and they take their instructions directly from the Lord. Fallen angels are angels who have become twisted, so
that they are fixed only upon themselves. Nephilim, partaking of both human and angelic nature, must become fixed upon some outward thing. Because God is not visible to them, they pick some other being or element from
their environment.

"Historically, most nephilim have fixed upon Lilith, which is what led
to their great excesses and, subsequently, the Flood."

"God's teeth!" Theo slapped the ice beside him. "Then, Miranda is not
under a spell at all! She's merely 'fixed'—'imprinted,' perhaps, would be a
better word—upon Father!"

Cornelius spoke softly. "If Miranda is indeed such a creature, it is likely
that Father consecrated her to Eurynome in hopes that she would imprint
upon the Unicorn. Perhaps, he was too late."

"Well, that makes me feel better." Theo laughed as if a burden had suddenly been lifted from his shoulders. "I hated thinking Father had done her
harm."

A sudden rush of joy filled me. I recalled the hope that had come when
the little silver star had balanced on Mab's palm. Astreus, as both himself
and the false Ferdinand, had spoken of how I might be like the angels, who
never swerve from their duties because they see only the virtuous course.
Certainly, such a fate would be preferable to being ensorcelled.

I had experienced so many twists and upsets lately that I hesitated to rejoice. Still, I felt very glad that I had never quite stopped believing in Father.

Gregor stood with his hands clasped behind his back. "It pains me to
bring up an unpleasant subject, but can we trust Miranda?"

"I beg your pardon?" I asked, quite astonished.

Gregor inclined his head to me, "I mean no disrespect, Sister, nor do I
doubt your intention. It is your heritage that concerns me. Do we know for
certain that Lilith does not have some kind of control over Miranda? If Miranda obeys Father, and Father is gone, will she obey his order to listen to her
brothers? Or will she revert to some earlier childhood memory and begin listening to the commands of her vile mother?"

"This is ridiculous," Theo interrupted. "Miranda is not a doll!"

"Isn't she?" Logistilla asked. "Why else did she haunt the *castello* for fifteen years without talking to anyone? I think she's very much like a wind-up
toy. Gregie-Poo is just asking: 'Who is winding her up?'"

"I wish you would not call me that," Gregor sighed, resigned.

"I am not a doll!" I insisted. "Nor am I going to do anything that would
betray my family—no matter who my mother is!"

"You mean, 'not on purpose,'" Erasmus said.

"You're one to talk," I spat back at him.

"I may be an ass, true, but that doesn't mean you're not something
worse. I saw your face when that horrid plant was trying to eat me. You were
glad. You just stood there and watched me get dragged down, laughing."

"That's not true!" Mab leapt to my defense. "Miss Miranda jumped
right in after you, as did Mr. Gregor!"

"Yup, that's right," Mephisto chimed in. "She grabbed Soupy's tail and
went right into the soup—only it was black, more like black bean broth.
Anyway, whatever it was, she went right in, while Mab and I took a nap. I
love you, too, Brother, but I was tired." He put his hands together, lay his
head against them, and made snoring noises.

I chuckled at Mephisto's antics and then turned to Erasmus. "I admit I
did not react immediately. It was not one of my best days. Especially, as you
had been so quick to save me. But in my defense, you are a seasoned war-
rior, while I am a woman who prays and plays a flute."

To my surprise, Erasmus threw back his head and laughed. "You have
me there. I've trained enough rookies to know that the skill of acting under
pressure is one that must be learned. I had no idea you dived in after me.
I'm touched." He did not look touched, but he kept smiling.

"She found you, too," Gregor said kindly. He did not add that he had
rescued Erasmus's arm.

"As to the Water"—Cornelius stood up; Erasmus moved to take his
arm—"it's up to Mephisto. He is currently the head of the family."

"That's right, Miranda!" Mephisto declared, "When Daddy's not here,
I'm in charge, and Daddy told Miranda to obey me . . . or her brothers
anyway, and that includes me. So, I've decided. We spend the wet and save
Daddy!"

"Wonderful." Erasmus turned to Caliban. "How much time do we have
left?"

Caliban inclined his head to the club. "What time is it?"

"Ten o'clock P.M. You have two hours until midnight," replied the voice of King Vinae.

Erasmus turned and smirked at me. "And just so that you don't need to worry about being left out because you mother's a demon, Miranda, you can be the volunteer."

WE rose to go to our places. The thought that we might be able to save Father after all brought hope to my heart and lent a lightness to my step. Maybe, things were just not as bad as I had feared.

All this time I had been assuming that my judgment was faulty.

What if it was not?

I believed Father was innocent of any wrong against me. I was right. I believed Ferdinand's sincerity by the hearth. Now I knew that had been Astreus, and he had been sincere. Even my family, whom I had believed in and then doubted, had been loyal and stalwart all along—well, except for Ulysses and Logistilla, and they had to be compelled to act against us. They were not willful traitors, like Uncle Antonio.

An eerie chill ran up my spine. I chafed my arms, as if against the cold. What had Astreus told me? *It is the calling of demons to breed mistrust and discord.* And Mephistopheles the demon had told me, on Erasmus's roof in Boston, that the denizens of Hell had no power to damn anyone but could only lead people to damn themselves. The whole purpose of demons, then, must be to cast aspersions upon us and upon the things we hold dear, until we no longer trust God, each other, or ourselves.

Well, it had worked with me.

I had ceased trusting both my father and myself. No wonder the angel on the balcony had urged me to start trusting my heart.

But Father had not betrayed me. None of the terrible claims that had been made against him were true. At worse, I could object that he had not corrected me when I jumped to the conclusion that his human wife was my mother. Or that he had told Erasmus and me different things in the matter of giving water to Maria. As for my former assumption that I had been his cherished companion . . . well, that had been an assumption. He never told me that it was so.

So, what was left? What had I been made to doubt in recent weeks that, ordinarily, I would have never questioned?

My mother. No, more precisely: my father's great love, the love that had touched his heart and transformed his life.

Because something had transformed him.

He had been a callous youth bent upon the pursuit of arcane knowledge with no thought for others. He had sought knowledge, secrets, and King Vinae had offered him everything he desired. Yet, something had caused him to turn his back on the gifts King Vinae offered, to break with his brother Antonio—whom he loved—and to flee into exile with the magic tomes, rather than to allow the demons to be released.

Who could have worked this transformation, in the short time—between when King Vinae gave him the great summoning spell as a bribe for agreeing to release the demons, and when Father fled into exile? It must have been whomever he called with that first summoning.

But whom had Father summoned?

Maeve? Would not Lilith have urged him to free the demons as quickly as possible?

Sycorax? Despite Uncle Antonio's endorsement, the idea was laughable. Sycorax may have had a few impressive spells, but her power was as nothing compared to King Vinae. Nor was she the virtuous type who would have urged him to turn his back on the demon's gifts.

Father's mystery love had to be a woman of virtue. She convinced him to break with his brother Antonio for the sole purpose of protecting mankind. No elven queen, witch, or denizen of Hell would have made such a request. So, maybe Shakespeare's description of my mother was accurate. Yet, Father had called Shakespeare "overly wordy." What could have he meant?

I searched for additional clues that might give me some insight into this puzzle. I recalled the words King Vinae had spoken almost to himself: *For what else could have enticed him, to whom I had offered all, except the one thing no demon could offer?*

According to Vinae himself, the one thing no demon could offer was . . . love.

If love transformed Father, and love was the one thing demons did not have, then Father's great love—assuming she actually existed—could not have been Lilith. And yet, my mother was not Lady Portia. Father had admitted that much today.

So, who was she?

Imitating Mab's style, I listed to myself what I knew about her. She must be virtuous. She must be supernatural. Otherwise, Malagigi's star would have rested upon my hand with ease. And she must have once dwelt in Heaven. Otherwise, I would not be a nephilim with wings of emerald light.

I recalled the radiance that always shone in Father's eyes when he talked of my mother, and how that radiance had spread to me and directed my life. I recalled sitting beside him on the bluffs, watching the waves and listening to him talk about the wonders of my mother. He loved talking about his love for her. He even liked to see me pretend to speak to her.

He had been so pleased the time he found me playing with my dolls by the mouth of the Eridanus, the same two wooden dolls that still graced my mantelpiece. Usually, I pretended the dolls were my mother and myself, or perhaps, my mother and an angel. This particular day, however, I had invited Caliban to play with me. When Father came upon us, I explained how the woman was Caliban's mother, while the angel was my mother, who had wings because she was up in Heaven.

Father's fierce blue eyes had softened with warmth and love, and he had said, "What a perceptive little girl you are."

Do you not know me, My Child?

I started and looked around, but the voice had spoken only in my memory.

Oh. Of course.

Tears of joy welled up in my eyes. But it was so extraordinary, so utterly glorious, that I could not believe it.

"Father was right: Shakespeare was overly wordy," I whispered, apparently not as quietly as I had hoped.

"Excuse me?" Logistilla said.

I swallowed and got control of my voice. "The Elf Queen is not my mother. I am not Lilith's daughter."

"What? 'Thy mother was a piece'?" Erasmus chuckled, smirking. "Don't quite know what to make of that, but it makes more sense than your mother was a . . ." His face went strangely blank.

"Erasmus." I grabbed his arm. "You're a lot like Father, devoted to knowledge and pursuing secrets. Imagine you were in his position, a young *Orbis Suleimani* member who has just been handed the great spell of summoning. Who would you summon?"

Erasmus shrugged my arm off. "O that's easy! As an *Orbis Suleimani,* I am always most eager to question our . . ."

I saw the exact moment when he realized what I was driving at; the exact moment when the truth struck home.

Erasmus's body rocked back. His face contorted into a disbelieving scowl, but his eyes were filled with awe. "No . . . it could not . . . but it . . ."

Almost as if he did not realize he was doing it, he reached out and passed his fingers through the emerald light of my wings. " 'Thy mother was a Virtue!' "

"I beg your pardon?" Theo looked up from where he had been intent upon a quiet conversation with Mephisto.

Erasmus pivoted slowly toward the others, his face as pale as the glacier underfoot. "Father's first summoning. We have figured out who he must have called."

"Who, my brother?" Cornelius asked eagerly, tapping toward us with great interest.

"Why is this important?" Ulysses looked up from where he was playing marbles with small balls of ice.

Mephisto piped up, "Because the first being Daddy ever summoned is Miranda's mother."

"Oh, right!" Ulysses leaned forward with interest. "Bully. Go for it, Erasmus. Who?"

Erasmus seemed to have some trouble answering. "Who else would he call: Solomon's angel, the one who brought him wisdom."

I said, "Of all beings Father knew of to call, only she could have offered him more than King Vinae; for the demon king could *tell* him secrets, but the angel of Heaven could make *him* wise."

My brothers and sister stared at me, expressions of incredulity and wonder frozen upon their faces. Then, they began all talking at once.

"No, it can't be!"

"But angels don't . . . do they?"

"Of course! Miranda's wings are exactly the color of Muriel Sophia's robes!"

"Shhh. Do not speak that name aloud!"

"Go, Daddy! He 'pooned an angel!"

"But how astonishing! Who could have expected such a thing?"

"I've always known Miranda was an angel." This last, quietly, from Caliban.

"So have I," said Theo. He and Caliban exchanged a brief, brotherly grin.

"No wonder you did everything Father told you!" Erasmus cried, aghast. "You weren't under a spell! Angels lack free will!"

"We already figured that out," Logistilla replied tartly.

Caliban added, "And Master Prospero . . . Father . . ."—Caliban's face broke into a smile—"He consecrated her to the Unicorn in hope that the Lady of Spiral Wisdom could set her will free."

"I think I missed something." Mab came back from where he had been pouring salt into the outermost circle. "Who'd Prospero summon?"

"His 'Fair Queen M.'" I laughed. "The angel, Muriel Sophia."

"The same angel you all just betrayed to Seir? Geesh!" Mab whistled. Then his eyes grew big. "Mr. Prospero was shooting a lot higher than we gave him credit for, wasn't he! No wonder he turned his back on what the demons had to offer! Angels of Wisdom are big stuff!"

"The Angel of Bitter Wisdom," volunteered the Club. *"My great nemesis. Miranda is her daughter."*

"Do not volunteer information," Caliban commanded mildly.

"Dear God!" Erasmus took a stumbling step back. It was one thing to conjecture. It was another thing to hear King Vinae confirm it. "All my life . . . I've been torturing a baby angel?"

"I hate to break up a party," Mab muttered, "but the spell's ready, and we don't got much time."

"I'm ready." I stepped forward.

Erasmus seemed to be in shock. I was not sure he had actually heard me until he murmured absently, "No . . . no, I don't need you anymore. I'll do it myself."

Alcestis's Bargain

"Okay, let's get moving!" Mab clapped his hands. "Everyone to their places, then I'll close the wards. Seeing as we're already in Hell, and all the bad spirits are already here, we've decided not to waste Water paying the guardians of the four directions, so you won't see triangles for them. Besides, Professor Prospero did not think the angels of the four directions would come anyway, even if he called them. Not having guardians definitely makes the spell more dangerous, though. So, from this point forward, no one but Professor Prospero had better talk!"

Mab herded each of us into one of three circles drawn in salt that Mab and my brothers had brought along for just such purposes. The three were set equidistantly about a central circle, which contained only a single triangle. The triangle held one of Erasmus's shoes, into which he had instructed me to pour the ounce of Water of Life. The scent from the Water was glorious, and the black shoe had already begun to sprout little green buds. If the spell failed, and we had to walk out of here, Erasmus was going to have a hard time making it back across the mountains and out of Hell with a single shoe.

As we took our places, Mab went about with a jar of salt from one of his many trench-coat pockets, closing the openings through which we had entered the wards. He saved for last the circle where I stood, stepping within and closing it from the inside. Then, he nodded to Erasmus, indicating everything was ready.

The wind moaned as it raced across the barren glacier, diffusing the heady fragrance that emanated from the Water of Life–drenched shoe. It hung in the air, filling our nostrils. I was reminded of our last dinner on New Year's Day, when we had drunk nectar-laced wine together. How long ago that event now seemed!

The ice beneath my feet trembled as, in the distance, the giant slammed his fist against the glacier.

Erasmus stood at the center of the inner circle with his head bowed, as if gathering the wherewithal to begin. He was dressed in his dark green justacorps and breeches. With his lank dark hair pulled back from his face, tied into a queue with a piece of black warding ribbon, he might have stepped off a stage production of *1776*. He looked handsome and sad, very different from his normal languid self.

Raising his hands, he cried out: "Spirits of the Inferno, I call your attention to the ancient laws of Sympathy and Contagion. The law of Sympathy declares: *Once touching, always touching.* From this follows the principle that the father and the son are one—for having touched once, at the time of engendering, they must always be together. I call upon you, Spirits, to witness this fact.

"Psychopomp, Lord of Messengers, he who conveys the souls of the dead, I call you by your secret name: Hermes Tristmegistes. I command, conjure, and compel thee to come and do my bidding! Come to me, drink of the nectar within this homage to your fleet-footedness, and carry out my will.

"The father and the son being one, I call upon you, Great Tristmegistes, to uphold the precedent set by Alcestis."

Mab clamped his hand over my mouth before I could scream. Some of the others were watching calmly, but the magicians in the family understood all too well what was about to come. Logistilla had gone deathly pale. Theo held both his hands over his own mouth, and Mephisto, his Cavalier's hat in hand, took several steps forward silently mouthing: "No! Let me. . . ." He paused at the edge of his salt circle, his face a twisted mask of sorrow.

I was not a magician, but I knew the story of Alcestis, who volunteered to take her husband's place when it came his time to die. It had never occurred to me to wonder about Alcestis's family. Did she have brothers, sisters, and parents who mourned her after her selfless sacrifice? How they must have rejoiced when she was rescued from Hades by Hercules.

Only there would be no Hercules to rescue Erasmus.

The wind stopped, and there came a flash. Bones, then organs, then skin and garments—all formed from white light—swirled together within the central triangle, forming a ten-foot-tall figure. There was no sound associated with this; the entire phenomena was silent.

The light faded. A youthful man with dark curling hair and beard stood in the central triangle beside Erasmus's shoe. He had lithe, bronzed limbs over which he wore a short tunic, a winged *petasos,* and winged sandals. In his hand, he carried the black and white Caduceus, its two snakes flicking their black tongues as they glanced this way and that. Father told me once that Hermes's Caduceus was the first of all magician's wands, and that he had patterned our staffs after it.

The god was brighter and more colorful than the landscape, as if a Technicolor character had stepped into a sepia film. Some invisible essence cast its influence all around him, so that we Prosperos appeared more graceful and quick in his presence. Our staffs and clothes gleamed, and the ice of the glacier beneath our feet seemed more valuable, as if you could mine it and sell it as gemstones. Erasmus, who was closest to the effect, took on a dashing, handsome aspect that reminded me of a movie star. His teeth sparkled when he smiled.

The god of merchants breathed the fragrant air and smiled lazily. His lazy smile died, however, as he took in his surroundings, noting the Mountains of Misery, the glacier, and the Tower of Thorns. He averted his eyes quickly, raising his arm, as if to shield his gaze. Apparently, even the gods feared the pain thorns.

"Lower Tartarus!" The god raised a dubious eyebrow, "It has been some time since I came this way."

Leaning upon the Caduceus, he examined us, pausing to wink at Logistilla and me, his eyes lingering upon my wings. When his gaze fell upon Gregor, they flickered respectfully over the Seal of Solomon.

"Fell Fiend," my brother Gregor called, "answer a question for me."

The rest of us started, horrified that Gregor had spoken during a spell. A sly amused smile played about the god's lips, and he began to take a step forward. My heart leapt into my mouth. Gregor had violated his ward. Why had he done such a thing? He knew the rules of magic.

Then, the Swift God paused. He took in the Seal of Solomon, my brother's crimson cardinal robes, and the halo of holiness that currently shone like a golden light above Gregor.

Hermes inclined his head. "Your Grace."

My brother spoke in his gravelly voice. "Tell me, what is your place in the war between Heaven and Hell?"

"I serve the same King as you," Hermes gestured upward, pausing to frown at the steely gray sky. "Why not throw in with the winning side, I always say."

"Then, you know His will?" Gregor leaned forward as if extremely curious to hear the god's response.

"I should smite you for speaking to me," the god spoke casually, raising his Caduceus. The snake wrapped around it lifted its head and hissed at us. We recoiled, drawing back within our protective circles. Hermes flipped the staff around like a baton, placed it on the ground, and leaned on it. "But I am the god of communication, and I do love to talk. I know as much and as little of the Divine Will as you do, Oh Twice-Pope. I follow Him as I think is best, as do you."

"So you serve our Lord Jesus Christ?" my brother pressed.

The look the god gave my brother was akin to pity. "You have a narrow view of the world, Twice-Holy Father. Do you think that the Alcreate loves only his human children? Yeshua Ben Josef was his messenger to mortal men. We gods have been sent our own divine messenger, who is different in specifics but not in purpose."

"What is the name of this savior of deities?" Gregor asked, intrigued.

The Swift God laughed. "You would not have heard of him. He does not concern himself with the mortal realms. There are other saviors as well, for other peoples, though the prophesied Savior of the elves has not yet been born. There are events that must happen before that can come to pass. It is said that he will be the distant offspring of a marriage between an elf and a mortal maid. Many take this to mean that he will be the descendant of Fincunir and Oonagh, but there are those who believe otherwise." He gazed directly at me.

My heart began to hammer as if it was a caged bird desperate to escape. But it was all foolishness, of course. The future implied by the god's glance was impossible.

I looked around at the others. No one else seemed to have caught the god's implication, for which I was supremely grateful. Gregor and Theo frowned suspiciously at the deity. Logistilla looked bored. Ulysses was filing his nails. Mephisto, Erasmus, Titus, Cornelius, and Caliban all attended with great interest, but it was Mab who was most fascinated. His jaw gaped open in astonishment. Twice, he moved his mouth as if to speak—presumably to ask if the Swift One knew whether there was a savior for his race—but his prohibition against speaking during magic rituals was too strong. He held his tongue.

Gregor was not so forbearing. He frowned severely. "But how can Our

Divine Father approve of you? You are a pagan god, a devil! Does not your very existence violate the First Commandment?"

The Swift God snorted. "You are lucky, Twice-Pope, that you amuse me, or you would be but a cinder now. We divine beings who serve the All High-est are forbidden from inciting mortals to worship us. This is why, since our conversion—which came after the visit of your Savior—we no longer have priests and keep up temples on the earth. But that was ever a small part of our nature. We have our tasks to perform, our spheres of influence to over-see, such as my duties as a messenger." He nodded at the person who had summoned him. My brother barely came to his waist. "Erasmus?"

"Trist." Erasmus inclined his head.

I gawked. My brother was on a first-name basis with the Psychopomp?

"Compel?" The god arched an eyebrow. "By what authority?"

"Do not toy with me, Great Tristmegistes! I have spoken the spell as was required and intend no harm. And I have paid thee well!" Erasmus gestured at the shoe. "When is the last time anyone gave you a whole ounce of nec-tar?"

"A whole ounce!" Hermes asked, impressed. He picked up the black leather shoe, from which roses and lilies were now blooming. He held it up to his nose and sniffed, inhaling the perfumed aroma of Water and flowers. He smiled.

"Very well. Where is . . ." The god glanced about the central circle and then looked with some surprise at Erasmus. "You?"

Erasmus nodded.

"Are you certain?"

Erasmus clasped his hands behind his back and raised his chin. "I am."

The god of magicians looked faintly sad. "I have known you a long time, for a mortal, Erasmus Giovanni Prospero Sforza. But if you insist. . . ."

Hermes stepped across the wards and, leaning down, laid his hand upon Erasmus's chest, over his heart. Erasmus dissolved into light—first, his clothing, then his skin, then his organs, and finally his skeleton. Then, there was a flash, and he was gone. It all happened so quickly that an un-trained eye would have seen only the brightness, but, over the years, I had had ample opportunity to watch the *Staff of Transportation* in action, and it used the same method.

There was a pause, like the eye of a storm, during which the god stood as motionless as a statue in the empty circle, shining and glorious, his hand still extended. Even the snakes on his Caduceus seemed frozen. My brothers and sister and I stood in silent shock as well. Then, another flash, and the effect happened in reverse: bones, organs, skin, ripped and tattered clothing.

Father—haggard and bedraggled with thorns tangled in his long beard—stood where Erasmus had been a moment before, the messenger god's hand resting upon his breast. Hermes Tristmegistes straightened and tipped his winged *petasos* to Father. Then, he vanished in yet another flash of white light.

"Well, Children! This *is* a surprise!" Though tattered and weary, Father stood erect, smiling faintly. Then, he saw our expressions and instantly realized what must have happened. "Who?"

Leaving our wards, we raced to embrace Father, welcoming him. Our joy was tinged by the sorrow of Erasmus's noble sacrifice. I felt particularly bad for having thought so poorly of my brother—until it occurred to me that, when my brother had suggested I volunteer, he had been intending to trade me for Father.

WE gathered around Father and embraced him. He was cheerful and keen-witted but weak from hunger and exposure. We brought him over to our camp and helped him to sit down on a sleeping bag.

Some of the others were in tears over the loss of Erasmus. I had trouble feeling particularly sorry for the brother who had come so close to sacrificing me. If someone had to go for Father, I would much rather it was him than any of my other siblings. Erasmus was an angry hateful man, consumed by malice, who had lived to make my life miserable. Uncle Antonio's magic had ruined him, and our uncle's revelations had destroyed him. Even after he learned the truth—even when Uncle Antonio's revelation gave him an op-portunity to forgive me—he had refused to give up his malice. Apparently, the last straw for Erasmus had been learning that, since my mother was not a monster, his persecution of me had been entirely unjustified.

All my brothers, even Gregor—who I had rather come to like during this desperate journey—were dearer to me than Erasmus. Especially since I realized that, had it not been for a sudden attack of self-pity, he would have sent me to my death. Hermes would have asked me to confirm that I was willing, of course, but I would have agreed. I could not have left Father stranded if there were a chance of my saving him—and Erasmus knew this.

For an instant, I was almost glad he was gone.

Then I turned and saw Cornelius standing alone. He was a living por-trait of sorrow. He had taken off his bandana and was using it to pat at the torrent of tears that drenched his cheeks. As I looked across the rocks into his pale sightless eyes, I suddenly felt as if I was the one who had lost the person most important to me—the brother who looked out for and showed concern for me, who was both family and friend, without whom I felt I probably would have been left languishing in Dis forever. What little light there remained in my dark lonely life seemed suddenly diminished, and I wished bitterly that it could have been me who went instead of him.

It had happened again!

I blinked and drew back. What did this mean? As I thought this over, I remembered what Astreus had said about those who belonged neither to the choir of angels nor the company of men, who were outside the sympathy that each race shared with its fellow members.

And, finally, I realized what was happening to me.

It was not an attack. It was not a spell. It was not even a sign of impending Sibylhood—though it might have, in fact, been a necessary prerequisite.

It was merely sympathy.

After so many centuries of living in solitude, with no concern for the emotions of others, I was joining the Company of Men.

I was becoming human.

As I contemplated the nature of humanity and human compassion, it occurred to me that it was not at all nice to gloat over the death of my brother, even if he was my least-favorite one. I remembered Caliban's comment to me back on the Island about how Erasmus blamed himself for the attack on me. *You may not be his favorite sister,* he had said, *but you are* his *sister.* And now that same brother, who had dived into the Swamp so quickly to save me, was trapped amidst those terrible thorns, and about to be slain by the Queen of Demons.

Suddenly, I felt very sorry indeed.

"I was just thinking about Erasmus," Titus said slowly. He sat guarding the pile of staffs. "What a decent fellow he was. Always showed up on time. Never let a fellow down. Always knew where to find the answer to a question. I remember when I was young, back in my student days, he would take time away from whatever project he was working on to teach me about the library, how to find books, how to look things up. He taught me to read, you know."

"He did?" Logistilla looked up in surprise from where she sat by Father. "You know, I know so little about your childhood. I always pictured you all as adults, the way I first met you."

Titus shook his head. "I was a stubborn lad. My tutor despaired of me. Said I could not be taught to read. Erasmus just laughed and took me under his wing. Within a few months, I was reading Aristotle and Chaucer."

"I did not know that about him," I said.

"His eldest son Sebastian and I were the best of friends." Gregor paced back and forth to fight the cold. "What a cheerful house they had, Erasmus and Maria. I adored her. They always welcomed me, made me feel at home. I am not surprised he still misses her." Gregor looked down at his hands, frowning. "He was a fine man when he wanted to be. Unfortunately, he seldom wanted to try. I see now, though, that it was because he had lost heart."

"I wish I had realized how hard things were for him." Theo sat with his head in his hands. "He did such a good job being clever and snide, it never occurred to me that he might be suffering. He did so much: taught, cast spells, investigated medicine."

"He drove himself very hard," Mephisto whispered. He sat on the bare ice, his face wan and dejected. "I used to watch him do things, one after another after another."

"It was probably his only way of keeping himself going," Ulysses said. "Some blokes are like that." He chafed his cold arms, especially his elbow, where he had bitten a hole in his shirt. "Wish I'd taken the time to get to know him better."

I sat still, thinking. Did I have any good memories about Erasmus? Of course I did. He was one of the three who had saved me from the Unicorn Hunters, the day they staked me down during a thunderstorm in an effort to trap my Lady. Three brothers had come to my rescue: Theo, Mephisto, and Erasmus.

FROM across our camp, I saw Mab watching me. A strange tremor traveled up my spine, and I remembered Mab's suggestion for outwitting Lilith's trap. For Father, I might have done such a thing. To ask me to make a sacrifice of such proportion to save Erasmus, of all people, was insane. And besides, we could never approach him now. The demons would be gathering to see his death. They would stop us from reaching him.

A motion in the distance caught my eye. I leaned forward, peering. Suddenly, I knew how to reach Erasmus.

No. I could not do it.

Sitting, I pressed my cool hands against my face. My whole body was shaking. It would be a noble gesture, true. One worthy of the "grand compassion" of a Sibyl. "Yet, I could not find within myself the wherewithal to perform such an act of charity. I just did not love Erasmus enough.

If it were anyone else, even quiet Cornelius or silly wayward Ulysses, I would have done it. But I could not give up the only thing of worth that was left to me to save, of all people, Erasmus.

Besides, I had no hope of becoming a Sibyl now, so there was no more need for me to live up to such a high standard.

Only . . . I lifted my head and gazed across the camp at Caliban's club, recalling something King Vinae had said to me: *So you have lost your rank. Have you turned your back upon your Mistress, as well? . . . Then, you are still her servant. . . .*

Was I not still Eurynome's servant? Did I not love Her as much as I ever had, even if I could not feel Her or hear Her voice? If all demons did was breed lies and deceit, even the darkness that I felt, where once my Lady's guidance had been, might be a deception. A veil drawn over me by Osae. How could Love, who was everywhere, damn me for being the cacodemon's victim?

Slowly, shakily, I rose, and, wiping away tears for the umpteenth time this day, made my way toward Father.

THE wind had shifted direction and was now blowing down from the mountains, bringing with it the scent of rotting flesh. The cries and moans of the creatures trapped in the cages atop the glacier had grown quieter, but the ground still shook whenever the giant banged his great fist. As I crossed our small camp, a lone harpy screamed.

I walked over to where the rest of my family was huddled. My father sat with a sleeping bag wrapped about his shoulders eating a carrot and a small handful of nuts that had been discovered in Titus's bag. Theo and Gregor flanked him, while Logistilla sat at his feet. Her dark head rested against his knee as he stroked her hair. My other siblings crowded around as well, except for Cornelius, who sat alone, mourning.

"Father, I can save Erasmus!" I declared.

Father raised his head and regarded me with his fierce penetrating gaze. Joy illuminated his features. "Can you?" Then, his face became inscrutable, as if a hood had been put over a candle. "And how many children am I going to lose in the process?"

"No children, Father. Just . . ." I bit my lip. "No children."

"How many demons will be released?"

"None!"

"Indeed?" Father arched a bushy eyebrow. "And yet, one never receives something for nothing. What, then, is the price?"

I swallowed. "Human lives."

Father frowned. "How many?"

"I don't know," I faltered. "A few dozen. A hundred? Maybe millions. It depends upon how quickly my brothers can act afterwards. But if we have everyone working together . . ."

Father pressed his fingertips against each other, clearly divided in how he wished to answer. He closed his eyes for a time, though whether praying, contemplating, or merely resting, I could not tell.

Standing, he paced back and forth, his steps firm and vigorous, despite his weakened state. Several times, he stopped and turned toward us, but each time he shook his head and began pacing again, as if hoping to come to a different conclusion.

Finally, he joined us again. Taking my hands in his own, he spoke to me gently: "Child, no one loves Erasmus more than I! And no one shall miss him as dearly. But the price is too high."

Cornelius tapped his way forward. "Father, how many men has Erasmus saved down through the years? How many more will die if Erasmus is not around to protect them?"

Father stroked his tangled beard. "That is a good point, Cornelius." He turned and addressed the club, "Vinae, what is the time?"

"Eleven thirty-six. You have twenty-four minutes until midnight," came the voice from the Club.

"Do not volunteer information," Father replied tersely. Turning back to me, he took my hands in his. "It is nearly midnight. Nothing you can do could help him in time. Recasting the spell Erasmus cast might take longer than twenty minutes, and I certainly do not want to switch one lost child for another."

"But Father, I can do it!" I insisted.

My father smiled sadly, "What a tangled world we live in that you, of all people, are arguing to save Erasmus, and I am counseling abandoning him." He touched my face, and I gave him a wan smile.

"Child, do not think that this decision is a frivolous one on my part," Father continued. "It is no easy thing to lose a son, especially when there is still a shadow of hope." Father held out his arm and moved it as if he hefted an invisible weight. "I remember when Erasmus was so small that he could fit in my hand, and when I lifted him, he would open his tiny mouth and laugh—such a cheerful noise as I have never heard before or since.

"I worried during his awkward years, when he wanted to be like his eldest brother but could not competently compete with Mephisto in any area. I watched with pride as he grew into a fine man, talented and quick of mind. And then, I watched with sorrow and more pride, as his confidence gave way to despair, and yet he did not allow himself to surrender to hopelessness but continued to fulfill his duties, regardless. I do not know how I can do without Erasmus, any more than I could do without you, Miranda.

"Erasmus is the one who thinks like me, who dreams the dreams I dream and seeks the secrets I seek. He has long been my right hand on my most important projects—the only magician among my children willing to put in the long hours of work and study it takes to accomplish our work. I do not know how I can continue without him."

Father lowered his head. I squeezed his hand. He smiled and, pulling me close, embraced me, laying his cheek against my hair. Then, putting me gently aside, he gestured to the others until they came together before him.

Father addressed us all. "Listen, My Children, and I will share with you what little wisdom my recent trials have taught me. I have learned a great deal from my stay here in Hell. Along with all the harm, some small good has come from my internment. Those terrible thorns chipped away a bit of the hubris under which I labor. Perhaps because of my regret at the schism that developed between myself and my brother Antonio, I have put family loyalty before all other things. I have stressed this, and I have taught it to all of you, feeding it to you along with your mother's milk. It took this terrible chapter of my life to teach me that even family loyalty must be tempered by wisdom.

"All that you have endured, all the hardships you have suffered upon my behalf, all this has happened because I could not leave well enough alone when one of my children was lost. And what did it gain me? Nothing. Gregor lives, but Erasmus shall die. No. I have learned my lesson. We will return home and pray for Erasmus's soul until the angels assure us they have rescued it from this terrible place and taken him home to Heaven."

"If Erasmus is welcome in Heaven . . ." Gregor murmured under his breath.

Father gave him a sharp look, frowning.

Cornelius came to join us, his cane tapping on the rocks as he walked. "Father, what of your staff? If we somehow retrieved it, could we resurrect Erasmus?"

"Only if we had his body," Father replied. "Unfortunately, Lilith knows this and will not return his corpse. Speaking of my staff, though . . ."

He raised his hand. From the distance, there came a whistling. The whistling grew louder and louder. Then, a length of bare wood, with leaves and dogwood flowers growing from it, fell out of the sky and landed on his outstretched palm.

"Now, that's a staff!" Father smiled. "I should have made them all able to do that."

"Mine does," Titus smiled proudly. Then, he frowned. "Only it's not mine anymore. I gave it to Gregor."

"Interesting!" Father glanced from Titus to Gregor. Then, he peered more closely at his own staff. "Hmm! Look at this! These flowers are new! Last time I saw it, it was bare. Seems to be resurrecting itself." Leaning on the staff, he lowered himself, until he was seated on the sleeping bag again. He laid the length of wood down beside him.

A cheering warmth radiated from the flowering staff. We all moved closer.

"Father, what are we to do?" asked Logistilla. "We'll never make it home in this condition. No food. No water, and you can hardly walk."

"We will wait a time, until we are certain Erasmus is dead, and then we will use Ulysses's staff," Father replied. "It is pointless to consider trekking out of here without the staffs to help us. We would never make it."

"Father, won't you even consider Miranda's plan?" Cornelius pleaded.

Father furrowed his bushy brow and fixed his keen eyes upon me. "Without telling me the details—Lilith may have set spies—what would your plan require?"

"I would need some help to pull it off," I replied. "We have to go to where Erasmus is, use a plan of Mab's devising to free Erasmus and then come back safely. I would need Ulysses for that last part, since we'd be free to use our staffs the moment Erasmus was released."

Mab's head shot up as I spoke, unexpected hope kindling in his dark eyes.

Father considered my words, his hands resting on his thighs. Then, he shook his head. "It's not worth the risk, Daughter. I would rather lose one child than several. As it is, we need only wait half an hour, and everyone who is still here will make it home alive. I am sorry, Cornelius. I love Erasmus, too, and I will miss him terribly. Yet, my final answer must be: No."

I breathed a sigh of relief and sat down next to Father, who leaned over and kissed me on the cheek. Father was back. He was in charge again. I did not need to worry any longer. If he did not want me to save Erasmus, I need not feel guilty about not making the sacrifice.

Cornelius slowly tapped his way across the snow until he found a ledge of ice, some dozen feet from the rest of us. He sat down there and bowed his head, weeping bitterly.

I CANNOT describe the battle that then raged within me. All my logic, all my reason, all my sanity screamed to listen to Father and obey his pronouncement. But, I now knew the truth. The part of me that wished to obey Father so blindly could do nothing else but obey Father's will.

I could not go to it for counsel.

What my heart said was very different. It said the pain Cornelius felt at the loss of Erasmus was even greater than what I would have felt had Theo died. For I merely loved Theo as a brother. I did not need him to live a decent life. Cornelius loved Erasmus, but he also depended upon him. Cornelius was so quiet, so subtle in his dealings, that he had made himself nearly invisible. Father and Titus and Theo all loved him, but how often did they stop to take thought for him? How often did they phone him or drop by his house to visit? Mephisto might check up on him, but only Erasmus actually cared about Cornelius. Only Erasmus led him through the dark paths of his life.

For years now, I had not particularly liked Cornelius, but compassion is a strange thing. Once I knew how he felt, I could not pretend otherwise. All I could think was: how would I have felt if someone else in the family could have saved Theo, and they had chose not to?

Even if the price was high, even if there was a chance that others would die. My own opinion aside, Cornelius was right. In the long run, Erasmus would save more people than might be harmed.

I stood up and planted my feet squarely on the ice. "YES!"

Father looked up at me, quite astonished. "I beg your pardon?"

"I am going to save Erasmus."

Father frowned. "No, Miranda, you are not."

Every fiber in my body yearned to obey him. I actually started to sit down. Gritting my teeth, I held my ground. "I can save Erasmus! But we have to hurry, and I cannot do it alone!"

"Miranda, I order you to sit down!"

In all my long life, the hardest thing I have ever done was to remain standing when Father told me to sit.

Instead, I stared back at Father. "No!"

Father stood, his tattered robes flowing, his hair billowing like Moses'. With his stern visage and outstretched, pointing finger, he looked like a Renaissance painter's idea of God himself.

"You will obey me!" he roared.

Father was right! If I tried this, people would die. Was Erasmus worth the lives of so many humans? No! Maybe, my plan to have Theo and Titus help me would turn out well in the long run, but if I did this, men, women and even children would die in the interim.

What if those people ended up here? What if even one of them might have been redeemed in years to come but ended up here instead because my action cut off his life?

On the other hand, was I to abandon my brother to be tormented in Hell, perhaps eternally, because of what might happen?

No, that was not right, either.

Rejoice and fear not, for it is the Father's good pleasure to give you the Kingdom.

My memory of my mother's voice resounded in my ears. *My mother.* My eyes filled with tears again, but this time they were tears of joy. What had she said? As the heirs of Solomon, we were the guardians of mankind. The earth had been given into our hands.

I turned to Mephisto to ask for his support, then paused. Why? Would I abandon Erasmus if he said no? The decision was mine. I could slay Erasmus or save him. I had to decide.

I had let Erasmus down so many times during our long life, inspired by Uncle Antonio–induced hate. I would not fail him again.

"No, Father," I struggled to get the words out of my mouth. "I will not obey you."

Father rubbed his temples and leaned upon his staff. "Miranda, I have waited all your life for the day you would disobey me, and I cannot deny that I am delighted to see you assert your independence. But this is neither the place nor the time."

He had been waiting for me to disobey him? Waiting? Why had he not told me . . . oh.

I wanted to laugh or cry. Instead, I crossed my arms and raised my chin. "Nonetheless, I am going to save Erasmus!"

"I am with Miranda, Father!" Cornelius rose to his feet.

"And I!" Theo leapt up as well, unlimbering his staff.

"And I," echoed Gregor.

"And me, oh pick me!" cried Mephisto, raising his hand. "Pick me!"

Theo stepped forward, his staff humming. "I'm coming with you!"

I hugged him but shook my head. "Thank you, Theo! But you had better not. If we should not return, the rest of the family will need you and your staff to have any chance of getting home alive."

His internal struggle showed in his eyes. The thought of me running off into danger without him seemed unthinkable. Yet, he could see the wisdom of my position. Finally, he slung his staff back in its holster and said fiercely, "They also serve who only stand and wait."

"Only Brother Theo could make waiting sound daring," Logistilla laughed. She sat up and put her arms about her knees. "So, let me guess the plan. Miranda and the boys run along, while I stay here with Father and Theo and pretend to hold horses?"

"You know"—Mephisto turned on her suddenly—"I'm fed up with that complaint! I've heard it one too many times. Logistilla, the reason you were holding the horses was because no one but you could have done the job! Pyroeis and Xanthos would not have stood still for anyone else. They liked you!"

"Finally!" Logistilla threw up her arms in a gesture of victory. "At last, somebody has noticed. At long last, someone has given me my due!"

Titus rolled his eyes. "Woman, do you mean all your complaining all these years has just been an attempt to have us acknowledge how important your part was?"

"Yes!" Logistilla exulted.

Mephisto stuck out his tongue. "If Erasmus were here, he'd tell you," Mephisto lowered his voice to sound more like Erasmus, " 'Logistilla, you are truly pathetic!' "

"Actually, Logistilla," I interjected, "you are one of the people I need, you and Ulysses."

Ulysses sighed, resting his forehead against his staff. "Frankly, I'd rather not go. In fact, given my druthers, I'd prefer to run away entirely. However, I've been a coward for a long time now. None of this would have happened, were it not for my foolhardiness. If Father and Erasmus can make such great sacrifices, I can, at least, lend a hand."

"Good!" I picked up my bag and slung it over my shoulder. "Mab will probably want to come, too."

Mab dusted off his hat and slid his hand into his pocket, checking his lead pipe. "Wouldn't miss it for the world, Ma'am."

"Mutiny! From my own family!" Father exclaimed, but his eyes were shining with pride. "If you must go, Miranda, God go with thee! But, before you depart, take a moment to discuss your plan with Caliban's club."

"I already know, and I have anticipated your question." The voice spoke from the club. *"Here is what we shall do . . ."*

The Queen of Air and Darkness

My hands bound behind me, I stumbled across the ice. To my left, Logistilla, Ulysses, and Caliban walked casually. To my right strode my uncle Antonio. His bearers and the rest of the procession surrounded us with their raucous, off-key music.

Somewhere within their midst, Mab lurked, trying to pass himself off as one of the dead.

"A wise decision, bringing your prisoner to me," my uncle addressed my siblings. "Lilith will make certain your master, Abaddon, knows of your loyalty."

"It was a natural choice," Ulysses replied airily, twirling his staff like a baton. Beside him walked Caliban. He had my flute resting on his shoulder next to his club. Despite the cold, he had shed his shirt and hunched his shoulders, deliberately transforming himself into the Caliban of old, a mindless brute. "While it's true we never met, we are family. Besides, who else could help forward our interests down here?"

"True." Uncle Antonio nodded. "And there may be things you can do for me, as well. We will talk after the event."

"We will look forward to it," Logistilla replied in her huskiest voice. She lowered her lashes and gave Antonio a come-hither smile. To my disgust, he did, or rather he gestured for her to walk on his far side, where she put her arm through his, the material of her enchanted blue gown allowing them to touch. "Miranda has been nothing but a pain in the unmentionable her whole life. I for one shall rejoice to be rid of her!"

"My feelings exactly. How lucky that we find ourselves with a meeting of minds." Antonio inclined his head so that his lips drew close to Logistilla who blushed prettily.

I wiggled my wrists surreptitiously, making certain that Mephisto's handcuffs had not mysteriously tightened, but all was well. There was still room to slip my hands free. So far, everything was going according to plan. I just hoped that my siblings did not get so caught up in playing their roles that they forgot our real purpose!

WE arrived back at the cage where Father had been held. Stands of seats had been erected on three sides. Glancing about, I felt like a star attraction in the Circus Maximus. Here to watch the spectacle of my brother Erasmus's demise were hordes of demons, demi-goblins, lilim, imps, ouphe, incubi, evil peri and cacodemons, all hooting and beating their leathery wings. Torturers in their brown robes, with their mist-gray sickles, stood to either side of Erasmus's twisted thorn-cage. The Torturers gave off a strange odor, musty yet sickly sweet.

Within the cage, my brother screamed. He must have been screaming for some time, for his voice was hoarse. Blood ran out of his eyes, blood ran down his face, blood ran from his arms and chest. Seeing him thus, I realized Father must have had supernatural help protecting him from the worst of the thorns, else he would not have been able to talk with us so calmly.

Erasmus, however, had no such help.

Above him and slightly to the right, the beautiful and deadly Queen of Air and Darkness hovered above the stadium that overflowed with her hordes. She rode in her black chariot pulled by skeletal lions. Long, slender bone spikes stuck out from their heads, indicating their missing manes. Lilith herself was a picture of loveliness, crowned in icicles. Her body was as slender and pretty as a girl of sixteen. Her face still bore the charming pout of youth. Her eyes, however, were ancient and old and terrible. No one could mistake them for the eyes of an innocent child.

"Oh, look! A present!" Lilith clapped her hands with glee. "How considerate, Antonio! You will be well rewarded for this!" She stroked a large gray cat that lay curled upon her lap. "Look, my sweet, a present for you! I'll let you play with her for a time, before I give her to the Tower. But, you must promise to be bad with her!"

The cat raised its head and glanced down. Its eyes were a reddish-orange, like the coat of an Irish setter. A shudder of revulsion shook my body.

Osae the Red!

Was Seir here, too? And, if so, was there any chance that he would rescue me? Not very likely after the last time with the evil bird-things! Still, it embarrassed me that I had to stop myself from scanning the crowds in search of blood red eyes in a sable face. Seir was not Astreus. Astreus was dead—even if my heart, deceived by the dreams the incubus sent me, wished otherwise.

Only, if I had been right about my father, and his love for my mother, could I perhaps trust my judgment after all? If so, what did I really think about the elf I danced with in a dream? Was he Seir or . . .

"As for Abaddon's loyal minions . . ." Lilith regarded Ulysses and Logistilla and giggled. "Eager to see your brother die, are you? I so look forward to your master's reaction when he learns your brother Gregor still lives. Perhaps, he will allow me to watch while he makes you eat your own eyeballs."

Logistilla smiled and waved. Under her breath, she huffed, "He cannot make me do anything! I merely swore to keep secrets!" She sighed. "Though even that cost me dearly."

Ulysses raised his staff as if he were about to disappear. At the last minute, however, he remembered that to do so would kill Erasmus and so he restrained himself.

A frisson of fear cut through me. We had nearly been abandoned. Without Ulysses, we would never escape alive. In retrospect, the choice of Logistilla and Ulysses as companions for this mission seemed like a bad idea. Yet, without them we had no chance at all. Was I throwing my life away attempting to save, of all people, Erasmus?

"And Mab!" Lilith laughed. "How polite of you to come all the way to me. Now, I will not need to call you to Mommur when the time comes to pay the next tithe!"

The dead Milanese parted around Mab, who shook his fist at the flying chariot. "I'm not afraid of you. You murderess!"

"You should be," replied the Queen of Air and Darkness.

Turning to the Torturers, she pointed at me. "Bind Prospero's brat! Put her where she can watch our prisoner as he gasps out his last breath!"

One of the brown-robed Torturers glided forward with the noise of many feet tapping against the crusted snow. The musty-sweet odor was overwhelming and evoked memories of my brief dream-stay in the Tower of Pain. Panicking, I bolted, only to be stopped by Antonio, who caught me, either because he could touch my gown or because I was upset enough to be solid to his touch.

He was not strong enough to hold me, but with the help of his bearers, they kept me from fleeing until the Torturers arrived, though two of the bearers cried out, burned by my emerald wings.

The Torturer seized me with many crablike claws that closed around my upper arms like vises, causing numbness. I twisted my shoulders, but my wings did not faze the Torturer. It did not matter now that my handcuffs did not actually bind me; I was trapped.

"Crikey Moses! This is not good!" whispered Ulysses. Logistilla and Caliban looked alarmed as well, so much so that I feared they would betray themselves. Mab's hand stole into his pocket where he kept his lead pipe, and he eyed the Torturer carefully, but there was no way for him to get near me undetected.

Instead, Mab stomped forward and threw down his hat. "Queen Maeve . . . why? Lesser spirits admired you. We looked up to you. Why must you do these terrible things?"

"You do not remember Heaven, Mab Boreal," replied the Queen of Air and Darkness, "but we do. You do not know what it is like. Men have the blessing of the Lethe. It lets them forget God's glory, so they can live for a time on earth. We demons have no such blessing. We remember Paradise with crystal clarity, as if we were there yesterday. Nor will this memory ever dim or grow distant.

"Can you imagine what it is like?" Lilith continued. "To remember Paradise, and know you are banned from it forever? No, you could not even begin to envision! We long for it. We remember its beauty and its glory. We are reminded of it every day and of all that we have lost. If we can't have it, then the mortals shan't either! We shall all suffer together. God wants us to share. We are sharing!"

"Can't you drink of the Lethe, too?" Mab asked.

"What?" Lilith cried, horrified. "And forget Paradise! Never!" She spread her slender white arms. "See our plight? We cannot forget, and we cannot bear to forget. Instead, we keep Paradise from the rest of you."

Mab narrowed his eyes, pulling out his notebook and Space Pen. "What exactly do you do?"

Despite the anxiety that ate at me, I could not help being amused at his audacity. Only Mab would pull out his notebook to interrogate the Queen of Air and Darkness. Out of the corner of my eye, I noticed that Ulysses had taken advantage of the fact that Lilith was distracted to walk over to Erasmus's cage and casually tap the butt of his staff against the snow next to the least-warped bar.

"What do we do, Little Wind?" Lilith spread her arms wide. "We breed hatred, conflict, and lies. We weaken men's morals. This current generation has proven especially prone to our influence, so we have made great strides of late." She bowed to the gathered hordes, who cheered and hooted. "Of course, the *Staff of Persuasion* has been a great help to us. We've used it surreptitiously for years." She gestured at Logistilla and Ulysses. "Without Cornelius's knowledge, we used it to increase his sister's envy, until it goaded her to consent to serve Abaddon. We did even better with his cowardly brother, Ulysses. When he followed the suggestion that brought him to Hell, Abaddon snared him and turned him into a weapon to destroy the Family Prospero, and, in particular, the members of that family who were the greatest threat to our plans: Gregor the Witchhunter who slew our human servants, and Theophrastus the Demonslayer, who sent in all-consuming fire to the agents whom we sent out upon the earth.

"But this is only a little part of our great overall triumphs! While you Prosperos—Solomon's so vigilant heirs—have been worrying your little heads over the spirit world, we demons have carried off the souls of humanity. In the last century and a half, we have done more for our cause than in all previous centuries combined. We have banished God from the minds of men, from the schools, from the public places. The great cathedrals of Europe are nearly empty. Russia and China have no religion at all. Even the churches of God-fearing America are often half empty.

"No one of us can take all the credit, mind you. Each of us has done our part. Belphagor has made sloth a favorite pastime—couch potatoes are celebrated instead of scolded, and every day there is another wonder that makes it even less necessary to get up from your chair. Asmodeus has sung his siren song until lust is lauded, and chastity despised. Lewdness is celebrated in art, in song, and upon billboards so large that they can be seen miles away. Beelzebub wins on two fronts: those not bloated from their gluttony obsess over faddish diets—neither the obese nor the skinny giving a single thought to the Will or Works of our Unaccursed Enemy. Also the drugs that decimate today's youth are his doing. Never has Hell had friends as dear as opium and its many, many imitators.

Around me, Logistilla looked unnerved, and Ulysses's face had an odd green tinge. I wondered what sin of his the Queen of Demons had just taken credit for. As for myself, I felt strangely disoriented, as if a thousand little things that had always seemed innocent and frivolous to me had suddenly snapped together like puzzle pieces to form an extremely disturbing picture.

"She's exaggerating, right?" Ulysses whispered as Lilith paused momentarily to answer a question put to her by a flying imp. "The demons are not really responsible for all this. Are they? They can't be that powerful!"

Mab pulled his hat down very far and lowered his head, so that the demon above him could not see his lips. "I don't know."

Ulysses blinked owlishly. "But . . ."

"She's a demon. Demons lie. Some of it has to be lies or at least blatant exaggeration," Mab said, but he looked uncomfortable, as if he feared that the demons' hold on the daylit world might be far more powerful than he had previously supposed.

Lilith finished speaking to the imp and turned back to Mab. "Where was I? Oh yes. Mammon, my servant, rules the markets and the hearts of men, who strive day and night for ever more trinkets and gadgets, each one more useless than the last. Satan himself rages, encased in ice, but his top minions have enflamed love of wrath, until rudeness rules, while politeness is ridiculed. And Lucifer, my great love and hated enemy, has made pride the glory of the known world.

"As for me, I am personally responsible for the weakening of the sacred rite of marriage, something of which I am rightly proud." She lowered her eyes demurely and gestured gracefully at herself. The crowds of imps, *lilim*, and demons went wild, hooting and cawing. "Wedding vows mean so little these days that young maidens are encouraged to eschew chastity, and their loss of virtue is met with celebration. When public figures are caught in the very act of adultery, no one even cares. Every type of carnal excess is applauded, and the perpetrators are urged to greater excess. And every day the Swamp of Uncleanness grows larger!

"But the true marvel, the crowning jewel of our achievements, is Abbadon's work." Lilith laughed, a noise that sounded pretty at first but then grew raucous and harsh. "Nothing in our Adversary's kingdom is more sacred than motherly love—personified by the love of the unaccursed Virgin for her precious Son—and yet, Beelzebub has convinced millions of your innocent young would-be mothers that it's no sin to slaughter their own children.

"Oh, the numbers of souls we've pulled in on that one alone! It's brilliant! Even more cunning than my previous victory, when I convinced all the known, civilized cultures of the ancient Middle East to practice temple prostitution!

"If we cannot go back to Paradise . . ." Lilith raised her white arms, haranguing the gathered crowds. Her face shone with such glory and sorrow that, for an instant, I felt as if I had been granted a glimpse of what she might have been like, back when she was an angel. "Then we shall make sure no one goes! We shall not lose our place to clay worms or a one-horned mare! We shall destroy mankind's champion, the Unicorn, and all that she stands for. Rip the Horn of Life from her head and drag everyone into the darkness, where they can squat in the squalor with us.

"After all, once everyone is in Hell," the Queen of Air and Darkness said, her voice suddenly breaking. "God will have to lower His impossibly high standards and accept us as we are, won't He?"

There was a pause, a momentary lull, during which the denizens of Hell ceased their eternal yowling and muttering—as if the curtain had been pulled back upon their pretense of pleasure in debauchery, and they felt exposed.

"I say!" Ulysses murmured under his breath. "That's rather pathetic, really."

The Queen of Air and Darkness was all seamless beauty again, as if no crack in her wickedness had appeared. She clapped her hands twice. "It is midnight. The time has come for Erasmus Prospero to die! Antonio, unsheathe the ceremonial knife. Here lies your victim!"

Antonio, who had been gazing worshipfully at Lilith, when he was not exchanging sly, flirtatious glances with Logistilla, looked toward the cage for the first time and started, appalled.

"My Fair Queen," my uncle called. "What is the meaning of this? Why is my nephew here? Where is my brother whose life you have promised to me?"

Lilith scowled, gesturing at the incoherent Erasmus. "This whelp stole him from us. We will have to make do with him."

"No!" cried Antonio. "You promised me my brother Lucretius! I feel no ill will toward my nephew. He once did me a good turn!"

"The great magician Lucretius Prospero has escaped us. Fear not, we will capture him again in time, but for the nonce, here lies your victim. Show us the knife!" She raised her hands, and the crowd responded, hooting and roaring.

"I will not!" Antonio declared. "I have no desire to slay Erasmus! I love my nephew!"

"A pity"—Lilith folded her hands and rested her pretty chin upon them—"for I was so hoping not to have to put you back where I found you. But," she spread her hands, "you are of no use to me now—since your connection to your nephew will do us no more good. Back to the ice for you."

"No! Wait! This is unfair! Did I not just bring you Miranda, whom you have yearned to have as your prisoner?"

"That is true. . . ." Lilith tapped upon her cheek with one slender finger.

"Very well, I will allow you to stay by my side and serve me, but you must show your devotion to me by slaying your nephew."

Antonio moaned and grabbed his head dramatically. Slowly, his hand inched toward the hilt of a cruel knife which he wore on his hip.

"Oh, for Heaven's sake, Uncle!" I declared. "Show some backbone!"

Antonio backhanded me, but I was calmer now. His hand passed through my face. "How dare you talk to me, wench!"

I lifted my chin and said nothing.

"Don't you understand? If I do nothing, she'll put me back in the ice!"

Glaring, I continued to say nothing.

"Don't you judge me! I cannot afford to live up to your lofty ideals!"

Even though I continued to say nothing, Uncle Antonio let out an inarticulate cry and buried his face in his hands. Perhaps, there was a drop of decency left within him somewhere.

"I am waiting, Antonio," Lilith called sweetly, tapping her fingers on the edge of her chariot.

"*Stop!*" King Vinae's voice rang out across the ice.

"Who speaks?" Lilith glanced about.

"*It is I, King Vinae. These mortals are under my protection.*"

That was unexpected!

A great deal of our plan hinged upon whether or not the *Club of Wisdom* had told us the truth. So in many ways, we staked our lives upon King Vinae's word. But I had not expected him to come to our defense himself.

"Yours?" Lilith gestured toward Caliban. "You are stuck in a flute!"

"*I am the master of thirty-six legions, nor have my rights and perquisites been stripped from me. I am still recognized here,*" the voice issuing from the *Club* replied. Caliban kept the club and the flute together, so that there would be no opportunity for Lilith to discover her mistake and anticipate our plan.

Lilith pursed her rosy lips. "What do you want?"

"*I call upon the right of last request. By ancient law, I cannot be refused.*"

"King Vinae!" Lilith frowned. "Whose side are you on?"

"*I am on their side—the side of Solomon's Heirs,*" replied the demon's voice.

There was a protracted gasp across the entire makeshift stadium. In all my long life, I had never been so surprised. I gawked at the club. Was this a trick? Could he . . . could the demon actually mean it?

The Queen of Air and Darkness laughed. "Fool! You will never be welcomed back into Heaven!"

"Heaven?" snorted the club. *"Who said anything about Heaven? If they win, you lose. As long as I am doomed to live in the eternal darkness forever, you might as well be as miserable as I. Besides,"* King Vinae added, *"I have become fond of them. I would suffer my torment more cheerfully knowing they had made it to Paradise."*

Lilith gnashed her teeth, screaming with rage at the mention of Paradise. Then, she regained her self-control and smiled charmingly.

"Shall I allow their brother his last request as Vinae asks?" Lilith addressed the crowd. "It is more pathetic that way!"

There was a roar of approval and more hoots. Lilith waved a hand at the Torturers, and they made several passes over Erasmus and his cage with their sickles. Erasmus's screams ceased, and he hung limply against the thorns. Logistilla broke from the rest of us and, running to him, wiped the blood from his face. Erasmus raised his head and recognition came into his eyes. He seemed very surprised to see her.

"What is the meaning of this?" my brother cried. There was a faint glimmer of hope in his eyes. "How did you get here so quickly?"

"I have come to play you one last song," I said, struggling against the Torturer's grip.

The hope died in Erasmus's eyes, and he gave a shaky laugh. "Came to kill me by your own hand, have you? Quite sporting of you to travel all this way just for that. You could just as easily have killed me from the camp . . . though I suppose that would lack the added pleasure of being able to rub it in." He tried to raise his hand, but could not. "That was not gracious of me. Please forgive me. I've had a hard day."

Erasmus's eyes narrowed as he took in me, Logistilla, Ulysses, Caliban, and Mab. "Odd bunch to send to see me off."

Moving closer, Logistilla hissed through the bars, "How could you do this, Erasmus? You of all people! I thought you wanted to live more than any of us."

"Only because I feared I'd end up here." Erasmus tried to shrug and then winced. Apparently, even with the supernaturally painful effect dampened, the thorns were still sharp. "But I am already here, so what is there to be afraid of now? I have failed everyone in my life! Father, Maria . . ." his voice trailed off.

"Not everyone," I replied softly. "You have never failed Cornelius."

Erasmus looked up, puzzled. Before he could speak, Caliban loped forward until he was in the center of the ring of demons. Head thrust forward and shoulders hunched, he looked the image of a wild brute. He scratched his chest and his armpits.

"What funny creature is this?" Lilith leaned over, her interest piqued.

He spoke in the slow slurred speech of an idiot. "Great Queen. I am Caliban, whose rightful island Prospero stole and made his own. I salute you and offer to lay my club at your feet, if you will but raise me up as you have done unto Antonio."

"Sounds intriguing. Tell me more."

"Great Lilith, you promised pretty Miranda to your cat. I, too, will be your cat and lap at your feet, if you will give her to me as well. Surely, there will be something left of her once your servant is done with her. Long have I longed to beget little Calibans upon her."

My skin crawled, and I felt suddenly weak and clammy. This, too, was part of our plan, or rather, Caliban's distraction was—King Vinae had predicted that Lilith and her minions would be amused by crude antics. Nothing had been said, however, about what Caliban should say.

Only now, when I was helpless and trapped, did I realize the flaw in our plan. With a word, Caliban could reveal our plot and deliver us all into Lilith's grasp. If he was loyal to us, to Father, to Mephisto, all was well.

But, could we trust him?

A cold sweat now coated the back of my neck. What if Caliban betrayed us? After all, he was not fam . . .

But he was family. He was my half-brother, the son of my father, as much my family as Ulysses, or Titus, or Theo. Silently, I committed my life into his hands, convinced that he was worthy of my trust.

Lilith laughed, "We might enjoy seeing that, mightn't we, my subjects?" The crowd roared. "You are an entertaining thing; what else can you do?"

"I can sing." Caliban danced about before Erasmus's cage, belting out words Shakespeare had written for him:

> *No more dams I'll make for fish*
> *Nor fetch in firing*
> *At requiring;*
> *Nor scrape trencher, nor wash dish*
> *'Ban, 'Ban, Cacaliban*
> *Has a new master: get a new man.*
> *Freedom, hey-day! hey-day, freedom! freedom,*
> *hey-day, freedom!*

"I can tell stories, too! Would you like to hear one?" Turning toward Erasmus's cage, Caliban declared in a loud voice, "And the cat in the boots said to the young man, 'Behold, if you wish to make your fortune, you must do exactly as I say!'"

As he said this, Caliban looked directly into Erasmus's eyes and extended his club in a dramatic flourish. I heard nothing, but Erasmus started and looked rapidly from the club to me.

Caliban had done it! He had given King Vinae a chance to fill Erasmus in on the plan. The hardest part had been accomplished! From here on, everything would go smoothly—unless someone betrayed us.

It was out of my hands. I would have to trust my family.

Caliban babbled on a bit, mixing lines from various fairy tales. Lilith yawned. "Enough! The time has come for Erasmus Prospero to die."

"Remember. Last request," King Vinae's voice called, as Caliban quickly moved the club next to the flute again.

"Ah. Right." The Queen of Air and Darkness directed her attention toward my brother. "Erasmus Prospero, do you have a last request before we kill you—which is when the real torture will begin?" The hordes of demons and goblins cackled gleefully. Lilith continued, "You may ask for anything you desire, except for your release. Do you wish us to allow one soul out of Hell? I will escort the lucky person myself. You could grant freedom to your uncle Antonio here. Then he would not be constrained to sully his soul further by striking the blow against you, for he would no longer need to fear what I could do to him. He would be free to spend eternity in Limbo.

"Or, you could ask that your own soul be escorted to Limbo. Or that your body be returned to your father, who could then use his new *Staff of Eternity* to resurrect you, undoing all our wicked work.

"Or, you may ask for the life of your son Fiachra. Otherwise, seven years after Mab here takes the Last Walk, Fiachra Swan-Lord will be the next denizen of Fairyland to be tithed."

"Rather decent of her," Ulysses murmured to Mab and Logistilla, "to make cracking suggestions. That idea about letting us take his body back is the dog's bollocks! We'd get Erasmus back, and everything would be fine."

"Not really," Mab growled back. "She's got Miss Miranda!"

"Oh! Bloody Hell!" Ulysses exclaimed. "That's no good!"

Erasmus hesitated, torn. He glanced at the carved length of wood in Caliban's hand, as if debating whether or not to trust King Vinae's advice.

Would he do as the Club had instructed? Or would he request some other boon?

I waited, my heart hammering. Silently, I prayed, "Please, Erasmus! Please!" For, if he did not choose to have me play for him, I would surely die . . . or worse.

Beside me, I saw Mab's eyes quickly flicker over the various objects in the environment. He clearly reached the same conclusion I had just reached. If Erasmus chose his own freedom, in any form, Ulysses, Logistilla, Caliban, and Mab could still escape. They were close enough to one another that they could successfully flee using the *Staff of Transportation*. I, on the other hand, would be trapped in the numbing grip of the Torturers. Unless Lilith instructed them to release me, I would never leave Hell again.

Even if my brother made a choice that did not benefit himself, such as the freedom of his son, if Erasmus failed to request that I play—requiring the Torturers to let go of me—my life as I knew it would be over.

Looking across the snow, I met Erasmus's gaze. His dark eyes stared mockingly back at me, and I realized Lilith had outwitted me.

She had offered my brother everything he desired. Erasmus merely had to ask that Ulysses and Logistilla be allowed to take his body back to Father, and, most likely, he would one day live again. He would be home, with Father and all his family, and the only price paid would be me—exactly the outcome he had been plotting for when he suggested I be the volunteer for his spell. As to his son, if Erasmus were alive and free, he could find a way to save Fiachra.

On the other hand, if he chose to go along with our plan, he would be trading a sure thing for the unknown. No, it was not that our plan was unknown that was holding him back. It was me. If he chose our plan, he would have to trust me, just as I, moments ago, had been forced to trust Caliban.

But, Erasmus did not trust me.

Uncle Antonio had won. The Queen of Air and Darkness had won. The Family Prospero was going to be undone by demon-sown mistrust.

Would I have come had I known what was at stake? That I might lose everything and be handed over to Osae the Red as his plaything before being dragged off to the Tower of Pain?

I recalled a thousand offenses Erasmus had committed against me: how he had mocked me ceaselessly; how he had ridiculed me in public; how he

364   L . J a g i   L a m p l i g h t e r

had called me unwomanly before the other ladies of the English court, provoking a duel with Theo, which led to my learning to embroider and to the coat-of-arms I sewed for Theo; how he had withered my hair and scalp, leaving my hair permanently white—he had not known at the time that I could restore its vitality using Water of Life; how he had dangled his shares of Prospero, Inc., before me just to yank them away again, resulting in the deaths of over a hundred thousand people when I was not present to mitigate the effects of the worst typhoon in recorded history.

And I was willing to make such a sacrifice, to give up everything of worth left to me, to risk the lives of my family and those of countless people on earth for this man?

Across the ice, our eyes met.

For an instant, it was as if I was Erasmus, as if I suffered despair such as I had not previously thought possible; as if it were I who had lost all hope—lost my love, been betrayed, and wasted my life in hatred.

It was as if I was the one who had loved Maria, who loved Father more than my own life, who loved Cornelius, despite his shortcomings, loved him for his intelligence, his wit, and his refusal to bow to despair, despite the mountain of challenges afflicting our blind brother.

I felt such sorrow, such self-loathing. Nothing in my previous experience prepared me for such depth of anguish.

I stumbled back, my heart pounding. The Torturer's claws tore into my shoulder. I managed to stifle my scream.

It had happened again. This time, I had seen a glimpse of the inner heart of my brother Erasmus. No wonder my brother had volunteered to take Father's place. The comeuppance he had suffered at Uncle Antonio's hands, and then again upon learning that I was not what he had taken me to be, was far worse than anything Hell might devise.

I could not hold him fully responsible for his rancor toward me. Some of it had been Uncle Antonio's doing. When it came down to it, Erasmus was not the enemy. He was a man whom Cornelius loved, and he was my brother.

Closing my eyes, I forgave him.

Opening them again, I met Erasmus's gaze and hope leapt in my heart. Then, a sneer curled his lip, and I knew that I was lost. Tears blurred my vision, as sorrow for vanished opportunities swelled my throat. I could barely breathe. Silently, I prayed that Mab would be able to get the flute out of Hell before his entire race fell under the sway of the Queen of Air and Darkness.

How different my life had turned out from what I had dreamt it might be when, as a maid of fifteen, I journeyed from Prospero's Island to Milan. What great hopes I had had for the wide world beyond our island, that brave new world. I did not feel that I had wasted my time; yet, I had never become a Sibyl, never become a wife, or a mother, and my two chances at love had been so fleeting that I could hardly say I had loved at all.

Both of the men were now dead; both killed by treachery.

My one consolation was that my epitaph would not bear the cold inscription that the dream Astreus had predicted. I had trusted my family. That was what had brought me to this impasse. Perhaps, instead, it might read: "She was loyal."

No, even that was robbed of me, for my very last action had been to disobey my father. Father had been right, of course.

Oh what a fool I had been to come!

My brother turned his head what little he could until he could see the beautiful Queen of Air and Darkness in her black chariot. She nodded prettily, awaiting his request.

Erasmus raised his voice: "Oh, Great Lilith, my last request is that my sister Miranda play one last song for me upon her flute."

I gasped. Ulysses and Caliban grinned. Logistilla sagged in relief. Mab let out a strangled cheer.

"And risk having her slay you herself? For, if the *Staff of Winds* is one of the tighter bars, her first note will kill you." Lilith clapped her hands. "Oh, that is splendid. Rather like Russian roulette, only with thorn bushes." A tiny furrow appeared between her lovely brows as her eyes paused upon my emerald wings, but it did not dampen her enthusiasm. "Let the concert begin."

The Torturer released me. I slipped my hands free of the handcuffs, and Caliban offered me my flute. My upper arms felt numb where the crab-like claws had pinched me, but I was able to move my shoulders. I took the flute and walked forward.

My brother watched me intently from where he waited in his warped cage. Some of his dark hair had pulled free of his queue and again hung in his eyes. His face was pale, except where it bled from multiple scratches.

Still sneering, Erasmus looked straight at me, his gaze defiant, as if daring me to slay him. He spoke in a soft, almost menacing voice. "I would rather be damned for trusting my family than redeemed for doubting them."

"Good for you, Sir," Mab murmured, taking off his hat and holding it in front of his chest.

"Before, I play, I would like to make a dedication," I announced.

Lilith nodded and waved her hand, encouraging me to add to the entertainment of her hordes.

"This song is for my Lady Eurynome," I began. There was a flash of lightning in the far distance. The ice beneath us shook, making a noise like thunder.

"You better not say Her name again," Logistilla hissed, "and shouldn't you be dedicating this to Erasmus?"

Drawing myself up, I chanted: "In the beginning, Eurynome moved across the face of Chaos, but found no place to rest her feet. Dancing upon the dark waters, she found the wind behind her had become a serpent, the great Ophion. Eurynome danced, and Ophion coiled about her divine limbs. Thus was the universe conceived."

I then told a succinct version of the tale Father Christmas told us at Landover Mall, about the demons and their garden and how the Divine Infinite breathed life into the first of men. Each time I spoke my Lady's name, my infernal audience cringed, Lilith scowled, and a lightning bolt snaked across the sky.

"As the woman sat beneath the blessed tree," I concluded, "a fruit fell into her hand, and she bit into it. Some say that it fell by its own volition, but others claim that Ophion, the Serpent of the Wind, moved through its branches, disturbing them; for he was ever a champion of mankind and an enemy of all demons.

"Many eons have passed since that long ago time," I finished, ignoring the hisses of my disgruntled audience, "but still Eurynome dances, bringing forth life and trampling Chaos beneath Her feet. This song, I dedicate to Her and to Her consort, the mysterious Serpent of the Wind, wherever he may have wandered. May they find their way back to each other. For while Love may be postponed or delayed, it can never truly be denied . . . or bound." I bowed my head. My audience hooted and booed.

I stood in their midst, holding the *Staff of Winds* in my hands. Never had its four-foot length of pale, polished pinewood seemed so precious to me. I recalled the last time I had played it, how its sacred music had soothed the creatures who were tortured here, giving them a moment's respite from their millennia of torture. Tears rose in my eyes. I longed to play it one more time, to hear its voice, to let it, just once more, transport me beyond this mortal coil into some realm more sublime.

But it was not to be.

Raising my flute, I touched my lips to its polished wood one last time. Then, I brought it down upon my thigh with all my supernatural strength, courtesy of the Water of Life.

The flute snapped in two.

CHAPTER TWENTY-EIGHT

The Serpent of the Winds

A stillness fell upon us, like the quiet clarity before the storm. It lasted just long enough for me to take in the expression of unadulterated joy upon the face of Mab and that of triumph on the face of Lillith, who leaned forward eagerly, expecting the release of King Vinae. Then, like a living hurricane, the Serpent of the Winds welled up out of the broken flute.

"Logistilla! Now!" I cried, as one of the thorny bars trapping Erasmus went limp and fell away from the cage. "Ulysses!"

Logistilla raised her staff. Eerie green iridescent light danced across the ball that topped it. It shot out and touched Erasmus, who had just enough leeway—due to the missing bar—to draw away from the sharp point of the thorn driving toward his heart. Then, he was a toad, and Ulysses grabbed him. With a bright flash, they were both gone—leaving the rest of us stranded.

The wind whipped around me, rising out of the two broken halves of the flute. It grew, blowing up the ice about us into a small blizzard. It threw imps, ouphe, and demi-goblins to and fro. It tossed the Torturers across the glacier like dry leaves, their long cloaks flapping in the hurricanic breeze.

The winds spread. Gathering together, they formed a great serpentine shape that undulated back and forth as it snaked through the nearby cages. The triangular head, as large as a bull elephant, rose up, poised to strike. Slitted serpent eyes, delineated by swirling ice, stared down at me.

I stood, petrified. I had risked everything on the fact that Ophion had not obeyed when Baelor called upon him to turn against me. I had chosen the words of my speech carefully, wishing to remind the great serpent where his loyalties originally lay. I was hoping he had remained loyal because, despite his captivity, he still preferred mankind to demons.

If I was wrong, then I had just done something terrible indeed.

I spread my arms and called, "Ophion, you are free. Forgive me, for I knew not who you were. Spare us, I beg you, and return to your Lady, whom you love."

The serpent remained poised above me, staring hypnotically. Then, as swiftly as a gale wind, he swept down upon me.

The Serpent of the Winds caught me up in his coils, drawing me some two hundred feet into the air. As he wound around me again and again, his head slithered past my ear.

"It is true," whispered a voice that sounded like the winds themselves speaking.

"What?" I cried, terrified. "What is true?"

As the great head of wind slipped by my other ear, it answered, "We do love you."

AS gently as a summer breeze, he placed me back on my feet. Then, he turned his fury against the demons.

Incubi and peri, demons and cacodemons flew through the air; horns and wings and tri-spiked tails all rolled together into great snowy balls. Terrified, the denizens of Hell fled, crying and cawing and wailing like babies.

There was another flash, and Ulysses appeared beside Logistilla, Mab, and Caliban. As he held out his hand, Uncle Antonio grabbed Logistilla's enchanted garment-clad arm, crying, "Please! Take me with you!" The five of them disappeared in a swirl of white light.

"Stop!" Lilith held up her hand.

The great serpent of wind paused, raising up like a cobra performing a rope trick. All the winds ceased. A slow smile spread across her girlish face. "We have had enough of this. Servants, grab the girl."

The sky cracked opened, and lightning struck the Tower of Thorns. The accompanying thunderbolt shook the glacier. The thorny tower trembled and tottered. As if in slow motion, it tumbled over before crashing to the snow beneath it.

All across the glacier, the captives gave a great cheer as the bars of their cages snapped and they ran out, free. Only the giant, who was trapped in the ice, remained restrained.

Overhead, the broken sky was lit from beyond by a brilliant glow, and a golden shaft of light fell from the hole in the sky to the snow. Angels circled about the opening, staying within the beam of golden light. I could not see them clearly, just glimpses of wings and gowns; but what a sound they made, like a thousand doves beating their wings in unison!

Then, I saw Her.

She came across the ice leaving a trail of wildflowers in Her wake, a slim white creature, horselike but as graceful as a deer, with silver cloven hooves and a slender tail with a puff at the end, like a lion's. Her lavender eyes were flecked with gold. Out of Her brow sprang a horn of spiraled ivory.

She had come!

The air now smelled of fragrant ozone, and a warmth was spreading across the valley, melting the snow up to a mile away. All about her, violets and forget-me-nots spread like wildfire.

"Great Queen!" roared a demon I recognized as Prince Sitri. "It is Her! Your dreaded enemy! This is your moment of glory! The moment for which we, your humble servants, have waited. Save us from Her as you have saved us from her consort! Destroy and demean Her, as you have so often told us you long to do!"

All eyes turned to Lilith, imploringly.

The Queen of Air and Darkness's face grew as pale as ash. Drawing back upon the reins of her carriage, she fled.

Terrified, the demon hordes rushed to follow, but they were too late. The Serpent of the Wind struck, and they were whirled away across the now-melting Glacier of Hate.

Of those who had been released from the cages, some ran, but others stopped and were drawn upwards. A host of angels, singing together in glorious chorus, flew down to greet them.

The Unicorn turned Her lovely delicate head and regarded me. In Her lavender eyes, I thought I saw pity, love, and understanding.

Then, She lowered her horn and charged.

The sharp point of Her horn struck my forehead and pierced my skull. I screamed.

Sparks flew everywhere.

GREATER *than the universe, greater than all universes, which I held in my arms, cradling them as a mother cradled a tiny infant, I danced within the void. My silver hair fell about me like a mane, and, from my brow, a beam of light spiraled up like a horn. The Alcreate's Regard, which showered down upon me like a resplendent, silvery-white ray, sustained me, and I, in return, shared it with all—the thousand-million galaxies that whirled and spun within my gentle embrace. I knew them all and loved—with equal and eternal love—each individual point of life, whether it be a living galaxy-spiral, whose* million light-year-long body consisted of a thousand-billion stars, or a single-celled ameoba wriggling its way through a solitary raindrop.

As I danced, I knew the secret that was no secret at all: ALL THE WORLD WAS MADE FOR LOVE.

As I woke to myself, Eurynome asked me if there were some iota of eternity I wished to take back with me, some specific question I wished answered.

I asked, "If the demons are so corruptive, why did God put mankind in this terrible position? Why did the Divine Infinite breathe life into the homunculi the demons had created in the garden? Or if that story is not the true one, why did God put the Tree of the Knowledge of Good and Evil into the garden in the first place? Why did he damn us to this mortal existence from which we cannot escape?"

My Lady laughed, a sound like the ringing of a galaxy of bells: *All those who came were volunteers.*

"Volunteers?" I cried. "Volunteering to do what?"

Save the demons.

"What?" I cried.

Do you think the Alcreate could do less than love all his children? Mankind is comprised of souls who volunteered to leave High Heaven on the mission to rescue the fallen angels, who are also His beloved children.

"Fallen angels are redeemable?"

Have you not read your Bible, where it says in the Book of Jude: "And the angels which kept not their first estate, but left their own habitation, He hath reserved in everlasting chains under darkness unto the judgment of the great day."

"Yes . . ." I replied.

It is the dearest wish of all in High Heaven that, upon the Day of Judgment, the fallen ones—having by then redeemed themselves and cleansed away their stains—shall be judged and not found wanting.

REENTERING the world after my sojourn with my Lady was a shock. All my senses reeled from the return of sensation. The light before me seemed too dull. Sound rushed back to my ears in a roar. Goosebumps formed upon my limbs from the chill. My mouth felt cottony and dry, and I nearly choked as the mingled fragrance of ozone, lavender, and the dust of corruption filled my nostrils.

I stood by myself. Instead of a glacier, a field of flowers spread out around me. In the distance, I saw the tumbled Tower of Thorns. It still hurt my eyes, so I quickly glanced away. Beyond that, however, more flowers stretched.

Nowhere did I see cages.

There was no sign of Ulysses, either.

I was alone in Hell. My family had deserted me. My Lady had departed. My precious flute lay broken. All I had with me—to help me make my way back over the glacier, up the Mountains of Misery, across the Plain of Wasted Lives, back through the lava, and . . . and after that I did not even know where to go, for we had flown on the back of the swan—was an enchanted dress and a very sharp fan. I did not even have Mab for company.

I shook myself and forced a laugh. Ulysses would come back, of course. I was only on my own for a minute, while I waited for him to drop the others off.

But he did not return.

I stood there, growing colder and colder. A single tear meandered down my cheek. Unable to bear it any longer, I knelt and prayed.

A golden cast fell across the flowers, and I breathed in a beautiful scent, even more glorious than the fragrance of the wild blossoms. Turning, I beheld a Virtue, her five pairs of seagull wings outstretched. She smiled down at me, the light of her five halos glinting off her silver slippers and off the pearls that trimmed her robes. Where her aura encountered any bare portion of the ice, not already converted to flowers by my Lady's presence, the glacier burned with a cherry-gold flame that bubbled and warped the hellish landscape about us, as if the very substance of Hell could not abide the angel's presence.

The angel bent toward me and touched my head. The green of her gown was the exact color of my wings.

"*Rejoice!*" Muriel Sophia spoke in her heavenly, melodious voice.

"Mother?" I jumped to my feet.

"*My daughter.*"

Hesitating only briefly, I threw my arms around the angel.

Heavenly wings enfolded me. Feathers as soft as the dreams of happy children brushed my cheek and the back of my neck. A glorious warmth flowed through my veins. The tension drained out of my limbs, and my whole body relaxed. I felt like a newborn kitten nestled under the wing of a giant swan, as if I were as far from the ravages of the Inferno as Paradise itself.

My face buried in feathers that smelled of sea spray and springtime after a rain, I asked, "When Eurynome spoke about redeeming the demons, did she mean something like what has happened to King Vinae?"

"He is the first, but there will be others." My mother stroked my cheek. Joy skittered through me. Her gentle touch made me feel whole, like fitting the final pieces to a long-slaved-over puzzle, where that puzzle was my heart.

"Will Vinae be able to return to Heaven?" I asked.

"That is not known yet. He has far to go, but he is on the right path. Once anyone values Love above other things, the Gate to Heaven cannot but open."

"Mankind's purpose is to save the demons, and, in the millions of years during which we have dwelt upon the Earth, we've only saved one?"

"Eurynome does not see the world the way we do." Muriel Sophia spread her wings, except for one pair which she kept snugly around me. She looked like a white peacock with a black trim, or a woman standing before a giant fan made of seagull feathers. *"Mankind has as many purposes as there are individuals, for the Divine Infinite weaves all things together for the good of those who love Him—and yet, it has but one purpose: to glorify Him. Saving the demons is one of those many purposes, and it is a purpose to which I am devoted.*

"This is why I sent my servant, Solomon, into Hell, so that he could bring some of the stronger demons up to where they could behold men as they really are, not merely the twisted version that they are familiar with from below. So that the demons could see mankind at their best: loving each other, struggling over adversity, and, most important, facing temptation and resisting.

"King Vinae is a step or two ahead of the rest because he saw, first hand, your father's fall and how the power of my love redeemed him. But, every time your siblings are kind to each other, the demons in their staffs learn a little more about love. Every time someone in the Family Prospero resists the temptation offered by the demon in his staff, that demon learns a little more about virtue and resolve, a little more about how to resist temptation and find the pathway back to Heaven."

"You mean the whole point of our having staffs is to do to the demons what Mephisto does to monsters? Win them over and tame them?"

"Indeed," my mother replied. I noticed her silver slippers did not quite reach the ground. *"That is why they would not turn and rend you, despite the urgings of Baelor of the Baleful Eye back at Erasmus's mansion. He persuaded them not to attack him, but he could not convince them to turn on their masters, whom they had grown to respect. Of them all, only Paimon has not made progress, but only because his binding was done incorrectly, and he could still hear the whispered voices of his demonic comrades."*

"And just living with our staffs was enough to bring about this change?" I asked. "I would have thought that the demons trapped within would have become more rancorous the longer they were imprisoned."

"Your family is particularly suited to this task," my mother explained. *"The soul of each of your father's children was sent from Heaven for the purpose of aiding in this project. But the task is hard. The weight of the demons' sins dragging upon their souls is so great that even the most resolute of heroes may falter."*

Horripilations of awe danced up and down my limbs. "We were born to bear staffs? Is that my purpose, too?"

My mother gazed at me with such tender love that, for an instant, I felt as if I were the sweetest, most beautiful woman to ever walk the earth. *"Yours is to serve Eurynome, and to free the elves from their tithe to Hell."*

"A purpose I have failed. . . ." I choked. I tried to swallow, but it felt as if a massive boulder blocked my throat. I could not continue speaking.

The angel pressed her shining hand against mine. It was like having the warm springtime sun emerge from behind a cloud just to light one's private bower. My heart rose, and even something as grave and final as the utter failure of my life's purpose could not entirely dismay me. One tiny chamber of my heart still felt hope.

"Why, Mother?" I cried, "All those years, why was it I did not become a Sibyl? Was it because I kept slaves?"

"No," my mother the angel replied, *"though in freeing them, you did resemble Her more fully."*

"Then . . . what was it?"

"To be a Sibyl, you must be like Eurynome. You must think like her. See as she sees."

My knees grew weak as everything finally made sense. I leaned upon the angel. "The grand compassion Uncle Antonio mentioned?"

"Exactly so." Her wings supported me.

She stroked my hair with a gentle soothing gesture. It made me faintly sad that the locks beneath her hand were midnight black instead of the pale silver I pictured in my imagination. How ridiculous the petty things that plague us when our mind should be focused upon the exalted.

"So . . . this thing that's been happening to me—where I understand someone else's experience as if it were mine—that is what was missing?"

"Yes. Your angelic nature kept you separate from men. You had to bridge that gap before you could be of service to our Lady," Muriel Sophia explained. *"Many times, an opportunity for compassion has been presented to you, a*

doorway through which you could have chosen to go. But, in the past, you did not make that choice."

"And it all changed when I saw the old lady on the bridge?"

"Not then. Before. Think back."

My thoughts reeled backward. "Mab? In the Great Hall?"

"When you made the choice to save Mab Boreal, rather than stones and books, you finally stepped through the open door that had been waiting for you from the beginning."

The pain of unshed tears pricked at my eyes. "A door I started through as a maiden, when I gave my heart to Ferdinand, and then backed away from." Sorrow filled my mouth, and I could not continue.

"Ferdinand was killed by Antonio, who was still under the influence of Paimon. All the horror and bareness of your life has been orchestrated by the Ruling Seven—by Abaddon and Lilith."

All those years. All those long wasted years. To think that the very isolation and coolness I so valued, thinking in my vanity that they made me better than other people, had been the obstacle to my fulfilling my dreams. My besotting sin truly was pride.

It all changed because of Mab—Mab who had done so much for our family, so much more than we would have expected of a spirit servant. A pang of sorrow grabbed my heart and squeezed. The only time I ever told Mab outright how much I appreciated and trusted him, I had been talking to Osae. I made a mental note to correct this error.

A raucous caw sounded from above us. Overhead, Prince Sitri and his minions circled. They were dark, bat-winged monstrosities, some with the heads of leopards, others with the heads of crocodiles. More joined them every moment, their flock growing greater and greater. Seeing my mother, the demon prince lowered his scepter, signaling to his legions to attack.

I grabbed my fan and prepared to fight, but my mother stopped me with a hand. She drew me against her side and surrounded me with a single soft, fluffy, white seagull wing. As its warmth wrapped around me, I again felt safe, protected, as if hid in the secret place of the most high.

The hordes of demons dived toward the single five-winged angel, cursing and shouting. A legion contains five thousand individuals. Prince Sitri reigned over sixty legions, according to Mab, though no more than half a dozen could have been currently present. Still, the sky grew black with beating wings.

Had it been my family and I with all our magic, we would have been hard-pressed to fight off such an assault!

Only, the moment the golden light shed from Muriel Sophia's top-most halo fell upon the winged monstrosities, they burst into flame. Screaming, they writhed. Some wheeled away. Others plummeted to the ground, burning. They dived toward us and then plummeted from the sky like shriveled black rain. The field of wildflowers near us grew black with their bodies.

Snarling, Prince Sitri called a retreat. His minions turned and fled.

When the skies were again clear, my mother drew back her wing and glided over to where the fallen demons lay. Most of their form had burnt away, leaving only a glossy, black, wormlike thing, such as what had remained after Theo blasted Osae.

Her face shining with compassion, my mother the Virtue knelt and gave a comforting stroke to each shriveled black thing. Lifting one, as a mother might cradle a child, she whispered to it: *"Rejoice!"*

For an instant, the burden in her arms turned a brilliant gold. Then, it grew black and ugly again. My mother lay it gently back among the flowers.

"They are not ready for heaven yet," she sighed, rising. *"The day will come."*

I gazed around us, my jaw dangling slackly. In my mind's eye, I could see what this scene would have looked like if it had been my family and our staffs who faced Sitri's legions—the destruction, the carnage, the glassy craters, and the drops of Water of Life spent to heal our wounded. An entire legion of demons, maybe even several legions, had been vanquished without a single weapon being lifted.

"But, M-mother," I struggled to find my tongue, "You can destroy them! Just like that! Why don't the angels sweep through here and conquer the demons?"

Humor and sorrow danced together in my mother's emerald eyes. She gestured across the plain toward the Mountains of Misery. *"We did defeat them. That is why they are here."*

"Oh!" I felt immeasurably foolish. "Right . . . of course."

"We could attack again, but to what end? Why should we destroy the home they have forged from their own desires and replace it with a prison of our making? What would they learn from that? Besides, no one can be touched here unless they consent. Occasionally, even some demons remember this."

"Couldn't you at least . . . I don't know . . ."

"Help the innocents?" She shook her head. *"There are no innocents here."*

"Ah." I nodded. "Good point."

"We do harrow these lands from time to time. As souls burn off their sins,

we bring them Heavenward. Also, the Hellwinds will deposit lighter souls in Limbo. The Hellwinds are the work of one of the half-fallen."

"Half-fallen?"

"Men call them elves. Come!" The angel took my hand. Together, we took a single step.

We were in Limbo, standing outside the Gate of False Dreams. Mother pointed at the words carved into the black, adamantium wall.

"You ask if the suffering and sorrow is worth it, if you have only managed to save one demon?" her beautiful voice sang, a lone soprano from the Heavenly choir. *"Only one is needed."*

"You mean, the success of one will give the others hope?" I asked.

She nodded.

Another step, and we stood beside a similar gate, only it was flanked by horn rather than ivory. Atop the gate were engraved the words:

THROUGH ME IS TRUTH.

ENTER AND HOPE.

"The Gate of True Dreams," my mother said. *"Behold."*

Gazing through the door, I saw a vast hollow cavern that stretched as far as the eye could see in all directions. Everyone, everywhere, lay sleeping, both the mortals and the demons. The sleepers twisted and turned. They writhed, flailing and thrashing, as if they fought off unseen assailants, yet nothing threatened them. Over each slumbering soul hovered its own great, enormous being of light. The immensely tall bodies of these beings stretched upward, farther than my eye could see. These guardians stood guard over both the men and the fallen angels, comforting them and softly calling them to awake.

"They are all sleeping!" I cried.

"Did not you enter through the Gate of False Dreams? What else could it be?" the Angel of Bitter Wisdom replied.

"Why was it that I could see through the illusions we came upon, but no one else could?"

"Because of the angelic portion of your nature, you saw part of the truth— that there was no good, no pleasure to be had below. But because of your human nature, your eyes were still deluded, and could not see that the pain, too, was an illusion. These beings are all here because they have chosen false dreams

over true. The moment they change their minds, they awake, and we whisk them off to Heaven—though they seldom wake so completely as to glimpse this version of things."

I swallowed twice, astonished and unable to find words to express my surprise.

"But . . . how . . ." I cried. "So, the churches are just wrong. Hell is not eternal?"

"The Church is not wrong." My mother's voice was as gentle as a spring zephyr, and yet an uncomfortable tingle spread up my spine. *"This is not Hell."*

She spread her hand, and the earth beneath us became transparent. Far, far below, flames burned, but not flames of light and brightness, as I was used to, but cold, lifeless, flames of nothingness. As if the nothingness were coming into being, consuming itself, and ceasing to exist, all in an instant of conflagrated horror.

My entire being rebelled. I felt as if my very innards were repulsed and fleeing my body.

"That," the angel intoned, *"is Hell."*

"Take it away!" I screamed, covering my eyes. "Make it stop."

The earth returned, and the terrible vision was gone.

"What . . . what was that?" I cried. "I mean, I know you said it was Hell, but . . . why was it so horrible?"

"Because the Alcreate is Good, as in goodness itself. If good is present, in any form, the Alcreate is there. Only where there is no good, nothing of any worth at all, could He be absent." She spread her five pairs of wings. It sounded like a thousand fans opening. *"Hell is the absence of God."*

"But . . . why are . . . the . . . who . . ." I paused and caught my breath. "What poor wretched souls were so vile that they are down there?"

"No one."

"Wha-what?"

"No one. Many do not see God. Many are not ready to approach his face. Many are sent here, in the hopes that they will change their ways. But no one, not even the Fallen Angels themselves, has ever abandoned God—abandoned love, abandoned affection, abandoned hope—so completely as to deserve to be put down there."

"So, Hell . . . real Hell is empty?"

"Yes."

"And nobody knows this?"

"As to that, you must ask your brother, the Churchman. There are a select few among the clergy who hope it might be so."

Disorientated, I took a step away. I turned in a circle and then peeked through the Gate of True Dreams again, gazing once more at the tall beings of light who so lovingly guarded the dreamers.

"Then . . . if what you just showed me is real Hell," I pointed at the dreamers, "where are they?"

"In a cavern beneath the mountain of Purgatory, much as Dante described it."

"You mean . . . that's why the tunnel at the bottom of Hell comes out at the foot of Mount Purgatory?"

"Exactly."

"So." I felt strangely disorientated, as if I were floating or spinning. "Hell is nothing. It is empty for all eternity?"

Sorrow clouded the shine of my mother's beautiful face. *"Only if the Fallen Ones repent. The place you just saw, the real Hell, will become their home, should mankind fail to save them."*

Stricken, I turned away and peered off into the dark mists of Limbo. What strange disorienting things my mother was saying. I was not sure what their significance was, or even if I believed them. I felt shocked and somewhat numb . . . until it occurred to me that, if it were true, it was a very good thing indeed.

After all, I had known that Eurynome intended to save everyone—including the damned and their fallen masters. Had I not believed it was possible?

The longer I thought about it, the more proud I was of my family for our part. It made all our suffering seem worthwhile.

Beyond the mists on the Limboside of the door, something caught my eye. A single figure dressed in black armor with a Greek helmet sat upon a throne, the same one I had glimpsed on our way down, just before we went through the Gate of False Dreams. There was something disturbing, something horrible, about this dark-clad form. A chill ran down my spine.

"I thought everything here was an illusion." I shivered. "He's real."

"The First Born?" asked Muriel Sophia. *"He received forgiveness at Calvary and now seeks to make reparations for his past misdeeds."*

"Hades? What terrible past does he have?"

"Cronos's first born stepped down long ago, passing his titles, station, and wife on to this one."

Another chill assailed me as I realized whose first born son must now sit upon the throne of Limbo. Shivering, I drew back, stepping closer to my mother. She wrapped her sea gull wings around me again, and for a moment, it was as if I was upon the ocean, surrounded by salt and sea spray, warm and joyful.

"There is much work to be done. You must return to your family." My mother spoke in her beautiful melodious voice, but her tone was as stern and relentless as the tides. *"Angels will strive to limit the harm being done to mankind by the Aerie Ones whom you let free when you selflessly sacrificed your flute to save your brother. But not all upon the earth can hear us or will heed our counsel. Go quickly now and bring the Family Prospero back to the mortal world, where they belong."*

"How ironic," I said softly. "We have saved only one demon, and that work was done by the basest of us. I am so ashamed of my former opinion of Caliban."

"Credit goes as well to Mephistopheles, who first did to Caliban what Caliban then did in turn to Vinae."

"Mephisto?" I asked, "He works for you, doesn't he?"

She smiled and nodded. *"Though sometimes wayward, he is sincere and loyal. A true servant of Heaven."*

"And it was you who helped Father while he was imprisoned, wasn't it?" I asked. "You who made it so that the pain thorns could not harm his spirit?"

The angel nodded again. *"Yes, Child. Your father is a brave and noble hero whom all Heaven honors."*

"One last question!" I cried, the words ripping unexpectedly from my throat. "Why did I never see you? Why did you never come to me?"

"Nonsense, Child." My mother cupped my cheek in her shining palm. Joy radiated from it, like heat radiates from the sun. *"I came every time you called me. And now you must go. But fear not, Child, for I am with you always, even unto the ends of the world."*

I FOUND myself alone, kneeling in flowers—violets and daisies, bluebells and buttercups, forget-me-nots and snowdrops, and Queen Ann's Lace. The lavender plume of an immortal amaranth poked up here and there, where Eurynome's foot had actually touched the ice. Giddy with joy, I pressed my face to cool petals, inhaling sweet perfume.

I raised my hand to wipe my face and encountered something sharp upon my brow. Drawing my hand away quickly, I found blood on my fingertip. My stomach clenched painfully as I recalled how my Lady had pierced my skull. Was there a hole in my head with jagged, broken bone sticking out?

I raised my hand again, and my heart skipped a beat, then two, then three.

Upon my forehead was a hard, smooth spiral about the size of a dime. It grew larger under my touch until it was as large as a quarter. The center rose to a point, the tip of which was still so sharp that it had cut my finger. Moving down, the arms of the spiral opened outward, ending in five curving pieces, like the petals of a flower, or a starfish that had curled all its limbs so that each one pointed at the next. Touching it caused a joyous sensation to run through my arm.

The mark of the Sibyl!

I touched the mark again, and a sensation of vitality and strength ran through my arm and down into my body. The sharp point at the center had already grown blunter; it now had a smooth nub for a tip. I put my injured finger in my mouth.

At long last, it had happened,

I was a Sibyl.

Sitting up, I glanced across the field of wildflowers to the glacier far beyond. To my great surprise, flowers sprang up in the wake of my gaze. I tried it again, looking off in another direction. Again flowers followed my line of sight.

What was happening?

I recalled what the *Book of the Sibyl* had said about the Gift of Visions. I did not know what *"closing my mortal eyes and opening Eurynome's eyes"* meant, but I tried closing my eyes and picturing the scene in my mind, imagining my Lady was with me.

In my mind's eye, I saw an image of the scene, just as it looked with my eyes open, only a white light, like a search beam, came from the mark on my forehead. I raised my hand and put it in the way of the beam. It was like touching love. A warmth spread through my body, and I felt stronger, more wholesome. I recognized that feeling! It was like drinking Water of Life, only more so.

Wherever I looked, a beam of my Lady's love came from my forehead and struck the object I was beholding. It tingled and sweetened the air, so that I felt as if I were in a holy place. When I paid attention to the flowers, they leaned toward me, as if I were the sun. When I looked across the landscape, the gleaming beam struck the snow of the remaining glacier and brought life, flowers, where previously there had been only ice.

So that was what the *Book of the Sibyl* meant by: *Where the Sibyl looks, love flows!*

And that was what flowed from my forehead: Love! A hundred things I had read about Sibyls over the years, a thousand subtle references, all came together and made sense at last. This energy, this invisible, liquid light, was Eurynome! Or rather Her spirit, Her love, flowing forth at the Sibyl's bidding. It drew from the endless reservoir of Her heart—a never-ending stream of joy upon which a Sibyl could call, assuming she could maintain the right state of mind. It was the very stuff of which souls were made.

I had to keep my heart filled with joy for this to occur. If I started thinking about mundane things, the beam diminished, and flowers ceased springing up. On the other hand, the more I loved, the more I thought about joy, and gratitude, the wider the beam and the more quickly the blooms spread.

I knelt there, laughing and spelling out words in wildflowers by tracing letters along the bare ice: "Truth," "Joy," and "Astreus Stormwind," which I wrote in long looping letters much like his own handwriting from my copy of the *Book of the Sibyl*.

Blushing, I quickly blotted out the last by glancing rapidly back and forth, until new blooms sprang up over the whole area.

The wonder of it—to be able to bring life out of nothingness, even in Hell—awed me. Despite having yearned for this for centuries, I could hardly believe such a gift had been granted to me.

In the distance, a minotaur cavorted among the flowers. Beyond that lay the fallen Tower of Thorns. Summoning up all the love and joy I could muster, I focused the white beam on its dreadful thorns.

They did not hurt my eyes. The entire length of the tower that had once so terrified me burst into brilliant red roses.

When Ulysses found me, I was laughing, surrounded by flowers.

CHAPTER TWENTY-NINE

Seir of the Shadows

Ulysses and I appeared amidst a sea of arms, all reaching for the *Staff of Transportation*. Somewhere in the mass of family, I caught sight of Mab. With a quick gesture, I pulled out the pins that held my hair up. Shaking my tresses over my face, I grabbed Mab and drew him over beside me.

"Psst," I whispered. "Can I borrow your hat?"

Mab gave me a long odd stare, but he handed the fedora over without a word. I put it on, pulling it low, so that it covered the mark. It was too much to talk about right now, too much to explain.

There would be time enough to share this with my family once we were all safely home.

"Ready?" Father called. "Let's go!"

Ulysses tapped his staff. A moment later, I was sinking into the Swamp of Uncleanness. The great adamant structure of the Gate of False Dreams towered over us.

"Sorry," Ulysses called cheerfully. "Forgot about this. This happened last time, too, and when I was fleeing Abaddon. Really gave me the heebie-jeebies, because I thought, having renounced hope and all that, I could never get out, but it's really all right. We just have to walk through the gate on foot, and we can teleport again on the far side. . . . Oops!"

"Oops?" asked Logistilla. "Oops, what?"

A rising sense of panic threatened to consume me. Before I had sunk very far, however, Titus picked me up and threw me over his shoulder. Holding me began to affect him, and he began to sink as well.

"Hurry, ye wee man!" Titus boomed. "Get us out of here!"

"Can't!" Ulysses called back. "The gate is locked! It was locked when I tried to bug out during the battle with Abaddon, too, but I forgot about it.

Or rather, I thought it might be open again, because Mephisto was able to summon his creatures."

"Can't you go around?" Erasmus asked. He looked pale. His face had been raked by thorns and was now marred by bloody scratches.

"No good. My staff doesn't work that way."

Theo's voice boomed from behind us. "Here, allow me."

Stepping forward, he drew out a long golden key from beneath his breastplate. "Abaddon dropped this when I blasted him. I thought it might come in handy."

So that was what he had been carrying all this time. He inserted the golden key into the keyhole. The giant black door slowly swung open. Immediately, Titus charged forward, carrying us both successfully through the gate, and I found myself in the vast, dark, mist-filled cavern of Limbo.

Erasmus limped forward. He looked tired but happy. He put his hand on my shoulder. Then, to my utter shock, he laughed and threw both arms around me, hugging me.

"I owe you my life," he whispered in my ear. "You are a better man than I—human, or whatever it is you are." He ran a hand through my wings, producing an odd ripple of pressure on my shoulder blades. "Thank you."

I squeezed him back. It felt weird, but there was no familiar rush of animosity, such as I had felt in the days before we destroyed Antonio's spell. In fact, now that I had forgiven him, he seemed quite different: part wise, part foolish, and rather dear.

The others filed through behind us. I turned to greet them, smiling, and was surprised by their long faces and the lack of bounce in their step. Why were they not celebrating?

"It was that Cavalier hat, Ma'am," Mab said sadly. "Should have warned him not to put it on until we were safely outside."

"Until who was safely outside? What are you talking about, Mab?"

"We lost Mephisto," Father replied, he leaned upon his staff, from which leaves and flowers grew. His face looked lined and worn. "Lilith had some hold on his soul. She pointed her finger, and the ground gaped beneath his feet." He shook his head in disgust. "All this effort, and there has been no net gain. We are still down one member. Let us go home and lick our wounds. Perhaps, with time and contemplation, we can discover a way to save my wayward son."

The mists of Limbo blew a pack of whirling souls against us. One passed through Ulysses, who screamed and disappeared in a flash of light, leaving the rest of us stranded in Limbo.

"Oh, that boy!" Father growled, shaking his head.

"I knew we should have marked the hole that led to that crate!" Logistilla wailed.

In the midst of this confusion, someone touched me on the shoulder. Turning, I found myself looking into a black sable face framing blood red eyes.

"I came to say one last goodbye," his golden-tongued voice whispered, "unless you wish to stay and come with me to my nest of love where we can bask in the carnality of our passion forevermore?"

Standing so close, I could not help but notice again how extraordinarily handsome he was. His intoxicating demon-scent wafted my way, and a tingling began in my forehead. Closing my eyes, I pictured the beam coming from my forehead touching the place from which the tingle seemed to originate. The tingling stopped, and I remained unaffected by the incubus's proximity.

I nearly laughed aloud. Apparently, the incubus's effect counted as a "poison." By removing his noxious influence, I had successfully used another of the Gifts of the Sibyl. Behind me, I heard Mab and Cornelius sniffing the air; apparently they had caught a whiff of the heavenly scent. Luckily, they did not glance this way. Seir himself seemed disturbed. He looked about in wary puzzlement.

"Lilith has stolen Mephisto," I whispered. "Can you bring him back?"

His eyes went a dull red, the color of dried blood. "Have I not done enough for Mephistopheles?"

My heart beat so loudly I feared my family would hear it. His eyes had changed color! Seir's eyes never changed; they had always been that same unchanging, bloody crimson. Could my dream have been true? Had the incubus really called up Astreus, only to be unable to put him down again?

"It's you!" I whispered in spite of myself.

He laughed. "And why do you think that? Because I sent you a false dream, and you believed it? No, he is dead. Deader than dead."

I frowned. Now, that seemed odd. Why would an incubus try to *decrease* my trust in him? Why would he mock me? That did not even sound like an incubus talking.

It sounded like an elf.

A cold terror laid a single silencing finger upon my heart. No! I was not going to walk down that path! I was not going to risk my heart, or my family, again. From my point of view, Astreus was dead and gone, no matter what this womanizing shadow might say.

A high-pitched *whir* sounded from over my left shoulder. Seir's eyes widened, and he vanished.

"Incubus!" Theo's voice barked out. My family immediately came to attention, staffs in hand, and began surveying the area warily.

I, meanwhile, stood stock still and trembled. If only I had not lost the crown, or we still had Mephisto's hat! If Astreus was in there at all, even as a ghost or a memory, I might have been able to convince him to make Seir rescue Mephisto.

I did not have the crown, but I did have something else.

Kneeling, I drew the figurine of Astreus that Mab had returned to me from my pocket and placed it on the ground.

With a second flash of light, Ulysses returned from wherever he had fled to, looking sheepish. "Sorry, folks, reflexes. Shall we tootle-loo along?"

"Let us depart! Immediately!" Father commanded striding toward Ulysses and grabbing his staff before my brother could flee again. "Any additional efforts to save Mephisto can be done from the safety of a landscape fit for mankind!"

The others grabbed hands. I did not rise.

"Ulysses, can you come back for me?" I asked. "I have an idea."

"Are you crazy?" Theo burst out, waving his hands. "Do you think we're going to abandon you in Hell the moment after that incubus tried to attack you?"

"I might—just might—be able to save Mephisto."

"I'm staying with you," Theo announced immediately.

"And I," said Titus.

"And me," said Mab.

"Me, too," offered Caliban.

"I as well," Gregor leaned upon the *Y* atop the *Staff of Silence.*

"And, I, I suppose," Erasmus said with a sigh. He could barely stand upright; he was still a mass of cuts, and his eyes were not quite focused. "I'm not really feeling my best, but it would be unsporting of me to leave now."

"Oh, pooh!" Logistilla stamped her foot. "Now we all have to stay, or we'll look like boobs."

"I will stay if someone will lead me in the right direction," Cornelius said. He stood with his hand on Erasmus's shoulder, and he was smiling.

Father's bushy eyebrows drew together but he did not object. He kept a hand on Ulysses's staff, though.

"Can't it wait?" Father asked. "I will remind you that there is a storm brewing."

My heart skipped a beat. I had forgotten about that. My family needed to rush back immediately to stop the Aerie Ones I had freed. I should wait, as Father suggested.

On the other hand, the window of time during which any remnant of Astreus might remain awake in Seir might be quite short. If I called him later, would he recall at all? I would have to trust that my mother and the angels could mitigate the damage a little longer.

"No. It can't wait." I frowned. "I appreciate the support, but really, the rest of you should rush back."

My siblings, to the man, shook their heads.

I sighed. "Very well, but if you are going to stay, you all have to stand together in a ward. And no shooting at the incubus when I call him up."

"Call him up?" Theo cried. "Do you mean Seir of the Shadows? The same tricky demon who hunted me for twelve years and tricked you into thinking he was Ferdinand?"

My head hurt. This was never going to work. All that elf-talk was certainly a trick as well.

Yet, why would the incubus mock me for trusting him. He had come as himself. He had not been pretending to be Astreus. It made no sense.

I stood up and turned on my brother. "Theo, are you going to trust me or not?"

Theo looked taken aback.

Erasmus lay a calming hand on Theo's shoulder. "Bro, just this once—just as a lark—why don't we all try trusting Miranda, hmm?"

"Er . . . right." Theo lowered his staff, whether because he agreed or because of the sheer irony of having Erasmus defend me against him, I did not know.

"Mab, draw a ward around everyone else, would you?" I knelt again and put my finger on the head of the figurine. Behind me, I heard Mab shuffling around, pouring out salt and the like that he had pulled from yet more of his ubiquitous pockets.

"All ready, Ma'am," he said finally.

My stomach churned. I tapped the figurine upon the head. For a moment, nothing happened. Then, Seir of the Shadows was standing before me, his tattered opera cape swirling about in the mists of Limbo.

Before I could so much as rise, there came a *whirring* hum from behind my back. Seir vanished again.

"Theo!"

"Sorry," my brother grumbled, shouldering his staff. "Habit."

I tapped the figurine again and stood.

Seir appeared again, gazing at my family warily.

"Don't go!" I called.

"Ah, an invitation from a maid? For that I will brave any danger."

I closed my eyes briefly, using my mark to dispel all the oogly incubus tingles.

"I want a favor." I touched his shoulder. He stared at my hand, as if mesmerized.

"You know what I want in return," he replied with honeyed words. "I want to carry you off to my love nest near the stars and pay my respects to your luscious sweet body until you grow faint from passion. I want us to become one and never to be parted. I want you!"

"I thought you might like something else." I whipped off Mab's hat and pushed my hair aside. My family currently stood behind me; only Seir could see the mark of my Lady's favor.

The incubus's eyes grew wide indeed. It may have been a trick of the light, but for an instant, it seemed as if his whole body had lost some of its sable darkness, becoming a papery gray. But then that instant was over, and he was the same as ever.

"Darling Miranda," Seir cooed. "Long have I desired to have you as my own, but that joy will be nothing to the pleasure and riches Lilith shall shower upon me when I deliver you to her now."

Behind me, Theo stirred, but he restrained himself and did not unlimber his weapon.

"I can offer you your freedom," I whispered very low.

"Freedom?" Seir spread his hands airily. "From what?"

I put the hat back upon my head. It was no good. Astreus was truly gone, and Mephisto—bless his dear soul—was lost to us, too.

Seir leaned toward me and reached out his hand. "You want me to risk my life, my position here in Hell, to rescue your brother? I will do it . . . if you come with me."

His eyes were red, and his sable features had not changed, but gone was the lust and longing. In its place was something both wild and calculating. It was an expression I had seen once before, as I fell from the back of a giant black swan toward a balcony of the palace of Hyperborea.

Mortal Maid, I have but to release you now, and you will fall and break apart upon the spires, speeding your way to Heaven. Is this your desire?

No! It was a trick! Remember Ferdinand . . . and Osae!

I took a step back. "I don't think so. You bring Mephisto to me."

He shook his sable head. "Only if you come with me. Otherwise, why should I risk Lilith's wrath?"

"What assurance do I have that you will not turn me over to Lilith, as you just said you would?" I asked, my voice rising.

"None at all, Miranda Prospero." His red eyes were strangely intent. Seir extended his hand again and chanted. "Choose you this day whom ye will serve: the deceits of the world, or the truth you can see only with your heart."

I pressed my hand against my chest as if to keep my hammering heart from breaking out of my rib cage. My breath had fled; I wondered if I would ever draw it again. The terror that grabbed ahold of me was so black, that I was surprised when my eyes could still see. I could not trust him. Only a fool would . . .

What was I afraid of? Betrayal? Losing myself? Humiliation? Erasmus had trusted me. He had done it when all the wisdom of the world would have counseled against it. Should I not be willing to do as much?

But I was Erasmus's sister, and this was a demon. The two cases were not the same.

I thought of Eurynome and of the glimpse my mother had shown me of Hell through the Gate of True Dreaming. If even the demons could be saved, what of elves?

I looked into his face once more, at the wild, laughing, living dare that stood before me. Then, for the first time in my life, instead of waiting for someone to prompt me, I followed my heart.

"Nooo!" Theo's voice followed us as, hand in hand, Seir and I disappeared.

INKY darkness embraced us, swirling about us like living shadows. Then, we stood in a dark alcove behind a rack, which blocked our view of the large chamber beyond. The floor, walls, and ceiling were made of gold. The scent of incense and rotting corpses filled the air, and screams and moans came from the main chamber.

On the other side of the rack, a large black demon with bat wings and many intertwining horns was bound to it with chains made of some black metal I did not recognize.

"Quick!" hissed the incubus. "Free him!"

"How?" I stared blankly at the heavy chains. The incubus merely stared at me as if I were an idiot. When I still did not respond, he pointed at my forehead.

"Oh!"

I slipped forward and knelt before the first lock. Pushing back Mab's hat, I touched the ivory mark upon my forehead to the latch.

The lock sprang open!

Mephistopheles's bonds were fastened in four places. Moving quickly from one to another, I opened the next two locks with ease. The last one, however, was above my head. I grasped one of the bars and put my foot on the lowest rung of the rack, intending to climb.

Pain! Fiery, scorching pain shot through my arm and foot.

I screamed.

An instant later, we were surrounded by demons. Seir met my eyes and shrugged. Then, he took my arm and dragged me from behind the rack out into the main chamber, displaying me for Lilith and her minions to see.

"Great Queen." He gave a courtly bow. "I have brought you a prize."

The throne room of the Queen of Air and Darkness looked just as Mephisto had portrayed it upon the wall mural in his Canadian mansion. It was a place of luxury and horror. All about the enormous chamber, demons, incubi, succubi, and *lilim* lounged on huge silken pillows. Some nibbled on dead corpses, as if upon delicacies; others engaged in vast orgies. The moans and screams came from this last group.

Mosaics set into the wall celebrated the reign of Lilith and her consort Cain who sat enthroned, flanked by the many monsters they had begotten together. Beneath these murals, stone statues ringed the chamber, portraying women with their heads dragged back as if by their hair; their stomachs ripped open; their faces masks of horror and shock. On some statues, a half-formed fetus climbed the woman's leg. Others reached imploringly toward stone images of squalling infants impaled upon pikes, their little mouths opened wide in agony.

Perhaps, there were still worse things, but I could no longer look. I lowered my gaze and stared at the golden floor, only then noticing that it crawled with maggots. My stomach churned. It must have shown on my face, for

Lilith laughed, a pretty tinkling sound, like a young girl enjoying the antics of her friends.

From my position, I could see out the door. We were high in the air. A sloping ramp of silver led from the door to the ground far below, descending along the side of a golden many-tiered structure that resembled the Ziggurat of Ur in Sumeria, where Lilith had first been worshiped by mankind. Lilith had placed her royal seat at the top of the ziggurat, in the room known as the "bedchamber of the god," where, if tradition was to be believed, a different maiden had been sent each night to serve as "the god's companion." A fitting throne room for the patroness of temple prostitution.

Lilith gave a screech of delight and sat forward on her throne, which was woven from black bones, clapping her slender hands. She sat garbed in a gown of scarlet owl feathers with dark crimson tips. A belt of pale white leather—probably human skin—circled her waist, clasped by a huge ruby.

Another ruby, carved into a spiral flower, dangled in the midst of her forehead, suspended by a golden chain—so that she seemed to have a Unicorn mark the color of blood.

She looked so young and delicate; it was hard to believe that something so lovely could be wicked.

"Look, the servant of the One-Horned Slut. Not so high and mighty now, are you? What a treat for us!" She laughed gaily. Turning to one of the long-haired and buxom *lilim,* her dark daughters who held an enmity with my Lady's Handmaidens, she instructed, "Meurex, call the Torturers. Tell them that the repair of their Tower can wait; they aren't getting anywhere anyway with those flowers everywhere. I have a prisoner for them."

Fissions of terror zipped through me as the *lilim* ran eagerly to complete her charge. I struggled, but Seir was no longer the only demon holding me. Another incubus, also extraordinarily handsome, restrained my arm with one hand while he stroked my side and hip with his other, dodging my attempts to elbow him. A big, burly cacodemon held my shoulder in his clawed grasp, threatening to sink his sharp talons into my flesh should I attempt to flee.

I had been betrayed. I supposed it was only what I deserved for trusting a demon.

"Incubus, you have pleased me," Lilith purred. "Name your reward."

"Great Queen." Seir bowed. "I would like this maiden to do with as I like."

I glanced at Seir curiously, trying to discern whether this was some stratagem intended to rescue me or merely an attempt to carry me off. If he meant me well, he did not give any indication.

From the midst of the servants who gnawed upon the corpse, a familiar voice shouted mockingly, "That one is a maiden no longer!"

I caught sight of Osae's spiky red hair amidst the crowd and shivered with revulsion. The imps and incubi laughed and hooted.

"Nonetheless," Seir replied mildly.

"Then, it shall be so," Lilith replied graciously. "When the Torturers are done with her, you may have what is left."

My legs were trembling now, and my throat felt dry. My hands and foot smarted where I had touched the rack, and my pride smarted as well: first because I had screamed and revealed our presence and second because I was displayed thus before Osae.

My face burned like a second inferno.

Worst of all, I had failed to free my brother. Had I succeeded in opening the last lock, Mephisto might have gotten free. Dear, charming Mephisto who acted so foolishly and yet, all that time, had been looking out for the rest of us.

Had I managed to set my brother free, there would have been a chance that—even with me lost to him—Seir might have returned him to our family, once Lilith's attention was distracted. Instead, Mephisto and I were both prisoners.

I had gambled one too many times in this infernal place and lost.

"Surely, Great Queen, you would not mar such beauty?" Seir objected. Other incubi in the chamber added their voice to his.

"Very well, Sweet Incubus, I will tell them only to break her mind and not to mar her pleasing body."

Seir opened his mouth, as if to object, but Lilith cut him off with a graceful gesture of her hand. "Enough. I grow weary of your petitions. Go now, or I will reconsider my gracious gift to you. There are many others who would be happy to enjoy even a damaged ex-Handmaiden."

Seir bowed.

He did not depart, but he did not continue to stand and defend me, either. He released my arm and stepped away, abandoning me to the whims of the Queen of Air and Darkness.

Immediately, two other incubi took his place; one caressed me while the other kissed my neck. When I squirmed, the cacodemon sunk his claws further into my shoulder, though I noticed he carefully avoided my wings.

The indignity of it was almost too great to bear.

I could resist, even fight. With the help of my wings, perhaps, I could get away from my current captors. But then what? Unless Seir came to my aid to whisk me away from here, I was trapped in the depths of Hell. Hardly a place I could fight my way out of single-handedly.

The incubus to my left—a handsome creature of living ivory—froze and began sniffing, as if scenting the air. He sniffed at my neck, my ear, the side of my head, and then knocked Mab's hat upward.

A collected gasp rose from the chamber.

"What is this?" the Queen of Air and Darkness cried aghast. "A Sibyl?"

Lilith curled up in her great throne and covered her face, her body shaking. After a moment, it became clear that she was giggling. Leaping lightly to her girlish feet, she addressed her people: "What fools these mortals be! Here I am, upon the eve of victory, great victory such as Hell has not seen since the days before Solomon! Within a hundred years, the Prospero Family will fall, their covenants will be undone, their plans fail, and all mankind will fall into a state of chaos and havoc.

"Only one thing could stand in my way, and that was if Miranda Prospero became a Sibyl. Only that could ruin my perfect work." She turned to me. "And you, with that unaccursed mark upon your forehead, come waltzing, of your own volition, up to one of my incubi, delivering yourself into my hand." She giggled, jumping up and down in her delight. "You have brought your own doom upon yourself!"

To my right, the great black demon stirred where he hung upon the rack of pain. Lifting his head, Prince Mephistopheles mocked Seir softly, "So much for your boast of being able to stand up to Lilith."

Lilith overheard him and giggled some more. "Stand up to me? Who, Seir?" She addressed Seir. "You can no more defy me, Little Incubus, than the tides can defy the moon."

"As you say, Great Queen," Seir bowed humbly.

Beyond the door, I could see the Torturers beginning their ascent of the long silver walkway, their brown robes blowing about them. Even from here, the mist gray blades of their sickles stung my eyes. They would take me to their broken tower and submit me to tortures worse than those I dreamt of when Astreus touched me. My legs began to tremble uncontrollably.

"As I know. And you shall prove it!" Lilith drew a cruel-looking bronze knife from her boot. "Gather round, my children, and we shall see such sport as we have not seen in many a day. Such entertainment as will more than make up for not getting to see that broken fool Antonio kill his own brother." She threw the bronze knife to Seir. "Incubus, slit Miranda Prospero's throat."

I did not wait for Seir's reaction.

Twisting my shoulders, I swept my emerald wings over the cacodemon and the incubi who had been pawing me. All three demons fell backward, screaming and clutching their burns. I drew my fan and sprang toward the Demon Queen.

"Malifaux! Pin her!" Lilith commanded, leaping atop her throne, the feathers of her gown fluttering about her.

One of the demons near her, a hulking ugly creature with twisted horns that poked out to either side, pointed a warty, taloned finger at me. Immediately, I was thrown across the chamber and slammed into the wall, my body pressed so hard against the gold, that I could neither move nor speak.

"Lower her, so the incubus can reach her lovely throat. Or shall we have him disembowel her?" inquired the Queen of Air and Darkness.

No one answered, but I slid down the wall until my feet were just above the floor.

How ironic.

I had failed to slit Astreus's throat, and now he would slit mine.

Seir stood in the midst of the chamber, a slender figure of sable in his black opera cloak. His red eyes gleaming, he held the jagged bronze knife in his hand, turning it this way and that, as if examining a novelty.

Lilith purred, "Now, Seir, we are all waiting."

"I apologize, Great Queen, but I must decline your kind offer," Seir replied with a bow, and he tossed the knife to the ground.

A murmur spread through the crowd, and a spark of something, some distant thing akin to hope began fluttering in my chest. To my left, my brother stirred and began watching Seir with great interest.

"Decline?" Lilith snorted, "Since when can an incubus decline the order of a queen? You are but a shadow, a servant of no accord."

"So I was . . . until you promoted me."

"Promoted you?" Lilith laughed mockingly. "I have done no such thing."

"Ah, but you have," Seir replied. "Tell me, Queen of Air and Darkness, you remember Heaven: what were you before you fell? A Virtue? A Dominion?"

Lilith flinched at the mention of Heaven, but she drew herself up and spoke to her minions. "I was a Throne, of the Seventh Choir! Of those who

fell, none but Seven were of the highest orders. Even the greatest of the Kings
of Hell, such as Vinae, Paimon, and Beliel, had never been more than Do-
minions of the Sixth!"

The demons in the chamber—incubus, succubus, imps and dark peri—
murmured in awe. They were impressed by their mistress's former rank.

Seir replied mildly, "Once, it is true, Seir of the Shadows was a mere
incubus, a minor messenger in the skein of life. But then he was killed by
Theophrastus Prospero.

"It was you, O Great Queen, who chose his replacement. But you did
not replace him with another minor messenger, oh, no . . ." Seir's eyes flared
with golden light, and Astreus's voice boomed from his mouth. "But with
one who, before Heaven's Gates were barred against him, was of the Eighth
Choir of Cherubim!"

A rustle of astonishment passed through the infernal crowd. Some muttered. Some drew back in fear and awe. A cunning gleam came into the
eyes of a few incubi and cacodemons as they glanced back and forth between the two.

As for me, that distant thing, hidden in my heart, bloomed into real
hope. I could not help it.

For the first time, a shadow of uncertainty crossed Lilith's face. She sat
down quickly, assuming a regal pose.

From his position on the rack of pain, Prince Mephistopheles laughed,
a deep rumbling sound. "Finally spotted a flaw in your plan to tithe the
Lord of the High Council, did you, O Queen of Air and Darkness?"

Seir tilted his head and gazed at Lilith. "Foolish, envy-riddled Demon
Queen. Thanks to your meddling, I am now your superior in both strength
and power."

Recovering her aplomb, Lilith laughed mockingly. "Perhaps, you are
more powerful than I suspected, but it matters little. A bull can be led by a
ring through his nose as easily as a calf. Your great power does you no good,
because you must still obey me, for your oath to Hell compels you."

"An elf took that oath. That elf is dead," Seir replied.

"Fool! Do not play games with me. Kneel and retrieve the knife!"

Seir's knee bent, but he did not kneel.

I strained against my invisible bonds, held in place by the mind of the
warty demon across the room. I tried to catch every word, every nuance.
How was Seir doing this? Why was he doing it? Answers occurred to
me based on King Vinae's explanation—wonderful, glorious answers that

made my heart soar and sing, despite the horror of my current situation—but they were merely speculations, phantoms of hope I dare not clutch at too tightly.

"I command you by your oath!"

Still, Seir resisted, standing in a half crouch.

"How can you keep resisting?" Lilith cried.

Seir's knees continued to bend, but each time he began to collapse, he resisted and rose again.

"Kneel!" the Demon Queen cried, "Kneel, now, or regret it for eternity! All Hell will turn against you. You shall be delivered to the Torturers and, as soon as the Tower of Pain is rebuilt, you will be its first inhabitant. Do you recall what it was like, when you dwelled there before?"

Seir's knees buckled, and the audience laughed. But he did not fall to the ground. Instead, he stood now in a low crouch.

"I recall that I was the equal of their torments," he replied in a voice that did not even remotely sound like that of an incubus. "It was not fear of torture but pity that wrung the cursed oath from me."

"This is impossible!" Lilith cried, alarmed. "Kneel! If you do not, the Queen of the Elves will begin tithing your people again—and only your people. Who were your favorites? Ah, yes, as soon as the Prospero Family fails, Boreas, Caurus, and Mab Boreal will be sentenced to take their Last Walk!"

Seir's strength gave out, and he fell to the floor. His hand reached, as if against his will, for the cruel bronze knife. But he did not pick it up. Instead, by dint of great strength, he withdrew his arm and rose, slowly, to his feet again.

"This cannot be happening!" the Queen of Air and Darkness cried. "You cannot resist me!"

Seir replied, "Behold how I slip through your fingers, O Great Queen! I am only the beginning. You vaunt of victory at hand, and yet it is your defeat that awaits. Have you not seen it?

"All Hell has turned its strength against the Family Prospero," he continued, "and yet they have not faltered. I speak not of whether their magic will sustain them, but of their spirits, their souls—all our efforts have been bent upon seducing and corrupting them, but instead of obliging us, they become more virtuous. Our efforts brought out the best in them. They have risen to the occasion, banded together, and overcome the obstacles that we were certain would destroy their spirit.

"When they perish, not a single one of them will find their final resting place here Below."

Moaning and gnashing of teeth interrupted him. Seir waited until it died down.

"But that is not the worst of it for you, O Great Queen," he continued. "For it is not merely that they have failed to fall, but that we demons are rising. Or did you fail to notice that King Vinae, once one of the worst of us, has taken their side? Look at me! Rather than us pulling them down, they are dragging us up!"

The demon and incubi in the audience chattered in agitation. Seir's words were affecting them. They looked to their queen in consternation.

My heart filled with a bubble of joy. My mother was right! Eurynome's plan was working! Even if it merely helped one wisdom demon and one ex-elf, it was worth all our pain and sorrow!

And how, how glorious he made us sound!

"Nonsense!" Lilith cried, "What you say is impossible!"

"Is it? When we see so clearly that you have failed, and they are winning? Of all our projects with the Family Prospero, none received more attention than the matter of Erasmus and Miranda. All of the malice of Hell was bent upon creating enmity between them—and yet, behold, not only did Miranda not rejoice at her brother's downfall, she sacrificed all that was precious to her to save him."

"You saved Erasmus!" Mephistopheles cried in a great voice. "Good for you, Miranda!"

"What you say, Incubus, makes no sense!" Lilith objected. "What could the Prosperos offer you—a fallen spirit consigned forever to Hell."

Seir stood and faced her. "That one thing with which escape from Hell is inevitable."

"And that is?"

"Hope. To remain Below, hope must be abandoned."

I blinked, surprised. His words gave a whole new twist to *all hope renounce, ye lost, who enter here.*

"But what could give a damned spirit hope?" Lilith cried, her voice rising.

"The knowledge that there is a power greater than Hell," replied Seir. "The Prospero Family has taught us the Great Secret: the secret that allows mankind to escape the maw of the Infernal Pit."

Lilith scoffed. "There is no such secret!"

"Certainly there is . . . Love. *All the world was made for Love.*"

Of course. He could not have copied the *Book of the Sibyl* without reading it.

"Love? That weak dove whom I crush beneath my heel? You are a fool's fool, Astreus Stormwind!" Lilith threw her head back and laughed. "In reality, it is only Power and Strength that matter."

My heart leapt in my chest like a winged thing whose cage door had been unexpectedly thrown open. Lilith had called him Astreus! Even she believed the Elf Lord was winning over his infernal counterpart!

"Is that so? Then, have you not heard," he opened his mouth: "*'Though I speak with the tongues of men and of angels, and have not love, I am become as sounding brass, or a tinkling cymbal. And though I have the gift of prophecy, and understand all mysteries, and all knowledge; and though I have all faith, so that I could remove mountains, and have not love, I am nothing.'*"

His words rang throughout the throne room. His opera cape whipped around him. He seemed taller, though his face remained Seir's, and his skin remained the color of pitch.

Everything within the sound of his voice suddenly seemed tawdry and hollow, as if its true nature had been revealed and found wanting. The chamber became so flimsy that, for a tiny instant, for a fraction of a split second, I saw right through it to the other version, where everyone lay sleeping with tall, glorious beings of light leaning over them in concern, whispering words of comfort and hope. Even Lilith slept. She lay curled in a ball, a stream of tears running down her cheeks and forming a pool on the ground around her.

Prince Mephistopheles chose that moment to move. With a roar, he struck with his glowing red claws at the rack that held him, which now seemed weak and insubstantial. The bars broke. He pulled the chain that still looped his wrist free of the bar. "Stop!" screamed Lilith. "Those holy words defile my court! Cease! I order you, by your oath to the Rulers of Hell, which you must obey, and you, Mephisto, by the oath you took to the Elf Queen to be my slave! Kneel!"

Seir's voice fell silent, and Mephistopheles sank to his knees, though slowly, as if he were fighting it.

The Torturers were coming closer. I could hear the eerie clicking of their feet upon the silver. Across the room, I could see the demon Malifaux concentrating on me, pinning me in place.

Seir and Mephistopheles were doing their best. Now, it was my turn.

My flute was broken. My fan was useless, for my arms were trapped—and even if they were not, I could hardly fight my way out of a chamber full of demons. But I was not without resources; for, at last, I was a Sibyl!

I closed my eyes and pictured the beam of white light coming from my forehead. If it could make the glacier burst into flowers, what might it do to demons?

It took me three tries to feel love in my heart while I regarded the huge warty demon with his twisted horns. The first two times, I shivered with revulsion, and the white beam failed. Finally, I kept my eyes closed and recalled what my mother had told me: that everything, even this vile creature, could be saved.

I heard an odd gargling sound and opened my eyes. The demon had fallen to its knees. A moment later, his fellows swarmed over him, sniffing him, licking him, biting him. Then, they began consuming the one I had drenched in the white beam of love. Released, I slid to the ground.

My entire body crawled with horror. The wrongness of what was happening was indescribable, and there were maggots everywhere. But I could not afford to succumb to revulsion.

As soon as I could move my arm, I touched the mark upon my forehead and pointed at my brother. "By the power invested in me as a Sibyl of the White Lady of Spiral Wisdom, I absolve you, Stefano Mephistopheles Prospero Sforza, from any and all oaths you have sworn. Rise up! You are free!"

A terrible noise like the scream of a screech owl issued from Lilith's throat, and she began to transform into something quite different from a young girl.

Mephistopheles yanked his arm, breaking the last chain. In a single jump, he leapt over the heads of the demons who swarmed toward me and landed beside me, lifting me up to sit upon his obsidian-like arm. He raised his ruby-tipped claws and swiped, rending a cacodemon and several peri.

Then, we were cloaked in inky darkness.

CHAPTER THIRTY

The Battle of Limbo

Mephistopheles and I found ourselves standing back in Limbo, to the immense joy of our family. I glanced about but saw no sign of our incubus. Before we could cross the distance to where the others stood, the hordes of Hell descended upon us.

Rank upon rank of incubi, ouphes, imps, goblins, skeletal warriors, and shambling ghouls now stretched as far as the eye could see. Above flew several of the superior lords. Great Prince Sitri, with his fanged beast head, led the airborne troops. Apparently, he had survived his attack on my mother, even if many of his minions had not.

Ulysses screamed and vanished in a bright flash, taking Cornelius and Caliban with him. The rest, who had not been touching the staff at the moment that he departed, were stranded . . . again.

Mephistopheles ripped the manacles from his wrists, slicing through the metal with his glowing ruby claws. Theophrastus threw him the *Staff of Summoning*.

With his staff in one hand, Mephistopheles threw out his arms. "Demons and demi-demons, I call upon you to recognize me as a Prince of the Sixth Circle. Beware, it shall go badly for those of you who fail to do so, should Lilith lose!" The demons and monstrosities glanced dubiously at my brother. Mephistopheles gestured at Theo. "I have Theophrastus the Demonslayer on my side!"

To my great surprise, about a third of the enemy host knelt and bowed their heads. Prince Sitri spat curses at them, but they remained resolute.

"Well, look at that," rumbled Prince Mephistopheles. "They did recognize me!"

Of those who had bowed, nearly half rose and began to retreat from the field of battle. The others merely stood again, prepared to fight nonetheless, having recognized Mephistopheles as a Prince of the Sixth Circle, but not as their own superior.

High in the gloom above—I could not tell if it was a ceiling or a sky— flew a black chariot pulled by what now appeared to be sleek golden lions with thick black manes. Within sat the Queen of Air and Darkness in her war gear.

"Halt!" Lilith cried, her voice echoing across the vast host. "Do not depart yet. I propose a challenge. Single combat! If Prince Mephistopheles wins, you may depart in peace. If our champion wins, you will all continue to fight with me!"

Mephistopheles, Prince of the Sixth Circle, yawned and patted his mouth. "Bring 'em on!"

"Er, Mephisto, is this wise?" Theo hissed. "How do you know you will win?"

My brother the demon just snorted derisively.

Erasmus spoke up from where he stood surrounded by fat red imps who were poking at him with pitchforks, which he withered to dust. "Can we ask for more? If you win, the whole host goes home?"

"No good," Mephistopheles replied. "Those not beholden to me would just betray me afterward, anyway."

"Father?" Theo asked.

"I do not see that we have much to lose," Father said in a low voice. "Ulysses will come back eventually. If we can stall long enough, the rest of us may not need to fight. Son, are you willing to do this?" From his dubious expression when he pronounced the word "Son," I gathered that Father had only recently discovered Mephisto's demon side. He fixed Mephistopheles with a piercing gaze. "Are you sure you can win?"

My brother the demon snorted again. "Of course."

He strode forward calling out, "I accept! Bring out your champion."

The crowd parted, and another demon came forward. It had two cruel black horns rising from its head. Its garments were doublet and hose of rich browns in the Italian Renaissance style. The rapier it carried gleamed with a wicked sheen, as if it were coated in poison.

Of course, poison no longer frightened me. I concentrated; there was a tingle in my forehead, and the sheen grew less ominous.

Mephistopheles's opponent bowed. In the midst of his demon head, he had a perfectly normal human face. It was a face I recognized. The denizens of Hell had given this demon the face of Our Savior.

No, not the Savior, the man who modeled for his portrait.

"Cesare Borgia!" Gregor cried out, his voice dripping with hatred. Titus put a calm but restraining hand upon his shoulder.

It was he. I recalled him from my youth, though I doubt Cesare and I had ever spoken to each other. I recalled that once, when my stepmother had summoned me to a party to parade me in front of my Gardelli relatives— whom, I now realize, were not my relatives after all—Cesare had made a rather crude pass at me. Ordinarily, this would be unusual behavior toward the daughter of a duke, except that as the son of the pope, he seemed to think he was omnipotent. Luckily, Theo had come to my rescue, slamming him in the face and then ushering me away before young Borgia could regain his feet.

After that, I asked Father to have the Aerie Ones carry him to some high height and drop him, but Father merely nodded and continued reading his books, murmuring something about Cesare receiving his just punishment in due time.

Apparently, he had. For now, he was in Hell.

Cesare strutted forward like a peacock. "Finally, we meet again, old friend-foe. While you have been dawdling above, I have been studying with the masters here below—for those who rule here understood that the day would come when my expertise would again be needed. Prepare now to meet your final end."

Mephistopheles grinned, his sharp teeth gleaming and his sapphire eyes glinting with mirth. "Eager to be defeated again, are you? Step forward. I will oblige you."

"Wait!" Father shouted, his arm raised, palm out. "Halt! Pause!"

"Yes?" Lilith purred.

"How do we determine the winner?" Father asked.

"I beg your pardon?"

Father stroked his beard. "Your champion is already dead. What is more, he's probably been given magic to sustain his well-being as well." Lilith pouted prettily. Apparently, Father was correct about that. "If you want this battle to take place, you have to make it possible for either of them to win."

Lilith rested her elbows on the edge of her chariot and leaned on them, still pouting. She tipped her head prettily, thinking.

"Oh, very well," she rose and tossed two pale lilies toward the contestants. "Wear these. Whomever first yields or whose lily is depetaled loses. Agreed?"

Father nodded, though I noted that while his head was inclined, and only then, he was smiling. "Agreed."

Cesare saluted Mephistopheles with his blade. My brother returned the gesture. The two squared off and began to circle. The other spirits and shades nearby moved back, giving them room. My father motioned to all of us. We moved forward until we all stood together, ready to grab Mephistopheles and escape as soon as Ulysses and the others returned.

With Cornelius and Caliban with him, Ulysses was sure to come back soon. I wondered what was taking him so long.

Slowly at first, then more quickly, they traded blows, until their swords moved at lightning speed, the tips of their blades flying too fast for my eyes to follow. They were not too fast for Theo, however, he understood what he was seeing. He stood beside Mab and me, pointing.

"A fencer's success or failure depends nearly entirely on his footwork," he explained. "Notice how they're both bouncing on their toes, not even putting their whole foot down. That's good. Oh! Look at that lunge! Meph really knows his stuff! Unfortunately, Cesare has reach on him. His sword is not made of ordinary matter; it keeps stretching beyond what would be possible up above."

Quick as striking serpents, the two opponents clashed. Their blades engaging, circling, parrying, striking. *Shing-shing* rang out again and again in the misty gloom. Both men—both demons—were light on their feet, but Mephistopheles was quicker to retreat, so as to keep the distance between them. To me, it looked as if my brother was on the run, but Theo was grinning and nodding his head in encouragement.

Cesare charged my brother, slashing as he ran by. His attack looked terrifying. I gasped. Theo, however, snorted with disapproval.

"Fleches look showy, but I have yet to see one pay off. Look, Meph got a hit in on his back before he could come around again."

"Maybe," Mab said uneasily, "but considering how quickly your brother won the other two fights he was in—Baelor and that corroding demon, Focalor—this Borgia guy must be good. Really good."

Theo stopped smiling. "He is very good. He was good in life, nearly as good as Mephisto. He's even better now . . . I hope Mephisto knows what he's doing."

The two continued to circle, stinging like bees. Occasionally, one got a hit, usually on a part of the body that was nearest. Their arms and hands were soon bloody. Cesare's demon body bled a thick black ichor. Mephistopheles, though a demon, still bled red.

Cesare kept my brother on the retreat. Mephistopheles lunged forward repeatedly, leaping huge distances, his wings allowing him to glide, but since Cesare's telescoping sword gave him reach, my brother quickly retreated again.

Cesare flourished his blade and lunged. Mephistopheles counterparried; his weapon whipped around his opponent's and struck at Cesare's shoulder. Grinning, the other demon dropped his head, parrying with his horns, knocking my brother's sword aside.

Theo snorted with derision. A moment later, I saw why. Mephistopheles's blade, as quick as the blink of an eye, struck Cesare's unprotected head while it was still bowed. It was only a small nick, but head wounds bleed profusely. Ichor ran into the other demon's eyes in a steady stream. My brother got in more than one hit while Cesare paused to wipe his face.

Cesare's moves were becoming more sloppy. Three times, he feinted, but Mephistopheles did not fall for it. Cesare was forced to straight-arm his attack through, which meant that my brother got several hits on him. He even stabbed his opponent's foot once, which, to gauge from Theo's cheer, was a difficult maneuver. After that, Cesare limped.

My brothers were cheering now, especially Erasmus and Theo, who best understood what we were seeing. Mab grinned, too, but whether from pleasure or from some other emotion, I could not tell. I breathed more easily, buoyed by my brother's success.

But it was Gregor who cheered the loudest, grinning all the while like a twelve-year-old boy. His red cardinal robes billowing around him, he leapt, punching the air and shouting, "Come on, Big Brother! Get that Borgia bastard!"

Our elation was short-lived. Cesare's wounds suddenly knitted themselves back together. He straightened and roared like a lion. Then he charged.

Lunging forward, Cesare's sword curled like a snake and bit Mephistopheles. I stared at the spot, willing myself not to lose track of it. Was there poison there? Sure enough, I felt a tingle in my forehead, as if the love flowing from Eurynome sensed some vile thing. I thought of the Gift of Curing Poison and concentrated on the spot. I felt energy flow from my forehead to my brother. The tingling stopped. Apparently, the poison had been denatured and was no longer harmful.

This all took place in an instant. My brother did not falter. The move proved a mistake for Cesare, for his flexible sword, while in its snake form, could not block my brother's thrust. Mephistopheles stabbed him through the heart, repeatedly.

Cesare staggered back. Mephistopheles lunged, stabbing him through the shoulder.

"The flower!" Father yelled. "Cut the flower!"

It was too late. Cesare's wounds healed again, and his sword returned to its rigid form. He grinned and pressed forward. Mephistopheles did not have Cesare's supernatural advantage. His wounds were beginning to take their toll.

But wait. Water of Life healed. Normally, we could not spare enough to heal wounds on the spot without Erasmus's help. I suddenly realized that those limits no longer restricted us. I concentrated upon my brother, thinking of everything lovable about him, his guardianship of the family, his good nature, his willingness to fight for the rest of us, even his scatter-brained cheer. A wave of love for my brother enveloped me, and warmth flowed from my forehead.

For a moment, I worried that this was interfering, but if it was legal for Cesare to use supernatural healing, then why not Mephistopheles?

On the field of combat, Mephistopheles straightened. Some of his cuts closed. Others ceased bleeding. His grin became more ferocious, his step lighter. He charged.

"What! No. That's not fair!" Cesare glanced over his shoulder, up toward Lilith. "You told me he couldn't do that."

"Keep your eyes on the battle, you fool!" Lilith cried.

The fighting grew more keen. Cesare did not use the snake move again, or block with his horns, or even try a fleche. His face became grimmer and more set. Now, he was fighting with all his strength.

Rapiers flashed. The opponents danced. My brothers watched in rapt fascination. I began to suspect that they had forgotten our dire surroundings, so entranced were they by the display of sportsmanship before them.

And then, it happened.

Cesare feinted right. Mephistopheles did not fall for it. Disengaging his blade, he pressed through and sliced the lily from Cesare's chest, its petals falling like snow upon the dull black earth of Limbo.

"It cannot be!" Cesare panted, huffing. "I cannot lose! I have studied so hard. I have learned everything!"

"From the wrong people," Mephistopheles chuckled, though he was panting as well.

"What do you mean?"

"You studied down here. I studied on earth."

"What difference does that make?" Cesare panted. "I have had centuries to perfect my art, to do nothing but study with the very best!"

"Not the very best," my brother corrected him, grinning. "You only studied with the best of those who came to Hell after they died. I studied with them all—both those condemned to Hell, and those who ascended to Heaven. Which group do you think worked harder at their art?"

Cesare's look of dawning horror was priceless.

The crowd roared. Lilith's forces hissed, but the fiends and foes beholden to Prince Mephistopheles bowed and withdrew, as promised.

I was impressed. Honor even among demons; who would have thought? My brother must have made a good master—probably a very rare thing in Hell.

Overhead, Lilith scowled, her pretty face twisting into an ugly mask. As I gazed at her, I wondered what drove her to do the terrible things that she did. While I had heard her speech by the Tower of Thorns, I could not sympathize. I could not understand how someone could become what she was.

I did not believe I could *ever* grasp what motivated someone like her.

And then, I did.

For the first time I recognized the Great Compassion as it struck me. Suddenly, I was seeing the world from Lilith's point of view: How would I feel if I disobeyed my father—as I just had, to save Erasmus—and in return, he had banished me from his presence forever?

A painful, terrible sympathy constricted my chest. What would it be like if I could never go home again? Could never see my books? Never walk through the Great Hall and see what remained of our statues? Never again breathe the air of the enchanted garden or pass through the pine trees to visit the Chapel of the Unicorn? What if it were all forbidden to me?

And what if my father owned, not just a mansion and some books, but everything: blue sky, rich earth, air, the stars, people, sunlight. What if I was cast from my home and all those things were forever forbidden to me—not for a week, or a year, or a century, but for eternity?

Still, that was nothing, nothing at all.

The real sorrow, the sheer agony, was knowing that no matter what I did, no matter how hard I labored, no matter how patiently I waited, I could never again achieve the only thing worth having: my father's approval.

Poor Lilith!

Even as my heart ached, however, I laughed. If I had reached the point where I could feel Grand Compassion for such a miserable creature as the Queen of Air and Darkness—who had done such harm to my Lady, my fellow servants of Her will, and my family—perhaps I was finally worthy of being a Sibyl.

How tremendously far I had come from a cold, isolated creature, concerned only with family and duty, that I had been only a month ago. Looking back, I was appalled at my former self, who had cut herself off from mankind, preferring to dwell in her own solitary, icy cocoon.

Had I really almost left Mephisto alone in Chicago? Had I really allowed a little dragon fire to keep me from saving my hapless brother from the chimera even if he had not really been in danger? What could I have been thinking? Water of Life cures burns. Why had I not rushed in to save him, letting nothing stand in my way? Had I truly considered saving the Great Hall rather than Mab?

Mab?

What an unpleasant person I had been!

I realized with a start that I felt more sympathy for the wretched demoness who had nearly destroyed my family than I did for my former self. I had forgiven Erasmus. I had forgiven Caliban. Whether or not I had forgiven the Queen of Air and Darkness, I at least understood her better now. Only one person remained whom I had yet to forgive.

Myself.

It was surprisingly hard. Pride held me back—the pride of angels. I cast it aside. The result was painful. I staggered, shocked at the torrent of fault-finding, as more and more of my defects became obvious to me. Looking over my past behavior, I found myself sympathizing with Erasmus. No wonder he thought so badly of me. It was amazing that anyone could have seen me as anything other than glacial and loveless.

But pursuing such thinking would do me no good. Admitting my flaws to overcome them was a virtue, wallowing in them was a vice.

If my Lady had felt that I was worthy of her service, there must have been something good about me. If nothing else, I had been utterly loyal. Resolving that I would never return to my old ways, I forgave my old self.

A horrible screech came from overhead. Above, Lilith's chariot had burst into bloom: red lilies, white datura, and purple nightshade grew from its black body. Lilith herself screamed and held her head, while hundreds of small imps swooped around her, biting her and pulling her hair. The chariot careened out of control and spun off into the gloom.

I laughed aloud again. My moment of sympathy had formed a bridge between her and my forehead. My Lady's touch, so uplifting to me, affected Lilith as it had her servant—the one who had trapped me with his mind before he was devoured by his fellows. She could not bear its sacred touch.

Using love as a weapon seemed mildly distasteful, but the results were delightful.

"ATTACK!" Prince Sitri waved his forces forward.

Across the vast empty cavern of Limbo, demons lifted great horns taken from the brows of Leviathans and blew upon them. As their deep calls sounded, the hosts of Hell charged.

"Fall back! Regroup!" cried Mephistopheles. With a violent gesture, he threw the crystal ball that had led us so faithfully through Hell into the front ranks of Lilith's army. It smashed against the ground and an enormous ball of fire and multi-colored sparks threw demon-parts far and wide.

"I recognize those sparks," Father said, startled. He raised his staff before him. "I saw them the day we raided the Vatican. All these years, I have wondered where they came from."

"That was Mephisto throwing the Seeing Sphere of John Dee," I replied. "He just neglected to mention that the thing reformed afterward."

"Ah." A glint of understanding lit Father's keen eyes. "Much that has puzzled me through the years is now explained."

We drew together, the nine of us who were still in Limbo, taking advantage of the momentary lull caused by the explosion. With Theo as our general and Titus as his lieutenant, we readied our weapons and took our positions before the gate. Theo unlimbered his staff and took the front, placing Titus to the right of him and Erasmus to the left. Behind them came Mephistopheles the demon and Logistilla, the sphere atop her staff already glowing its eerie green. Then came Father and I, with Mab standing guard on one side, trusty pipe in hand. Gregor stood guarding our back, facing the other way. He had the *Staff of Silence* in one hand and Solomon's Ring on the other. If worse came to worst, we could retreat into Hell—not an option we were eager to advantage ourselves of, true, but better than being cornered.

Theophrastus lowered his goggles, set his stance, and fired the *Staff of Devastation,* creating an enormously brilliant blast, then another, and then another. The rest of us ducked, turning away as the wind from the explosions blew back over us. Within moments, Theo had reduced the enemy ranks by roughly a fifth. The imps and demons, eager to escape his blasts, rose into the air, where Theo's staff was less effective. We all watched, horrified, as the enemy hordes dived at us from above.

"Sorry, Ma'am, I don't like doing this, but . . ." Mab muttered apologetically. I handed him his hat back. He put it on his head. Then, he opened his mouth and blew.

Freezing gale-force winds came out of his mouth and lifted the incoming attackers, throwing them through the air and coating them with ice as they went. Mab's body fell backward and lay on the ground, eyes vacant, mouth opened wide. A few shades tried to enter the body, but Gregor swiped at them with the Seal of Solomon, and they backed off. They whispered the word *priest* and fled, wailing.

As soon as the majority of the airborne troops had been cleared away, the wind returned, formed a tight vortex, and funneled itself back into Mab's mouth.

"Merciful God!" Erasmus gaped at Mab. "You're Caekias!" He turned to me. "Are you telling me that we've been traveling with the god of the Northeast wind all this time?"

Mab dusted himself off and chuckled. "Thought I was a hapless gust, did ya? Just goes to show that you cannot judge from appearances."

"Especially when our sister Logistilla created the appearance." Mephistopheles stiffened, sniffing. "Beware! The enemy returns! Behind us!"

"About face!" yelled Theo.

Thanks to Mephistopheles's warning, we were prepared when a squadron of imps, goblins, and skeletal warriors poured through the Gate of False Dreams. They came shouting and gibbering, and stinking of brimstone and rotting flesh.

Logistilla let out an ear-piercing scream. She raised the *Staff of Transmogrification* and began turning demons into toads, rats, fish, and ravens left and right. When some of the ravens swooped at our eyes, she turned them to pigs in midair. They fell and struck the ground with a satisfying *splat*.

As Theo could not shoot at such close range, he concentrated on the larger body of troops, while Mephistopheles, who was guarding his back, tapped his staff to call his many friends to help him. Titus came to the front to lead the rest of us, moving Father and me to one side. He charged into the midst of the force that poured through the Gate, cracking heads and smashing wings with his staff.

Behind him, Gregor followed suit with the *Staff of Silence*. Those he hit could no longer hear their own thoughts. They wandered aimlessly until he touched them with his ring, popping the resulting withered things into a quickly filling glass vial he pulled from under his robe.

Erasmus came forward, smiling his languid half-smile, his dark hair free of the ribbon and hanging in his eyes again. Many of the demons were immune to the ravages of time, but the skeletal warriors collapsed into piles of pale ash as soon as the *Staff of Decay* grew near. Over the din of the battle, I caught snatches of my brother's words.

> *Art-magicians and astrologes,*
> *Rhetors, logicians, and theologes,*
> *Them helpes no conclusions sly;*
> Timor Mortis conturbat me.

> *In medicine the most practicions,*
> *Leeches, surgeons, and physicians*
> *Themselves from death may not supply;*
> Timor Mortis conturbat me.

A group of ugly, fanged demi-goblins ran at Father and me. Father spoke a word, and none of their weapons struck us. Mab leapt forward and cracked one and then another over the head, flattening them. A third one grabbed his arm and sank his jagged fangs into Mab's shoulder. Mab screamed. Titus struck the creature, and its head flew from its body and went bouncing across the misty ground.

More demons came toward us, as if they were pouring out of some endless dark cornucopia of demonkind. I reached for my flute—but, of course, I had no flute, only two broken pieces of pine. Instead I drew my razor-sharp fan.

Strike! came my Lady's voice in my mind.

My Lady's voice! I could hear it in my mind so clearly.

Even better, She was back.

I swung my fan and sliced through the neck of an ouphe who had sneaked up behind me. Two more followed, menacing me with their long claws. With a roar and a puff of flame, Mephistopheles's chimera pounced on my attackers. The lion head mauled one, while the dragon head roasted the other. The goat head swept back and forth, looking for something to butt.

More of Mephisto's friends leapt into the fray. The winged lion scattered goblins. The great roc carried off a high-ranking demon. The mammoth and a boar trampled and gored the enemy. The cockatrice struck imps with its terrible poison, and Donner, the reindeer that had led us through the snow to Father Christmas's house, ran through the air, impaling flying monstrosities upon his antlers. The poisonous butterfly fluttered over and landed on the head of a cacodemon that fell silently to the ground. The butterfly then fluttered on to the next demon, who collapsed just as silently.

Farther off, the Loch Ness monster floundered on its flippers before vanishing again, as Mephistopheles tapped the *Staff of Summoning* to send the gentle beast back to its lake. The Horror from the Deep Abyss shambled across the battlefield, ripping arms from evil peri with the tentacles that protruded from under its hooded robe. Even at a distance, in spite of everything else, I could smell the horrible stench it exuded. The fabric of Limbo warped as it passed through, bubbling and collapsing upon itself.

The enemies were impressive, too. Balam, a great and powerful King of Hell, with flame in the eyes of all three of his heads—bull, man, and ram—and the tail of a serpent, came riding across the field of battle on a cave bear the size of an elephant. Around him, his minions began to turn invisible and vanish from our sight. Titus held up his staff and thick clouds of shadow drifted from it, enough that we could see ripples in the low swirling darkness as the invisible enemies moved. Titus, Erasmus, and Mephistopheles then leapt forward to rend them with staff and glowing ruby claw.

A white flash heralded Ulysses's return. My wayward brother arrived, pistol in hand, and immediately started shooting. Cornelius and Caliban were with him; both were eating doughnuts. Cornelius looked impatient and annoyed. Caliban held a white bag, which presumably held more doughnuts. He raised his hand cheerfully to offer a doughnut to the rest of us. Upon seeing the situation, however, he stuffed the bag into Cornelius's hands and waded into the fray, whacking demonic minions with his club.

A hart with a fiery tail bounded across the battlefield. This one I recognized: Furfur, a storm demon I had fought several times in the past. Desperately, I wished I had my staff, so I could keep its power at bay. Before it had an opportunity to call upon any of its magic, however, Ulysses took it out with three bullets: one hit the eye, one penetrated the forehead, and one pierced the heart.

Prince Sitri flew above the infernal troops. He flapped his wings, and all around demons on his own side unwittingly fell under his spell. They threw off what garments they wore and danced naked, declaring their love for Lilith. Ulysses, too, began stripping out of Gregor's turtleneck, crooning a love song. Cornelius waved his staff in the general direction of Ulysses, who, glassy-eyed, now turned and began shooting into the enemy ranks again.

Cornelius then waved the *Staff of Persuasion* toward the enemy. The amber stone set into the top twinkled like a star. Within the sound of his voice, imps, peris, and lesser hellions stopped in their tracks and turned, rending their masters.

A giant red demon, twice as tall as any of his fellows, strode through the sea of enchanted imps and peri, kicking them aside when needed. He strolled up behind Cornelius, who could not hear my shouts for I was still in the zone of silence, and conked him on the head with his huge scarlet fist. Cornelius fell, and his body disappeared beneath the enemy hordes.

The siren's song came lilting over the fields. Logistilla threw her staff down and ran toward the music, screaming, "My children! I can hear my children! Edwardo! Ricardo! Marisa! Marisa, I'm coming!"

Gregor tapped the *Staff of Silence,* and the battlefield fell quiet. Logistilla blinked and, straightening, leapt for her staff. A cacodemon, grinning an impossibly wide grin, pounced upon it, growing fangs and claws as she approached. Logistilla grabbed the demon, attempting to throttle him, while it scratched her face and chest, sending a spray of blood up like a fountain. Logistilla's scream made no noise.

Titus, swinging his staff like a golf club, silently knocked the cacodemon into the air. Putting an arm around the wounded Logistilla, he kicked her staff up into his hand and, charging through the enemy ranks, brought her to where Father and I stood back to back, within a protective circle

Mab had drawn with chalk. He laid her at my feet and gestured for me to help her.

I smiled at her and pictured the world from my Lady's perspective. Sure, enough, in my mind's eye I could see a soft white beam of living love flowed from my forehead into her. Her bleeding slowed.

I shouted to Titus to save Cornelius but, of course, he could not hear me. To my relief, I saw that my blind brother had risen again, though he looked woozy.

Father gestured abruptly to Gregor, who approached and temporarily lowered his Silence effect.

"Please keep your effect to a minimum. I cannot use my charm to deflect weapons without speaking," Father said tersely.

The voice of King Vinae spoke from nearby where Caliban was bashing a demi-goblin with the *Staff of Wisdom*.

"*Gregor, order your staff to make a hollow sphere. It will keep out much evil, but allow you to hear one another within.*"

"Can it do that?" Titus gaped at the rod in Gregor's hands, so recently his.

Gregor commanded, "Staff, do as he has instructed."

The noises of the greater battle fell silent. Theo fired, and we watched the expanding blossom of white flame unfold soundlessly among the enemy, slaughtering an untold number. The wind from the explosions swept back upon us, blowing some of the smaller imps and goblins away.

Titus shook his head, chuckling. "Why do they even bother when Theophrastus is against them?"

A large demon with the head of a reptile leapt over Mab's barrier. Titus took him out with a single powerful swing.

Agares, the Duke of the East, an old man on the back of a giant crocodile carrying a goshawk, came riding out from amidst the enemy's ranks. He raised his fist, and all the imps and cacodemons near him froze in place, as did Theo, Cornelius, and Ulysses. When the ripple of Agares's effect struck the wall of silence, it stopped. Angry, the old man stamped his foot, and the ground shook. Before him, the earth parted, and a fissure came rumbling toward us, splitting Mab's chalk circle. Father and I jumped to safety. Mab and the others were nowhere to be seen, separated from us by the motion of the battle.

A giant black wolf leapt across the chaotic battlefield. On its back sat the Marquis Andras, a winged man with the head of a black raven, who flourished a shining saber. My heart grew cold. I knew that sword, recalled it from battles fought against demonic enemies long ago. Its name was *Discord*.

I watched, helpless, as the wolf-mount loped toward my frozen brothers. The demon Andras rode straight at Theophrastus, his great enemy; for Theo had sent him back to the inferno the last three times Andres dared to show his raven face upon the daylit world. But Theo was frozen, standing motionless amidst ranks of immobile demons. He held his staff with both hands, his head thrown back in furious laughter.

I screamed and started running forward, but there was no way to reach him in time. Nor could I call to Mephistopheles, who was near him in the fray, because the wall of silence stopped my voice from reaching that far.

After all we had gone through, I was going to lose Theo!

I stood, screaming with fury. How I missed my staff! Without it, there was nothing I could do. As the Marquis Andras raised the sword *Discord* to slice my beloved brother's head from his shoulders, I glared at the demon, all my hatred, pain, and frustration rising in my heart.

Andres opened his bird mouth and fell from his mount to the ground, where he lay writhing in spasms. Amazed, I touched my forehead and then yanked my fingers away again, for they now felt slightly numb. Closing my eyes, I "saw" the beam coming from my forehead had taken on a reddish hue. Instead of life and strength flowing from the mark into the demon, its life and strength were being sucked out and flowing into the mark on my forehead.

So this is what the *Book of the Sibyl* had meant by: *Where the Sibyl disdains, Love is withdrawn. Without Love, life flees.*

I glared at another demon near Theo, a great horned creature with bat wings and a scorpion's tail. His face contorted in horror, and he slumped upon his mount, a fiery dragon. A demon with peacock wings fell writhing to the ground. Another, with the head of an owl, exploded into a puff of razor-sharp feathers.

Any demon who came near my frozen brothers, I destroyed by the force of my wrath alone. Elation bubbled up within me as my enemies fell.

Only a fool would anger a Sibyl indeed!

As my wrath turned to joy, I concentrated upon my love for my brother Theophrastus, thinking about what the battle must seem like from his perspective. Sure enough, Theo twitched and began to move. Using the same method, I quickly freed Ulysses and Cornelius as well. Immediately, Ulysses began to slaughter the demons frozen around them, putting a bullet directly between each target's eyes.

My brothers looked terrible. Sweat dripped down their faces. Theo had a head wound that poured blood into his eyes. Ulysses was holding his right arm at an odd angle, as if he could not move it. Luckily, he could shoot just as well with his left hand. Gregor was bleeding from multiple wounds. Something had chopped through his enchanted red robes. Caliban was limping, his left leg a bloody mess.

Nor was it just us. The noble mammoth who uncomplaining had carried us across the Glacier of Hate lay upon its side, hamstrung. The chimera's dragon head had been nearly severed; it hung from its body by a mere thread. Brave Pegasus had lost a wing, and the magnificent roc lay unmoving upon the battlefield.

We were doing so well . . . but we were losing.

Rapidly, I looked from one dear wounded soul to another, a rush of affection flowing through me. My brothers breathed deeply and fought with renewed strength. Mephisto's friends stirred and sought to rise. Their wounds did not vanish, but at least any who were not already dead would not perish from these wounds.

The invisible beams of unicorn love filled the battlefield with a holy fragrance, driving the denizens of Hell crazy. Here and there, wildflowers sprang up in the dull substance of Limbo.

Before I could finish, something slithered against my enchanted gown. A dagger held in what must be an invisible hand tried again to stab me. I raised my fan against my attacker, but another invisible demon caught me from behind. Together, the two unseen opponents knocked me sideways, tossing me into the fissure Agares had created.

I was falling.

The walls of the fissure rushed pasat me. I reached for my flute to call for a wind to save me, but, of course, I no longer had a flute. I whistled hopefully, but no one came. Beneath me, rushing ever more quickly toward me, flames danced.

"Seir! Seir!" I shouted.

He did not come.

Panic gripped me. My enchanted tea gown would not protect me from the impact of the fall or from burns to my hands, face, and legs. If this was the same lava that burned Theo and Caliban, remaining calm would help. But we were in Limbo now, not Hell; I did not know if the rules were the same.

I tried flapping my wings but could find no way to manipulate them. I was out of options. Touching my forehead, I thanked my Lady for raising me to the rank of Sibyl before I perished and felt Her love and warmth flow through me in return. I felt certain my family would now be able to regroup and escape. My only regret was I had not had a chance to set Astreus free.

Strong arms embraced me from behind. I caught whiffs of brimstone and an intoxicating masculine scent. My forehead tingled.

"I have caught you, my sweet." Seir of the Shadows's laughter suddenly cut off. "Argh! Your wings are burning me."

"You came!" I whispered.

"Of course, my love, how could it be otherwise? Were you to perish, it would be as if my very self had died."

I twisted about until I faced him. This seared him briefly but put my wings behind me. Leaning closer, the sable incubus whispered in my ear, "I rescued your brother as you requested. Now, I have come to claim my reward."

We fell together, plummeting toward the flames. The world turned to darkness, and then, I was standing amidst the swirling mist of Limbo again, to one side of the battle, with the incubus's arms still wrapped tightly about my waist.

He gestured at my forehead with his head. "This is the reward I seek. To be free."

"Astreus! I thought you were dead!"

"Love saved me." The incubus spoke with Astreus's voice. "Love is stronger than any curse or oath. It is stronger than the waters of the Lethe. Love is the strongest thing in the universe, and nothing in Hell can dim it."

I looked up into his laughing green eyes and, for an instant, I felt as if I was the one who had resisted the Torturers a thousand years lest I lose my chance at Heaven; as if I was the one who had pursued the White Lady through field and forest, hill and dell, on the faint glimmer of a suggestion that there might be a way to freedom; as if I was the one who had fallen in love with the young woman who bore within her the hope of this promise; as if I was the one who had waited over three hundred years to bring her the key that could set us both free.

Coming back to myself, I would have stumbled backward had he not been holding me so tightly. I swayed in his embrace, a strange tingle running up and down my limbs and making them weak.

All this time, all these years, I had completely misunderstood him. I had ascribed to him every elvish and quixotic motive I could invent. I had doubted his every action, his every word. When all the time, his motives had been entirely plain and straightforward.

Hope and *love*.

Within me, my heart took flight. It swelled until it seemed too large for my body, too large for the unending cavern of Limbo, too large for all of space and time. Only Heaven was large enough to encompass it now.

Touching two fingers to my forehead, I tapped his shoulder. He jerked, startled. I declared: "I call upon the Sixth Gift of the Sibyl! Astreus Stormwind, I release you from any and all oaths you have ever sworn, to anyone. You are free!"

A cloud of dark snow rose about Seir, accompanied by a faint scent of brimstone. Within the darkness, he grew taller. Then, the air cleared, and Astreus stood in Seir's ripped opera cloak, his eyes a triumphant violet. We embraced and, laughing, he kissed me again, this time with his own lips, which were as cool and fresh as a winter's breeze. And I was still there. I had not fallen away into dreams.

Pulling away, I looked up at him from the circle of his arms—for suddenly an idea had struck me, a terrible, wonderful idea. It was an idea so awe-inspiring that just thinking of it caused tremors of heat and cold to shoot across my limbs.

"Astreus," I asked slowly, "how many elves have been tithed?"

"Altogether?" He tilted back his head, calculating. "Hundreds of millions, if not more."

"Where are they?"

"Most of them work for Lilith."

I regarded the hellish host. "Really? You mean they are right here?"

"Many of them, yes."

"What would happen if I picked one, say that one"—I pointed at an ouphie who was jumping up and down on the back of Mephisto's Mammoth—"and freed him from his oath to Hell."

Astreus gazed at me, his attention arrested. His eyes had turned that eerie angelic gold. "He would go free, I expect."

"Has any Sibyl ever freed an elf?"

"Occasionally. They only seem to stay free for a time. There is some trick to it that I do not know."

"But they do go free at first?"

"Yes. They do."

Staring at the raging horde, I whispered hoarsely, "It *couldn't* be that easy."

"But what if it is?"

"Well . . ." I gulped. "There's only one way to find out."

Touching my forehead, I pointed at the field of battle. In a loud voice, I cried: "By the power invested in me as a Sibyl of Eurynome"—a lightning bolt flashed across the gloom overhead—"I release all elves, servants of the High Council, fairies, sylphs, bwca, dwarves, salamanders, undine, djinn, oreads, ouphie, oni, and all other elementals and denizens of Fairyland, everywhere, from their oath to the Infernal Powers! *There shall be no more tithe to Hell!*"

Puffs of darkness rose everywhere at once. The smell of brimstone hung thick in the air. Evil peris became pixies. Imps transformed into fairies and winged sprites. Ouphe became sylphs and Aerie Ones. To my left, Mab let out a whoop and threw his hat into the air.

"Hey, look!" he cried, pointing in the direction of the general jubilation and waving with great enthusiasm. "It's my cousin!"

Not all the troops transformed, but most of those who did were from Lilith's personal retinue. The newly restored faery folk wreaked havoc with the lines of battle. Laughing, singing, and turning cartwheels, they tumbled away in all directions, dashing about randomly and tripping their comrades.

Astreus threw back his head and laughed with joy, a sound that was very different from the laughter of mortals. "For longer than your sun has burned have I dreamt of this day! Surely, this . . ."

His voice trailed off as he looked down, frowning. Light streamed from his finger tips.

Raising his hand, Astreus stared in puzzlement at the beams of golden light that sprouted from each finger. As he moved his hand, the five beams were visible against the mists of limbo. Then, holy golden light began to radiate from his eyes, from his mouth, and from every pore of his skin. The opera cloak split down the back as wings unfolded from his shoulders.

Then, a second pair.

And a third, and a fourth, and a fifth, and a sixth and a seventh—until eight pairs of wings had sprouted. By this time, Astreus was fifteen feet tall and clothed in splendor. His face was glorious. In his eyes, I could see the majesty of the night sky, as if the universe itself was contained within him, but one of his many secrets.

Awe paralyzed me. My limbs trembled as if pricked by needle points of holy fire. The bones of my face and jaw vibrated like the plucked string of a harp. I could no more speak or move than I could have melted the ices of Pluto and sent the planet careening from its orbit by an act of will.

On the battlefield, lesser demons and denizens of Fairyland alike turned and fled. Running randomly in their panic, they screamed, "Angel!"

A distance away to the left, my brother Mephisto smacked himself on the forehead. "D'oh! Of course!"

He was in his smaller human form again, bruised and bloody, with all his clothes ripped; however, I could not see any open wounds. He tapped his staff, and I began to imagine a glorious sight.

The imagined became reality: The Archangel Uriel, Regent of the Sun, Protector of Earth, and Lord of the West Quadrant, strode across the battlefield.

Towering more than twenty feet tall, Uriel was clad in armor of shining Urim, too bright to look upon, and a surcoat of purest gold. Over his arm, he carried an enormous shield, which I recognized as the *Shield of Virtue*. Nine pairs of eagles' wings sprang from his back, and nine halos shed illumination above his head: a golden circle, a ring of blue sky, a ring of fire, moons, stars, a circle of starlight, comets, a ring of sunlight, and constellations. Beholding his face was like beholding the face of God.

Nor was it merely the eye that saw the glory of his coming. Rays of spiritual warmth the eye could not behold radiated from this Servant of High Heaven. Like the first crocus bud of spring raising its head out of the snow to unfold its pale lavender petals toward the warmth of the life-giving sun, my heart, my very being, was lifted out of the dreary darkness.

One could not look upon the Seraph and not rejoice.

Uriel drew his flaming sword and stepped up beside Astreus. The two of them strode across the battlefield. All Limbo trembled in the angels' wake, and the dark mists of which it consisted began to disperse. Some shades rushed away pell-mell. Others paused their endless chase for the first time in what might have been a century, or a millennia. Their wispy bodies took upon themselves form and substance where the light that shone from the Regent fell upon them. Raising their heads like men, they fell in step behind Uriel, marching and singing hymns in unison.

An undulating wail rose from the combatants. The demons and their cohorts, both high ranking and low, dropped their weapons and fled. They stampeded toward the Gate of False Dreams, knocking each other down and running over their cohorts. We gave way quickly, letting them go.

And that was that. The battle had ended. We had won.

We stood there stunned, watching the angels in awe. Mephisto was the first to recover. He tapped his staff numerous times, sending away the healthier of his creatures, one after another. Then, he grabbed my arm and dragged me from one to another of the wounded ones. I smiled at his brave furred and feathered friends, and felt warmth flow from my forehead toward them. We were able to save all but the magnificent roc, whose vast body lay stiff and lifeless. Mephisto sat down on its wing and cried.

My family was now scattered across the vast emptiness of Limbo. Those who had been on the outside of Gregor's barrier of silence stood at some distance. Eventually, we regrouped near the two empty thrones—I gave the one on the left wide berth.

I made my way back to my brothers. Titus, Theo, Gregor, and Caliban were bleeding profusely: Titus from his thigh wound where he had been gored by a horned demon; Theo from the gash across his forehead; Gregor from deep cuts in his shoulder, arm, and hip; and Caliban from a slash across his chest as well as slashes on his legs. Blood still oozed from Logistilla's many cuts on her face and neck, though they were healing quickly, thanks to the Water of Life I had given her. Ulysses moved stiffly, massaging his hurt arm.

Erasmus was sunburned on one side of his face. Apparently he had gotten too close to Theo's blast. Mab had that ugly wound in his shoulder where the demi-goblin had bitten him, and Father had taken a bad blow to the back of the head. I had a scratch or two, though I was basically unharmed.

Only Mephisto was entirely unscathed.

As my family drew back together, I imagined the world from the point of view of each one and felt the living love stream from my forehead into their weakened bodies. Smiles replaced scowls, and they all stood straighter and began to walk with more ease, except for Caliban, who continued to limp.

Of the enemy, the only ones left were several dozen fish, who flopped helplessly in the drifting mist, unable to flee. In the distance, the two angels had stopped to converse. The taller one was arrayed in nine glorious halos. The second angel, only slightly shorter, bore no halo at all. I watched them with heavy heart, realizing that I had freed Astreus, or maybe I should say Astriel, only to lose him to Heaven.

At least, I could take joy in his triumphant return to Heaven. I truly had granted his heart's desire.

Erasmus halted suddenly and began glancing about.

"Where is Cornelius?" he asked.

Tears for the Living

We found Cornelius upon the battlefield standing over a prone body. He gazed down at it, puzzled. As I grew closer, my stomach did an odd kind of flip. The body at Cornelius's feet had a bandana wrapped about its head, but the Cornelius standing above it wore no bandana. Instead, he looked around in astonishment, gazing at his hands, glorying in his new-found sight.

"So, here you are!" Erasmus came up and slapped Cornelius's shoulder. His hand went right through Cornelius. Erasmus's face crumpled in horror. "High Holy God! You are dead!"

Cornelius smiled. "Yes, but my sight has been restored. Oh, the beauty, the wonder of color and shape! I had forgotten how much I had been missing!"

"If you think Limbo is spectacular, you should see the world above."

"Or the one above that," said Cornelius, "for I believe that is where I am headed."

Two angels with wings of purest white descended a single golden ray that split the darkness of Limbo. They were not as brilliant as the Regent of the Sun, who still strode across the battlefield in the distance, with Astreus at his side, but they radiated a holy glow that made me feel as if I had just awakened, refreshed, upon a warm summer morning. Most of the wraiths fled from the brightness, but a few began circling the ray, as if attempting to climb it.

The angels alighted on either side of Cornelius. If a tongue were granted to a harp, it would have sounded much like their voices. Upon hearing them, my spirits lifted and I felt as if I could dance with weightless grace or even fly.

"Come, Child of the Earth, we are here to bring you to Heaven."

"Stop! Leave him!" Father brandished the *Staff of Eternity.* "You may not take him!"

Some of the leaves and flowers had been damaged in the fight, and bits of demon ichor still clung to it, but it was already repairing itself. The broken blossoms and branches straightened more quickly when the angels' radiance shone upon them.

Reaching Cornelius, Father touched his staff to Cornelius's body. A bridge of rosy and azure light sprang up arching from the body to Cornelius's spirit.

"Father, please . . ." Cornelius bowed his head. "Let me go."

"What do you mean?" Father asked sharply. "Is all our work to be for nothing, again?"

"Cornelius, don't be a fool!" Erasmus insisted. "Get back in your body!"

"Please," Cornelius begged again. "Don't ask me to go back into the darkness."

Father drew back and put his hand on his chest, across his heart. Erasmus let out a long wordless moan. Titus limped over, tears in his eyes. The rest of us stood helplessly, torn with sorrow. Logistilla turned away, crying.

"Come with us, Cornelius." The angelic voices swelled like a choir, though there were only two. *"We shall bring you to your long awaited reward in Paradise."*

Cornelius's face lit up. He straightened, as if the weight of the world had been lifted from his shoulders. He resembled a different person, the man he might have been had secrecy and lust for power not corrupted his generous nature—a man I might have loved as dearly as I loved Theo.

Nor was Cornelius the only one affected. Around me, the faces of my other siblings were bathed in the light of Heavenly joy. While in the presence of the Messenger of the Gods they had sparkled with cleverness and wit; now, in the presence of angels, they seemed young and fresh, as if the centuries of distrust and toil had never happened, and they were still unfallen and whole.

I, too, felt uplifted, as if I had been wallowing in the mud, crying, my face buried in my hands, and some vast and glorious presence had come and helped me up, lifting me out of both my squalor and my sorrow.

"Cor-Cornelius is going to Heaven!" Theo cried. His face was slack with shock and relief.

"Of course." Cornelius's shade patted Theo's hand kindly. "I did my duty."

"And *I* was worried? I have been a greater fool than I thought!" Theo gave a burst of joyful laughter, and Cornelius laughed with him.

We all laughed with them. I stepped forward and, leaning toward Cornelius, whispered, "Finally, you get your wish."

"My wish?" Cornelius inclined his head, just as he had done when he could not see.

"The one you made on New Year's," I reminded him. "You finally get to retire."

Cornelius closed his eyes and his spirit body sagged, as if shouldering a great burden. Opening his eyes again, he turned to the divine emissaries.

"Thank you, kind Messengers of Heaven, but I must decline. My sister is right. To go now to my final reward—when Father's staff would allow me to remain—is no different than choosing retirement. I must stay, for the battle is not yet won and much remains for me to do."

"No!" I cried, immediately regretting my words. "Cornelius! Don't stay. You have a chance to go to Heaven! Isn't that what this is all about?"

Erasmus opened his mouth, stopped, opened it again, and stopped again. Finally, he said, "I cannot advise you. I cannot urge you either to eschew Heaven or to give up on life if you can continue to lie."

"Come with us." One of the angels extended a shining hand toward Cornelius. Just hearing the angel's voice brought a feeling of serenity. Its voice rippled like a sacred harp. *"Years, centuries, you have labored in darkness, bearing far more than most are ever asked to bear; even the hardest mortal life ordinarily lasts but the blink of an eye. There is no need for you to return to the darkness. Come with us into the Light."*

Cornelius's gaze rested on the heavenly messenger, his face full of longing. He looked like a shipwrecked man who had been dragged out of the ocean into paradise and was now contemplating diving back in.

"Go, My Son," my father said finally, his voice breaking. "You have earned your rest. Though . . . though, nothing. Go with my blessing."

"Come. All the Choirs of Heaven wait to sing your praises." The angel extended his proffered hand.

Cornelius's eyes locked on that hand as if it were the last hope of a drowning man, almost totally submerged, before he went under.

"No." He shook his head firmly. "The Heavenly Choir will just have to wait a bit longer. There is still work to be done here." He looked down at his body. "Really, the darkness isn't so bad. . . ." His voice trailed off.

"We shall await the glorious day when you return for your final reward," the angels sang in unison. They flew once over the battlefield before rising back up the white beam. As they went, their wings swept up the wraiths who had been circling about their golden light and those more substantial shades who had fallen into step behind Uriel, who ascended singing hymns.

The bright ray slowly faded.

Cornelius stared at his body, lost and dejected. The lightness of spirit the angels had brought seeped away. My heart felt as if it were rising into my throat and swelling, as if it would soon block my windpipe so that I would be unable to breathe due to sorrow and regret. I felt such remorse for having spoken.

"Please, Father"—my brother held up a hand—"give me just one minute to see before returning me to my dark cell."

A hush fell over the family. We drew around Cornelius, and he gazed from one face to another, staring at each of us in wonder. He took a step closer to our youngest brother.

"You must be Ulysses." Cornelius reached up and ran his immaterial fingers over Ulysses's face. "I have never seen you before."

"It's a shame you couldn't see me in my fancy duds," Ulysses replied sheepishly. "I look a great deal spiffier that way."

"It isn't your finery I'm interested in," Cornelius replied gently, stretching out his immaterial hand as if to touch Ulysses's face. "I know what fine clothing looks like."

Cornelius turned to the tallest of us and bowed solemnly. "And you must be Caliban."

Caliban stepped back, stammering, "P-please, I-I am—"

"Our eldest brother," Cornelius intoned.

Caliban stared at him, gawking. Then, suddenly, a huge grin split his face. "I am, aren't I! Thank you, younger brother! I'm glad you are staying!"

"Well, then . . ." Cornelius glanced from the bleary Limbo landscape to the body laying at his feet. "I guess I must . . ." His voice trailed off.

"Here!" Mephisto tapped his staff. I began to imagine that a kangaroo hopped beside him. Then it did, and Mephisto pulled the crystal ball from its pouch, as whole and solid as before he had thrown it in amid Lilith's troops. "Look at everything you like!"

Cornelius gazed into the ball for some time, different intensities of light illuminating his ethereal face as he asked it to show various places: his house, the face of his young guide back in Boston, parks he loved, cities he had visited, museums that held some of the finest works of mankind, his favorite fishing hole.

Finally, turning away from us, he walked over to where flowers were growing. He knelt in the wildflowers without picking them and gathered some in his arms. Burying his nose in the blooms, he sniffed their perfume. He sat for a while, just admiring the beautiful shades of color. Then, he rose and came back to stand by his body.

"I am ready."

Father touched the *Staff of Eternity* to Cornelius's prone form. The glowing rosy and blue arch sprang up again from either side of the staff. Cornelius stepped onto the shining bridge, slid down the staff, and lay down atop his body. For an instant, there were two of him laying supine, then his spirit sank into his body, and he sat up, blind behind his bandana again.

Erasmus bent down beside him to help him rise, and Cornelius smiled as he accepted the aid, saying, "The darkness is not so bad, if one has loved ones about." Yet his voice sounded so weary, so sad.

Tears stung my eyes, yet again before pouring forth and running down my cheeks. Who would have imagined I would weep because one of my brothers had *not* died?

"WHAT about him, Father?" Logistilla pointed at where a lone shade stood. He seemed more substantial than the waiflike wraiths that flew through the mists. Logistilla gestured, and he came slowly forward. It was Uncle Antonio.

Of course, he had been with my siblings when Ulysses rescued them. He must have followed us here.

Uncle Antonio fell to his knees before Father. "Save me, Brother, as you saved your son! Let me see the sunlit world once more. I swear I shall do no harm from this day forth!"

Father stared into the face of his brother, the man who had once been his best friend, his closest companion, whom he had betrayed—albeit for a good cause—and by whom he had been betrayed in return.

"Brother," Father replied gently. "I forgive you. And I will continue to forgive you, even if you offend me seventy times seven times; for it is our job upon the earth to forgive, even as it is Christ's duty to dole out justice." My uncle looked vastly relieved, then faltered as Father's tone became stern.

"However, in this case, Antonio, forgiveness is not mine to grant or with-hold. It is Miranda and Erasmus whom you have offended, and Miranda and Erasmus who shall decide your fate."

Turning to Erasmus and me, Father asked, "What shall we do with him, Children? Shall I travel to Milan and search for some remnant of his body, so that I might resurrect him and give him another chance? Or shall we have Theo here blast him back to the depths of Hell?" Father patted Theo on the back.

Erasmus turned to me. "This whole situation is quite awkward, my ow-ing you my life, and likely to make us both uncomfortable over time. How about I give you a life to do with as you please—Uncle Antonio's—and we settle for me just being grateful to you in my normal, mildly irritating kind of way, hmm?"

Erasmus's words made me smile, and yet his offer gave me pause. Was I ready to decide the fate of a man's soul?

Yesterday, I might have refused, doubting my judgment. Today, I was a Sibyl. Harder tasks than this would be presented to me.

I nodded and turned to face Uncle Antonio. "Uncle, you have done me great harm in my life, for no cause. You killed Ferdinand, you betrayed Milan to the French, and you bent your magic to turn Erasmus against me, which almost led to the destruction of our family. Why should I forgive you?"

Uncle Antonio rose slowly to his feet, the rotted portion of his face in shocking contrast with his handsome features. He tried to meet my gaze coolly but could not entirely hide his fear. He had never liked me. He had never gone out of his way to hide the fact, and he had done me great wrong.

"It is the station of a Sibyl to be merciful?" he offered hopefully.

"It is the station of a Sibyl to love virtue and hate iniquity," I responded severely.

"Please!" The shade of my uncle fell to his knees again and embraced my legs, kissing the hem of my gown. "Don't send me back there. I'll do anything! Anything!"

"Will you?" I considered the matter. The answer, when it occurred to me, was obvious.

"Uncle Antonio had his day upon the earth," I declared. "Nor has any-thing he has done since convinced me that he has reformed to the degree that his services would be of use to our cause above."

Theo turned the collar of his staff; it began to hum. I held up my hand.

"But neither can I countenance deliberately sending our uncle to Hell. He may be a scoundrel, but he is still part of *our* family." I nearly said "our flesh and blood," but that hardly seemed appropriate under the circumstance.

"Thank God!" cried Uncle Antonio.

"Exactly," murmured Gregor. "Amen."

"Then what are we going to do?" asked Logistilla. "Just leave him wandering around here in Limbo?"

"No, we will let Uncle Antonio rise or fall on his own behalf. All we can do is help him get started." I bowed my head and prayed as we had been instructed to do. "Now, we wait."

In the distance, a tiny silver star cut through the mist. As it grew closer, we saw that it was carried upon the palm of Malagigi. He pushed back the hood of his blue robe and winked at Logistilla, who smiled and blushed.

"Greetings, Old Friends," he said. "I hear you are victorious this day and congratulations are due. And I also express gratitude, upon my own behalf, for my brother has been found and, even now, is conversing with one of our higher members. For this, I thank you from the bottom of my heart."

I gestured. "This is my uncle Antonio. He would like to enter your Brotherhood and learn how he might turn away from Hell and begin the long slow process of purifying himself."

"Antonio! My old friend!" Malagigi laughed and embraced my uncle, who looked stunned. "Do you not recall? I am the French sorcerer you hired to sack your hometown."

"The solitary sorcerer of Charlemagne's Brood!" Uncle Antonio gasped, astonished. "And now you are . . . what?"

"I, too, made many mistakes, but now I am finding my way upward again, toward the light, with the help of an organization called the Brotherhood of Hope. You, too, can join and, in time, earn a full redemption." Malagigi put his arm around my uncle's shoulder. "Worry not. I shall take him and introduce him to our ways. We are fellow magicians, he and I. We will understand each other."

Wagging his finger, Malagigi added, "But only upon his own merit will he rise or fail."

The shade of my uncle trembled. "Then you think there might be hope for me?"

Malagigi glanced at Uncle Antonio and seemed to see something that the rest of us could not. He shook his head disparagingly. "There is always hope. But with that black load of sins, it will be hard going indeed. A shame you could not be shriven and start again clean."

Uncle Antonio hung his head, then suddenly a hope lit his eyes. He shuffled forward upon his knees until he clung to the enchanted cloth of Gregor's ripped scarlet robes. "Nephew, you were pope. Can you not take my confession?"

Gregor stroked his beard. "I have read three treatises from the Vatican vaults on the absolution of sins of the incorporeal dead, and their conclusions were inconclusive."

"Someone wrote treaties on that?" Erasmus laughed. "Three of them?"

"Churchmen must be prepared for every eventuality," Gregor intoned. To Uncle Antonio, he said, "I shall take it upon myself to decide the issue. Come, Uncle, let us withdraw that you may have privacy for your confession."

Gregor strode away with Uncle Antonio rising and hurrying after him. We could not hear what was said, but we saw Gregor's red cardinal robes billow about him and a halo of golden light hovering above his head. Uncle Antonio's expression entirely changed, as if a great burden had been lifted from his shoulders as well.

Malagigi came over to me. He was smiling. "Stretch out your hand."

I did so. He dropped the little silver star onto my palm. I flinched, preparing to concentrate. But it was not necessary. The star stayed upon my palm with no effort upon my part.

"Voila! Your soul has been repaired!" Malagigi exclaimed softly. Retrieving the star, he led my uncle away, whistling.

"UM, Daddy?" Mephisto poked Father's arm hopefully. "While we are waiting, can you use your new staff on my roc?"

Father smiled wearily but nodded. He followed Mephisto to the great bird's corpse and put his staff against its feathers. A bridge of light left the body and arched off into the distance. A gigantic roc-shaped shade descended along the beam and settled upon the corporeal bird. The great creature stirred. Mephisto yelped with joy and gave it a fierce hug. Mab and I cheered.

As Mephisto sent the roc away, Logistilla, who had been watching, blew her nose, an act that made her yelp in pain. When Erasmus raised an eyebrow, she sniffed.

Erasmus chuckled. "You old softy."

Logistilla raised her head with regal dignity. "Women are allowed a touch of sentimentality now and then." She stepped over and took Father's arm. "About your staff, Papa . . . I happen to recall the location of several graves . . ."

Father patted her shoulder gently. "All in good time, Logistilla. We'll discuss this all in good time . . . but be warned. If the spirit is long departed, the chance of my staff being of use is very small."

FROM above, Lilith approached us in her flying chariot, from which she had removed most of the wildflowers. A single blood red lily still bloomed from one of the wheel spokes.

Pulling her black-maned lions to a stop, she laughed triumphantly. "Clever trick, freeing them all, but it won't work. Only a few will benefit. No elf can be free unless he acknowledges and accepts the offer of freedom, and, by ancient law, you only have a year and a day to reach them!"

Father fixed her with his keen eyes. He stood leaning on the *Staff of Eternity*. Leaves and dogwood flowers sprouted from its length. His hair and beard were unkempt and tangled with thorns. His face was scratched, and his once-handsome robes were torn and dilapidated. Yet, he bore about him a regal air that harkened back to his days as Duke of Milan.

"A year and a day," he said. "And then what?"

"And then the Sibyl's authority will end, and any who have not accepted their release will remain bound. As long as any remain with us, we can always recapture the ones you have freed. Only if you free all the elves will any of them truly be free." Lilith stepped down from her seat and began stroking one of the lions who pulled her chariot. It made a deep, rumbling, growling sound that might have been a growl or an un-lionlike purr.

"Yes, yes, I understand all that." Father gave a dismissive wave of his hand. "But what next?"

"What do you mean?"

"In a year and two days, what is to keep my daughter from releasing them all again?" asked Father.

Lilith pushed the lion away, frowning. "That is not how the laws of magic work."

"But my daughter is not bound by the laws of magic," Father replied mildly.

"Perhaps not when she was a mortal, but now she is a Sibyl."

"Even still, she is bound by higher laws."

Lilith regarded me, again taking in the green wings of light that sprang from my shoulders and the mark on my forehead.

"A Nephilim Sibyl! The prophecy has come true!" She gnashed her teeth and wailed. "No! It cannot be!"

My brothers and I grinned at one another. How clever Father was. How much we enjoyed watching Lilith meet her comeuppance. Doubly so, on my part, for I realized that this must have been what Father and my mother's plan had been since the very beginning, the reason for my being.

A cold voice, which sent shivers through the depths of my bones, spoke from the darkness. "Who troubles the sleep of the dead?"

The voice was not loud, yet we all heard it clearly. The Archangel Uriel stopped just before the Gate and turned toward the thrones, his flaming sword burning in his hand. Around and behind him, the dark mists of Limbo were melting away, and I caught a glimpse of some bright and glorious place, with trees and flowers formed from living flame. They burned in brilliant colors I had never beheld, colors beyond those in our mundane rainbow.

Mephisto hastily tapped his staff, and the Seraph vanished like a dream. Before it left, it nodded graciously at my brother, as if it were leaving as a courtesy to him, rather than because of the necessity of the magic. With the departure of the Regent of the Sun, the hole into some far more glorious realm faded until only swirling mists remained.

Astreus crossed his arms and lowered his head, much as Mephistopheles the demon had done when he wished to revert to his smaller size. The light pouring from Astreus's angelic form dimmed, and he returned to his normal height and appearance. Eight pairs of enormous wings, shaped like those of the swallow, the swiftest of birds, still spread out behind him. He folded them away into a cloak of feathers and came across the misty battlefield to join the rest of us.

I looked toward the source of the voice. In the empty darkness, near the dais with the two black thrones, I began to make out the figure of a man pulling a Greek horse-plumed helmet from his head. He was tall and imposing, some ten feet in height, with shoulders as broad as a bull's. His features were Arabic or perhaps Levantine, but his skin was black as pitch and looked as if it were made of obsidian. He stared at Lilith, a hint of sarcastic masculine humor glinting in his eyes.

"Ah . . . Lady Lilith."

"Lord Hades!" The Queen of Air and Darkness cried, delighted. The lovely demoness stroked her long auburn hair and lowered her lashes, casting him a pretty sidelong glance. I recalled the carvings in her throne room that depicted the history between these two—now that my mother had made it clear to me who he really was—when they had reigned together with their monstrous children. That she was still so pleased to see him was not a good sign for us. "These interlopers have invaded our kingdom and are attacking my people. Thousands, they have slaughtered, sending them down to the fires of Tartarus."

He shrugged his solid black shoulders. "And this is of interest to me . . . why?"

Lilith pouted. "But they are mortals, Milord. Mortals using trapped demons against their fellows!"

He frowned down at her, a fearsome sight, and said softly, "You forget who I am."

Lilith's pretty girlish face grew pale, yet she refused to back down. "But they are oath breakers, Milord. We all know how strongly you feel about oath breakers. Should not their sins be punished?"

"Oath breakers, I abhor," the god of the dead replied, "but these are not oath breakers, for their oaths have been forgiven by the White Lady, whose glance brings joy and whose breath brings salvation, even here in the dark of Limbo. I have no quarrel with them."

"You can't just let them go!" objected Lilith.

"Are they dead?" asked Hades.

"No . . ." she began.

"Then what business of mine are they?" He turned his back on her and regarded Father, who still leaned upon the *Staff of Eternity*. Hades snorted. "Besides, they are family."

"I beg your pardon?" the Demon Queen asked, taken aback.

The Unseen One, his horse-plumed helmet still tucked under one arm, gestured toward Father, who had his hand upon his beard, partially covering his smile. "The magician Prospero is my brother-in-law and his whelps, my nephews. My wife would not take kindly to any harm done to them."

"What are we women, chopped liver?" muttered Logistilla. Hades turned his intimidating gaze upon her, and she shrank back behind Titus, clearly regretting having spoken.

"Huh, look at that!" Mab whispered to me, awed. "All that Eleusinian stuff must have worked! Demeter really did adopt Mr. Prospero, which makes him the brother of the Maiden." He jerked his head in the direction of the death god. "This guy's wife!"

"And you let your wife rule you?" The Queen of Air and Darkness gave him a long sultry look. "I remember you being made of more manly stuff back in our day."

He crossed his arms. "Your point being . . . ?"

Exasperated, she let out a stream of curses.

"You are undone, Lilith," Father spoke kindly. "Leave while you can still do so with dignity."

"Damn you, Prospero! And damn your family!"

"No, thank you." Father bowed respectfully, a twinkle in his eye. "We'll stick with Heaven."

Turning her back on us, the Queen of Air and Darkness stormed to her chariot and drove away.

"Thank you, Brother-In-Law." My father addressed the armored death god. "We will depart now and not impose on your hospitality any longer. Come, Children!"

The others, including Astreus, moved quickly to Father's side, but I hesitated, trying to catch a glimpse of the god's forehead. He caught me looking and pushed back his hair, showing me a smooth sable brow.

"I see you know who I really am. Sibyls always seem to know more than is good for them. Keep it to yourself!" He glared at me, an intimidating experience. "My mark vanished when Our Savior forgave my sins at Calvary, but you would not have cared to see it. It was not pretty like yours."

I blushed, embarrassed to have been caught staring, and started to turn away, but I could not let the opportunity slip by entirely. Moving closer to him, I asked softly, "I've always wanted to know . . . Which story is real? What really happened in the Garden?"

He crossed his arms again. At close range, his shoulders were huge. It was like standing next to a bull or a very large wolf. "I wouldn't know. It was before my time."

I lowered my head, chastened.

"But I will tell you this . . ." A gleam of humor came into his sardonic eyes. "My Lady Mother's tale never quite agreed with the story told by my Lord Father, and—like all things—the real events were far more complicated than any fable." He leaned forward, towering over me. "Now, White Maiden, take your people and go. Your blessedness disturbs my sullen kingdom."

I fled, quickly returning to where my family stood. We put our hands on Ulysses's staff.

"Nice to have met you, Hades." Mephisto held up his free hand, spreading his thumb and his third and fourth fingers. "Live long and Prospero!"

The god of the dead snorted. Returning his great plumed helmet to his head, he vanished from view. Though whether he stayed or left, no mortal could say.

CHAPTER THIRTY-TWO

Into the Tempest

In the twinkling of an eye, Ulysses transported us back to the courtyard on Father's island. Immediately, gale force winds dragged us across the orchids. Rains drenched us; our wet clothes stuck to our bodies. Ulysses screamed and vanished again, taking those who were still holding on with him, which happened to be Logistilla and Gregor. The rest of us had already let go of the *Staff of Transportation* and were now pushed along by the winds until we reached the trees, where we grabbed onto their trunks and held on for dear life.

Overhead a storm raged as violently as even I had never seen. The heavens clashed. Fire and pitch rained from the sky. Forty-five-foot waves crashed against the shore, and, as far as we could see, the surface of the ocean was entirely white with foam and spray. A mix of rain and seawater blew in our faces; the air smelled of ozone.

With a horrific grinding noise, the tower at the top of Father's house tumbled off, crashing down into the ravine where the Eridanus flowed, the river Father had named after the constellation. It was awe-inspiring and terrifying.

"Now, that's a storm! The way I remember 'em from the old days!" Mab grinned furiously as he clung to the bole of a pine.

"What is happening?" Father shouted. He had his back pressed against a wide oak, his arm up to shield his face from the winds. "Miranda, quickly! Put a stop to this!"

"She can't!" called Erasmus. "She broke her flute to save me."

Father cried in horror. "Miranda! What were you thinking!"

"I was thinking that it did not contain a demon!" I shouted back, most of my words carried away by the storm. Looking over my shoulder, I noticed that my wings were no longer visible. "I was thinking about the Great Fire of London!"

"Excuse me?" Father knit his brow.

"The Great Fire of London! When Erasmus stopped the salamanders from killing the people?" I shouted over the roar of the storm. "I thought if we worked together, we could stop any supernatural threat! But if one of us were dead, how could we work together?"

Father looked faintly surprised, but before he could respond, Astreus's voice cut through the driving winds.

"Enough!" Astreus still stood in the center of the courtyard amidst the orchids. The feathers of his wings billowed, and his hair whipped about his face, but he himself seemed untroubled by the storm. "Winds, obey your lord! Carry our words and do not constrain our persons, both myself and my fair companions."

Immediately, we were free to move. The winds did not lose their ferocity nor did the moaning and roaring lessen, but we were no longer being crushed and dragged about, and we could now hear each other clearly.

"Astreus!" Mephisto's face lit up with joy. "You're okay! You have wings!"

He dashed across the intervening distance and threw his arms about the Elf Lord, hugging him. Astreus's wings *whooshed* opened in surprise, but he laughed and returned the embrace.

"Mephistopheles? And you are free as well?" The elf grabbed my brother by his shoulders and looked down into his face. Mephisto nodded. "Centuries of sorrow have I endured waiting to hear these joyful tidings! For this, all my suffering has been worthwhile!"

"Yup! Except I still have to wear this stupid hat if I want to remember anything." My brother put the hat on his head, and he and Astreus conversed in soft voices. They looked like two prisoners who had suddenly burst free of their cells, comradery and relief mirrored on both their faces.

Back by the trees, the rest of us righted ourselves and brushed at the sticky pine sap on our clothing.

"The Aerie Ones! You mean Miranda let them free?" Cornelius cried aghast, as he brushed at the orchid petals that were plastered to his face. "There is nothing controlling them?"

"You have undone a fourth of Solomon's work. You have freed the King of the Air!" Father shouted, as a bolt of lightning struck the tallest oak on the island, splitting it in two. "Planes will fall out of the sky. Air need not remain breathable! What will become of mankind?"

Closing my eyes, I spoke to my Lady, whom—now that I was a Sibyl—I could reach directly. *If I call him, will he come?*

He will come.

I whistled a trill I used to play often upon my flute.

A third of the force of the storm broke away and began twisting about itself, forming a long sinuous length of wind, rain, and spray that stretched as far as the eye could see. Down from the sky came a great triangular serpent head with long slitted eyes of mist. It encircled us, wrapping once about the courtyard, a second coil about the house, and a third about the island itself, before trailing off through the sky into the horizon.

"Ophion!" I cried. "To me!"

"Miranda!" the Serpent of the Winds hissed as he buffeted me with his head. It was like being pushed by a cyclone.

"Great Serpent," I said, realizing with a sudden joyful lurch that this great being was my flute—that the love I had lavished upon my beloved instrument had been accepted and returned, just as I had always imagined. "You must re-swear your oath to Solomon. You must swear to uphold the laws of nature."

The great snake head drew back and hissed with the force of a tornado. I would have been blown from my feet and smashed against the trees, were it not for Astreus's magic. Instead, I faced him calmly.

"I am free! Why should I put my head back into the noose?"

"For the love of mankind."

"Mankind? What are they to me?"

Softly, I replied, "Should you not ask, rather, what are they to your Lady?"

Ophion writhed, his long body twisting and shaking. Part of him struck Father's house and more of the tower tumbled into the ravine. Then, he lowered his head down beside me.

"Not for mankind, nay. I have given them their due. But for love of you and of She who stands behind you, I will do it."

I stroked his giant triangular nose. The shape of it pushed back against my hand. It was like patting a wind tunnel. "Thank you."

Titus came forward and pushed the *Staff of Darkness* against the King of the Air's snout. Erasmus, who had the words of Solomon's oath memorized, instructed the Serpent of the Winds as to what he should say.

When, it was done, Eurynome's voice spoke in my mind: *Tell him to come to Me among the stars.*

"Your Lady has need of you." I stroked the Serpent's head. My hand kept buffeting off of him, as if I were trying to push against the jets of water in a Jacuzzi. "She asks that you join Her among the stars."

"Then, there I shall go. Take care, Little Miranda. Whistle for me if you need me." The Serpent of the Winds circled once more about me, then swept across the island, over the side of the ravine and dived into the Eridanus. Immediately, the fury of the storm lessened. It was now merely a hurricane, instead of something more.

In awe, I watched the tail of the Serpent go over the edge of the ravine. "Is there really a connection between our little Eridanus and the Milky Way?"

"According to the Laws of Sympathy and Contagion, the similarity of the name would be enough to make a connection for a spirit being." Erasmus walked back to the courtyard where Astreus stood. "I must say that was pretty impressive, Miranda! Guess he came to like you during all those years of having you toot on his tail."

"Miranda, sacrificing your flute to save your brother was noble indeed, especially as I know you are not very fond of Erasmus." Father lay a hand on my shoulder. "Noble, but not wise. Many shall die today. Somehow, we must bind up the Aerie Ones!"

"Silence, Slaver!" Astreus stepped up to Father and glared down from his greater height, his eyes a deep midnight black. "I have given my word to help the Lady Miranda control my people." He looked to me and gestured upward. "Shall we put a stop to this display of playful spirits?"

I nodded, my heart leaping at his glance.

Astreus whistled then, and a long, flowing cloak of silver tinged with an indigo hue floated out of the sky. It hung in the air before him, and he regarded his reflection within its indigo-mirrored surface. Within, he appeared garbed in raiments of sapphire and storm gray with a coronet of stars upon his brow. Astreus reached out and touched the cloak, which rippled like the surface of a pond. As if it was actually made of water, he stepped into it and emerged on the far side of the cloak, garbed and crowned as his reflection had been. The mirrored cloak rolled up into a pearl. He put it in his pocket.

Turning, he offered me his hand, which I accepted. All eight pairs of wings opened with a *shoosh* and upward we soared.

WE flew into the storm. The winds parted before us. Rain soaked our faces and ozone-tinged air blew all about us. Twice the sky lit as thunderbolts ripped the clouds. High in the thunderclouds, Astreus called out in a strong voice:

"Boreas!"

A face appeared in the sky, not a human face, but a face of wind and cloud; yet it resembled the Russian face Boreas had worn these last decades.

"Lord Astreus!" His eyes flashed. "I rejoice to see that you have returned."

"Fair Boreas, it does my heart good to see you, too," Astreus replied.

Boreas cried, "The great days of yore have come again! Let us join together and wreak havoc upon this mortal world, as we have done in ages past! Let us toss ships and break masts and scatter the splinters of great vessels across the white waves!"

Astreus's expression changed, his eyes growing brighter, "And knock down towers and carry off chariots . . ."

"And blow planes from the air and smash skyscrapers . . ." Boreas chanted.

"And rip off roofs and tumble water towers!"

Astreus's eyes were now blood red, the same red as Seir's. The wind tossed his storm-gray hair so that it seemed to leap about his face like a living thing. An eerie light transformed his features, until he looked the epitome of a wild elf lord bent on strife and mischief.

I was hundreds of feet in the air supported by the whim of a mad elf. Would he even remember I was here before he joined Boreas on their course of mayhem and destruction? Or would he forget me and let go?

Astreus threw back his head, laughing; his wings springing upward. The motion seemed to startle him. He glanced at them in surprise and, for an instant, so quick that I could hardly be sure I had seen it, his eyes turned a brilliant gold.

He drew me closer, wrapping a wing or two around me, and gave me an encouraging smile. His eyes had returned to the dark gray of an undisturbed lake. It was soft and warm beneath his feathers and smelled of stardust. The speed of my heart began to drop.

Astreus said, "Greatly do your words call to me and stir my heart, Boreas. And yet, were I to do as you suggest, it would bring this lady sorrow, and that my heart could not endure."

Astreus drew back his wings, so that Boreas could see me.

"Hello, Boreas," I cried over the tremendous roar of the storm, waving.

Boreas eyed me coldly and opened his mouth as if to blow me away. Remembering the lessons of our last encounter at the eyrie, when I had ruled him through firmness rather than through force, I refused to be daunted. I met his gaze squarely and spoke in a stern voice. "Boreas, what are you doing?"

His face swelling with bluster and wrath, he boomed, "I am asserting my independence!"

"Boreas, you've worked for my family for years. You were our enforcer. You've seen the other unruly spirits forced into obedience by my brothers: the oreads, the nymphs, the oni, the phoenixes. Is that the fate you desire? How long will you enjoy your freedom, if you carry on thus?"

Boreas glared at me, furrowed his brow, and blew five-hundred-mile-an-hour winds from his nostrils. There was a blast of terrible cold, but the torrential winds did not even so much as ruffle Astreus's feathers. My hand was still firmly clasped in his, and his protection continued to extend to me. Unmoved, I gazed evenly at Boreas, waiting.

Then, he saw me, really saw me. The great Lord of the North Wind beheld the mark of Eurynome upon my brow, and his icy eyes widened in awe and astonishment. His head of wind bowed.

"Mistress . . ." He breathed a gentle cold sigh. "You are a Sibyl! You can make Water of Life! That which gives us heart and strength and makes us great!"

"I can." I touched my forehead. "Now listen carefully, Boreas. Spread this message; I know you are good at that. Every wind who calms his people, I shall reward with Water of Life: a dozen drops for himself and one drop for each minion who obeys him. Any minion who disobeys and continues to rage shall not be rewarded. In addition, I shall reward you similarly upon the birth of each new year. With time, those who are obedient will receive more Water and grow stronger than those who are unruly.

"What is more," I continued, "any Aerie One who wishes to continue working for Prospero, Inc., will receive a regular salary of Water. Also, any Aerie One who returns to work will have access to a fleshy body such as you and your fellow Northerly have worn." I leaned toward him, smiling. "By wearing such a body, Caekias has developed a soul!"

"Caekias? But he is the worst of us!"

"*Was* the worst," I replied.

Boreas let out a frigid gasp of wonder. "Lady, I beg your pardon for my previous impertinence. I will be returning to my body now."

The cloudy face dissolved, and Boreas was gone. Moments later, another face formed slightly to the left. This one had a long nose and wisps of cloud indicating a scarf.

"Congratulations, Milady!" Caurus cried in his Scandinavian accent.

"Boreas told me the splendid news. A Sibyl, at last. We all have received our heart's desire!"

"Except the innocent mortals harmed by this storm."

"Not to worry, Milady. I and mine have not taken part in any storms over the continents. Neither has Ariel, Afer, Eurus, or Notus; we understand what will become of us if we betray mankind. We may have tipped a few ships in our celebrations, though, and for that I apologize. I will send my servants and winglings to scoop up the sailors and carry them safely to dry land.

"Boreas and Zephyrus have been a bit more exuberant, as has Zetes and Calias, the sons of Boreas who have been filling in for Caekias and myself while we were incarnated. By the way, where is Caekias?"

"He is below." I pointed down toward where I thought the courtyard to be. I could not see through the storm clouds.

"Wonderful! I would not wish him to miss all this. Father!" Caurus addressed Astreus. "I did not recognize you with your wings! How splendid you look!"

"My thanks, Caurus." Astreus inclined his head. "Go, spread this word: I have returned, and I am lending the strength of my authority to the Lady Miranda. Who offends her, offends me!"

"I shall tell all straightaway!" Caurus promised, and his cloud face dissolved into wind and rain.

The winds above us slowly died down to the speeds of a tropical storm. Astreus drew me to him, wrapping his arms about my waist. With the merest motion of his wings, he waltzed us through the clouds. The warmth of his body was a wonderful contrast to the chill of the winds.

"I was dead, and you rekindled my life." He stared down at me, his changeable eyes a deep fascinating blue. "Every moment of my life, hereafter, is a gift from you. And to that end, I lay my people at your feet. No longer shall I whip up their fury, urging them to rage and storm and crush the ships and homes of mankind. I see now the harm I did when I walked that path. For I have walked the roads of Hell, and I would not send so much as one mortal there before his time.

"I am yet still an elf, and my people still capricious winds. I cannot promise that all will swear again, or that there will be no terrible storms in years to come. But what I can do, I shall do, and all for love of you."

His eyes reflecting the fury of the tempest, he lowered his head and kissed me.

I entwined my arms about his neck, my lips yielding willingly beneath his mouth. He clasped me to him, and his wings enfolded me, sheltering me in a soft feathery embrace. Breathing the air about my elvish love, I dreamt we danced together in the sky, twirling and spiraling through cloud and wind and storm. Only, this time, it was not a dream at all. Or perhaps, the dream and the reality were one.

When we parted again, still dancing and gazing into each other's eyes, I asked, "Will you answer a question for me? Something I have been curious about?"

"For you? Anything," his eyes flashing green, "so long as it suits my elvish fancy."

"In your pact with Mephisto, where you promised to help him with Queen Maeve, what did he promise you?"

Few mortals have ever seen an elf blush. I now joined that lucky elite.

"We made a solemn oath that"—he spun me about—"if I helped him win the affection of the Elf Queen, he would help me win yours. At first, I must admit, I sought merely dalliance, for you were lovely to behold, like a rainbow over the morning dew, or the light of a newborn star piercing a cloudy night. However, Mephisto made it clear you were a vestal virgin and not to be trifled with. After that, the hope grew in my breast that, by bringing you the *Book of the Sibyl,* I might win both my freedom from Hell and you for myself."

And he kissed me again.

The clouds parted around us briefly, and I could see Father's island beneath us. I felt a stab of sadness as I saw that the lightning-damaged oak was the one in the Grove of Books, from which Theo's staff came.

"The poor oak! Remind me to go by and give it a drop of Water."

Astreus touched the ivory mark upon my forehead. "Cannot you help it right now, from here?"

I gazed at it, picturing what the world might be like from an oak's point-of-view. As the warmth began to flow from my Lady's mark, a thunderbolt ripped across the sky, following the invisible beam coming from my forehead. Quickly, I averted my gaze, and the bolt struck the first thing my eyes fell upon, a high plinth of rock.

Again and again, I picked some object beneath me, the tip of a wave, a ledge of rock, an open field. Each time, lightning flashed across the sky, striking the place I had chosen.

I threw back my head, laughing.

After five hundred years, I had become a Sibyl of Eurynome, and it was even more splendid than I had imagined!

"The Gifts of the Sibyl!" I shouted. "Command the Lightning!"

Astreus touched the mark on my forehead and smiled. "Indeed, and even more wonderful gifts await you, the secondary gifts. Did you not read the book I so laboriously copied for you? *The very elements themselves rejoice in Her love, standing firm or fleeing as She requires.* I have seen Sibyls run across the waves and sink fleets, make quagmires firm and rocks porous, dance in the midst of flames, and fly."

"Fly!" I cried joyously, clapping a hand to my forehead. A joyous jolt of strength passed through my arm. "You mean, with this I can fly?"

Astreus drew me close. "We are birds of a kind, you and I." His eyes still sparkled a merry green. "Perhaps we should form a flock."

CHAPTER THIRTY-THREE

Prospero's Secrets

My family had repaired to the library, a great cavern of a chamber with a
vaulted cathedral ceiling and book stacks over twenty-five feet high. Most
of the vast shelf space was empty or contained a smattering of modern volumes, paperbacks, and hardcovers with brightly colored dust jackets, as the
majority of Father's books were in Prospero's Mansion in Oregon or at
Erasmus's. The place was both drafty and musty, but this was preferable to
the torrents of rain currently drenching many of the house's other cham-
bers, now that the great glassless windows no longer had Aerie Spirits to
keep the elements at bay. The library had a few skylights set among the
arching vaults of the ceiling, but they had been installed recently and were
made of glass.

A few massive tomes still rested upon their custom-made pedestals, one
or two of which I recalled from my childhood. These books were enormous
and fascinating to behold. One had the ages of man etched into its white
leather cover, so that as one watched, a babe seemed to grow into a child
into a youth into a man into an old man and back to a babe again. Another
had as its cover a mirror that reflected the sky of other worlds. Yet a third
bore a demonic face that grimaced menacingly, hissing and growling,
whenever any of us came near. This last one was bound up with a thick iron
chain.

Near the center of the library stood a table surrounded by straight-
backed chairs. Food from many nations, in variously shaped cardboard and
Styrofoam boxes, littered its teak surface. I gathered this bounty had been
provided by Ulysses, for he and the others who had vanished with him were
now present again, as were Logistilla's and Titus's children, who munched
on Happy Meals. Stacks of plates, silverware, and napkins stood to one
side.

At the head of the table, my father sat in his old armchair eating dough-nuts and Chinese takeout. His hair and beard had been brushed and trimmed, and he was garbed in his enchanted gold robes with their royal purple trim, which, like our garments, had been woven by Logistilla. Though he was still gaunt, he looked much more like his old self. The thorn wounds were already healing, thanks to the Water I had given him. He smiled at the rest of the family who were already seated around the table.

I came to join the others after landing and visiting the oak tree, to which I gave a liberal dose of Water of Life. Then Astreus headed skyward again, and I went to see my family.

As I came into the library, the first thing I did was touch two fingers to my forehead and point first at Ulysses, who was sporting a black eye I did not recall having seen after the battle, and then at Logistilla, who was tend-ing Titus's wounds, her face covered with a mass of bandages.

"By the power granted to me as a Sibyl of Eurynome," I announced, "I free Ulysses Reginald Prospero and Logistilla Violante Prospero from their oaths to Abaddon, the Angel of the Bottomless Pit, and from any other foolish promises or vows undertaken in times past."

My younger siblings were not Sforza, our family having officially changed our name to Prospero during our years in England.

"Jolly good!" Ulysses leapt up and punched the air. His voice echoed throughout the mostly empty library. "Miranda, you are literally the best sister a guy could have!"

Logistilla breathed an audible sigh of relief. "Thank you, Sister. That is one nightmare I am happy to have behind me! You cannot imagine . . ." She shuddered and held up a hand. "No, I shan't speak of it!"

"The fake Seal of Solomon!" Ulysses blurted out. "Now that the geas is gone, I can tell you! It's an imp in disguise. I was supposed to smuggle it into Father's mansion so that it could let other demons in past his wards."

"Which explains how Seir of the Shadows got into the Vault." Mab flipped open his notebook and made a note of this, crossing off yet another unanswered question. "And how he got onto the grounds of the Oregon mansion in the first place. I wager it helped that the demons had Mr. Pros-pero's blood and could pass the wards, right?"

"Yes." Father inclined his head. "Lilith was 'kind' enough to inform me when they cast the spell to let Seir into the mansion. I suppose she hoped it would weaken my resolve. Make a note, Mab, to remove that fake piece first thing when you return to Oregon."

Mab scribbled obediently in his notebook.

My stomach rumbled. The mingled smells of the many cuisines all warred for my attention. Realizing that I was very hungry indeed, I quickly served myself from the various boxes and sat down.

"We've settled the storm, for now," I explained between bites. "Some of the Aerie Ones will be coming back to work, and Caurus has gone to scoop up sailors who would otherwise drown at sea."

"A worldwide storm." Cornelius shook his head sadly. He sat at the table between Ulysses and Theo, his staff resting beside him, his shoulders slumped, and his expression dejected. "It is going to take a great deal of work to clean this up in the history books."

His voice seemed flat, as if it echoed from a great distance away, as if his soul were elsewhere, far from us, and resented being dragged back in order to speak.

Again, I felt a pang of sharp regret and wished that it had not been my words that had convinced him to forgo Heaven.

"Nonsense!" Erasmus did not bother looking up from where he knelt treating Theo's head wound. "Just blame it on global climate changes. People blame all sorts of things on global climate changes—earthquakes, the losses of their favorite rugby teams—and everyone believes it."

Father looked around the table, his eyes traveling from one of our faces to the next, until he had studied each of us.

"Miranda has learned a great deal in the short time I have been away," he said. "I expect to discover the rest of you have done as well."

"I could wax poetic about life as a bear." Titus sat with his leg out so that Logistilla could treat his wound.

"You were a bear? No wonder my servants could not find you!" Father's eyes narrowed as he regarded Logistilla speculatively. "I see there is much I have not yet heard."

"I was a leopard for over fifty years," Gregor volunteered, raising a hand. He turned to Titus. "You and I should swap tales. One interesting thing I discovered—"

"Before we go telling you all our little secrets, Father," Erasmus interrupted, "or fill you in on our new plan for family-wide, periodic, staff rotation, perhaps it is time for *you* to answer a few questions of ours."

We all looked at Father with great interest, but he gave a curt shake of his head.

"That would not be wise," he explained. "Our enemies are very danger-ous. It is best you ask me your questions later, one at a time."

Erasmus shrugged and went back to applying bandages, though some of the others looked quite disappointed. I sighed. Apparently, everything was going right back to the way it had been. Somehow, I had hoped things would be different.

Mab had been sitting at the far end of the table, eating a Boston Cream doughnut. He came forward to stand politely before Father, his hat in his hand.

"Begging your pardon, Mr. Pros . . ." Midword, Mab halted and threw down his hat. "Beggin' nothing! I'm a free agent now!" He jabbed a finger at Father. "You listen to me, Lucretius, and listen well! I'm far older than you and a good lick wiser. So take it from me: secrecy breeds distrust, and distrust is a primary weapon of our enemy! True, it was useful that the de-mons did not know about the *Staff of Wisdom*—but look at the price you paid!"

Father appeared quite taken aback. It had been a long time since some-one had addressed him by his given name. I wondered if he had forgotten he had one.

"I beg your pardon." He drew his bushy brows together and frowned, quite an intimidating sight. "How so?"

Mab refused to be daunted. "If you had encouraged Miss Miranda to be honest about being jilted by Ferdinand, Mr. Erasmus would not have come to distrust her. If Mr. Erasmus had not distrusted her, your brother Antonio would never have gotten the hold on Mr. Erasmus that he did. If Antonio had not gotten his claws into Mr. Erasmus, he would not have been able to cast his spell, and Miss Miranda and the Professor would not have bickered so much. If they had not bickered so much, Mr. Ulysses would not have gone off on his own to be captured by Abaddon, which led to no end of mess.

"What's more, if Mr. Ulysses and Madam Logistilla had known about the antidemonic effect of the *Staff of Silence,* Mr. Ulysses could have writ-ten out his plea for help back in 1921, before Mr. Gregor spent most of a century in prison and Mr. Theophrastus nearly died from the influence of the *Staff of Persuasion,* which had fallen under the influences of the de-mons." As Mab spoke, Father looked rapidly from Cornelius to Theo, and I realized how many things we had not yet told him.

"Secrecy has harmed your family a great deal," Mab concluded, "nearly costing several lives. I, for one, say the time has come to do away with it!"

Titus lifted his hands and brought them together with a resounding *crack,* once and then again. Moments later, the rest of us joined in, until we all clapped furiously. Mab looked faintly embarrassed, but he winked at me.

"Whatever answer you give, Father, I'd give it politely." Erasmus finished off Theo's bandage. He leaned forward and announced in a stage whisper, "This Mab fellow is secretly the god of the Nor'easterly, and he doesn't work for us anymore."

Father stroked his beard, regarding us without saying anything for quite some time. Finally, he replied, "Very well. I will answer one question from each of you. After that, you will have to wait until I have rested and regained my strength before you quiz me further. For I have endured more than any man who has ever descended into the Inferno and returned to the sunlit lands, and I am very weary."

He turned to me, where I sat to his right. "Miranda, you are the heroine of the hour. You may go first. After that, I will take one question each, in order, from eldest to youngest."

"Will you really answer, Father?" I asked hopefully and then, grinning, quoted Shakespeare's lines for my alter ego. "For 'You have often begun to tell me what I am, but stopp'd, And left me to a bootless inquisition, Concluding "Stay: not yet." '"

"You cannot best me with the Bard." Father chuckled. Smiling, he quoted back. " 'The hour's now come; The very minute bids thee ope thine ear; Obey and be attentive.' "

I asked without hesitation, "Why didn't you tell us that there were demons in our staffs?"

"I told each of you what I felt you needed to know," Father replied. "There was no demon in your staff, Daughter, so I did not see the need to explain the matter to you. The more people I told, the more chance of the information falling into the wrong hands."

"Did you tell my siblings about how, if they resisted the demons in their staffs . . ."

"Shhhh!" Father raised his finger to his lips, cutting me off. "*They* are present in this room." He pointed his elbow at Cornelius's staff. "They will hear you."

"Oh!"

"We'll discuss that later, Child," he promised.

Mephisto jumped up and down waving his hand. "Me! Pick me! I'm next."

"No, Mephistopheles," Father replied mildly, "Caliban is next."

"Oops!" Mephisto covered his mouth with both hands. "Your turn, Calvin."

Caliban grasped his club, turning it in his lap. "I don't have many questions that haven't been answered by . . ." He looked down at his club. "But there is something I would like to ask you . . .

"Master . . . Brother Mephisto told me that Erasmus had spoken of a place in your journal where you wrote of Sycorax's child. I know you spoke to this matter in Hell, but I wanted to hear it again, directly from your lips, when we were not being overheard by enemies, so that you do not have a reason to be hiding anything or, perhaps, lying."

Father colored faintly. He glanced at Erasmus, his eyes narrowing. "I didn't know you had that journal."

I snorted with irony and self-amusement. And to think that I had been jealous.

Erasmus smiled and shrugged. "You said I could take any journal I found in the teak chest. This one was next to the chest. I figured that counted."

"Indeed." Father's eyes glittered with amusement. "And from reading it, you learned that I had a child by the witch Sycorax. Ah, I see now: you thought it was Miranda." Pushing his food aside, Father reached out and clasped Caliban's shoulder. "Yes. I am your father, and you are my son."

Caliban gazed at us all with worshipful delight. He had already known, but he, who had lived in such solitude, seemed overwhelmed, to be joining such a large, noisy family. He probably would probably always be closest to Mephisto, yet he was already establishing relationships with my other siblings, particularly Cornelius and Ulysses, whom he had toted around in Hell. This was a good thing, I decided. Ulysses could use a little exposure to wisdom.

"That's right," Erasmus laughed. He stood and came over and slapped Caliban on the back. "You are our older brother, now. Next time Father disappears, you'll be the one in charge."

"Oh, no!' Caliban gasped. "T-that's Master Mephisto's job!"

"Oh-ho-ho!" Mephisto chortled. "You're the eldest now! I'm off the hook!" He immediately plopped his head down on the table and pretended to snooze making *konk-feewww* noises. He opened one eye. "Besides, I'm Little Brother now. Not Master."

"He's right," Titus rumbled. "You're our eldest brother, and there's no getting out of it." He grinned and gave Caliban a friendly punch on the shoulder. "Nice having another big 'un around to help me with the heavy lifting."

Caliban smiled, touched. The others grinned at him. Ulysses gave him a thumbs-up. He blushed under all the attention.

I reached out and lay my hand on his arm. "Welcome to the family, brother. You're really one of us now."

Tears came into his eyes. He opened his mouth but could not speak.

Father cleared his throat. "Please. Stop choking the boy up. He can't finish his question."

"How come you treated him so much more badly than you treated the rest of us?" Logistilla asked archly, giving Caliban a sisterly smile.

"Do not think me too heartless, Daughter," Father replied. "I treated Caliban as my son until his attack on Miranda. After that, I admit I was less than fatherly. As soon as Mephisto was up to the task, I sent him to take care of Caliban, which he has done admirably over the years."

"There were a few rough spots when Mephisto first lost his wits." Caliban wiped sauce from his face with his sleeve. Mephisto *tsked* at him and handed him a napkin. "But he has been a good master . . ."—he grinned—". . . brother to me. Who were the 'A.T.' I hear that I terrorized?"

"Angelikon Teknon," Father replied, "Angel Child."

"You mean that passage meant Caliban was troubling Little Miranda?" Erasmus hit his forehead with a resounding *slap*. "Oh, Lord! Did I get that one wrong!"

"Who's next?" Father pointed his finger and moved it around the room until it fell upon Mephisto. "Mephistopheles. You're the next eldest, and you have your hand up."

Mephisto indeed did have his hand up. He waved it wildly, grinning his happy, goofy smile. I could not help chuckling. Of all my brothers, Mephisto had surprised me the most. I never would have guessed, back when we first found him singing on a tomato crate, dressed in a filthy poncho, that he had been looking out for the rest of us. I felt quite ashamed.

I was particularly touched by the care he had taken of Theo. While I had sat at home bemoaning Theo's situation, Mephisto, of all people, had been out there doing something. Theo seemed chagrined, too—especially since he learned that the warning Voice he heard so often came courtesy of Mephisto. His former irritation with his elder brother seemed to be giving way to a grudging respect.

Leaping up, Mephisto cried out, "What was it like, Daddy, 'pooning an angel?"

My father flushed. "Unions with angelic beings are not as unions between mortals. It was more a meeting of hearts."

"You mean you've been in love with an angel all these centuries, and you've never even boinked her?" Rising, Mephisto came over and patted Father on the shoulder. "That must have been difficult for you!"

Father turned as red as his glass of wine. He cleared his throat. "Hmph, right. Moving right along . . . Theophrastus?"

Theo's face was now a deep tan, except for the white raccoon mask around his eyes where his goggles had been. Nothing we had accomplished, not even realizing my long-cherished dream of becoming a Sibyl, pleased me as much as seeing Theo's youthful and healthy face. In amazed delight, I realized that my plan to drag him out of that cozy old farmhouse had worked. I had saved Theo, and the world was a better place for it.

"Father, during the period when Miranda was under the spell . . . I mean, lacking in free will . . . how come nobody else noticed?" Theo asked.

"Mephisto noticed, and Titus," Father replied.

I glanced in surprise at both brothers. Titus ducked his head, embarrassed; Mephisto winked and gave me a thumbs-up.

"They helped me keep an eye on her. They did not believe I was the one behind it, so they did not hesitate to come to me." Father fixed his keen gaze on Theo who flushed. "As for the rest, they believed Erasmus."

"Excuse me?" Erasmus glanced up from his food.

Father fixed his keen gaze on him. "Every time Miranda acted oddly, Erasmus gave her behavior a malicious spin, accusing her of having some malevolent motive, such as callousness or spite. Since this offered an explanation for her behavior, the rest of you looked no deeper."

"Well, I feel like an even bigger idiot! That's me: Erasmus, the Baby Angel Torturer. If you need me, I'll be here banging my head against this table." Erasmus banged his head against the table with an audible *crack*.

"Stop that!" Logistilla cried. "This is an antique table."

"Thanks so much for your sisterly concern," drawled Erasmus, rubbing his head.

Theo leaned forward, a discerning glint in his eye. "And you didn't set him straight because you thought that it was better that she be misunderstood than that she be understood and mistreated."

"Exactly," Father replied. "In my mind, it was the lesser of two evils. If

others had known, they might have found ways to order her around like a
servant. That Erasmus's dislike of Miranda might lead to evil in and of
itself, I fear I did not take into consideration."

The tome containing the demonic face began to howl and thrash about
in its chains. Father made a gesture, but nothing happened. He made it
again, more impatiently, then looked chagrined as he recalled there were no
airy servants left to obey his commands. Instead, he nodded to Titus, Erasmus, and Caliban, who wrestled the thing off its pedestal and into the back
of the library, where it could carry on howling and wailing without inter-
rupting our conversation.

As we waited, I told Gregor and Theo about seeing my mother and
what she had told me about the fallen angels and the nature of Hell. Theo
balked, unwilling to believe such heresy. He pointed out that since I had
woken up in the field of flowers next to the tumbled Tower of Thorns afterward, there was no evidence that my visit with my mother had really happened. Perhaps, I had dreamt it. Gregor, however, nodded, as if my words
confirmed a theory.

"We of the Church have long debated this question. There are those
among us who believe that, since God can save a man's soul right up to the
last minute—far after life seems to have fled to the mortal observer—it was
possible that everyone had repented, and Hell was empty, because no one
had ever gone there. During my second term as pope, I had a good friend,
a Franciscan friar, who held this position and would debate it with me at
length. He held that we of the Church should all pray that his theory was
the true one, for who would wish it to be otherwise. I, on the other hand,
thought that I knew better because of our family's dealings with demons
and the like."

Gregor smiled with weary sheepishness, "Apparently, Brother Laurence
was right."

Mab sat beside me, a second doughnut in hand. Seeing his craggy face
brought a sudden pang of sorrow. Our time together was coming to an end.
Mab had realized his greatest wish. He was now free. He could leave. He
could even go back to his previous state as a bodiless spirit. The thought of
him giving up his life as Mab and returning to being the Northwest Wind
made me unexpectedly sad, as if I had just learned that a friend was going
to die. I had come to rely upon him so. How would I run Prospero, Inc.,
without him?

Since Erasmus was not back from wrestling the book yet, Father moved on to the next eldest. "Cornelius, do you have a question for me?"

Cornelius nodded slowly, his face impassive behind the royal purple swath of cloth that again bound his useless eyes.

I wondered, suddenly, why we had brought a blind man to Hell with us. And yet, Cornelius had managed to hold his own, an astonishing feat. Of all my brothers, he was still the greatest cipher to me, the one with whom I had the least in common.

And, yet, it had been for love of Cornelius that I had broken my staff to save Erasmus. He had more than paid back my sacrifice when he had turned down his chance to enter Heaven, choosing instead to remain on Earth to help the family and serve mankind. I watched him, speaking softly to Ulysses, who was helping him choose dishes he wished to eat, and I felt quite grateful that I had been given the opportunity to save his favorite brother.

I just wished that he would regain his normal composure. He looked so haggard, so listless, like a mere shadow of his former self.

"Father," Cornelius said softly, his voice strained. "I have a request, rather than a question. My staff needs to be rebound. It has been acting on its own, at the prompting of its masters in Hell."

"*Oh, Please! Let me speak with Paimon!*" the voice from Caliban's club said. "*I shall set him straight!*"

Father replied tersely to the *Staff of Wisdom*. "Vinae, you must stop speaking up without being spoken to! Otherwise, I shall rebind you, too. Whose side are you on, anyway?"

"He's on our side," Logistilla had finished tending Titus's wounds and now sat gingerly upon a pillow, wincing slightly as if her rump pained her, sipping soup. "He told Lilith so to her face."

"Really!" Father's face lit up. "Good work, Caliban! As for you, Vinae, be silent. We shall discuss your idea of speaking to King Paimon later. Anything else, Cornelius?"

My blind brother shook his head. Father's brow furrowed. He gazed at him with concern. Reaching forward he lay his hand on Cornelius's shoulder and squeezed his arm. Cornelius nodded and forced a smile, but his heart was not in it. Father tightened his grip on his shoulder one more time and then turned back to the rest of us.

"Next question, Titus?" Father asked.

Titus had come back when it became clear that three people were too many to carry the groaning tome. Now, he sat again, chewing on his meal. As he looked up, his mouth full of stew and his younger son hanging upon his back, my heart went out to him.

His period as a bear or, perhaps, changing staffs with Gregor, had done him good. He responded much more quickly than he had when last I saw him, a decade ago. Back then, he had seemed to be in a slothlike stupor. He looked so happy now, seated with Logistilla and their younger son—the older one had gone off exploring the library—I prayed he and his family would be granted many happy years together.

Swallowing his stew, Titus said, "I'm still confused about Miranda's mother. Is she really an angel, and if so, why was it such a secret?"

Father pressed his fingertips together. "Yes, Miranda's mother is the Virtue Muriel Sophia, the patron angel of the *Orbis Suleimani*—as I believe you all have surmised."

"But why keep this secret?" Titus repeated.

"This was kept secret for two reasons," Father replied. "First, because of a prophesy about a nephilim Sibyl freeing the elves from their tithe to Hell. Those who wished to prevent that prophesy from being fulfilled would have come after her, had they known. Second, as I just said to Theo, I feared that if Miranda's true nature was known, people might try to manipulate her. It would be easy enough to present her with instructions that appeared to have come from me, and to prompt her to do any number of things. I had such bad experiences with her accidental misinterpretation of my commands, I did not wish to have her abused maliciously."

"Why didn't you tell me?" I asked. "That I should not obey you?"

Father shook his head. "I could not be the one to tell you, Child. If you heard it from me, your mind would have interpreted it as an order. You might have tried to act as if you were free, but you would have been doing so under orders, not because of free will. Rather like someone who has been told 'Go have a good time,' spending the day at an amusement park they don't particularly enjoy. I discussed this with your mother a great deal over the years. We both concluded that we had to wait for you to discover the truth on your own."

"But why didn't you at least tell her that her mother was an angel?" Theo asked.

"Because that was the greatest secret of all . . . that Miranda was a candidate for the nephilim Sibyl of prophecy. I could not risk that secret to anyone, not with demons such as Baelor of the Baleful Eye wandering the earth."

I thought of my mother, the angel, and breathed a long-delayed sigh of relief. Finally, I could step off the roller coaster that had swept me along ever since that day, a mere week ago, when Erasmus had informed me that Portia Lucia di Gardello was not my mother. For a time, I had felt rudderless and lost, yet the truth, when it finally came out, had proved more glorious than even my wildest hopes.

Oddly enough, though, discovering my mother was an angel did not seem as significant as it might have in the past. In the space of seven days, I had gone from believing my mother was Lady Portia, to Sycorax, to Lilith, to Muriel Sophia. Yet, in the end, it did not matter whether my mother was a mortal, a half-ogre witch, a demon, or an angel. I was still myself, and my strengths and weaknesses were mine alone.

Still, I was deeply grateful to know that Father had not lied when he spoke of his admiration for my mother, and I felt honored to be the child of such great love.

Mab raised a hand. "Will you allow follow-up questions?"

Father nodded. "Be my guest."

Mab flipped through his notebook and, finding the place he was looking for, pulled out his space pen. "If it was a secret that Miranda was the one fulfilling the prophecy, why was Lilith so bent on keeping Miranda from becoming a Sibyl?"

"Lilith was not taking any chances," Father replied. "She created the Unicorn Hunters in an effort to slay all the Sibyls, and she bound up all the nephilim, both the wicked and the harmless ones. I believe you saw some of them in the cages around me."

"So, Lilith was out to get Miranda on principle?" Mab asked.

"Exactly," Father replied. "Had she known the truth, she would have bent much more of her twisted will to harming Miranda."

"Makes sense," agreed Mab.

"Gregor?" Father asked.

Gregor looked up from where he sat in his ripped scarlet cardinal's robes, watching the family with an indulgent smile. I had hardly wept during Gregor's funeral; that would not be true today. His time on Mars had changed him. While he was still a man of principle, he had acquired a kindness that had been lacking in his youthful self. I recalled how impressive he had looked with his robes flying about him as he drove off the demons in Infernal Milan or when he had blessed Malagigi and shriven Uncle Antonio and tried to reconcile this with my old image of Gregor the Brute. I could not.

He was a good man, Brother Gregor.

Gregor chuckled. "Father, I have so many questions, I have missed so much, that I do not feel it is worth my asking any particular question now. Rather, I would like to take this time to say thank you. I am so very happy to be home again!"

"There is much I do not know as well." Father also chuckled. "I still have only the vaguest idea of where you were or why you are alive. I shall look forward to a long, cozy conversation with you, anon. Next? Logistilla?"

Logistilla looked up from her Vietnamese soup and smiled with mock sweetness. "I don't have a question for Father," she purred. "He's always told me what I want to know. But I do have a question I'd like to ask of somebody: what will happen to all those creatures who escaped in Hell? The ones who the Serpent of the Wind let out of their cages?"

"Oh, oh! Me! Can I answer? Me!" Mephisto bounced up and down on his chair, spilling Theo's coffee. Theo glared at him and then sighed, resigned.

"Certainly. Answer away." Father gestured at Mephisto and took advantage of the momentary lull to get in a bite of his beef and broccoli.

Mephisto leapt in cheerfully. "The Hellwinds will catch most of them—those that were evil—and bring them back there, once a new set of cages has been built. Those who were merely prisoners of Lilith's, and there were a few, might escape, if they're lucky. Might help if Gregor prays for them."

"You can pray too, Mephisto." Gregor glanced sideways from his meal.

Mephisto shrugged. "Maybe, but you're better at it."

"Speaking of freedom and prayer, I wonder how Uncle Antonio is faring," Logistilla opined.

"Let's look!" Mephisto replied cheerfully. He whipped out the crystal ball and announced, "Show me Uncle Antonio!"

The mist within the crystal cleared to show a large building of dark gray stone, much like a prison. Within, Uncle Antonio knelt in a small cell that contained a bed, a table, and a chair and nothing more. It must not have been a jail, though, for the cell door was open. Uncle Antonio wore the blue robe and yellow belt of the Brotherhood of Hope. Upon his shoulder was the emblem of the anchor and star.

"Let us pray for him," Gregor intoned. Obediently, we all lowered our heads and prayed.

When we looked up again, Logistilla gasped and pointed at the cell. "Look at that!"

On the table lay three intertwined rings. Unlike the dull gloomy objects in the cell around them, these rings were made of gold so bright that they seemed to shine. I recognized them, of course; they were the Borromean rings, one of the emblems of the House Sforza, of which we and Uncle Antonio were members.

"How did they get there? They weren't there a moment ago," Erasmus asked. He had just returned from his mission to move the demonic tome. He leaned over Mephisto's shoulder, staring into the crystal sphere.

"They are a concrete symbol of our prayer," Gregor replied. "A sign to remind him not to lose his way. Let us hope that he follows it."

As Mephisto put the ball away, I caught one last glimpse of Uncle Antonio, rising from where he knelt to gaze in astonishment at the golden rings, their light lending substance and solidity to his features.

"Ulysses, I believe you are next." Father had also been gazing into the ball. His face was calm, but the barest smile crinkled the corners of his eyes as he watched his brother. He sat back down again and regarded our youngest sibling.

I smiled as I realized that I had even grown fonder of Ulysses in this past month, despite his foibles. His easy airy charm, which I had found annoying in the past, now seemed well-meant and appealing. And, while he had abandoned us in times of trouble again and again, he had screwed up his courage and come back to rescue us.

Ulysses asked, "Why didn't you tell anyone what I was up to—about my acquiring talismans, I mean?" To the rest of us, he said, "I like to think of myself as in the Indiana Jones line of work." He patted his pistol. "No, perhaps more the Lara Croft line of work, really, except without huge gazang . . ." He looked from Logistilla to me and fell quiet, muttering, "Right-o!"

"Who?" Gregor whispered to Theo.

"A female Allan Quartermain," Theo whispered back.

Gregor frowned. "How quaint."

I felt a moment of sympathy for Gregor, who had dropped out of sight the year after American women got the vote. Modern life would be quite a surprise.

"Yes, I'm quite curious about this, too." I turned to Father, eager to hear how he would answer my brother's question. "When I complained about Ulysses, you did not breathe a word about what he was doing."

"Ah, that's the rub, isn't it?" Father sat quietly for a time, massaging his temples. I suspected I knew what was to come: he was about to tell us that he had kept us apart because he did not want us to spill secrets to each other and thus to the enemy. Still, I would like to hear it from his own mouth.

CHAPTER THIRTY-FOUR

O Brave New World

"Perhaps you all think working for an angel is easy," Father said, when he finally began to speak. "Well, take it from me: it is not! It takes tremendous faith and courage to follow Divine Will. The angel comes and says, 'Put Aerie Ones into bodies so they will develop souls.' And you think: that idea is crazy! We'll lose control of them. And what kind of souls? Not all souls are good, you know.

"It took great courage upon my part to go forward with the plan to try to give the Aerie Ones souls. It went against many things I believed in, putting spirits into bodies, letting them interact with mankind," Father continued. I saw Cornelius and Mab both nodding. "However, once I had done it, I could not help thinking . . . If I was brave enough to give the Aerie Ones freer rein, what about my children?

"Miranda has often berated me for allowing you all to leave Prospero, Inc., but during the period when we ran the company together, I controlled everything. I made the decisions, chose our projects, enforced good behavior, mediated disputes—marshaling you all like a good general with his troops. And you all acted like good soldiers, obedient but with little initiative.

"So, I decided to take a risk. I set each of you about separate tasks and slowly withdrew my oversight. There were some frightening moments there." Father frowned at Ulysses. "More frightening than I had realized, apparently. But look at the benefits I have reaped. Each of you has flourished and grown. Without my help, you went to Hell, rescued me, rescued your brothers who were in need, and all came back again—only eight have ever made it to Hell and come back alive, before this." He turned to me, a twinkle in his keen eyes. "Besides, I figured if you were really interested in what your brethren were doing, you might take the trouble to ask them."

I blinked in astonishment, my head spinning as I tried to absorb all that

Father had revealed. I put my hands on my temples, as if that could stop the feeling of vertigo.

Had I known a month ago what I knew today, the Three Shadowed Ones would have been no more successful at making me doubt Father than they had been at convincing me Cornelius blew up our warehouse. So, all my guesses had been wrong; Father had not acted from secrecy and suspicion.

He was something quite unusual, my father: a man whose hidden motives were more noble than his outward façade. I would never have guessed he had stepped aside, not out of a longing to return to his orchid-strewn island, but so that the rest of us could finally come out from under his shadow. How funny that Logistilla, of all people, had put her finger on the matter when during our dinner at her island home she pointed out how Father was hardly any older than the rest of us.

And yet, during these last few days, I had lost something as well.

While I still loved my father dearly, I no longer looked up to him in the worshipful way I had done previously. I did not know if this came from having a freer will, or from seeing that Father could be put into a peril from which he could not extricate himself without our help. Either way, it was as if he was now more of an equal and less of a master. The old me missed the old Father who had been so wise and could do no wrong.

Mab scratched his stubble. "Do I get a question?"

"Certainly, Caekias." Father nodded.

Mab tilted his squashed and stained fedora, lowering the brim. "Actually, if it's all the same to you, I'd rather be called Mab."

"Mab, then."

As Mab flipped through his notebook, a spark of cheer glowed in my heart. So he was not renouncing his time as "Mab." I was glad of it.

I cleared my throat. "Before Mab goes, I have something to say." Mab looked up from his notes. "Mab, on behalf of my family and myself, I wanted to thank you for your loyalty, your tireless work, your sharp insights, and for putting up with bullheaded employers who did not listen to you, even when your advice was really very good."

Mab attempted a disapproving frown, but his mouth kept sneaking upward into a smile. "Thank you, Ma'am. About time someone noticed. Just wish you had noticed that my advice was trustworthy when it mattered."

"Actually, I did tell you I trusted your word once before," I said, "but the you I told turned out to be Osae."

"Danged demon getting my praise," Mab muttered, but he was still grinning a big, wide grin. "Back to my question. I just looked over the questions I'd written down, and I was able to cross off every one: what happened to Mephisto, why did Logistilla have the knife—I assume Ulysses gave it to her after taking it off Mr. Thompson's corpse." Mab glanced at Ulysses, who nodded. "Whether Cornelius had Theo under a spell—that's all cleared up now, right?" He looked up again. Theo, who was tearing at barbecued spare ribs with his teeth, gave him a thumbs-up. "Whether Astreus had tithed Mephisto, all that stuff. However, I do have a question of my own." He shot me an apologetic look. "I guess you could say it's another version of a question you and Miranda have heard quite often . . . but it is the first time you've heard it from me. . . .

"If Lord Astreus is so eager to help keep us Aerie Ones in line, why couldn't you have enlisted his aid a long time ago and let us free then?"

Father arched a bushy brow. "What, in our time together, Mab, would lead you to believe I had any interest in letting your people free one millisecond before their allotted one thousand years had passed? I have not my daughter's soft heart." A smile tugged at the corner of Father's mouth. "Beside, just imagine I had suggested the idea to you: 'Mab, I'm off to negotiate with the elves.'"

"Don't do it, Sir!" Mab answered quickly. He made a negating motion with his hand, and I recalled the wild look in Astreus's face when Boreas tempted him to *Sturm und Drang*. In the past, before the return of his wings gave him a new hope of Heaven, the Elf Lord would have joined in the fray, urging the Aerie Ones on rather than calming them down. That was hardly the kind of help upon which Father—and mankind—wished to rely.

Mab continued, "Isn't worth it. Elves and humans just don't mix! I make an exception for Miss Mir—" He paused and then said deliberately, "For Miranda, of course, seeing as she isn't really human."

"Exactly." Father nodded. "Despite this, I did consider the option of approaching Lord Astreus, if the Aerie Ones were not showing more restraint by the time the thousand years were up, but I fear no good would have come of it." He smiled at me, his eyes twinkling. "It is not I whom the quixotic Lord of the Winds seems so eager to help. Next?" Father looked around the table. "I believe I skipped you, Erasmus, as you were off wrestling with my recalcitrant book. Did you have a question?"

Erasmus brushed his lank hair from his eyes and stood. His habitual lazy smile was still in place, but his face was rather pale. "Father, why did you tell Miranda not to give Water to Maria?"

A great sadness came over Father's face. He suddenly looked old and very weary, as if his time in Hell had taken a heavy toll upon him. "Erasmus, my son. I beg your forgiveness. Maria was one of the great mistakes of my life. I sincerely misjudged how much she meant to you."

"But you told me it was up to Miranda?" Erasmus asked again. "And Miranda said you told her not to do it."

"I was hoping Miranda would disobey me," Father said slowly.

"Maria died because of that?" Erasmus choked.

Father rubbed his temples. "It's not so simple. You see, Miranda did disobey me once—back on our island, when I forbade her to speak with young Prince Ferdinand. That's why I gave my blessing for them to marry. I thought it would be only a matter of weeks before she became a Sibyl and would be free to marry—for Muriel Sophia had told me that Miranda could not be elevated to Sibyl until she demonstrated her own free will. And clearly she was making her own choices when it came to the handsome Prince of Naples!"

"So, that was it! All this time . . ." I whispered, recalling suddenly how Father had ordered my youthful self not to speak with Ferdinand. Shakespeare had that one right after all.

"Then Ferdinand died." Father rested his head in his hands. It was a while until he began speaking again. All was quiet except the *pit-pat* of rain on the sky lights and *thump-thump* of Titus's younger son as he jumped on his father's back. Finally, he continued, "All the ground we had gained was lost. Worse than lost, she became almost like an automaton, obeying me down to the littlest detail or in the most exaggerated fashion. Antonio dealt us a far worse blow than he knew, the day he killed the young Prince of Naples."

Father raised his head and met Erasmus's gaze. "Miranda was fond of Maria. She liked her and spoke well of her. I thought—I hoped—she would disobey me and save Maria . . . but she did not."

"Antonio told me Maria came back to earth several times more and each time he manipulated me into rejecting her." Erasmus's voice was barely audible. "Finally, she gave up on me. She lives on Earth today, somewhere in Poland."

"Is this true, Vinae?" Father inclined his head toward the *Staff of Wisdom*.

"It is true."

"I am truly sorry, Son."

A period of quiet followed during which we ate in silence. Theo came and sat beside me, squeezing my hand fondly. I smiled and laid my head against his shoulder.

"I have a question for you all," Father addressed us. "If Gregor was alive all this time, whom did we bury?"

"Eli Thompson." Mab handed Father the wrinkled, water-stained printout with the article about Mr. Thompson's television appearance.

"What do you know!" Father smiled. "My new staff worked! That was the first time I tried it on a human being. Before that I had only resurrected squirrels." As he scanned the article, he began to frown. "Cornelius?"

"I'm on it, Father." Cornelius nodded wearily, a spoonful of curried rice suspended before his mouth. "We of *Orbis Suleimani* will make certain this man's story does not make it into the history books."

Gregor looked up from where he sat, examining the boxes the food had come in. "I have a grave?"

"Oh, yeah, and we had a funeral and everything. Very sad." Mephisto made as if to wipe a tear away. "We all cried, even Daddy. Ulysses gave a very touching speech."

"Did he?" Gregor eyed his younger brother.

"Quick, someone change the subject before I get beaten to a pulp, again!" begged Ulysses.

I nearly laughed aloud. The implication of Ulysses's new black eye finally dawned on me, as well as those of Logistilla's apparently tender seat. When they teleported away from the storm, Ulysses and Logistilla had found themselves alone with Gregor. Apparently, my long-imprisoned brother had taken the opportunity to express his displeasure at their treatment of him upon Ulysses's face and Logistilla's rear end.

Good for him!

"Hey, speaking of your staff, Daddy," Mephisto cried, "if I go dig up my dead cat, can you bring him back to life?"

"Your cat?"

"Someone hit Schrödinger with a car," I explained.

"That's right," Logistilla sniffed, "don't ask your sister, the sorceress who makes bodies. After all, she couldn't possibly know how to incarnate a familiar!"

Mephisto ran over to Logistilla and, falling on his knees, put his hands together, pleading, "Please! Please! Oh, please!"

"Don't beg, it's pathetic." She raised her nose and sniffed again. "I'll do it if the mood strikes me."

"Wonderful!" I laughed. "Tybalt will be so pleased!"

Logistilla turned to Father. "How come Mephisto is not sane again, now that he's been released from the oath he took?"

"I still drank from the Lethe," Mephisto replied.

"Well, that was stupid, Brother!" she sniffed. "Why don't you wear your hat then, the one you were showing off to Father when the Demon Queen snagged you?"

"It makes me talk funny. As soon as I put it on, I start thinking like I used to before I lost my memory—saying *thee* and *thou*—and I have trouble remembering everything that has happened since then."

"There is a river called the Eunoe in Purgatory that restores memory," Erasmus said. "Perhaps, our sister the Sibyl could find her way there one of these days."

"Or he could take up studying the Ancient Art of Memory again," Cornelius offered. For the first time, his voice almost sounded normal. "Now that there is no longer a reason for him not to do so."

Mephisto shook his head quickly, indicating that he did not cherish the idea of returning to the rigors of that discipline. Father glanced pointedly from Cornelius's dejected face to Mephisto, his bushy eyebrows jutting above his glaring eyes like great, gray beetles.

Mephisto flinched back and started nodding quickly. "Yeah, sure, Cornelius! Great idea!"

Logistilla sniffed a third time, then turned to watch her sons fondly. She seemed more relaxed with her children than she had been a week ago, more pleased to be their mother. I wondered if meeting Galeazzo had affected her more than she let on. Perhaps, she did not want any more of her children to end up in Hell.

A skylight opened, and Astreus flew into the library, closing the window behind him. Landing, he shook out his wings, spraying the rest of us with water. From the bright gleam of his eyes and the smile dancing about his lips, I suspected he had done this on purpose. Apparently, it amused him to drench us mere mortals.

"Off to Heaven, then?" asked Father.

I looked down at my food but found myself unable to eat. When Astreus had spoken of forming a flock, I had hoped . . .

Astreus strode across the chamber, stopping beside Father. Despite that he was soaking wet, he looked splendid in his sapphire and charcoal garments. The coronet of stars twinkled upon his brow.

"Uriel explained to me that the way to Heaven is open to me now, but I am not yet worthy to travel it," Astreus said. "I must earn back my halos. My first task is to aid my fellow elves in freeing themselves from the yoke of Hell. Tomorrow, I shall depart to pass among them, spreading the word of our freedom."

He was not running back to Heaven, but he was off anyway, was he?

I could not claim to be too surprised. I had known that was how it would be. I wondered if he would return and visit me occasionally, or if his words of love had been a passing fancy, a wind that blew my way and then changed its course again.

Worse, if he did return, would I be able to bear it?

Astreus was departing and I would return to my work at Prospero, Inc. Funny, I had so looked forward to getting back to the company, and yet, now, the thought of it seemed unbearable, as if I were a butterfly trying to crawl back into my cocoon. I had come so far, I had learned so much . . . surely the future had something more to offer me than just a repeat of my past?

Intellectually, I knew that, once I returned to work, the urgency of the problems the world currently faced would draw me out of my sorrow. And, yet, I knew as well, that it would take years, perhaps decades, for my former good spirits to return.

Broken hearts were like that.

Then, just when I regained my equilibrium, he would burst like the sun upon my life, and the whole thing would begin again.

How many times could I bear that cycle? Could I bear it even once? Better to make a clean break now, than to suffer so eternally, with no hope of succor or release. I turned away, waiting for him to depart. Instead, Astreus came around until he was in front of me and offered me his hand.

"Come with me!" Glowing a rosy-gold, his eyes shone with love. "Surely the elves will accept their newfound freedom all the more quickly if the Sibyl who made it possible travels in my company!"

Time stopped. Space ceased to exist. My heart paused midbeat and did not pick up its rhythm again. I sat there, everything around me as still as if it had been a scene painted upon glass.

Had I heard him correctly?

I pictured us flying through the starry sky, traveling on the backs of

giant swans, visiting the courts of Fairyland, and seeing wonders upon
which no mortal eye had ever laid.

What could be more wonderful?

With all my soul, I yearned to go with him. Then, I thought of the split
oak and the tumbled turret. The damage on the mainlands, where mankind
dwelt, must be even more terrible, and Prospero, Inc., would be needed to
help keep matters from getting even worse. With the majority of my Aerie
Ones departing, the company would be in disarray. It would take all our
strength and effort just to service our Priority Contracts. How we were going to perform all the damage control that was needed, I had no idea.

All this had happened because of my broken flute; I could hardly run
away and abandon the mess I had created.

"I can't," I replied softly, my voice filled with lingering sadness. "All the
damage. The Aerie Ones have fled. If I went, who would run Prospero, Inc.?"

I expected Astreus to look disappointed. Instead, he tapped his temple
thoughtfully. "Who indeed?" He spread his hands, indicating my family.
"Why, right here stands the Magician Prospero and his lively sons, a whole
parcel of them! Who better to run Prospero, Incorporated?"

"But they can't. They're busy. They . . . I . . ." I stuttered.

In all my dreams of a future life with Astreus, I had never even considered walking away from Prospero, Inc. I had never once thought of going
to live with him to Fairyland. And yet . . . and yet, was that not exactly
what I wanted: to explore, to visit places unknown, to soar through the sky,
hand in hand, unfettered by earthly fears?

Astreus leaned close to me and gazed directly into my eyes, his eyes a
brilliant, piercing, deep blue. "Are you trying to talk yourself out of coming
with me, my love?"

He had called me *his love*, right here, in front of my family. My heart
soared with joy, leaping as if it could fly through a skylight, up into the
stormy heavens.

Father, smiling, addressed my brothers. "What do you say, sons? Shall
we take up the task before us and free your sister to wander the world with
this elf?"

"I suppose it should be my duty," Erasmus drawled, "considering all
this"—he gestured up and outward, as if to indicate the storm—"happened
on my behalf."

"But, you can't!" I cried, watching as all my hard work, over which I had
slaved for so many years, was yanked from me. "Prospero, Inc., is mine . . ."

Flashes of green merriment darted through Astreus's eyes as my voice trailed off. Taking my hand, he kissed it without removing his gaze from mine.

"Oh, so it is to be a Boys Club, is it?" Logistilla turned her back with a huff. "And I thought we had made such progress with the horses!"

"Do you think you could do better?" Erasmus asked Logistilla.

"Indeed I could!" Logistilla shot back. "I've discovered of late I have rather a head for business. Since Cornelius stopped helping me, I've had to run all aspects of my enterprise myself, and I've done rather well, thank you!"

"Then, it has been decided," Father announced. "Logistilla is to be the new C.E.O. of Prospero, Inc. Among her first tasks will be to provide bodies for Aerie Ones who want them."

"But . . . I . . ." Logistilla sputtered.

"You don't want to be C.E.O. of Prospero, Inc.?" Father asked.

She rose to her full height. "Certainly, I do!" "So long as we can find room at the Mansion for all my pets."

"Your pets will be going back to their former shapes," growled Titus.

"Oh, pooh!" Logistilla replied, pouting. More cheerfully, she added, "Surely, there won't be enough identities yet for all the Aerie Ones who'll want one. Maybe, I'll be able to interest a few airy spirits in an internship as a dingo or a vicuna."

In the brief span of time it took my family to reach this conclusion, my life was utterly transformed. What had been impossible, suddenly became possible indeed.

I felt so happy that tears welled up.

As to my sister, if my memory of her management of her son's dukedom sufficed, Logistilla was being modest. She had always had a talent for business and management. What she needed was a chance to do something worthwhile—something that would draw her out of herself and away from the little games she had been playing with her pets and the *Staff of Transmogrification*. She would make a capable leader for the family company. With some chagrin, I realized I would be doing her a favor.

I realized something else, too. Logistilla, whose great complaint in life was that she went unappreciated by her family, deserved to know that I appreciated her ability.

Aloud, I said, "You will make a wonderful C.E.O., Logistilla. You're a natural. You will probably do better than I did."

Logistilla was so shocked that she did not know how to respond. She tried to swallow but could not. Eventually, she sputtered, "Why t-thank you, big sister Miranda. That is the nicest thing you have ever said to me."

"Then, it shall be so! Logistilla will run Prospero, Inc., and Erasmus will be her lieutenant," Father announced. Logistilla crowed with delight and Erasmus sighed.

"I suppose this is only what I deserve, but . . . oh, Father, the humiliation!" Erasmus hung his head in mock shame. Father chuckled.

Rising, Father came toward me and took my hands, giving me a loving, fatherly smile that reminded me of so many wonderful talks we had shared, including our chats upon the bluffs of Prospero Island, where he first told me about my mother and how great love had altered the course of his life.

"Go, Miranda, with my blessing." Father said. "The way will be difficult, for not all the faery folk will welcome your news, and all the powers of Hell shall rise to stop you. But if you are brave, and true to each other, you will prevail."

He embraced me, kissing my forehead gently. A warm tingle spread through my body. "You are my dearest child. So long have you been beside me, that I hardly know what I shall do without you . . . and yet," he stroked my hair and then, drawing me in close, embraced me—"and yet, I would not have it any other way—for now I know that you are finally and truly free!"

So, it was decided.

Part of me was petrified, trembling with terror like a leaf in a hurricane, but it was a small part. Far greater was the utter joy of venturing out to see all the wonders I had longed to visit. And, best of all, we would not just be traveling . . . we would be flying!

I hugged my father tightly, pressing my cheek against his chest, my eyes brimming with tears. He squeezed me back for a time. When we finally parted, Father turned and pointed his staff at Astreus, fixing him with his fierce gaze.

"But you, elf lord," he declared. "Know this: you shall not keep my daughter under a roof with you or under the sky for so much as a single night until full and holy rites of marriage have been performed, and she is your lawful wife!"

I blushed and started to object, but my brothers were already reaching for their staffs. Erasmus slipped on his Urim glove, and Theo's began its rising hum. Even Caliban was hefting his club. They closed in upon Astreus, menacingly, ringing him, except for Mephisto, who stepped beside him, staff in hand, as if to guard him. When Astreus threw Mephisto a grateful look, the latter leaned toward the elf lord, whispering, "Psst, remember? You promised."

The Elf Lord threw up his hands, pleading, "No objection do I make to your geas, Dread Prospero, and yet when I did question Mephistopheles about matrimony, so long ago, he assured me that this blessed state takes time to achieve, involving kneeling and three years of affianced bliss."

"Nonsense." Gregor stood, his robes swishing about his legs. "I can marry you immediately. Am I not a priest?"

Astreus spread his wings, forcing my brothers to retreat or be struck in the face with feathers. He held out his hand to me again. "Then, come, Fair Miranda! Let our love be sanctified by this holy ceremony, that we might be made one before the eyes of the Most High, our hearts intertwined and our purposes forever united! From our loins shall spring a race of terrestrial angels, like unto nothing that yet walks or breathes. They shall be a new race, born of the union of Heaven and earth, from which shall spring saints, poets, and heroes who, by dint of their fierce spirit, shall change the face of the world, even as the Family Prospero has done!"

My family cheered and thumped the floor with their staffs. Even Father clapped. Mephisto, who was particularly ecstatic, cartwheeled back and forth across the chamber.

Rising, I placed my hand in Astreus's.

THE wedding ceremony was short but sweet. Logistilla stood up with me and Mephisto stood up with Astreus, alternating between hat-on and hat-off. Astreus pulled matching rings from his indigo cloak, bands of sapphire with a tiny star burning upon each. Mine fit perfectly. After slipping it on, Astreus taught me how to hide the light, should I want to move about stealthily. Then, he kissed me, and for a time, we danced in dreams amidst bonfires and starlight.

AFTERWARD, Father sent Gregor and Erasmus to fetch bottles from the wine cellar. When they came, I held up the bottles and let Life flow from my forehead into the liquid. A familiar pearly golden-white spread throughout the dark red of the wine. When I pulled the cork and the smell of it escaped the bottle, a chorus of "oohs" sounded throughout the chamber. I poured out a glass for each of us.

"That scent!" Cornelius cried, half-rising. "So beautiful."

"Dear God!" cried Theo. "Miranda, you really did it! You made Water of Life! Or Wine of Life, in this case."

"We are saved!" breathed Erasmus. "Mankind is saved! And you can make an infinite supply. We could make all mankind immortal!"

"One thing at a time, Son," Father chided. "One thing at a time. Let us free the elves first. Heaven may have other plans for mankind than eternal life trapped on earth."

"Could you see but a glimpse of Heaven," laughed Astreus, "you would not yearn for immortal life on earth, and yet"—he swirled the iridescent liquid in his glass—"with this, mankind's days upon the earth could be healthy and whole. No need for him to sweat with fever or suffer crippling wounds. Those ills are Hell's invention. We elves do not suffer them. They are not part of Heaven's greater plan. Had illness been the work of the Most High, would not your White Christ have refused to heal it?"

"Interesting . . ." Gregor frowned. "Though I'm not sure that is theologically sound."

"Perhaps." Erasmus gazed into his wine. "But, ah, the possibilities!"

And, of course, Erasmus was right.

We were immortal again. We Prosperos would be around to see that the spirits did not break their oaths and escape their bonds. Mankind would not lose their modern marvels and be plunged back into the Dark Ages—a time of torment and misery. Hell would not win after all.

And, in time, maybe even the spirits themselves could be set free—with souls!

Theophrastus propped his feet upon the end table and raised his glass, proposing a toast to our future happiness, which was quickly echoed by the others. My heart expanded with joy every time I saw him looking so young and strong. He met my eyes and smiled in return.

"Was it really only a month ago when you came looking for Father, Miranda?" Theo asked. "It seems like a lifetime!"

"God works in mysterious ways." Gregor took a sip from his glass. "In a matter of days, we have gone from elation to desperation and back to elation. Who would have thought, when Miranda lost her Handmaidenship, the night you all rescued me, that six days later our lives would be so much grander than they had previously been?"

"Who knows what the future may bring?" Father's fierce blue eyes glanced from Astreus to Erasmus. "Free elves no longer bound to Hell?

Mankind no longer prey to disease and famine? Or things more wondrous still?"

"I sense an apropos moment for our favorite Miranda quote," offered Erasmus, raising his glass.

"Say it! Oh! Oh! Say it!" Mephisto jumped up and down. The others soon joined in the chant.

Raising my own glass, I recited the immortal words the Bard had written for my namesake: *"'O wonder! How many goodly creatures are there here! How beauteous mankind is! O brave new world, That has such people in 't.'"*

EPILOGUE

I rose the next morning from my marriage bed, feeling both refreshed and giddy with wonder, and—after kissing my elvish husband with all the sweetness I could muster—went to gather my things. Coming down the hallway, I ran into Erasmus, who carried his travel bags upon his staff, which rested over his shoulder, so that he looked like a medieval vagabond taking off for a journey with suitcases hanging from his bindle stick.

"Well, I'm off to Poland. Ulysses's bringing me as far as Warsaw. After all," Erasmus said with a smirk and patted his staff, "what does 'sixty-three years' matter to me?"

"And you think you can find Maria in a reincarnated body with only the instructions, 'She's in Poland'?"

"Father let me talk to the *Club O' Wisdom*. He gave me an address."

"Oh, Erasmus, that's wonderful!" I cried. "I wish you all the luck in the world winning her back!"

I took his free hand and pressed it fondly, thinking how strange it was to feel so charitably toward Erasmus. That alone attested to the tremendous difference between the present me and myself of a month ago!

Of all of us, Erasmus had suffered the most during this last week. Like me, he had seen all his comfortable illusions ripped away, but unlike me, he had not found something of worth waiting on the far side. That he had undergone so much and still kept his spirits up, resisting the despair that accompanied his staff, showed tremendous strength of character. I hoped the demon in his staff—the Great Duke Vepar if I recalled Baelor correctly—had taken note and was duly impressed. With such determination, Erasmus could not fail to win back the woman he so loved, even if he had to learn Polish first.

"I never got to thank you properly, Miranda. You—of all people!" Erasmus shook his head wryly. "You saved my life and at such a terrible cost."

He laid his free hand upon his staff and shuddered. "I would not have done the same for you."

"I don't know." I laughed. "I remember a certain brother who jumped into the Swamp of Uncleanness without a second thought. Besides," I added, "I didn't do it for you. I did it for Cornelius."

"Cornelius? I didn't know you even liked Cornelius."

I brushed aside escaped strands of my raven black hair, which still seemed jarring and unfamiliar to me. "It's a long story." I looked him in the face a moment and suddenly thought of something. "Erasmus! Wait here, just a moment!"

I ran off and came back with an old tin canteen wrapped in a Mac-Laren plaid. I thrust it at him.

"What is this?" He opened it and sniffed the wondrous aroma that escaped from the bottle. His breath caught in his throat, and his face went slack. He stared at the canteen for a time, as if he was afraid to trust his senses. Finally, he looked up at me, his face agog with joy. "Water of Life! A whole canteen!"

"I thought you might need some. It's not a Urim container, so the holy essence will eventually leak out, but—"

"It's all right." He cut me off, his dark eyes dancing with an inner light. "I know how to make it last long enough to serve my purposes. I'll ward the canteen with that black cloth we prepared to keep Paimon quiet during our trip."

He put down his staff and bags and pulled me into his arms, hugging me tightly. I squeezed him back, laying my head against his shoulder. I searched my memory, but could not recall that he had ever willingly embraced me before, except in Limbo, when he thanked me for saving him.

Stepping back, he smiled at me sideways though his dark hair, which, as always, hung in his face. He picked up his staff again, leaving the bags on the floor. "I'm not entirely certain this Elf Boy is good enough for you, though. If any part of him gives you trouble, you tell me." He hefted his staff. "I'll see it won't bother you in the future!"

I started to smile then blushed furiously as possible implications of his threat occurred to me.

"You need not fear having Osae's bastard for a nephew," I replied in a rush. "My Lady assures me I have escaped that doom."

"Wonderful news!" Erasmus exclaimed. "I shall look forward to the *pitter-patter* of little elvish feet, Madam Stormwind."

His use of my new title caught me by surprise and caused me to blush all the more. For he was right. I was now Miranda Stormwind. I put my hands over my mouth to suppress a girlish giggle.

Erasmus shook his head, chuckling. "Nothing makes a bride giddier than to remind her of the gravity of her new position." Lowering his staff through the handles, he picked up his bags again. "A Sibyl. After all these years. And now you can talk to Eurynome directly, can't you?"

I smiled. "Yes. Which is wonderful . . . but not as important as I once thought it was."

"How so?"

"I have learned how to make my own decisions."

"How glorious, Sister," Erasmus bowed, smiling though his hair.

As he turned to go, I watched him fondly. I realized that I now had trouble recalling why I had so disliked him.

"Erasmus!" I called as he walked away. He paused and arched an eyebrow. I hesitated and then blurted out, "My hair, can you . . . would you turn it back to silver?"

Erasmus threw his head back and laughed. "Certainly, Sister," he replied when he could speak again. "Always happy to wither a family member."

I WENT down to the Eridanus and, after showering the life and love that poured from my forehead upon a still pool, washed my newly withered hair in Water of Life until it shone like spun silver. It was a pleasure to see my reflection match my mental image of myself, and an even greater joy to see the spiral ivory mark upon my brow. I hoped Astreus would like my pale locks.

The little feylings gathered around the Water, sipping it and dancing, until the whole glade sparkled with tiny lights. Several Aerie Ones who were still on the island swooped down to drink as well, caressing me with gentle gusts to show their gratitude.

When I came back to the house, I found my family gathered in the music room. An Aerie One—who had accepted my offer of employment—stood by, muting the tremendous roar of the waterfall. Beyond the sheet of falling water, I could see Astreus soaring above the island, laughing as he glided and dove. Closer at hand, Logistilla and Titus talked with their children. Teleron had put his book aside, and Typhon leaned his head happily against Logistilla, who was stroking his hair. Gregor and Ulysses sat at the small table in the center of the room, sipping wine and playing cards with Father's antique *tarocco* deck.

Theo stood beside the piano with a cavalier-hat-wearing Mephisto, who was trying to master modern language. Near them, Schrödinger, in her new, Logistilla-designed, brindle cat body, batted playfully at Tybalt, Prince of Cats. Ulysses had fetched my familiar from Prospero's Mansion, along with the gem that held Mab's "cousin" in it, which I had found on my breakfast tray.

On the far side of the room, Father, Cornelius, and Caliban listened as the *Staff of Wisdom* conversed with the *Staff of Persuasion*. Cornelius's shoulders still slumped dejectedly, but Caliban's face had a calmer, more steady quality: more like a professor, less like a servant.

"Where's Mab?" I asked.

I FOUND him in Father's workroom amidst swirling sawdust. He had my flute in a vise and was slicing it into slim rings with the electric saw. My stomach clenched, and I had to look away.

"Won't be enough for us all," he commented over the *whirr* of the saw, "but, heck, at least some of us can enjoy 'em. Maybe we can take turns. Thought I'd keep the mouthpiece myself. Seems fitting, somehow. Kind of like the idea of dancing to my own tune for a change."

I held out the gem that Ulysses had brought from Prospero's Mansion. Mab's face lit up.

"My . . . well, you'd call him a cousin!" A big grin split Mab's craggy face as he accepted the jewel in which some airy spirit flitted hither and yon. "Ah, Ma'am, you remembered! You kept your word."

Mab started to peer into the gem and then seemed to think better of it. He stuffed it into his pocket to work on later and went back to sawing.

"Oh, Mab!" Tears rushed to my eyes. "Father's servants are all leaving. Five hundred years, they've been with us, yet they're leaving. Ariel will be gone when Logistilla gets to Oregon. I have no idea how she'll run that house without him. Or Prospero, Inc! Though Mustardseed is staying on as head of Priority Contracts, bless him! That sacrifice alone may save mankind. Wh-what will you do?"

Mab left off sawing and cocked his head, tilting up the brim of his hat. "Well, Ma'am, the truth is I've gotten to rather like this mortal body. Figure I'll stick with it a while longer. Besides, Lord Astreus's a fine elf, but he doesn't know squat about this mortal world. A half-angel like yourself, Ma'am . . . Well, someone's got to stand by to keep you out of trouble. Might as well be me." He fidgeted with the pile of new rings he had cut from what had, for so long, been my precious flute. "That is, if you'll have me. Don't want to be intruding on your honeymoon or nothing."

"Mab!" I cried joyously. Leaning forward, I gave him a kiss on his scratchy cheek. Straightening up, I added, "Looks like we'll have some exciting times ahead, with all these elves to contact and Gifts of the Sibyl to explore."

"Exciting is not the word I'd choose," Mab muttered, as he went back to sawing, "but, that's just me, Ma'am."

⚜

The End

⚜

ACKNOWLEDGMENTS

Thank you to Mark Whipple, Dave Eckstein, and Catherine Rockwood, without whose encouragement, this novel would have been abandoned in its infancy.

To Von Long, Bill Burns, Erin Furby, Kirsten Edwards, Dave Coffman, Donna Royston, Don Schank, James Hyder, Anna MacDonald, and Diana Hardy for their support and advice, and to Danielle Ackley-McPhail and the Yesterday's Dreamers for all their useful ideas concerning the craft of writing itself.

To my brother, Law Lamplighter, for recounting his vision of the City of Dis, which I reproduced to the best of my ability.

To Peter Atkins, for permission to reprint his poem, "Expectant Father to His Unborn Son."

To Father Laurence and Brother Gerard for the idea about the nature of Hell, which they shared under a circumstance so strange that it would not be believed if I tried to explain it.

To my gracious editor, Jim Frenkel, and my dashing and knightly agent, Richard Curtis.

To Milton, whose title this one hopefully honors.

And, most important, to my mother, Jane Lamplighter, without whose selfless devotion to her grandchildren this book literally could not have been written.

ABOUT THE AUTHOR

L. Jagi Lamplighter is the author of the novels *Prospero Lost, Prospero in Hell,* and *Prospero Regained,* and sundry short stories. She lives with her husband and children in northern Virginia. For more information, visit her Web site at www.ljagilamplighter.com.